HEROES
BLOCKBUSTER
—2024—

B.J. DANIELS

REGAN BLACK

BRENDA JACKSON

SUE MacKAY

MILLS & BOON

Published by
Mills & Boon
An imprint of Harlequin Enterprises (Australia) Pty Limited (ABN 47 001 180 918), a subsidiary of HarperCollins Publishers Australia Pty Limited (ABN 36 009 913 517)
Level 19, 201 Elizabeth Street
SYDNEY NSW 2000
AUSTRALIA

FSC
MIX
Paper | Supporting
responsible forestry
FSC® C001695
www.fsc.org

Printed and bound in Australia by McPherson's Printing Group

CONTENTS

Cowboy's Redemption
B.J. Daniels

I N T R I G U E

Seek thrills. Solve crimes. Justice served.

This one is for Stelly, who even at four loves stories where the heroine gets to help save herself.

CHAPTER ONE

RUNNING BLINDLY THROUGH the darkness, Lola didn't see the tree limb until it struck her in the face. It clawed at her cheek, digging into a spot under her right eye as she flung it away with her arm. She had to stifle the cry of pain that rose in her throat for fear she would be heard. As she ran, she felt warm blood run down to the corner of her lips. The taste of it mingled with the salt of her tears, but she didn't slow, couldn't. She could hear them behind her.

She pushed harder, knowing that, being men, they had the advantage, especially the way she was dressed. Her long skirt caught on something. She heard the fabric rend, not for the first time. She felt as if it was her heart being ripped out with it.

Her only choice was to escape. But at what price? She'd been forced to leave behind the one person who mattered most. Her thundering heart ached at the thought, but she knew that this was the only way. If she could get help...

"She's over here!" came a cry from behind her. "This way!"

She wiped away the warm blood as she crashed through the brush and trees. Her legs ached and she didn't know how much longer she could keep going. Fatigue was draining her. If they caught her this time...

She tripped on a tree root, stumbled and almost plunged

headlong down the mountainside. Her shoulder slammed into a tree trunk. She veered off it like a pinball, but she kept pushing herself forward because the alternative was worse than death.

They were closer now. She could feel one of them breathing down her neck. She didn't dare look back. To look back would be to admit defeat. If she could just reach the road before they caught up to her...

Suddenly the trees opened up. She burst out of the darkness of the pines onto the blacktop of a narrow two-lane highway. The glare of headlights blinded her an instant before the shriek of rubber on the dark pavement filled the night air.

CHAPTER TWO

Major Colt McCloud felt the big bird shake as he brought the helicopter low over the bleak landscape. He was back in Afghanistan behind the controls of a UH-60 Black Hawk. The throb of the rotating blades was drowned out by the sound of mortar fire. It grew louder and louder, taking on a consistent pounding that warned him something was very wrong.

He dragged himself awake, but the dream followed him. Blinking in the darkness, he didn't know where he was for a moment. Everything looked alien and surreal. As the dream began to fade, he recognized his bedroom at the ranch.

He'd left behind the sound of the chopper and the mortar fire, but the pounding had intensified. With a start, he realized what he was hearing.

Someone was at the door.

He glanced at the clock on his bedside table. It was after three in the morning. Throwing his legs over the side of the bed, he grabbed his jeans, pulling them on as he fought to put the dream behind him and hurry to the door.

A half dozen possibilities flashed in his mind as he moved quickly through the house. It still felt strange to be back here after years of traveling the world as an Army helicopter pilot. After his fiancée dumped him, he'd planned to make a career out of the military, but then his father had died, leaving him a working ranch that either had to be run or sold.

He'd taken a hundred-and-twenty-day leave in between assignments so he could come home to take care of the ranch. His father had been the one who'd loved ranching, not Colt. That's why there was a for-sale sign out on the road into the ranch.

Colt reached the front door and, frowning at the incessant knocking at this hour of the morning, threw it open.

He blinked at the disheveled woman standing there before she turned to motion to the driver of the car idling nearby. The engine roared and a car full of what appeared to be partying teenagers took off in a cloud of dust.

Colt flipped on the porch light as the woman turned back to him and he got his first good look at her and her scratched, blood-streaked face. For a moment he didn't recognize her, and then it all came back in a rush. Standing there was a woman he'd never thought he'd see again.

"Lola?" He couldn't even be sure that was her real name. But somehow it fit her, so maybe at least that part of her story had been true. "What happened to you?"

"I had nowhere else to go." Her words came out in a rush. "I was so worried that you wouldn't be here." She burst into tears and slumped as if physically exhausted.

He caught her, swung her up into his arms and carried her into the house, kicking the door closed behind him. His mind raced as he tried to imagine what could have happened to bring her to his door in Gilt Edge, Montana, in the middle of the night and in this condition.

"Sit here," he said as he carried her in and set her down in a kitchen chair before going for the first-aid kit. When he returned, he was momentarily taken aback by the memory of this woman the first time he'd met her. She wasn't beautiful in the classic sense. But she was striking, from her wide violet eyes fringed with pale lashes to the silk of her long blond hair. She had looked like an angel, especially in the long white dress she'd been wearing that night.

That was over a year ago and he hadn't seen her since. Nor had he expected to since they'd met initially several hundred miles from the ranch. But whatever had struck him about her hadn't faded. There was something flawless about her—even as scraped up and bruised as she was. It made him furious at whoever was responsible for this.

"Can you tell me what happened?" he asked as he began to clean the cuts.

"I... I..." Her throat seemed to close on a sob.

"It's okay, don't try to talk." He felt her trembling and could see that she was fighting tears. "This cut under your eye is deep."

She said nothing, looking as if it was all she could do to keep her eyes open. He took in her torn and filthy dress. It was long, like the white one he'd first seen her in, but faded. It reminded him of something his grandmother might have worn to do housework in. She was also thinner than he remembered.

As he gently cleaned her wounds, he could see dark circles under her eyes, and her long braided hair was in disarray with bits of twigs and leaves stuck in it.

The night he'd met her, her plaited hair had been pinned up at the nape of her neck—until he'd released it, the blond silk dropping to the center of her back.

He finished his doctoring, put away the first-aid kit, and wondered how far she'd come to find him and what she had been through to get here. When he returned to the kitchen, he found her standing at the back window, staring out. As she turned, he saw the fear in her eyes—and the exhaustion.

Colt desperately wanted to know what had happened to her and how she'd ended up on his doorstep. He hadn't even thought that she'd known his name. "Have you had anything to eat?"

"Not in the past forty-eight hours or so," she said, squinting at the clock on the wall as if not sure what day it was. "And not all that much before that."

He'd been meaning to get into Gilt Edge and buy some groceries. "Sit and I'll see what I can scare up," he said as he opened the refrigerator. Seeing only one egg left, he said, "How do you feel about pancakes? I have chokecherry syrup."

She nodded and attempted a smile. She looked skittish as a newborn calf. Worse, he sensed that she was having second thoughts about coming here.

She licked her cracked lips. "I have to tell you. I have to explain—"

"It's okay. You're safe here." But safe from what, he wondered? "There's no hurry. Let's get you taken care of first." He'd feed her and get her settled down.

He motioned her into a chair at the kitchen table. He could tell that she must hurt all over by the way she moved. As much as he wanted to know what had happened, he thought she needed food more than anything else at this moment.

"While I make the pancakes, would you like a hot shower? The guest room is down the hall to the left. I can find you some clothes. They'll be too large for you, but maybe they will be more comfortable."

Tears welled in her eyes. He saw her swallow before she nodded. As she started to get to her feet, he noticed her grimace in pain.

"Wait."

She froze.

"I don't know how to say this delicately, but if someone assaulted you—"

"I wasn't raped."

He nodded, hoping that was true, because a shower would destroy important evidence. "Okay, so the injuries were…"

"From running for my life." With that she limped out of the kitchen.

He had the pancake batter made and the griddle heating when

he heard the shower come on. He stopped to listen to the running water, remembering this woman in a hotel shower with him months ago.

That night he'd bumped into her coming out of the hotel bar. He'd seen that she was upset. She'd told him that she needed his help, that there was someone after her. She'd given him the impression she was running from an old boyfriend. He'd been happy to help. Now he wondered if that was still the case. She said she was running for her life—just as she had the first time they'd met.

But that had been in Billings. This was Gilt Edge, Montana, hundreds of miles away. Didn't seem likely she would still be running from the same boyfriend. But whoever was chasing her, she'd come to him for help.

He couldn't turn her away any more than he'd been able to in that hotel hallway in Billings last year.

Lola pulled out her braid, discarding the debris stuck in it, then climbed into the steaming shower. She stood under the hot spray, leaned against the smooth, cool tile wall of the shower and closed her eyes. She felt weak from hunger, lack of sleep and constant fear. She couldn't remember the last time she'd slept through the night.

Exhaustion pulled at her. It took all of her energy to wash herself. Her body felt alien to her, her skin chafed from the rough fabric of the long dresses she'd been wearing for months. Stumbling from the shower, she wrapped her hair in one of the guest towels. It felt good to free her hair from the braid that had been wound at the nape of her neck.

As she pulled down another clean towel from the bathroom rack, she put it to her face and sniffed its freshness. Tears burned her eyes. It had been so long since she'd had even the smallest creature comforts like good soap, shampoo and clean towels that smelled like this, let alone unlimited hot water.

When she opened the bathroom door, she saw that Colt had

left her a sweatshirt and sweatpants on the guest-room bed. She dried and tugged them on, pulling the drawstring tight around her waist. He was right, the clothes were too big, but they felt heavenly.

She took the towels back to the bathroom to hang them and considered her dirty clothing on the floor. The hem of the worn ankle-length coarse cotton dress was torn and filthy with dirt and grime. The long sleeves were just as bad except they were soiled with her blood. The black utilitarian shoes were scuffed, the heels worn unevenly since she'd inherited them well used.

She wadded up the dress and shoved it into the bathroom wastebasket before putting the shoes on top of it, all the time feeling as if she was committing a sin. Then again, she'd already done that, hadn't she.

Downstairs, she stepped into the kitchen to see Colt slip three more pancakes onto the stack he already had on the plate.

He turned as if sensing her in the doorway and she was reminded of the first time she'd seen him. All she'd noticed that night was his Army uniform—before he'd turned and she'd seen his face.

That he was handsome hadn't even registered. What she'd seen was a kind face. She'd been desperate and Colt McCloud had suddenly appeared as if it had been meant to be. Just as he'd been here tonight, she thought.

"Last time I saw you, you were on leave and talking about staying in the military," she said as he pulled out a kitchen chair for her and she sat down. "I was afraid that you had and that—" her voice broke as she met his gaze "—you wouldn't be here."

"I'm on leave now. My father died."

"I'm sorry."

He set down the plate of pancakes. "Dig in."

Always the gentleman, she thought as he joined her at the table. "I made a bunch. There's fresh sweet butter. If you don't like chokecherry syrup—"

"I love it." She slid several of the lightly browned cakes

onto her plate. The aroma that rose from them made her stomach growl loudly. She slathered them with butter and covered them with syrup. The first bite was so delicious that she actually moaned, making him smile.

"I was going to ask how they are," he said with a laugh, "but I guess I don't have to."

She devoured the pancakes before helping herself to more. They ate in a companionable silence that didn't surprise her any more than Colt making her pancakes in the middle of the night or opening his door to her, no questions asked. It was as if it was something he did all the time. Maybe it was, she thought, remembering the first night they'd met.

He hadn't hesitated when she'd told him she needed his help. She'd looked into his blue eyes and known she could trust him. He'd been so sweet and caring that she'd almost told him the truth. But she'd stopped herself. Because she didn't think he would believe her? Or because she didn't want to involve him? Or because, at that point, she thought she could still handle things on her own?

Unfortunately, she no longer had the option of keeping the truth from him.

"I'm sure you have a lot of questions," she said, after swallowing her last bite of pancake and wiping her mouth with her napkin. The food had helped, but her body ached all over and fatigue had weakened her. "You had to be surprised to see me again, especially with me showing up at your door in the middle of the night looking like I do."

"I didn't even know you knew my last name."

"After that night in Billings… Before I left your hotel room, while you were still sleeping, I looked in your wallet."

"You planned to take my money?" He'd had over four hundred dollars in there. He'd been headed home to his fiancée, he'd told her. But the fiancée, who was supposed to pick him up at the airport, had called instead with crushing news. Not only was she not picking him up, she was in love with one of his best friends, someone he'd known since grade school.

He'd been thinking he just might rent a car and drive home to confront the two of them, he'd told Lola later. But, ultimately, he'd booked a flight for the next morning to where he was stationed and, with time to kill, had taken a taxi to a hotel, paid for a room and headed for the hotel bar. Two drinks later, he'd run into Lola as he'd headed from the bar to the men's room. Lola had saved him from getting stinking drunk that night. Also from driving to Gilt Edge to confront his ex-fiancée and his ex-friend.

"I hate to admit that I thought about taking your money," she said. "I could have used it."

"You should have taken it then."

She smiled at him and shook her head. "You were so kind to me, so tender..." Her cheeks heated as she held his gaze and remembered being naked in his arms. "I'm sure I gave you the wrong impression of me that night. It wasn't like me to...with a complete stranger." She bit her lower lip and felt tears well in her eyes again.

"There is nothing wrong with the impression you left with me. As a matter of fact, I've thought of you often." He smiled. It was a great smile. "Every time I heard one of those songs that we'd danced to in my hotel room that night—" his gaze warmed to a Caribbean blue "—I thought of you."

She looked away to swallow the lump that had formed in her throat before she could speak again. "It wasn't an old boyfriend I was running from that night. I let you believe that because I doubted you'd have believed the truth. I did need your help, though, because right before I collided with you in that hallway, I'd seen one of them in the hotel. I knew it was just a matter of time before they found me and took me back."

"Took you back?"

"I wasn't a fugitive from the law or some mental institution," she said quickly. "It's worse than that."

He narrowed his gaze with concern. "What could be worse than that?"

"The Society of Lasting Serenity."

CHAPTER THREE

"THE FRINGE RELIGIOUS cult that relocated to the mountains about five years ago?" Colt asked, unable to keep the shock from his voice.

She nodded.

He couldn't have been more stunned if she'd said she had escaped from prison. "When did you join that?"

"I didn't. My parents were some of the founding members when the group began in California. I was in Europe at university when they joined. I'd heard from my father that SLS had relocated to Montana. A few years after that, I received word that the leader, Jonas Emanuel, needed to see me. My mother was ill." Her voice broke. "Before I could get back here, my mother and father both died, within hours of each other, and had been buried on the compound. According to Jonas, they had one dying wish." Her laugh could have cut glass. "They wanted to see me married. Once I was on the SLS compound, I learned that, according to Jonas, they had promised me to him."

"That's crazy." He still couldn't get his head around this.

"Jonas is delusional but also dangerous."

"So you were running from him that night I met you?"

She nodded. "But, unfortunately, when I left the hotel the

next morning, two of the 'sisters' were waiting for me and forced me to go back to the compound."

"And tonight?" he asked as he pushed his plate away.

Lola met his gaze. "I escaped. I'd been locked up there since I last saw you within miles of here at the Montana SLS compound."

Colt let out a curse. "You've been held there all this time against your will? Why didn't you—"

"Escape sooner?" She sounded near tears as she held his gaze.

He saw something in those beautiful eyes that made his stomach drop.

Her voice caught as she said, "I had originally gone there to get my parents' remains because I don't believe they died of natural causes. I'd gotten a letter from my father right before I heard from Jonas. He wanted out of SLS, but my mother refused. My father said he feared the hold Jonas had on her and needed my help because she wasn't well."

"What are you saying?"

"I think they were murdered, but I can't prove it without their bodies, and Jonas has refused to release them. Legally, there isn't much I can do since my parents had signed over everything to him—even their daughter."

Murder? He'd heard about the fifty-two-year-old charismatic leader of the cult living in the mountains outside of town, but he couldn't imagine the things Lola was telling him. "He can't expect you to marry him."

"Jonas was convinced that I would fall for him if I spent enough time at the compound, so he kept me there. At first, he told me it would take time to have my parents' remains exhumed and moved. Later I realized there was no way he was letting their remains go anywhere even if he could convince me to marry him, which was never going to happen."

Maybe it was the late hour, but he was having trouble making sense of this. "So after you met me..."

"I was more determined to free both my parents and myself from Jonas forever. I wasn't back at the compound long though, when I realized I was pregnant. Jonas realized it, too. I became a prisoner of SLS until the birth. Then Jonas had the baby taken away and had me locked up. I had to escape to get help for my daughter."

"Your daughter?"

She met his gaze. "That's why I'm here... She's *our* daughter," she said, her voice suddenly choked with tears. "Jonas took the baby girl that you and I made the first night we met."

Colt stared at her, too shocked to speak for a moment. *What the hell?* "Are you trying to tell me—"

"I had your child but I couldn't contact you. Jonas kept me under guard, locked away. I had no way to get a message out. If any of the sisters tried to help me, they were severely punished."

He couldn't believe what he was hearing. "Wait. You had the baby at the compound?"

She nodded. "One of the members is a midwife. She delivered a healthy girl, but then Jonas had the child taken away almost at once. I got to hold her only for a few moments and only because Sister Amelia let me. She was harshly reprimanded for it. I got to look into her precious face. She has this adorable tiny heart-shaped birthmark on her left thigh and my blond hair. Just fuzz really." Tears filled her eyes again.

Colt ran a hand over his face before he looked at her again. "I'm having a hard time believing any of this."

"I know. If Jonas had let me leave with my daughter, I wouldn't have ever troubled you with any of this," she said.

"You would never have told me about the baby?" He hadn't meant to make it sound like an accusation. He'd expected her to be offended.

Instead, when she spoke, he saw only sympathy in her gaze. "When I met you, you were on leave and going back the next day. You were talking about staying in the Army. Your fiancée had just broken up with you."

"You don't have to remind me."

"What you and I shared that night..." She met his gaze. "I'll never forget it, but I wasn't fool enough to think that it might lead to anything. The only reason I'm here now is that I need help to get our daughter away from that...man."

"Don't I have a right to know if I have a child?"

"Of course. But I wouldn't be asking anything of you—if Jonas hadn't taken our daughter. I'm more than capable of taking care of her and myself."

"What I don't understand is why Jonas wants to keep a baby that isn't his."

She didn't seem surprised by his skepticism, but when he looked into her eyes, he saw pain darken all that beautiful blue. "I can understand why you wouldn't believe she's yours."

"I didn't say that."

"You didn't have to." She got to her feet, grabbing the table to steady herself. "I shouldn't have come here, but I didn't know where else to go."

"Hold on," he said, pushing back his chair and coming around the table to take her shoulders in his hands. She felt small, fragile, and yet he saw a strength in her that belied her slim frame. "You have to admit this is quite the story."

"That's why I didn't tell you the night we met about the cult or the problems I was having getting my parents' remains out. I still thought I could handle it myself. Also I doubt you would have believed it." Her smile hurt him soul deep. "I wouldn't have believed it and I've lived through all of this."

He was doing his best to keep an open mind. He wasn't a man who jumped to quick conclusions. He took his time to make decisions based on the knowledge he was able to acquire. It had kept him alive all these years as an Army helicopter pilot.

"So what you're telling me is that the leader of SLS has taken your baby to force you to marry him? If he's so dangerous, why wouldn't he have just—"

"Forced me? He tried to…join with me, as he put it. He's still limping from the attempt. And equally determined that I will come to him. Now that I've shamed him…he will never let me have my baby unless I completely surrender to him in front of the whole congregation."

"Don't you mean *our* baby?"

Lola gave him an impatient look. Tears filled her eyes as she swayed a little as if having trouble staying upright after everything she'd been through.

He felt a stab of guilt. He'd been putting her through an interrogation when clearly she was exhausted. It was bad enough that she was scraped, cut and bruised, but he could see that her real injuries were more than skin deep.

"You're dead on your feet," he said. "There isn't anything we can do tonight. Get some rest. Tomorrow…"

A tear broke loose and cascaded down her cheek. He caught it with his thumb and gently wiped it away before she let him lead her to the guest bedroom where she'd showered earlier. His mind was racing. If any of this was true…

"Don't worry. We'll figure this out," Colt said as he pulled back the covers. "Just get some sleep." He knew he wouldn't be able to sleep a wink.

Could he really have a daughter? A daughter now being held by a crackpot cult leader? A man who, according to Lola, was much more dangerous than anyone knew?

Lola climbed into the bed, still wearing his too-large sweats. He tucked her in, seeing that she could barely keep her eyes open.

"Dayton." At his puzzled look, she added, "That's my last name." They'd shared only first names the night they met. But that night neither of them had been themselves. She'd been running scared, and he'd been wallowing in self-pity over losing the woman he'd thought he was going to marry and live with the rest of his life.

"Lola Dayton," he repeated, and smiled down at her. "Pretty name."

He moved to the door and switched off the light.

"I named our daughter Grace," she said from out of the darkness. "Do you remember telling me that you always loved that name?"

He turned in the doorway to look back at her, too choked up to speak for a moment. "It was my grandmother's name."

Lola thought she wouldn't be able to sleep. Her body felt leaden as she'd sunk under the covers. She could still feel the rough skin of Colt's thumb pad against her cheek and reached up to touch the spot. She hadn't been wrong about him. Not that first night. Not tonight.

She closed her eyes and felt herself careening off that mountain, running for her life, running for Grace's life. She was safe, she reminded herself. But Grace...

The sisters were taking good care of Grace, she told herself. Jonas wouldn't let anything happen to the baby. At least she prayed that he wouldn't hurt Grace to punish her even more.

The thought had her heart pounding until she realized the only power Jonas had over her was the baby. He wouldn't hurt Grace. He needed that child if he ever hoped to get what he wanted. And what he wanted was Lola. She'd seen it in his eyes. A voracious need that he thought only she could fill.

If he ever got his hands on her again... Well, she knew there would be no saving herself from him.

Colt kicked off his boots and lay down on the bed fully dressed. Sleep was out of the question. If half of what Lola had told him was true... Was it possible they'd made a baby that night? They hadn't used protection. He hadn't had anything. Nor had she. It wasn't like him to take a chance like that.

But there was something so wholesome, so innocent, so guileless...

Rolling to his side, he closed his eyes. The memory was almost painful. The sweet scent of her body as she lay with her back to him naked on the bed. The warmth of his palm as he slowly ran it from her side down into the saddle of her slim waist to the rise of her hip and her perfectly rounded buttocks. The catch of her breath as he pulled her into him and cupped one full breast. The tender moan from her lips as he rolled her over to look into those violet eyes.

Groaning, Colt shifted to his back again to stare up at the dark ceiling. That night he'd lost himself in that delectable woman. He'd buried all feelings for his former fiancée into her. He'd found salvation in her body, in her arms, in her tentative touch, in her soft, sweet kisses.

He closed his eyes, again remembering the feel of her in his arms as they'd danced in his hotel room. The slow sway, their bodies joined, their movements more sensuous than even the act of love. He'd given her a little piece of his heart that night and had not even realized it.

Swinging his legs over the bed, he knew he'd never get any rest until he checked on her. Earlier, he'd gotten the feeling that she wanted to run—rather than tell him what had brought her to his door. She hadn't wanted to involve him, wouldn't have if Jonas didn't have her baby.

That much he believed. But why hadn't she told him what she was running from the night they'd first met? Maybe he could have helped her.

He moved quietly down the hallway, half-afraid he would open the bedroom door only to find her gone and all of this like his dream about being back in Afghanistan.

After easing open the door, he waited for his eyes to adjust to the blackness in the room. Her blond hair lay like a fan across her pillow. Her peaceful face made her appear angelic. He found himself smiling as he stared down at the sleeping

Lola. He couldn't help wondering about their daughter. She would be three months old now. Did she resemble her mother? He hoped so.

The thought shook him because he realized how much he wanted to believe her. A daughter. He really could have a daughter? A baby with Lola? He shook his head. What were the chances that their union would bring a child into this world? And yet he and Lola had done more than make love that night. They'd connected in a way he and Julia never had.

The thought of Julia, though, made him recoil. Look how wrong he'd been about her. How wrong he'd been about his own mother. Could he trust his judgment when it came to women? Doubtful.

He stepped out of the room, closing the door softly behind him. Tomorrow, he told himself, he would know the truth. He'd get the sheriff to go with them up to the compound and settle this once and for all.

Colt walked out onto the porch to stare up at the starry sky. The air was crisp and cold, snow still capping the highest peaks around town. He knew this all could be true. Normally, he would never have had intercourse with a woman he didn't know without protection. But that night, he and Lola hadn't just had sex. They'd made love, two lost souls who'd given each other comfort in a world that had hurt them.

He'd been heartbroken over Julia and his friend Wyatt. Being in Lola's arms had saved him. If their lovemaking had resulted in a baby...a little girl...

Yes, what was he going to do? Besides go up to that compound and get the baby for Lola? He tried to imagine himself as a father to an infant. What a joke. He couldn't have been in a worse place in his life to take on a wife and a child.

He looked across the ranch. All his life he'd felt tied down to this land. That his father had tried to chain him to it still infuriated him—and at the same time made him feel guilty. His father had had such a connection to the land, one that Colt had never felt. He'd loved being a cowboy, but ranching was more about trying to make a living off the land. He'd watched his father struggle for years. Why would the old man think he would want this? Why hadn't his father sold the place, done something fun with the money before he'd died?

Instead, he'd left it all to Colt—lock, stock and barrel, making the place feel like a noose around his neck.

"It's yours," the probate attorney had said. "Do whatever you want with the ranch."

"You mean I can sell it?"

"After three months. That's all your father stipulated. That you live on the ranch for three months full-time, and then if you still don't want to ranch, you can liquidate all of your father's holdings."

Colt took a deep breath and let it out. "Sorry, Dad. If you think even three *years* on this land is going to change anything, you are dead wrong." He'd put in his three months and more waiting for an offer on the place.

When his leave was up, he was heading back to the Army and his real job. At least that had been the plan before he'd found Lola standing on his doorstep. Now he didn't know what to think. All he knew was that he had to fly. He didn't want to ranch. Once the place sold, there would be nothing holding him here.

He thought about Lola asleep back in the house. If this baby was his, he'd take responsibility, but he couldn't make any promises—not when he didn't even know where he would be living when he came home on leave.

Up by the road, he could see the for-sale sign by the gate into the ranch. With luck, the ranch would sell soon. In the meantime, he had to get Lola's baby back for her. His baby.

He pushed open the door and headed for his bedroom. Everything was going to work out. Once Lola understood what he needed to do, what he had to do…

He lay down on the bed fully clothed again and closed his

eyes, knowing there was no chance of sleep. But hours later, he woke with a start, surprised to find sunlight streaming in through the window. As he rose, still dressed, he worried that he would find Lola gone, just as she had been that morning in Billings.

The thought had his heart pounding as he padded down to the guest room. The door was partially ajar. What if none of it had been true? What if she'd realized he would see through all of it and had taken off?

He pressed his fingertips against the warm wood and pushed gently until he could see into the dim light of the room. She lay wrapped in one of his mother's quilts, her long blond hair splayed across the pillow. He eased the door closed, surprised how relieved he was. Maybe he wasn't a good judge of character when it came in women—Julia a case in point—but he wanted to believe Lola was different. It surprised him how *much* he wanted to believe it.

Lola woke to the smell of frying bacon. Her stomach growled. She sat up with a start, momentarily confused as to where she was. Not on the hard cot at the compound. Not locked in the claustrophobia-inducing tiny cabin with little heat. And certainly not waking to the wonderful scent of frying bacon at that awful prison.

Her memory of the events came back to her in a rush. What surprised her the most was that she'd slept. It had been so long that she hadn't been allowed to sleep through the night without being awakened as part of the brainwashing treatment. Or when the sisters had come to take her breast milk for the baby. She knew the only reason, other than exhaustion, she'd slept last night was knowing that she was safe. If Colt hadn't been there, though...

She refused to think about that as she got up. Her escape had cost her. She hurt all over. The scratches on her face and the sore muscles were painful. But far worse was the ache in her heart. She'd had to leave Grace behind.

Still dressed in the sweatshirt and sweatpants and barefoot, she followed the smell of frying bacon to the kitchen. Colt had music playing and was singing softly to a country music song. She had to smile, remembering how much he'd liked to dance.

That memory brought a rush of heat to her cheeks. She'd told herself that she hadn't been in her right mind that night, but seeing Colt again, she knew that was a lie. He'd liberated that woman from the darkness she'd been living in. He'd brought out a part of her she hadn't known existed.

He seemed to sense her in the doorway and turned, instantly smiling. "I hope you don't mind pancakes again. There was batter left over. I haven't been to the store. But I did find some bacon in the freezer."

"It's making my stomach growl. Is there anything I can do to help?"

"Nope, just bring your appetite." He motioned for her to take a seat. "I made a lot. I don't know about you, but I'm hungry."

She sat down at the table and watched him expertly flip pancakes and load up a plate with bacon.

As he set everything on the table and took a chair, he met her gaze. "How are you feeling?"

"Better. I slept well." For that he couldn't imagine how thankful she was. "On the compound, they would wake me every few hours to chant over me."

"Sounds like brainwashing," Colt said, his jaw tightening.

"Jonas calls it rehabilitation."

He pushed the bacon and pancakes toward her. "Eat while it's hot. We'll deal with everything else once we've eaten."

She looked into his handsome face, remembered being in his arms and felt a flood of guilt. If there was any other way of saving Grace, she wouldn't have involved him in this. But he had been involved since that night in Billings when she'd asked for his help and he hadn't hesitated. He just hadn't known then that what he was getting involved in was more than dangerous.

Once Jonas knew that Colt was the father of her baby... She shuddered at the thought of what she was about to do to this wonderful man.

CHAPTER FOUR

COLT PICKED AT HIS FOOD. He'd lied about being hungry. Just the smell of it turned his stomach. But he watched Lola wolf down hers as if she hadn't eaten in months. He suspected she hadn't eaten much. She was definitely thinner than she'd been that night in Billings a year ago.

But if anything, she was even more striking, with her pale skin and those incredible eyes. He was glad to see her hair down. It fell in a waterfall of gold down her back. He was reminded again how she'd looked the first time he'd seen her—and when he'd opened the door last night.

"I've been thinking about what we should do first," Colt said as he moved his food around the plate. "We need to start by getting you some clothing that fits," he said as if all they had to worry about was a shopping trip. "Then I think we should go by the sheriff's office."

"There is somewhere we have to go first," she said, looking up from cutting off a bite of pancake dripping with the red syrup. "I know you don't trust me. It's all right. I wouldn't trust me, either. But don't worry, you will." She smiled. She had a slight gap between her two front teeth that made her smile adorable. That and the innocence in her lightly freckled face had sucked him in from the first.

He'd been vulnerable that night. He'd been a broken man and Lola had been more than a temptation. The fact that she'd sworn he was saving her that night hadn't hurt, either.

He thought about the way she'd looked last night when he'd found her on his doorstep. She still had a scratch across one cheek and a cut under her right eye. It made her look like a tomboy.

"You have to admit, the story you told me last night was a little hard to believe."

"I know. That's why you have to let me prove it to you."

He eyed her suspiciously. "And how do you plan to do that?"

"Do you know a doctor in town who can examine me?"

His pulse jumped. "I thought you said—"

"Not for that. Or for my mental proficiency." Her gaze locked with his. "I need you to know that I had a baby three months ago. A doctor should be able to tell." He started to argue, but she stopped him. "This is where we need to start before we go to the sheriff."

He wanted to argue that this wasn't necessary, but they both knew it was. If a doctor said she'd never given birth and none of this was real, then it would be over. No harm done. Except the idea of him and Lola having a baby together would always linger, he realized.

"I used to go to a family doctor here in town. If he's still practicing…"

Dr. Hubert Gray was a large man with a drooping gray mustache and matching bushy eyebrows over piercing blue eyes.

Colt explained what they wanted.

Dr. Gray narrowed his gaze for a moment, taking them both in. "Well, then, why don't you step into the examination room with my nurse, Sara. She'll get you ready while I visit with Colt here."

The moment Lola and Sara left the room, the doctor leaned

back in his office chair. "Let me get this straight. You aren't even sure there is a child?"

"Lola says there is. Unfortunately, the baby isn't here."

The doctor nodded. "You realize this won't prove that the child is yours—just that she has given birth before."

Colt nodded. "I know this is unusual."

"Nothing surprises me. By the way, I was sorry to hear about your father. Damn cancer. Only thing that could stop him from ranching."

"Yes, he loved it."

"Tell me about flying helicopters. You know I have my pilot's license, but I've never flown a chopper."

Colt told him what he loved about it. "There is nothing like being able to hover in the air, being able to put it down in places—" he shook his head "—that seem impossible."

"I can tell that you love what you do, but did I hear you're ranching again?"

"Temporarily."

A buzz sounded and Dr. Gray rose. "This shouldn't take long. Sit tight."

True to his word, the doctor returned minutes later. Colt looked up expectantly. "Well?" he asked as Dr. Gray took his seat again behind his desk. Colt realized that his emotions were all over the place. He didn't know what he was hoping to hear.

Did he really want to believe that Lola had given birth to their child to have it stolen by some crazy cult leader? Wouldn't it be better if Lola had lied for whatever reason after becoming obsessed with him following their one-night stand?

"You wanted to know if she has recently given birth?" the doctor asked.

"Has she?" He held his breath, telling himself even if she had, it didn't mean that any of the rest of it was true.

"Since she gave me permission to provide you with this information, I'd say she gave birth in the past three months."

Just as she'd said. He glanced at the floor, not sure if he was relieved or not. He felt like a heel for having even a glimmer of doubt. But Lola was right. He'd had to know before he went any further with this. It wasn't like he really knew this woman. He'd simply shared one night of intimacy all those months ago.

There was a tap at the door. The nurse stuck her head in to say that the doctor had another patient waiting. Behind the nurse, he saw Lola in the hallway. She looked as if she'd been crying. He quickly rose. "Thank you, Doc," he said over his shoulder as he hurried to Lola, taking both of her hands in his. "I'm sorry. I'm so sorry. You didn't have to do this."

Her smile was sad but sweet as she shook her head. "I just got upset because Dr. Gray is so kind. I wish he'd delivered Grace instead of..." She shook her head. "Not that any of that matters now."

"It's time we went to the sheriff," he said as he led her out of the building. She seemed to hesitate, though, as they reached his pickup. "What?"

"Just that the sheriff isn't going to be able to do anything—and that's if he believes you."

"He'll believe me. I know him," he said as he opened the pickup door for her. "I went to school with his sister Lillie and her twin brother, Darby. Darby's a good friend. Both Lillie and Darby are new parents. As for the sheriff—Flint Cahill is as down-to-earth as anyone I know and I'm sure he's familiar with The Society of Lasting Serenity. Sheriff Cahill is also the only way we can get on church property—and off—without any trouble."

She still looked worried. "You don't know Jonas. He'll be furious that I went to the law. He'll also deny everything."

"We'll see about that." He went around the truck and slid behind the wheel. As he started the engine, he looked over at her and saw how anxious she was. "Lola, the man has taken our daughter, right?" She nodded. "Then I don't give a damn how furious he is, okay?"

"You don't know how he is."

"No, but I'm going to find out. Don't worry. I'm going to get to the bottom of this, one way or the other."

She looked scared, but said, "I trust you with my life. And Grace's."

Grace. Their child. He still couldn't imagine them having a baby together—let alone that some cult leader had her and refused to give her up to her own mother.

Common sense told him there had to be more to the story—and that's what worried him as he drove to the sheriff's department. Sheriff Cahill would sort it out, he told himself. As he'd said, he liked and trusted Flint. Going up to the compound with the levelheaded sheriff made the most sense.

Because if what Lola was telling him was true, they weren't leaving there without Grace.

Sheriff Flint Cahill was a nice-looking man with thick dark hair and gray eyes. He ushered them right into his office, offered them a chair and something to drink. They took chairs, but declined a beverage.

"So what is this about?" the sheriff asked after they were all seated, the office door closed behind them.

Colt could see that Lola liked the sheriff from the moment she met him. There was something about him that exuded confidence, as well as honesty and integrity. She told him everything she had Colt. When she finished, though, Colt couldn't tell from Flint's expression what he was thinking.

The sheriff looked at him, his gray eyes narrowing. "I'm assuming you wouldn't have brought Ms. Dayton here if you didn't believe her story."

"I know this is unusual." He glanced over at her. Her scrapes and scratches were healing, and she looked good in the clothes they'd bought her. Still, he saw that she kept rubbing her hand on her thighs as if not believing she was back in denim.

At the store, he'd wanted to buy her more clothing, but she'd insisted she didn't need more than a couple pairs of jeans, two shirts, several undergarments and hiking shoes and socks. She'd promised to pay him back once she could get to her own money. Jonas had taken her purse with her cash and credit cards. Her money was in a California bank account. Once she had Grace, she said she would see about getting money wired up to her so she could pay him back.

Colt wasn't about to take her money, but he hadn't argued. The one thing he'd learned quickly about Lola was that she didn't expect or want anything from him—except help getting her baby from Jonas. That, she'd said, would be more than enough since it could get them both killed.

At the time, he'd thought she was exaggerating. Now he wasn't so sure.

"I believe her," Colt told the sheriff. "What do you know about The Society of Lasting Serenity?"

"Just that they were California based but moved up here about five years ago. They keep to themselves. I believe their numbers have dropped some. Probably our Montana winters."

"You're having trouble believing that Jonas Emanuel would steal Lola's child," Colt said.

Flint sighed. "No offense but, yes, I am." He turned to Lola. "You say your only connection to the group was through your parents before their deaths and your return to the States?"

"Yes, they became involved after I left for college. I thought it was a passing phase, a sign of them not being able to accept their only child had left the nest."

"You never visited them at the California compound?" the sheriff asked.

"No, I got a teaching job right out of college in the Virgin Islands."

Flint frowned. "You didn't visit your parents before you left?"

Lola looked away. "By then we were…estranged. I didn't agree with some of the things they were being taught in what I felt was a fringe cult."

"So why would your parents promise you to Jonas Emanuel?" the sheriff asked.

She let out a bitter laugh. "To *save* me. My mother believed that I needed Jonas's teaching. Otherwise, I was doomed to live a wasted life chasing foolish dreams and, of course, ending up with the wrong man."

"They wanted you to marry Jonas." Flint frowned. "Isn't he a little old for you?"

"He's fifty-two. I'm thirty-two. So it's not unheard-of."

The sheriff looked over at Colt, who was going to be thirty-three soon. Young for a major in the Army, he knew.

"I doubt my parents took age into consideration," Lola said. "One of the teachings at the SLS is that everyone is ageless. My parents, like the other members, were brainwashed."

"So you went to the compound after you were notified that your parents had died," the sheriff said.

"I questioned them both dying especially since earlier I'd received a letter from my father saying he wanted out but was having a hard time convincing my mother to leave SLS," she said. "Also I wanted to have them buried together in California, next to my older sister, who was stillborn. My parents were both in their forties when they had me. By then, they didn't believe they would ever conceive again."

"So you had their bodies—"

"Jonas refused to release them. He said they would be buried as they had wished—on the side of the mountain at the compound. I went up there determined to find out how it was that they had died within hours of each other. I also wanted to make him understand that I would get a lawyer if I had to—or go to the authorities."

"That's when you learned that you'd been promised to him?" the sheriff asked.

"Yes, as ridiculous as it sounds. When I refused, I was held there against my will until I managed to get away. I'd stolen aboard a van driven by two of the sisters, as they call them. That's when I met Colt."

"Why didn't you go to the police then?" Flint asked.

"I planned to the next morning. I'd gone into the back of the hotel when I saw one of the sisters coming in the front. I ducked down a hallway and literally collided with Colt. I asked for his help and he sneaked me up to his room."

The sheriff looked at Colt. "And the two of you hit it off. She didn't tell you what she was running from?"

"No, but it was clear she was scared. I thought it was an old boyfriend."

Flint nodded and looked to Lola again. "You didn't trust him enough to ask for his help the next morning?"

"I didn't want to involve him. By then I knew what Jonas was capable of. This flock does whatever he tells them. The few who disobey are punished. One woman brought me extra food. I heard her being beaten the next morning by her own so-called sisters. When I had my daughter, they took her away almost at once. I could hear her crying, but I didn't get to see her again. The women would come in and take my breast milk, but they said she was now Jonas's child. He called her his angel. I knew I had only one choice. Escape and try to find Colt. I couldn't fight Jonas and his followers alone. And Jonas made it clear. The only way I could see my baby and be with her was if I married him and gave my life to The Society of Lasting Serenity."

Flint pushed back his chair and rose to his feet. "I think it's time I visited the compound and met this Jonas Emanuel."

CHAPTER FIVE

COLT FOLLOWED THE sheriff's SUV out of town toward the Judith Mountains. The mountains began just east of town and rose to the northeast for twenty miles. In most places they were only about ten miles wide with low peaks broken by stream drainages. But there were a number of peaks including the highest one, Judith Peak, at more than six thousand feet.

It was rugged country. Back in the 1950s the US Air Force had operated a radar station on top of the peak. The SLS had bought state land on an adjacent mountaintop in an isolated area with few roads in or out. Because it was considered a church, the SLS had rights that even the sheriff couldn't do anything about.

So Colt was nervous enough, but nothing compared to Lola. In the pickup seat next to him, he could feel her getting more agitated the closer they got to the SLS compound. He reached over to take her hand. It was ice-cold.

"It's going to be all right," he tried to assure her—and himself. If what she'd told him was true, then Jonas would have to hand over the baby. "Jonas will cooperate with a lawman."

She didn't look any more convinced than he felt. He'd dealt with religious fanatics for a while now and knew that nothing could stop them if they thought they were in the right.

"Jonas seems so nice, so truthful, so caring," she said. "He's fooled so many people. My parents weren't stupid. He caught them in his web with his talk of a better world." She shook her head. "But he is pure evil. I hate to even think what he might have done to my parents."

"You really think he killed them."

"Or convinced my mother to kill herself and my father."

Colt knew that wouldn't be a first when it came to cult mania.

"Clearly the sheriff wasn't called when they died. Jonas runs SLS like it's his own private country. He told me that his religious philosophy requires the bodies to be untouched and put into the ground quickly. Apparently in Montana, a religious group can bury a body on their property without embalming if it is done within so many hours."

The road climbed higher up the mountain. Ahead, the sheriff slowed. Colt could see that an iron gate blocked them from going any farther. Flint stopped, put down his window and pushed a button on what appeared to be an intercom next to the gate. Colt whirred down his window. He heard a tinny-sounding voice tell him that someone would be right down to let them in.

A few minutes later, an older man drove up in a Jeep. He spoke for a few moments with the sheriff before opening the gate. As Colt drove through, he felt the man's steely gaze on him. Clearly the SLS didn't like visitors. The man who'd opened the gate was wearing a gun under his jacket. Colt had caught sight of the butt end of it when the man got out of his rig to open the gate.

As they passed, he noticed something else interesting. The man recognized Lola. Just the sight of her made the man nervous.

Lola felt her body begin to vibrate inside. She thought she might throw up. The memories of being imprisoned here for so long made her itch. She fought the need to claw her skin, remembering the horrible feel of the cheap cloth dresses she was forced to wear, the taste of the tea the sisters forced down her throat, the horrible chanting that nearly drove her insane. That wasn't all they'd forced on her once they'd quit coming for her breast milk. There'd been the pills that Sister Rebecca had forced down her throat.

She felt a shiver and hugged herself against the memories, telling herself she was safe with Colt and the sheriff. But the closer they got to the compound, the more plagued she was with fear. She doubted either Colt or the sheriff knew who they were dealing with. Jonas had gotten this far in life by fooling people. He was an expert at it. At the thought of what lies he would tell, her blood ran cold even though the pickup cab felt unbearably hot.

"Are you all right?" Colt asked, sounding worried as he glanced over at her.

She nodded and felt a bead of perspiration run down between her shoulder blades. She wanted to scratch her arm, feeling as if something was crawling across it, but feared once she started she wouldn't be able to stop.

Just driving up here brought everything back, as if all the crazy they'd been feeding her might finally sink in and she'd be a zombie like the other "sisters." Isn't that what Jonas had hoped? Wasn't that why he was just waiting for her return? He knew she'd be back for Grace. She couldn't bear to think what he had planned for her.

By the time they reached the headquarters and main building of the SLS, there was a welcome group waiting for them. Lola recognized Sister Rebecca, the woman Jonas got to do most of his dirty work. Sister Amelia was there, as well, but she kept her head down as if unable to look at her.

Lola felt bad that she'd gotten the woman in trouble. She could still hear Amelia's cries from the beating she'd received for giving her extra food. She could well imagine what had happened to the guards after she'd escaped. Jonas would know that she hadn't been taking her pills with the tea. Sister Amelia would be blamed, but there had been nothing Lola could do about that.

Flint parked his patrol SUV in front of the main building. Colt parked next to him. Lola felt her body refuse to move as Colt opened his door. She stared at the two women standing like sentinels in front of them and fought to take her next breath.

"Would you feel better staying out here in the truck?" Colt asked.

She wiped perspiration from her lip with the back of her hand. How could she possibly explain what it was like being back here, knowing what they had done to her, what they might do again if Colt didn't believe her and help her?

Terrified of facing Jonas again, she thought of her baby girl and reached for her door handle.

Colt wondered if bringing Lola back here wasn't a mistake. She looked terrified one moment and like a sleepwalker the next. What had they done to her? He couldn't even imagine, given what she'd told him about her treatment. They'd taken her baby, kept her locked up, hadn't let her sleep. He worried that was just the tip of the iceberg, though.

One of the two women, who were dressed in long simple white sheaths with their hair in braided buns, stepped forward to greet them.

"I'm Sister Rebecca. How may we help you?" Appearing to be the older of the two, the woman's face had a blankness to it that some might have taken for serenity. But there was something else in the eyes. A wariness. A hardness.

"We're here to see Jonas Emanuel," the sheriff said.

"Let me see if he's available," she said, and turned to go back inside.

Colt started to say something about Jonas making himself available, but Flint stopped him. "Let's keep this as civilized as we can—at least to start."

The second woman stood at the foot of the porch steps, her fingers entwined and her face down, clearly standing guard.

A few moments later, Sister Rebecca came out again. "Brother Emanuel will see you now." She motioned them up the porch steps as the other woman drifted off toward a building in the pines where some women were washing clothes and hanging them on a string of clotheslines.

"Seems awfully cold to be hanging wash outside this time of year," Colt commented. Spring in Montana often meant the temperature never rose over forty in the mountains.

Sister Rebecca smiled as if amused. "We believe in hard work. It toughens a person up so a little cold weather doesn't bother us."

He thought about saying something about how she wasn't the one hanging clothes today in the cool weather on the mountaintop, but he followed the sheriff's lead and kept his mouth shut.

As Sister Rebecca led them toward the back of the huge building, Colt noticed the layout. In this communal living part of the structure, straight-backed wooden chairs were lined up like soldiers at long wooden tables. Behind the dining area, he could hear kitchen workers and the banging of pots and pans. An aroma arose that reminded him of school cafeterias.

What struck him was the lack of conversation coming from the kitchen, let alone any music. There was a utilitarian feeling about the building and everything in it—the workers included. They could have been robots for the lack of liveliness in the place.

Sister Rebecca tapped at a large wooden door. A cheerful voice on the other side said, "Come in." She opened the door and stood back to let them enter a room that was warm and cozy compared to the other part of the building.

A sandy-haired man, who Colt knew was fifty-two, had been sitting behind a large oak desk. But now he pushed back his office chair and rose, surprising Colt by not just his size, but how fit he was. He had boyish good looks, lively pale blue eyes and a wide, straight-toothed smile. He looked much younger than his age.

The leader came around his desk to shake hands with the sheriff and Colt. "Jonas Emanuel," he said. "Welcome." His gaze slid to Lola. When he spoke her name it was with obvious affection. "Lola," Jonas said, looking pained to see her scratched face before returning his gaze to Colt and the sheriff.

"We need to ask you a few questions," Sheriff Cahill said, introducing himself and Colt. "You already know Ms. Dayton."

"Please have a seat," Jonas said graciously, offering them one of the chairs circled around the warm blaze going in the rock fireplace to one side of the office area. Colt thought again of the women hanging wet clothes outside. "Can I get you anything to drink?"

They all declined. Jonas took a chair so he was facing them and crossed his legs to hold one knee in his hands. Colt noticed that he was limping before he sat down.

"How long have you known Ms. Dayton?" Flint asked.

"Her parents were founding members. Lola's been a member for the past couple of years," Jonas said.

"That's not true," she cried. "You know I'm not a member, would never be a member."

Colt could see that she was even more agitated than she'd been in the truck on the way up. She sat on the edge of her chair and looked ready to run again. "Just give me my baby," she said, her voice breaking. "I want to see my baby." She turned in her chair. Sister Rebecca stood at the door, fingers entwined, head down, standing sentry. "My baby. Tell her to get my baby."

Colt reached over and took her hand. Jonas noticed but said nothing.

"As you can see, Ms. Dayton is quite upset. She claims that you are holding her child here on the property," the sheriff said.

Jonas nodded without looking at Lola. "Perhaps we should speak in private. Lola? Why don't you go with Sister Rebecca? She can make you some tea."

"I don't want any of your so-called tea," Lola snapped. "I want my child."

"It's all right," Flint said. "Go ahead and leave with her. We need to talk to Jonas. We won't be long."

Lola looked as if she might argue, but when her gaze fell on Colt, he nodded, indicating that she should leave. "I'll be right here if you need me." Again he could feel Jonas's gaze on him.

After Sister Rebecca left with Lola, the leader sighed deeply. "I'm afraid Lola is a very troubled woman. I'm not sure what she's told you—"

"That you're keeping her baby from her," Colt said.

He nodded sadly. "Lola came to us after her parents died. She'd lost her teaching job, been fired. That loss and the loss of her parents... We tried to help her since she had no one else. I'm sure she's told you that her parents were important members of our community here. On her mother's death bed, she made me promise that I would look after Lola."

"She didn't promise Lola to you as your wife?" Colt asked, and got a disapproving look from the sheriff.

"Of course not." Jonas looked shocked by the accusation. "I had hoped Lola would stay with us. Her parents took so much peace in living among us, but Lola left."

"I understand she ran away some months ago," Flint said.

"A year ago," Colt added.

Again Jonas looked surprised. "Is that what she told you?" He shook his head. "I foolishly suggested that maybe time away from the compound would be good for her. Several of the sisters were making a trip to Billings for supplies. I talked Lola into going along. Once there, though, she apparently became turned around while shopping and got lost. In her state of mind, that was very traumatic. Fortunately, the sisters found her, but not until the next morning. She was confused and hysterical. They brought her back here where we nursed her back to health and discovered that while she'd been lost in Billings, she'd been assaulted."

Colt started to object, but the sheriff cut him off. "She was pregnant? Did she say who the father was?"

Jonas shook his head. "She didn't seem to know." The man looked right at Colt, his blue eyes giving nothing away.

"Where is the baby now?" Flint asked.

"I'm afraid the infant was stillborn. A little boy. Which made it all the more traumatic and heartbreaking for her since we all knew that she had her heart set on having a baby girl. I'm not sure if you know this, but her mother had a daughter before Lola who was stillborn. I'm sure that could have played a part in what happened. When Lola was told that her own child had been stillborn, she had a complete breakdown and became convinced that we had stolen her daughter."

"Then you won't mind if we have a look around," the sheriff said.

"Not at all." He rose to his feet, and the sheriff and Colt followed. "I'm so glad Lola's been found. We've been taking care of her since her breakdown. Unfortunately, the other night she overpowered one of her sisters and, hysterical again, took off running into the woods. We looked for her for hours. I was going to call your office if we didn't hear from her by this afternoon. When she left, she forgot her pills. I was afraid she'd have another psychotic event with no one there to help her."

"Don't you mean when Lola *escaped* here?" Colt asked.

Jonas shook his head as if trying to be patient. "Escaped?" He chuckled. "Do you see razor wire fences around the compound? Why would she need to escape? We believe in free will here at Serenity. Lola can come and go as she pleases. She knows that. But when she's in one of her states…"

"What kind of medication is she on?" the sheriff asked.

"I have it right here," Jonas reached into his pocket. "I had Sister Rebecca bring it to me when I heard that you were at the gate. I was so glad that she had come back for it. I believe Dr. Reese said it's what they give patients with schizophrenia. I suppose she didn't mention to you that she'd been taking the medication. It helps with the anxiety attacks, as well as the hallucinations."

"Dr. Reese?" Flint asked.

"Ben Reese. He's our local physician, one of the best in the country and one of our members," Jonas said.

"I'd like to see where the baby was buried," Colt said.

"Of course. But let's start with the tour the sheriff requested."

Colt memorized the layout of the buildings as Jonas led them from building to building. Everywhere they went, there were people working, both men and women, but definitely there were more women on the compound than men. He saw no women with babies as most of the women were older.

"Our cemetery is just down here," Jonas said. Colt followed Jonas and the sheriff down a narrow dirt path that wound through the trees to open in a meadow. Wooden crosses marked the few graves, the names of the deceased printed on metal plaques.

He spotted a relatively fresh grave and felt his heart drop. It was a small plot of dark earth. What if Jonas was telling the truth? What if Lola had had a son? *His* son? And the infant was buried under that cold ground?

"It is always so difficult to lose a child," Jonas was saying. "We buried him next to Lola's parents. We thought that would give her comfort. If not now, later when she's...better. We're waiting for her to name him before we put up the cross."

"I think I've seen enough," Sheriff Cahill said, and looked at Colt.

Colt didn't know what to think. On the surface, it all seemed so...reasonable.

"Sister Rebecca took Lola to the kitchen," Jonas said. "Lunch will be ready soon. I believe we're having a nice vegetable soup today. You're welcome to join us. Some of the sisters are better cooks than others. I can attest that the ones cooking today are our best."

"Thank you, but I need to get back to Gilt Edge," Flint said. "What about you, Colt?"

He knew the sheriff wasn't asking just about lunch or returning to town. "I'll see what Lola wants to do," he said, after taking a last look at the small unmarked grave before heading back toward the main building.

"If Lola is determined not to stay with us, I just hope she'll get the help she needs," Colt heard Jonas tell the sheriff. "I'm worried about her, especially after your visit. Clearly she isn't herself."

Lola shoved away the cup of tea Sister Rebecca had tried to get her to drink. She'd seen Colt and the sheriff go out to search the complex with Jonas. "I know you hid her the moment the sheriff punched the intercom at the gate. Please..." Her voice broke. "I just want to see her so I know she's all right."

Sister Rebecca reached over to pat her hand—and shove the tea closer with her other hand.

Lola jerked her hand back. "You can't keep her. She's mine." Tears burned her eyes. "Keeping a baby from her mother..."

"You aren't taking your medication, are you? It makes you like this. You really should take it so you're more calm."

"Brain-dead, you mean. Half-comatose, so I'm easy to manipulate. If you keep me drugged up, I won't cause any trouble, right?"

"You wouldn't have left here if you'd been taking your medication." Sister Rebecca shook her head. "You know we were only trying to help you. I should have been the one giving you your medication instead of Sister Amelia. She let you get away with not taking it and look what's happened to you, you poor dear."

Lola scoffed. "As if you care. And Sister Amelia didn't know anything about what I was doing," she said quickly, fearing that the next beating Amelia got could kill her. "I was hiding them under my tongue until she turned away."

The woman nodded. "Well, should you end up staying here, we won't let that happen again, will we."

"I'm not staying here."

Sister Rebecca said nothing as the front door opened and Colt came in. Through the open doorway, Lola could see Jonas and the sheriff standing out by the patrol SUV. She could tell that Jonas had convinced the sheriff that she was crazy.

Standing up too quickly, Lola knocked over her chair. It clattered to the floor. Dizzy, she had to hang on to the table for a moment. When the light-headedness passed and she could let go, she started for the door. But not before she realized Colt had seen her having trouble standing.

She swept past him, determined not to let the sheriff leave. Her baby was hidden somewhere in the complex. Jonas had had one of his followers hide her. The sheriff had to find her. Lola had to convince him—

At the sound of a baby crying, she stumbled to an abrupt stop. "Do you hear that?" she called down to the sheriff from the top of the porch steps. "It's my baby crying." He looked up in surprise. So did Jonas. Both seemed to stop to listen.

For a moment, Lola thought that she had imagined it. Fear curdled her stomach. She felt Colt's hand on her shoulder as he reached for her. She could see that they believed Jonas. Her eyes filled with tears of frustration and pain.

And then she heard it again. A baby began to squall loudly. The sound was coming from the laundry. She shrugged off Colt's hand and ran down the steps. Jonas reached for her, but she managed to sweep past him. Grace. It was her baby crying for her. She knew that cry. She'd heard it in the middle of the night when the sisters had come for her breast milk. Somehow Grace had known she was here.

"Lola, don't," Jonas called after her. "Sister Rebecca, help Lola. She's going to hurt herself."

She could hear running footsteps behind her, but she was almost to the laundry-room door. Sister Rebecca had set off an alarm. As Lola burst into the room, a half dozen women were already looking in her direction. Lola paid them no mind. She ran toward the woman holding the baby.

Inside this room with the washers and dryers going, though she could barely hear the baby crying, all Lola could think about was getting to the woman before they hid Grace away again. Reaching the woman, she heard the infant let out a fresh squall as if the mother had pinched the poor thing.

Lola grabbed for the baby, but the woman swung around so all she got was a handful of dress cloth from the woman's shoulder.

"Lola, stop." It was the sheriff's voice as he stepped between her and the woman with the child. "May I see your baby?" he said to the woman.

CHAPTER SIX

COLT WATCHED THE woman with the infant look at Jonas standing in the doorway. The leader nodded that she should let the sheriff look. Colt held his breath as the woman turned so they could see the baby she held. The infant had stopped crying and now looked at them with big blue eyes fringed with tear-jeweled lashes.

"Grace?" Lola whispered as she tried to see the baby.

"May I?" the sheriff asked, and held out his arms.

After getting Jonas's permission, the woman released the baby to Flint. He carefully pulled back the knitted blanket the infant was wrapped in. Colt found himself holding his breath.

The sheriff peeked under the gown the baby wore. Colt knew he was looking for the small heart-shaped birthmark that Lola had told him about. He checked under the baby's diaper. His shoulders fell a little as he looked up at Lola and shook his head. "It's a little boy."

"No," Lola cried. "I heard my baby. This isn't the baby I heard crying. It can't be. Sister Rebecca pulled the alarm. She warned them to hide my baby." She looked from the sheriff to Colt and back again before bursting into tears.

Colt stepped to her and pulled her into his arms. She cried against his chest as he looked past her to the sheriff. He'd watched the whole thing play out, holding his breath. The baby the sheriff had taken from the woman was adorable and about the right age. Was it possible Lola was wrong about the sex of the infant she'd given birth to? Maybe the baby hadn't died.

But Lola had been so sure it was a little girl. She'd convinced him. And there was the tiny heart birthmark that Lola had seen on their daughter. But what if she was wrong and Jonas was telling the truth about all of it?

Now he felt sick. He thought of the small grave next to Lola's parents'. He felt such a sense of loss that it made him ache inside. He pulled Lola tighter to him, feeling her heart breaking along with his own.

As the sheriff spoke again with Jonas, Colt led Lola out of the laundry and down the path toward his pickup.

"I heard her," she said between sobs. "The first baby I heard. It was Grace. I know her cry. A mother knows her baby's cry. Sister Rebecca pulled the alarm to warn them so they could hide her again." She began to cry again as he led her to the truck and opened the passenger-side door for her. "Please, Colt, we can't leave without our baby."

He tried to think of what to say, but his throat had closed with all the emotions he was feeling, an incredible sense of loss and regret. It broke his heart to see Lola like this.

Lola met his gaze with a look that felt like an arrow to his chest before she climbed into the pickup. As he closed the passenger-side door, the sheriff walked over. "You all right?" Flint asked.

All Colt could do was nod. He wasn't sure he would ever be all right.

"I think we're done here," the sheriff said. "If you want to take it further..."

He shook his head. "Thanks for your help," he managed to get out before walking around to the driver's side of his pickup. As he slid behind the wheel, he saw that Lola had dried her tears and was now sitting ramrod straight in her seat with that same look of surrender that tore at him.

He started the engine, unable to look at her.

"You don't believe me. You believe…" She stopped and he looked over at her. She was staring straight ahead. He followed her gaze to where Jonas was standing on the porch of the main building. There was both sympathy and pity in the man's gaze. "He's lying." But Lola said it with little conviction as Colt started the pickup and headed off the compound.

Lola closed her eyes and leaned back against the pickup as they headed down the mountain road. What had she expected? That Jonas would just hand over Grace? She'd been such a fool. Worse, she feared that they'd made things worse for Grace—not to mention the way Colt had looked at her. Leaving them alone with Jonas had been the wrong thing to do. She knew what that man was like. Of course the sheriff would believe anything the leader told him. But Colt?

"What did Jonas tell you?" She had to ask as she squeezed her eyes shut tighter, unable to look at him. "That I'm crazy?"

"He said your baby died. That it was a little boy. He showed me the grave."

She let out a muffled cry and opened her eyes. Staring straight ahead at the narrow dirt road that wound down the mountain, she said, "Is that what convinced you I was lying?"

"Why didn't you tell me you were on prescription medication?" Colt asked.

She let out a bark of a laugh. "Of course, my *medication*. What did he tell you it was for?"

"He hinted it was for schizophrenia and that after your breakdown—"

"Right—my breakdown. What else?"

He glanced over at her. "He said you were fired from your teaching job."

Tears blurred her eyes. She bit her lower lip and drew blood.

"That at least is true. I resisted the advances of the school princi-
pal. When some materials in my classroom went missing, I was
fired. Three days later, I heard that my parents had died. Perfect
timing," she said sarcastically. "I'm not a thief. I wouldn't give
in, so she did what she said she would, she fired me, claiming I
stole the materials. It was my word against hers—even though it
wasn't the first time something like that had happened involving her. I had planned to fight it once I took care of getting my
parents remains returned to the California cemetery. So what
else did Jonas tell you about me?"

"That you're a troubled young woman."

"I am that," she agreed. "Given everything that has been
done to me, I think that is understandable." Ahead she could
see Brother Elmer waiting at the gate for them. Elmer was her
father's age. When she'd first arrived at the compound, she'd
asked him what had happened to her parents and Elmer had
been too terrified to talk to her. She'd only had that one opportunity. Since then Elmer had kept his distance—just like the
rest of them.

"Stop up here, please," Lola said, even though the gate was
standing open.

Colt said nothing and did as she asked.

She put down the truck window as Colt pulled alongside the
man. Elmer met her gaze for a moment before he dropped his
head and stared at his feet. "Elmer, you know I'm not crazy.
Help me, please," she pleaded. "You were my father's friend.
Tell this man the truth about what really goes on back there in
the compound."

Elmer continued to focus on the ground.

"Okay, just tell me this," she said, her voice cracking with
emotion. "Is Grace all right? Are they taking good care of her?"
She didn't expect an answer. She knew the cost of going against
Jonas. Everyone did. If she was right and Jonas had had her
parents killed...

Elmer raised his head slowly. As he did, he grabbed hold of

the side of the truck, curling his fingers over the open window frame. His fingers brushed her arm. His gaze rose to meet hers. He gave one quick nod and removed his hands.

"You should move on now so I can close this gate, Sister Lola."

Colt blinked, telling himself he hadn't just seen that. His heart beat like a war drum. He swore under his breath. He'd seen the man's short, quick nod. He'd seen the compassion in Elmer's eyes.

Jonas Emanuel was a liar.

Colt wasn't sure who he was more angry with, Jonas or himself. He'd bought into the man's bull. He'd *believed* him. But the man had been damned convincing. The grave. The pills. The crying baby that wasn't Grace.

Shifting the pickup into gear, he felt as if he'd been punched in the gut numerous times. He kept seeing that tiny grave, kept imagining his son, their son, lying in a homemade coffin under it—just as he kept seeing Lola sobbing hysterically in his arms after hearing what she thought was her baby crying.

"Lola."

"Please, just leave me alone," she said as she closed her window and tucked herself into the corner of the pickup seat as he pulled away, the gate closing behind him. When he looked over at her a few miles down the road, he saw that anger and frustration had given way to emotional exhaustion. With the sun streaming in the window, she'd fallen asleep.

Colt was thankful for the time alone. He replayed everything Lola had said, along with what Jonas had told him. He hadn't known what to believe because the man was that persuasive. Jonas had convinced the sheriff—and Flint Cahill was a shrewd lawman.

But as he looked over at the woman sleeping in his pickup, he felt his heart ache in ways he'd never experienced before. He would slay dragons for this woman. He wanted to turn around and go back and...

He couldn't let his emotions get the best of him. He never had before. But this woman had drawn him from the moment he'd met her. He thought about the fear he'd seen in her eyes that first night. There'd been no confusion, though. If anything, they'd both wanted to escape from the world that night and lose themselves in each other. And they had. He remembered her naked in his arms and felt a pull stronger than gravity.

Would he have believed her if she'd told him on that first night what was going on? Probably not. Look how easily he'd let Jonas fool him. Colt was still furious with himself. He would never again question anything she told him.

Glancing in the rearview mirror, he wasn't surprised to see that they were being followed. Everything she'd told him had been true.

So where was the child he and Lola had conceived? He couldn't bear the thought of Grace being in Jonas's hands. But he also knew that they couldn't go back there until they had a plan.

As he slowed on the outskirts of Gilt Edge, Lola stirred. She shot him a glance as she sat up.

"Before we go back to the ranch, I thought we'd get something to eat," he said, keeping his eye on the large dark SUV a couple of car lengths behind them.

"There is no reason to take me back to the ranch. You can just pull over anywhere and let me out."

"I'm not going to do that."

"I can understand why you don't want to help me, but I'm not leaving town until—"

"You get Grace back."

She stared at him. "Are you mocking me?"

"Not at all," he said, and looked over at her. "I'm sorry. I should have believed you. But I do now."

Tears welled in her eyes and spilled down her cheeks. "You believe me about Grace?"

"I do. I saw that armed guard who let us through the gate. I saw him nod when you asked him about Grace."

She wiped at her tears. "Is that what changed your mind?"

"That and a lot of other things, once I had time to think about it. That first night, you were scared and running from something, but you weren't confused. Nor do I think you were confused the next morning. You checked my wallet to see who I was. You considered taking the four hundred dollars in it, but decided not to. Those were not the actions of a troubled, mentally unstable woman. Also, we're being followed."

Lola glanced in her side mirror. "How long has that vehicle been back there?"

"Since we left the compound."

She seemed to consider that. "Why follow us? If they wanted to know where you lived…"

"I think they are more interested in you than me, but I guess we'll find out soon enough. That's the other thing that made me believe you once I was away from Jonas's hocus-pocus disappearing-baby act. I saw guards armed with concealed weapons around the perimeter of the compound. While there might not be any razor wire and a high fence, that place is secure as Fort Knox."

"So how are we going to find Grace and get her out of there?"

"I don't know. I haven't worked that out yet."

She looked at him as if afraid of this change in his attitude. "The sheriff believes Jonas."

"I don't blame Flint. Jonas is quite convincing. He certainly had me going."

Lola let out a bitter laugh. "How do you think he got so many people to follow him to Montana? To give him all their money, to convince them that to find peace, they needed to give up everything—especially their minds and free will."

"Why wasn't he able to brainwash you?" he asked as he glanced in the rearview mirror. Their tail was still back there.

"I don't know. The meditation, the chanting, the affirmations on the path to peace and happiness? I blocked them out, thinking about anything else. Also, I didn't buy into any of it. I was surprised my father did. It's one reason I didn't see them for so many years. My father wrote me and I spoke with my mother some on the phone, but there was no way I was going to visit them on the compound and they never left except to move to Montana with SLS."

"How was it your father was one of the founding members if it wasn't like him to buy into Jonas's propaganda?"

"My father would have done anything to make my mother happy. That's why he didn't leave after he quit believing in Jonas. He wouldn't have left her there alone. I'm sure he finally saw what my mother couldn't. That Jonas was a fraud. I feel terrible for those lost years."

"The man at the gate…"

"Elmer? He and my father were friends. It's possible that, like my father, he has doubts about SLS and Jonas. Also, not everyone is easily brainwashed into believing everything Jonas says. They might believe he has a right to my child because he says so. But that doesn't mean some aren't sympathetic to a mother losing her baby, our baby, to Jonas."

"I still don't understand how Jonas thinks he can get away with this."

"Because he has."

He glanced over at her, seeing that she was right. Jonas did rule that compound like it was his own country, and because his society was considered a church, he was protected.

"He has Grace," she said. "He knows I can't live without her. Except he's wrong if he thinks I'll let him keep my child, let alone that I would ever be his wife."

Colt glanced over at her. "So he knows we'll be back."

CHAPTER SEVEN

LOLA LOOKED OUT the side window as the road skirted Gilt Edge. Her heart beat so loudly that she thought for sure Colt would be able to hear it. Tears stung her eyes, but this time they were tears of relief.

Colt believed her.

The liberation made her weak. She'd seen his face earlier in the laundry when the baby had turned out not to be hers. She'd seen the heart-wrenching sympathy in his gaze, as well as the pain. He'd been so sure at the moment that she was everything Jonas had told him. A mentally unstable woman who couldn't accept the death of the baby she'd carried for nine months. *His* baby.

But Colt had seen the truth. He'd seen Elmer's slight nod, and when he looked at everything, he knew she was telling the truth.

She wiped at her tears, determined not to give in to the need to cry her heart out. They still didn't have Grace. Her stomach ached with a need to hold her baby. Jonas had Grace and that alone terrified her. Would he hurt the baby to get back at her?

No. He'd fooled the sheriff. He would feel safe and superior.

He would simply wait, knowing, as Colt said, that they'd be back. Or at least she would. Jonas thought he'd fooled Colt, too.

She tried to assure herself that Jonas wouldn't hurt Grace just to spite her. The baby was his only hope of getting Lola back to the compound. She'd looked into Jonas's eyes as they'd left. He hadn't given up on her being his wife. He would need Grace if he had any hope of making that happen.

At least that must be his thinking, she told herself. It would be a cold day in hell before she would ever succumb to the man. And only then so she could get close enough to kill him.

"Do you think Jonas knows I'm Grace's father?" Colt asked, dragging her out of her dark thoughts. "He looked me right in the eye and told me that you swore you didn't know who the father was."

"I did. I was afraid he'd come after you. Or send some of his men to hurt you—if not kill you. He was quite upset to realize I was pregnant. I told him I didn't know your name. You were just someone who'd helped me."

"Helped himself to you. Isn't that what Jonas thought?"

She shrugged. "He was so angry with me. I'm not sure when he decided he wanted my baby. Our baby."

"Well, he can't have her."

"We will get her back, won't we?"

He reached over and took her hand.

"I mean, if you dig up the grave and prove that—"

"Lola, that would take time and be very iffy. First off, that is probably what Jonas is expecting us to do. Second, even if we had proof that your baby didn't die, I'm not sure we could get a judge to send up an army to search the place for Grace."

"Then what do we do?" She felt close to tears again.

"The problem is that it is hard for the authorities to get involved in these types of pseudo-religious groups, especially when, according to Jonas, you're a member—and so were your parents. It's your word against Jonas's. So I'm afraid we're on our own. But that's not a bad thing." He smiled at her. "I'll do everything in my power and then some to bring Grace home to you."

She smiled and squeezed his hand, knowing that she could depend on Colt.

Colt pulled up in front of the Stagecoach Saloon on the outskirts of Gilt Edge. The large dark SUV that had been following them drove on past. He tried to see the driver, but the windows were tinted too dark. The license plate was covered with mud, no accident either, he figured.

But it didn't matter. He knew exactly where it had come from.

"The sheriff's brother and sister own this place," Colt said as he parked and turned off the engine. "They serve some of the best food in the area. I thought we'd have something to eat and talk. It shouldn't be that busy this time of the day."

Lola's stomach growled in answer, making him smile. "I thought I would never eat after Grace was taken from me. But soon I realized that I needed my strength if I had any hope of getting her back. Not that I was given much food on the compound."

They got out, Lola slowing to admire the place. "I love this stone building."

"It was one of the original stagecoach stops along here. Lillie Cahill bought it with her brother Darby, to preserve it." He pushed open the door and Lola stepped in.

"Something smells wonderful," she whispered to Colt as they made their way to an out-of-the-way table by the window. All this time eating nothing but the swill that had come out of the compound kitchen had left her ravenous.

There were a few regulars at the bar but other than that, the place was empty. A man who resembled the sheriff came over to take their orders. He had Flint's dark hair and gray eyes and was equally good-looking. "Major McCloud," the young man said, grinning at Colt.

"Just Colt, thank you."

"I heard you were back. Welcome home. Again, so sorry about your father."

"Thanks, Darby." All of the Cahills had been at the funeral. Colt's father would have liked that. He'd always respected their father, Ely Cahill, even though a lot of people in this town considered him a nut. "This is my friend Lola."

Darby turned to Lola and said, "Nice to meet you."

"Congrats on the marriage and fatherhood. How's your family?" Colt asked, since that's what small-town people did. Everyone knew everyone else. He was sure Darby had heard about Julia and Wyatt since they'd all gone to school together.

"Fine. Lillie's married and now has a son, TC. She married Trask Beaumont. If you're sticking around for a while, you'll have to meet Mariah and my son, Daniel. Don't know if Flint mentioned it, but his wife, Maggie... Yep. Expecting."

Colt laughed. "Must be somethin' in the water. Which reminds me. Ely still kickin'?"

Darby laughed. "Hasn't changed a bit. Still spends most of his time up in the mountains when he's not hanging around the missile silo." He sighed. "So what can I get you?"

"What's cooking today? Something smells delicious."

"Our cook, Billie Dee, whipped up one of her down-home Texas recipes. Today it's shrimp gumbo. Gotta warn ya, she's determined to add some spice in our lives and convert us Montanans."

"I'll have that," Lola and Colt said in unison, making Darby chuckle.

"Two coming up. What can I get you to drink?"

Colt looked at Lola. "Two colas?" She nodded and Darby went off to place their order.

"What was that about... Ely?"

"The Cahill patriarch. Famous in these parts because back in 1967, he swore he was abducted by aliens next to the missile silo on their ranch." Colt explained how the government had asked for two-acre plots around the area for defense back in the 1950s. "You might have seen that metal fence out in one of my pastures? There might be a live missile in it. No one but the government knows for sure."

"The missile silos on your property would be scary enough, but aliens?"

He laughed and nodded. "What makes Ely's story interesting to me is that night in 1967 the Air Force detected a flying-saucer type aircraft in the area. Lots of people saw it, including my father."

"So it's possible Ely is telling he truth as he knows it," she said, wide-eyed.

He shrugged. "I guess we'll never know for certain, but Ely swears it's true."

Darby brought their colas, and they sat in companionable silence for a few minutes.

"It feels so strange to be in a place like this," Lola said. "It's so…normal. I haven't had normal in way too long."

"How long had you been held at the compound before I met you in Billings?"

"Almost a month. The first week or so I was trying to get my parents' remains released to a mortuary in Gilt Edge. Jonas had been kind enough to offer me a place to stay until I could make arrangements. I didn't realize that he was lying to me until I tried to leave and realized there were armed guards keeping me there. At least I wasn't locked up in a cabin that time. I had the run of the place, or I would never have gotten away in the back of the van when the sisters drove to Billings."

And Colt would never have met her. They would never have made love and conceived Grace, Colt thought. Funny how things worked out.

Darby put some background music on the jukebox. The sun coming in the window gave the place a golden glow. Colt had been here a few times when he was home on leave. He was happy for Lillie and Darby for making a go of the place.

"How did you manage to get away this last time?" he asked.

"I'd been hiding my pills under my tongue until Sister Amelia left my cabin. I would spit them out and poke them into a hole I'd found in the cabin wall. The night I escaped, I pretended to be sick and managed to distract Sister Rebecca. When she wasn't looking, I hid the fork that was on my tray. She didn't notice that it was missing when she took my tray and left. I used the fork to pick the lock on the window and went out that way."

Darby returned a few moments later, accompanied by a large woman with a Southern accent carrying two steaming bowls of shrimp gumbo.

"Billie Dee, meet Colt McCloud," Darby said as he joined them. "Colt and I go way back. He's an Army helicopter pilot who's finally returned home—at least for a while, and this is his friend Lola."

"Pleased to meet you," the woman with the Texas accent said. "Hope you like my gumbo."

"I know we will," Colt said, and took a bite.

"Not too spicy for you?" the cook asked with a laugh.

"As long as it doesn't melt the spoon, it's not too spicy for me," Colt said, and looked to Lola.

She had tasted the gumbo and was smiling. "It's perfect."

Billie Dee looked pleased. "Enjoy."

Darby refilled their colas and gave them pieces of Billie Dee's Texas chocolate sheet cake to convey both "welcome home" and "glad to meet you."

Left alone again, Colt asked, "How are you doing?"

Lola realized that she felt better than she had in a long time. Just having food in her stomach made her feel stronger and more able to hold off the fear and frustration. She needed her baby.

But Colt believed her, and that made all the difference in the world. That felt like a huge hurdle given how convincing Jonas could be. Even more so, she was glad that she hadn't been wrong about Colt. They'd only been together that one night, but she

hadn't forgotten his kindness, his tenderness, his protectiveness. Just having someone she could depend on… Her heart
swelled as she looked over at him. "We're going to get Grace
back, aren't we?"

Jonas stood at the window of his cabin. He'd had his cabin built
on the side of the mountain so he could look down on the compound. For a man who'd started with nothing, he'd done all right.
He often wished his father was still alive to see it.

"Look, you sanctimonious old son of a bitch. You, who so
lacked faith that I would accomplish anything in my life. You,
who died so poor that your congregation had to scrape up money
to have you buried behind the church you'd served all those
years. You, who always managed to cut me down as if you
couldn't stand it that I might do better than you. Well, I did!"

Thinking about his father made his pulse rise dangerously.
He had to be careful not to get upset. Stress made his condition
worse. So much worse that some of his followers had started
to notice.

He stepped over to the small table where he kept his medication. He swallowed a pill and waited for it to work. He tried
not to think about the father who had kicked him out at sixteen. But it wasn't his old man who was causing the problem
this time. It was Lola.

"Lola." Just saying her name churned up a warring mix of
emotions that had been raging inside him for some time. Over
the years, a variety of willing women had come to his bed in the
night. He'd turned none of them away, but nor had he wanted
any of them to keep for himself. Until Lola.

Her mother had shown him a photograph of her daughter
back when Maxine and her husband, Ted, had joined SLS. The
Society was just getting on its feet in those days. The Daytons'
money had gone a long way to start things rolling.

Jonas had especially liked Maxine, since he knew she was
the one calling the shots. Ted would do anything for his wife.

And had. All Jonas had to do was steer Maxine in whatever direction he wanted her to go and Ted would come along as a willing participant. If only they were all that easy to manage, he thought now with a sigh.

The photo of Lola had caught him off guard. There was a sweetness, a purity in that young face, but it was what he saw in her eyes. A fire. A passion banked in those mesmerizing violet eyes that had made him want to be the one to release it.

He'd done everything he could to get the Daytons to bring Lola to the California ranch. But the foolish girl had taken off right after high school to attend a college abroad. She'd wanted to become a teacher. Jonas had groaned when Maxine told him, and he'd conveyed his thoughts.

I think she could be anything she wants to be with my help. I really want to help her meet her potential. Lola is destined to do so much more than teach. She and I could lead the world to a better place. She might be the one person who could bring peace to the world.

Maxine had loved it, but Lola hadn't been having any of it. Right after college she'd headed for the Virgin Islands to teach sixth-grade geography at a private school down there. What a waste, he'd thought, not just for Lola but for himself. He had imagined what he could do with a woman like that warming his bed at night. They could run SLS together. Lola would bring in the men. He'd bring in the women. They could build an empire and live like royalty.

He'd known that Ted wasn't happy after the move to Montana. Jonas had heard him trying to get Maxine to leave. That was the first time that Jonas had realized that Ted had held out on him. Ted hadn't bought into SLS either mentally or financially. He hadn't turned over all his money. He'd set some aside for Lola, and no small amount, either.

Ted's dissatisfaction and attempts to get Maxine to leave hadn't fitted into Jonas's plan. He suddenly realized there was only one way to get Lola to come to him. Maxine and Ted would have to die—and soon.

Getting Maxine to sign a paper of her intentions to persuade Lola to marry him had taken only one private session with her. Maxine had bought into SLS hook, line and sinker. If she wanted to save her daughter... He'd promised to give Lola the kind of life her mother had only dreamed of. Then he'd had Ted and Maxine disposed of and, just as he'd planned, Lola flew to Montana, bringing all that fire inside her.

But he'd underestimated her. She was nothing like her mother. He'd thought that his charm, his wit, his sincerity would work on the daughter the way it had on her mother. That was where he'd made his first mistake, he thought now as he watched dusk settle over the compound.

There'd been a series of other mistakes that had led to her getting pregnant by another man. That was a blow he still reeled from. But it hadn't changed his determination to have Lola, one way or another. Not even some Army pilot/rancher could stop him. No, he had the one thing that Lola wanted more than life.

She would be back. And this time, she wouldn't be leaving here again.

CHAPTER EIGHT

AFTER SHRIMP GUMBO at the Stagecoach Saloon, Colt took them to the grocery store. He and Lola grabbed a cart and began to fill it with food. He loved her enthusiasm. After being locked up and nearly starved for so long, she was like a kid in a candy store.

"Do you like this?" she would ask as she picked up one item after another.

"Get whatever sounds good to you."

She scampered around, quickly filling the cart with food she obviously hadn't had for a while as he grabbed the basics: milk, bread, eggs, butter, bacon and syrup.

"I suspect you can live on pancakes," she said, eyeing what he'd added to the cart.

He'd only grinned, realizing that he'd never enjoyed grocery shopping as much as he had with her today. They felt almost like an old married couple as they left the store. He found himself smiling at Lola as she tore into a bag of potato chips before they even reached the pickup. He unloaded their haul and had started to replace the cart in the rack when he heard someone call his name.

"Colt?"

He froze at the sound of Julia's voice. Somehow he'd managed not to cross paths with her since he'd been back in town, but only because he'd shopped either very early or very late. He'd picked a bad day to run out of groceries, he thought now with a grimace.

"Colt?"

Lola set her potato chip bag in the back of the pickup bed and walked over to join him. He could feel her looking from him to Julia, wondering why he wasn't responding. With a silent curse, he turned to face the woman he'd been ready to marry a year ago.

Julia looked exactly the same. Her dark hair was shorter, making her brown eyes seem even darker. She looked good, slim and perfect in a dress and heels. Julia always liked to dress up—even to go to the grocery store. Gold glittered at her ears, her neck and, of course, on her ring finger, along with the sizable diamond resting there. The one he'd bought hadn't been nearly as large.

He swore under his breath. As many times as he'd imagined what it would be like running into her again, he'd never imaged this. Lola was watching the two of them as if enjoying a tennis match.

Colt had hoped that he wouldn't feel anything, given what Julia had done to him. But he'd believed in this woman, believed they would share the rest of their lives; otherwise, he would never have asked her to marry him. It had taken him almost three years to pop the question. He'd wanted to be sure. What a fool he'd been.

"I heard you were back," Julia said, and glanced from him to Lola beside him. "I was so sorry to hear about your father. I was at the funeral..."

He'd seen her and managed to avoid her.

"How are you?" she asked, sounding as if she cared.

As if sensing who this woman was and what she'd meant to him, Lola reached over and took his hand, squeezing it gently.

"I'm good," he said, squeezing back. "And you?"

"Fine." She looked again at his companion, her gaze going to their clasped hands.

"I heard you've put the ranch up for sale." Julia hesitated. She brushed a lock of her hair back from her forehead, looking not quite as confident. "Does this mean you're going back into the military?" His joining the Army's flight program had been a bone of contention between them.

He shook his head, as if what he planned to do was any of her business.

"I was just wondering," she said, no doubt seeing him clenching his teeth. "I was hoping that if you were staying around Gilt Edge we could..." Again she hesitated. "Maybe we could have a cup of coffee sometime and just talk."

Just talk the way they had before she'd had an affair with Wyatt? Or talk the way they had when she hadn't shown up at the airport to give him a ride home?

"Our last conversation..." Julia looked again at Lola for a moment. "It went so badly. I'd left you messages. I had no way of knowing you hadn't gotten them or the letter I sent."

"You were clear enough on the phone the last time we talked," he said, wishing she would just say whatever it was she needed to say so he didn't have to keep standing there. He could tell that she was waiting for him to introduce her to Lola, but his heart was beating too hard. Julia and Wyatt had hurt him badly. Her and one of his friends? Equal amounts of anger and regret had him shaking inside.

But he didn't want to get into an argument here in the grocery store parking lot in front of Lola. He didn't want Julia to know just how much she and Wyatt had hurt him. And he feared that if he started in on her, he wouldn't be able to stop until all of his grief and rage and hurt came pouring out.

"I'm glad you're home." Julia looked from him to Lola again and forced a weak smile. "It was good to see you. If you change your mind about that cup of coffee..." She stood for a moment, looking awkward and unsure, something new for Julia, he thought. And he realized that she needed him to tell her it was okay, what she'd done. That he forgave her. That he wanted her and Wyatt to be happy. Julia was struggling with the guilt.

That alone should have made him feel better, he thought as she turned and left them standing there. Instead, he felt as if he'd been ambushed by a speeding freight train.

"I'm sorry," Lola said as she let go of his hand.

He couldn't speak so merely nodded as he took the cart to the rack and quickly returned to the pickup. Lola grabbed her potato chips out of the back and joined him in the cab. He'd expected her to be full of questions.

Instead, she buckled up, holding the bag of potato chips as if she'd lost her appetite, and quietly let him process what had just happened. He was thankful to her for that. And for taking his hand back there.

"Thanks," he said, after he got the truck going and drove out of the parking lot.

"It was the first time you've seen her since...since the breakup." It wasn't a question, but he answered it anyway.

"I've managed to avoid her. Just my luck..." He shook his head.

"I can see how painful it is."

"I'm more angry than hurt."

Lola looked out the side window. "Betrayal is always painful." She hugged herself.

He glanced over at her, thinking what a strong, determined woman she was. Not the kind who would give up when things got a little tough.

"Julia turned out not to be the woman I thought she was," he said. "I'm better off without her."

Lola said nothing, no doubt sensing that no matter what he said, he wasn't completely over his former fiancée or what she had put him through.

It made him angry that his heart hadn't let go of the hurt. The anger he didn't mind living with for a while.

* * *

What would Lola do now? That was the question Jonas knew he should be asking himself as he stepped back inside his warm, elegantly furnished cabin.

She must think him a complete fool. Her great escape. He let out a bark of a laugh. Did she really think she could have gotten away unless he'd let her? Sure, he'd had his men chase her with instructions to make sure that she got away.

He'd known she would run straight to the father of her baby. As if he hadn't known she was lying about not knowing who she'd lain with. He scoffed at the idea. Sister Rebecca had seen her with a man near the hotel bar that night. Unfortunately, Lola and the man had disappeared on the elevator too quickly.

But Rebecca had managed to get the information. Major Colt McCloud. An Army helicopter pilot. Jonas would ask what she could see in a man like that, but he wasn't that stupid. The man was good-looking, part cowboy, part flight jockey. He had just inherited a large ranch.

Not that Jonas had been certain Colt McCloud was the man who'd knocked Lola up. No, he hadn't known that until today when the man had shown up with Lola and the sheriff.

Lola was too bound up from her conservative upbringing to go to bed with just anyone. So she'd seen something beyond Colt McCloud's good looks. Jonas swore under his breath as he moved to the fireplace to throw on another log. Just the thought of the cowboy pilot made his blood boil. How dare the man come up here making demands.

Jonas thought he might have convinced Colt that Lola was unstable and not to be believed. She'd certainly played into his plan perfectly when she'd lost it in the laundry room. But he couldn't be sure about Colt. The man was probably smitten with Lola and would want to believe her.

At least the sheriff wouldn't be returning. He'd been sufficiently convinced. Law enforcement always backed off when it came to churches. Just like the government did. He smiled at the thought of how he'd been able to build The Society of Lasting Serenity without anyone looking over his shoulder.

Until now.

"You could return the baby," Sister Rebecca had dared to say to him before the dust had even settled earlier today. "You know she'll be back if you don't."

"Mind your place," he'd snapped. He'd seen how jealous the older woman was of Lola. He suspected she'd been mean to her, cutting her rations, possibly even being physically abusive to her. He hadn't stopped it, wanting Sister Rebecca's loyalty.

But now he wondered how much longer he might be able to count on Rebecca. Once Lola was back—and she would be back—Sister Rebecca might have to be taken down a notch or two. Then again, maybe it was time to retire her. Not that she would ever be allowed to leave. She knew too much.

Strange how a valuable asset could so quickly become a liability.

As soon as he had Lola... Yes, he would dispose of Sister Rebecca. It would be almost like a wedding gift for his new wife. Not that he would tell Lola what had really happened to the older woman. Let her believe he'd given Rebecca a golden parachute and sent her off to some island to bask in the sun for the rest of her days.

He stared into the flames as the log he'd added began to crackle and spark. If he was Colt McCloud, what would he do? Jonas smiled to himself, then picked up the phone. "We're going to need more guards tonight, especially around the cemetery."

After running into Julia, Colt had known it was just a matter of time before he and Wyatt crossed paths. He'd promised himself that when it happened, when he finally did see his traitorous, former good friend, he would keep his cool. He wasn't going to lose his temper. If Wyatt wanted Julia, a woman who would betray her fiancé while he was fighting a war oceans away, then she was all his.

He'd visualized seeing both of them, but even in his imagination, he hadn't known what he would do. He'd told himself that he would tell them both off, make them feel even more guilty, if possible, hurt them the way they had hurt him.

But look what had happened when he'd seen Julia. He'd been boiling inside, his heart pounding, anger and hurt a potent mixture. And he'd said none of what he'd planned. Instead, he hadn't wanted them to know how much they'd hurt him. Or even how angry he still was.

After seeing Julia, it made him wonder when it could happen with Wyatt. How would Wyatt react? He just hoped Lola wouldn't have to witness it again. Colt thought that Wyatt must be dreading the day when they would come face-to-face again as much as he was. Colt hoped he'd given Wyatt a few sleepless nights worrying about it. Because, in a town the size of Gilt Edge, a meeting had to happen.

But Colt was sorry that it had to happen at this moment as he stopped to get gas on the way out of town. Lola had gone inside the convenience mart to use the ladies' room.

As he stood filling the pickup with gas, Wyatt drove up, pulling to a pump two away from him.

Colt froze, his heart in this throat, as he watched Wyatt get out of his pickup and step to the fuel pump. He thought about staying where he was, pretending he never saw him. But that was way too cowardly. Anyway, he wanted to get this over with.

He finished fueling his truck and walked down the line of gas pumps. Wyatt looked up and saw him and seemed to freeze. They'd grown up together, hung out with many of the same friends since grade school. It was only after college that Colt, needing to do something more with his life, had enlisted in the Army helicopter program.

Wyatt had tried to talk him out of it. "Why do you need to go so far away? You're going to get yourself killed and for what?"

Colt hadn't been able to explain it to him. So he'd left to fly and fight while Wyatt had stayed on his family ranch and stolen Julia.

He took a step toward the man he'd thought he'd known better than himself. As he did, he wondered what he would come out of his mouth or if he would be able to speak. His pulse thundered in his ears as he advanced on his former friend.

"Colt." Wyatt was a big, strong cowboy. He put up both hands in surrender but held his ground. "Colt, whatever you're thinking—"

Colt hit him hard enough to drive him back a couple of steps. Wyatt banged into the side of his pickup.

"I don't want to fight you," Wyatt said as one large hand went to his bleeding nose.

"That's good," Colt said. "Since you'd probably take me." He knew that might be true since Wyatt had a few inches on him and a good twenty pounds, but as angry as he was, he'd fight like hell.

His hands were balled into fists, but he didn't hit him again. Wyatt's bleeding nose looked broken. Colt was reminded of the time Wyatt had taken on the school bully, a kid twice his size back then. His former friend was tough and had never backed down from a fight in all the time Colt had known him.

He took a step back, hating that he was remembering the years of their friendship. His eyes burned with tears, but damned if he was going to cry. Looking at Wyatt, he realized that losing Julia had hurt; losing someone he'd considered a close friend, though, had ripped out his heart.

He turned on his heel and walked back to his pickup before he made a complete fool of himself. His knuckles hurt, but nothing like his heart as he listened to Wyatt get into his truck and drive away.

Lola had seen everything from the front window of the convenience store when she'd come back from the restroom. The "fight" had ended quickly enough.

She didn't have to ask who the man had been.

Wyatt Enderlin. When she'd asked Colt about him, he'd said they'd been friends. "It's a small town. We make friends for life here." She could imagine how much Wyatt's betrayal hurt Colt.

She pushed open the door and walked out to Colt's truck, climbing in without a word. Out of the corner of her eye, Lola saw him rub his skinned and swollen knuckles before he climbed behind the wheel.

It wasn't until they were in the pickup headed toward the ranch that Colt said, "You saw?"

She hesitated, forcing him to look over at her. "I wanted you to hit him again."

He smiled sadly at that. "I hadn't planned to even hit him once."

"Do you feel better or worse?"

Chuckling, he said, "Better and worse."

"Well, you got that out of the way."

"Right, I got to see them both on the same day. Lucky me." He drove in silence for a few minutes. "Wyatt and I were like brothers at one point growing up. I'd always wanted a brother..." He shook his head.

"He was your friend."

"*Was* being the key word here. My other friends like Darby Cahill never would have done that."

"Which hurts worse?" she finally asked.

Colt shot her a glance before turning back to his driving. "Wyatt."

"Maybe one day—"

"I don't think so. Being in the military you learn which men you can trust in battle. Those are the men you want watching your back. Wyatt, as it turned out, isn't one of them."

"I'm sorry." She let the words hang in the air for a moment. "Do you believe in fate?"

They were almost at the turnoff to the ranch. Ahead she could see the for-sale sign. They hadn't talked about it. She doubted they would because she already knew from the first time they'd met how Colt felt about flying the big birds in the military.

"Fate?" he asked, glancing at her for a moment before he slowed for the turn.

"Maybe it was fate that has brought us all to this point in our lives."

Fate? Lola couldn't be serious. If his fate was having his fiancée hook up with his good friend behind his back, then he'd say he was one unlucky bastard. He said as much to Lola.

"I was thinking more about the way we met."

Instantly he hated having rained on her parade like that.

"If Julia hadn't broken up with you and had met you at the airport like she was supposed to, then you wouldn't have been in that hotel that night and I wouldn't have…"

Would some other man have saved her? Or taken advantage of a young woman who was obviously inexperienced and desperate? The thought made him sick to his stomach, but he wouldn't have known because he would never have laid eyes on Lola Dayton.

Nor would he be worrying about how to get their baby away from a madman at an armed and dangerous cult compound at the top of a mountain, he thought as he parked in front of the house at the ranch and shut off the engine.

But as he looked over at Lola, the anger he'd been feeling ebbed away. "You're right," he said, softening his tone as he reached over and squeezed her hand. "It definitely was fate that brought us together." Damn fickle fate, he thought, realizing with growing concern how much Lola was getting to him.

He put Julia, Wyatt and the past out of his mind and concentrated on what to do next. He knew what he was going to have to do. It went against his military training. A man didn't go in alone with no backup. Nor did he take matters into his own hands. He went through proper channels.

But there was no way the sheriff was going to be able to get a warrant to have whatever was buried on the church grounds exhumed—even if Colt could talk Flint into doing it. Jonas would fight it and drag out the process. Meanwhile, that madman had their baby. Baby Grace, the daughter he had yet to lay eyes on.

After helping put the groceries away, he went into the ranch office. The maps were in a file—right where his father had kept them. He found the one he needed and spread it out on the desk.

"We need proof that Jonas is lying," Lola said from the open doorway.

"Proof won't do us any good. We need to find Grace and get her out of there."

"But that grave. If you dig it up—"

Colt shuddered at the thought. "That's exactly what Jonas will expect me to do." He recalled a shortage of manpower on the compound. But a woman could be just as deadly with a gun, he reminded himself. "While they're busy guarding the cemetery, I'll find Grace."

"I'm going with you," she said, stepping into the small office.

He shook his head, hating how intimate it felt with her in here. "It's going to be hard enough for me to get onto the grounds—and away again—without being caught."

"Exactly. They will expect you and will have doubled the guards. You're going to need me."

He started to argue, but she cut him off. "I have lived there all this time. I know the weakest spots along the perimeter. I also know the guards. And, maybe more important, I know where to look for Grace."

Admittedly, she made a good argument. "Lola, if we are both caught, no one will know we're up there. If Jonas is as dangerous as you think he is, we'll end up in the cemetery."

"If one of us is caught, then the other can distract them while whoever has Grace gets away."

He hated that her argument made sense, more sense than

him trying to find Grace on his own. "Can you draw a map of the place?"

She nodded.

"Good. We leave at midnight."

Lola hadn't dared hope, but as she watched Colt studying the web of old logging roads around the mountain compound on the map, she let herself believe they could succeed. They would get in, find Grace and slip back out with her. Once she had Grace in her arms, no way would she let anyone rip her out again. Especially Jonas.

"I'll need paper and a pen," she said as she leaned over the desk. Their gazes met for a moment, his gaze deepening. She felt goose bumps ripple over her skin. Heat rushed to her center. Then he quickly looked away and began searching for what she needed.

She drew a map of the compound buildings, marking those that were used for housing. "I know you got a tour, but I thought this would help. As you can see there are two women's dorms, one for the women with babies. There is only the one men's dorm on the opposite side the main building."

"What's this?" Colt asked as he moved to her side to point at a large cabin away from the others and at the top of her diagram.

"Jonas's. He likes to look down on his followers."

"And this one at the bottom right?" His fingers brushed hers.

A shiver ran the length of her spine. She felt her nipples harden to pebbles under her top. "That's the storage room, shop and health center." Her voice cracked with emotion.

"And this one bottom left?" There was no doubt. He'd purposely brushed against her as he pointed to the only other structure. The bare skin of his arm was warm. His touch sent more shivers rippling through her. Her nipples ached inside her bra.

"Laundry." She turned enough to meet his eyes. What she saw made her molten inside. His gaze was dark with desire as his fingers trailed up her arm to brush against the side of her breast.

* * *

What the hell are you doing? As if he could stop himself. He looked into Lola's beautiful violet gaze and knew he was lost. He wanted her. Needed her. Thought he would die if he didn't have her right now. This had been building inside him all day, he realized. Maybe since the first time he'd met her.

"Colt?" she breathed, and shuddered as his fingers brushed over the hard tip of her nipple. She moaned softly, her head going back to expose her slim silken neck.

He bent to kiss her throat, nipping at the pale skin, and felt her shiver before trailing kisses down into the hollow between her breasts. "Yes, Lola?" he asked, his muffled voice as filled with emotion as hers had been.

When she didn't answer, he raised his head to look into her eyes. He held her gaze, seeing the answer in all that lovely blue.

Cupping her other breast, he backed her up against the office wall and dropped his mouth to hers. Her lips parted and he took the invitation to let his tongue explore her as his free hand found the waistband of her jeans and slipped inside.

She let out a gasp as he found the sweet cleft between her legs. "Colt." This time it was a plea. She was wet. He began to stroke her, drawing back to look into her eyes. Her head was back and her mouth open. Tiny sounds escaped her lips as he slowly stroked, until he could feel her quiver against his fingers and finally cry out.

Withdrawing his hand, he swung her up into his arms and strode to his bedroom. He didn't want to think about later tonight when they would go up the mountain. Nor did he want to think about the future or even why he was doing this right now.

All he knew was that he wanted her more than his next breath. The only thing on his mind was making love to this woman who had captivated him from the first time he'd laid eyes on her.

CHAPTER NINE

JUST BEFORE MIDNIGHT, Lola and Colt loaded into his pickup and headed toward the SLS encampment. Colt had programmed his phone with the latest GPS information and had mapped out their best route up the mountain.

They'd both dressed in dark clothing. Lola had borrowed one of his black T-shirts. Her blond hair was pulled up under one of his black caps.

Earlier, after making love several times, they'd showered together, then sat down again with the map. His plan was to approach this like a battle.

Lola had showed him on her diagram what she thought was the best way in—and out again. The layout of the compound was star shaped, with the large main building at its center. It was where everyone ate, met for church and meetings, and where Jonas had his office.

From it, the other buildings formed the points of a star. At the top was Jonas's cabin, on the left center were the women's two dorms and on the right, the men's dorm. At the bottom was the laundry to the left and the health center, shop and storage building to the right.

"Once we grab Grace, someone will sound the alarm. Everyone will get a weapon and go to the edge of the property."

"The SLS is sounding less and less like a church by the moment," Colt had said.

"If the intruder or escapee is caught, a second signal will sound announcing the all clear," she'd said.

Colt had studied her for a moment. He couldn't help thinking of her earlier, naked in his arms. He wondered if he could ever get enough of this woman. "You're sure about this?"

She'd smiled, nodding. She really did have an amazing smile. "Whichever one of us has Grace gets out if the alarm goes off. Whoever doesn't have her distracts the guards to give them a chance to escape."

"Who will have Grace?" he'd asked.

"I guess it will depend on who finds her first. Once we approach the housing part, someone is bound to see us."

Colt would have preferred a more comprehensive plan. "You must have some idea where they are keeping Grace."

"Normally, she would be in the second women's dorm where the other babies are kept," she'd said. "But Jonas will know that I haven't given up. He might have ordered that Grace be kept in the other women's dorm."

"Where were they keeping you before you escaped?"

She'd drawn in a tiny box. "That's the cabin. It serves as the jail."

"And you could hear Grace crying when they came to pump your breast milk?" She'd nodded. "You're thinking they had our baby in this dorm, the farthest one to the west and closest to the cabin where you were being kept. I'll take that one, then head east to the second women's dorm if I don't see you. They won't expect us to come in from different directions."

"We'll meet up there. Or if the alarm goes off, just try to meet back at the pickup"

Now, as the road climbed up the mountain, he looked over at Lola. She appeared calm. Her expression was one of determination. She was going after her baby. *Their* baby. Her last thought was her own safety.

His heart ached at the thought of their lovemaking. He couldn't let anything happen to this woman. Grace needed her. He needed her, he thought and pushed the thought away. What he needed was to get himself, Lola and their baby out of that compound alive tonight. Later he'd think about what he needed, what he wanted, what the hell he was going to do once Lola and Grace were safe.

The night was thankfully dark. Low clouds hunkered just over the tops of the tall ebony pines. No stars, let alone the moon, shone through. Colt thought they couldn't have picked a better night.

Still, he was anxious. So much was riding on this and he felt they were going in blind. What he did know had him both worried and scared. If Jonas or any of his followers caught them...

He couldn't let himself go down that trail of thought. If they wanted to get Grace out of there, they had no choice but to sneak in like thieves, find her and take her. Isn't that what Jonas had done?

Lola had been lost in thought when Colt pulled the pickup over, cut the engine and doused the lights. She'd been thinking about the ocean and the time she'd almost drowned.

Her father had saved her, plucking her from the depths and carrying her to the beach. She remembered lying on the warm sand staring up at the sky and gasping for breath as her father wept in relief over her.

She had no idea why that particular memory had surfaced now. Anything to keep her mind off what was about to happen once they reached the compound. She'd learned to let her mind wander during Jonas's attempts to brainwash her. She would think of anything but what was happening—just like now.

With the headlights off, they were pitched into blackness. She listened to the tick, tick, tick of the cooling engine, her heart a hammer in her chest.

"You ready?" he asked, his voice low and soft.

She nodded and locked gazes with him. Colt looked as if there was something he wanted to say. She'd seen that same look earlier after they'd made love.

Earlier, she'd put a finger to his lips. She hadn't wanted him to say the words that he thought he needed to say. Colt was an honorable man, but she couldn't let him say things that he'd later regret. Nor had she been able to bear the thought of him pouring his soul out to her at that moment. Just as now.

There was too much riding on what they were about to do. Emotions were high and had been since she'd appeared at his door in the middle of the night. There was no need to say anything then or now, though she understood his need. She too wanted to open her heart to him because both of them knew how dangerous this mission was. Neither of them might get out of this alive.

Just as he started to speak, she opened her door and stepped into the darkness. She gulped the cold spring-night air and fought her fear for Colt and their daughter, a gut-wrenching fear that made her eyes burn with tears.

Colt sat for a moment alone in the cab of the dark pickup. What had he been about to say? He shook his head. Lola had cut him off—just as she had earlier.

He sighed, wondering at this woman.

Then he got out, and the two of them headed through the dark pines for the hike to the compound.

They moved as silently as they could once their eyes adjusted to the darkness under the towering pines. A breeze stirred the boughs high above them, making the pines sigh.

Colt led the way until they were almost to the SLS property. The whole time, he'd been acutely aware of Lola behind him.

Now he stopped and motioned her forward. They stood inches apart for a long moment, listening.

Lola had suggested entering the property on the opposite

side of the cemetery and the farthest away from any main road up to the mountaintop.

The main road was gated, so Jonas wouldn't be expecting them to come that way. That was also the most visible, so they'd opted for this approach.

But now it was time to separate. Colt could feel the tension in the air, as well as the tension between them. Lola had made it clear that she didn't want any words of undying love. But, after everything they'd shared, he felt the need to say something, do something.

He drew her close, looked into her violet eyes and kissed her.

"What was that?" she demanded in a whisper. "It felt like a goodbye kiss."

He shook his head and leaned close to whisper, "A promise to see you soon." As he drew back, he saw her smile. "Good luck," he whispered, and turned and headed in the opposite direction, his heart in his throat. If things didn't go well, he didn't want his last memory to be of her standing in the darkness, looking up at him with those big blue eyes and him not doing a damned thing.

Now he thought of her slightly gap-toothed smile and held it close to his heart for luck. Ahead he saw the no-trespassing sign and knew a guard wasn't far away.

Lola touched her tongue to her lower lip as she made her way through the pines. Just the thought of Colt's kiss made her heart beat a little faster. If she'd been falling for him before that moment, well, she'd just fallen a little further. She warned herself that this wasn't any way to go into a relationship.

Her mother would have called it "going in the back door." Maxine would not have approved of Lola having a baby out of wedlock when she could have married Jonas and given Grace a father.

But Grace did have a father. A fine father. Lola just didn't see them becoming a family. She shook the thought from her head and tried to concentrate. Getting Grace back, that was all that mattered.

She hadn't gone far when she saw a faint light bobbing through the trees ahead of her.

Ducking down, she watched as Elmer made his way along the edge of the property. She waited until he was well past her before she rose and sneaked onto the compound. The only lights were the ones outside the buildings that illuminated parts of the grounds.

Lola edged along the pines until she reached the edge of the men's dorm. Only one light shone at the front. She moved cautiously along the back, keeping to the dark shadows next to the building and being careful not to step on anything that might make a sound.

She had no desire to wake anyone, though she thought the men's dorm was probably fairly empty. All of the men would be on guard duty tonight and maybe even some of the women.

Elmer would be turning back soon on his guard circuit. If she hurried, she should be able to reach the closest women's dorm and slip inside the nursery before he started back this way.

Before the first time she'd escaped, she'd had the run of the place, including the one women's dorm, where she'd stayed with the sisters. She'd even helped with the babies a few times. Because of that, she knew where to find the main nursery.

"If I find her first, how will I know her?" Colt had asked.

She'd smiled and said, "You'll know her and she'll know you."

"No, seriously."

"There were two babies born in the past six months that I know of. The boy we saw in the laundry and Grace."

At the end of the men's dorm, Lola stopped to listen. She heard nothing on the breeze. The distance between her and the women's dorms was a good dozen yards—all of them in the glow of the men's dorm light.

She looked for any movement in the darkness beyond. Seeing

none, she sprinted the distance and dropped back into the shadows. Her heart pounded as she waited to see if she'd been spotted by one of the guards. The only one she'd seen was Elmer, but she knew there were others stationed around the compound, more than usual, just as she'd told Colt.

As she caught her breath, she thought of Colt and wondered where he was. Saying a silent prayer for his safety, she crept along the edge of the building to the door to the main nursery and grasping the knob, turned it.

Colt recognized the guard as one he'd seen here yesterday. The man looked tired and bored as he moved along the edge of the property and fiddled with the handgun holstered at his hip.

The guard had only gone a few feet when he stepped into the shadows and suddenly drew his weapon like an Old West gunfighter. He took the stance for a moment, pointing the gun into the darkness ahead of him and then holstered his weapon again as he moved on to practice his fast draw a few yards later.

Colt had been startled for a moment when the guard had suddenly drawn his weapon. He'd been more than a little relieved to see that the man's gun was pointing only at some imaginary person in the dark.

He slipped behind the man, closing the distance from the dense pines to the edge of the closest women's dorm. Stopping to listen, he heard a sound that froze him in place.

A low growl followed by another. This part of the country had its share of bear from black bear to grizzly. But the low growling sound he'd just heard wasn't coming from the darkness, he realized. Instead, it floated out of the open window on the back side of the women's dorm. Someone was snoring loudly.

It gave him good cover as he moved cautiously along the dark side of the building. Only a dim light shone inside. Staying as far back as possible, he peered in. The large room was filled with bunk beds like a military barrack. He recognized the woman in the closest lower bunk. Sister Alexa, a woman Colt had met in passing the day Jonas gave him the tour.

She let out a snort and stirred. He saw her eyes flicker and he froze. She blinked for a moment before her eyes fluttered shut and her snoring resumed.

Colt ducked away from the window and made his way down to the end that Lola said could house a second nursery. The outside light high over the front door of the main building cast a circle of golden light.

He watched from the dark shadows at the edge of the light. He'd only seen two guards so far, one on the way in and another crossing the complex, before he'd made his way to the far end of the building where he would find the nursery.

From where he stood, he could see toward the cemetery where Lola's parents were buried. He wondered about the small mound of fresh dirt next to them. Was something buried under there?

Jonas seemed like a man who didn't take chances. At the very least, he would have buried a small wooden casket. Colt remembered seeing the shop on his tour of the complex. Followers made wooden crosses in the shop that they sold when they went into town to raise money for the poor, Lola had told him. She said she doubted the poor ever saw a dime of it.

"I think it's Jonas's way of keeping them busy and making a little extra cash. The crosses are crude, but I think people feel sorry for the followers and give them money."

He thought now about the small casket he'd seen in one corner of the shop during his tour and swallowed hard. What if Jonas had filled the casket under that mound of dirt since their visit?

The thought made his stomach roil. He pressed his back against the side of the women's dorm and waited for the guard he'd seen earlier to cross again.

From inside the women's dorm, he heard a baby begin to cry. His heart lodged in his throat. Grace?

* * *

Lola turned the knob slowly. The door creaked open an inch, then another. A small night-light shone from one corner of the room, illuminating four small cribs. In one of the cribs, a baby whimpered.

She looked toward the doorway into the sleeping room with its bunk beds. She could hear someone snoring softly, heard the rustle of covers and then silence.

Her heart pounded as she slipped through the door and into the nursery. The first two cribs were empty. She moved to the third one. The baby in it was small. A newborn. Sister Caroline's baby, she realized. Caroline had been due when Lola had run away from the compound that night.

She stepped to the last crib, looked down at the sleeping baby and felt her heart begin to pound.

Colt stood against the wall in the darkness outside the nursery. Inside, he heard the sound of footfalls as someone awakened in the dorm and headed for the nursery.

A few moments later, he heard a woman talking soothingly. The baby quit crying. He could hear the woman humming a tune to the child, but he didn't recognize the song.

Then again, he knew no children's songs. He tried to imagine himself getting up in the middle of the night to calm his crying infant and couldn't. It was so far from what he'd been doing for the last eleven years.

What kind of father would he make when he didn't even know a song he could sing a child? Or could even imagine himself doing something like that? In all his years he'd never held a baby. He'd be afraid he would drop it with his big clumsy hands.

He could see the woman's shadow as she'd come into the room and now watched her swaying with the infant in her arms, singing softly, willing the baby back to sleep. Was the baby Grace?

He waited, staying to the dark shadow of the building as,

in the distance, he saw the guard come back from making his rounds. The man was headed for the men's dorm. Change of shift? He hadn't anticipated that and realized he should have.

Where he was standing, the man would have to pass right by him. Colt had no chance of going undetected. Nor could he move away from the building without being seen.

Inside the nursery, he saw the shadow of the woman move. The singing continued as she seemed to lay the infant back into its crib. The man was getting closer now. His head was down. He looked tired, bored, ready to call it a night.

Where was his replacement? For all Colt knew, there could be another guard headed from the opposite direction.

He realized the music had stopped inside the nursery. Reaching over, he tried the door. The knob turned in his hand.

He had no choice. He could stay where he was and be seen by the guard, or he could chance slipping into the nursery and coming face-to-face with the woman tending the baby.

He slipped into the nursery to find it empty except for four cribs lined up against one wall. As the door closed behind him, he heard voices outside. Two men. And then silence.

Colt waited a few more seconds before he approached the cribs and saw that all but one of the cribs was empty.

He moved quietly to the crib being used and looked down at the sleeping baby. The infant lay on its back, eyes closed. He carefully reached in and pulled up the homemade shift the baby wore.

For a moment, Lola couldn't move or breathe. Her heart swelled to bursting as she looked down at the precious sleeping baby. She would have recognized her baby anywhere, but still, with trembling fingers, she lifted the hem of the infant's gown.

There on Grace's chubby little left thigh was the tiny heart-shaped birthmark. A sob rose in her throat. She desperately wanted to lift her daughter from the crib. For so long she'd yearned to hold her baby in her arms.

She tried to get control of her emotions, knowing that once she picked up Grace, she would have to move fast. With luck, Grace wouldn't cry. But being startled out of sleep she might, and it would set off an alarm that would awaken the women in the dorm, if not the whole complex.

Lola wiped at the warm tears on her cheeks as she stared at her daughter. Grace was beautiful, from her tiny bow-shaped mouth to her chubby cheeks. As if sensing her standing over the crib, Grace's eyes fluttered and she kicked with both legs.

Lola grabbed two of the baby blankets stacked next to the cribs. Reaching down, she hurriedly lifted her daughter. Grace started, her eyes coming wide-open in alarm.

Quickly wrapping her infant in the blankets, Lola turned toward the door and felt a hand drop to her shoulder.

CHAPTER TEN

LOLA HAD BEEN in midstep when the hand dropped to her shoulder. The fingers tightened, forcing her to stop. She turned, terrified of who she would find standing behind her.

Sister Amelia put a finger to her lips before Lola could speak. Their gazes locked for what seemed an eternity. Neither looked away until Grace stirred in Lola's arms.

"Go," Amelia whispered, and pushed her toward the door. From back in the dorm came the sound of footfalls. "Go!"

Lola stumbled out the door, Grace wrapped in a blanket and clutched to her chest. Behind her, she heard Sister Amelia say something to the woman who'd awakened. Then the door closed behind her and she was standing out in the dark of the building.

Run! The thought rippled through her, igniting her fight-or-flight impulse. She had Grace. If she could get her off the compound...

From the dark, she heard a sound. A whisper of movement. A dark shadow emerged and she saw it was one of the guards. She recognized him by the arrogant way he moved. Brother Zack. She'd seen the way the former military man looked at her when he thought no one was watching. She'd heard that he'd been drummed out of the service but could only guess for what. He'd struck fear in her the nights when she knew he was the guard working outside the cabin where she was being held.

If Sister Rebecca hadn't been in charge of her "rehabilitation" and had sisters coming every hour or so to chant over her, Lola feared what Brother Zack might have done.

Now she watched him move through the darkness, her heart in her throat. Had he seen her? He appeared to be headed right for her. From inside the baby blankets, Grace whimpered.

Colt checked the baby. No heart-shaped birthmark on either chubby leg. The moment he lifted the thin gown, the baby began to kick. Its eyes came open. Colt froze, afraid to breathe. The baby's gaze became more unfocused. Its eyes slowly closed.

He took a breath and let it out slowly. Grace wasn't here. He stepped toward the door. The floor creaked under his boot. He froze again, listening. With a glance over his shoulder, he stepped to the door, pushed it open a few inches and slipped outside.

The dark night felt like a shroud over the complex. Only circles of golden light from the outside lamps illuminated a few spots around the complex. He waited for his eyes to adjust, keeping himself tucked back against the shadow of the building. Nothing seemed to move but the pine boughs in the breeze.

Off in the distance, an owl hooted, then the night fell silent again. He had no idea how long he'd been inside the nursery or where the guards might be now.

On the way in, he'd thought they'd been changing shifts. That meant the new ones might be more alert, having just started. He thought of Lola. She'd gone to the other women's dorm. Had she found Grace?

His fear was that Jonas would want the baby closer to him, knowing Lola wouldn't give up. But wouldn't he want one of the sisters watching over her? Jonas didn't seem like a hands-on father figure. Colt wondered if he, himself, was. He could only hope that Lola had already found Grace.

He looked around, but saw no one. It appeared that most of the guards were out by the cemetery. Jonas had thought Lola would try to get evidence to take to the sheriff. He had thought no one believed her—not even Colt. Maybe especially Colt.

He spotted one of the guards moving slowly through the pines out on the perimeter. He wanted desperately to go look for Lola, but they'd agreed that the best plan would be for them to meet at the pickup. That way if one of them was caught, the other could go for help rather than walk into a trap that would snare them both.

As soon as the guard was out of sight, Colt crossed between the buildings and worked his way along the dark side of the second women's dorm.

He reached the end of the building and looked to the expanse of open land he would have to cross to reach the dark safety of the pines.

As he started to take a step, he heard a sound behind him and spun around to come face-to-face with Lola. One glance at her expression told him that the bundle in her arms was Grace.

She took a step toward him, smiling, tears in her eyes, and suddenly the night came alive with the shrill scream of an alarm.

Lola felt Grace start at the horrible sound. From inside the blankets, the baby began to cry. Lola tore the blankets from the crying baby and thrust Grace's wriggling small body at Colt. "Take her and go!" she cried. "Go! I'll distract them." She could see that he wanted to argue. "Please."

He grabbed the now-screaming baby and, turning toward the pines, ran.

Lola felt a fist close on her heart as she looked down at the empty blanket in her hand. She didn't have time for regrets. She'd gotten to see her daughter, hold her for a few priceless minutes, but now she had to move, and she knew the best way to make the alarm stop.

Grabbing up several large stones lying along the side of the building's foundation, she quickly wrapped them in the baby blankets, then hugged the bundle against her chest. It wouldn't fool anyone who got too close, but it might work long enough to get her where she needed to go.

Turning, she hurried back toward the center of the compound. She desperately needed to distract the guards and give Colt a chance to escape with Grace.

SLS members poured out of the dorms in their nightwear. She half ran toward Jonas's cabin, screaming at the top of her lungs. Guards came running from all directions.

Zack saw her and charged her. He would have taken her down, but Jonas had come out of his cabin. Seeing what was happening, he shut off the alarm with his cell phone.

"Leave her alone, Brother Zack!" he yelled down. "Don't hurt the baby."

Zack stopped just inches from her. She could see his disappointment. He hadn't cared if he hurt the baby. He had been looking forward to getting his hands on her.

"Bring her to me," Jonas ordered.

Zack reached for her, but she jerked back her arm. One of the rocks shifted and she had to grip her bundle harder.

"Never mind, Brother Zack," Jonas called down. "Lola, I know you don't want to hurt the baby. Come up to my cabin. I promise I won't hurt you or the child."

As if she believed a word out of his mouth. But she walked slowly up the hill, holding the bundle of rocks protectively against her breast.

She listened to make sure that none of the guards had stumbled across Colt and Grace. But there'd been no more activity at the edge of the complex, no shouts, no gunshots. Jonas had sounded the all clear siren. His followers were slowly wandering back to either their beds or their guard duty.

Before she reached the steps to the cabin, Jonas told Zack to leave only a few guards on duty. The rest, he said, could go to bed for what was left of the night.

Clearly he thought that the danger was over and that Lola had acted alone.

She stopped at the bottom of the porch steps and looked up at Jonas. He had a self-satisfied look on his face. He thought he'd won. He thought he had her and he had Grace.

"How did you get here?" Jonas asked suddenly, looking past her.

"I stole his pickup."

"Colt McCloud's? I thought he was your hero?" he mocked.

"Some hero," she said. "But that doesn't surprise you, does it? You knew he'd believe you and not me."

Jonas almost looked sorry for her. "The man's a fool."

She hugged the bundle tighter.

"You should come in. It's cold out here," he said. "Is the baby all right?"

She knew he had to be wondering how Grace had been able to sleep through all of the racket. He had to be getting suspicious.

"She is so sweet," Lola said, glancing down for a moment to peel back of the edge of the blanket so only she could see what was inside. She smiled down at the rock. "She really is an angel." She wanted to give Colt as much time as possible to get away with Grace, but she knew she couldn't keep standing out here or Jonas was going to become suspicious.

"As I've said all along," he agreed as she mounted the steps. He reached for the baby, but she turned to the side, holding the bundle away from him.

"Please, let me hold her just a little longer." Tears filled her eyes at just the thought of the few minutes she'd had Grace in her arms and the thought that they might be all she was going to get.

Jonas relented. "Of course, hold her all you want. There is no reason you should be separated from your child. If you stay here, you will have her all the time. Imagine what your life could be like here with me."

"I have." She hoped she kept the sarcasm out of the voice as she moved to the middle of the room, giving herself a little elbow room.

"We could travel. Europe, the Caribbean, anywhere your heart desired. We could take Angel with us."

"Her name is Grace."

He ignored that as he started to close the door. He froze and cocked his head, taking in the bundle in her arms again. "It really is amazing she slept through all of that noise," he said again.

"She knows she's with her mother now. She knows she's safe."

Jonas looked out the still-open doorway as if suddenly not so sure about being alone with her. She saw Zack watching them.

Lola knew she had no choice. Zack was watching, expecting trouble, and Jonas was getting suspicious. She had no choice.

"Europe? I love Europe," she said, and saw Jonas relax a little. He waved Zack away and closed the door. She looked around, remembering the last time she'd been brought here. Jonas had told her that he would make her his wife—one way or another. He'd tried to kiss her and she'd kicked him hard enough in the shin to get away and, apparently, given him a permanent limp.

Behind her, she heard him lock the door and limp toward her.

CHAPTER ELEVEN

COLT REACHED THE PICKUP. All the way, he'd hoped that he would find Lola waiting for him even though he knew there was little chance of that.

Still, he was disappointed when he got there to find he was alone. Grace had quit crying not long after they'd left the compound. He was grateful for that since he was sure it had helped him get away.

He opened the passenger-side door, the dome light coming on as he laid the bundle Lola had given him on the seat to get his first look at his daughter.

A pair of big blue eyes stared up at him. He lost his heart in that moment. He touched the perfect little cheek, soft as downy feathers. She did resemble Lola, but he thought he could see himself a little in her, too.

"Hi, Grace," he whispered, his voice breaking. Tears welled in his eyes. He swallowed the lump in this throat. He had the baby, but what now?

He turned off the dome light, realizing that if someone had followed him, they would be able to see him through the pines. He stared into the darkness, willing Lola to appear.

He had to assume that Jonas had her by now. He'd heard the alarm go off and then another signal, which he'd assumed must be the all clear. Why would Jonas sound it unless he'd thought there was nothing more to fear?

Which meant he had Lola. She'd sacrificed herself to save her daughter. Their daughter.

He looked toward the dark trees, silently pleading for that not to be the case. He needed her. Grace needed her.

They had Lola. He couldn't leave without her. But he couldn't go back for her with the baby for fear of getting caught.

Nor could he stay there much longer. If Jonas suspected she hadn't come alone...

"What are we going to do, Grace?" he asked as he wrapped her in his coat and watched her fall back to sleep.

With her back to Jonas, Lola reached into the baby blanket with her free hand and slowly turned to face him.

"What really happened to my parents?"

He had been moving toward her but stopped. "They were getting old, confused toward the end. Your mother came down with the flu. It turned into pneumonia. Your father stayed by her side. She was getting better and then she just...died."

She nodded, knowing that it happened at her mother's age, and not believing a word of it. "And my father?"

"I think he died of grief. You had to know how he was with your mother. I don't think he could live without her."

That too happened with people her parents' age who had been married as long as they had. "You didn't have them killed?" She said it softly so he wouldn't think it was an accusation. It wasn't like she expected the truth.

"Lola." There was that disappointing sound in his voice again. He took a step toward her. "Why must you always think the worst of me? Your parents believed in me."

Well, at least her mother had—until he'd had her killed, Lola thought. She wondered if he'd done it himself and realized how silly that was. Of course, he hadn't. Her heart went out to her parents. She couldn't bear thinking about their last moments.

"I took care of your baby for you. I wouldn't hurt a hair on that sweet thing's head. Or on yours. Let me see her." He was close now, and she feared he would make a grab for the baby.

She loosened her hold on the baby blanket bundle a little and faced him, her hand closing tightly around the rock inside.

"Thank you for taking care of her," she said, letting her voice fill with emotion.

"I will take care of you, too—if you give me a chance." He was getting too near—within reaching distance.

She took a step toward him, closing the distance between them as she pretended to hold out the baby for him to take. She had to be close. She had to make it count. It was her only hope of getting out of here and being with Grace.

As Jonas opened his arms for the baby, she pulled out the rock and swung it at his head. He managed to deflect the blow partially with his hand—just enough to knock the rock from her hold.

But she'd swung hard enough that the rock kept going. It caught him in the temple. He stumbled back. She pulled out the second rock, dropping the baby blankets, as she swung again.

This time, he didn't get a chance to raise an arm. The rock connected with the side of his head. His blood splattered on the rock, on her hand. He stood for a moment, looking stunned, then he went down hard on the wood floor.

Lola didn't waste any time. For all she knew he could be out cold—or only momentarily stunned and soon sounding the alarm so the whole cult would be on her heels.

She ran just as she had before. Only this time, she wasn't leaving her baby behind.

Colt had never had trouble making a decision under duress. He'd been forced to make quick ones flying a chopper in Afghanistan. But one thing he'd never done was leave a man behind.

He couldn't this time, either. He'd purposely not taken a weapon into the compound earlier. They'd needed to get Grace out clean, and that meant not killing anyone—even if it meant getting themselves killed.

Now he took the weapons he would need. He was changing the rules—just as he was sure Jonas was. Wrapped in his coat, he laid Grace down on the floorboard of the pickup. She would be plenty warm enough—as long as he came back in a reasonable amount of time.

Locking the pickup door, he turned back toward the woods and the SLS compound. He wasn't leaving without Lola. And this time, he was armed and ready to fight his way in and out of the place if he had to.

Lola felt a sense of déjà vu as she ran through the woods. Her pulse hammered in her ears, her breath coming out in gasps. And yet she listened for the sound of the alarm that would alert the SLS members to fill the woods. Jonas would not let her get away if he had to run her to ground himself.

If he was able.

She had no idea how badly he'd been hurt. Or if he was already hot on her heels.

She crashed through the darkness, shoving away pine boughs that whipped her face and body. Colt had said how important it was for them get in and out of the compound without causing any more harm than was necessary.

"We're the trespassers," he'd told her. "We're the ones who will get thrown in jail if we fail tonight. We need to get in there and out as clean as possible."

She thought about the blood on the rock and could see something staining her right hand as she ran. Jonas's blood. She hadn't gotten out clean. She might have killed him. A cry escaped her lips as her ankle turned under her and she fell hard.

She struggled to get up as she hurriedly wiped the blood on the dried pine needles she'd fallen into. But the moment she put pressure on her ankle, she knew she wasn't going far. She didn't think it was broken, but she also couldn't put any weight on it without excruciating pain.

Grace. Colt. She had to get to them. They would have left by now, but she couldn't stay here. She couldn't let Jonas or one of his sheep find her. If Jonas was still alive. The thought that she might have killed him made her shudder. It had been one thing to wish him dead, to think she could kill him to save her daughter, but to actually know that she might have killed the man…

She crawled over to a pine tree and used the trunk to get to her feet. As she started to take a step, she saw a figure suddenly appear out of the blackness of the trees.

Lola felt a sob rise in her throat. She'd never been so glad to see anyone in her life. Colt. He seemed just as overwhelmed with joy to see her. She'd thought he would have left—as per their plan. But he couldn't leave her.

Another sob rose as he ran to her, grabbed her and pulled her to him, holding her so tightly she could hardly breath. "Lola," he kept saying against her hair. "Lola."

She couldn't speak. Her throat had closed as she fought to hold back the tears of relief. As he let go, she stepped down on her bad ankle and let out a cry of pain.

"You're hurt. What is it?" he asked, his voice filled with concern.

"My ankle. I'm not sure I can walk."

He swung her up in his arms and carried her through the trees to the truck. She hadn't realized how close she was to where they'd parked it earlier.

She looked around, suddenly scared. "Grace? Where's Grace?"

He unlocked the passenger side of the pickup, opened the door and picked up a bundle wrapped in his coat. She heard a sound come from within the bundle as Colt helped her into the pickup and put Grace into her arms. The tears came now, a floodgate opening. No longer could she hold back.

Tears streaming down her face, she turned back the edge of

Colt's coat, which was wrapped around the infant. "Grace," she said as Colt slid behind the wheel, started the truck and headed off the mountain.

Lola held her baby, watching her daughter's sweet face in the faint light as Grace fell back asleep. She thought she could stare into that face forever. For so long she'd feared she'd never see her again, never hold her. She wiped at her tears and looked over at Colt. He smiled and she could see the emotion in his face.

"Have you met your daughter?" she asked.

"I have," he said, his voice sounding rough. "We got acquainted while we were waiting for you, until I couldn't wait any longer and had to come looking for you."

"I'm so thankful you did."

"Let's go home," he said, his voice breaking.

Tears filled her eyes again as she looked from him to their daughter. She pulled Grace close as they left the mountain and headed toward the ranch. Home.

CHAPTER TWELVE

JONAS CAME TO, lying on his back in a pool of his own blood. His hand went to the side of his head and came away sticky. He stared for a few moments at his fingers, the tips bright red, before he tried to sit up.

His head swam, forcing him to remain where he was. He couldn't remember what had happened. Had he fallen? He'd been meaning to have one of the brothers fix that rug to keep the corner from turning up.

But from where he lay, he could see that the rug wasn't to blame. Not twelve inches from him sat a rock the size of a cantaloupe. A dark stain covered one side of it. Nearby was a baby blanket and another rock of similar size.

Memory flooded him along with a cold, deadly rage. The pain in his skull was nothing compared to the open wound of Lola's betrayal. His heart felt as if it had been ripped out of his chest.

He thought of those moments when she'd been holding what he thought was her infant in her arms. They'd been talking and she had made it sound as if she was weakening toward him. His heart had soared with hope that she was finally coming around. He had so much to offer her. Had she finally realized that she'd be a fool to turn him down?

He'd been so happy for those moments when he'd thought things were going to work out with her and even the baby. That other man's baby, but a baby Jonas was willing to raise as his own as long as Lola became his wife and submitted to him.

The shock when she'd pulled the rock from the baby blankets was still painfully fresh. It had taken him a moment, his arms outstretched as he'd reached to take her and the infant to his bosom. The shock, the disappointment, the disbelief had slowed his movements, letting the rock get past his defenses and stun him just long enough that she was able to pull out the second rock and hit him much harder.

He closed his eyes now. He was in so much pain, but a thought wriggled its way through. His eyelids flew open. His mind felt perfectly clear, making him aware of the quiet. He recalled the alert alarm going off. When Lola had come to him with the baby... Yes, he recalled. He'd sounded the all clear signal.

Why hadn't there been another alert? He had to assume that Lola had gotten away. Gotten away with the baby. If she'd been caught, she would have been brought to him by now. And if Sister Rebecca had checked the crib and found the baby missing...

For a moment, he thought the alarm must have sounded while he'd been unconscious. But if that was true, then Brother Zack would have come to check on him and found him lying here, bleeding to death.

Two things suddenly became crystal clear. Even through the excruciating pain, he saw now that Lola couldn't have acted alone. She would have had help to get the baby off the compound. And her showing up at his door with what he thought was the baby was only a diversion.

He let out a bitter laugh. As persuasive as he'd been, it was just as he'd feared. He hadn't convinced Colt McCloud that the woman was unbalanced, that their baby boy had died, that he should leave Lola while he could.

Apparently, she'd been more convincing than he had been. He

grimaced at the thought. Admittedly, he had to give her credit—her plan had worked. Or had it been Colt McCloud's plan? He closed his eyes, cursing the man to hell. Colt was a dead man.

But so was he, he realized, if he didn't get help. He was still bleeding and even more light-headed. He felt around for his cell phone to activate the alarm.

He had to turn his head to find it. The pain was so intense that he almost passed out. He closed his hand around the phone and, leaving bloody fingerprints, hit the button to activate the alarm.

His hand holding the phone dropped to his side as the air filled with the shrill cry of the alert. Any moment Brother Zack would come bursting through the door. He could always depend on Zack.

Unlike someone else, he thought, remembering his second realization. If he was right, Colt had taken the baby while Lola had pretended to be acting alone. The alarm had sounded and she had known that she couldn't get away. So she'd come up to Jonas's cabin with the rocks in the baby blankets.

But wouldn't someone have checked the baby's crib? And then wouldn't Sister Rebecca, who was responsible for the infant, have realized the baby was gone and summoned help? Pulled the alarm again?

As Brother Zack burst through the front door and rushed to him, Jonas felt the steel blade of betrayal cut even deeper. One of his flock had betrayed him.

CHAPTER THIRTEEN

COLT WOKE TO find Lola and the baby sleeping peacefully next to him. He felt his heart do a bump in his chest. The sight filled him with a sense of joy. A sense that all was right in the world.

Last night on the way down the mountain he'd felt like they were a family. It was a strange feeling for a man who'd been so independent for so long. They'd been exhausted, Lola barely able to walk on her ankle. He'd gotten them both inside the house and safe as quickly as he could.

With Grace sleeping in the middle of his big bed, he'd taken a look at Lola's ankle. Not broken, but definitely sprained badly. He'd wrapped it, both of them simply looking at each other and smiling. They'd done it. They'd gotten Grace back.

He had questions, but they could wait. Or maybe he never had to know what had happened back at the compound. He told himself it was over. They had Grace. That was all the proof they needed against Jonas should he try to take either the baby or Lola back.

They'd gone to bed, Grace curled between them, and fallen asleep instantly.

At the sound of a vehicle, Colt wondered who would be coming by so early in the morning as he slipped out of bed and quickly dressed.

Someone was knocking at his front door by the time he reached it. He peered out, worried for a moment that he'd find Jonas Emanuel standing on his front step.

"Sheriff," Colt said as he opened the door.

"A moment of your time," Flint said.

Colt stepped back to let the sheriff enter the house. Flint glanced around, clearly looking for something.

He'd been wondering how Jonas was going to handle this. He'd thought Jonas wouldn't call in the sheriff about the events of last night. He still didn't think he would. But this was definitely not a social call.

"What can I help you with, Sheriff?"

Flint turned to give him his full attention. "Jonas reported a break-in at the SLS compound last night. I was wondering if you knew anything about that."

"Was anything taken?"

Flint smiled. "Apparently not. But Jonas was injured when he tried to apprehend one of the intruders."

That was news. Colt thought of Lola just down the hall still in bed with Grace. Last night when he was wrapping her ankle, he'd seen what looked like blood on her sleeve. But he hadn't want to ask what she'd had to go through to get away.

"He see who did it?" Colt asked.

"Apparently not," Flint said again.

Just then the sound of a baby crying could be heard down the hall toward the bedroom.

Flint froze.

"So nothing was taken," Colt said. "Jonas's injuries..."

"Aren't life-threatening at this point," Flint said as Lola limped down the hall from the bedroom, the baby in her arms.

Lola spotted the sheriff and stopped, her gaze flying to Colt. She looked worried until Colt said, "You remember Lola. And this is our daughter, Grace."

Colt moved to her to take the baby. He stepped to the sheriff, turning back the blanket his daughter was nestled in.

Every time he saw her sweet face his heart swelled to over-flowing. She was so precious. Having never changed a diaper in his life, he'd learned quickly last night.

Now he lifted the cotton gown she'd been wearing when Lola had taken her from the crib last night at SLS to expose the tiny heart-shaped birthmark.

"Our baby girl," Colt said. "We'll be going to the doctor later today to have her checked over—and a DNA test done, in case you were wondering."

Flint nodded solemnly, and Colt handed Grace back to Lola. As she limped into the kitchen with the baby, the sheriff said, "I'm not going to ask, but I hope you know what you're doing."

"That little girl belongs with her mother."

The sheriff met his gaze. "And her father?"

"I'm her father."

Flint sighed. "I was at the hospital this morning taking Jonas's statement. He isn't filing assault charges because he says he doesn't know who attacked him. I see Lola is limping."

Colt said nothing.

"You sure this is over?" the sheriff asked.

"It is as far as I'm concerned."

Flint nodded. "Not sure Jonas feels that way. Got the impression he's a man who is used to getting what he wants."

Colt couldn't have agreed more. "He can't have Lola and Grace, but I don't want any trouble."

The sheriff shook his head at that. "I'm afraid it won't be your choice."

He knew a warning when he heard one. Not that he had to be told that Jonas was dangerous. "He's brainwashed those people, taken their money and keeps them up on that mountain like prisoners."

Flint nodded. "A choice each of them made."

"Except for the children up there."

"You think I like any of what I saw on that mountain?" Flint swore. "But you also know there is nothing I can do about it.

That's private property up there. Jonas has every right to keep trespassers off. Not to mention it is church property, holy ground under the law."

"I have no intention of going up there."

"I wish I thought it was that simple." The sheriff had taken off his Stetson when he'd come into the house, and now he settled his hat back on his head. Turning, he started for the door. "You know my number," he said over his shoulder. "I'll come as quickly as I can. But I fear even that could be too late."

"Thanks for stopping by, Sheriff."

At the door, Flint turned to look back at him. Lola had come out of the kitchen carrying the baby. She was smiling down at Grace, cooing softly.

Flint's expression softened and Colt remembered that Darby had mentioned the sheriff's wife was pregnant. "Have a good day," Flint said, and left.

Jonas listened to the doctor tell him how lucky he was. He had a monster headache and hated being flat on his back in the hospital when he had things that needed to be done—and quickly.

"You lost a lot of blood," the doctor was saying. "If your... friend hadn't gotten you here when he did..."

"Yes, it is fortunate that Brother Zack found me when he did," Jonas said. He didn't need the doctor telling him how lucky he was. He was very aware. But a man made his own luck. He'd learned that when he'd left home to find his own way in life.

Not that he discounted what nature had given him—a handsome, honest-looking face, mesmerizing blue eyes and snake-oil-salesman charm. But he was the one who'd taken those gifts and used them to the best of his ability. Not that they always worked. Lola, a case in point. They'd worked enough, though, that he was a very rich man and, until recently, he would have said he had very loyal followers who saw to his every need. What more could a man ask for?

"You're going to have a headache for a while, but fortunately, you suffered only a minor concussion. A fall like that could have killed a man half your age. Like I said, lucky."

"Lucky," Jonas repeated. "Yes, Doctor, I was. So when can I be released?"

"Your laceration is healing quite nicely, but that bandage needs to be changed regularly so I'd prefer you stay in the hospital at least another day, maybe longer."

That was not what he wanted to hear. "One of the sisters could change my bandage for me. Really, I would be much more comfortable in my own home. I have plenty of people to look after me."

The doctor wavered. Jonas knew that the hospital staff would be much more comfortable with him gone, as well. A half dozen of the brothers and some of the SLS sisters had been coming and going since his "accident." He'd seen the way the hospital staff looked at them, the men in their black pants and white shirts, the woman in their long shapeless white dresses.

"I'd prefer you stay another day at least. I'll give instructions to one of your…sisters for after that. We'll see how you're doing tomorrow."

"I'm feeling so much better. I promise that when you release me, I will rest and take care of myself." His head ached more than he had let the doctor know. He didn't want any medication that would make his brain fuzzy. He needed his wits about him now more than ever.

"Like I said, we'll see how you are tomorrow," the doctor said, eyeing him suspiciously. The man knew Jonas couldn't be feeling that good, not with his head almost bashed in. He also knew the doctor had to be questioning how he could have hurt himself like this in a fall.

Jonas just wished he would go away and leave him alone.

"I need to ask you about these pills you've been taking," the doctor said, clearly not leaving yet. "One of your church members told me they were for a bad heart, but that's not the medication you're taking."

"No, it's not for a heart ailment," Jonas had to admit. "I'd prefer my flock not worry about my health, Doctor."

"If you're suffering from memory loss at your age, then we need to run some tests and see—"

"I have early-onset Alzheimer's," Jonas interrupted.

The doctor blinked.

"It is in the beginning stages, thus the pills I'm taking. I can assure you that I'm being well taken care of."

The doctor seemed at a loss for words.

"I believe Brother Zack is waiting in the hall," Jonas said to the doctor. "Would you ask him to step in here? I need to talk to him."

Realizing he was excused, the doctor left. A few moments later, Zack stuck his head in the door.

Jonas motioned him in. "Close the door. Have you seen Sister Rebecca?"

"Not since last night."

"Who was on duty at the second nursery last night?" he asked.

Zack frowned. "Sister Alexa." His eyes widened as he realized what the leader was really asking. "Sister Rebecca was taking care of the...special baby."

The angel. That's what Jonas had told his flock. That he'd had a vision and Lola's baby was a chosen one.

"Sister Rebecca." Jonas nodded and closed his eyes for a moment. He'd known it, but had needed Zack to verify his suspicions. Rebecca had been with him since the beginning. If there was anyone he knew he could trust, could depend on, it was her. He slowly opened his eyes and stared up at the pale green ceiling.

Zack stood at the end of the bed, waiting. Rebecca and Zack had never gotten along. Jonas blamed it on simple jealousy. Both were in the top positions at SLS. He knew how much Zack was going to enjoy the task he was about to give him.

"Go back to the complex," Jonas told him. "I want Sister

Rebecca—" if she was still there "—restrained. Use the cabin where Sister Lola stayed. Guard it yourself." He finally looked at Zack, who nodded, a malicious glint in his gaze even as he fought not to smile.

"I'll take care of it."

After the sheriff left, Colt stepped to Lola and Grace and pulled them close. He knew the sheriff was worried and with good reason. Jonas was an egomaniac who enjoyed having power over other people. He ran his "church" like a fiefdom. He would be incensed to have lost Lola and the baby, but there was really nothing he could do. At least not legally. Once the DNA results came back, once they had proof that Grace was Colt's daughter...

He tried to put it out of his head. Jonas was in the hospital. He'd lied to the sheriff. It was over. Hopefully, the man would move on with some other obsession.

Colt cooked them breakfast while Lola fed Grace. He loved watching them together. It made his heart expand to near bursting.

Their day was quickly planned. First the DNA tests, then shopping for baby things. Never in his life had Colt thought about buying baby things, but now he realized he was excited. He wanted Grace to have whatever she needed.

At the doctor's office DNA samples were taken, then Colt took Lola and Grace to the small-box store on the edge of town. He was amazed at all the things a baby needed. Not just clothing and a car seat, but bottles and formula, baby food, diapers and wipes.

"How did babies survive before all of these things were on the market?" he joked, then insisted they get a changing table.

"It's too much," Lola said at one point.

"It's all good," he'd said, wanting only the best for his daughter. At the back of his mind, like a tiny devil perched on his shoulder, a voice was saying, "What are you doing? You are going back on assignment soon."

He shoved the thought aside, telling himself that he'd cross that bridge when he got there. He still had time. But time for what? There hadn't been any offers on the ranch. It was another thought that he pushed aside. Instead, he concentrated on Lola and Grace, enjoying being with them. Enjoying pretending at least for a while that they were a family.

He didn't even need the DNA test. That was all Lola. "We need it for Jonas should he ever try to take Grace again," she'd said. "Also, I don't want you to have doubts."

"I don't have any doubts."

She'd given him a dubious look. "I want it settled. Not that I will ever ask anything of you. And I will pay you back for all the baby things you bought. I called this morning and am having some money wired to me."

"That isn't necessary."

But she said nothing, a stubborn tilt to her chin. He hadn't argued.

Instead, he took them back to the Stagecoach Saloon where, the moment they walked in, he knew that Billie Dee was cooking up her famous Texas chili.

Lillie Cahill Beaumont just happened to be there visiting her brother, along with Darby and his wife, Mariah. They oohed and aahed over Grace and Lola did the same with their babies.

By the time they got home, Colt was ready for a nap, too. After Lola put Grace down, she came into the bedroom and curled up against him. He held her close, breathing in the scent of her. He'd never been more happy.

CHAPTER FOURTEEN

THE NEXT DAY, Jonas couldn't wait for the doctor to stop by so he could hopefully get out of the hospital. He knew that Zack was taking care of things on the complex, but he worried. He still couldn't believe that Rebecca would betray him. It shook the stable foundation that he'd built this life on. Never would he have suspected her of deceiving him.

When the doctor finally came by, he hadn't wanted to send Jonas home yet. It took a lot of lying to get the doctor to finally release him. It was late in the day before he finally got his discharge papers.

Elmer picked him up at the hospital and drove him to the compound. He liked Elmer, though he'd seen the man's faith in their work here fading. He and Lola's father had been friends. Jonas suspected Elmer only stayed because he had nowhere else to go. But that was all right. Jonas still thought that when the chips were down, he could depend on Elmer.

Once at the compound, Zack was waiting, Excusing Elmer, Jonas let Zack help him inside. He was weak and his head ached, but he was home. He had things that needed to be taken care of and had been going crazy in the hospital.

Three of the sisters entered his cabin, fussed over him until he couldn't take it any longer and sent them scurrying. The pain in his head was better. It was another pain that was riding him like a dark cloak on his shoulders.

As soon as he was settled, Jonas asked Zack to bring him Sister Rebecca. "She's still detained in the small cabin, right?"

"She is," Zack said.

"How is her...attitude?"

"Subdued."

Jonas almost laughed since it didn't seem like a word Zack would ever have used. "Subdued? Is she on anything?"

"No, but I've had the sisters chanting over her every few hours. I thought it was something you would have done yourself had you been here."

He was both touched and annoyed by Zack taking this step without his permission. But he needed Zack more than ever now so he let it go. "You did well. Thank you."

Zack beamed and Jonas saw something in the man's eyes that gave him pause. Zack wanted to lead SLS. The man actually thought he had what it took to do it. The realization was almost laughable.

"Bring Sister Rebecca to me," he said, and closed his eyes, his head pounding like a bass drum. He wondered if he shouldn't have put this off until he was feeling better.

Zack hurried out, leaving him peacefully alone with his thoughts. Lola had made a fool out of him by sleeping with Colt McCloud. To add to his embarrassment, she'd gotten pregnant. That child should have been his.

Instead, he'd put aside his hurt, his fury, his embarrassment and offered to raise the baby as his own. Still, she'd turned him down. How could she have humiliated him even more?

He let out a bark of a laugh. What had she done? She'd almost killed him—after giving him hope that she was weakening. The latter hurt the most. Offering hope was a poisonous pill that he'd swallowed in one big gulp. And now even his flock was turning against him.

Was he losing his mind faster than he'd thought? Could he trust his judgment?

He started at the knock on the door, forgetting for a moment that he'd been expecting it. "Come in."

The moment Rebecca walked through the door, he could see the guilt written all over her face. Brother Zack stood directly behind her. He started to step into the cabin, and Jonas could tell Zack thought he was going to get to watch this.

"That will be all, Zack."

The man looked surprised and then disappointed. But it was the flicker of anger he saw in Zack's eyes that caused concern.

Jonas watched his right-hand man slowly close the door, but he could tell he'd be standing outside hoping to hear whatever was going on. Was Zack now becoming a problem, too?

He saw Sister Rebecca quickly take him in. In her gaze shone concern and something even more disturbing—sympathy, if not pity. His head was still bandaged, dark stitches under the dressing, but his headaches were getting better. Stuck in the hospital, he'd had plenty of time to think over the past two days.

It was bad enough to be betrayed by Lola, even worse by Sister Rebecca, because he'd come to depend on her. She had to have known that Lola's baby had gone missing. It would have been the first thing she would have checked. Seeing the baby missing, she should have come to him.

He was anxious to talk to her, but as he looked at her standing there, he felt a loss of words for a moment. He kept telling himself that he was wrong. Sister Rebecca had been with him for years. She wouldn't betray him. Couldn't. He'd always thought she was half in love with him.

Which was probably why she hadn't come to him to let him know the baby wasn't in her crib. Even if she'd seen Lola with that bundle in her arms entering his cabin, she should have come to him. If she had, his head wouldn't be killing him right now. But he suspected Rebecca had wanted to be shed of Lola and the baby he was so determined to make his.

Since Zack had locked up Rebecca, she would know she was in trouble. He wondered what story she would tell him and how much of it he could believe?

Colt almost changed his mind. Things had been going so well that he didn't want or need the interruption. He enjoyed being with Lola and Grace. If he said so himself, he'd become proficient at diaper changes and getting chubby little limbs into onesies. He liked the middle-of-the-night feedings, holding Grace and watching her take her bottle. Her bright blue eyes watched him equally.

"I'm your daddy," he'd whispered last night, and felt a lump rise in his throat.

So when Julia had called and said it was important that they meet and talk, he hadn't been interested.

"If this is about you needing me to forgive you—"

"No. It's not that," she'd said quickly. "I doubt you can ever forgive me. I know how badly I hurt you."

Did she? The news had blindsided him. Hell, he'd been expecting her to pick him up at the airport—not break up with him to be with one of his friends. He still couldn't get his head around how that had gone down. No warning at all. He'd thought Wyatt hadn't even liked Julia. He knew that Darby didn't think she was right for him. Not that Darby had ever said anything. But Colt had been able to tell.

He could laugh now. He used to think that Darby just had his expectations set too high. But then Colt had met Mariah and realized that his friend had just been holding out for the real thing. Darby had done well.

"Julia, I can't see what meeting you for coffee could possibly—" It had been Lola who'd insisted he meet with Julia. She'd walked in while he was on the phone. As if gifted with ESP, she'd motioned to him that he should go.

"Fine," he'd said into the phone. "When and where?" He had just wanted to get it over with.

Now he drove past the coffee shop, telling himself that there was nothing Julia could say that would change anything. But she'd sounded...strange on the phone. He suspected something was up. Did he care, though?

He circled the block, saw a parking space and pulled his pickup in to it. For a moment he sat behind the wheel debating what he was about to do. And why had Lola been all for him seeing his ex? Was she worried that he wasn't over Julia? Or was she hoping to hook the two of them up again?

He'd heard her on the phone calling a car dealership to order a vehicle. "You don't have to do that. You can use my pickup whenever you want."

"I need my own car, but thank you," she'd said.

He thought of the discussion they'd had after he'd hung up from Julia.

"I knew that was Julia on the phone," Lola had said. "I wasn't eavesdropping. You talk to her in a certain way." She'd shrugged.

"A certain way?"

"I can't describe it, but you owe her nothing."

"Then why should I meet with her?"

"Because it won't be over until you tell her how you feel," Lola had said.

He had laughed. She made life seem so simple, and yet could her life have been any more complicated when he'd met her? "Okay, I'll meet with her with your blessing."

"You don't need my blessing."

He stepped to her and, taking her shoulders in his hands, pulled her close. "All I care about is you and Grace. You have to know that."

"So you'll talk to her. You'll be honest. You'll see if there is anything there that you might have missed. Or that you want back."

He'd wanted to argue the point, but she'd put a finger to his lips.

"You should go. She'll be waiting."

Let her wait, he thought now as he glanced at his watch. Let her think he wasn't coming—look how she'd treated him at the Billings airport.

Then, just wanting to be done with this, he climbed out and walked down to the coffee shop. It was midafternoon. Only a few tables were taken. Julia had chosen one at the back. Where no one would see the two of them together and report back to Wyatt?

As he pushed open the door, he saw her frowning down at her phone. Checking the time? Or reading a text from Wyatt?

She looked up as if sensing him and motioned him over. "I got you a coffee—just the way you like it."

Except he'd never liked his coffee that way. Julia had come out to the ranch when they'd first started dating with some caramel-mocha concoction. When he'd taken a sip, he'd had to force a smile and pretend he'd liked it. His mistake.

"It's good, huh. I thought you'd like it. You always have the same boring coffee. I thought we'd shake things up a bit," she'd said. And from then on, she'd decided that was the way he liked his coffee.

"Thanks," he said now, without sitting down, "But I never liked my coffee that way. I'll get my own." He moved to the counter and ordered a cup of black coffee before returning to the table.

She looked sullen, pouting like she used to when he'd displeased her—which was often enough that he knew this look too well.

"So what is it you want?" he asked as he sat down but didn't settle in. He didn't plan to stay long and was regretting coming here, no matter what Lola had said. He couldn't see how this could help anything.

Julia let out a nervous laugh. "This is not the way I saw this going."

"Oh?"

She seemed to regroup, drawing in a long breath, sitting up

a little straighter. He was suddenly aware that she'd dressed up. He caught a hint of the perfume she used to wear when they were together because he'd commented one time that he liked it. He frowned as he realized she hadn't been wearing it the day they'd accidentally run into each other.

"What's going on, Julia?"

She looked away for a moment, biting down on the corner of her lower lip as if nervous. He used to think it was cute.

"I've made a terrible mistake. I didn't mean to blurt it out like that, but I can tell you're still angry and have no patience with me. Otherwise, you wouldn't have been so late, you would have drunk the coffee I ordered you and you wouldn't be looking at me as if you hated me."

He wasn't going to try to straighten her up on any of that. "Mistake?"

Julia looked at him as if she thought no one would be that daft. "Wyatt. I was just so lonely, and it looked as if you were never going to quit the military and come home…"

"How did you two get together? I always thought Wyatt didn't like you."

She mugged a face at him. "You don't need to be cruel."

"I'm serious. He never had a good word to say about you. Or was he just trying to keep his feelings for you from me?"

"I have no idea. And I don't care. He probably didn't like me. Maybe that's why we aren't together anymore."

Colt realized he wasn't surprised. Julia hadn't gotten him to the altar. He remembered that had been the case with an earlier boyfriend, too. Looked like there was a pattern there, he thought but kept it to himself.

"That's too bad."

"I can tell that you're really broken up over it."

After the initial shock had worn off, he'd actually thought Julia and Wyatt wouldn't last. Julia was beautiful in a classic way, but definitely high maintenance. He could see that clearly after being around Lola. As for Wyatt, well, he'd never had a serious girlfriend. He'd always preferred playing the field, as he called it.

"I'm sincerely sorry it didn't work out. Is that all?"

"Colt, stop being so mean." She sounded close to tears. She glanced around to make sure no one had heard her. "I feel so bad about what I did to you."

"You shouldn't." He realized he meant it. For a while, he'd hoped she choked on the guilt daily. Now he didn't feel vindictive. He realized he no longer cared.

"I know how hurt you must be."

"I was hurt, Julia. That was one crushing blow you delivered, but I've moved on."

"With that woman you were with the other day? Are you in love with her?"

Now there was the question, wasn't it? "It's complicated."

"It doesn't have to be." She reached across the table and covered his hand.

He pulled his free. "Are you suggesting what I think you are?"

She looked at him as if to say, *No one can be this dense.* "I want you back. I'll do anything." She definitely sounded desperate.

Colt had played with this exact scheme in his mind on those long nights in the desert after she'd dumped him. It had been like a salve that made him feel better. Julia begging to come back to him. Him loving every minute of it before he turned her down flat.

Now it made him feel uncomfortable because he no longer wanted to hurt her. If anything, he felt indifferent and wondered what he'd ever seen in this woman. He couldn't help comparing her to Lola. Julia came up way short.

"Julia, you and I are never getting back together. Truthfully, I doubt we would have made it to the altar."

"How can you say that?" she demanded. "You asked me to marry you."

"I did. But I didn't realize then how wrong we were for each other. I overlooked things, thinking they would change once we were married. Now I know better. I'm sure it was the same for you. Otherwise, how could you have fallen so quickly in love with another man?"

She seemed at a loss for words.

"So I imagine we both would have realized we weren't right for each other before we made a huge mistake."

Julia stared at him as if looking at a stranger. "I don't believe this."

Had she expected him to take her back at the snap of her fingers? The flutter of her eyelashes? She really hadn't known him. Even if he'd never met Lola, he wouldn't have taken Julia back. She'd proved the kind of woman she was—not the kind a man could ever trust.

Colt got to his feet. "You should try to work things out with Wyatt. Now that I think about it, you two belong together."

Her eyes widened, then narrowed dangerously. "Do you realize what you're throwing away? And for what? That…that… woman I saw you with the other day?" She made a distasteful face.

"Easy, Julia," he said, lowering his voice. "You really don't want to say anything about the mother of my child."

"What?" she sputtered.

"Lola and I have a beautiful daughter together."

Openmouthed, she stared at him. "Lola? That's not possible. You can't have known her long enough to… Are you going to *marry* her?"

"I haven't asked her yet, but you know me. I like to take my time. Also, I'm a little gun-shy after my last engagement."

Julia pushed to her feet. He'd never seen her so angry. It made him want to laugh because he realized, with no small amount of relief, that had he married her, he would have seen her like this a lot.

The one thing he did know was that he was completely over

her. No hard feelings. No need for retribution. No need to ever see this woman again.

"This never happened," she said with a flip of her head. "You hear me? You're right. Wyatt and I are perfect together. We're going to get married and be happy."

He smiled. "So you and Wyatt aren't broken up." He let out a bark of a laugh. "Good to see that you haven't changed. Give Wyatt my regards."

Julia stormed out. Colt finished his coffee and threw away the cups Julia had left behind. He smiled as he headed for the door. He couldn't wait to get home to Lola and Grace.

CHAPTER FIFTEEN

LOLA SAW THE change in Colt the moment he walked in the door. It was as if a weight had been lifted off his shoulders. He was smiling and seemed...happy.

"I guess I don't need to ask how it went." Her heart had been pounding ever since Julia's phone call. A woman knows. Julia wanted more than Colt's forgiveness. A woman like that would try to hold on to him, to keep him in the wings—if she didn't already want him back.

Colt met her gaze. "She wants me back."

It felt as if a fist had closed around her heart, but she fought not to let him see her pain. "That must seem like a dream come true."

He laughed. "I'll admit at one time it would have been. But no," he said with a shake of his head as he stepped to her. "It would never have happened even if I hadn't met you. But now that I have..." He leaned down to kiss her softly on the mouth. As he drew back, he saw that she was frowning.

"I don't want you giving up the woman you love because of me and Grace," she said quickly. "I told you. We can take care of ourselves."

"That wasn't what I meant." His blue-eyed gaze locked with

hers and she felt a bolt of heat shoot to her core. "Julia is the last person on earth that I want."

She swallowed. "But you asked her to marry you."

"I did." He chuckled. "And I have no idea why I did. Honestly, I feel as if I dodged a bullet. But I don't want to talk about her. I want you," he said as he drew her close again. "Is Grace sleeping?"

While he'd been gone, Lola had practiced what she was going to say to him. But when she looked up into his blue gaze and saw the desire burning there, it ignited the blaze inside her.

She told herself that they could have a serious talk later. There was time. Colt was in such a good mood, she didn't want to bring him down. She cared too much about him. But that was the problem, wasn't it? She was falling in love with him. And that was why she and Grace had to leave before Colt did something stupid like ask her to stay.

Later, after making love and falling into a sated sleep, Colt heard Grace wake up from her nap and slipped out of bed to go see to her. "Hi, sweetheart," he said as he picked her up and carried her over to the changing table. As he changed her, he talked to her, telling her how pretty and sweet she was.

She was Lola in miniature, from her pert nose to her bow-shaped mouth to her violet eyes. And yet, he saw some of himself in the baby—and knew it might be only because he wanted it to be true. They hadn't gotten the DNA results, not that he was worried.

What bothered him was how much he wanted to see himself in Grace. How much he wanted to tell her about all the things he'd teach her as she grew up. What he wanted to do was talk about the future with Grace—and Lola.

Getting Lola's baby back was one thing, but seeing himself in this equation? He would have said the last thing he needed was a family. He was selling the ranch and going back into the service. That had been his plan and he'd always had a plan.

Now he felt rudderless and aloft, not knowing if he was up or down. What would he do if not go back to flying choppers for the Army? Ranch?

He stared into Grace's adorable face, feeling his heart ache at the thought of being away from her. He picked her up, holding her as he felt his heart pounding next to hers. Fatherhood had always been so far off in the future. But now here it was looking back at him with so much trust... He thought of his own father, his parents' disastrous marriage, how disconnected he'd felt from both of them.

He knew nothing about being a father or a husband. A part of him felt guilty for asking Julia to marry him. True, he'd put her off for years. It had come down to break up or marry her. He'd thought it was what he'd wanted.

Now, though, he knew his heart hadn't been in it. What he'd told Julia earlier had been true. He doubted they would have made it to the altar. After he'd put that diamond—she'd picked it out herself—on her finger, all she'd talked about was the big wedding they would have, the big house, the big life.

He'd let her talk, not really taking her seriously. He should have, though.

While Lola... Well, she was different. Her heart was so filled with love for their child that she'd risked her life numerous times. He'd never met anyone like her. And Grace... She smiled and cooed up at him, her gaze meeting his, and he felt her steal another piece of his heart if she hadn't already taken it all.

"Does she need changing?" Lola asked from the doorway.

"All taken care of. She just smiled at me."

Lola laughed. "I saw that." She'd been watching from the doorway, he realized. He wondered how long she'd been there. She was wearing one of his shirts and, he'd bet, nothing under it. She couldn't have looked sexier.

His cell phone rang. Lola moved to him to take the baby.

After pulling out his phone, Colt felt a start when he saw

that it was Margaret Barnes, his Realtor, calling. He'd forgotten about her, about listing the ranch. All that seemed like ages ago.

"Hello?" he said as he headed out of the nursery.

"Colt, I have some good news for you. I have a buyer for your ranch."

For a moment he couldn't speak. He looked back at Lola and Grace from the doorway. Lola was rocking the baby in her arms, smiling down at her, and Grace was cooing and smiling up at her mother—just as she had done moments before with her father.

"Colt, are you there?"

"Yes." He saw Lola look up as if she heard something in his voice.

"You said to find a buyer as quickly as I could. If you have some time today, stop by my office. I can get the paperwork all ready. The buyer is fine with your asking price and would like to take possession as soon as possible."

He felt as if the earth was crumbling under his feet. Yes, he'd told her to find a buyer and as quickly as possible. But that had been before. Before Lola had shown up at his door in the middle of the night. Before he'd known about Grace.

"What is it?" Lola asked, seeing his distress as she joined him in the living room. "Bad news?"

He stood holding his phone after disconnecting. "That was the Realtor."

Lola hadn't asked about the for-sale sign on the road into the ranch and he hadn't brought it up. But Lola knew what his plans had been months ago. The night they'd met he'd told her he was going to accept another Army assignment rather than resign his commission, like he'd been planning before that night, to marry Julia.

"Does she have a buyer for the ranch?" Lola asked, giving nothing away.

He wasn't sure what kind of reaction he'd been expecting. His gaze went to Grace in her arms. He felt his heart breaking. Lately, his only concern had been protecting Lola, getting Grace back and making sure that horrible Jonas didn't have either of them.

He hadn't thought about the future. Hadn't let himself. "I think we should talk about—" His phone rang again. He checked it, hoping it was the Realtor calling again. He'd tell her he needed more time.

It was the doctor calling. He glanced at Lola and then picked up. "Doc?" he said into the phone.

"Your test results are back. You're welcome to come by and I would be happy to explain anything you didn't understand about DNA testing."

"Let's just cut to the chase, Doc."

Silence hung on the other end of the line for a long few moments. "The infant is a match for both Lola and you, Colt."

"Thanks, Doc." He looked to Lola, who didn't appear all that interested. Because she'd known all along.

"Are you all right?" she asked.

He nodded, but he wasn't. Grace had fallen back to sleep in her arms. Had there ever been a more beautiful, ethereal-looking child? No wonder Jonas had wanted her. Wanted her and Lola.

If he looked like a man in pain, he was. Lola and the baby had taken his already topsy-turvy life and given it a tailspin. All he'd wanted just days ago was to get out of this town, out of this state, out from under the ranch his father had left him and the responsibility that came with it.

Now, though, he no longer wanted to run. He wanted to plant roots. He wanted to make them a family. "I think we should get married." The words were out and he wasn't sorry to hear them. But he should have done something romantic, not just blurted them out like that.

To his surprise, Lola smiled at him. "That's sweet, but...it's too early, isn't it?"

Too early? Like in the morning or—

"We hardly know each other."

"I'd say we know each other quite well," he said as he picked up the tail end of his shirt she was wearing.

She laughed and playfully slapped his hand away as she headed for the spare room that they'd made into a makeshift nursery. "You know what I mean."

He followed her and watched as she put Grace down in the crib. "We have a daughter."

"Yes, we do. But we can't get married just for Grace. You know that wouldn't work."

"But neither can I let the two of you walk out that door," he said.

"Colt, that door will soon be someone else's."

She had a point.

"I won't sell the ranch."

She gave him a pointed look. "I owe you my life and Grace's. But I also owe you something else. Freedom. Grace and I can take care of ourselves now. Jonas is no longer a problem. He isn't going to bother us, not after the sheriff saw our daughter and knows that Jonas lied about keeping her from me. My parents set aside money for me should I ever need it and I saved the money I made teaching. Grace and I will be fine."

"But *I* won't be fine."

She looked at him, sympathy in her gaze.

"Lola, I need you. I need you and our daughter. I want us to be a family."

Tears welled in her eyes as she tried to pass him. "Colt."

He took her in his arms. "I know we haven't known each other long. But the night we met, we connected in a way that neither of us had before, right?" She nodded, though reluctantly it seemed. "And we've been through more than any couple can ever imagine, and yet we worked together and pulled it off against incredible odds. If any two people can make this work, it's you and me."

She smiled sweetly, but he could tell she wasn't convinced. "We're good together, I won't deny that. But, Colt, you don't want to ranch. You admitted that to me the first night we met. Now you're talking about keeping the ranch just to make a home for me and Grace? No, Colt. You would grow to resent us for tying you down. I see how your eyes light up when you talk about flying helicopters. That's what you love. That's where you need to be."

He wanted to argue, but he couldn't. She'd listened to him. She knew him better than even he knew himself. "Still—"

"No," she said as she moved down the hallway to the room that they now shared. She began to pick up her clothing. "This is best and we both know it."

It didn't feel like the best thing to do. He'd come to look forward to seeing Lola's face each morning, hear her singing to the baby at night and spending his days with the two of them.

"Promise you won't leave just yet," he said, panicking at the sight of her getting her things ready.

She stopped and looked at him. "I'll stay until the ranch closes so you can spend as much time with Grace as possible. But then we have to go."

"It isn't just Grace I want to spend time with," he said as he drew her close. He kissed her and told himself he'd figure out something. He had to. Because he couldn't bear the thought of either of them walking out of his life.

Jonas studied the woman before him, letting her wait. Sister Rebecca was what was known as a handsome woman. She stood almost six feet tall with straight brown hair cut chin-length. Close to his own age, she wasn't pretty, never had been. If anything, she was nondescript. You could pass her on the street and not see her.

That was one reason she'd worked out so well all these years. She didn't look dangerous. A person hardly noticed her. Until it was too late.

Studying her, Jonas admitted that he'd come to care very deeply for her. He had depended on her. Her betrayal cut him deeper even than Lola's. Fury gripped him like fingers around his throat.

Along with guilt, he saw something else in her face now. She knew that he knew what she'd done.

"Rebecca?"

She raised her gaze slowly. The moment she met his eyes, her face seemed to crumble. She rushed to him to fall to her knees in front of his chair. "Forgive me, Father," she said, head bowed. "Please forgive me."

He didn't speak for a moment, couldn't. "For almost getting me killed or for letting Lola get away with the baby?"

She raised her head again. While pleas for forgiveness had streamed from her mouth, there was no sign of regret in her eyes.

"You stupid, foolish woman," he said with disgust, and pushed her away.

She fell back, landing hard. He watched as she slowly got to her feet. Her dark eyes were hard, her smile brittle. Defiance burned behind her gaze, a blaze that he saw had been burning for some time. Why hadn't he seen it? Because he'd been so consumed with Lola for so long.

"I have done whatever you've asked of me for years," she said, anger making her words sharp as knives hurled at him.

"As you should, as one of my followers," he snapped.

She let out a humorous laugh that sent a chill up his spine. "I wasn't just one of your followers."

He felt for his phone and realized he'd left it over on the table, out of his reach. Zack had said he would be right outside the door. But would he be able to get in quickly enough if Rebecca attacked? Jonas knew he wasn't strong enough to fight her off. Rebecca probably knew it, too.

"Many times you were wrong, but still I did what you asked without question," she continued as she moved closer and closer until she was standing over him. "All these years, I've followed you, looked up to you, trusted that you were doing what was best for our community, best for me."

He swallowed, afraid he'd created a monster. If he was being honest, and now seemed like a good time for it, he'd let her think that one day the two of them would run SLS. He'd trusted her above all others, even Zack.

"You didn't sound the alarm when you found the crib empty," he said, trying to regain control and get the conversation back on safer ground.

She shook her head. "No, when I found Sister Amelia standing next to the empty crib, I told her to go back to bed and let me handle it. I thought about sounding the alarm, but then I didn't. In truth? I was overjoyed to see the brat gone, along with her mother."

"That wasn't your decision to make."

She smiled at that. "You would destroy everything for that woman? You would take her bastard and raise it as your own? I thought of you as a god, but now I see that you are nothing but a man with a man's weaknesses."

The truth pierced his heart and he instantly recoiled. "You will not speak to me like this or there will be serious consequences."

A chuckle seemed to rise deep in her, coming out on a ragged breath. "Will you have the sisters chant more over me? You've already locked me up. Or..." Her gaze was hard as the stone Lola had used to try to bash his head in. "Will you have me killed? It wouldn't be the first time you've had a follower killed, would it?"

The threat was clear in her gaze, in her words. Rebecca knew too much. She could never leave this compound alive, and they both knew it.

He grabbed for his phone, but she reached it first. She held the phone away from him, stepping back, daring him to try to take it from her.

"This is ridiculous, Sister Rebecca. You would throw away everything we have worked so hard for out of simple jealousy?"

She raised a brow, but when she spoke her voice betrayed how close she was to tears again. This was breaking her heart as much as his own. "I know you. After all these years, I know you better than you know yourself. You'll go after her and that baby. You'll have her one way or another even if it means destroying everything."

He stared at her, hearing the truth in her words and realizing that he'd let her get too close. She *did* know him.

She looked down at the phone in her hand, then up at him. She pushed the alarm. The air on the mountaintop filled with the scream of the siren.

When Zack burst through the door, she threw Jonas his phone and, with one final look, turned and let Zack take her roughly by the arm and lead her back to her prison.

She wouldn't be locked up there long, Jonas thought. He owed her that at least, he thought as he sounded the all clear signal. But things weren't all right at all and he feared they never would be again.

CHAPTER SIXTEEN

COLT HAD BEEN worried that the sheriff was right, that Jonas wasn't going to take what had happened lying down. Hearing that Jonas had been released from the hospital, he'd almost been expecting a visit from the SLS leader.

He'd been ready, a shotgun beside the door. But the day had passed without incident and so had the next and the next.

The days seemed to fly by since he'd signed the ranch papers and deposited a partial down payment from the buyer. He'd kept busy selling off the cattle and planning the auction for the farm equipment. He tried not to think about the liquidation of his father's legacy, telling himself his old man knew how much he hated ranching. It was his own fault for leaving Colt the ranch.

He was in the barn when he heard footfalls behind him and turned to see Lola. "So the buyer doesn't want any of this?" she asked.

"No, I believe he plans to subdivide the property. It won't be a ranch at all anymore."

"And the house?"

"Demo it and put in a rental probably."

Lola said nothing, but when he saw her looking out the barn door toward the mountains, there was a wistfulness to her he couldn't ignore.

"I'm not leaving Montana. This will always be my home. I'm just not ranching. With what I got from the sale, I can do anything I want." But that was it. He didn't know what he wanted. His heart pulled him one way, then another.

"How long has your family owned this property?" she asked.

"My great-grandfather homesteaded it," he said. "I know it must sound disrespectful of me to sell it."

She shook her head. "It's yours to do with whatever you want, right?"

"Yes." He didn't bother to tell her that the three-month stipulation his father had put on it was over. "You were right. I'm not a rancher. I have no interest."

"But you're a cowboy."

He laughed. "That I will always be. I'm as at home on a horse as I am behind the controls of a helicopter. Ranching is a different animal altogether. Most ranchers now lease their land and let someone else worry about the critters, the drought, the price of hay. Few of them move cattle on horseback. They ride four-wheelers. Everyone seems to think ranching is romantic." He laughed at that. "It's the most boring job I've ever done in my life."

"That's why you're selling," she said with a smile. "It's the right thing."

He hadn't needed her permission, but he was thankful for it. As much as he denied it, there was guilt over selling something his father had fought for years to keep.

Nor had he contacted the Army about his next assignment, putting that off, as well. He still had plenty of leave, so there was time.

He'd also put off his Realtor about when the new owners could take possession. It sounded as if they hoped to raze the house as soon as he moved out.

He knew he couldn't keep avoiding giving a firm date and time, but once that happened Lola and Grace would be gone.

"Where will you go?" he asked Lola.

"Probably back to California. At least for a while." The car she'd ordered had come, and she'd been able to get to her funds and make sure Jonas couldn't access them. She'd had to get a new driver's license since Jonas had taken her purse with hers inside, along with her passport and checkbook and credit cards.

Colt had heard her on the phone taking care of all that. No wonder he could feel the days slipping away until not only this ranch and the house he'd grown up in were gone, but also Lola and the baby. He worried that once he went back to the Army, this would feel like nothing more than a dream.

Yet, he knew that he would ache for Lola and Grace the rest of his life—if he let them get away. He'd always see their faces and yearn for them.

He'd never felt so confused in his life. What would he do if not go back to the Army? He was almost thirty-three. He couldn't retire even if he wanted to, which he didn't. He wanted to fly. But he couldn't ask Lola and Grace to wait for him for the next two to five years. He couldn't bear the thought of her worrying about him, or the worst happening and him never making it back.

His cell phone rang. Margaret again. "I'd better take this," he said to Lola. As she walked back toward the house, he picked up. "Margaret, I might have changed my mind."

Silence. "It's too late for that and you know it. Colt, what is this about?"

A woman and a child. The rest of my life. Regrets.

"If you're having second thoughts about selling the ranch—"

"I'm not. I just need a little more time to get off the property."

More silence. "I'll see what I can do but, Colt, they are getting very impatient. I need to tell these buyers something concrete. I can't keep putting them off or they are going to change their minds or fine you, which they can under the contract you signed." She sounded angry. He couldn't blame her.

As he looked out at the land, he had a thought. "I'll be in first thing in the morning."

"What does that mean?" she asked after a moment.

"I have an idea."

She groaned. "Could you be a touch more specific?"

"I'm selling the ranch, but there's something I need."

"Okay," she said slowly. "Why don't we sit down with them in the morning, if you're sure you won't change your mind."

He pocketed his phone and watched Lola as she slipped in the back door of the house. Taking off his Stetson, he wiped the sweat from his brow with his sleeve. "Do something," he said to himself. "Do something before it's too late."

"She's staying on the ranch with Colt McCloud," Zack told Jonas later that afternoon.

"Is the baby with them?"

"I've had the place watched as you ordered. They took the baby into town the next morning, bought baby clothes and supplies, and returned to the ranch."

So they were settling in. They thought it was over. "What kind of security?"

"No security system on the house. But I would imagine he has guns and knows how to use them since he's a major in the Army."

"I'm sure he does." That's why they would strike when the cowboy least expected it. He looked past Zack toward the main building below him on the hill. "You led church this morning?"

He nodded.

"What is the mood?"

Zack seemed to consider that. "Quite a few of them are upset over Sister Rebecca."

He'd suspected as much. "I'll lead the service tonight." Zack didn't appear to think that was going to make a difference. Jonas thought about the things that Rebecca had said and ground his teeth. He still had a headache, and while his wound was healing, it was a constant reminder of what Lola had done to him.

Worse, she'd bewitched him, put a spell on him as if sent by the devil to bring him down.

Did he really want her back, or did he just want to retaliate? Did it matter in the long run? His memory was getting worse. The pills didn't seem to be working. He couldn't be sure how long he had until he was a blubbering old fool locked up in some rest home.

He shook his head. He wasn't going out that way. "I don't want Lola or the baby injured."

"What about McCloud?"

"Kill him and dispose of his body. I know the perfect place. If possible, leave no evidence that we were there."

Colt left the barn headed for the house, suddenly excited that his idea just might be the perfect plan. "Lola?" he cried as he burst through the back door.

"Colt?" She was standing in the kitchen wearing an apron that had belonged to his mother. He hadn't seen it in years. She must have found it in a drawer he and his father had obviously never bothered to look in.

"What?" she asked, seeing the way he was looking at her.

"You look so cute in that apron, that's all." He stepped to her. "I'm selling the ranch."

"I know."

"You were right. I'd make a terrible rancher, always did. This was my father's dream, not mine. I'm a helicopter pilot."

She nodded. "I thought we already knew this. So you're going to take the commission the Army is offering you."

"No."

She tilted her head. "No?"

"No," he said, smiling. "For years, my friend Tommy and I have talked about starting our own helicopter service here in the state. We're good at what we do. With the money from the ranch, I can invest in the birds we'll need."

"That sounds right up your alley. But are you sure?"

He nodded. "Come here." He put his arm around her waist and ushered her over to the window. "Look out there. See that."

"Yes? That mountainside?"

"Imagine a house in that grove of aspens and pines. The view from there is incredible. Now imagine an office down by the road and a helipad. The office would be just a hop, skip and a jump from the house. We'd have everything we need for Grace and any other children we have."

Lola smiled at him, caught up in his enthusiasm. "Isn't that land part of the ranch?"

He grinned. "I'm going to buy it back."

"Aren't you being a little impulsive?"

"Not at all. I've been thinking about this for years." He seemed to see what she meant and turned her to face him. "And I've been thinking about being with you since that first night. With you and Grace here... Lola, I've fallen for you and Grace..." He shook his head. "It was love at first sight even before I knew for certain that Grace was mine. I want you to stay. I want us to be a family."

"Colt, do you know what you're saying?" But it was what he wasn't saying that had her stomach in knots. She knew he wanted her and Grace, but she wouldn't let herself go into a loveless marriage just to give her daughter a home.

She said as much to him.

He stared at her. "Damn it, Lola, I love you."

She blinked in surprise. All their lovemaking, their quiet times together, those moments with Grace. She'd waited to hear those words. Well, maybe not the "damn it, Lola" part. But definitely the "I love you" part. Her heart had assured her that he loved her and Grace. And yet, she wouldn't let herself believe it was true until he finally told her.

"I love you," he repeated as if they were the most honest words he'd ever spoken. "I've only said those words twice to a woman. With Julia, it was over two years before I said them. I don't think it was a coincidence that I held off. With you... I've been wanting to say them for days now."

"Oh, Colt, I've been waiting to hear them. I love you, too."

He reached into his pocket and pulled out a small velvet box. Lola gave a small gasp.

"This ring was handed down from my great-great-grand-mother to my great-grandmother to my grandmother. When my grandmother gave it to me, she made me promise only to give it to a woman who was my equal." He opened the box.

She looked down at a beautiful thick gold band circled in diamonds. "Oh, Colt." Her gaze went to his. "I don't understand. Julia—"

"I didn't give it to her."

"Why?"

He shrugged. "I don't know. It didn't seem...right for her. She picked out one she liked uptown."

Her heart went out to him. Julia had hurt him badly in so many ways, only proving how wrong she was for him almost from the start.

"Now I realize that I was saving this ring so I could live up to the promise I made my grandmother," he said. "I want you to wear it." He dropped to one knee. "Will you marry me, Lola Dayton, and be my wife and the mother to my children?"

She smiled through the burn of tears. "Yes."

He slipped the ring on her finger. It fit perfectly. "Now what is the chance of that?" he said to her, only making her cry and laugh at the same time.

Swinging her up into his arms, he spun her around and set her down gently. "For the first time in so long, I am excited about the future."

She could see that he'd been dragged down by the ranch, Julia and the past, as well as his need to do what he did so well—fly.

Colt kissed her softly on the mouth. She felt heat rush through her and, cupping his face in her hands, kissed him with the passion the man evoked in her.

He swung her up in his arms again, only this time he didn't put her down until they reached the bedroom.

That evening, Jonas held church in the main building. He'd gathered them all together to give them the news. He could feel the tension in the air. There'd been a time when he'd stood up here and felt as if he really was a god sent to this earth to lead desperate people looking for at least peace, if not salvation.

As he looked over his flock, though, all he felt was sad. His father used to say that all good things end. In this case, the preacher was right.

"Brothers and sisters. I have some sad news. As you know, Sister Rebecca has chosen to leave us. It is with a heavy heart that I had to let her go." He wondered how many of them knew the truth. Too many of them probably. He was glad he'd had Zack bury her far away from the compound.

"But that isn't the only news. I have decided that it is time to leave Montana." His words were followed by a murmur of concern that spread through his congregation. "As many of you know, I'm in poor health. My heart… I'm going to have to step down as your leader."

The murmurs rose. One woman called out, "What's to become of us?"

He'd bilked them out of all their money. A lot of them were old enough now that they would have a hard time getting a job. He didn't need this crowd turning on him as Sister Rebecca had.

"Brother Zack will be taking those who want to go to property I've purchased in Arizona. It's farmable land, so you can maintain a life there. Each of you will be given a check to help with your expenses."

The murmur in the main building grew louder. "If you have any questions, please give those to Brother Zack. I trust him to make sure that each and every one of you will be taken care of." That quieted them down, either because they were assured or because they knew how Zack had taken care of other parishioners who'd became troublesome.

"It is with a heavy heart that I must step down, but I know that you all will be fine. You will leave tomorrow. Go with Godspeed." He turned and walked away, anxious to get back to his cabin and pack. The sale of his property would be enough to pay off his followers—not that he would be around to hear any complaints after tonight.

He rang for Zack. Since he'd told Zack of his plan, the man had been more than excited. Jonas had recognized that frenzied look in Zack's eyes. He'd seen it in his own. Zack would be Father Zack. God help his followers.

"I need you to pick about six brothers and a few sisters for a special mission," he told Zack. It would be one of their last missions under him.

Zack nodded, clearly understanding that he needed to pick those who would still kill for their leader.

"Make sure one of them is Brother Elmer."

"Are you sure? I mean—"

"Already questioning my authority?" he asked with a chuckle.

"No, of course not."

"Good. I have my reasons."

"I'll get right on it," Zack said, and left him alone.

Jonas looked around the cabin. He'd had such hopes when he'd moved his flock to Montana. He couldn't get maudlin now. He had to think about his future. He stepped to the safe he had hidden in the wall, opened it and took out the large case he kept there full of cash and his passport. Next to it was Lola's purse.

He took that out, as well, and thumbed through it even though he knew exactly what was in it since he'd often looked through it. He liked touching her things. He found her passport. Good, it was up-to-date. He'd deal with getting the baby out of the country when it came time.

After putting Lola's passport beside his own into his case, he closed the safe. There was nothing keeping him here after tonight. He would have everything he'd ever dreamed of, including a small fortune waiting in foreign banks across the world.

He thought of his father, wishing he could see him now. "Go ahead, say it. You were right about me, you arrogant old sanctimonious fool. I was your worst nightmare and so much more. But you haven't seen anything yet."

CHAPTER SEVENTEEN

COLT WOKE TO the sound of both outside doors bursting open. The sudden noise woke the baby. Grace began to cry in the room down the hall. Lola stirred next to him and Colt, realizing what was happening, grabbed for his gun in the nightstand next to him.

Moments before he had lain in bed, with Lola beside him.

They were on him before he could draw the gun. They swept into the room, both men and women. Colt fought off the first couple of men, but a blow to the back of his head sent him to the floor and then they were on him, binding his hands behind him, gagging him, trussing his ankles and dragging him out of the house.

He tried to see Lola, but there was a group of women around her, helping her dress. In the baby's room, he heard Grace quiet and knew they had her, as well.

The strike had been so swift, so organized, that Colt realized he'd underestimated Zack—the only ex-military man in SLS. Clearly he had more experience at these kinds of maneuvers than Colt had thought.

Still stunned from the blow to his head, he was half carried, half dragged to a waiting van.

"Take care of him, Brother Elmer," he heard Zack say, the

threat clear in the man's tone. Zack must have known that Brother Elmer was a weak link. "Brother Carl will go with you to make sure the job is done properly."

The van door slammed. Elmer started the engine and pulled away. The whole operation had taken less than ten minutes.

"Don't hurt him!" Lola had cried as Colt was being dragged from the bedroom. Three women blocked her way to keep her from going after the men.

"Dress!" Sister Caroline ordered.

"My baby?"

"Grace will be safe as long as you do what we ask," Sister Amelia said. But there was something in Amelia's tone, a sadness that said not even she believed it.

Lola had no choice. They had Colt. They had Grace. She dressed quickly in a blouse and jeans, pulled on her sneakers and let the women lead her outside to a waiting van.

Sister Shelly was already in the van and holding Grace.

"Let me hold her," Lola said, steel in her voice.

The women looked at one another.

"Give the baby to Lola," Sister Amelia said and Shelly complied.

She sat holding the now-fussing Grace as the van pulled away. "Where are they taking Colt?"

No one answered. Her heart fell. Hadn't she feared that Jonas would retaliate? He'd be humiliated and would have to strike back. Isn't that what the sheriff had warned them about?

But what could he hope to achieve by this? The sheriff would know who took them. The first place Flint Cahill would look was the compound.

She remembered something she'd overheard while a prisoner at SLS. Some of the women had been worried that Jonas wasn't himself, that his memory seemed to be failing him. He often called them by the wrong names, got lost in the middle of a sermon. They questioned in hushed voices if it was his heart or something else, since they'd seem him taking pills for it.

"What is going on?" Lola asked, sensing something different about the group of women.

"We're leaving Montana," Sister Amelia said, and the other sisters tried to hush her. "She'll know soon enough," Amelia argued. "Father Jonas announced it earlier. He's selling the land here. Some are going to a new home in Arizona. Others…" Her voice broke. "I don't know where they're going."

Lola realized that their leader wasn't here. "Where is Sister Rebecca?" The question was met with silence. "Amelia?"

"She's gone."

"Everyone is leaving," Sister Shelly said, sounding near tears. "Father Jonas… He's letting Brother Zack lead the group in Arizona. He will be Father Zack now."

Lola couldn't believe what she was hearing as the van reached the highway and headed toward the compound. "He's putting Zack in charge?" She knew that the women in this van must feel the same way she did about Zack. "Did Jonas say what he is planning to do?"

Silence. Lola hugged Grace to her, her fear mounting with each passing mile as the van turned onto the road up to the mountain. Lola saw no other taillights ahead. No headlights behind them. Where had they taken Colt?

Colt couldn't see out, but he could tell that Elmer and Carl weren't taking him to the compound. He had a pretty good idea what their orders had been when Zack had told Elmer to take care of him.

He was furious with himself. He'd thought Jonas would have no choice but to give up. He should have known better. He should have taken more precautions. Against so many, he knew he and Lola hadn't stood a chance.

When they'd gone to the compound and rescued Grace, he'd thought this could be settled without bloodshed. It was why he hadn't taken a gun to the compound the first time that night. He didn't want to kill one of Jonas's sheep. They were just following orders, though blindly, true enough. But he hadn't wanted trouble with the law.

Now, though, he saw there was no way out of this. Jonas had taken Lola and Grace. Nothing was going to stop him. He was going to end this once and for all no matter whom he had to kill.

Colt rolled to his side. They'd bound his wrists with plastic ties. He worked to slip his hands under him. If he could get a foot into the cuffs, he knew he could break free.

As he did, he watched the men in the front seat. Neither turned around to check on him. He got the feeling they didn't like being awakened in the middle of the night for this any more than Colt had. And now they had been ordered to kill someone. They had to be questioning Jonas and the SLS. He already knew that Brother Elmer had a weak spot for Lola and her baby.

He managed to get his hands past his butt. He lay on his back, catching his breath for a moment before he pushed himself up. Once he had his hands in front of him...

The van slowed. Elmer shifted down and turned onto a bumpy road that jarred every muscle in Colt's body. Colt caught a glimpse of something out the back window and realized where they were taking him. The old gravel pits outside of Gilt Edge. He caught the scent of the water through the partially opened windows up front. It was the perfect place to dump a body. Weighted down, there was a good chance the remains would never be found.

He felt his heart pound as he worked to free his wrists. The plastic restraints popped—but not louder than the rattle of the van on the rough road. Colt went to work on the ones binding his ankles.

As the van came to a stop, he resumed his original position, his hands behind him, feet together as he lay on his side facing the door.

Both men got out. He waited, wondering if either of them was armed or if the plan had been simply to drown him.

The van door opened noisily. "Can you get him out?" Elmer asked his companion.

Carl grunted but reached for him.

Colt swung his feet around and kicked the man in the chest, sending Carl sprawling in the dirt. He followed with a quick jab to Elmer's jaw. The older man stumbled and sat down hard on the ground.

So far, Colt hadn't seen a weapon, but as he jumped out, he saw Carl fumbling for something behind him. The man came up with a pistol. Right away, Colt saw that he wasn't comfortable using it. But that didn't mean that Carl wouldn't get lucky and blow Colt's head off.

He rushed around the back of the van to the driver's side. Grabbing open the door, he leaped in and started the van. As he threw the engine into Reverse, he saw Carl trying to get a clear shot. Elmer had stumbled to his feet and was blocking Carl's way—either accidentally or on purpose.

Colt didn't try to figure out which as he hit the gas. The van shot back. He cranked the wheel hard, swinging the back end toward the two men.

Carl got off two shots. One bullet shattered the back window of the van. The other took out Colt's side window, showering him with glass, and just missing his head before burying itself in the passenger-side door.

Elmer had parked the van close to the edge of the gravel pit, no doubt to make unloading his body easier.

As Colt swung the van at the two men, they tried to move out of the way. But Elmer was old and lost his footing. He was the first to go tumbling down the steep embankment and splash into the cold, clear water.

Carl had been busy trying to hit his target with the gun so he was caught unaware when the back of the van hit him and knocked him backward into the gravel pit. He let out a yell as he fell, the sound dying off in a loud splash.

Colt shifted into first gear and tore off down the bumpy road, thankful to be alive. He hoped both men could swim. If so, they had a long swim across the pit to where they would be able to climb out.

If either of their cell phones still worked after that, they might be able to warn Jonas. Not that it would matter.

Colt sped toward his house to get what he needed. This time he was taking weapons—and no prisoners.

For Lola, walking into Jonas's cabin with the bundle in her arms felt a little like déjà vu. Only this time, there was a precious sleeping baby instead of rocks in her arms. As she entered, propelled by Brother Zack, she told herself that she would die protecting her daughter. Did Jonas know that, as well?

"Leave her," Jonas ordered. Zack started to argue, but one look at their leader and he left, saying he would be right outside the door if he was needed. The sisters scattered, and the door closed, leaving Lola and Grace alone with Jonas.

He still had a bandage on the side of his head, but she knew better than to think his injury might slow him down.

"You are a very difficult woman."

"Only when someone tries to force me into doing something I don't want to do or they take my child from me."

He glanced at the bundle in her arms. "May I see her?"

Lola didn't move. "What do you hope to get out of this?" she demanded.

"I thought I was clear from the beginning. I want you. It's what your parents wanted—"

"I don't believe that. I heard from my father before he…died. He wanted out of SLS. He was trying to convince my mother to leave. I believe that's why you killed them both."

Jonas shook his head. "Are we back to that?"

"You're a fraud. This is no church. And you are no god. All this is only about your ego. It's a bad joke."

"Are you purposely trying to rile me?"

"I thought maybe it was time you heard the truth from someone instead of Sister Rebecca telling you how wonderful you are."

"Sister Rebecca is no longer with us."

"So I heard. Did you kill her yourself or make one of your sheep do it?" She knew he could not let Rebecca simply walk away. She'd been with him from the beginning. She'd done things for him, knew things.

"Why do you torment me? I cared about Rebecca."

"And yet you had her killed. I don't like the way you care about people."

At the sound of vehicles and activity on the mountain below them, Lola moved cautiously to the window, careful not to turn her back on Jonas.

She frowned as she saw everyone appearing to be packing up and moving. Fear coursed through her. "What's going on? I thought they weren't leaving until tomorrow?"

"Our time in Montana has come to an end. We are abandoning our church here."

What Amelia had told her was true. "So they're scurrying away like rats fleeing a sinking ship. You're really going to let them go?"

"All good things must end."

She thought of Colt as she had on the ride to the compound. Something told her that he hadn't been brought here. "Where is Colt?"

Jonas shook his head. "As I said, all good things must end."

Tears burned her eyes. "If you hurt him—"

'What will you do? Kill me? They will put you in prison, take away your baby. No, it is time you realized that you have never been in control. You are mine. You will always be mine. I will go to any lengths, including having Grace taken away so you never see her again if that's what it takes to keep you with me."

Fear turned her blood to ice as she looked into his eyes and understood he wasn't bluffing.

"You have only one choice. Come with me willingly and Grace will join us once we are settled."

No, she screamed silently. She didn't trust this man. But she also knew she couldn't keep someone like Zack from ripping Grace from her arms. Just as she knew that Jonas wasn't making an empty threat. She'd known this man was dangerous, but she hadn't realized how much he was willing to give up to have her—and Grace.

"You have only a few minutes to make up your mind, Lola." He had his phone in his hand. "Once I push this button, Zack will take Grace. If you ever want to see her again, you will agree to go with me."

"Where?" She knew she was stalling, fighting to find a way out of this. Colt. If he was dead, did she care what happened to her as long as she had his baby with her?

"Europe, South America. I haven't decided yet. Somewhere far away from all this. I have money. We will live well. We will be a family."

She thought of the family Colt had promised her and felt the ring on her finger.

Jonas's gaze went to her left hand. His face contorted in anger. "Take that off. Take that off now!"

CHAPTER EIGHTEEN

COLT DIALED THE number quickly, knowing he had no choice even if he ended up behind bars. It would be worth it as long as Lola and Grace were safe from Jonas Emanuel once and for all.

"I need to borrow a helicopter," he said, the moment his friend answered.

"Mind if I ask what for?" Tommy Garrett asked, sounding like a man dragged from sleep in the wee hours of the morning. Tommy worked as a helicopter mechanic outside of Great Falls. Colt had served with him in Afghanistan and trusted the man with his life—and Lola's and Grace's.

"A madman has the woman I love and my baby daughter."

There was a beat of silence before Tommy said, "You planning to do this alone?"

"Better that way. I'll leave you out of it."

"Like hell. Tell me where you are. Outside my shop I have a Bell UH-1 Huey that needs its shakedown. The old workhorse is being used to fight forest fires. I'm on my way."

Colt knew the Huey could do up to 120 mph. But a safe cruising speed for helicopters was around a hundred. Without having to deal with traffic, road speeds or winding highways, the response time in a helicopter was considerably faster than anything on the ground. It was one reason Colt loved flying them.

So he wasn't surprised when Tommy landed in the pasture next to Colt's house thirty minutes later. The sun was coming up, chasing away the last of the dark. He could make out the mountains in the distance. Within a matter of minutes, they would be at the compound. He tried not think about what they would find.

"How much trouble is this going to get you in?" Colt asked his friend as he loaded the weapons in the back and climbed into the left seat, the crew chief seat.

"You just worry about what happens when we put this bird down," Tommy said in the adjacent seat at the controls.

As they headed for the mountaintop in the distance, Colt told him everything that had happened from that moment in the hotel in Billings to earlier that night.

When he finished, Tommy said, "So this woman is the one?"

For a moment, Colt could only nod around the lump in this throat. "I've never met anyone like her."

"Apparently this cult leader hasn't, either. Tell me you have a plan." He swore when Colt didn't answer right away.

"There will be armed guards who are under the control of the cult leader, Jonas Emanuel. But we don't have time to sneak up on them. You don't have to land. Just get close enough to the ground that I can jump," Colt said as he began to strap on one of the weapons he'd brought. "Did I mention that these people are like zombies?"

"Great, you know how I love zombies. Except you can't kill zombies."

"These are religious zealots. I suspect they will be as hard to kill as zombies."

"This just keeps getting better and better," Tommy joked.

Colt looked over at him. "Thank you."

"Thank me after we get out with this woman you've fallen in love with and your daughter." He shook his head. "You never did anything like normal people."

"No, I never did. There's the road that goes up to the compound."

Tommy swooped down, skimming just over the tops of the pines, and Colt saw something he hadn't expected.

"What the hell?" As they got closer to the mountain, Colt spotted the line of vans coming off the mountain. He felt a chill. "Something's going on. Fly closer to those vehicles," he said to Tommy, who immediately dipped down.

Inside the vans, he saw the faces of Jonas followers. There were a dozen vans. As each passed, he saw the pale faces, the fear in their eyes.

"Where do you think they're going?" Tommy asked.

"I have no idea. Leaving for good, from the looks of it. What is Jonas up to? Are these people decoys or are they really clearing out?" He thought of Lola and the baby. How crazy was Jonas? Would he kill them and then kill himself, determined that Colt would never have either of them?

"Up there," Colt said, pointing to the mountaintop. Tommy swung the helicopter in the direction he pointed. Within a few minutes, the buildings came into sight. Colt didn't see any guards. He didn't see anyone. The place looked deserted. Had everyone left?

Not everyone, he noticed. There was a large black SUV sitting in front of Jonas's cabin.

"Think you can put her into that clearing in front of the cabin?"

"Seriously?" Tommy said. "You forget who you're talking to. Give me a dime and I can set her down on it." Colt chuckled because he knew it was true.

Lola looked down at the antique ring that Colt had put on her finger. She swore she would never take it off. It felt so right on her finger. Colt felt so right.

Jonas moved faster than she thought he could after his injury. He grabbed the baby from her arms and shoved her. She fell back, coming down hard on the floor. "I told you to take if off. Now!"

"Give me Grace."

"Her name is Angel, and if you don't do what I say this moment..."

Lola pulled off the ring. She knew it was silly. Colt was probably dead. She'd lost so much. What did a ring matter at this point? The one thing she couldn't lose was Grace, and yet she felt as if she already had in more ways than one. Jonas had them captive. He could do whatever he wanted with Grace. Just as he could do whatever he wanted with her now.

"Happy?" she asked, still clutching the ring in her fist.

"Throw it away." He pointed toward the fireplace and the cold ashes filling it.

She hesitated again.

"Do as I say!" Jonas bellowed at her, waking up Grace. The baby began to cry.

Lola tossed the ring toward the fireplace. It was a lazy, bad throw, one that made Jonas's already furious face cloud over even more. The ring missed the fireplace opening, pinged off the rock and rolled under the couch. She looked at Jonas. If he really did have a bad heart, she realized his agitation right now could kill him. She doubted she would get that lucky, though.

He seemed to be trying to calm down. Grace kept crying and she could tell it was getting on his nerves.

She got to her feet. "Let me have her. She'll quit crying for me."

He shook his head. "I'm not sure I can trust you," he said slowly.

Colt was gone. The ring was gone. But Jonas had something much more precious. He had Grace. But Lola wasn't giving up.

"How do I know I can trust *you*?" she said.

The question surprised him. He'd expected her to cower, to promise him anything. She knew better than to do that. Jonas was surrounded by people who bowed down to him. Lola never had and maybe that's why he was so determined to have her.

She approached him. "You hurt my baby and I will kill you. I'll cut your throat in your sleep. Or push you down a flight of stairs. Or poison your food. It might take me a while to get the opportunity, but believe me, I will do it."

He chuckled as his gaze met hers. "I do believe you. I've always loved your spirit. Your mother told me what a headstrong young woman you were. She wasn't wrong."

It hurt to have him mention her mother. Was it possible that Jonas could get away with the murders he'd committed? She feared it was. She thought of Colt and felt a sob rise in her throat. She forced it back down. She couldn't show weakness, not now, especially not for Colt. She had to think about Grace.

"We seem to be at an impasse," Jonas said. "What do you suggest we do?"

"I suggest you give me my baby and let me leave here."

He shook his head. "Not happening. Neither you or your baby will be leaving here—except with me."

"So what are you waiting for?" she demanded.

Jonas chuckled as he tilted his head as if to listen. "We're waiting for Colt. I just have a feeling he will somehow manage to try to save you one more time."

Lola listened as her heart thumped against her rib cage. Colt? He was alive? She thought she heard what sounded like a helicopter headed this way.

"I believe that's him now."

Colt fought the bad feeling that had settled in the pit of his stomach. Jonas was playing hardball this time. He wasn't going to let Lola and Grace go—not without a fight to the death. That's if they were still alive.

"Change of plans," he said to Tommy. He felt as if time was running out for Lola and Grace. "Put us down and wait for me," he said, fear making his voice sound strained as he passed Tommy a handgun. "I hope you won't have to use this. It appears that the guards have left, but I've already underestimated Jonas once and I don't want to do it again. I'm hoping this won't take long."

As Colt started to jump out, Tommy grabbed his sleeve. "Be careful."

Colt nodded. "You, too."

"I'll be here. Good luck."

Colt knew that if there was anyone he wanted on his side in a war it was Tommy Garrett—and this was war. These soldiers would die for their leader. They were just as devoted to dying for their cause as the ones he'd fought in Afghanistan.

The moment the chopper touched the ground, he leaped out and ran up the mountainside to where a large black SUV sat, the engine running and Brother Zack behind the wheel. Behind him, he heard Tommy shut down the engine. The rotors began to slow.

Colt looked around. The only person he'd seen so far was Zack, but that didn't mean that another of the guards hadn't stayed behind.

As he approached the SUV, he could hear the bass coming from the stereo. Closer, he saw that Zack had on headphones and was rockin' out. He must have had the stereo cranked, which explained why he hadn't heard the helicopter land. Nor had he heard him approach.

Colt yanked open the door. A surprised Zack turned. Colt grabbed him by his shirt and hauled him out. Unfortunately, Zack was carrying and he went for his gun. Zack was strong and combat trained. But Colt was fighting for Lola's and Grace's lives.

Colt managed to get hold of the man's arm, twisting it to the point of snapping as they struggled for the weapon. When the shot went off, it was muffled—just like Zack's grunt. Blood blossomed on the front of Zack's white shirt. The gun dropped, falling under the SUV.

As the man slumped, Colt shoved him back inside the vehicle, shut off the stereo and slammed the door before turning to Jonas's cabin. He'd seen suitcases in the back of the SUV and suspected the sheep weren't the only ones fleeing.

Colt pulled his holstered gun and climbed the steps. He had another gun stuck in the back of his jeans under his jacket. He always liked to be prepared—especially against someone like Jonas Emanuel.

He could still hear the sweep of the helicopter's rotors as they continued to slow. The wooden porch floor creaked under his boots. He braced himself and reached for the doorknob.

Before he could turn it, Lola opened the door. Her face had lost all its color. Her violet eyes appeared huge. He could see that she'd been crying. The sight froze him in place for moment. What had Jonas done to her? To Grace?

"Where is Jonas?" Colt asked quietly. Suddenly there wasn't a sound, not even a meadowlark from the grass or a breeze moaning in the pines. The eerie quiet sent a chill up his spine. "Lola?" The word came in a whisper.

"I'm leaving with Jonas," she said.

"Like hell." He could see that Jonas had put the fear into her and used Grace to do it. He'd never wanted to strangle anyone with his bare hands more than he did the cult leader at this moment.

"Please, it's what I want." Her words said one thing; her blue eyes pleaded with him to save Grace.

He pushed past her to find Jonas sitting in a chair just yards away. He was holding Grace in such a way that it stopped Colt cold.

Jonas relished the expression on Colt's handsome face. It almost made everything worth what he was going to have to give up. The cowboy thought he could just bust in here and take Lola and the baby? Not this time.

"Lola is going with me and so is her baby," he said as he turned the baby so she was facing her biological father and dangling from his fingers. He wanted Colt to see the baby's face and realize what he would be risking if he didn't back off.

"I don't think so," Colt said, but without much conviction.

Jonas was ready to throw the baby against the rock fireplace if Colt took another step. The cowboy wasn't stupid. He'd figured that out right away. But he'd been stupid enough to come up here again. The man should have been dead.

Idly, Jonas wondered what had gone wrong at the gravel pit. He'd known he couldn't depend on Elmer, but he was disposable. Brother Carl had inspired more faith that he would get the job done. Jonas had assumed that Carl would have to kill both Elmer and Colt. Clearly, the job had been too much for him.

"Has he hurt you?" Colt asked Lola.

She shook her head.

Jonas was touched by the cowboy's concern, but quickly getting bored with all this. "Elmer and Carl?" he asked, curious.

"Swimming, that is, if either of them knows how," Colt answered.

"And Brother Zack?"

"No longer listening to music in your big SUV."

So he couldn't depend on Zack to come to his rescue. Another surprise. Everyone was letting him down. Just as well that he was packing it all in. He'd grown tired of the squabbling among the sisters and the backbiting of the brothers. Human nature really was malicious.

Still, he would miss Zack. And now who would lead his people to the promised land of Arizona? He chuckled to himself since he didn't own any land in Arizona. But they wouldn't know that until they got there, would they?

He saw the cowboy shoot a look at Lola. She was standing off to Colt's left as if she didn't know what to do. He could see the tension in her face. She wasn't being so smart-mouthed now, was she? As much as he was enjoying this, he didn't have to ask what she was hoping would happen here.

But, this time, she'd been outplayed. The cowboy was going to lose. It was simply a matter of how much he would have to lose before this was over. Did he realize that he wasn't getting out of here alive? At this point, Jonas wasn't sure he cared if

Lola and the baby survived either, though he still wanted the woman, and damned if he wouldn't have her—dead or alive. The thought didn't even surprise him. His father used to say that one day he would reach rock bottom. Was this it?

"Why would you want a woman who doesn't love you?" Colt asked conversationally, as if they were old friends discussing the weather—and took a step closer.

"Because I can have her. I can have anything I want, and I want her. The baby is optional. I guess that's up to you."

"How's that?"

"You can't reach me before I hurl your baby into the rock fireplace. But if you try, I will, and then we will only be talking about Lola. The thing is, I don't think she will love you anymore, not after you got her baby killed," Jonas said. "Want to take a chance on that? Take another step..."

Colt could see that Jonas's arms were tiring from holding Grace up the way he was. He was using the baby like a shield. There was no way Colt could get a shot off with Jonas sitting and the baby out in front of him. Nor could he chance that, as he fired, Jonas wouldn't throw Grace into the rocks.

One glance at Lola and he knew that what they both feared was a real possibility—Jonas could drop the baby at any moment. Or, worse, throw Grace against the rock fireplace as he was threatening.

"Colt, I'll go with him. It's the only way," Lola pleaded as she stepped to him, grabbing his arm.

It was a strange thing for her to do and for a moment he didn't understand. Then he felt her reach behind him to the pistol he had at his back. She must have seen the bulk of it under his shirt. She freed the gun and dropped her hands to her sides, keeping turned so Jonas couldn't see what she held. Then she began to cry.

"You heard her," Jonas said. "Leave before someone gets

hurt. Before you get hurt." His arms were shaking visibly. "If you care anything about this child…"

Jonas knew Colt wasn't leaving without Lola and Grace. Saying he could walk away was all bluff. Did he have a weapon handy? Colt suspected so.

Lola was still halfway facing him so she could keep the gun in her hand hidden. Colt feared what she planned to do, but he could feel time running out. Jonas was losing patience. Worse, his arms were shaking now. He couldn't hold the baby much longer—and he couldn't back down. Wouldn't.

"Tell him, Jonas," she cried, suddenly running toward the cult leader and dropping to her knees only feet from him after sticking the gun in the waist of her jeans. "Tell him I'm going with you, and that it's true and to leave."

The cult leader hadn't expected her to do that. For a moment, it looked as if he was going to throw the baby. Before he could, Lola grabbed for Grace with her left hand. At the same time, she pulled the pistol from behind her with her right. She had hold of Grace's chubby little leg and wasn't letting go.

Everything happened fast after that. Colt, seeing what Lola had planned, took the shot the moment Lola managed to pull the baby down and away from Jonas's smug face. Colt had always been an expert shot. Even during the most stressful situations.

He missed. Jonas had fallen forward just enough that the shot went over his head and lodged in the back of the chair. Before he could fire again, he heard Lola fire. She'd taken the shot from the floor, shooting under Grace to hit the man low in the stomach. He saw Jonas release Grace as he grabbed for his bleeding belly.

Lola dropped the gun and pulled Grace into her arms. They were both crying. As Colt rushed to the cult leader, his gun leveled at the man's head, Lola scrambled away from Jonas with Grace tucked in her arms.

Jonas was holding his stomach with one hand and fumbling for something in the chair with the other. Colt was aiming to shoot, to finish Jonas, when he saw that it wasn't a gun the cult leader was going for. It was the man's phone.

He watched Jonas punch at the screen, his bloody fingers slippery, his hands shaking. It took a moment for the alert to sound. Jonas seemed to wait, one bloody hand on his stomach, the other on his phone. He stared at the front door, expecting it to come flying open as one of the guards burst in.

Seconds passed, then several minutes. Nothing happened. Jonas looked wild-eyed at the door as if he couldn't believe it.

"They've all left," Colt said. "There is no one to help you."

Jonas looked down at his phone. With trembling fingers he made several attempts to key in 9-1-1 and finally gave up. "You have to call an ambulance. It's the humane thing to do."

"This from the man who was about to kill my baby daughter?"

"You would let me bleed to death?"

Colt looked over at Lola, huddled in the corner with Grace. Their gazes met. He pulled out his own phone and keyed in 9-1-1. He asked to speak to the sheriff.

When he was connected with Flint, he said, "You were right. Jonas hit us in the middle of the night. He sent two men to kill me. I left them in the old gravel pits. He took Lola and Grace, but they are both safe now. Unfortunately, one of his guards tried to shoot me. He's dead outside here on the compound and Jonas is wounded, so you'll need an ambulance and a—" He was going to say *coroner*, but before he could get the word out, the front door of the cabin banged open.

He spun around in time to see Zack bleeding and barely able to stand, but the man could still shoot. He fired the weapon in his hand in a barrage of bullets before Colt could pull the trigger.

Lola screamed. Grace wailed. It happened so fast. She'd thought it was all over. Finally. She'd thought they were finally safe. And so had Colt. He hadn't expected Zack to be alive—let alone come in shooting—any more than she had.

Colt threw himself in Grace's and her direction. As he did,

he brought up the weapon he'd been holding on Jonas. The air filled with the loud reports of gunfire.

Lola laid her body over Grace's to protect her, knowing that Colt had thrown himself toward them to do the same. It took her a few moments to realize that the firing had stopped. She peeked out, terrified that she would find Colt lying dead at her feet.

Colt lay on his side, his back to her. She put Grace down long enough to reach for him. He was holding his leg, blood oozing out from between his fingers. He looked up at her.

"Are you and Grace—"

"We're fine. But you're bleeding," Lola cried.

"It's just a flesh wound," Colt said. "Don't worry about me. As long as you and Grace are all right..." He grimaced as he tried to get to his feet.

In the doorway, Zack lay crumpled on the floor. Lola couldn't tell if he was breathing or not. Her gaze swung to Jonas. He had tumbled out of his chair. He wasn't breathing, given that the top of his head was missing. She looked away quickly.

Grace's wailing was the only sound in the room. She rushed to her. As she did, she saw Colt's cell phone on the floor and picked it up. The sheriff was still there.

"We need an ambulance. Colt is wounded. Zack and Jonas are dead."

"Tommy," Colt said, trying to get to his feet. "He would have seen Zack heading for the cabin..." He limped to the door and pushed it open. Beyond it, he saw Tommy slumped over the controls of the helicopter. "There isn't time to wait for an ambulance. Tell the sheriff we'll be at the hospital."

As she related to the sheriff what Colt had said, she hurried to the couch. Squatting down, she fished her ring from under it. Her gentle toss of it hadn't hurt the ring or the diamonds. She slipped it on her finger, feeling as if now she could face anything again. Then, holding Grace in her arms, she ran after Colt to the helicopter sitting like a big dark bird in the middle of the compound.

* * *

Colt ignored the pain as he ran to the helicopter. When he reached Tommy, he hurriedly felt for a pulse. For a moment, he thought his friend was dead, and yet he didn't see any blood. He found a pulse and felt a wave of relief. He'd dragged his friend into this. The last thing he wanted to do was get him killed.

On closer inspection, he could see a bump the size of a goose egg on Tommy's head. He figured Zack must have ambushed him before coming up to the cabin to finish things.

"Is he...?" Lola asked from behind him. She held a crying Grace in her arms and was trying to soothe her.

"He's alive, but we need to get him to the hospital. Come around the other side and climb in the back with Grace." Colt helped them in and then slid into the seat and took over the controls. He started up the motor. The rotors began to turn and then spin. A few minutes later, he lifted off and headed for Gilt Edge.

The helicopter swept over the tops of the pines and out of the mountains. Colt glanced over at Tommy. He seemed to be coming around. In the back, Lola had calmed Grace down and she now slept in her mother's arms.

He told himself that all was right with the world. Lola and Grace were safe. Tommy was going to make it. But he was feeling the effects of his blood loss as he saw the hospital's helipad in the distance. He'd never lost a bird. He told himself he wasn't going to lose this one—especially with the precious cargo he was carrying.

Colt set the chopper down and turned off the engine. After that, everything became a blur. He knew he'd lost a lot of blood and was light-headed, but it wasn't until he'd shut down the chopper and tried to get out that he realized how weak he was.

The last thing he remembered was seeing hospital staff rushing toward the helicopter pushing two gurneys.

CHAPTER NINETEEN

COLT WOKE TO find Lola and Grace beside his bed. He tried to sit up, but Lola gently pushed him back down.

"Tommy is fine," she told him as if knowing exactly what he needed to hear. "A mild concussion. The doctor is having a terrible time keeping him in bed. We're all fine now."

Colt relaxed back on the pillows and smiled. "I was so worried. But everyone's all right?"

She nodded. "I was worried about you." She pushed a lock of hair back from his forehead and looked into his eyes. "You lost so much blood, but the doctor says you're going to be fine."

He glanced over at the IV attached to his arm. "I remember flying the chopper to the hospital but not much after that." He took her hand and squeezed it. "How is Grace?"

"Sleeping." Lola pointed to the bassinet the nurses had brought in for her. "I refused to leave until I knew you were all right." They'd also brought in a cot for Lola, he saw. "I've just been going back and forth from your room to Tommy's."

Colt smiled, took her hand and squeezed it. "I almost lost you. Again."

"But you saved me. Again. Aren't you getting tired of it?"

He shook his head. "Never." He glanced down at the ring

on her finger. When he'd come into the cabin, he'd seen her rubbing the spot on her left hand where it had been. He hadn't been surprised Jonas hadn't liked seeing the ring on her finger. "When are you going to marry me?"

"You name the day. But right now you're in the middle of selling your ranch and holding an auction, and the doctor isn't going to let you out of here for a while. The bullet missed bone, but your leg is going to take some time to heal. Also, I believe you missed your appointment with your Realtor."

Colt grimaced. "Margaret. She is going to be furious."

"I called her. Apparently, ending up in the hospital bought you some time."

"I need to talk to Tommy, but I want to talk to him about my plan for the future, for *our* future."

The hospital-room door opened and Sheriff Flint Cahill stuck his head in. "Our patient awake? I hate to interrupt, but I need to talk to Colt if he's up to it."

Colt pulled Lola down for a kiss. "I'll talk to the sheriff. You can leave Grace. If she wakes up, I'll take care of her."

She nodded. "I know you will." She said hello to the sheriff. "I'll just be down the hall."

Flint took off his Stetson and pulled up a chair. "I've already spoken with Tom Garrett and Lola. I have their statements, but I need yours. I have two dead men up on the mountain, two suffering from dehydration and two more in the hospital. Elmer and Carl have been picked up. They both said they were the ones who almost got killed, not you." He pulled out his notebook and pen. "Said you knocked them into the gravel pit."

Colt nodded. "After they took me from my house in the middle of the night, tied me up and planned to kill me and dump me in the pit. They probably didn't mention that."

"Actually, Elmer confessed this morning. They're both behind bars." The sheriff sighed. "Just give me the basics. You'll have to come down to the office when you're released."

Colt related everything from the time he was awakened by the cult members breaking into the house until he landed the helicopter at the hospital.

"It would have been nice if you'd given me a call," Flint said.

"Jonas would have killed them. He was so close to hurting Grace..." His voice broke. "If Lola hadn't acted when she did..."

"Jonas had one bullet in him from a gun registered to you, but all the others were from a gun registered to Jonas himself. We found it next to Zack's body. Why would Zack kill his own leader?"

Colt shook his head. "He came in firing. When I jumped out of the way, he kept firing..."

"He's the one who wounded you?"

"Yes. And the one who knocked out Tommy, but he might have already told you that."

"Actually," the sheriff said. "He didn't see who or what hit him."

"Zack was the only guard left. Everyone else vacated the property."

"Lola said that most of them were headed to Arizona, where Jonas had promised them a place to live, but we can't find any property owned by him or SLS," Flint said. "We did, though, find a variety of places where he has stashed their money, a lot of it. I would imagine there'll be lawsuits against his estate."

"Lola thinks he murdered her parents. They're buried on the compound."

The sheriff raked a hand through his hair. "We saw that there is a new grave in the woods. We were able to contact a couple of SLS followers who didn't make it any farther than town. They said they think he killed Sister Rebecca and that she is buried in the new grave." He shook his head. "He had me fooled."

"Me, too. For a while," Colt admitted.

Grace began to whimper next to his bed.

The sheriff put away his notebook and pen as he rose. "I'll let you see to your daughter." He tipped his Stetson as he left.

* * *

The story hit the local paper the next day. SLS members were spilling their guts about what had gone on up at the compound. A half dozen had already filed lawsuits against the fortune Jonas had amassed.

The article made Colt and Tommy sound like heroes. Colt figured that was Lola's doing since she'd told him she'd been interviewed by a reporter. She'd said she was anxious for her story—and that of her parents—to get out.

"Maybe it will keep other people from getting taken in by men like Jonas," she'd said. "He caught my parents at a vulnerable time in their lives. But if they could be fooled, then anyone can."

Lola picked him up after the doctor released him from the hospital.

He sat in the passenger seat of the SUV she'd had delivered to his house. The woman was damned independent, but he liked that about her. Grace grinned at him from the car seat as they drove out to the ranch. Drove home. Well, home for a while anyway. All he'd been able to think about was getting back to that old ranch house that had felt like a prison before Lola. Now it felt like home.

Not that he was going to get sentimental and hang on to the house. Or the ranch. He wanted a new start for his little family.

They'd been home for a while when Tommy stopped by the house to see how he was doing before taking his helicopter home.

"You've met Lola," Colt said.

Tommy nodded.

"We got to know each other while we were waiting on you to get well. I had to thank him for all he did in helping us." She turned to the man from where she was making cookies in the kitchen. "We owe you. If you can stick around for twelve minutes, I will have a batch of chocolate chip cookies coming out of the oven. It's not much, given what you did for us."

"I'm just glad you're all right," Tommy said, looking bashful. "Anyway, I owe your husband. He saved my life. I'd do anything for him. I got to tell you, I think our boy Colt has done good this time," his friend said, grinning at Lola, then Colt. "You got yourself a good one," he said with a wink. "So what's this plan you wanted to talk to me about?"

"You're not mad at me for almost getting you killed?" Colt asked.

Tommy looked embarrassed. "I let some cult member sneak up on me."

"Zack was ex-military."

"That makes me feel a little better, but let's keep it to ourselves, okay? So what's up?" he asked as he took the chair he was offered at the kitchen table. Lola checked the cookies. Grace was watching her from her carrier on the counter. Colt liked watching Lola cook. He just liked watching her and marveling at how lucky he'd gotten.

"Colt?" Tommy said, grinning as he drew his attention again.

He laughed, then got serious. "Remember all the times we talked about starting our own helicopter service?" Colt and Tommy had spent hours at night in Afghanistan planning what they would do when they got out of the Army. Only Colt had stayed in, so their dream of owning their own flight company had been put off indefinitely.

"You still thinking about it?" Tommy asked.

"I know you're doing great with your repair business. I know you might not be interested in starting a company with me, but I've sold the ranch. I have money to invest. You don't have to answer right now. Take a few days to—"

"I don't need a few days. Absolutely," his friend said. "Where were you thinking of headquartering it?"

"There's a piece of land close by I'd like to build a house on. Right down the road from it would be the ideal place for the office, with lots of room for the shops and landing any number of birds."

Tommy laughed. "You really have been thinking about this." He glanced past Colt to Lola, who was busy taking the cookies out of the oven. "What about the military?" he asked, his gaze shifting back to Colt.

"I've decided not to take the upcoming assignment and resign my commission. I'm getting married. I have a family now. I don't want to be away from them."

"I get it," Tommy said as he took the warm cookie Lola offered him. "How soon?"

"I can make an offer on the land and we can get construction going on the shops and hangers—"

"How long before you get married?" Tommy asked with a laugh and took a bite of the cookie, before complimenting Lola.

"In three weeks. That was something else I needed to talk to you about," Colt said. "I need a best man."

Lola wanted to pinch herself. She couldn't believe she was getting married. She'd never been so happy. She was glad they'd put off the wedding for a few weeks. There'd been a lot of questions about everything that had happened up on the mountain. The investigation, though, had finally ended.

It had taken a while for the bodies of her parents and Sister Rebecca to be exhumed. Just as she'd suspected, autopsies revealed that both of her parents had been poisoned. So had Rebecca. Lola made arrangements to have their remains flown to California and reinterred in the plots next to her sister's.

"You have nothing to feel guilty about," Colt had assured her.

"But if I'd come straight home after university and tried to get them out of that place—"

"You know it wouldn't have done any good. They were determined that you join them, right?"

She'd nodded. "But if I'd come right home when I got my father's letter, maybe I could have—"

"You know how Jonas operated. It wouldn't have made a difference. You said yourself that your mother adored Jonas. You couldn't have gotten her to leave and your father wouldn't have left without her, right?"

She'd known he was right. Still, she hated that she hadn't been able to save them. She was just grateful to Colt. If it hadn't been for him...

Lola looked down at her sleeping daughter. Yes, if it hadn't been for him there would have been no Grace.

Colt wandered through the days afterward, more content than he had ever been. He and Lola went horseback riding. She took to it so well that she made him promise he would teach Grace when she was old enough.

"I'll teach all of the kids."

"All of the kids?" she'd asked with one raised eyebrow.

He'd smiled as he'd pulled her to him. "Tell me you wouldn't mind having a couple more."

"You want a son."

"I want whatever you give me," he'd said, nuzzling her neck and making her laugh. "I'll be taking all girls if that's what you've got for me."

Lola had kissed him, promising to give him as many children as he wanted.

"And I'll teach them all to fly. Which reminds me, anytime you want to go for a ride... The helicopters will be coming in right after the wedding."

The new owners of the ranch had allowed Colt to stay on with his family until he was able to get a mobile home put on the land he'd bought back from them. "We'll live in it until the house is finished, then maybe use it for the office until the office building is done."

Lola seemed as excited as he was about the business they were starting with Tommy. She kept busy with her new friends Lillie and Mariah. They were actually talking playdates for the kids.

He ran into Wyatt a couple more times in town. He hadn't

wanted to slug him. Actually, he'd wanted to thank him. The thought had made him laugh.

Also, Colt hadn't been that surprised when Julia called. He almost hadn't answered. "Hello?"

"Colt, it's Julia. I saw your engagement announcement in the newspaper not long after that story came out. What a story."

He didn't know what to say.

"Wyatt and I are over. I know you don't care, but I wanted you to hear it from me first."

"I'm sorry." He really was. He no longer had any ill will toward either of them and said as much.

"I won't bother you again. I'm actually leaving town. But I had to ask you something…" She seemed to hesitate. "It's amazing what you did for this Lola woman. You really put up a fight to save her and the baby."

He waited, wondering where she was going with this.

"Why…" Her voice broke. "Why didn't you put up a fight for me?"

It had never crossed his mind to try to keep Julia from marrying Wyatt. She was right. He hadn't put up a fight. He'd been hurt, he'd been angry, but he hadn't made some grandiose effort like riding a horse into the church to stop the wedding—if it had ever gone that far.

"I hope you find what you're looking for," he said, because there wasn't anything else he could say.

"And I hope you're unhappy as hell." She disconnected.

He looked over at Lola and laughed.

"Julia," she said.

"Yep, she called to say she liked the article."

Lola smiled. "You're a terrible liar."

"She's leaving town."

"Really?" She didn't seem unhappy to hear that.

"She wished us well."

"Now I know you're lying," she said as he pulled her close.

* * *

The wedding took place in a field of flowers surrounded by the four mountain ranges. Colt had purchased the property just days before. He'd had to scramble to get everything moved in for the ceremony.

What had started as a small wedding had grown, as old and new friends wanted to be a part of it.

"Lola, I know this isn't what we planned," Colt had apologized. They'd agreed to a small wedding, and somehow it had gone awry.

She had laughed. "I love that all these people care about you and want to be there. They're becoming my friends, as well." Lillie and Mariah had given her a baby shower, the three becoming instant friends.

He kissed her. "I just want it to be the best day of your life."

"That day was when I met you."

Colt couldn't believe how many people had helped to make the day special. Calls came in from around the world from men he'd served with. A dozen of them flew in for the ceremony. The guest list had continued to grow right up until the wedding.

"Let us cater it for you," Lillie and Mariah had suggested. "Darby insists. And the Stagecoach Saloon is all yours for the reception, if it rains."

Lola had hugged her new friends, eyes glistening and Colt thought he couldn't be more blessed. Lola had accepted their kind offer and added, "Only if the two of you will agree to be my matrons of honor."

So much had been going on that the weeks leading up to the wedding had flown by. Colt wished his father was alive to see this—his only son changing diapers, getting up for middle-of-the-night feedings, bathing the baby in the kitchen sink, and all the while loving every minute of it.

Tommy always chuckled when he came by and caught Colt being a father. "If the guys could see you now," he'd joked. But

Colt had seen his friend's wistful looks. He hoped Tommy found someone he could love as much as Colt loved Lola.

She'd continued to amaze him, taking everything in her stride as the ranch auction was held and the sale of the ranch continued. She'd had her things shipped from where they'd been in storage and helped him start packing up what he planned to keep at the house.

He'd felt overwhelmed sometimes, but Lola was always cool and calm. He often thought of that woman he'd met in Billings—and the one he'd found on his doorstep in the middle of the night. Often he didn't feel he was good enough for her. But then she would find him, put her arms around him and rest her head on his shoulder, and he would breathe in the scent of her and know that this was meant to be.

Like standing here now in a field of flowers next to Lola with all their friends and the preacher ready to marry them. If this was a dream, he didn't want to wake up.

Lola couldn't believe all the people who had come into her life because of Colt. She looked over at him. He was so handsome in his Western suit and boots. He was looking at her, his blue eyes shining. He smiled as the preacher said, "Do you take this woman—"

"I sure do," he said, and everyone laughed.

Lola hardly remembered the rest of the ceremony. She felt so blissfully happy that she wasn't even sure her feet had touched the ground all day.

But she remembered the kiss. Colt had pulled her to him, taking his time as he looked into her eyes. "I love you, Lola," he'd whispered.

She'd nodded through her tears and then he'd kissed her. The crowd had broken into applause. Cowboy hats and Army caps had been thrown into the air. Somewhere beyond the crowd, a band began to play.

Lillie hugged her before handing her Grace. Lola looked up

from the infant she held in her arms, her eyes full of tears. Colt put his arm around both of them as they took their first steps as Mr. and Mrs. Colt McCloud.

* * * * *

Braving The Heat

Regan Black

Romantic **Suspense**

Danger. Passion. Drama.

Regan Black, a *USA TODAY* bestselling author, writes award-winning, action-packed novels featuring kick-butt heroines and the sexy heroes who fall in love with them. Raised in the Midwest and California, she and her family, along with their adopted greyhound, two arrogant cats and a quirky finch, reside in the South Carolina Low Country, where the rich blend of legend, romance and history fuels her imagination.

Visit the Author Profile page at millsandboon.com.au for more titles.

Dear Reader,

Welcome back to Philadelphia, PA, and the Escape Club! This riverside hot spot is *the* place to find both great music and a safe haven if you have a problem that doesn't fit within the framework of typical law enforcement.

Stephen Galway first appeared in *Safe in His Sight*, my debut book for Harlequin Romantic Suspense, and though I've written several novels in between, I've never been able to put this brooding man out of my mind. I've wanted him to have a happy-ever-after since the first moment he showed up on the page, grumbling at his brother.

Kenzie Hughes, a PFD firefighter, is in trouble and her options are dwindling when help comes from an unlikely source: Stephen. For some reason he sees right through her independent nature, which is currently propped up by little more than bravado and a big smile. Time after time he listens and then quietly steps up and does what's needed and all without trampling her pride.

Life has dealt Kenzie and Stephen some serious challenges and alone they found unique ways to cope and compensate. But now that they've met, it's time to make some hard choices about who they are, what they really need and how those revealing answers will shape their future.

Live the adventure,

Regan Black

For my friend Sam, a man who consistently stepped up as a sheriff's deputy, as an author and as my inspiration for Stephen's dad, Samuel Galway.

I am forever grateful for the light and laughter you added to my world.

CHAPTER ONE

Standing at a prep counter in the Escape Club kitchen, Kenzie Hughes stuffed the last bite of her sandwich into her mouth and added her plate to the rack loaded for the dishwasher. She thanked the cook and slipped the strap of her backpack over one shoulder. Pausing at the doorway to the main floor, she scanned the empty stage, looking for Grant Sullivan, owner of the establishment.

The extra personnel Grant had brought on for the summer concert series were resetting for the evening show. Leaving them to cover her workload through the afternoon changeover didn't sit well with Kenzie, but her landlord had called. She had only a few more hours to clear out whatever she didn't want exposed to termite fumigation and the dust and debris from the repair process.

If she hustled she could get to her apartment and back again before the doors opened for the evening session. That would please her as much as it would please Grant. It wasn't as if she had anything better to do with her time, other than finding an affordable place to crash for a couple weeks.

Though her pay from the Philadelphia Fire Department had continued during her current administrative leave, storage units and short-term room rentals added up fast. She'd asked both her union representative and her lawyer if she could visit her mom in Delaware while her apartment was out of commission, and been told she had to stay in Philly. Both the union rep and her lawyer implied that her leaving town could be perceived as an admission of guilt.

"Can't have that," she muttered to herself.

If there was anything Kenzie dreaded more than the potential outcome of her current legal trouble, it was having nothing productive to do while she waited out the process.

She had, in fact, been cleared of any wrongdoing during a PFD investigation that followed a complaint from a man she'd rescued from a fire. He'd claimed her incompetence had resulted in minor injuries that could have been avoided. Just when she thought she'd be back on the job, the victim had filed a civil suit against her personally. She knew she wasn't guilty of any error in the process of saving his life. The victim disagreed. Loudly, publicly and constantly.

Stop, she ordered herself. Dwelling on the negative situation only fouled up her mood. The jerk didn't have a case at all. If he had, the PFD would have fired her outright weeks ago. Her lawyer assured her most civil cases settled out of court; it was simply a matter of working the case and being patient with the system. Oddly enough, the only place Kenzie successfully exercised patience was while working emergency calls and fires.

Unable to find Grant, she tracked down Jason Prather at the bar. The latest full-time addition to the Escape Club, Jason was the closest thing Grant had to an assistant manager. Tall and wiry, bordering on skinny, he, too, had a few years with the PFD on his résumé. Whenever she looked at him, she thought he could pass as a front man for one of the bands that came through if he'd let his thick black hair grow out.

"If Grant asks, will you remind him I went to clear out my apartment? I should be back in time for opening tonight."

Jason gave her a long look over the tablet he was using to record inventory. "You need any help? I can send—"

"No, thanks. I've got it," she managed to reply. If she said anything else, she'd probably break down in a puddle of frustration. Grant was doing enough for her already, keeping her busy with this job. She refused to impose on anyone else.

Hurrying out of the club and across the street, she cringed at the sight of her road-weary compact sedan. Though the primer-and-rust color scheme was a fright, it ran, and that was the important thing. And it was paid for. She'd sold her car and paid cash for the rust-bucket sedan so she could redirect her previous car payment to her legal fees for the civil case. When she didn't have those extra expenses anymore, she could go back to a better car. One with a powerful engine and serious sex appeal, she thought, indulging in a quick fantasy of a classic American muscle car.

As if. Although owning a classic Camaro was on her bucket list, this case meant it would be a long time before she'd be able to make that kind of investment.

After unlocking the driver's door, she tossed her backpack into the passenger seat and slid behind the wheel. She turned the key in the ignition, expecting the sputter and catch of the small engine, but hearing silence instead.

"No." She dropped her head to the steering wheel, almost ready to give in to the threat of tears she'd been fighting off all week. Her apartment closing, if only temporarily, the civil suit claiming she was unfit for firefighting, and now a car that wouldn't start.

Crying over this heap of metal was pointless, but it was one obstacle too many right now. She ruthlessly swiped away the lone tear rolling down her cheek. It wasn't the potential expense of repairs, though cash was currently tight. No, what upset her more was the idea of asking another friend or family member for more help. Her independence had taken enough of a beating lately. Here she was at thirty years old, feeling less self-sufficient now than when she'd crossed the stage for her high school graduation. Unlike so many of her peers, back then she'd had clear goals and a clear path planned to reach them.

"This is not happening." She tried the ignition again, got the same result.

With a colorful oath, she removed the key and pulled the hood release. After slamming out of the car, she raised the hood and stared into the filthy engine. Her father, a car aficionado and passionate weekend race car driver, might have wept at the sight. He'd taught her everything he knew about cars and engines, and when she'd bought this one, it had been functional, if ugly. The new battery she'd installed after the purchase was the only clean thing in view. With a critical eye, she assessed the rest of the machinery, looking for an obvious problem.

"It has to get better," she said aloud, willing herself to believe the words.

Life hadn't been perfect. She'd experienced her share of sorrows to offset the celebrations and happy milestones of being an independent adult. Overall, she'd been content through both the highs and lows. Until the last fire she'd worked, three months ago, turned into a difficult rescue and ongoing nightmare. Though she tried to ignore it, a small voice inside her head wondered again if that would be the last fire she ever fought.

"All of this will pass." Just like every other pain, challenge and setback she'd faced. She calmed herself with the assurance that she'd be back at the firehouse, back with her crew on the truck soon. She couldn't afford to let her mind wander away from anything less than her ideal outcome.

Returning to the driver's seat, she turned the key again, listening for clues. Was it the alternator or starter? It couldn't be a broken fuel gauge. She'd just filled up with gas yesterday. "Come on, baby, tell me what's wrong," she said to the car. "We've got things to do."

If she didn't figure this out, she'd leave Grant shorthanded during what was sure to be a packed house tonight. She shook the steering wheel. Sure, Grant might understand, but that wasn't the point. Letting people down, shirking commitments wasn't how she operated. Besides, working at the Escape Club distracted her, filling all the empty hours while the PFD kept her off the job.

As tears threatened again, she jerked the rearview mirror around and glared at her reflection. "*You* are a firefighter," she said to the moody face in the mirror. She pushed the wisps of hair that had escaped her braid behind her ears. "You're one of the *best*," she said, willing away the doubt in the blue eyes staring back at her.

And if you lose the case and your career is over, who will you be?

She was really starting to hate that pesky negative voice that kept sounding off. Shoving the mirror back into place, she tried to start the car once more. Instead of getting anything out of the engine, she heard a knock on the window. She jumped in the seat, startled to see Mitch Galway on the other side of her open door. Her friend, part-time Escape Club bartender and fellow firefighter, Mitch had suggested she ask Grant for a job to help her through her current crisis. *Momentary* crisis.

"Car trouble?" he asked, tipping his head to the exposed engine.

"It won't turn over."

"Let me hear it." He signaled her to try again. Mitch knew cars and often helped his older brother with custom restorations at the Galway Automotive shop over in Spruce Hill. At the lack of response, he frowned and walked out of sight behind the open hood.

She silently prayed he could help as she checked the time. If she didn't make it to her apartment soon, all her belongings would be out of reach for at least two weeks. The last thing she needed was the expense of buying a new wardrobe.

"Any ideas?" she asked as she joined him. "I know it has gas in the tank."

He frowned at the engine. "In that case, my first guess is an alternator," he said. "You need a good mechanic?"

"I am a good mechanic," she reminded him. Or she had been when her dad was alive. With the right tools and time, she could probably sort this out on her own. Too bad she didn't have either.

"True." He dropped the hood back down and dusted off his palms. "You know I can hook you up," he said with a quick smile.

"What I need is a good car." She explained the dwindling time issue to Mitch. "I never should've waited until the last minute to do this." She didn't share the still more embarrassing fact that she had no idea where she would stay tonight or any night until she could go back to her apartment. Mitch had offered his spare room to her last week, but she'd turned him down. Newlyweds, he and his wife didn't need her underfoot.

Mitch tossed her the keys to his truck. "Go get your stuff," he said. "I'll call my brother and get your car towed to the shop."

Dollar signs danced through her head. Maybe she could trade labor for parts or something if his brother was amenable. "I'm not sure—"

"We'll figure it out," he said, waving off her concerns before she could name them all. "Get going."

"All right." Arguing with him to save a smidge of pride only robbed her of more time. "Thanks."

She grabbed her backpack and dashed over to Mitch's truck. She appreciated his generosity as well as his gracious acceptance of her circumstances. Everyone on the PFD knew she was in over her head with the civil suit and working every available hour at the Escape Club to pay for a decent lawyer to defend her.

A former firefighter himself, the plaintiff, Randall Murtagh, knew better than most people what *should* be done during a rescue. That he'd made it nearly impossible for her to save him didn't seem to have any relevance to his injuries, in his mind. A card-carrying member of the old guard who believed only men were capable of pulling people out of burning buildings, he made no secret of the fact that he wanted women drummed out of the ranks. If he couldn't get all the females off the PFD with this case, he seemed hell-bent on making her a prime example against equal opportunity employment.

And there she was dwelling on the negative again. She couldn't control his issues, only her response, and she wouldn't let a jerk like Murtagh take any more chunks of her life.

Fortunately, she was soon distracted, packing all the belongings she cared to take as swiftly as possible. She crammed clothing and linens into two suitcases, boxed up her stand mixer and kitchenware, and filled two more boxes with family pictures and hand-me-downs that were irreplaceable. Per the instructions from the landlord, she labeled her bed and dresser, the only furnishings she'd added to the apartment when she moved in, and locked the door.

An intense, inexplicable sadness came over her as she secured the last box in the truck bed. This wasn't an ending. It wasn't as if she'd been evicted. That would come later, if she lost her job. This was one more untimely circumstance in a life that had suddenly been filled with high hurdles.

With a final glance at the lovely old building she'd called home, she headed back to the club and a long shift that would keep her mind and body busy for the rest of the night.

At Galway Automotive the phone rang, a shrill sound interrupting the throbbing pulse of the heavy metal music filling the garage. Under the back end of a 1967 Camaro SS, Stephen Galway used the voice control to lower the volume on the music. At an hour past closing on a Friday, he wasn't obligated to answer the phone, but a heads-up for what problems might be showing up tomorrow never hurt.

"Pick up, Stephen. It's Mitch." His brother's voice wasn't nearly as soothing as the heavy metal had been. The oldest of Stephen's younger siblings, Mitch was the one who consistently refused to let him stay off the family radar for too long.

"I know you're there," Mitch pressed.

Where else would he be?

"He'll come through," Mitch promised in an undertone to someone on his end of the call.

"Not your job to make promises for me, little brother," Stephen muttered.

"Pick up," Mitch said, bossy now. "I've got a friend here at the club with car trouble. Tow it out of the employee parking lot and we'll come by and look it over when I have time tomorrow." He gave the make, model and license plate number of the car.

Huh. Stephen rolled out from under the Camaro, wiping grease from his hands. His brother knew as much about cars as he did. If Mitch couldn't get his friend's car rolling, there was a serious problem. Still, he didn't pick up, waiting to see if his brother would sweeten the deal.

Mitch swore. "Come on, Stephen. The club has your kind of group onstage tonight. I'll buy you a beer and help you hook up the car."

Stephen picked up the handset. "I'll head over." He glanced down at his stained T-shirt and jeans. The customer waiting on the Camaro wasn't in any rush, preferring this rebuild and restoration be done perfectly rather than by a specific date. *If only they could all be that patient*, Stephen thought. "Give me an hour or so."

Dropping the receiver back into place, he scowled at his stained hands and T-shirt. Promised beer or not, if he wanted inside the Escape Club during business hours he had to clean up. He put his work space to rights and lowered the bay door. The Camaro would be waiting when he returned.

He walked through the office and around to the refurbished camper he'd parked behind the building. Not that long ago, he would've headed to the house he once shared with Mitch, but his brother and Julia, his recent bride, had eventually settled there after their honeymoon.

Stephen had promised his mom he'd find a decent house

somewhere near the shop. It was a good neighborhood. Instead, he kept taking on more work, limiting his time to search. The last time he'd gone house hunting had been with his fiancée, Annabeth. Even after three long years he still couldn't walk a property without hearing in his head how she'd react.

Last year, when his parents had suggested he move back home with them, he'd bristled. He hadn't taken it any more gracefully when Mitch and Julia swore he wouldn't be in their way. The newlyweds didn't need a big brother crowding them. His parents didn't need him returning home when they could all but taste the empty nest. His youngest sister, Jenny, was almost ready to spread her wings.

Although they meant well, there were days when he was sure he'd drown under all the love and good intentions of his family.

Losing Annabeth before they'd had a chance to experience the life they'd dreamed of didn't make him an invalid. He maintained a successful business and supported the PFD and other causes in the community that mattered to him. Stephen continued to give special attention to the after-school program where his fiancée had worked, and where three years ago she'd been shot and killed for having the audacity to help kids avoid gangs and drugs.

He'd long since given up on shedding the melancholy that hovered like a storm cloud over his life. What his family wanted for him and what he knew he could handle were two different things. He didn't bother trying to convince them anymore. Work was all the sunlight he needed. Cars and engines he could understand, fix and make new again. People were too fragile, himself included. In his mind, that was all the rationalization necessary for the old Airstream trailer he'd purchased. After months of work, inside and out, he considered it home, though he wasn't yet brave enough to use the word within his mother's hearing.

As the oldest, he really should get more respect for his good judgment, if only by default.

Having washed off the pungent smells of the shop, he debated briefly about clothing. He'd prefer shorts on a summer night, but since he was going to hook up a car, he opted for jeans and a red polo shirt. When he finally reached the club, he found room for the tow truck near the back of the employee parking lot across the street. With the Escape Club perched at the end of the pier, few cars were granted the prime spaces on busy nights. No one emerged from a parked car or otherwise expressed any interest in his arrival, so he walked down to the club.

On the rare occasions his brother got him here, Stephen couldn't help but admire what Sullivan had made out of his forced early retirement and an old warehouse. He'd never heard anyone question Sullivan's choices, or express worry over what he was or wasn't doing with his life. Though admittedly, a club naturally was a more social environment than an auto shop. People came from all over for the bands the Escape Club drew to Philly.

Striding straight to the front of the line, Stephen realized maybe he had more in common with Sullivan than he thought. Galway Automotive was building a solid reputation and people were calling from all over the region to get their cars on his restoration schedule.

"Unless you hire a female mechanic, you'll never meet a nice girl under the hood of a car." His mother's voice broke into his thoughts. Myra Galway had a way of saying things that slid right past his defenses and lingered, mocking him with her maternal logic. If only his mom would admit there was more to life than filling lonely hours with pointless chatter with women who sneered at his stained fingernails and the rough calluses on his palms.

At the burly doorman's arched eyebrow, Stephen gave his name and was quickly waved inside.

The bold, heavy sounds of the metal band onstage slammed into him and battered away at the discontent that persistently dogged Stephen since his fiancée's death. He leaned into the music, weaving through the crowd until he reached Mitch's station at the service end of the bar, closer to the kitchen.

His brother eyed him and popped the top off a bottle of beer, setting it in front of him between serving other patrons. Good. Stephen wasn't in much of a talking mood. The delayed conversation was no surprise, considering the sea of humanity supporting the band from all corners of the club.

"Took you long enough," Mitch said at the first lull between customers. "You might be here awhile."

Stephen checked his watch. He'd said an hour or so and had hit the mark precisely. "How come?" he asked, though he didn't care about the time, since the band was as good as Mitch had promised.

"No way I can get out there right now. This set just started."

Stephen shrugged and swiveled around on the bar stool to watch the band. They were good, from the sound to the showmanship. He was enjoying the music, the process of being still and people-watching. Waitresses in khaki shorts and bright blue T-shirts emblazoned with the Escape Club logo brushed by him with friendly glances and quick greetings as they exchanged trays of empty bottles and glassware for the fresh orders Mitch filled with startling efficiency. From Stephen's vantage point everyone in the club seemed to be focused on excellent customer service. Sullivan had definitely created an outstanding atmosphere.

"Do you always ignore the signals?" Mitch asked when another waitress walked off, tray perfectly balanced.

"What are you talking about?"

Mitch shook his head. "Signals from *interested* women," he said. "If you'd pay attention, you'd see it for yourself."

"Please. Not you, too." Stephen glared at his little brother. "You know I've got too much work to spare time for dating."

"Uh-huh." Mitch slid another city-wide special across the bar to a customer and marked the tab. "Then I'm sorry I called you. Another beer?"

"Water," Stephen answered, then checked his watch again. The band would probably take a break soon. He drained the glass of water Mitch provided and pushed back from the bar. "Tell your friend I'm waiting out in the truck. No rush. Thanks for the beer."

"Stephen, wait."

Not a chance. What was it with married people? His parents and married siblings were ganging up on him lately, and being relentless about it. Was there some statute of limitations on grief he didn't know about? He'd tried believing that crappy philosophy of it being better to have loved and lost, and couldn't pull it off. He'd loved, he'd lost everything and it sucked.

They kept wanting him to be happy, checking in on him week after week, never letting it rest. Was he happy? He didn't know. At this point he wasn't sure he cared about happiness. Business was good. Booming, in fact. If that was enough happiness for him, his family should back off. Not everyone got a happy ending. He'd accepted that hard truth; why couldn't they?

"Hey! Stephen Galway?"

Nearly to the truck, he turned at the sound of his name. Recognizing the waitress uniform, he was tempted to ignore the slender blonde jogging his way with a long, ground-eating stride. His brother earned points for tenacity. Stephen made a note to punch him at the earliest opportunity.

"You are Stephen, right?"

"That's right. And you are?" The lamp overhead cast her features in shadow, illuminating pale hair pulled back from her face. He remembered seeing her in the bar. She was the one with the long braid that fell to the middle of her back, and great legs anchoring that willowy body.

"Kenzie Hughes." She stuck out her hand, then let it fall when he didn't reach out to meet her halfway. "You probably don't remember me."

"Should I?" The name wasn't ringing any bells.

"Guess not. I was in the same high school class as Mitch."

Stephen was ready to march back into the club and punch his brother right now for orchestrating this elaborate setup. He had work to do without dragging the tow truck out on a wild-goose chase. What bad idea or wrong impression had Mitch planted in her head? He stared at her, struggling for a polite way out of this. It wasn't her fault his brother was an idiot.

"Um, anyway," she continued, "I didn't mean to keep you waiting." She pulled keys from her pocket. "The car's right over here."

Now he felt like a complete jerk. Stephen had assumed he'd be helping out one of Mitch's male buddies. "Great." He fell in behind her and put his mind back in car mode. "Let's take a look."

He tried not to wince when he saw the vehicle. Not his business what people chose to drive, and people who drove rust buckets like this one made up a core segment of his business. He let her explain Mitch's opinion of the situation while he listened to a whole lot of nothing going on in her engine. Something didn't smell right under the normal scents of oil and gas.

"If Mitch couldn't get you running here, we're better off hauling it in." He dropped the hood, checked the latch. "Do you have a way to get home?"

She climbed out of the car and he noticed the interior was packed with boxes and suitcases. He couldn't imagine Sullivan allowing any of his employees to live out of their car, and if she was doing so, she hadn't left much room for herself.

"I'll be fine," she said, her gaze sliding to the crammed interior. "Here." She handed over the keys. "I'll get your number from Mitch and call you tomorrow."

"One second." *Hughes, PFD, female.* It all clicked into place and embarrassment flooded through Stephen. "You're Mackenzie Hughes."

Her entire body went on the defensive in one fluid movement. "Yes. Is that a problem?"

"No." He couldn't believe he didn't recognize her in the club.

Her name was at the center of a public debate about the ability of female firefighters. In person, her height and poise were evident and she looked far more capable than she did on television, where the images provided focused on her photogenic and fine-boned, feminine face.

"Of course not," he reiterated, when she cocked an eyebrow at his long perusal. He'd heard his brother rant more than once in Kenzie's favor. Like most people of his acquaintance, Stephen thought the gender bias was in the past. "I'll take good care of the car," he promised. "What's with all the boxes?"

Now her shoulders slumped. "Do I have to unload them for you to tow the car?" She looked around as if a storage shed would appear out of thin air. "I didn't think of that."

"If you don't have a problem with it, I don't. Things might get jostled as I load and unload the car."

"No. My stuff will be okay." She backed away. "Thanks so much. I'll pick up the boxes tomorrow."

He trailed after her as if someone had set him on automatic pilot. "How?"

She skidded to a stop. "Pardon me?"

"If I have your car, how are you getting around?"

She gave him a weak smile. "I'll figure it out."

He blamed it on having sisters. Only her car was his business, but he still felt compelled to get a better answer from her. "What time are you off tonight?"

"Two."

"Have Mitch bring you over to the shop."

She gaped at him. "You can't be serious. At two in the morning?"

Something about her response had him changing his mind. "Good point." His brother had a wife waiting at home. "I'll bring over a loaner car for you."

"At two in the morning?" she repeated, incredulous.

He rolled his shoulders and resisted the urge to shift under that intense blue gaze. "That's when you need it, right?"

"Well, yeah, but—"

"Then I'll be here. Unless you won't have time to drop me back at my shop on your way home?"

She snorted. "No, I can do that."

"Good. We're all set." He turned away before she could argue, and went to load her car onto the flatbed tow truck. Being near her put an odd pressure in his system, as if his heart was a half-beat too slow. He glanced back over his shoulder and caught her staring at him.

Couldn't blame her; he barely recognized himself in his actions since she'd caught up with him. For his own peace of mind, he chalked up his uncharacteristic behavior to Mitch's frustration on Kenzie's behalf. According to his brother, she'd had a rough time of it since the PFD put her on administrative leave after a victim blamed her incompetence and weakness as a woman for his minor injuries.

She hadn't looked the least bit weak to Stephen, and if Mitch vouched for her, she could handle the job. That must be why he was so determined to do more than the bare minimum of towing in her car for an evaluation and repair.

Kenzie worked the rest of the night with a little more spring in her step. Hope flashed bright and hot though her system at odd and unpredictable intervals. It was nice to feel a genuine smile on her lips. Maybe the recent circumstances hadn't permanently smothered her courage and optimism, after all.

As she cashed out and split her tips with the rest of the staff, she realized she'd earned enough on this shift to cover an economy motel for the night and give Stephen some money for the tow and repair. Every penny left over would go to the lawyer fund.

"Grant's looking for you," Mitch said, as he walked into the break room. "And I have a text for you." He held out his phone.

"For me?" Who would text Mitch to reach her?

"About your car," he said.

Belatedly, she realized she'd been in such a hurry to get back to the club that she'd forgotten to give Stephen her cell phone number. The text message asked Mitch to tell her he was waiting outside. Kenzie replied with her cell phone number and let him know she needed only a few more minutes. She rolled up her apron and shoved it into her backpack, then headed for Grant's office.

Rapping a knuckle on the open door, she stepped inside when Grant turned from his computer monitor. He smiled and waved her in, asking her to close the door. His constant energy belied the gray salting his hair. She suspected the creases bracketing his warm brown eyes were a result of laughter as much as the challenges he'd faced in his career as a cop and a nightclub owner. He reminded her of her dad, she realized with a prickle of nostalgia. Not in appearance—Grant had a barrel-chested, stocky build and her father had been tall and slim. The similarities were in the general demeanor of both men. Grant cared for his club and his employees with the fatherly affection and protectiveness she remembered her dad exhibiting every day of his life.

The chair squeaked as Grant leaned back. "Was it a good night?"

"Yes. Thanks again for giving me so many shifts."

"I prefer employing people who are willing to work," he said. "You know, you remind me of your dad in that way."

"I didn't realize you knew him." She knew she was over-tired and overstressed when tears stung behind her eyes. Fifteen years had passed since they'd buried him, and she usually didn't feel melancholy anymore unless it was the anniversary of the warehouse fire or Christmas. Her mother had been determined her daughters would smile with hearts full of happy memories when they remembered their father. She insisted living well was the best way to affirm all the love and gifts he'd given them.

Grant nodded. "There are few circles in Philly tighter than

those of us who worked the front lines." His thick eyebrows drew into a frown over his assessing gaze. "I heard about your car trouble."

The swift change of topic helped restore her composure. "Mitch called his brother for me. Stephen came out and towed it to his shop. He, ah, offered to loan me a car until mine is fixed." She still wasn't sure how she was going to cover the extra expenses.

"That's good." Leaning back in his chair, Grant drummed a quick rhythm on the edge of his desk. "Here's the thing. I just got off the phone with Stephen."

"About my car?" That didn't make any sense. "Why?"

"You may not know it, but he likes to stay busy," Grant said. "He took a look at your car as soon as he got back to his shop."

"Did he find the problem already?" She braced herself for the worst, assuming Stephen had mentioned parts, labor and prices.

"Yes. He says he can fix it fairly quickly, though he's not sure that's the wise choice since the car's a rolling wreck. His words, not mine." Grant sat upright suddenly and the chair squeaked a protest. He ignored the grating sound, massaging at the scar tissue in his shoulder, the way he often did when he was thinking. "Any chance you forgot how your dad taught you to care for a car and accidently dumped sugar into your gas tank?"

What? "Of course not."

Grant's intent brown eyes turned weary from one blink to the next. "Didn't think so." He blew out a breath and rubbed his temples. "Stephen can explain all the details, of course. I just wanted to be the one to give you the big picture."

"Which is?" she prompted when he hesitated.

"Everything Stephen found suggests that someone sabotaged your car."

"Sugar in the gas tank is hardly the problem people think it is," she said, latching on to the one factor she could comprehend in this bizarre situation. It was a fairly affordable fix to change the clogged filters and flush the tank and fuel lines. "Maybe the previous owner pissed off someone who didn't know keying a car was a better form of revenge."

"Maybe," Grant allowed. He looked as if he wanted to believe her theory as opposed to the evidence that contradicted it. "How long have you had the vehicle?"

She gripped the straps of the backpack, resisting the logic and implications he was forcing on her. "Three weeks." He arched an eyebrow. She didn't need him to say it for her. "If I'd bought the thing with sugar in the tank it would have given me problems long before now."

"So you bought the car at the same time you had to hire an attorney for the civil suit?"

"Yes," she replied, grudgingly.

"Then whoever dumped sugar in the tank was targeting you."

"Unless they didn't realize the car had been sold." She rushed on when Grant rolled his eyes. "It's an inconvenience, that's all." She could do the repairs, assuming Stephen would let her borrow space and the tools.

Grant glanced at the clock over the office door. "You need help, Kenzie. Support."

She understood it wasn't a question. Help was what Grant did. He'd never been able to depart from his inherent need to get involved from his days on the police force. He probably hadn't tried too hard.

She gathered the fraying remnants of her pride. "My attorney has it under control," she said. "He assures me it's a matter of wading through the system."

"I'm glad to hear it." Grant stood up, ending the meeting. "It's okay to remember you have friends willing to help, too."

"Thanks." She hated the idea of dragging her friends into her problems. Besides, there wasn't anything to *do* except let her lawyer handle the case.

She escaped the office and the club, relieved and troubled in equal measure. Outside, she paused and breathed deeply. The air at this hour was clear along the river and as cool and pleasant as Philly could be in the summer. The stars in the inky sky above were faint, the lights from buildings on both sides of the river offering more sparkle.

Only a few cars remained in the lot, and she assumed the small SUV parked next to Mitch's truck was the car Stephen had brought for her. Standing between the two, the Galway brothers turned to her as she approached. She sensed she'd interrupted something important.

"Hi," she said. "Sorry for the delay."

"No problem." Stephen opened the passenger door of the SUV for her. "I'll drive to the shop and you can take it from there."

"Okay." She glanced at Mitch. "Thanks for loaning me your truck today."

"No problem." Lines of tension bracketed the stern set of his mouth. It wasn't a look she often saw on his face. "Be careful, Kenzie."

"Always," she promised, before sliding into the seat. He couldn't be warning her about his brother. "You told him about the clogged fuel filter?" she asked, as Stephen slid behind the wheel and started the car.

"Saves him a trip to the shop tomorrow," Stephen replied, pulling away from the club.

"That's...thoughtful." So why did Mitch seem aggravated?

Stephen's gaze slid from the nearly deserted streets to her and back to the road. "Practical. I've got your car in pieces already, easier for me to put it back together. If that's what you want."

"It's what I need," she replied. When the case was settled she would take great delight in buying a better car. "You didn't have to give me a loaner this nice."

"This was what I had available." He shifted in the seat as if he wasn't comfortable with the conversation. "You needed something with better security."

She could argue the point, though the irritating sabotage spoke for itself. "We don't even know the prank was aimed at me. It could be someone who thought the car still belonged to the previous owner." A weak argument was better than none.

He snorted, clearly not any more convinced of that than Grant had been. "Better not to tempt fate again. This one has a tamper-proof tank and hood."

"Guess that limits someone to cutting the brake lines, slashing tires, rerouting exhaust, planting a GPS tracker or even an explosive," she said. She'd meant it all as a joke, but the list unnerved her.

"Your safety isn't a joke. Did you ask Grant for protection?"

"No." The idea was absurd. She could take care of herself. She leveled her toughest stare at him, the one she saved for those who aimed sexist comments at her when they heard she was a firefighter. There had been far too many opportunities to perfect the expression since Murtagh went public with his complaint and civil suit. "While I'm dressed as a waitress at the moment, you might recall safety is an essential aspect of my career."

"I only meant—"

"I'm an adult," she interrupted. "As a firefighter I'm trained to cope with any number of crises, including saving people and property. It's my job to put out fires." At least she put out fires whenever lawsuits didn't keep her on the sidelines. "I'm merely pointing out there's no way to prevent all forms of trouble. That, too, is an element of my career."

He didn't reply and in profile she noticed his jaw set in a hard line. She imagined if the radio were off she would have heard his teeth grinding.

"I'm sorry," she said. "That was really rude." Embarrassed, she toyed with the straps of her backpack. "You've gone above and beyond to help me today. Despite the rant, I do appreciate it."

"Forget it," he said. "I understand irritable."

He stopped in front of a wide gate barring the entrance to Galway Automotive. Plucking a key ring from the cup holder, he pressed a button on a fob that must have been connected to his security system. The gate slid back, rolling along the inside of the tall fencing surrounding the business. Rather than put the car in Park, he drove through the opening and the gate slid closed behind them. She caught the cameras mounted at the gate, assumed there were more around the property.

She wasn't sure what she'd expected, but it wasn't the well maintained blacktop pavement surrounding an L-shaped building. What must serve as his office jutted slightly forward from the line of bays stretching to the side. Several cars were parked on a strip of gravel at the far end of the building and the tow truck had been backed into a space near the gate where Stephen could leave quickly if necessary.

Bright security lights mounted around the property were aimed at the building and they came on as he drove by. The manufactured sunlight smothered any hope of shadows. Made of metal rather than stone, the garage didn't have much in common with a fairy-tale castle, yet Stephen had definitely created a fortress. The only things missing were a moat and a vigilant dragon.

A dragon? The whimsical thought was a clear sign the late hour had taken its toll. She felt a bizarre wish to stay right here in this sheltered place until her troubles went away. Too bad lawsuits didn't disappear if they were ignored.

He parked next to the office, away from the other cars, and the headlights glanced off the gleaming silver siding of a sleek, bullet-shaped camper.

"It's bigger than I expected," she said.

"The trailer?"

"No." She laughed now, giddy and definitely overtired. "The business."

He gave her a long look. "I own the block now."

Impressive. She managed to swallow several prying questions about the man and his work that were none of her concern.

"Do you need anything from your car?" he asked.

Feeling unsettled, she ducked away from his gaze and nudged

the backpack with her knee. "I'm set for tonight. Is there a good time for me to swing by and pick up everything tomorrow? I guess I mean today?" The clock on the dash showed it was already past three. "I can help with the repairs to my car, too."

He didn't jump on her offer. "Where will you take your things?" He cut the engine and held on to the key.

She had no idea. "I'll figure something out." Although she couldn't leave town, maybe her belongings could. Her mom had extended the offer. Kenzie just needed to make time to drive up there.

The burnished gold eyebrows flexed over his eyes. "You don't have anywhere to stay, do you?"

She was too weary to fib or bluster through. "I figure there's an available motel room somewhere in town." She waved a hand at the clock. "I only need a few hours of sleep. Tell me what time to come by."

His lips pressed together and he nodded once as if an internal debate had just been settled. "I didn't think so. You'll stay here tonight."

He got out of the car and walked to the camper. She gawked at him through the windshield, trying to make sense of his statement. Trying to catch up as her pulse went racing ahead of her at his abrupt declaration.

When he noticed she wasn't behind him, he came around to the passenger door and opened it. "Come on."

She gripped the edge of the seat. "No thanks. If you'll give me the car key and open the gate I'll see you tomorrow."

"As you said, it's already tomorrow," he said, completely ignoring the salient point that she would leave and handle her troubles on her own. He reached past her for the backpack, his forearm brushing across her bare knees.

"Hey, that's mine. What are you doing?" She shifted her leg, pinning his arm. *Mistake*, a small voice warned her too late. His skin was warm against hers and in this position his handsome face was close enough that the security lights sparked in the dark blond stubble shading his jaw.

The tough, callused palm of his free hand landed on her leg and he extracted his trapped arm and simply lifted her out of the car. He handled her as if she weighed nothing. Worse, he behaved as if he had the right to move her about at will. Where was her fight?

"You'll stay here tonight," he repeated, setting her on her feet. "I'll stay on the couch in the office. We'll sort out the rest in the morning."

She dug in her heels as he opened the camper door and waited for her to go inside. "Stephen, this isn't right. It's too much," she added, when he refused to agree with her.

He tipped his head. "Go on in and make yourself at home. We've both lost enough sleep as it is."

Nothing else he could have said would have convinced her to cooperate. Fully aware she'd been a big imposition already, she obediently walked up the steps. She glanced back before he could close the door. "Stephen, why are you doing this?"

He shrugged. "Good night, Kenzie."

She watched him disappear into the office, bewildered by his unexpected kindness.

Emotions she'd rather not examine churned inside her as she stood in his camper. It was neat and clean, and the evidence that he lived here was everywhere. The plain, heavy white mug stationed near the coffeepot on the narrow counter. The mail tucked into a slim wire basket next to a laptop computer on the shelf behind the table. She passed the bathroom and caught a whiff of the crisp, green scent she'd noticed on his skin.

Why would Stephen give his home to her, even for a night?

Her pride had taken a hard tumble in recent weeks and she'd been so consumed with the lawsuit that she couldn't ask her friends to let her crash on couches or in spare rooms. Requests like that left her too vulnerable. Her friends, with lives and concerns of their own, didn't need to hear her worries and fears about her future.

Her backpack slid from her grasp and hit the floor with a soft thud when she spotted the stack of clean towels at the foot of the perfectly made bed. He must have found the trouble with her car and then cleaned up in here, turning his home into a guest house. For her.

Gratitude swamped her. Everyone but Stephen had let her get away with her small fibs about having things under control. He didn't even know her. They were basically strangers. How had he seen through her defenses so easily?

It was a question she would never answer while she was exhausted. She stripped away the Escape Club uniform and readied herself for bed. As she slipped between the cool, clean sheets, she decided none of the whys and hows of Stephen's actions mattered as much as figuring out what she could do to make it up to him.

CHAPTER TWO

ALMOST THREE HOURS LATER, Stephen woke with the sun and a colorful vow to find something to cover the bare window on the back wall. He supposed he could board it up, but that seemed extreme for a temporary situation. He squinted at the window and considered planting a tree. That would have a lasting benefit even if it didn't help in the short term.

Short term, he reminded himself. Kenzie wouldn't be in his trailer for long. She gave off independent vibes as bright as the sunshine glaring in his eyes. He sat up, scooping his hair back from his face as his bare feet hit the cool vinyl flooring. At least it wasn't winter, when the freezing temperatures tried to climb right through the heavy-soled boots he wore in the shop.

With no hope of more sleep, he decided to get to work. He grabbed clean clothes from the pile he'd brought over last night and headed into the bathroom wedged between the office and the storage room. The cramped space didn't have an ounce of aesthetics, since clean, efficient and functional were all the design elements he'd cared about when he made the improvements.

Back in the office, he punched the button on the machine to brew coffee, and checked phone messages. Disappointment crept in when none of the callers asked about the restored Mustang he'd listed for sale last week. It had been in rough shape when they found it at an auction. He'd warned his brother that particular car would drain time and money. At least he had a better distraction today.

Turning, he opened the cabinet over the coffeemaker and pulled a foil-wrapped toaster pastry out of the box. Filling a stainless steel mug with fresh coffee, he carried it and the pastry into the shop and circled Kenzie's disassembled car while he waited for the caffeine and sugar to kick in. The poor excuse for transportation put a knot in his stomach as he debated where to start. So many options, and the best choice might be scrapping it for parts. Couldn't move forward on any of it until they discussed what she wanted. *Please scrap it*, he thought. It would be a public service.

He drank more coffee, savoring the jolt of caffeine, and shifted his focus to the far more appealing 1967 Camaro SS. This was the car that got Stephen out of bed every morning since the client, Matt Riley, had dropped it off. A total rebuild, inside and out, and despite the need for fresh paint, about as far from Kenzie's nondescript junker as a car could get. He'd cleaned every inch of the engine until a person could practically use it for a dining table, and now that the muffler was installed the Muncie four-speed transmission was ready for a second test drive.

Inside the Camaro, the upholstery was in decent shape, with only a few repairs and touch-ups needed. Same with the body. Stephen wondered where Riley had managed to find such a gem and if he'd share the source.

The Camaro wasn't the only thing waiting on him, just the most fun. Finishing the pastry, he dusted the crumbs from his fingers and trashed the wrapper. Time to get busy. With a sigh, he turned to the car parked in the last of his four service bays. His sister Megan had dropped off her minivan for new brakes and fresh tires. Naturally, she was hoping he'd deliver it when they were all at family dinner tomorrow.

Did none of them realize he could smell these setups a mile

away? Megan and her husband could pick up the minivan as soon as he was done this afternoon. By insisting on making the exchange tomorrow, they made sure he couldn't skip the dinner. He supposed he should be grateful for Megan's willingness to go without her beloved minivan for nearly forty-eight hours. Given half a chance, she'd tell him to appreciate her devoted-sister sacrifice, but he recognized his mother's influence at work. No one was better at keeping family together than Myra Galway.

With more affection than gratitude, Stephen turned up the music and put the vehicle on the lift to knock out the single straightforward job on today's agenda.

Kenzie came out of the recurring nightmare riding the hard wave of adrenaline and confusion. It always started with the same call to the row house fire. The same search protocol. When she found the victim, the nightmare shifted on her. The man was too heavy for her alone and the fire was burning too hot and fast, blocking every route as her team tried to reach her. The victim shouted at her, berating her until his throat went dry, yet none of his ideas was remotely plausible. Huddled in a corner, surrounded by smoke with flames marching toward them, she would wake up with the unbearable pressure of failure in her chest and the sheets tangled around her legs.

She had not failed that victim. Randall Murtagh was alive because she'd done the right things. She'd pulled him out of a terrible fire with minor burns that were probably healed already.

She tried to wriggle free of the sheets, nearly ripping them away before she remembered they weren't hers. Her skin clammy with the sweat of the nightmare, she found herself registering other details. This wasn't her bedroom. The space was too bright, the mattress too firm, and the scent of the laundry detergent on the linens was wrong.

Scrubbing at her face, she felt the rest of her situation crash over her like a bucket of ice water. At least the last wisps of the nightmare were gone. She untangled her legs from the sheets and paused as a variety of sounds and smells drifted by her waking senses.

For a moment she wallowed in the comfort and familiarity of clean motor oil, grease and new rubber tires. She heard the pulse of heavy metal music underscored by the whirr of power tools. All of it mingled with the promise of another hot and humid summer day in Philly.

She straightened the bedding and then headed for the bathroom, which was almost roomy, considering the limits of the camper. Fifteen minutes later she emerged refreshed and feeling human again. Dressed in denim cutoff shorts and a T-shirt sporting the logo of a local microbrewery, she made a cup of coffee and tried to figure out what to do with all the hours between now and her shift at the club tonight.

Her stomach growled, but she didn't feel right about helping herself to Stephen's groceries, despite his hospitality. Of course, with the loaner car he'd given her, she could restock his supplies easily. It still felt weird going through his cabinets for a bowl and cereal. She added milk and found a spoon in the basket of utensils on the counter. At the table she ate her cereal and used her cell phone to scroll through travel sites, looking for the best prices on decent motels near the club.

She knew she was hiding from Stephen, and life in general, when she'd washed her dishes and caught herself reorganizing her backpack. Stephen deserved better from her. For that matter, she deserved better. The sooner she got out there and helped him with her car, the sooner she could be on her way. She shoved her bare feet into her tennis shoes and headed over to the garage to say thanks again and refine her plans to get out of his hair.

The music crashed over her as she approached the garage through the open bay door nearest the office. Though her car was in pieces, she grinned, recognizing one of her favorite heavy metal bands doing a cover of one of the recent pop chart hits. She was about to follow the sound of an impact wrench to the other side of a champagne-colored minivan on a lift when the phone rang.

Stephen didn't seem to hear it over the tools and the music. Kenzie assumed he had a machine or service that answered calls for him. He might even have his calls forwarded to his cell phone during business hours. The phone kept ringing and, following impulse, she picked it up. "Galway Automotive."

"Hello?" a woman said, clearly startled. "Where's Stephen?"

Is this a girlfriend? "His hands are full changing a tire at the moment," Kenzie improvised.

"Who are you?"

Not as much jealousy as speculation in those three syllables. "I'm Kenzie," she replied, using her best polite-receptionist voice that she'd refined during her first week of administrative duty for the PFD. "May I take a message for him?"

"*Umm*, sure. This is his sister Megan. I was checking on my minivan."

Kenzie smiled. She'd heard a few typical big-brother stories from Mitch, but never met Megan. "If you can hold a moment, I'll see if I can get an update for you."

"Great."

The curiosity and confusion came through loud and clear and Kenzie had to stifle a chuckle. Stephen must not keep a receptionist around. The place did have the feel of a one-man operation. Accustomed to working with a team and having people around constantly, she couldn't imagine so much solitude. She didn't want to risk making a mistake with the hold button and cutting off Megan's call, so she placed the handset gently on the desk and hurried into the garage.

She saw her little rust-bucket in pieces, but her gaze locked for a long, reverent moment on the classic Camaro SS. A 1967, she knew. Oh *my*. Her hands tingled to peek under the hood. It would benefit from fresh paint and oh, that pure American muscle cried out for a touch. This was as close as she'd come to a car like this since her dad died. She hoped Stephen would be willing to show it to her and fill her in on the details later.

A classic Camaro was her dream car, if money weren't an object. It was a pipe dream at the moment, and likely would remain so for the next decade. *One day*, she promised herself, exerting significant willpower to stay on track with the minivan, when she would've happily gone exploring the Camaro.

From her vantage point only Stephen's legs and lower torso were visible under a minivan on the last lift. She failed in her attempt to ignore the appeal of those long legs and the T-shirt lifting to reveal toned abs when he stretched for something. *Whew.* She tucked away that little buzz of attraction.

Kenzie had no chance of getting his attention over the blaring music. It wasn't hard to find the speakers, but she didn't see the controls. She shouted. He didn't flinch. There were too many things in a working garage that might catch a finger or hand wrong if he was startled. She came around the front corner of the car and shouted his name again.

This time he froze. Slowly, he turned in her direction, and she could see the wire brush he was holding in hands darkened by brake dust.

He stared at her as if he couldn't figure out why he wasn't alone. "Kenzie."

She started to shout, pausing when he held up a finger and lowered the volume with a voice command. "Your sister Megan is on the phone," she said. "She's asking about her minivan."

He rolled his eyes and then glared down at his hands. "Give me a second."

"I can handle the call for you. You're doing both front and rear brakes?" she asked, when he didn't volunteer any information.

"No. Just rear brakes, and new tires all around," he replied.

Kenzie glanced about, judging his progress. "Do you want her to come by this afternoon?"

"Not really," he muttered.

Kenzie laughed, understanding the sibling dynamics. "When works for you?"

"She's such a nag," he grumbled. "When she dropped it off, she made me agree to deliver it for her at Sunday dinner tomorrow."

"No problem. Leave it to me." Kenzie returned to the office and picked up the phone. "Megan?"

"Yes."

"Thanks for waiting." Kenzie smiled as she explained Stephen's progress and his confidence that the minivan would be delivered on time to Sunday dinner.

"Great. Thanks, um, what was your name?"

"Kenzie."

"I'm so glad you're there. It's about time he hired good help," Megan said. "Have a good day," she added brightly.

"You, too." Replacing the phone in the cradle, Kenzie sat back in the chair and swiveled side to side gently. Maybe she could give Stephen some time in the office or the garage while she waited to return to her normal schedule at the firehouse.

"Was she rude?"

Kenzie smothered the reaction as the deep burr of Stephen's voice skimmed over the nape of her neck. He stood just outside the door frame, wiping dark streaks from his hands with a shop towel. Something about him sent her heartrate into overdrive. This was not the time for her hormones to take a detour.

"Not at all," she replied, she managed in a steady voice.

His eyebrows arched in disbelief. "She didn't do any wheedling to get her minivan back today?"

Kenzie shook her head.

"Huh. Thanks."

The man was pretty cute when he was baffled. "No problem." She was about to ask about her own car when the phone rang again. Stephen's face clouded over with a scowl. "Go on back. I'll handle it," she told him.

"Really? Thanks. Just take messages," he said, practically running back to the shop.

She handled the various inquiries for the rest of the morning. When her stomach was rumbling around noon, she wandered back into the shop with the intent of picking up lunch for both of them. Stephen wasn't in the garage. The bay where the minivan had been was empty and Kenzie followed the sounds of water running outside.

She found him power washing the brake dust off his sister's tire rims, and her first thought was that he should hire someone to handle that kind of thing. It would be a great job for some high school kid. Not her business how he wanted to run his garage.

Her second thought, and those that followed right after it, were centered on the way his T-shirt, damp from the spray of water, molded to his chest. When he turned that serious, brooding gaze on her she nearly forgot she was here about lunch.

"Keys are in the loaner," he added, after requesting a meatball sub from the pizza place down the block.

"They are?"

"Well, sure. It's yours to use whenever you need it. The key fob will handle the security gate for you."

She was still processing all the implications of his easy generosity when she returned with lunch. He'd finished the brakes and cleaned up the service bay during her brief absence, and she marveled at his efficiency.

A man who obviously appreciated solitude, he didn't want her hanging around while they ate, she assumed, but she didn't want his well-earned break interrupted by the phone. He'd seemed almost afraid of the thing earlier.

"So what's with delivery over having Megan pick up her minivan?" Kenzie unwrapped her sandwich and took a big bite. "This is amazing."

He nodded, his mouth full, too. When he'd swallowed, he said, "Delivery tomorrow isn't ideal, but I'm already doing the job for the cost of parts. If I do it in record time, they'll never let me rest. Do you know how many Galways there are?"

She did a quick head count. "You have four siblings, right?"

"Yes," he said between bites. "Add in parents and cousins and in-laws, and a man wouldn't have time for anything else."

"I thought Mitch helped you out."

"He does. He prefers the custom work more than the maintenance stuff," Stephen said.

"Don't we all?" There was an excitement in restoration, in breathing new life into quality machinery.

Stephen raised an eyebrow. "To be fair, he would've handled Megan's van if I'd been slammed."

"Based on the phone calls I managed this morning, I'd say you could be slammed at any given moment. If you can spare the bay, and time with the tools, I can fix my car on my own," she said. "After hours, so I can stay out of your way."

"You know cars?" he asked.

"My dad taught me more than enough to handle that particular car."

He lifted a bottle of water to his lips and Kenzie caught herself staring at his jaw and throat. It was as if he was carved from some substance that could shift between a solid and fluid state at will. He was almost too lean and the shadows under his eyes were a sure sign he didn't sleep as much as he should.

She belatedly recalled he'd been engaged a few years back, the woman murdered before the wedding. It put Kenzie's own issues into sharp perspective. Her career was at risk thanks to Murtagh, not her life.

"You think your car is overwhelming for me?"

"I think my car is a piece of crap and well beneath your level of expertise." She found herself on the business end of that inscrutable expression. What was going on behind the hazel eyes shadowed by those burnished gold eyebrows?

"I can spare the space and tools," he said. "Thanks for helping out with the phone. I usually just check messages at the end of the day."

"I didn't realize you had an answering machine," she said, trying to contain the happy urge to bounce in her chair. Working on a car, even the pitiful rust-bucket, would be a fabulous distraction until she was back on shift. "That makes me feel better about leaving you this afternoon."

His brow wrinkled. "You're leaving?"

"Yes," she replied. "I'm scheduled on the late shift again tonight at the club. Between now and then I need to find a place to stay." She pointed to the boxes he'd stacked for her near the storeroom. "I can't just leave all my stuff here in your way."

Stephen's hands stilled, the sandwich wrapper balled up between his palms. "You have a place to stay."

Finding herself the focus of his full attention made her mouth go dry. She felt like the proverbial deer in headlights. It took two attempts to get the right words past her lips. "Last night was too kind. I'm not kicking you out of your house."

"It's yours," he stated. "For as long as you need it." He stood up, as if that was the end of the conversation.

"But last night you said—"

He cut her off. "I said we'd sort it out today." He tossed his trash and leaned back against the counter, apparently waiting for her to say something else he could shoot down.

"That feels like way too much of an imposition."

"You're wrong." A muscle jumped in his tense jaw. "I know what firefighters make," he stated. "And I know what lawyers can charge. If it makes you feel better, keep answering the phone and taking messages when you can."

"That's hardly a fair trade for kicking you out of your home," she protested.

His fingers flexed around the edge of the countertop. The muscles in his forearm bunched and relaxed slowly. "If it's all I'm asking for, why argue the point?"

"Do logic and reason ring a bell?" Why was he insisting she stay here?

"Does *sabotage* ring a bell for you?" he countered, his gaze heating up.

This wasn't the conversation she'd planned on having with him, but it was too late now and she was too aggravated to successfully turn the topic to the Camaro. "I don't need protection."

He folded his arms over his chest. "Duly noted. Do you want to file a police report about the damage?"

That gave her pause and she took her time to think it through. As both Grant and Stephen had previously pointed out, someone had most likely targeted her with the sugar in her gas tank. At the moment she could think of only one person angry enough with her to try such a stunt. "No."

"Because you know who did it?" Stephen pressed.

"What good would it do to file a report? I have no idea when it happened."

"Based on the settling and filter damage, I would guess it happened within the last week," Stephen said, his voice as hard as his gaze now. "A police report is an official record. It could establish a time line or a pattern of behavior."

"Stop. Please." She held up a hand as she studied him. There was obviously a bigger issue on his mind than a disabled car. Filing a report would also mean suggesting Murtagh as a suspect, which could make her look like an idiot grasping at straws to undermine his credibility in the lawsuit. She had to trust her lawyer's advice that the truth would come out and clear her of any wrongdoing or errors.

"I hear what you're saying," she continued. "This was probably a prank gone wrong. Yes, the timing makes it unlikely, but it is possible this was a case of mistaken identity." Logic and odds aside, she couldn't risk giving voice to the outrageous theory that Murtagh had done it. "I've only had the car three weeks."

"It's paid for?" Stephen asked.

"Yes."

"Then I'll put it back together for you." He sighed and pulled such a grimace, she laughed, startling them both.

"That isn't necessary," she said. "I can handle the repairs, and help with the phone when I'm here."

He shot her a skeptical glance. "And you'll work at the club and jump through hoops for your lawyer, too?"

That image made her grin. "He keeps telling me he's the one jumping through hoops on my behalf."

Stephen rolled his eyes. "You've got a deal, *if* you agree to stay in the trailer."

She counted to ten. Slowly. "I don't like the idea of pushing you out of your place."

He shrugged that off. "You'll get over it."

It was such an unexpected reply she laughed again.

He pushed away from the counter and reached into the fridge for another bottle of water. Pausing at the desk, he skimmed the messages she'd taken, various expressions flitting across his stern features. He turned over one message slip and wrote out a short list.

"Can you get these parts ordered for me?"

She glanced at his neat, block-style printing. "Sure."

"Thanks." He looked her over head to toe and back up. "If you hit a snag, be sure to ask for help."

"I promise."

"I have coveralls you can borrow. What about better shoes?"

"There are steel-toed boots in one of the boxes over there." They were battered, but though she'd had few chances to use them in recent years, they still fit.

"All right." With one last look, he walked out. A moment later the music started pulsing again.

Sensations continued to fizz through her system long after he left the office. Part of it was the anticipation of getting her hands dirty and seeing the result of fixing something. Another part was pure lust over the opportunity to work near a man who was bringing that classic Camaro back to life. Both man and machine had her system revving, she thought with a wistful sigh.

She couldn't recall the last time any man as sexy as Stephen had studied her so thoroughly. Her face felt hot and her fingers trembled as she ordered the parts he'd requested.

With that task done, she rooted through her belongings and found her boots, then eyed the clock. Now that she didn't need to find a place and move her stuff, she could potentially get started flushing the fuel lines before heading to the club.

She was almost—no she was *definitely* relieved when a call came in for a tow truck and he agreed to go pick a vehicle up. Relieved. Yes. If she went out to the garage and tried to work beside him now, with all this fizz, there was no telling what kind of stupidity her hormones would talk her into.

Neither of them needed that kind of complication.

What the hell was *wrong* with him? Stephen wondered a few hours later, as he worked alone in the shop. Every time he thought he had his head on straight, the memory of Kenzie's laughter sent him spinning, the echo of the sound rattling through his head. Cranking the radio didn't help. He left the garage and went out to detail his sister's van. Spoiling her with that kind of surprise was probably a mistake and his mood soured further.

That mouth on Kenzie, he thought, so mobile and expressive. Her lips were quick with a smile and he couldn't keep the images out of his head. Her laughter astounded him, the merry sound full and loud and rich, as if she didn't care who heard her. He envied that wide-open spirit, even when it grated against the solitude he'd carefully built here.

How could Kenzie laugh at *anything* with a civil suit that threatened her career hanging over her head? He shot a glance back at the garage, fighting off the urge to get in there and just do the work for her.

She claimed she could handle it, and it wasn't a complex task to flush a little sugar out of a fuel system. If only that was all that junker needed. He was almost embarrassed to have such a sorry-looking car in the shop.

Not sorry to have Kenzie around.

The errant thought startled him and he shoved it away. He didn't like extra people milling about in his space, but having her answering calls had been a big help. Mitch was about the only other person he could work with. Even his dad got under his skin after a few hours.

At least she wasn't here tempting him into conversation just so he could hear her voice. The last time a woman intrigued him like this, he'd been engaged to her. Stephen fought back the unwelcome spark of interest. Kenzie was a temporary anomaly in his self-contained life. She needed a break and he could tolerate having her around for a few days as long as she didn't start in on him with questions about the business or why he was a loner.

Finished detailing his sister's minivan, he parked it next to the cars he was ready to sell. While he'd been out with the tow truck, Mitch had called, claiming to have a buyer lined up for the Mustang. Stephen hoped his brother closed the deal on that one soon. The upholstery and paint alone had cost them a small fortune.

He tried to work up irritation over having it sit here and failed. The car looked amazing and they'd get their asking price eventually. The swell of pride in the work drained enough of the persistent tension out of his neck and shoulders that when his mom's sassy red sedan pulled through the open gate, he managed a rare smile.

"Happy Saturday, sweetheart," she said, drawing him into a hug. "You look good."

Her hugs never changed, no matter what was happening in his life. She must have just come from the salon, he realized, as a wave of feminine scents swept over him. Her hair was sleek and smooth and the gray effectively hidden by a perfect application of ash-blond color. "You look great, Mom."

"Nice of you to notice." A little pink warmed her cheeks as she beamed at him. "Hopefully, your father can be persuaded to take me out tonight."

Stephen didn't think it would be much of an effort. His parents were still in love after all this time and the challenges life tossed at them. While he knew that wasn't in his future, he valued the rare treasure of their relationship. "Car trouble?"

"Not a bit."

Her gaze slid past him toward the office and he realized his sister had tipped her off that a woman had been here. Answering phones and relaying messages. Stephen managed not to roll his eyes at his mother's obvious agenda. "If you're looking for someone in particular, she isn't here."

His mom's expression fell so fast he felt terrible for busting the bubble of hope wreathing her face. "What do you mean?"

"Please." He walked toward the office, urging her to come out of the heavy, late afternoon heat. "Megan called you, right?"

Myra nodded.

"There's nothing to it, Mom. I'm just helping out one of Mitch's friends. She had car trouble."

"You're helping Kenzie Hughes," she stated.

"Nothing gets by you," he said. It had been that way all his life. Myra Galway had a mysterious, maternal inside track on information involving her children. Wishing he had a better explanation for the stack of boxes near the wall and the folded linens at the end of the couch, he offered her something to drink.

"Water, please."

He handed her a bottle of water from the fridge and waited for her to explain her visit. It didn't take long.

"Kenzie was Mitch's classmate all through school," Myra told him. "You probably don't remember her at all."

"No." He was tempted to ask what his mom might know about Kenzie's dad, but that would only stoke her persistent hope that he would eventually open his heart to a relationship again. *Not a chance.* He couldn't handle that kind of vulnerability again.

"Well, the poor girl's name has been splashed all over the news lately."

Stephen was very selective about when he turned on the news. Sometimes knowledge wasn't power, only more pain. "Mitch told me some of it."

"Your brother says she's one of the best firefighters around. He's convinced the suit will fall apart." His mother's gaze took in all the things that were out of place in his office. "You let her sleep here?"

He chose not to explain the precise definition of "here." "Her landlord is fumigating or something. Her stuff was in her car." He gestured toward the boxes. "Her car was here. It was late…" He pushed his hand through his hair. "Made sense to me at the time."

Her smile, a mix of maternal delight and concerned tenderness, put him on edge. "You turned out all right," she said, clearly satisfied with her parenting skills. "Here's another bit of sense for you. Bring her to Sunday dinner tomorrow."

No. "Mom." He set his jaw against the persistent lance of pain searching for his heart. "She probably has plans," he added. Kenzie at Sunday dinner was a terrible idea.

"You'll ask and find out," she said breezily. "There's always room for one more at the table."

Did she practice these careless phrases that eviscerated him? By now he and Annabeth should have been working on their first baby and joining his married siblings in testing their mother's theory about room at the table. A lousy drug dealer had decided Annabeth had done enough good in this life, and snuffed her out with a cowardly ambush at the community center.

Three years after her death there were still nights when Stephen was convinced he'd heard those gunshots. The community center was too far from the garage for that to be possible, but the sounds haunted him anyway. *I should have done more for her*, he thought, though there had been nothing within his power to do. Logic seemed to have no effect on overwhelming grief.

Stephen turned away, wishing the water in his hand was a beer or a whiskey. Conversations like this one were better with a whiskey close by. Distracted by those dark memories, he flinched when Myra touched her hand to his shoulder.

"I consider Kenzie a friend of the family," she said gently.

"Then you should be the one to extend the invitation." Though the churlish tone shamed him, he wouldn't take it back. She had to know she was asking too much of him.

"That is actually why I came by," she pointed out. "Since I missed her, I trust you'll handle it on my behalf. *Politely* and graciously as I would."

"Mom." He gazed down at her, wondering why thirty-two years hadn't been enough time for him to build up immunity to the mom voice. She wouldn't drop it until he agreed. "I'll text you if she can't make it."

His mother's eyebrows lifted and she tried and failed to suppress an amused smile. "Thank you." She rocked back on her heels. "Do you have time to show me the progress on the Camaro out there?"

He knew she was trying to put him back on his feet after dealing a blow, and he let her. "The engine is in and the transmission came together," he said, as he walked with her around the car. "It needs a test drive and I'm waiting on a few more original pieces I found from a dealer in Ohio. Then it's off for the finish work."

"Do you know what the color scheme will be?"

At some point in the past, the paint had been a metallic champagne. "Silver with black rally stripes. He's career army."

"Make sure you take pictures if I don't get over here before your client picks it up."

"Sure thing, Mom." She ignored the fact that he had a portfolio of before and after pictures online she could access anytime, insisting that he show her in person. He knew it was because she worried he spent too much time with the quiet thoughts in his head.

If she had any idea how disquieting his thoughts were she'd have real reason to worry.

Myra made a bit more small talk, and when she seemed convinced he wouldn't do something stupid like take the rest of the day off and wallow in grief and alcohol, she left him in peace.

Stephen closed the gate when she'd gone and set the emergency number to ring through to his cell phone. Too restless to work, he cleaned up his tools, gave Kenzie's car another hard look and went to move more of his things out of the trailer and into the office.

It felt rude to him to keep invading space he'd given her. Better to keep as much distance as possible between him and Kenzie. His gaze landed on the denim cutoffs and T she'd worn earlier, on a corner of the bed. A vision of her long, gorgeous legs filled his mind, followed closely by an echo of that bold laughter.

Basic human nature explained why her legs got under his skin, but the effect of her laughter baffled him. Maybe the happiness of it, a sound foreign in the shop, was what bugged him. That sound shouldn't fit in and yet something deep inside him wanted to make room for it. Damn, he needed more sleep.

He closed his eyes and brought Annabeth's serene face to his mind. A dark beauty with generous curves, his fiancée had had a steady, pleasant outlook underscored with integrity and grit that made her someone people trusted. The kids confided in her about things they were too scared to share with anyone else. On appearance alone, Kenzie was the polar opposite, not to mention the vast personality differences, and yet he had a random, discomfiting thought that they might have been friends.

Twice he picked up his phone to text Kenzie about dinner with his family. Twice he stopped, deleting the messages before he could send them. If his mother caught wind of him taking the easy way out, he'd get a lecture and a heavy dose of that sad disappointment she wielded so effectively.

He and his siblings agreed on one thing without fail: it was always better to make Myra Galway flat-out mad than to disappoint her.

To do this right, and avoid a mom lecture, Stephen would either have to go to the club or wait up for her. Resigned, he took a shower and changed clothes to go back to the Escape Club. He considered taking the Camaro, to get a feel for the clutch and the suspension, but he was too restless to listen to the car.

Instead, he grabbed a dealer plate, put the For Sale sign in the rear window of the Mustang they needed to move, and planned a route through the city that might spin up some interest. If that particular route took him by the community center where Annabeth had worked, that was just coincidence.

Right. Not even he believed that.

The community center was a central, positive influence working persistently to keep a toehold in a neighborhood framed with rough edges. The area was hard on the eyes and residents in broad daylight. Once night fell, those rough edges turned razor-sharp and mean.

Since losing Annabeth, Stephen continued teaching the basic automotive class despite the vicious ache in his chest every time he came near the building. After her killer was acquitted, he'd picked up the habit of frequently driving through the neighborhood in various vehicles. Occasionally, he parked a block out and walked in, daring any of the local thugs to take a swipe at him.

They often did.

His walks and drive-bys were random. Sometimes they paid off and he caught a picture of a drug deal that he forwarded to the police, or he caught wind of a name while he wandered past on foot. For all the good it did. The police would pick up one dealer and another stepped up, keeping business rolling. Once in a while he timed his visits or ended his classes so he could walk other staffers to their cars, as he should've done every day for his fiancée. Sometimes he just circled the block, letting the deep purr of a big engine serve as a warning to the petty criminals skulking in the shadows.

So far, the man he wanted to confront, the man who had killed his fiancée, had yet to make himself a target. Stephen didn't have anything better to do with his life than wait him out.

Tonight, he circled the block like a shark, generally being a nuisance and interfering with the fast deals that happened at the corner. The thugs tasked with backing up the dealer showed their guns on his third pass. The familiar dance put a kick in Stephen's pulse. He was aware they knew who he was and where to find him when he wasn't trying to interrupt their business. Just one reason he kept upgrading the security at the garage. He used to lie awake at night, praying someone with ties to Annabeth's murder would come by and get caught on his cameras.

Spoiling for a fight, he parked the Mustang under the floodlights and security cameras in the community center parking lot and went for a quick stroll. At this hour the facility, church and other buildings on this side of the street were deserted and locked up tight.

He walked around to the front of the building and sat on the steps. Although the building owners tried to keep security cameras operational, anything aimed in the general direction of the dealer on the corner was repeatedly disabled. Stephen had decided he had to stand in whenever possible.

Annabeth's blood had long since been washed away from the area, but the fresh paint they'd used on the railings was peeling again after three years of weather. He knew where they stored the paint and he had a key to the center. He'd almost decided to take care of it now under the glare of the streetlights when a rusty station wagon from the nineties pulled up to the corner. It made Kenzie's sedan look good by comparison.

Stephen raised his phone and hit the record button, making sure the video light caught the driver's attention. The car sputtered and rolled away, deal incomplete. From across the street, the thugs shouted a warning at him.

Stephen lowered the phone and gave them a wave without leaving his post. He scared off another two cars before the enforcers stalked across the street with orders to make him leave.

Finally.

He waited for them, his weight balanced and his knees loose. They could just shoot him. Luckily for him, they knew as well as he did that two innocent people dead on these steps might inspire someone to actually come through this neighborhood and clean it up for good.

"Get the hell outta here," the first kid said. He couldn't be more than twenty, probably younger. His T-shirt, emblazoned with a classic arcade game character wielding an AK-47, was partially tucked into dark jeans. Stephen noted the bulging biceps and the brands seared in faint patterns on the kid's dark skin.

At Gun-shirt's nod a second man walked to the base of the stairs to face Stephen. Bald, his pale head lit by streetlights, he wore a white undershirt and faded jeans that rode low on his hips, revealing the band of his boxers. Stephen assumed the open jacket must be hot in this weather. An unfortunate circumstance for Baldy, since the jacket did nothing to conceal the gun shoved into his belt.

"You need to leave," Baldy said. He drew the gun and took aim at Stephen's midsection. "Go willingly, or go permanently, your choice."

Stephen raised his hands. "Willingly," he replied, starting down the steps.

At the sidewalk, Gun-shirt grabbed Stephen's arm and drove a fist into his gut. Although Stephen was braced for it, the blow took a toll, stealing his breath. He gasped, doubling over, hands on his knees. When Gun-shirt leaned close to make more threats, Stephen punched him in the throat. The thug staggered back into the street, bouncing off the hood of a slowly passing car before he caught his balance.

The bald man swore and aimed his gun once more, but Stephen was quicker. He kicked out, connecting with the guy's knee. Baldy crumpled into a whimpering heap.

Across the street, the furious dealer called for reinforcements. Stephen shouted out a crude suggestion before he ran for the parking lot. He knew none of these criminals wanted to get caught chasing an innocent civilian by those cameras.

Safely in the Mustang, Stephen drove off. He was several blocks away before the pain started seeping through the adrenaline rush. He kept to the rest of his planned circuit, cruising through much nicer streets filled with people out for the evening at restaurants and posh bars. Hopefully, the sign in the rear window would attract some positive inquiries.

The sooner they moved this car the better. He had other builds in mind and more plans to keep himself busy through the summer.

CHAPTER THREE

THINGS WERE HOPPING at the Escape Club tonight and tips were already weighing down Kenzie's apron pockets. It was a good feeling, although waitressing wasn't nearly as much fun as fighting fires. Here, no one seemed to care about her gender or build as long as she kept the drinks coming. The lively atmosphere and the pulsing music were a bonus, filling the space with an energy that made the hours fly.

Onstage Grant was taking a turn on the drum set while the band's real drummer stood back, grinning and working the crowd. Kenzie laughed, enjoying the sight of her boss having a blast as she weaved through the crowded dance floor to call out her orders at the bar. Mitch was on duty at the firehouse tonight, a fact she did her best to push to the back of her mind as she waited for Jason to fill her tray with longneck beers and two fancy cosmopolitans.

The PFD was a typically tight-knit community and Kenzie had first met Jason when he was teaching at the academy. He couldn't be much older than her, and she'd never heard what had led him to the academy so early in his career. Now, he was a full-time assistant to Grant. As much fun as she had with most of her shifts here at the Escape, she couldn't imagine choosing this over the real challenge and sense of accomplishment that came with fighting fires.

"Any word from your lawyer today?" he asked, as he added curls of lemon peel to the pale pink cosmopolitans.

She shook her head. "The last email claimed no news is good news. I just have to be patient."

"Easy for him to be patient—he's doing his job while you're stalled out on the sidelines. Not that we aren't happy to have you here," he added with a friendly wink.

Kenzie hefted her tray to her shoulder and gave him a warm smile. "Thanks. Not many people understand that."

She moved through the crowd, delivering drinks and taking more orders in her section. The summer concert series was a huge success, padding the bottom line for the Escape Club as well as the rest of the businesses along the river. It helped that Grant made a habit of pairing local bands on the rise with established regional groups vying to get onto this stage in front of music lovers.

When she approached the bar again several minutes later, Grant and Stephen were talking near the doorway that led to the kitchen. She felt that sizzle at the sight of the oldest Galway brother. The sensation was quickly followed by curiosity when she realized the men were embroiled in an intense conversation. Pressure simmered through the air as Grant crowded Stephen.

She called out her drink orders and told herself the two men had better things to discuss than her. Besides, she was stable now that Stephen had insisted she stick around, and had given her time to fix her own car. Though it couldn't possibly be any of her business, she kept sneaking glances at them.

Stephen turned slightly, blocking her view of Grant's face. A moment later, Grant was all but hauling Stephen back to his office. Kenzie stared after them for a long moment.

"What's all that?" she asked Jason.

"Don't know. I get the impression Stephen has a few issues," he replied. "Grant's been in his face for a few months now."

She swallowed the urge to ask why. If Stephen wanted her to know something about him, he would share. She wouldn't abuse his hospitality by snooping around for details like a high school gossip girl with a crush on the star quarterback.

Crush? Her mind locked on the word and wouldn't let go as she kept up her circuit between her customers and the bar. Sure, he was attractive and he added plenty of sex appeal to that intense broody look. Huh. She hadn't realized she was into that. Maybe it was just his proximity to that soon-to-be-stunning Camaro.

By the time her break rolled around, she was more than ready for a breather from the crowd and noise in the club. She grabbed a bottle of water from the kitchen and a power bar from her backpack and went outside for some fresh air.

The muted sounds on the river always fell over her like a silk curtain. Though she was only a few paces from the club, with businesses thriving up and down the waterway, the immediate peace and dark enveloped her, tempting her to linger well past her allotted fifteen minutes.

"What are you doing out here?"

The gruff demand startled her as she sipped the water and she choked. Sputtering, she turned to face Stephen. Oh, the man had broody and sexy in spades. Kenzie made a mental note to use some of this unexpected free time to find a date. This was a big city. She could find some neutral and friendly guy to hang out with, someone who didn't dare her hormones to rise up and take control of her common sense.

"I'm on my break," she said, when her throat finally cooperated.

"Alone." Stephen glared at the dark river behind her. "Out here."

"Not alone anymore," she said, with as much patience as she could muster. Until this particular moment, the man had shown her remarkable kindness. She supposed it was his turn to be rude.

"It isn't safe out here," he said, shoving his hands into the pockets of his jeans.

"For who?" she asked carefully.

"For you." He glared across the river as if New Jersey was on the verge of launching a fleet to invade Pennsylvania and take her captive.

"You'll notice I'm fine," she replied, deliberately taking a step closer to the river, distancing herself. Something was troubling him and she felt compelled to draw out an explanation if possible. She watched him lingering at the blurry edge of the shadows near the building. "You and Grant were intense. Everything okay?"

"You'll notice I'm fine," he replied.

Normally having her words tossed back in that bored tone would irritate her. Stephen made her laugh. "So we both have things we don't want to talk about." She turned her back on the river, preferring the view he offered. That stoic, immovable stance dialed up the fizz factor in her system whenever he was near and she reveled in it. "That's fair. I'm surprised to see you here two nights in a row."

"I'd rather be at the garage."

She understood that perfectly. She worked to hide her grin. "I bet. Please don't tell me you're here to keep an eye on me." Grant had a tendency to call in favors or hand out orders as needed, with the idea of protecting people he cared about. Still, a pleasant, happy warmth slid through her to be a person Grant wanted to keep safe. He was one of the world's good guys.

"Not exactly." Stephen crossed his arms and then uncrossed them, shoving his hands into his pockets again. He took a deep breath and met her gaze. "I came by tonight to let you know my mother would like you to join us for Sunday dinner tomorrow."

Wow. The darkness hid the scowl on his face, but she heard it in his voice. Through Mitch, she knew Mrs. Galway expected her children to gather once a week unless they were on shift or out of town.

"Thought it would be better to do it now, rather than after your shift," he added under his breath.

He would have waited up for her two nights in a row? No one other than family had done that for her. She wanted to assign some significance to it, though she really didn't know him well enough. She studied him as closely as the dim light allowed. What did he want her to say?

He shuffled his feet. "You can think about it and let me know in the morning."

"Your mother's worried about me feeling left out?" A trademark Mrs. Galway move. She'd always been one of Kenzie's favorite parent volunteers when she and Mitch were in school. The woman had a way of making everyone she met feel as if they mattered.

"That's my guess," he said.

"Thanks." The idea of sharing a meal with the Galways sounded like fun. "The invitation is a thoughtful gesture."

"Is that a yes?" he asked.

"Would you like me to refuse?" Thanks to Mitch, Kenzie was aware that when the Galway kids brought a guest to Sunday dinner, it was assumed that person was significant. That wasn't the case for her and Stephen and she didn't want to make the situation difficult for him. "It wouldn't bother me at all to have Sunday to myself."

"Do you have something else to do tomorrow afternoon?"

"No," she answered. "I'm off tomorrow. I was going to work on my car."

He stepped back, as if he found that news distasteful. "Then I'll tell her you'll join us."

"Only if that's okay with you," she insisted.

"It's fine." He pulled out his cell phone.

She didn't quite believe him, but she didn't want to argue the point and make this conversation any more difficult than it was. "Great. Thanks."

Family dinner hadn't been a regular occurrence with Hughes

women, even before her mother and little sister had moved to Maryland. In recent years, the three of them tended to do more family bonding over spa days, shopping trips and the occasional beach weekend.

Stephen slipped his phone back into his pocket and stood there. As awkward moments went, this had to rank in the all-time top ten. "I should get back to work," she said. "Did you enjoy the band?" she added.

"They're a local favorite."

She was about to call him on the evasion when he reached to open the door for her and grimaced. She recognized pain when she saw it. "What's wrong?" She shifted, taking the weight of the door off him.

"Nothing," he said, following her into the club.

"Liar." She looked him over, head to toe, not seeing any obvious injury. "Something's hurting you," she pressed.

His eyebrows shot up. "It's not a big deal. I slipped on a step."

"Landing on your side?" On reflex, she reached for his rib cage, then pulled back, curling her fingers into her palms.

"Pretty much," he replied. "Nothing's broken," he added before she could ask.

"You're sure about that?"

"I've had a broken rib before," he told her, without elaborating on how it had happened.

"All right." Pain would explain the general discomfort he projected, though she sensed there was still something more lurking under the surface. "If you're sticking around, have Jason pour you a beer. My treat."

"I'll just get going. Unless you have another break coming."

She grinned. He seemed determined to keep an eye on her. "I'll be safe," she said, backing toward the club noise spilling into the hallway.

"Have someone walk you out tonight," he called after her.

"Yes, sir."

Kenzie decided Grant must have asked Stephen to keep an

eye on her, after all. No other reason for Stephen to make that request. Rather than getting bent out of shape about it, she welcomed the sweet sensation that life was giving her a little upswing, a boost to help her over the other muck she was trying to navigate.

Hours later, as she closed out the shift and waited for Jason to walk her out to the car, Grant offered to take on the role of safety escort.

"I need a favor," he said, as soon as they were away from the club.

"Of course. You've certainly done plenty of them for me." She appreciated that the Escape Club had been an option for her, bridging the gap and keeping her busy while she waited to get back on shift at the PFD.

"Can you keep an eye on Stephen?"

"What?" She couldn't have heard him correctly. Grant made no secret of the fact that he helped people tangled up in difficult situations, but Stephen seemed capable of handling himself.

"You are staying at his place, right?" Grant asked.

"I am." She didn't add that Stephen had practically insisted on it. "On top of the loaner car, he's letting me stay in his camper until I can get back into my apartment."

Grant snorted. "He told me he's lending you space and tools to fix your car, so that will give you more reason to stick close. Try not to fix it too fast."

"What is this about? Stephen doesn't strike me as the type to enjoy having people looking over his shoulder."

"You're right, but someone has to do something and you're already in." Grant's bushy, salt-and-pepper eyebrows dipped low over his dark brown eyes. "Can you please try?"

She had a sudden image of Stephen's face twisted with pain. "He didn't fall down the stairs, did he?"

"Not without help," Grant muttered. "Since his fiancée was murdered and the killer acquitted, Stephen has struggled to stay on track."

A chill of unease trickled down her spine. "Meaning what, exactly?" What sort of situation was she signing on for? Grant had to know she didn't need more life complications that Murtagh's legal team could use against her. Though Stephen didn't give off the vibe of a man using drugs or alcohol, he was so reserved she couldn't be sure.

"A buddy of mine in Narcotics tells me Stephen sends in pictures, tips, and occasionally names of drug dealers near the community center where his fiancée worked," Grant said. "Tonight, they got another tip and the undercover officer in the area caught a few pictures of Stephen in the community center lot before and after the tip came in. I think he's hurting from a fight."

Stephen didn't have a substance abuse kind of habit; he had vigilante tendencies. *Great.* "Is he trying to get himself killed?"

"Can't answer that one," Grant said. "I do know if he doesn't lay off he runs the risk of blowing a major drug bust in the area."

At the car, she shoved her rolled-up apron into her backpack and pulled her keys out of the smaller pocket. "And here I thought you'd told him to keep an eye on me."

"I did." Grant's unrepentant grin flashed across his face. "He wasn't excited about it, but I'm hoping such an impossible and unnecessary task will distract him from the troubles near the community center."

She rolled her eyes. His flattery amused her and blended with his fatherly concern into a comforting warmth that soothed her tired mind and body. "It's a tall order, but I'll do my best," she said, unlocking the car. "Does Mitch know anything about this?" She didn't want to stick her foot in her mouth at Sunday dinner.

"If he does, he didn't hear it from me," Grant said. "I've been trying to guide Stephen away from this habit quietly."

"All right." If Grant hadn't enlisted any of the Galway family's help on this issue, she wouldn't, either. It was always better to know where she stood. She opened the door and pushed her backpack into the space behind the driver's seat.

"And Kenzie?"

She glanced up. Grant was still leaning on the passenger side of the car. "Don't let Stephen run you off."

"Not a chance," she assured him. "His camper is the most affordable place in town." Keeping it light, she gave her boss a confident wink and settled behind the wheel of the loaner car.

Though Stephen valued his privacy and solitude, working at his garage was no hardship for her. She enjoyed getting her hands dirty and had already planned to help him out as much as he'd allow just as payback for letting her stay. Now she had to rethink how to dig in deeper, and keep him closer to the garage without driving either of them crazy.

Just past noon the next afternoon, Stephen waited by Megan's minivan, wondering if he should go check on Kenzie. They had plenty of time to get to the house, but he hadn't seen her since her break last night.

When he'd returned from the club, he couldn't recall if he'd told her what time to be ready today. Frustrated and sore from the scuffle at the community center, he'd taped a note to the camper door for her. Though he'd waited up until she returned from her shift, he didn't go outside when she arrived. The note hadn't been there when he checked this morning and he had to assume she'd seen it. Or he could just go knock on the door and make sure she was up.

No. He wouldn't nag her. She might have changed her mind or decided she'd rather sleep after her crazy-late hours.

Running on fumes from lack of sleep, he might have downed too much coffee while he dealt with invoices and paperwork as the clock on the wall crept closer to Sunday dinner time. Maybe they should just take two cars over, though he didn't want her to think he would leave without her. Exasperated with himself, he tried to sigh and only managed to swear at the pain in his ribs when he inhaled.

He couldn't get past how *wrong* this felt to be taking someone other than Annabeth to the Galway weekly ritual. Sure, his mother considered Kenzie a family friend, but she would be arriving with *him*.

His palms went damp and guilt fogged his mind as memories slammed into him from every angle. The last time he'd brought a woman to Sunday dinner he and Annabeth were in the thick of wedding plans. His mom had surprised everyone at dessert, bringing out samples from three bakeries vying for the wedding cake and reception contract. The family voted in favor of a rich berry cake, insisting it was the best choice for a summer wedding.

If he closed his eyes, he could almost see Annabeth's delighted face as she savored a bite of fluffy, light lemon cake. He hadn't had a preference between the samples until that moment. As soon as her favorite was obvious, he wanted her to have whatever made her happiest. Wouldn't settle for anything else.

It had been his job to make her life better in every way possible. *Epic fail*, he thought. And it was only getting worse. No matter what he did at the community center during or after hours, Annabeth's memory kept drifting further into the back of his mind.

He tugged at the open collar of his button-down shirt. The humidity was already unspeakable. What had they been thinking? Summer was too hot for formal occasions. Except with Annabeth, getting married in July, the anniversary month of their first date, had seemed perfect.

They'd had big plans for that summer and all the ones that would follow as husband and wife. Four days after that cake tasting, his life and all their plans were shattered when the phone rang and the cops told him she was dead.

Carefully, he took a slow, deep breath, mindful of the bruised ribs this time. He wasn't going to get out of this dinner and he needed to pull himself together or he'd be on the receiving end of pitying glances and smothering concern all afternoon.

"Hey!" Kenzie waved as she crossed the yard. "Have you been waiting long?"

"No." Mentally, he shook off the melancholy and forced a smile onto his face. She wore strappy sandals, and a dress in a blue patterned fabric that tied behind her neck and flowed over her body, down to points just past her knees. Her hair was braided differently today, across the top of her head rather than straight back. It looked softer and left her shoulders bare. She was a punch of sex appeal with a girl-next-door smile, and he struggled to find two words to fit together into a coherent thought.

"Why don't I follow you over in the loaner?" she suggested.

If it wasn't so hot, he would have suggested they walk back to the shop after dinner. "Mitch and Julia will give us a ride back. He wants to be here when the potential buyer for the Mustang stops in."

"Oh. I didn't realize you had an appointment today."

Stephen shrugged and walked over to open the passenger door for her. The fluttering fabric of the dress played peekaboo with her knees as she hopped into the minivan. He jerked his gaze away. "Mitch sent me a text message from someone curious about it after I drove it around last night. I'm hoping it's a legitimate offer."

He felt her watching him as he rounded the hood of the car and climbed into the driver's seat. "Are you feeling all right?" she asked.

"No," he admitted, before he caught himself. He couldn't put the brakes on any of the feelings knocking around like bumper cars in his gut.

"Your family would understand if you skip dinner because you're hurt. Just give your mom a call."

Hardly. They all thought he dwelled in the past too much. Although they respected his grief, too often they suggested Annabeth would want him to move on. Previous attempts to move on had been too much like boxing up their shared memories and giving up on justice. "Not Mom. Besides, she's eager to see you." He managed a weak smile as he twisted to back out of the space.

He made the mistake of glancing Kenzie's way and the concern in those blue eyes stopped him. Looks like that should be illegal. "What?" he demanded.

"Stephen, the pain is etched on your face," she said, with far too much compassion.

"Gee, thanks," he muttered. Surely he'd gotten better at hiding his raw emotions by now. He resumed the task of driving as if his life depended on it. The sooner they got over there the sooner it would be over.

"Did you do anything helpful when you got home?" she pressed.

Stephen wasn't following the subject change, but he refused to risk another glance at her. "What are you talking about?"

"Your *ribs*. It's obvious you're sore from falling last night. Are you sure nothing's broken?"

He nearly laughed with relief, except that would hurt too much. "I'm all right."

"If you say so." She didn't sound the least bit convinced.

"Thanks for the concern," he said sincerely. He'd forgotten how it felt to have someone other than family take an interest in his welfare. Well, Grant cared enough to tell him to stay away from the dealers near the community center. It wasn't something he could stop. Annabeth deserved more than an acquittal arranged by a fast-talking lawyer.

He couldn't articulate any of that to Kenzie, not without revealing far more than she needed to know. "In my experience nothing helps bruised ribs but time," he said, as he parked on the street in front of the house he'd grown up in.

The door opened and Megan hurried out to see her minivan. "You washed it for me." She beamed at him. "James will be grateful."

"Part of the full package," Stephen replied. As he moved to open the door for Kenzie his sister got in the way.

Megan scoffed. "Since when?"

Stephen dropped the keys into her hand. "I had time." He gave her a gentle, one-armed hug with his good side.

She stepped back and glared at him. "Who told you?"

He ignored her question in favor of introducing Kenzie, pleased when his voice didn't crack in the process.

"Hi." Megan gave a halfhearted wave. "You were in Mitch's high school class."

"I was," Kenzie replied with an easy smile.

As the two women bonded over fashion, Stephen wondered why *he* didn't remember Kenzie from high school. Apparently back then being the oldest meant he'd had zero interest in his younger siblings.

"Julia and Mitch are already here," Megan said. She turned back to Kenzie. "Are you on his side when it comes to the Marburg law firm?" She pointed at Stephen.

He rolled his eyes. "Leave her alone, Megan." His family acted like he had no common sense. Just because Marburg got Annabeth's killer acquitted didn't mean he hated his new sister-in-law for working there.

"Everyone knows Marburg is representing the plaintiff against her," Megan replied in a stage whisper. "I was only going to give Julia fair warning if Kenzie turned out to be as moody as you."

"Megan." He urged them up the walk toward the house.

"I've met Julia at the firehouse," Kenzie interjected. "And no, I don't blame her that the law firm she works for represents the guy suing me."

Stephen gestured for Megan to go inside first, then pulled the door closed behind her. He held firm when Megan tried to open it again. "For the record, I'm okay with Julia, not with Marburg." He swallowed, searching for the right words. "If there's anything I can do to help you beat the lawsuit, count on me."

Her blue eyes went wide, then sparkled as she squished that big laugh of hers into a quiet chuckle. "Thanks for the offer, Stephen. According to my lawyer we just have to wait out the process, but it's good to have a friend right now. Better than good. Thanks," she said again.

Part of him appreciated being safely labeled as a friend while another part of him rebelled at the idea. The door opened before he could decide on a suitable response, and Stephen was ready to snap at Megan when he realized it was his mother. She stared him down.

"Hello, Mrs. Galway," Kenzie said.

His mom drew Kenzie inside and gave her a big hug as she aimed an "I taught you better" glare at Stephen.

Disappointing his mother was the worst and an excellent distraction from the unexpected turn his thoughts were taking with Kenzie. Being attracted to a pretty woman was normal, though not at all welcome. Why couldn't she have worn shop coveralls to dinner? He walked in and closed the door, trying to focus on tattling little sisters and the other details of life that never seemed to change.

Megan's little ones came at him first and he quickly sheltered his bruised side from their boisterous greetings. He was glad he and Kenzie had arrived last, subjecting them to less predinner chitchat. He lingered in the foyer with the kids while his mom reminded the rest of the family of how they all knew Kenzie.

He was inching toward the kitchen when Mitch and Julia walked in from the dining room, their hushed conversation cut short when they spotted him.

Stephen tried to pretend he didn't have a care in the world. He turned Julia's hug to the side as he'd done with Megan, but Mitch clapped him hard on the shoulder and caught him wincing.

"Again?" Mitch said under his breath.

Julia looked back and forth between them. "Do I want to know?"

"No," the brothers said in unison.

"All right." She slipped into the family room and joined the conversation there.

"You two probably should've finished that discussion in the car," Stephen said, "or waited until you were home."

"How much did you hear?" Mitch asked, his gaze aimed at the family room as if he could keep an eye on his wife through the wall.

"None of it," Stephen assured him. "Trouble is stamped on your face."

"I'll fill you in at the shop," Mitch said. He forced his lips into a dreadful excuse for a smile. "Is this better?"

"Better than my version usually is."

"You can fill me in on that later, too," Mitch said.

Stephen didn't dignify that with an answer. It was bad enough Mitch had outgrown him by a couple inches. He wasn't about to relinquish his role as the oldest brother and all the perks that came with it. Not even for the duration of a conversation. He didn't need a keeper, didn't need any reminders that harassing drug dealers was a dangerous hobby. He had to assume Mitch heard about his afterhours treks to the community center from a friend on the police force, the same way Sullivan had heard about it.

Thankfully, the family gathered around the dining room table, and Stephen let the voices flow around him, blotting out the ache in his side and the thoughts of last night. He tried to stay quiet so no one heard the grief lodged in his throat or accused him of being cynical. Though he offered comments and answered questions when necessary, he preferred hearing what was going on in their lives. What could he say? His life had frozen three years ago and his existence revolved around the garage, with the same routine day in and day out, week after week.

To his vast relief his family included Kenzie in the conversation as if she were a weekly fixture without expressing any hint of pushing her at him in a personal capacity. He picked up on the details that her mother and little sister, Courtney, had moved to Maryland five years ago. She made it sound like they got together only a few times a year.

He briefly entertained the idea of that much freedom, but shut down the vision when it felt as if he'd been cut loose to float away. When his lips parted to ask about her dad, he dug into his potatoes. Not his business and definitely not smart to ask her anything personal in front of his mother and sisters.

She and Julia got along easily enough, proving Kenzie was a better person than him. He'd been rude, hating Julia simply because she was an attorney. Well, he'd wanted to hate her and couldn't quite manage it, since it was so obvious his brother had seen something more under the woman's employment with the notorious Marburg law firm.

"The lawsuit Murtagh filed against you has been all over the news, Kenzie," his father said. "How are you holding up?"

"Being sidelined is a challenge," she admitted. "The shifts at Escape Club are a great distraction. No one there seems to recognize me." She sent Stephen a glowing smile that hurt more than his rib cage. "Stephen has been more than generous about giving me time and space at the shop to fix my car."

Weakness more than generosity, he told himself. He liked her company and already he knew he'd miss her when she left."Your dad would be tickled to hear you talk like that," Samuel said with a chuckle. "The two of you were sure something."

Kenzie only nodded, as if some emotion had her choked up. Stephen swallowed more questions along with the urge to give her an outward sign of support. His mom would leap on any glimmer of interest he showed as hope for something more than a platonic association. He was surprised to realize he didn't want her to run Kenzie off too soon.

"He might have a proper guest room to offer, too, if he ever bought a house," Myra said.

The gentle reprimand underscoring her words only poured more salt in that wound. What did a workaholic bachelor need with a house? Stephen cut into his ham and shoved a big bite into his mouth, preventing him from saying something he'd regret.

"The camper is plenty comfortable," Kenzie said. "Stephen did a great job with it."

Crap, he thought, as Myra's eyebrows arched and her gaze met her husband's across the table. Kenzie seemed oblivious to the way she'd drawn full attention from every adult at the table. He caught a gleam in his youngest sister's eye and blurted out the first thing that came to mind before Jenny could open her mouth.

"Dad, you knew Murtagh. Do you think he'd sabotage her car? Someone put sugar in her gas tank."

Samuel's face clouded over, his jaw set. "Murtagh always was an a—a jerk," he said, correcting his language for the grandkids just in time. "If your lawyer wants to depose any of us who worked with him, we're every last one of us willing."

Kenzie's lips pressed together, holding back the surge of emotion welling in her eyes. "Thank you," she said quietly.

The sight of those tears she wouldn't let fall was like a metal splinter under his skin. He wanted to take her away from anything that dimmed her sparkling laughter. What was wrong with him?

From his side of the table, Stephen caught the look of concern Julia aimed at Mitch. They must have been talking about Kenzie earlier. He couldn't imagine that Marburg would assign Julia, Mitch's wife, to Murtagh's legal team. Once they reached the privacy of the garage, it would be Stephen's first question.

Conversations resumed and his dad asked him about his current project.

"I'm finishing up the rebuild of a 1967 Camaro SS for Matt Riley," Stephen replied.

"General Riley's oldest?" Samuel asked.

"That's right." Stephen nodded.

"I didn't realize that one was for Matt. We haven't seen them

in years," Myra said. "It sounds like they're becoming good clients," she added, with a hefty dose of maternal pride.

"And they have excellent taste in classic American muscle
cars," Mitch added. "I still want to know where he found it. It's
in such good shape."

Megan's oldest asked what a muscle car was, drawing Stephen back into the conversation. He happily explained, in the
simplest terms, that a muscle car earned the name because of
how it was styled and built, and had an engine geared for performance. "The cars that are classics now were new when Grandpa
was your age."

"Show some respect," Samuel grumbled with a grin.

Kenzie looked down the table at his wide-eyed nephew. "My
dad taught me muscle cars growl when you're going slow and
purr when you drive fast. I bet Uncle Stephen will teach you
all about it when you're older."

Stephen gave her a long look. Classic cars were one interest
his fiancée hadn't shared with him. Oh, she'd admired and respected his work, but she didn't know cars or parts and hadn't
been inclined to learn. That had been fine with him. She'd trav-
eled with him to a few car auctions, hanging out at the hotel pool
while he conducted business. He thought of Kenzie answering
the phone and managing the customers. Annabeth would never
have been comfortable stepping into his space that way.

Stephen couldn't figure out how that made him feel. Done
with his dinner, he helped Jenny clear as the others finished.
As his mom served up thick slabs of cherry cobbler for dessert, he caught Megan and James exchanging cryptic glances.
Happy to get even for earlier, he called her on it. "Something
you'd like to share with the rest of the class, Meg?"

She wrinkled her nose at him. "Who told you?"

"You did," he said.

Her eyebrows snapped together a moment. "No, I didn't. We
haven't told anyone."

James draped an arm across the back of her chair and Stephen

felt a sharp pang of resentment over the gesture. He missed sharing intimacies like those looks and small touches. He checked
his watch, wishing for an excuse to get out of here before the
surly mood took over and he said something stupid.

"We were saving the news," James said.

"News?" Myra set dessert in front of her husband and leaned
in when he wrapped his arm around her waist.

As James gave Megan's shoulder a squeeze, Stephen gritted
his teeth. He knew what his sister would say before the words
came out of her mouth.

"We're expecting again," Megan said at last. When the first
chorus of happy congratulations died down, she added, "It's
twins."

Laughter and groans filled the room and Samuel offered
James his sympathy. "Good luck with that," he said with a heart-
felt sigh. "One to two is enough challenge." He nodded at Ste-
phen and Mitch in turn. "Going from two to four overnight?"
He gazed up at his wife, eyes sparkling with humor and love.
"Good luck," he repeated.

"You'll have all the help you need." Myra paused to kiss the
top of Megan's head as she returned to her chair.

"Meg and I weren't that bad," Andrew declared, defending
himself and his twin sister.

"None of us slept for weeks," Stephen said, as if it had been
agony.

"Years," Samuel said, teasing them all.

Mitch said, "I remember helping Mom all the time."

Myra cackled. "Please. You rescue people now in less chaos
than I faced daily with four children. I cried tears of joy when
Stephen started kindergarten. And then Jenny came along."

"And being a perfect angel, I quickly became the favorite,"
Jenny said with a wink.

To prove he could do something of value other than marry
well and procreate, Stephen retreated to the kitchen. They
tended to rotate the cleanup chores, but he needed some breath-

ing space. He was happy for his sister. Delighted, he assured himself as he rinsed plates and loaded the dishwasher.

"You okay?"

Mitch. He kept his back to the sympathy in his brother's voice.

"Fine," he said. Anything more than one syllable would push the envelope of his control.

"I've told everyone we need to get over to the garage to meet the potential buyer for that Mustang. Julia and Kenzie are ready when you are."

Stephen finished loading the dishwasher and returned to the dining room. "Ready." When the conversation paused, he ordered Andrew and James to finish the cleanup for his mom. He made quick work of the goodbyes and finally made it through the door. Julia and Kenzie were trailing Mitch to his car.

"Hang on." Megan was on his heels, preventing a clean escape. "How did you know I was pregnant?"

"Why are you so convinced I did?"

"You only do the half-hug thing when I'm pregnant. Did I leave something from the doctor in the van?"

"Just a lucky guess," he said. Ignoring his griping ribs, he pulled her in for a real, two-armed hug and she cinched her arms tight around his waist.

He grunted. "Come on, Meg."

"Well, this one has to last, since I'll be big as a house with twins soon."

"Right." He let her squeeze all she wanted. "Love you, sis."

"Love you, too," she said against his shoulder. "Go be happy," she added, her gaze sliding toward Kenzie.

"Shut up," Stephen protested. "We're friends." Again, something unfamiliar inside him rebelled at that label.

Megan only twinkled in that way of women overflowing with happiness. "So was James."

Stephen was more than a little relieved to escape to Mitch's gleaming Dodge Charger. Only a few years old, it served as an advertisement for Galway Automotive. Julia and Kenzie had taken the backseat, giving him more leg room up front.

"Tell me about this buyer," Stephen demanded, needing to put the family and talk of babies out of his mind. "You think he can really afford it?"

"I've told him we don't do financing, if that's what you mean," Mitch replied. "I think he can make the deal. Don't tell me you've got another buyer on the hook."

"I wish." A bidding war could be fun, although if they wanted to do that, they should take it to auction. Stephen struggled to hide the deep despair clamping around his rib cage like a vise. He wanted to blame the pervasive discomfort on the altercation last night or Megan's hug, but he knew this pain was emotional. "Is he willing to pay cash?"

"Well, I didn't ask him for stacks of unmarked twenty-dollar bills," Mitch joked.

In the backseat, Julia and Kenzie were talking in low tones. Kenzie was definitely a better person than he was. Given a choice, he'd rather see the notorious law firm dismantled and their historic building on Walnut Street removed from existence brick by brick. That little fantasy kept his mind off dinner, Kenzie and the thousand other stupid things bothering him like a swarm of bees.

"What's wrong with you?" Mitch asked, when they reached the garage and the women were out of the car. "You're grouchier than normal."

"I'm fine." Stephen reached for the door, paused. "Did you promise this buyer a deep discount or something?"

Mitch called him on it. "You're hurt again." He swore. "You ask all kinds of stupid questions when you want to smother the pain."

"Go to hell."

Mitch grabbed him before he could get out of the car. "You can't keep this up. It's time to get some help."

He didn't dignify that with a reply. Besides, he was far more interested in what Mitch and Julia had been talking about before dinner.

"Megan's pregnant and you can't dredge up any real happiness," Mitch continued. "The misery is obvious to everyone."

Stephen bristled. "I'm happy for them." What kind of jerk wouldn't be happy for them? "End of story." He glanced out the window and saw Julia and Kenzie still looking chummy. Maybe Julia was filling her in on what had upset them.

Mitch drilled a finger into Stephen's shoulder. "It's me. I was there, remember?"

Yes, Stephen remembered. How could he forget that his brother had responded to the 9-1-1 call that a woman, Stephen's fiancée, had been shot? His brother had been there while Annabeth bled out on those cursed steps, well beyond the help of the paramedics on the scene. Stephen would never forget how he'd failed to protect the woman he'd planned to grow old with. Mitch had been the one who'd called him. Mitch had held him when grief and denial dropped him to his knees in the ER.

"You're wrong. I fell, that's all," Stephen lied.

"Like hell. You need to talk with someone. You can't hide under cars alone all day and go looking for fights all night. You deserve better."

"I had better," Stephen shot back. "And you've got better things to worry about than me." His gaze drifted to Kenzie. "Plus I'm not alone." She was all the interference he could handle in his routine right now. "You're a good brother for caring, but I'm fine."

Mitch swore again. "Come on—"

Stephen swiveled around as a car pulled to a stop in front of the gate. "Your buyer?"

Mitch nodded, the scowl on his face smoothing out as he climbed from the Dodge to greet the newcomer. Stephen envied that ease his brother demonstrated, and tried his best to smile at the man, who seemed vaguely familiar.

"Jason?" Kenzie's lips curved into a grin as she hurried over to join them.

Something clicked for Stephen. This was one of the full-time bartenders from the Escape Club. A weird ripple of irritation chased through him as Kenzie and Jason fell into an immediate, friendly conversation.

Clearly, she knew how to get along with anyone in any circumstance, he decided, as she turned the conversation to the car. Had he ever been that easy with people?

Having had more than a week's worth of conversation over family dinner, Stephen let the others chat. He leaned back against the trunk of another car-in-progress and let Mitch handle the dealing. His little brother enjoyed the bargaining as much as he enjoyed the hands-on work.

Although... Stephen slid a glance at Julia. Would Mitch still want to be as involved when they started a family?

Kenzie, a smile on her face, walked over. He tried to keep his eyes on her face rather than that teasing hem of her dress.

"You're not into the art of the deal?" she asked.

"He's better at it," Stephen answered. He could smell the sunshine in her hair and something tangled with it that reminded him of a summer-ripe peach.

"What about the Riley Camaro in there? Did you negotiate that deal?"

He looked toward the bay where the Camaro was hidden by the lowered door. "That's different."

Her bare shoulder rubbed faintly against his biceps. "Come on. Tell me more."

"It's more like a commission." He glanced down to her shining face and knew she wouldn't let it rest. Talking was overrated and he always seemed to get tangled in the wrong details of the conversation. He folded his arms over his chest, the movement pressing his arm to hers. He swallowed, holding his ground rather than jumping away from her. "The Riley family brings us the car, a list of priorities, and gives me the budget," he said at last.

"Interesting." She was eyeing that bay door as intently as he had been.

He told himself he didn't want to know if she'd aimed that "interesting" at the customer's methods or him. "I need to take it out for a test drive," he said before he thought better of it. "You could ride along," he suggested, startling them both.

"Right now? You sure you're up for it?"

"Once we're done here." And he could drive with far worse injuries than bruised ribs. He lifted his chin toward Mitch and Jason. "Unless you'd rather join him?"

"I'm surprised Jason's looking at a car with that kind of price tag." Kenzie's nose wrinkled as she studied the Mustang.

"You don't like it?" he challenged. He and Mitch had brought that thing back to mint condition. "It's a '70." In theory, it could get upward of a hundred grand at the right auction. He had confidence that Mitch would work a profitable deal. Stephen was eager to get it off his lot and churn the profits into another project.

"I know," she said. "I can *appreciate* the car," she added quickly. She did her best to suppress the smile and failed. "And it's excellent workmanship. Still, there is something about the lines of a classic Camaro."

Her soft murmur of longing gave him a jolt, as if he'd touched a loose live wire. Stephen couldn't reply. His passion for cars ran the gamut from classic to quirky to cutting edge. He loved them all, and the challenge and ongoing learning kept him sharp. Cars didn't need conversation. Engines and tires and mufflers didn't demand he talk about feelings. The garage was a place to get things done. In a world that had frozen three years ago, the night his fiancée died, the garage gave him tangible progress and rewarded honest efforts equitably.

The Mustang's beefy engine roared to life and Jason, Mitch and Julia took the car for a short test drive. When they returned, the deal was settled in the office, payment and delivery arranged, and at last Stephen was alone again.

Well, almost alone.

He changed from the button down to a Galway Automotive T-shirt and joined Kenzie in the bay where the Camaro waited. She'd changed into denim shorts, a faded red, sleeveless cotton top and canvas shoes. She'd redone her hair, the thick braid falling straight down her back. He told himself he didn't miss the dress.

"My dad would have loved this one," she said, her voice soft and wistful.

He recognized the nostalgic nuance in her tone. "How long ago did he die?"

"I was fifteen," she said, her hand sweeping over the rise of the rear fender. "Our dads worked together," she added, caressing the tail fin. "Did you know that?"

"Vaguely." She was thirty and death had neatly divided her life in two parts, yet she remained so vibrant, completely alive. For the first time in recent memory Stephen wanted to ask how to manage that full recovery. Watching her, he realized the sorrow was still there, deep in her eyes, the tug at the corners of her lips. He wondered how her dad had died. He couldn't recall any deadly fires around that time. "Back then, the fire department was low on my list of priorities."

She met his gaze, her blue eyes sparkling. "Girls, right?"

"Cars." *Girls followed*, he thought, with an inward smile. "Engines made sense to me, and to my mother's dismay street racing was my preferred adrenaline rush."

She stopped at the front of the car, her eyes wide. "Seriously?"

"Young and stupid." He flipped the Camaro's keys around his index finger. "Sure you want to be seen with me in this?" The lines and body of the car were in decent condition, but although the factory color had once been crisp champagne, the years and a little rust gave it an unsightly coppery patina.

"That could be embarrassing," she teased. Stepping back, she planted her hands on her hips. "Better let me hear the engine first."

Mechanically, the car was nearly done. He needed to test the suspension and make sure the manual transmission was good to go. Curious how she'd react, he kept his gaze on her as he reached in and turned the key.

The engine roared to life.

Her expression absolutely lit up and she threw her head back in one of her big laughs. If he'd felt sucker punched earlier, seeing her in that dress, her reaction to the car might as well have been a knockout.

He had no idea how to cope with all the reactions she stirred inside him. Thankfully, she wouldn't be sticking around more than a week or two.

CHAPTER FOUR

Settled into the passenger seat, Kenzie could tell her heart was still running a little fast as Stephen drove the Camaro away from the shop, and not just because of the big block engine under the hood. Oh, that sound had been like magic, sending her straight back to those days of helping her dad in the garage. Just like her father always said, in the lower gears, this kind of motor growled, ready to leap at the first opportunity to open up.

Sure, the car had given her pulse a jump start, but it was the man behind the wheel that kept her system amped up. His hard jaw set in concentration made her want to reach out and see what kind of touch would soften him up. The flex and motion of his working hands and forearms as he shifted gears posed a ridiculous temptation to reach out, to feel that sinuous movement under her fingertips. Not smart to go there just because she was feeling lonely.

Keeping her mouth shut and her thoughts and hands to herself, she sank into the experience of watching Stephen handle the car. He needed to listen to and feel what the car was doing under him. She made her own mental notes, just in case he asked her opinion later.

As they cruised through the neighborhood, she tried to divert her attention with the Sunday evening activities around them.

Summertime in this part of town was a throwback to an idyllic era. With the car windows rolled down, the scent of burgers and hot dogs on backyard grills drifted through, backed by the soundtrack of delighted shrieks of children dashing through sprinklers.

"What was your favorite part of summer as a kid?" she asked abruptly.

"Catching fireflies," he replied, the stern line of his mouth easing with the memory. "Though burying my little brothers in the sand when we went up to Ocean City in Jersey is a close second."

"They really let you do that?"

His lips twitched, though he didn't smile. "Let's just say they always managed to draw the short straw."

She chuckled. "Being oldest does have its advantages."

"A few," he agreed.

He wound his way out of the neighborhood and let the car open up a bit more, then picked up Interstate 95 and aimed north, away from the city. She didn't care where they were going because the driving was plenty of fun. Shedding the city and her recent troubles gave her a sense of relief, despite knowing she'd have to go back and ride out the lawsuit.

Once he was in fourth gear the engine sounded good to her, but she felt a lag in the clutch whenever he shifted from second to third. She didn't mention it; this was his project, and he had to be feeling it more than she did.

The low purr of the engine filled the space where most people would want to talk, and she enjoyed the companionable silence as the miles slipped by. She'd been doing so much talking, defending and justifying her decisions in the Murtagh fire, that Stephen's quiet tendencies were a refreshing reprieve. So focused on the professional ramifications, she hadn't realized how the case was consuming her personally. The only thing no one wanted to discuss with her was what she was going to do if Murtagh won his case against her.

She glanced at Stephen again. It wasn't as if firefighting was the only thing she could do. She was a quick learner, tenacious, good with her hands, and she had decent skills with computers, too. If Stephen hired her to manage the office, she could build on that, giving him a hand with the basic maintenance tasks. Combined with waitressing at the club, she could make ends meet.

She sighed, frustrated and more than a little discouraged by how that life looked in her mind. Her career as a firefighter couldn't be over. Not like this. She had turned her gaze to the passing scenery. Positive thinking was essential. She had to keep a strong vision of the result she wanted.

"What do you think about the car?" Stephen asked, drawing her away from the less pleasant thoughts.

"The engine loves the highway," she said.

His lips tilted into a faint smile. "Riley will have his hands full keeping her in check in town."

"About that," she said.

He shot her a quick glance.

"Is there a hiccup between second and third gear or do you enjoy abusing a clutch?"

He laughed, a rusty sound that seemed to surprise them both. "I took an oath as a mechanic not to abuse any machinery."

The joke made her smile. "What a relief," she teased.

"I think I know what to look for when we get back," he said. "I'm glad you noticed it, too. But you weren't thinking about the car."

She didn't appreciate his observation skills. "I wasn't *only* thinking about the car." It was as far as she wanted to go on the subject. They barely knew each other, and though he wasn't the only person trying to help her though this rough patch, something in his quiet intensity slipped past her defenses. She wasn't sure she could deal with that kind of invasion. Not now, anyway.

Before she could ask what he'd meant by the earlier offer to help her beat the lawsuit, he was turning off the interstate to a less-traveled side road.

"Would you like to just think about the car?"

She stared at him, almost afraid to hope. "Are you offering to let me drive?"

"Yes."

That single word sent a thrill of anticipation rolling through her. It was all she could do to sit still when she wanted to bounce in her seat like one of his siblings' children had done at the sight of him.

He stopped to fill the car with gas, but didn't turn over the keys when she hopped out and held out her hand.

"Five minutes," he told her.

She took in the trees lining the road and something clicked. She hadn't been up this way in a long time. More than fifteen years, in fact. Her weekend trips out of Philly had come to an abrupt halt when her dad died. "Where are we going?"

"Be patient." His lips twitched again.

That bemused expression made her want to tease him for hours and hours with more than words. She pulled herself back from that slippery slope. Neither of them was in the market for a fast fling. He was doing her a big favor letting her stay in the camper, and she didn't dare screw that up by letting her hormones call the shots.

He continued down the access road until the trees cleared away to reveal an old oval racetrack. She sat a little forward in her seat. "I have been here."

"You have?"

"Yes!" The grandstands looked weary and forlorn now. She remembered when bright racing team flags had flown from the poles along the top rail. She could almost smell the popcorn blending with the pungent scents of hot tires, oil and gasoline. "Ages ago when my dad did some racing on the weekends," she replied. "I was probably twelve or thirteen the last time."

"How did I not know about that?" Stephen asked.

"It's not like he was some racing celebrity or anything," she pointed out. "He had to give it up when he got sick."

Stephen parked the car and climbed out, to punch a number into the security panel at the gate. She was reminded of the security measures at his garage when the fence rolled back. Once they were through, he waited until the fence closed behind him.

"Did you buy this track?" She couldn't believe her good luck. "Are you going to open it up again?" All the wonderful memories with her dad came rushing back. This evening just kept getting better and better.

"No. I couldn't quite justify that, but I know some of the right people."

"I can't believe I'm about to drive this beauty on this track."

"Me first," Stephen said.

"Right, right. Of course." As he worked through the lower gears, she sat back, getting a feel for the track, impatiently waiting for him to open it up.

Then he did and she laughed again as the engine responded, the vibrations coming up through her feet on the floorboards, surrounding her in a delicious sensation. He leaned into the corners, weaved back and forth on the straightaways, testing the Camaro's responses. Then he opened it all the way for a few exhilarating laps.

As he slowed down, she nearly begged him for one more lap before she remembered it was her turn to drive. Her palms went damp when he stopped at the start/finish line, and she swiped them across her shorts. Releasing her seat belt, she scrambled out of the car.

The moment the car stopped she raced around the hood, reaching the driver's door before he was all the way clear. She skidded to a stop before colliding with him and instantly regretted it, imagining what those strong hands would feel like on her.

"Eager?"

"You have no idea," she admitted. Stephen had her fired up more than the car. She didn't bother trying to contain her excitement. At one time she and her dad had dreamed of her doing the driving, racing her way up through the ranks from tracks like this one to bigger venues.

"Promise me one thing." He stopped her with a light touch at her elbow.

Her skin warmed all over under his touch and the intensity in his hazel eyes sent an extra spark through her system. One question answered. "I'll be careful." He had to know she would never do anything stupid with someone else's car. Or with him.

"That's not it."

"Then what?" Impatient, she rocked up on her toes and back again.

"Give me time to buckle in before you hit the gas?"

She laughed, the only outlet for so much excitement. "I promise." His hand slipped away. "You'd better be quick about it."

Kenzie adjusted the seat and took a few calming breaths before she placed her hands on the wheel. When they were both ready, she familiarized herself with the clutch, shifting and accelerating and then slowing and downshifting, as Stephen had done when they started out.

"This is smooth as glass everywhere but second to third."

"Just drive," he muttered.

She spared him a long glance as she came up on the start/finish line again. "You ready?"

"Eyes on the road," he said.

"Yeah, the traffic is awful out here." She goosed the gas, watching his face.

"Kenzie."

"No worries," she assured him. "I've got it under control." Thanks to her dad, driving was as natural to her as walking or breathing.

Stephen made a noise loaded with skepticism.

She accelerated on the next lap, familiar now with the track surface, the car's responses. "This track is in great condition," she said.

"Better to maintain it than let it rot and then have to rebuild if they decide to open it again," he replied.

"True." She pushed the speedometer past eighty. "Reopening here would be amazing."

She knew better than to push a new engine too hard too soon, and she behaved herself, though the motor would have given her more. At just over ninety miles per hour, the rush was incredible. The Camaro hugged the turns and prowled over the front and back straightaways. It was almost as much fun as watching her dad win races when she'd been a kid.

"You've got skills," Stephen said. His voice was full of clear admiration and far more relaxed than it had been on the short drive to dinner.

"Thanks." She shifted through another turn. "If only I'd been a boy I might've done more racing."

"Girls can drive," Stephen pointed out.

She grinned when she wanted to melt into a wistful puddle. For a quiet guy, he had a knack for knowing just what to say. "Fifteen years ago, without Dad in my corner, it was an uphill battle I wasn't ready for. There were too many other details to handle."

She took the next lap slower, and when she finally rolled to a stop, the melancholy of missing her father had her heart in a crushing grip.

"Need a minute?" He rested his hand on the back of the seat and his thumb brushed lightly across her shoulder. "Or another lap?" he teased.

Shaking off the unexpected sadness, she climbed out of the car before she begged him to hold her and gulped in the evening air mingling with the heat of the car.

"Thanks, Stephen," she said brightly, when she trusted her voice again. "That was a blast." It was good to make new memories in an old, familiar place. Careful to keep her distance so she wouldn't do something dumb like hug him, she moved back to the passenger side.

"You're welcome." His eyebrows were flexed in a thoughtful frown as he resumed his place behind the wheel.

They'd topped off the gas tank and were back on the highway when he finally spoke. "You decided not to race cars, but you followed his footsteps and became a firefighter?"

"That was also a bit of an uphill battle," she said. "Though there was more support in place. The gender bias decreases every year." It would be nice if someday she and other female firefighters wouldn't have to cope with people who shared Murtagh's outdated views.

"Racing is really how I got interested in firefighting," she continued. "Dad was an inspiration, of course. Watching the safety crews and the pit crews in action really convinced me," she added, thinking of the time when her father's engine had roared to life and promptly exploded into a ball of flame.

Inexplicably content, she watched the evening light fade to dusky blue velvet over the river as they returned to the city. Summer twilight always left her nostalgic for dirt racetracks with her father and camping trips with the family.

"Thanks for a great time," she said, when he'd parked the Camaro back inside the bay so he could make the adjustments to the clutch. She knew it hadn't been a date, though it had been one of the best evenings she'd had in recent memory. She stretched her arms overhead, wishing it could last just a little longer. Still, rejuvenated and relaxed, her body thrumming from the car and the man, she walked over to the bay where her car waited.

Beside the classic muscle car, her disassembled compact looked more pitiful than ever. If only she could buy the loaner car from him, she'd tell him to scrap the weary car for parts, assuming there was anything of value left in it. Murtagh's mottled face flashed into her mind and she fought back a wave of resentment over his frivolous lawsuit. Refusing to let trouble creep in and spoil her mood, she started toward the camper.

"Kenzie, hang on."

She suppressed the little shiver that went through her at the sound of his low voice as she turned back toward him.

"I like the way you drive and the way you listened to the car. If—" His cell phone rang, cutting him off. "Hold that thought," he said, before he answered.

She knew something was wrong when what she'd come to consider his normal scowl deepened into a troubled expression, shadowing his hazel eyes. Concerned, she took a step closer to him.

"She's fine," Stephen said to the caller. "Yes, I'm *sure*. I'm looking right at her." Another pause. "Consider it done." He ended the call and tucked his phone into his back pocket.

"That was Grant," he said, as he moved to lower the door on the open bay, closing them in the privacy of the shop.

"What happened?"

"Someone vandalized a car in the Escape Club parking lot. The customer was naturally upset and called the cops."

"Good," she interjected. "Was there more?" she prompted, when he didn't move or explain anything else about the call. "Was he phoning for a tow truck?"

Stephen ran his hand through his hair, mussing it, and her fingers twitched as if she had a right to smooth it back into place. She forced her eyes away from the way his T-shirt rode the flex of his biceps.

"Yes, they needed a tow truck, but Grant called someone else." Stephen's gaze locked with hers and a chill slid down her spine.

There was more. "Just say it."

"The vandalized car is nearly identical to your loaner."

Her knees wanted to buckle, though she refused to show it. Her stomach twisted. "Murtagh."

Stephen's chin jerked in a brief nod. "Grant's thinking the same thing. He wants you and me to stay alert."

She shuddered at the idea of Murtagh following her and watching her so closely. No amount of willpower or resolve could restrain her reaction. Stephen reached out and rubbed the goose bumps from her bare arms.

"What if...?" She stopped herself a half second too late. All the ways Murtagh could hurt someone, thinking he was getting even with her, flashed through her mind in a blur. As a first responder, she'd seen plenty of the mishaps, accidents and deliberate injuries people suffered. She covered her mouth with a hand, trying to regain her composure. Stephen didn't need her going to pieces.

"No one got hurt," he said. "Grant says it was only property damage."

Kenzie stepped back from him and tucked her hands into her back pockets before she could give in and lean into all his quiet strength. "No witnesses?"

"He didn't mention anyone coming forward. You can ask him next time you're over there. But you won't be going to and from the club alone."

"Stephen, you have a business to run. You can't trail after me everywhere I go." That kind of hovering would give Murtagh's threats too much validity and erode what was left of her confidence. Where was her spine? What had happened to the courage and defiance that had gotten her over every other hurdle life dropped in her path?

"Fine." He leaned back against a workbench. "You can take a different car every time you leave."

"Stop." She waved off the offer. "The vandalism at the club might very well be a complete coincidence. You know the loaner is a fairly common model."

He rolled his eyes and folded his arms over his chest. "Right. Grant Sullivan is known for jumping to outrageous conclusions."

Her temper spiked and she swallowed the rude retort on the tip of her tongue. Stephen wasn't the problem. He was only trying to help. "That's not it. I don't want to be more of an imposition. The depositions don't even start for another week," she managed. She glanced again at the heap of parts that were once a car. "I'll take care of that between my shifts at the club this week and find a different place to stay. You don't need my drama in here."

"This is the safest place for you and you know it."

True. "Hotels have security," she pointed out.

"For a price," he shot back.

Frustrated, she wanted to kick something. There had to be some way to get control of the mess that was her life. *Temporary mess.*

"I could take care of your car in my sleep. Let me."

"No." She couldn't handle more of his kindness right now. "It's my responsibility. Let me know what else you need me to do around here in trade for the time and space. Something more than the phone."

"Fine." His gaze narrowed.

He didn't sound all that fine about it. "Thank you," she whispered, through the tangle of emotions. Anger at Murtagh, gratitude for Stephen's unflagging generosity and concern for some unknown person who'd been caught in the crossfire of her troubles twisted her up inside.

"Your car, your repair," Stephen said. "But you're staying in the trailer. That part isn't up for further discussion."

"Okay." She turned away and headed to the camper. If she stuck around, she'd start crying. Stephen did *not* need that.

It had been such a wonderful day with the Galway family, topped with the treat of her first time taking real laps on the same track where she and her dad had enjoyed themselves all those summers ago. Did Murtagh's actions have to poison everything? For the first time she gave serious consideration to leaving town against legal advice. It might be worth risking the "appearance of guilt" to get away for a few days.

Her nose stung and for a split second tears blurred her vision. Give up Philly and her place in it because some whiny jerk didn't like the way she'd saved his life?

No. She yanked open the camper door and turned on the lights. She would *not* give Murtagh that kind of power over her life. Although he might take her career, he couldn't have a single one of the intangibles that made her the Kenzie Hughes her family and coworkers respected.

"Kenzie?"

She glanced over her shoulder to find Stephen watching her from the corner of the building. Was a man supposed to look that sexy with a scowl on his face? Studying him, she realized she couldn't just leave. Not after Grant had asked her to keep an eye on Stephen. She'd given her word and she took that type of promise seriously. Besides, it would be so much better to think of something other than her problems.

"More trouble?" she asked, coming back down the steps. Why couldn't Murtagh be satisfied wrecking her career with the lawsuit? Petty behavior like vandalism didn't make any sense to her.

"No." Stephen crossed to her with a few ground-eating strides and the light from the camper window washed over his face, revealing the depth of concern in his gaze. "You're safe here behind this fence, with me. I promise."

Standing on the bottom step, she was eye level with him. His words smoothed over all her prickling nerves. She almost gave him those same words back, except her protecting him wasn't supposed to be obvious.

He looked so earnest, so determined to tolerate her invasion of his space until everything in her world was back to normal. "I appreciate that." Knowing how much he preferred his solitude, she felt the gesture unravel something within her.

Leaning forward, Kenzie brushed her lips to his cheek. A light, friendly, platonic gesture was all she intended. Instead, he caught her as if he thought she'd lost her balance, his hands hot on her waist. Then his lips touched hers. By accident or design, the spark of contact set her body humming. She braced her hands on his strong shoulders, wanting to sink a little deeper, explore his taste as his masculine scent and the summer night enveloped her.

It would be reckless to fall into that sweet fantasy. She eased back, forced her hands to come along with the rest of her. "Thanks again, for everything today." She darted into the camper on quivering legs.

Whoa. That had been an eye-opener.

She moved away from the door and clapped a hand over her mouth before the nervous laughter bubbling up could burst free. Her lips felt as though she'd tasted something too spicy. She'd had plenty of real dates in the past that didn't end with a kiss as enticing as that one. There was some *serious* heat simmering under all that calm, cool and collected that Stephen projected.

Heat that ignited a tantalizing jolt of desire in her bloodstream.

Don't go there, she scolded herself. That kiss had been a happy accident. She had to put it, and all the hot-summer-night fantasies the feel of his lips on hers stirred up, out of her mind. It was the only sane way forward.

Stunned, Stephen felt his feet grow roots, holding him in place as Kenzie disappeared behind the trailer door. She'd kissed him. No. He'd kissed her. Did it matter who'd started it? He licked his lips, catching the faint taste of her strawberry lip gloss. *Strawberry.* That was a surprise.

When his feet were finally ready to cooperate, he turned and walked away from the trailer, if only because he wanted to climb those steps, throw open the door, pull her into his arms and kiss her again.

Not the best move after he'd just told her she was safe with him here on his property. What had he been thinking? He hadn't been thinking at all, obviously, but acting on impulse.

He wasn't supposed to be kissing Kenzie or anyone else. Reality doused him as effectively as a cold shower. His last first kiss had been with Annabeth. Kenzie hadn't meant anything romantic by the gesture. She'd aimed for his cheek and something inexplicable had him taking advantage of the moment.

Back in the office, he closed the door but didn't lock it, just in case she needed something in the night. His conscience demanded to know what he thought she might need. Did he expect her to run in and ask him to comfort her after a nightmare? Yeah, that would happen. Maybe she would need shelter from an intruder? Not a chance. His security system would alert him long before a trespasser could cause any trouble.

He glared at the dead bolt and couldn't make himself turn it to lock her out.

For the first time he thought maybe his mom and sisters had a point about him needing to dive back into the dating pool. Unfortunately, that didn't feel right, either.

Kissing Kenzie was proof he wasn't ready. He'd chosen the wrong response to a friendly gesture and now he was overreacting and overanalyzing the mistake. He could only imagine the blunders he would make on a real date.

So why was he still reliving those few seconds of her lips on his as if he'd never been kissed before?

"Man up," he muttered, double-checking the status of the security system at the desk.

She's a friend of the family, he reminded himself as he changed into a T-shirt and gym shorts for the night. She might as well be another little sister. As if the two sisters he had weren't enough to worry over on any given day. When he added in the two sisters-in-law, even he could see the last thing he needed was another woman in that category.

Yet thinking of Kenzie in any other type of relationship held far more risk. He wasn't ready to date, wasn't looking for a receptionist or even a tenant for the trailer. Draping a sheet over the couch, he squeezed the pillow between his hands, trying to wedge Kenzie into the sister category.

She just wouldn't go.

Maybe it was the big blue eyes or the soft lips or that ironclad willpower that kept her going forward no matter what bomb-shells life dropped on her. Stretched out on the couch in the darkness, he could admit part of his attraction to her might be tied to the way she'd handled the Camaro on that track. The woman could *drive*. Her delighted grin had been infectious and the way her small hands worked the gearshift and steering wheel slid right under his defenses.

He caught himself rubbing his shoulder where her hands had touched him, and punched the pillow under his head. Dwelling on any aspect of her as a woman was the wrong thing to do. He should be working on regaining some sense and perspective.

Logically, he knew she wasn't over there in the trailer sa-voring the feel of that kiss the way he was. She was probably annoyed—and rightfully so—that he'd taken advantage of the moment. Then why did the taste of her hold him with such an unbreakable grip?

Because he never planned to leave himself open to that kind of longing and need again.

His mother had tried a couple times to set him up with some-one new. That last attempt had been a miserable night, he re-called, with some regret for the woman involved. He suspected his mom frequently sent single women and their car troubles his way, with her fingers crossed that one of them would break through the grief that kept him locked up in his work.

Her well-meaning attempts to see him happy again only made him feel more broken inside, drifting further beyond repair.

Desperate for sleep, he forced his mind back to what he'd felt and heard while test-driving the Camaro. He wasn't satis-fied with the clutch performance from second to third. He sus-pected the most likely root of the problem and would tweak it tomorrow. Any other concerns and solutions evaporated as the memory of Kenzie's dazzling happiness when she took the wheel played across his closed eyelids.

Letting her stay here was a mistake, yet he was committed now. Instead of taking her to Sunday dinner and kissing her, he should have been asking why she didn't have a boyfriend help-ing her out. He'd sat up and reached for his phone to text Mitch and ask about Kenzie's personal life when he realized there was no good way for his brother to interpret that kind of question.

She didn't strike him as a woman who would let him steal a kiss while she was in a relationship with someone else. Kenzie radiated integrity and loyalty.

No. Just like everything else lately, he'd have to deal with his hang-ups on his own. Mitch worried about him enough al-ready. No sense giving his brother more cause to come around and pester him. He was being an idiot, and he'd given Kenzie his word that she could stay. If she felt inclined to answer the business phone and repair her car by herself, he should shut up and let her.

Attempting to get comfortable in his makeshift bed again, he closed his eyes and kept them closed until he fell asleep.

All too soon, sunlight through the window brought him awake and he dragged himself to the shower to face Monday. If he was working, with the music amped up and power tools running, maybe she wouldn't bother asking him what he'd meant by kissing her. He could hope. And if he was working he'd be too preoccupied to do something dumb and try to kiss her again.

Thankfully, when Kenzie walked into the garage with her coffee and an easygoing smile, she didn't seem annoyed or in-clined to hold that kiss against him. She didn't seem inclined to chat, either. He noticed the dark smudges under her eyes, but kept his concern to himself as she pulled coveralls over her tank top and shorts. After lacing up her steel-toed boots, she started in on her pitiful junker, pausing whenever the phone rang.

Over the next several days they fell into a surprisingly com-fortable routine. In the mornings they worked side by side. He found and fixed the clutch issue on the Camaro and sent it off for the interior and exterior work, returning to the more typi-cal maintenance tasks. Kenzie booked service appointments, searched for and ordered parts, did an inventory on a whim and fielded calls for the tow truck, as well as potential restoration clients.

He stayed away from the community center, telling himself the neighborhood would survive his absence for a few more days. Without a good reason for leaving, he couldn't take the chance she would discover his unpredictable and unpleasant hobby. Instead he worked late or researched cars he might want to restore. Although he was tempted to do his drive-bys while Kenzie was working at the club, he resisted the urge. Security system or not, he didn't want Kenzie coming home from a shift to find the garage empty.

When she wasn't scheduled early at the Escape Club, she ordered lunch and they would sit down in the office and eat together before she headed to her evening shifts. Although Kenzie's sunny demeanor was usually at odds with his perpetual solitude, he found himself enjoying those conversations more than he anticipated. She loved sharing stories about working on cars with her dad, and she never lectured him about his lacking social life. He eventually realized she was deftly avoiding the topic of anything related to Murtagh or the lawsuit, and Stephen found himself happy he could help her, even if it was only to serve as a small distraction.

Happy in any capacity wasn't something he'd ever expected to feel again.

Though she was eager to return the loaner, he'd convinced her not to stop with a new fuel system, but to go ahead and take care of the long list of potential troubles with her car. During her shifts at the club, Stephen hustled to get the parts she would need into his storeroom, for her to find at the right time.

She had excellent skills as a mechanic, and if he needed extra hands around the shop, she would have been at the top of his new-hire list. He told himself it wasn't just because it was pure pleasure watching her peel off the oversize coveralls whenever she had to leave. Though he tried, he couldn't kick that fascination of her long-limbed body out of his head, not even when he reminded himself Kenzie needed a friend more than a pseudo boss hitting on her.

Between the GPS tracker on the loaner car and the constant communication between him and Grant and Jason, Stephen didn't feel the need to tail her to and from the club or blow up her phone with check-in requests. If Kenzie had any idea how many text messages were exchanged regarding her safety on any given day she'd be furious with all of them.

It wasn't that they didn't believe in her ability to hold her own, but rather a general unease about the guy suing her. They hadn't heard anything out of him after the car had been vandalized at the club, and though the security cameras hadn't offered a conclusive ID, everyone assumed the vandal had been Murtagh.

As Stephen finished up an oil change service for Mr. Cartwright, a faithful customer from the neighborhood, he was waiting for the phone to ring with a Kenzie update. She'd put in two hours at the shop before her midmorning appointment with her lawyer. Apparently he wanted to give her an update on the deposition process and schedule. After that she was supposed to go straight to the Escape Club for a double shift.

"That's a sorry excuse for a man right there," Mr. Cartwright said from his typical waiting place, near the doorway between the shop and the office.

Stephen glanced up from the tire pressure gauge. "What's that?"

"Old" Mr. Cartwright had lived in the neighborhood, a block down from his parents' place, for as long as Stephen could remember. His hair had gone white and wispy and his shoulders were stooped, but his mind was sharp as ever. One of Stephen's first customers, he brought his car in for maintenance every three months like clockwork, had a cup of coffee and shared his opinion on everything from the weather to global politics. With a wry chuckle, he always claimed waiting while Stephen tended to the car got him out of his wife's hair and saved their marriage.

He raised his paper coffee cup toward the television Stephen had installed in the small customer waiting area he'd carved out of the office space when he'd bought the place. "That man is alive and walking around thanks to the Hughes girl. He should be on his knees thanking her, not suing her."

That brought Stephen to his feet and he hurried over to the television. The cameraman chose that moment for a close-up shot of Randall Murtagh's red-cheeked face, while a ticker at the bottom of the screen ran a summary of how he'd come to file a civil suit against Kenzie.

Stephen couldn't hear anything Murtagh said because Mr. Cartwright had hit his stride, rattling off a litany of opinions about trial-happy lawyers, community heroes and bitter old men until at last the interview was over. As soon as he had a break, Stephen meant to ask Julia why Murtagh's legal team allowed him to do public interviews before the case even got rolling.

His concentration fractured, he turned to the checklist posted on the wall to help him tick through the last details of Mr. Cartwright's service. He sent the older man on his way with a hearty handshake.

Alone in the garage, Stephen sent Grant a text message as a heads-up. He didn't want Kenzie getting blindsided by this while she was on shift. She was popular among the club staff and probably equally liked by regular customers. He knew some-one would mention it to her.

With time to spare before his next appointment, he closed the driveway gate and retreated to the office to search the web for a replay of the interview. He decided it was a good thing Mr. Cartwright had talked throughout the interview because Ste-phen wouldn't have been able to control his language.

The accusations and outrageous claims Murtagh aimed at Kenzie and the PFD had to qualify as slander. Someone needed to give the jerk a serious wakeup call. As Mr. Cartwright said, the man was alive and well when he might just as easily have been dead.

Stephen groaned when the interview showed pictures of the man's burns. He wouldn't presume to judge another man's pain, but those burns were mild enough that they had to be completely healed by now.

"Vindictive bastard, aren't you?" he said to the monitor when the interview finished.

Stephen pushed back from the desk as a familiar wave of helplessness surged through him. Other than quiz Julia or send a sympathetic text message to Kenzie, he couldn't do a damn thing for her. His temper reared up and he slammed his palms into the metal file cabinet, rocking it back against the wall. With an oath, he stalked out to the shop to find a better release valve before he did something irreparable in the office.

Mad as hell on her behalf, he cranked up the music as he debated his options. He could cruise by the community center, for all the good that would do around noon on a weekday. It was much easier to strike back at those useless drug dealers from the shadows, though reporting a few drug deals wouldn't help Kenzie. He sent a text to Mitch asking what the PFD was doing to protect Kenzie and their own reputation. No telling when his brother would have time in his shift to reply.

Stephen picked up a wrench, spinning it repeatedly in his hand, desperate for some kind of action. There had to be something to bleed off this pent-up frustration. He'd failed Annabeth. He wouldn't fail Kenzie, too. Staring at her car, he decided to start with that.

She might get pissed off when she discovered he'd taken over the project. Too bad. This wasn't about charity or generosity. The sooner this car was up and running, the sooner she could sell the thing and churn the profit into a better car. Assuming he could convince her that was her smartest option.

Decided, he set to work before his next maintenance appointment arrived.

CHAPTER FIVE

KENZIE LEFT HER lawyer's office feeling less than optimistic about the civil suit. The son of a firefighter, Paul Corrigan had been recommended by the PFD. She liked him well enough. He was young and smart and he was willing to roll up his sleeves and get creative. More than all that combined, he wasn't afraid to go up against the notorious Marburg law firm.

Paul had laid out what they had so far and what he expected Murtagh to do during the depositions next week. He was on the verge of explaining his plan to counter those moves when his assistant had interrupted them with the interview disaster. All of it echoed through her mind as she drove toward the pier for her shift at the Escape Club.

"She was too small for the task," Murtagh had said as the studio flashed her academy picture beside a picture of his burned leg. "And I'm not even a big man."

Big baby was more like it, she thought darkly, gripping the steering wheel while she waited for a traffic light to change. When Murtagh had first filed his complaint, she'd told everyone up the PFD chain of command how he'd fought her attempts to get him out safely. He'd argued with her long enough that the fire cut off the first clear escape route, putting them both at more risk.

Still, she'd amended her original plan and managed to get him clear of the blaze before the second floor dropped on top of them. The body-cam footage from a police officer on the scene proved Murtagh had walked to the ambulance on his own power. Of course, as the paramedics tried to treat him, he'd shoved away the oxygen mask so he could complain more loudly about her ineptitude. At the time, she'd chalked up his nonsense to smoke inhalation, and rejoined her crew as they put out the fire.

Both the PFD and her lawyer had statements from the police officer and paramedics and a few bystanders willing to step up in her defense. Those statements had been enough to ward off any disciplinary action against her on the original complaint, but Murtagh had kept on gunning for her.

Though Paul wasn't happy about it, he'd reminded her that Murtagh was getting this outrageous free publicity only because he'd given twenty years to the PFD. He served as his own expert and the media couldn't resist his controversial agenda to limit women in the PFD to desk roles.

Murtagh spouted off as if the women who had fought fires on the front lines as far back as the 1800s had never existed. Good grief, the academy—the same academy they had both attended—had pictures of women who'd stepped up as firefighters while most of the men in the area were serving overseas during World War II. Why wasn't anyone in the media asking his opinion on those women?

By the time she reached the club and parked in the spot near the kitchen at Grant's insistence Kenzie was furious all over again. She sat there trying to breathe through the temper and worry, to push all this to the back of her mind so she could be pleasant for the long hours ahead. Given a few minutes, she'd be able to smile again. Just as soon as she found something better to think about.

The feel of Stephen's lips against hers popped back to the front of her mind and she couldn't help reliving that sweet, tender moment. Not even that kiss was a straightforward happy thought to carry with her tonight. Not when she factored in his reaction. As eager as she'd been to see where something more personal might lead, it had been clear the following morning that Stephen wanted to pretend it hadn't happened.

Which was okay. His reaction was better than okay; it was the smart approach. Angling for a conversation about a kiss would have made her look needier than she felt already. Forgetting that kiss was for the best. She didn't need any more complications in her life right now, especially the sort that came in the form of a handsome, lean mechanic with a sexy scowl.

Getting nowhere, Kenzie left the car and walked in the back door of the club, nearly plowing into Grant, who was on his way outside.

"I was just coming to check on you," he said, with his easygoing smile.

Knowing his history, she wondered if he ever had to practice the calm, confident expression. Probably not. Grant maintained a pragmatic outlook when it came to adversity, and made a point of always looking ahead and moving forward.

"Here I am," she said. "Who's onstage tonight?"

He ignored her question. "You doing okay?"

"Sure." Though she tried to give him a warm smile, it felt stiff and awkward on her face.

"That's not your best look." Grant exaggerated the move as he leaned back. "Walk with me a minute," he said, turning her around. "If I let you clock in now, you'll scare off everyone inside."

"Your employees are tougher than that," she said, deliberately misinterpreting him.

He held open the door she'd just come through. "My employees need to have something to do and customers to serve, or the club is just another empty warehouse again."

"We don't want that," she said. Though it came out with an edge of sarcasm, she'd meant it sincerely. The Escape Club made a difference for customers, staff and the people who came by seeking "Alexander" to help them through various sticky situations.

She walked alongside Grant toward the river, the breeze teasing a few strands of hair from the twin French braids she'd woven it into this morning for the long day.

"I wanted to say thanks," Grant said.

Kenzie was lost. "For what?"

"Keeping Stephen out of trouble," he told her. "He hasn't been spotted near the community center in almost a week. Whatever you're doing, keep it up."

All she'd done was fill his schedule from open to close and keep him talking about cars. "I haven't done anything special." If Stephen had wanted to go out, he'd certainly had ample opportunity during her shifts here at the club. It made her wonder why he wasn't taking advantage of those hours.

"Well, keep it up anyway," Grant repeated, pulling her attention back to the conversation. "The narcotics unit is having an easier time without him in the way."

"Good to know." She suspected that if they cleaned up the area, he'd give up his dangerous hobby and everyone would be happier.

Grant turned away from the river to face her. "Now, let's go over the television interview this morning."

She didn't bother trying to smile. "I was with my lawyer," she replied. "He said he was heading to the courthouse to ask the judge for a gag order."

"I'm glad to hear that. This civil suit is the definition of frivolous."

"If only the judge agreed with you," she muttered, watching a tour boat chugging upriver. That recurring urge to leave town rose up again and she punted it away. She was sticking it out right here, for Stephen as well as for her case. "Paul keeps telling me these cases usually settle and often turn one way or the other on the smallest detail."

She just wasn't sure it would turn her way.

"Sounds right," Grant agreed. "I was given the option of filing a civil suit against the man who shot me."

She'd never heard that part of his story. "But you didn't, did you?"

"No." Grant sighed. "What was the point?" He shrugged. "Wasn't like a billionaire shot me," he quipped. "My expenses were covered and I wanted to find a new place to fit in. Felt like if I'd had to tell that story one more time I'd lose my mind."

She could sympathize with that. Unless Murtagh dropped the suit she was doomed to relay the events of the rescue a few more times, until the case was settled. "Stephen's bruised ribs are healing," she said, in an obvious change of topic. "He's moving better around the shop."

"Good." Grant's gaze followed the boat, as well. "I saw the Mustang Jason bought. If I have to invest in a car restoration to keep that boy in his garage, I'll do it. Just say the word and I'll convince my wife it's a midlife crisis."

Kenzie laughed, the sound accompanied by a grin that felt completely natural this time. "You're such a soft touch, Sullivan."

"You think so?" He arched his salt-and-pepper eyebrows. "Don't tell anyone."

She raised her hand as if taking an oath. "If news gets out, it didn't come from me."

They returned to the club and she felt remarkably lighter as she tied her apron and headed onto the floor to take care of customers. Although Grant didn't have live music lined up for this time of day, they were doing steady business, which kept her mind away from her troubles.

She was ready for her break when the first of the two bands on the schedule arrived for their setup. Carrying two sandwich platters to the end of the bar, she encouraged Jason to take a break with her and fuel up for what was sure to be a packed house tonight.

"How's the Mustang running for you?" she asked.

"It purrs," he said, a glint of pride in his eye. "Best invest-ment I've made in a long time. I love it."

"Mitch and Stephen do great work."

"And Mitch drives a hard deal," he agreed with a distracted smile.

She was curious what kind of a deal he'd worked with Mitch. She didn't want to snoop into Galway business, but wanted an opening to ask how Jason had come up with the money for such an exclusive car.

The female vocalist did a mic check and Jason watched her, mesmerized.

Kenzie glanced over her shoulder to the stage and then back to him. "You know her?"

"We've met once or twice," he said.

A story there, she thought, though she didn't pry. When Jason dragged his attention back to his food, she pulled up her courage and asked another question she'd been wrestling with recently. "Why did you move to the academy so early?"

"It was a chance to advance," he replied. "Not an easy choice, but the right one at the time."

"What made you decide to give it up to work for Grant full-time?"

"I still teach classes at the academy," Jason answered.

"You do?" Of course, she wouldn't have that sort of career option. If Murtagh won his case the PFD wouldn't risk taking her back in any capacity.

"You're a great firefighter, Kenzie," he said. "And I believe the civil suit will go your way. That said, there are plenty of other career options for you within the department and outside it. It's comes down to whether or not you *want* to look at them."

The only viable option she could see was at Stephen's ga-rage. Becoming a receptionist/mechanic didn't feel like a new career as much as it felt like hiding. And that was completely discounting Stephen's preference to keep his business limited most days to a one-man operation.

"Right now, I only want to get back to life as it was and forget Murtagh ever existed," she admitted, keeping her voice low.

Jason took a long drink of water, then reached over the bar to refill his glass. "That's understandable." His gaze drifted back to the stage and the petite vocalist with the dark, glossy hair gathered high on her head in a messy knot. "You have a good sense of self, Kenzie. If there comes a time when you need to make a change, you'll recognize it and it will feel right."

His sandwich half-eaten, he picked up his dishes and left the bar.

She finished her meal quickly. Yes, she had options. Firefighting wasn't her only career path, just the one that fitted her best. Despite the support from so many people, she didn't feel entirely whole during these days away from the firehouse. It wasn't all about missing the action of riding out to calls to the shrill music of the sirens. Her team was her family and she missed the camaraderie and unified purpose they shared.

Jason claimed she knew herself, but she wasn't so sure. Did she even have a purpose away from the PFD? The question drifted through her mind as the Escape Club filled with summer concert patrons. Soon she was too busy to think about the myriad what-ifs if the case went against her. The atmosphere was fantastic, with the music flowing over a teeming dance floor. The general lighthearted happiness was a wonderful balm after her stressful morning. And tomorrow, she worked only the night shift, so she'd be able to be at the garage all day.

Her mind on the progress she could make on her own car while enjoying the tantalizing views of Stephen working nearby, she was slow to recognize the middle-aged man standing at a high-top table at the end of her section.

She dutifully stopped to greet him as she would any other customer.

Randall Murtagh's eyes were mean as his gaze raked over

her from head to toe. "This is where you belong," he said. He wore a Hawaiian shirt splattered with obnoxious orange flowers, and loose cargo shorts that left the fresh scars from his burn visible on his calf. A complete departure from the understated charcoal suit he'd donned for his interview.

She held her body stiff when she wanted to squirm out of his view. She would not let him see her flinch or cower. "Welcome to the Escape Club," she repeated, determined to maintain her professionalism here as she had in the fire. "Would you like to hear the drink specials?"

Maybe if he had a drink or two, Grant could make sure he got pulled over once he left the club. Although if that happened, Murtagh would probably file harassment charges and pile that on to her civil suit somehow. Well, even the brief fantasy had been a nice respite.

He sneered at her. "I'll have a citywide special. Your treat, right, *honey*?"

"I'm sorry. According to club policy I can't treat you to anything but a glass of water, sir. Would you prefer water?"

"Sir." He gave a humorless chuckle and his beady eyes lit up in his fleshy face. "That sounds *good* coming out of your pretty mouth."

Kenzie barely suppressed a shiver. The way he'd said that, with his eyes on her mouth, creeped her out. She wanted to kick him and worse. It took every ounce of willpower to assure him she'd return momentarily with his order.

She managed not to break into a panicked run as she arrowed to the service end of the bar, prepared to report the situation to Grant. He was up onstage with the band. No problem. Jason could lend her a bouncer to escort her through her section until Murtagh got bored and left. She didn't want him tossed out; that would give him too much power. No, she just wanted someone to hang close so the man couldn't do anything other than toss insults at her. Although, if she asked for help, wasn't she proving Murtagh's point that she couldn't even handle a tough job as a waitress?

Logically, she knew that was baloney. Teamwork made everything work, from a busy nightclub to a three-alarm fire. He hadn't done anything more obnoxious than be himself, and if he was in here bugging her, he wasn't outside vandalizing someone's car. To cover her bases, she sent her lawyer a text message about the situation while she waited for Jason to give her the beer and shot Murtagh had ordered.

"Slow at the waitressing, too, I see," he said with a sneer when she returned.

Kenzie smiled and gave the man his drinks. "Would you like me to start a tab for you?"

"Not on my dime." He raised the shot of whiskey. "Let's consider this a good-faith marker for what you owe me."

There was no sense repeating the club policy on staff buying drinks for customers. Murtagh probably thought he could get her fired from this job, too. She started a tab, noting that the customer did not give her a credit card. Documentation would give Jason or Grant room to work if he became more belligerent or tried to leave without paying. "I'll need a credit card or permission from my manager, sir, before your second round," she said, with as much sweetness and light as she could squeeze into her voice.

Moving along, she worked through the rest of her section, clearing empties and taking new orders. As she passed him again, Murtagh caught her in a bruising grip, his hand a painful hook at her elbow. "You need to release me right now, Mr. Murtagh."

Kenzie noticed heads turning as customers nearby sensed trouble.

He jerked her back, hard enough to make her wince. "Can't you take the heat, tough girl?"

That he'd made her wince had her temper leaping into high gear. She refused to give him further satisfaction by struggling.

"This is the age of cell phones," she said with a tight smile. "If you make a scene, you undermine that woeful victim image you had going on TV this morning. Your legal team won't like that."

His fingertips dug into her skin before he let her go with a little shove. She caught her balance and walked away as quickly as possible. She gave brief reassurances to the few people who asked if she was all right. It wasn't easy to pretend the incident was nothing, but she managed. On her way back to the bar, she gave herself a mental pat on the back for not needing any help to put Murtagh in his place.

Her hands shook as she filled her tray.

Naturally, Jason noticed. "You okay?"

"I'm good." She took a deep breath, smoothing back a few strands of hair that had worked free of her braids. "You know jerks happen occasionally."

"Where?" Jason's gaze roamed through her section. She assumed spotting Murtagh was what made him swear. "How the hell did he get in?"

She shrugged. "Let him have his delusions of importance," she said. "It's not as if he can do anything to me here." Her arm would be bruised by morning, but that would be a problem for later.

"Grant would want him out of here," Jason said.

"Then tell him once he's done. It's not worth interrupting his set." She checked the orders on her tray. "He's claiming I'm buying his drinks. I've only served one round and I'll probably need some help with that issue before he leaves."

"You got it," Jason promised.

"Thanks." Coaching herself to keep calm, she picked up her tray and turned, coming face-to-face with Stephen.

She absorbed the view of him, let it ease the rough edges seeing Murtagh had caused. In dark khaki shorts and a pale blue untucked oxford shirt with the sleeves rolled back to his elbows Stephen was as tempting to her now as he was in his grease-stained work-clothes at the garage. She could tell he'd been running his hands through his hair and she almost reached up to smooth it into place.

"Hi," he said. His mouth tilted up at one side, as if his lips weren't sure about giving her a full smile or not.

"Hi." That half smile was nearly as sexy as the scowl she'd come to expect on his face. What was wrong with her?

His eyebrows dipped as he studied her face. "You're pale."

She rolled her eyes. "It's just bad lighting."

He stepped aside to let her pass. "Something happened."

"Nothing new," she replied. It wasn't exactly a lie. Murtagh had been a persistent problem in her life since the day she'd rescued him. "I wasn't expecting you," she added brightly, in an attempt to shift his focus. "How was your day?"

"Great." That underused, subtle smile made another appearance. "Which section are you in tonight?"

"I'm way out tonight," she answered. "This is a much better spot for you to enjoy the band." From this vantage point she almost couldn't see Murtagh's balding head. If Stephen sat down, he wouldn't see Murtagh, either. "I'll be back in a few minutes."

She didn't wait for a reply, eager to get the drinks delivered and get back to Stephen before this first band of the night finished. During the break there would be a flurry of people settling tabs, leaving, and new customers coming in. With luck, Murtagh would be one of them and she could enjoy the rest of her night in peace.

She purposely went the long way through her section. Deftly avoiding a difficult customer was part of doing the job well, by preventing trouble-causing opportunities. By the time she approached Murtagh, she had only a tray full of empty glassware and bottles. Pausing, she gave him the smile she saved for surly drunks. "Do you need another round, sir?" she asked, pitching her voice so he could hear her over the band.

"As long as you're buying, girl."

"That's against Escape Club policy," she reminded him

sweetly. Giving him his total for the special, she waited expectantly, her hand open to accept his cash or a credit card.

He grabbed her hand hard enough to have the bones grinding together. "One way or another, you're paying for what you did to me, little girl."

She barely suppressed the reflex to defend herself. A stomp on his instep, a kick to his knee and this would be over. That kind of negative reaction would likely play right into his hands. If she lost her temper, he would twist it to his advantage in the lawsuit.

"We do reserve the right to refuse service," she said. His grip on her hand tightened and the sharp pain brought tears to her eyes. She blinked them away, determined to hold her own. "You should leave, sir."

"If you're so damned capable of handling anything a man can do, *make* me leave." He upended her tray, smashing glassware against her body and sending the empty beer bottles to the floor.

"Allow me," a rumbling voice said from behind her.

She recognized it was Stephen a split second before his fist connected with Murtagh's jaw. The older man staggered back, releasing her hand. She shook it automatically, more concerned with stopping Stephen as he hauled Murtagh upright by his shirt and reared back to punch him again. Kenzie latched on to Stephen, holding him back as the muscles of his arms bunched and flexed, ready to dish out more punishment.

Cell phones were pointed at the scene from every angle and a few customers had pressed closer, protecting her. The expressions on the nearest faces behind Murtagh ranged from morbid curiosity to disgust. She understood the curiosity and hoped the disgust was aimed at Murtagh rather than her. The Escape Club didn't need any drama or bad publicity, and she knew her lawyer wouldn't want to give the Marburg legal team more ammunition.

A bouncer waded into the fray from his station near the door and Grant was coming from the direction of the stage, slicing through the crowd like a freighter through the water. The music skidded to a rough stop.

"Let him go," Kenzie said to Stephen. "Grant's here. He'll handle it."

Stephen stepped back, his hands raised in surrender as Grant and the bouncer took control of Murtagh.

Grant snapped orders for the mess to be cleared and Kenzie immediately got to work, but her left hand wouldn't cooperate. "Not you," Grant said, with far more gentleness than she'd ever heard. "Jason, take names and numbers of witnesses."

"On it, boss," Jason said.

"Galway, get her to the back. Take pictures first, then help her clean up."

Kenzie knelt down once more, ducking under the threats Murtagh was spewing, to pick up broken bottles and glassware. The pieces kept slipping from her grasp. The vocalist said something, a few patrons laughed and then the music flared to life. It all sounded fuzzy around the edges, as if she had cotton in her ears. What was wrong with her?

"Let the others do that," Stephen said, drawing her to her feet. He tucked her against his side, and she cradled her aching hand close to her stomach.

"But…" She noticed a trickle of blood on her arm as he guided her away from her section. If he didn't step back it was likely to stain his shirt. "Stephen…" Her voice trailed off. He wouldn't let her move away from him. "You should be careful," she murmured.

"I've got you," he said. "Lean on me."

"I'm fine." She willed it to be true. Every time she twitched a finger, pain lanced up through her arm, burning deep in her shoulder. It couldn't be unbearable pain because she was tough. "Do you know why I'm bleeding?"

Stephen swore as Kenzie swayed. Done playing around, he scooped her up and barked at people to clear a path. Though she protested, it was weak, and he didn't set her down until he reached Grant's office.

"Just sit here a second," he said. "Breathe." He took his own advice, struggling against the urge to go take another swipe at Murtagh.

"I'm fine." She stared at him, her blue eyes glassy.

"I know," he replied. "You're doing great."

Someone from the kitchen hurried in with the first aid kit and clean towels.

"Thanks," he said. "Just put it all on the desk."

Kenzie's hand was already starting to bruise. Stephen was pretty sure the jackass had broken a bone or two. Murtagh had at least a hundred pounds on Kenzie and though she was tough as nails, excessive force amplified by temper could do a great deal of damage. He swore.

"Where's your phone?" he asked her when they were alone.

Without a word, she reached for her back left pocket and winced. Stephen carefully extracted the cell phone for her. He snapped pictures with her phone and his, getting close-ups of her hand, as well as the scratches and splinters of glass piercing her skin from her collarbone to her elbow.

He did his best to keep his cool as a red haze pressed at the edges of his vision. If he ever saw Murtagh again, he wouldn't stop punching. *Later*, he told himself. Anger from any source wouldn't help Kenzie right now.

"Did he drug me?" she asked.

The idea alarmed him, but he kept his voice calm. "I doubt it."

"Then why am I so woozy?"

The question simultaneously worried and amused him. "Probably shock."

She snorted, then hissed as he started cleaning the first wounds on the delicate skin at the base of her throat.

"I can't be in shock," she said.

He supposed she'd know better than he would. "Pain, maybe?"

"No way. I'm tough."

He wished someone else with more experience was here. Some of these wounds looked deep. Surely someone on Sullivan's staff had more experience with this kind of thing. "You are tough," he agreed heartily. Would she stay tough when he started pulling out the shards of glass? Her arm looked like she'd gone a few rounds with a shattered window. "Maybe it was the sight of blood."

Her nose wrinkled as she peered at her arm. "I'm a firefighter. Blood happens."

"Uh-huh." Stephen knew some people could tolerate the sight of blood as long as it wasn't their own. Was she one of them? "Guess that leaves us with the logical conclusion that you're just a weakling."

"Am not." She tried to smack at him with her good hand and it bounced listlessly off his arm.

"Almost done," he said. "Then we'll go get an X-ray for that." And maybe stitches for the gash over her elbow, he thought, as he removed a chunk of glass and applied pressure to stem the bleeding. "Grant should call an ambulance."

"No."

He didn't think she was in any condition to decide, but he had his hands full at the moment.

Grant walked in and stopped short, the fierce expression softening as he looked at Kenzie. "How's she doing?"

"I'm fine," Kenzie replied.

"She's dazed," Grant said. "Sounds almost drunk."

"Won't argue with that." Stephen cleaned out the deepest of the wounds on her arm. "I think he might have broken her hand."

"I can hear you." Her nose crinkled again. She shifted a bit, sitting up straight. "He caught me by surprise is all."

The last part sounded a little stronger to Stephen. Pride was a powerful thing and Kenzie had plenty of it. He hoped the improvement he heard was more than just wishful thinking on his part.

"All of us," Grant said. "I'm sorry, Kenzie. He's in police custody right now and won't bother you again. I assume you'll want to press charges. We'll sort out how he got inside later."

"That's the best I can do for her." Stephen followed the trail of scrapes and bandaged cuts from her neck to her wrist. "She needs an X-ray on that hand. I'll take her over to the hospital."

Grant used his phone to take pictures of the glass fragments Stephen had removed. "This is my fault," he muttered. "I should have kept you off the floor," he said to Kenzie.

"Stop." She winced as she pushed herself out of the chair. "I'm here because the PFD benched me. What's the point of having a life if no one will let me live it?"

"Fair enough," Grant allowed.

Stephen was tempted to remind them both that she wasn't going about the general matter of living life out there. She'd been attacked and nearly passed out. Kenzie glared at him as if she knew exactly what he wasn't saying.

"We can't let a jerk like Murtagh think he can get away with that behavior," she said.

"He won't get away with it," Grant assured her. "Let me handle it from the business side. Go on and get X-rays of your hand and take tomorrow night off. The weekend if necessary."

"Tomorrow? But that's Friday night," she protested. "You need all hands on deck."

"Not yours, even if it isn't broken."

She tried to hide her injured hand behind her back, bumped it on her hip and groaned with pain. "Grant, if I don't work—"

"We'll keep you posted," Stephen said to him.

He could see the pain threatening to swamp her again and refused to waste another minute. Although he was nothing short of livid that Murtagh had orchestrated this assault and potentially caused a serious injury, he had to let Grant handle those details.

"Come on, Kenzie. You need to have that examined." He

guided her out of the office and down the hall to the break room to pick up her backpack and keys. Outside at the loaner car, he helped her into the passenger side and buckled her seat belt.

"You're treating me like a porcelain doll," she muttered, as he adjusted the driver's seat and then backed out of the parking space.

"Want me to promise it won't last?" he asked.

"Please," she said with great feeling. "If word gets out that Murtagh made me pass out, I'll never live it down at the station."

Stephen appreciated her assumption that she would eventually be back at work with the PFD. Her tenacity was one of her finest features. After this stunt he couldn't imagine a judge bothering with Murtagh's case.

"You didn't really pass out. Not completely," he said. "You could always say I overreacted, too eager to do the hero thing. They'd all believe that."

She snorted. "I won't throw you under the bus unless I have no other choice, deal?"

"Deal."

Fortunately for Kenzie, the wait at the emergency room was remarkably brief. The pain had cast a gray pallor over her skin and she couldn't seem to get comfortable in the chair. When the nurse called her name, Stephen had the irrational urge to go with her. He didn't want to let her out of his sight.

Instead, while Kenzie was back getting treatment, he paced the hallway near the waiting area, trying to make sense of the assault. He couldn't figure out why Murtagh would make such a scene in a public place. It was absolutely illogical, especially since he'd put his hands on her. On the interview this morning the former firefighter had come off as an expert victimized by Kenzie's natural limitations as a woman. It wasn't an accurate opinion, though he'd looked good delivering it. Could Murtagh just be that angry to have been rescued by a woman?

Stephen supposed it was possible. He considered calling his dad to get a better idea of the type of work Murtagh had done during his PFD career. Kenzie's lawyer might not like Stephen asking around, but a conversation with family shouldn't be a problem for her side of the lawsuit. He decided to check with Julia first, in the morning. His reputation as the family grump was bad enough already. He wouldn't make it worse by treating his sister-in-law like a legal expert on call.

What he couldn't resist was reviewing the images of Kenzie on his phone. He still had her cell phone, too, and he knew she'd want to see pictures. He didn't think it was a good idea. Not tonight, anyway. She had enough to process with the attack, pain and potential damage to her hand. As both the brother and son of firefighters, Stephen knew an injury could put her off the job, possibly forever.

Was that what Murtagh meant to accomplish with this stunt? Had he been trying to hurt Kenzie and end her career because he knew his lawsuit was weak? Stephen kicked around the theory and sent Grant a text message for a second opinion.

At last Kenzie emerged from the treatment area, her color a little better and a wan smile on her face when she spotted him. She raised her splinted hand, and he held his breath until he heard what she had to say.

"It's not broken," she said. "They gave me something for the pain and the swelling. The plan is anti-inflammatories, rest and some extra support for a few days and I should be good as new."

He smiled as an enormous weight of worry on her behalf lifted from his shoulders. "That's the best news I've heard all day." He bent his head to kiss her and caught himself just in time. They were a couple of friends, not a *couple*. "I'll, ah, go get the car."

Were they friends? he wondered as he jogged across the parking lot. Had to be, he decided. Although he didn't have many friends left since withdrawing into himself after his fiancée's death, he remembered the general concept. Friends weren't supposed to abuse the trust with inappropriate moves like kisses.

Though the woman challenged him and tempted him in turns, he could control himself.

Once he'd pulled into the patient pickup area and the nurse helped Kenzie into the car, she fumbled with the seat belt, eventually managing it on her own this time.

"I'll call Grant in the morning," she said, as he drove away from the hospital. "I'm sure I can work tomorrow night."

His first instinct was to back up Grant and tell her that wasn't an option, but he wasn't her keeper. "Is it the money?" He could spot her some cash if she needed it.

"A little," she admitted. "It's more because I'm on the schedule."

"Technically, Grant said you're not," he pointed out.

To his surprise, she laughed. "You're right. No one argues with Grant. Still, I'm going to try." She raised her splinted hand again. "I have to do something. It's not like I can do much around the garage."

She could keep him company and brighten his day with her stories and laughter, he thought. "You've got another perfectly good hand to answer phone calls," he joked.

"You're lucky they gave me something for pain," she said, chuckling. "Or I'd make you pay for slamming a glass ceiling over my head."

When they reached the garage, he helped her into the trailer and made sure she had what she needed for the night. He left her backpack on the table and hung on to her cell phone. Tomorrow was soon enough to send pictures to her lawyer.

Alone in the garage office, Stephen paced off more restless energy. Although she was safe and as comfortable as modern medicine could make her, he couldn't unwind. Murtagh's mean, glowering expression as he overpowered Kenzie kept flashing through his mind. There was no doubt that Murtagh had had a specific intention when he'd grabbed Kenzie. Stephen just couldn't be sure if it was to embarrass her or hurt her outright.

He hoped by morning Grant would have a plan to make certain something like that didn't happen again.

The office was suddenly too small. Stephen needed to get out and do something that mattered. His first instinct was to go to the community center and see if he could make life difficult for another drug dealer. He'd grabbed the keys for the car he'd loaned Kenzie before he remembered he couldn't leave her here alone. He trusted his security system, of course, but that was useless if she needed an extra hand.

He walked into the shop. There wasn't anything to do to keep his hands busy that wouldn't make a racket. Kenzie's car was mechanically sound now, despite still being an eyesore. Would she agree with his suggestion to have the little car repainted and the interior repaired for resale? He'd gone to the club on a whim and a bit of a completed-project high, hoping to ease the stress she hid so well behind that big smile. Of course, he hadn't been able to give her the news on her car or have any kind of discussion, thanks to Murtagh's nasty stunt.

Kenzie had incredible reflexes and fortitude; he'd seen it on the racetrack and around the shop. Though it had surely been the right response, it had to have been a struggle for her to stand there and let him humiliate her and hurt her that way. She was a woman used to holding her own, paving her own way.

Leaning back against the workbench, Stephen looked around his shop. He'd worked hard building this business and his reputation. He couldn't imagine a stranger coming in and forcing him out of it the way Murtagh was attempting to force Kenzie away from her career as a firefighter.

Stephen recognized it was more than a job to her. That kind of service and dedication was a calling. He'd seen the pride and commitment to community on his father's face through the years. That same gleam shone in his brother's eyes, too, as it had from day one. When Mitch had been on administrative leave, he'd been as miserable as Kenzie was now. And that was without the added pressure of a civil suit.

Stephen switched off the lights in the shop and, returning to the office, pulled a bottle of whiskey from the bottom drawer of the filing cabinet. He poured a shot and tossed it back. With luck, it would dull this edgy feeling so he could catch a few hours of decent sleep.

CHAPTER SIX

KENZIE DIDN'T MISS her phone until the next day, when she woke up to sunlight streaming through the wide window over the bed. Normally an early riser, she couldn't believe she'd slept so late.

Sitting up, she noticed the brace on her hand. The small tugs of her bandaged cuts and scrapes along her left arm brought the night back in an unpleasant rush. Better not to dwell on it any more than necessary. Once she found her phone, she'd tell her lawyer what had happened and possibly file a police report, depending on how Grant chose to handle the incident. After that, she wouldn't think about it anymore.

She set a cup of coffee to brew as she grabbed a shower and dressed in a loose peasant top that hid most of the marks Murtagh had left behind. Feeling steadier with the jolt of caffeine, she took a couple ibuprofen tablets and searched her backpack and the trailer for her phone, coming up empty.

Following the sounds of Stephen's blaring music and power tools to the garage, she hoped he had her phone. If not, she'd ask if she could use the business line to make a few calls.

The ringing phone in the office caught her attention and she picked it up before it went to voice mail. With luck it would be about the parts she needed for her car. Working on the vehicle would keep her mind off other things while she couldn't go to the club or the firehouse.

Instead the caller was asking about one of the cars Stephen had listed for sale. She handled the questions and checked the calendar she'd set up for him, arranging an appointment for the prospective buyer.

When she went out to tell him about the call, she stopped short in the office doorway, just admiring the way he moved as he worked. He had another rebuild project up on the lift and moved around it with a confident, loose-limbed grace. Her pulse did a tap dance as she enjoyed every lean inch of him packed with that hard, capable strength. And compassion, she thought, recalling the tender way he'd taken care of her last night.

He turned her way, his persistently stern expression softening with concern as his gaze swept over her.

That look had her thinking about kissing him again and doing it right this time. She tightened her abs to give the sudden swirl of butterflies less space for maneuvers.

He used a voice command to lower the volume on the music. "Did I wake you?"

"No." She smiled. "But you should have. All my alarms are on my phone. Do you have it?"

"Yes. Sorry about that." He crossed to the workbench that lined the back wall. "I kept it with me."

"Why?" she asked, joining him.

"Hold it." He held up a hand. "You'll trash your clothes in here."

"I know how to keep myself out of the grease for the span of a conversation," she replied. Though she supposed he wouldn't accept a hug while he was wearing work clothes. She'd have to save that for later. Anticipating that gave her system more of a jolt than the coffee had.

"Grant told me to take pictures," Stephen said, regret weighing down his voice. "I used both your phone and mine."

"Thanks." She was still embarrassed she'd gone woozy over

a minor altercation. "Lawsuits aside, I wish I'd fought back," she said. Playing it meek must have messed with her head and her confidence. "Grant tells us we can defend ourselves if necessary until a bouncer arrives."

"Not that simple for you," Stephen replied.

No, it wasn't. Although his understanding helped, she wished she could hit Rewind and handle last night differently.

"You did the right thing," Stephen said. "Grant called this morning to check on you and to make sure you sent the pictures to your lawyer as soon as possible." He wiped his hands clean and pulled her phone from his back pocket. "I almost did it for you. I'm not sure you should look at them."

She should feel annoyed that he'd considered taking over and yet she only appreciated this thoughtfulness more. She peeked up at him, tried to smile. "I'm feeling better, I promise." It was only a small fib. "I'll just select the right pictures and hit Send. I won't obsess over them."

"Okay." The rough pads of fingers brushed gently across her skin, leaving a trail of warmth behind as he returned her phone.

With the brace on her hand it was clumsy work sending the text message and attaching the pictures. Based on the throbbing beating through her palm to her elbow from merely getting showered and dressed, her hand wouldn't be much use for another day or two. As promised, she tucked the phone into her pocket, remembering too late to shift it to her right side rather than her left.

"Did you take a pain pill?" Stephen asked. "I left them on the nightstand for you."

She curled the tips of her fingers over the edge of the brace. "I must have overlooked that," she admitted. "I took ibuprofen instead. It's not unbearable."

He didn't appear to be convinced.

She handed him the message slip with the appointment on it. "You've got some interest in the Charger out there."

His gaze remained locked with hers. "That's great news."

"Have you heard about the progress on the Camaro?" Feeling a blush rising in her face as he studied her, she searched for another topic to distract him.

"It should be moving right along," he said. "They gave Riley the choice of restoring and repairing the original interior or going with all new seats." He rubbed at his cheek, leaving behind a smudge of dirt. "I'm not sure what he'll decide."

She wanted to reach up and wipe it away, and told her fingers to behave. They were quasi-coworkers and tentative friends. He didn't need her making another platonic move loaded with wishful thinking after being so amazing with her last night.

"Thanks for handling me and, well, all of that chaotic mess last night. Can't believe I passed out on you." The sense of utter security she'd felt in his arms would stay with her forever.

"You didn't really." His gaze drifted back to the vehicle on the lift and his mouth twitched at the corners. "Mitch backed a car over my foot once."

She grinned at his attempt to make her feel better. "Bet you didn't faint over the pain."

"No, I puked. Your way was *much* cleaner."

He was so matter-of-fact that she laughed. "I'll let you get back to..." Her voice trailed off when she saw her little rust-bucket wasn't in pieces anymore. She walked over, circling the reassembled car. This was her project, not his. She'd had it under control. "What did you do?"

"Um, yeah. About that."

Anger, mostly with herself, gaining steam, she spread her arms wide when he didn't complete the explanation. "Yes?"

"Well, that's why I went into the club last night."

And she'd been grateful for his surprise appearance. Who knew what he'd kept Murtagh from doing by charging in to help her? "I'm waiting, Stephen."

He looked to the rafters above and back to her. "I really needed to finish something."

"Was the car in your way?" There were four bays and only two were occupied right now.

"No." It was the only logical reply.

"Let me guess." She tried to fold her arms and the brace got in the way. "You didn't think I could manage the job."

"Of course not," he said. "You know what you're doing."

"Then why did you interfere?" She closed the distance between them. "It was *my* responsibility." She couldn't get her emotions under control. This was a ridiculous thing to argue over, but it had been her problem to solve. "I would've been done in a few days." Though the bum hand would have slowed her down.

"I'm sorry. Don't you ever need to see progress on something?"

"Yes." She looked back at the car. "Yes," she repeated with a weary sigh. "I understand that." Unfortunately, the car had apparently represented that tangible progress for both of them. She studied him now, the timing clicking into place. "You finished it before you came to the club."

He rolled his shoulders back, cocked his chin, daring her to react. If only she could decide whether to kiss him or smack him.

"You can take it apart and do it yourself if tightening every bolt means that much to you."

She bit back an oath. "Do I look dumb enough to undo the work of an excellent mechanic?" Two flags of color stained his cheeks at the compliment. She couldn't stay mad, not when he helped her at every turn. "I'll get it out of here and then you can finally sell the loaner car." Stalking over to the control panel, she raised the bay door.

"I was thinking maybe you'd rather sell this one." Stephen handed her the key. "My guy would give you a good rate on the paint and body work. Interiors for this car are easy to come by."

If only it was that easy. "Right idea," she admitted. "Wrong time. I don't have the disposable income to pay any kind of rate right now."

"So use my account. Pay me when you sell it."

Exasperated, she paused, half in and half out of the driver's seat. Why was he being so nice? "I pay my own way." She was already trying to figure out how many hours of office time she owed him for his labor.

"That's clear," he said. "I just thought if you invested a little now, you'd have more money in a week or two. That model and year, in working condition, will be perfect for a kid heading to college."

"Hardly your typical clientele."

"I buy and sell what I want here," he stated.

Unable to come up with any credible response to that, she got into the car and backed it out of the service bay. She couldn't line it up with the other cars that were ready for sale; it looked too pitiful with the rust-and-primer color scheme. Circling around back, she parked it along the fence, where none of his customers would have to look at it while she made up her mind about what to do next.

The car didn't sputter or rattle anymore and that shimmy in the left rear tire was gone.

She cut the engine and sat there a moment, collecting herself. He'd done more than she'd ever planned to do and now he'd given her a fair option. Minimal paint and body work would increase the resale value and make sure he got a decent return on what he'd pumped into it. Selling the car for a decent profit would go a long way to ease the financial stress she was under at the moment. And knowing Stephen, he probably had a buyer in mind already.

Did he have to do everything so well? It was petty for her to be upset with him for being a decent man. No, this was simply her overdeveloped pride rearing its ugly head. She'd been stressed out by the complaint and lawsuit, and feeling small after

Murtagh's interview, then harassment at the club. None of that gave her valid cause to be aggravated with Stephen.

Not wanting to accept help was different from not needing the assist in the first place.

Contrite, she walked back to the garage, feeling like a dork, ready to accept his offer to make the most of their invested effort, parts and time. In a rare moment, she found him watching the television, arms folded over his chest. She did a double-take when she realized the images were a cell phone video of last night's debacle at the club.

The angle, taken from over Murtagh's shoulder, showed her clearly, while hiding most of his face. Without an alternate view, Murtagh could almost claim it wasn't him hounding her at all. The audio was terrible and the expression she'd intended as professional came across the television as snarky, while a cultured male voice off-camera explained the situation for the viewers.

"It's quite clear that Miss Hughes does not handle stressful situations well," the man continued. "You'll see she does nothing to diffuse the customer's ire and allows herself to be bullied."

In the video, the tray slammed into her chest. Kenzie gasped, reliving it. "I look pathetic, just standing there like some damsel in distress." The video footage froze at that moment. Even knowing better, she could almost believe the woman on the screen was helpless.

Stephen blocked her view and turned it off. "Sorry." His gaze moved over her, leaving flickers of warmth in its wake as he tracked the resulting nicks and scrapes as if he could see through her top.

She waved off the apology. "At least now we know why he pulled that stunt."

"Your lawyer will have a plan to counter this," Stephen said.

"I hope you're right." She'd promised herself she wouldn't think about it anymore. "I'm sorry I was a twit about you doing the work for me," she said in a bold change of subject. "I like your idea of selling the car." She moved by him and into the office. "I'll go call your paint and body guy. And we'll split whatever profit we make," she said over her shoulder.

"Hang on. That's not fair."

She was done arguing. Dropping into the desk chair, she picked up the phone. When she finished making the arrangements, she found Stephen staring at her. "It is fair," she said. "You did all the labor."

"Not even close. You had a good start on it."

"What about all the parts? Answering your phone hardly evens that score."

"You'd be surprised." He scowled at the phone. "I hate that thing."

"I won't go through with your plan unless we agree to split the profit. And I mean the *profit*, not the gross from the sale," she added, anticipating his next likely maneuver.

He stalked over to the refrigerator under the counter and pulled out a bottle of water. "Fine. Write it up that way."

She swiveled the chair to follow his movements. "Why aren't you a cop or a firefighter?" Watching him, her pulse quickening, she thought he'd be a stunning addition to any fundraising calendar.

"I told you. I was too into cars to think about any other line of work."

"You've got this innate good-guy nature." And he employed it in his own way within his family and community. "Plus you're cool as a cucumber in a crisis."

His cheeks colored again. "You don't know that."

"Do too. You kept your head in the middle of my crisis last night."

He scoffed, started for the door. "I've got work to do."

Her cell phone chimed and the garage phone rang at the same time. "Me, too," she said with a big smile, letting him off the hook now that things felt steadier between them.

There were layers and layers to Stephen Galway and she had the ridiculous urge to peel back every one of them, polishing up all the rough edges along the way. Smitten, her father would have called it.

He would have been right.

Stephen worked through the remainder of the morning and into the afternoon, turning up the music so he wouldn't hear her voice in the office. Alone in the garage had always been his preference, and yet after mere days of Kenzie working alongside him, being alone out here felt wrong.

She had a way about her, smart and strong, with a sweetness under the tough exterior. He told himself to shut up. Thoughts like that led into dangerous territory. He'd get over this distraction, just like he got over everything else life tossed his way.

In the back of his mind he was assessing the new rebuild project as he dealt with the basic maintenance and repairs on the schedule. He had plenty of standard business to keep his business flush, but once he and Mitch had started with the restoration and rebuilds, Galway Automotive had swiftly earned a reputation in collector circles that had clients seeking them. It helped that they worked well together and had similar, though not identical, taste in cars.

Naturally, as soon as Kenzie drove off to take her car for paint, his concentration shattered. He didn't like her going out there without him, yet there was only so much hovering he could get away with. There had to be a way to kick this need to keep her safely within sight. Kenzie personified independence. While she was gone, he turned down the music and took advantage of her absence to give Grant another update.

"I've sent everything Jason collected from the other customers to her lawyer," Grant was saying. "You're sure she's feeling all right?"

"Seems to be." Stephen checked the clock. "Won't take the heavy painkillers." If she wasn't back in fifteen minutes, he'd call her cell and make sure she was okay.

"She's tough," Grant said. "Try to encourage her to rest."

Stephen gave a snort. "You've met Kenzie, right?"

"*Try*," Grant emphasized. "It's all any of us can do."

True. "I can't believe Murtagh's lawyers found a way to twist his assault on her in his favor." Although when it came to the Marburg firm, Stephen trusted only Julia to play fair.

Grant was equally displeased and baffled by the tactic. "I've reached out to a few reporters I know, making it clear she was following company policy."

"Won't matter much if they like his version better," Stephen pointed out. The unfairness of that had him hefting a socket wrench, wishing he could hold off every possible threat or danger to her.

"I'm not giving in. The man assaulted an employee," Grant said. "By the way, I've texted Kenzie her new schedule. She's off until Tuesday. That gives her recovery time for the hand and her deposition on Monday afternoon."

Stephen rubbed his temples, feeling the headache brewing. "You know, I really didn't need the extra challenge right now," he said.

Grant chuckled. "I believe you're up to it. Keep me in the loop and I'll do the same."

The call ended, Stephen stood in the quiet solitude of the garage, unable to focus. What was taking her so long? Ten more minutes and he'd call her.

Hearing a bigger engine idling nearby, he walked out to see a media van parked at the curb across the street. Apparently they'd discovered she was staying here. No big surprise. The Marburg law firm was familiar with Stephen. He'd made no secret of how he felt when they'd successfully defended Annabeth's killer. They probably recognized him immediately from the altercation at the club. He assumed Murtagh's legal team had given Kenzie's location to the media just to keep tightening the screws on her.

A low-slung, foreign street-racing car with a neon paint scheme and more power than anyone needed in the city rolled to a stop just outside the gate. Joey Garcia, owner of the shop Stephen preferred for the paint and interior details, was behind the wheel. He gave Stephen a wave as Kenzie hopped out of the passenger side, carrying a big brown paper bag. He waved back and pressed the button on the fob in his pocket to close the gate behind her, giving her as much shelter as possible from the media van.

"I brought lunch," she called as she walked up. "Better late than never, right?"

"Right." A good rule when applied to lunch. He opened the office door for her and failed in his gallant effort to ignore the tempting sway of her hips. The woman had legs that commanded attention.

She caught him scowling and raised an eyebrow. "What happened now?"

"You didn't see the news van out there?" he asked.

"I did," she replied. "I'm not sure it's wise to look like I'm hiding out."

"It is," he replied. "What's for lunch?" No point dwelling on what they couldn't change.

"I picked up your favorite." She held up a bag with the logo of a nearby sandwich shop.

How did she know his favorite?

She opened the bag and the rich aroma of a meatball sub filled the room. His stomach rumbled and she grinned. "It was the least I could do after getting mad over nothing."

With that expression on her face, he was suddenly hungry for more than the sandwich. He pulled himself together. She trusted him as a friend. He would not wreck that. "How did you convince Joey to stop for food?" he asked.

"I bought his lunch, too."

"Really? That guy never stops moving long enough to eat."

"Like someone else I know," she said with a grin. "He ordered enough to feed the whole shop," she said, "though he was the only one in sight when I dropped off my car."

Stephen shook his head in disbelief, digging into his sandwich while she pulled out an enormous chopped salad. "Did he give you a good price?"

"He gave me the same rate he gives you for the painting. Said he couldn't be sure about the body work until he had a better look at the rust damage."

"No rust on the frame," Stephen said. "It shouldn't be too bad."

She nodded, picking at her salad, but not really eating. He wondered if the pain was making her queasy. He'd keep an eye on her. There was a quart of his mom's chicken soup in the freezer. She'd brought it over when he'd had a cold around Easter.

"We chose a hot pink color scheme," Kenzie said.

Stephen choked on a bite of his sandwich, washed it away with some water. "Hot pink?"

"I knew it." She aimed her fork at him. "You already have a buyer in mind."

"Not anymore," he muttered.

"Stephen, I've been managing my life for over a decade now. I don't need you to stack the deck for me."

Someone should. She deserved better than what she'd been dealing with on her own lately. Better than the firestorm ahead of her if Marburg continued to work the media in favor of their client.

"Say *something*," she urged. "You know you want to."

That ornery sparkle in her big blue eyes made him want to say plenty, and not much of it had to do with cars and paint, or the civil suit. He wanted to make her promises to hold her close and keep her safe and happy. Promises he had no business making.

"If it is hot pink, I'll have to check with Mom about some better local prospects."

"I should have expected that unflappable calm to prevail."

She rolled her eyes. "There are moments when teasing you is no fun," she said, with a ghost of a smile on her generous lips.

It made him want to smile back. "So what color did you go with?"

"A neutral, medium-gray with enough metallic to keep it shy of boring," she replied.

"Easy-care color."

She agreed with a quick bob of her chin. "A factor I thought would hold great appeal for a college-bound kid."

"How long until it's ready?"

"I believe the direct quote from Joey was 'a week or so'."

"Sounds about right," he said. The conversation had veered back to the Charger and the new rebuild on the lift when someone buzzed the gate for entrance.

"New client?" he asked, pointing to the desk calendar under her salad.

"Not one I scheduled," she said.

Together they studied the luxurious, German-built black sedan through the monitor. Stephen didn't have a good feeling about it, but he opened the gate, anyway. The car rolled inside with little more than a murmur and stopped in front of the office door. A man emerged from the driver's side, his silver hair trimmed perfectly and his tailored, charcoal suit flawless. Despite the heat, he appeared as cool and immovable as an iceberg. Stephen could spot a Marburg attorney from a mile away and this one was carrying a slim leather briefcase.

He was here to offer her some sort of deal. Stephen had watched plenty of legal maneuvering during the trial for Annabeth's killer. Unlike the lawyers working with evidence to convict or clear a defendant, those cutting deals never carried an excess of paperwork.

"Miss Hughes, I'm Lance Webster. May I speak with you a moment?"

"You're with Marburg," Stephen interjected. "Her lawyer

should be present at any meeting." Turning to Kenzie, he said, "Call him right now. Use the office phone."

She ignored him, pulling out her cell and entering the number.

"This is a civil case, Mr. Galway. Although you're not *currently* involved, it's my pleasure to inform you Mr. Murtagh is considering filing assault charges against you."

"Oh, I look forward to it," Stephen said.

Kenzie stepped between them, her braced hand on his chest and her cell phone to her ear. "He doesn't mean that."

"Yes, I do." He glared at Webster. "I was protecting her from an assault. I'm confident most witnesses, and a jury if necessary, will see it my way once they have access to accurate footage of the incident." He drew her back just enough to make his point clear to the Marburg puppet. She was under his protection and this was his property. "If you want to talk to Miss Hughes, you'll have to set an appointment when her lawyer can be present," he said. "Please leave."

"We don't enjoy theatrics, Miss Hughes," Webster said. "Your attorney was informed of when and where we wanted to meet today."

"You invented theatrics," Stephen retorted, unable to contain the outburst.

Kenzie was staring at her phone. "He's not answering." She swiped up and down her call history. "There's no message from him, either."

"Guess you'll have to reschedule," Stephen said to Webster. "I recommend the next appointment take place at an office rather than my place of business."

Just when he thought he'd won this round for her, a car pulled in through the gate, stopping beside the black sedan with a brief squeal of the tires. Also a German sedan, this one was older and a deep red, but had clearly been well maintained.

"That's Paul, my lawyer." Kenzie rushed forward as a younger man scrambled out of his car without his suit jacket. His short dark hair and an elegant circle beard framed his dark complexion. Stephen relaxed when he noticed the temper banked in the man's deep brown eyes.

Stephen was close enough to Webster to catch the man's muttered curse. "Problem?" he challenged.

Webster ignored him.

"This is Paul Corrigan," Kenzie said.

Her lawyer extended a hand to greet Stephen and paid no attention to Webster. Stephen liked him already.

"Could we take this into the office?" Paul tipped his head to the street, where another media van had joined the first.

Though it aggravated him immensely to play host to anyone from Marburg besides Julia, Stephen led everyone into the office. The only benefit would be fewer witnesses if he decided to deck Webster.

"I don't believe you need to be here, Mr. Galway," the Marburg attorney said.

"On the contrary, you threatened me with an assault complaint. I'll stay."

Paul bristled. "For last night? Oh, that is rich."

Webster simply plowed forward with his agenda. "I'm offering your client a settlement. Mr. Murtagh isn't without compassion for her predicament. He is willing to drop the lawsuit if she voluntarily resigns from the PFD."

"No deal," Kenzie snapped.

Stephen nearly gave her a high five for stubbornness.

"The evidence is mounting, Miss Hughes. We can make it clear you are physically and emotionally incapable of doing your job," Webster continued. "You're a liability to the PFD and a risk to the greater community if you remain in your position. It's only a matter of time before someone gets hurt."

"Tossing around threats like confetti." Paul shook his head as if the development disappointed him. "The judge will love this."

"I'm tossing out facts, Mr. Corrigan. You can't argue with the video we have showing your client freezes in a crisis."

"There's more than one angle," Stephen began. "She didn't freeze, you son of a—"

"This case isn't a popularity contest or a publicity exercise," Paul interrupted. "I don't believe this is an offer you make unless you see the writing on the wall as well as I do. Your client's bizarre attempt to intimidate my client has put your case in jeopardy."

Stephen liked Kenzie's lawyer more with every minute.

Webster shifted his snooty gaze to Kenzie. "This settlement gives you a gracious exit from a difficult situation. Our client is only asking you to pay his legal fees. If our case moves forward the judgment against you will be financially devastating with legal fees, medical expenses, and pain and suffering factored in. And you'll still be out of work."

"He's bluffing," Paul said to Kenzie. "Don't give this a single thought."

Stephen agreed, though he managed to keep the opinion to himself.

The Marburg attorney handed over the documentation to Paul. "Our offer in full detail," he said. "It will remain open until the depositions begin."

He turned on his heel and left.

Stephen, Kenzie and Paul waited in a tense silence until the sleek black car backed out of the yard and drove out of sight.

"I'll let you two talk," Stephen said. He wanted to go pound something into dust. Dismantling the new rebuild would have to suffice.

"Wait." Kenzie caught his hand as he stalked by. "Stay, please?"

He jerked his chin in a quick affirmative, letting her lace her slender fingers through his.

Paul read through the settlement for them. It was remarkably brief, considering who had delivered it.

Kenzie groaned at the stated legal fees. "It would take me years to pay that off at my firefighter pay. As a waitress? Not a chance." She rolled her eyes. "And that doesn't even count what I'd owe you."

"Everything is negotiable," Paul reminded her.

"Not her career," Stephen stated. She squeezed his hand. "You both know she didn't do anything wrong. The PFD investigation cleared her when the initial complaint came in. You need to focus on why Marburg is trying to force a settlement now."

"My office has been fielding calls all day," Paul said. "Marburg controls the story in the public right now. If you'd give an interview we could—"

"What about the gag order?" she asked.

"No luck there," he admitted.

"I still won't do it," Kenzie said. "You said yourself it's not a popularity contest. The PFD cleared me. Pandering to the public isn't the answer to his harassment. I won't sink to Murtagh's level like we're trapped in some twisted reality television show. If I shared all the details of his rescue now, it would sound like I'm shaming the victim."

Knowing she was right didn't make hearing it any easier. "Let Grant work the media and counter Marburg's account of last night," Stephen suggested.

"What's that?" Paul asked.

"Grant Sullivan owns the Escape Club," Kenzie explained. "He told me he sent the other eyewitness videos of the altercation to you. He has friends in the media."

"My assistant is working through it," Paul said.

Kenzie narrowed her gaze at Stephen. "When did you talk to Grant?"

"You were picking up lunch," he replied. To Paul he added, "As the club owner he can explain her response and lack of reaction better than she can."

"Good, good. So unless you're interested in this sorry excuse for a settlement, I'll move forward with deposition prep."

Although that should have reassured her, Kenzie continued to cling to Stephen's hand and he felt the subtle tremble in her grasp. He stroked her finger with his thumb, trying to reassure her. "It will work out," he said.

"He lied in his initial complaint to the PFD," she said absently, as if that detail was the only thing in her favor. "They discovered it, of course, but they didn't pursue it according to the law, as a courtesy."

He knew she had plenty of valid reasons to be concerned, yet she was in the right and Murtagh was being a complete jerk with the civil case. "Marburg attorneys will sink as low as they need to in order to win a case," Stephen grumbled. At her long look, he added, "With a singular exception."

Her lips twitched, tempting him to steal another kiss.

Her lawyer rolled up the offer and tapped it against the desk. "Despite the lousy press and the blustering Webster, your case is solid, Kenzie. We'll get through this."

"Thanks, Paul."

She escorted the lawyer to his car and Stephen returned to the work waiting for him in the shop. He watched Kenzie reenter the office, thinking she looked as if the weight of the world rested on her shoulders. Her dejected expression was all wrong, muting her normally friendly sparkle and tugging at her lovely mouth. It was outrageous that such a good person had to go through this kind of crap. Quips and platitudes about life and lemons, hardship and strength were useless to someone in the middle of the storm.

He stalked into the office. "You have this under control."

"Thank you." She curled forward, resting her head on her folded arms on the desktop. "I don't think my life has ever been this out of control."

He thought about the inventory in the yard and the two open bays in the shop. "Come with me."

"Where?"

He motioned for her to get up and follow him as he went out to the yard. "Choose one," he said, when she came to a stop beside him, surveying the worn and shabby cars he and Mitch had picked up at the last auction.

"What?"

"You heard me." He tucked his thumbs into his back pockets and waited.

"I heard you, but you're not making any sense," she replied. "Choose a car for what?"

"When we buy cars, Mitch and I do an initial inspection and create a basic plan and parts list. It's tucked in the driver's side visor. Go through the inventory here and choose the one you want to work on." He started back to the shop.

"Seriously?"

He turned at the sharp tone and found himself on the business end of her annoyed gaze. "What did I say? You know this is what we do."

She waved the hand with the brace. "I'm not much use here."

"That's temporary." He stared her down. This was supposed to make her happy, and if happy was too much at the moment, he'd thought it would provide a good distraction. "Once you choose, you can move the car inside, take a closer look at it and get the parts ordered so we're ready to go when that brace comes off."

She made a noise in her the back of her throat. "Stephen, come on."

"Would you rather I started some fires so you can put them out?"

She sucked in a breath, her eyes blazing, and then she laughed, the sound rolling over him in waves that drained away all the tension of the past hour.

"I'm sorry." She walked up to him and wrapped her arms around his waist. "I'm being an idiot."

He didn't know what to do with his hands. He knew what he wanted to do. Stroking a palm over her braided hair and following her subtle curves from shoulder to hip probably wasn't the right move between friends. He settled for awkwardly patting her shoulder.

"Thank you." She gave him a little squeeze and stepped back. "For last night and for today. And for rebuilding my car."

"You had that under control," he said. A little grime from his shirt had transferred to hers. Hopefully, when she saw it, she'd remember she'd hugged him. "I just..." Just what? Trying to find a better explanation would only raise more questions about his feelings and intentions. He wasn't ready to face those answers.

"I'll let you get back to work," she said, moving toward the row of cars.

"Would it help to get out of here?" The fence blocked the nosy media, but as she'd said, she wasn't the type to hide from anything. "Later tonight."

She turned back, curiosity dancing in her vivid blue eyes. "What do you have in mind?"

"There's a drive-in theater. If you're up for a short road trip."

"What's showing?" she asked.

He had no idea. "Does it matter?" It would be a complete change of pace for both of them, with a pleasant, relaxing drive on either end of it.

"Not at all." The grin on her face lit her up from head to toe. There, that was the energetic, conquer-the-world Kenzie he'd met last week.

Telling himself he hadn't just asked her out on a date, he went back to the shop to wrap up the one brake job he had left on the day's schedule.

CHAPTER SEVEN

THE REST OF the afternoon flew by and Kenzie knew it was all because Stephen had put her back on even footing and given her a much-needed distraction. He really was a good guy under the gruff attitude. Of course, he was a Galway, and she suspected it might be in the DNA Mr. and Mrs. Galway had passed down to their kids.

She found herself able to concentrate on the details of supporting the garage and feeling useful in the process. After a long debate of the choices, she'd chosen to work on the 1966 Chevy Nova. Not her favorite of the classic muscle cars, but according to the paperwork, it was a relatively straightforward build. Though she'd been tempted by a Mustang fastback out there, knowing those were a favorite of Mitch's she'd steered clear of it.

When she'd pulled the Nova into the bay, Stephen had arched an eyebrow, then resumed his own work, making her wonder what he thought of her choice. Between calls for service appointments next week, she started searching for parts and pricing out what she thought it would take to restore the Nova. The time line could drag out and she wondered if Stephen would let her come by and stay involved on the project even after she returned to the PFD.

She *would* return to the PFD.

The scents and sounds of a working garage soothed her more than she expected, even though she wasn't out in the middle of it. There was comfort in this environment as memories of time with her father rolled through her mind.

She hadn't anticipated staying here on Stephen's property or leaning on him this way. She was so grateful for how he made her feel included and valued during this ordeal. The idea of going through the ups and downs of the civil suit, of dealing with Murtagh's antics while crashing in some anonymous motel room alone would have been overwhelming. Every time her lawyer mentioned working through the systems and processes she wanted to scream.

If she'd faced the Marburg attorney's intimidation on her own, she might have caved to the pressure, or said something that would have made her lawyer's job more difficult. Stephen had been a real friend, a steady, unflappable support when she'd most needed it.

She booked a few more appointments for the next week, all basic maintenance she could help with as her hand healed. Anything to keep herself busy next week as Paul dealt with the depositions.

Thinking about the evening ahead at the drive-in sent her mind back down memory lane. When she and her sister were little, their mother would pack sandwiches and their favorite junk food and cookies. To re-create that, Kenzie would need to make a grocery run. She glanced at the monitor that gave a view of the two media teams outside the gate. The idea of venturing out there beyond the privacy and security of Galway Automotive made her heart stutter. Who would have guessed reporters would mark the limit of her courage? She just couldn't bring herself to do it. Not today.

Though she was well aware tonight's outing wasn't a real date, she wanted to do something nice for him, as well. When he'd offered to help her last week, he couldn't have known she'd be this much trouble. Right now, all she could give back were little gestures. Calling one of Stephen's favorite delis, she placed an order for delivery and hid the food that arrived in the camper until they were ready to leave. Once she was back in her apartment, or back on shift where she had access to the firehouse kitchen, she would whip up something homemade.

He delivered the last car and closed the gate behind another happy customer. She vacated the office so he could clean up, and when he knocked on the camper door, she had to stomp out all the tingles of desire that went rushing through her system. The casual cargo shorts and graphic T-shirt emblazoned with a vintage Camaro emphasized the lean build honed by long hours of work.

"You ready?"

She nodded, not trusting her voice. Grabbing the cooler and tote she'd packed, she followed him outside and stopped short.

He was standing in front of a gorgeous convertible roadster in a gleaming midnight blue with a stunning white interior.

"Holy cow," she murmured. She was almost scared to put the cooler anywhere near it.

"I took my time with it," he said.

There was a story behind this restoration. She could see it in the wary, defensive glint in his eyes. "I can tell. It's beautiful." She wished he felt as safe with her as she did with him, just so she could hear the full story.

He took the cooler and tote from her, securing both behind the driver's seat. "I'd planned to pick up dinner for us on the way," he said.

"I was feeling nostalgic." She shrugged. "My mom always did this when we were kids."

He nodded in understanding as a faint smile toyed with his lips. "Mine, too."

"Think they'll follow us?" She tipped her head toward the media gathered outside the gate.

"Only until we lose them," he replied. "I made a dinner reservation for us down on Market Street. It will be easy to sneak away unseen."

His plan worked like a charm and the weather was beautiful as they left the city, the wind cool and swift, preventing conversation. The silence was fine with her. Her mind blanked as Stephen drove, and the tightness that had locked up her shoulders since the Marburg attorney's visit finally eased.

The drive-in was at about half capacity when they arrived. The marquis showed a double feature of two high-action blockbusters of summers past. Stephen found a great spot for them, middle of the row toward the front. He popped the trunk and pulled out a blanket to protect the pristine upholstery.

"I have a philosophical question for you," she said, unpacking the picnic of slider sandwiches, juicy peaches and junk food. "Can you watch a movie without popcorn?"

"Not at a theater," he said.

She blotted the corner of her mouth with a napkin, swallowing quickly. "Me, neither. I've never figured out how they make movie popcorn so addictive."

His lips twitched. "We'll get stocked up before the first movie."

"You're a good man, Mr. Galway."

His eyebrows dipped low, but didn't linger in a frown. She counted it progress, though why she felt it was her job to help him lighten up was beyond her.

They chatted about their favorite movie genres until the previews started and Stephen made a run for soft drinks and popcorn.

"Thanks for this," she said at the end of the first feature. "You were right about getting away from everything. It helps."

"I'm glad," he replied cautiously. "I try to get out here at least once a summer."

"Really?"

"Drive-in movies and summer go together."

She agreed, thinking back to long summer days of watching her dad race and late nights watching movies from the family car, giggling with her sister as they kept each other awake. As people milled about between features, she caught plenty of appreciative looks and murmurs as they passed the car.

"If you wanted to sell this one, you could probably manage it tonight."

"People make offers every time I take it out," he said. "This one will stay with me."

He didn't have to spell out his reasons for her to understand the sentiment. "Some cars are special," she said, twisting around to pull another bottle of water from the cooler.

"You get it." He sounded startled.

"Have you forgotten I was raised by a car-crazed man masquerading as a firefighter?" Perched as she was between the seats, she was close enough to catch him eyeing her legs. The pure male interest made her grateful for the great bone structure from her mom's side and the perfect fit of her favorite cutoffs.

"Not a chance. I've seen you work."

The compliment made her blush as she dropped back into the seat. "Why don't you hire full-time help?"

"I prefer the quiet."

She laughed at that, could hardly catch her breath long enough to explain, "Your heavy metal work music is a noise violation."

His mouth broke free of the habitual, stoic mold and the resulting grin was spectacular. She wanted to see more of that open, happy expression.

"Thanks for making me laugh during the worst week of my life," she said, a little breathless. "I truly appreciate everything."

"You're welcome." That sexy grin faded back to serious determination. "Marburg is known to use some nasty tactics to blur the facts, but I can't see them winning this case. Don't let their antics get to you."

She was moved, and inordinately pleased, by his support and belief in a positive outcome. He'd seen Marburg in action, when justice for his fiancée was on the line. "I hope you're right," she said with feeling. "I have other skills, but I already miss the firehouse and everyone there."

He reached over and opened the water bottle, his hand covering hers in the process. It seemed her entire body zeroed in on the sensations of the cool plastic under her palm and the heat of his hand on hers.

Suddenly, he sat back, taking that tender heat with him. "I bought this car for Annabeth a week before she died," he said. "Restoring it for her was supposed to be a wedding present. I finished it before what should have been our first anniversary."

The sorrow in his revelation gripped her heart like a vise. "She would've loved this," Kenzie said.

"I want to believe that." Stephen dropped his head back against the seat, gazing up at the sky. "Believe it. She loved you." Kenzie ran a hand over the beautiful finish on the dash, a safer move than touching him. "This is clearly the work of a man who put his heart into every inch of the restoration."

"I couldn't let it go." He raked his fingers through his hair and swallowed hard.

The previews for the second feature started, ending the conversation too soon for Kenzie. It seemed to her he wanted to talk about Annabeth, that he needed to do so. She vaguely recalled the general news reports about Annabeth's murder. Through Mitch she knew how deep the family concern for Stephen went.

It dawned on her as they watched the action on the screen that once more, inadvertently, she was doing as Grant requested and keeping Stephen away from the community center he typically haunted. Well, if some good came from the stupid civil suit and her interruption of Stephen's routine, then she'd call it a silver lining and be thankful.

When the second feature ended and they were on the road again, Kenzie contentedly watched the stars wheeling overhead. The roadster hugged the pavement and she wished they could keep going. It would be delightful to drive all night and wake up in a place without Stephen's traumatic past and her frustrating present. She wondered who they might be together without the baggage.

She braced herself as they neared the neighborhood, immensely pleased to find the media crews hadn't returned to their posts in front of the garage. "Thanks for a great night," she said, coming around the convertible for the tote and cooler moments later.

Stephen already had both in hand. "You get the door," he said.

She did, holding it for him as he walked in ahead of her and set the items on the table.

"This was fun," he said, tucking his hands into his pockets.

It seemed as if the admission made him uncomfortable. "It was precisely the distraction I needed," she said. "I owe you one."

"Not at all." He waved it off. "You need anything before I go?" he asked, with a pointed glance at the brace on her hand.

"No, thank you." She had to get a handle on this weird blend of affection and lust surging through her. It was probably a combination of proximity and loneliness. Everything about him turned her on, from the way he drove to the rare grins to the reluctant, rusty laughter. He had integrity, and he was a great guy whether or not he was scowling. She admired his clear view of what he wanted out of life and the way he worked to make it happen.

His chest swelled on a deep breath. "You really think Annabeth would've liked the car?"

The hope in his eyes made hers sting with tears she couldn't let him see. "I'm sure of it," she said with a smile.

"I felt cheated when she was killed." His voice was barely more than a whisper, but the grief in those words was an agonized shout. "Life just...stopped."

She'd experienced that same timeless pain. "It was like that when my dad died. There's life before and a yawning emptiness after." One day he was fine, the next the doctors gave him six months to live. As a family, they'd followed his courageous lead and made the most of every minute he had left. It had never felt like enough.

"How?"

"Cancer," she said. "He died five months after the diagnosis. No matter how it happens, I don't think we ever have enough time with the people we love most."

"But your laugh..." His voice trailed off, the corners of his mouth tightening around the emotion he held in check.

"I feel my dad with me when I laugh," she admitted. "Humor was his way of coping with everything." She wanted to give Stephen hope that he'd start living again when he was ready. "We all get through grief in our own way and at our own pace."

Stephen reached out and tucked a loose strand of hair behind her ear, his hand curling around the nape of her neck. Slowly, he drew her close, his hazel eyes warm and golden as he bent his head to touch his lips to hers.

Firm, warm, knowing, the arousing sensations of the kiss flowed all the way through her body. The rough texture of calluses on his palms, the summer-night scent of his skin, the hot, rich taste of his tongue stroking across hers. Her brace bumped clumsily into his shoulder and he tucked it close to his side. The fingers of her good hand found the thick softness of his hair as his strong arms circled her and brought her body flush to his. They kissed and explored until simply breathing became an erotic maneuver as her breasts rubbed along the hard planes of his chest.

"Kenzie." He whispered her name against her throat, his big hands flexing into her hips. His breathing ragged, he rested his forehead to hers. "I need to go."

"Okay." Indulging the urge, she traced the carved outline of his forearms as she pulled away from him.

He lifted his head and stepped back. "Mom will be expecting both of us again for dinner tomorrow." The familiar scowl shaded his gorgeous eyes. "I don't have a believable excuse for either of us to get out of it."

"It's fine," she said with a smile. He looked miserable. Once more she imagined the joy of driving away into the night, with him, toward a fresh start. "I'll be ready on time."

"That's not all."

She waited.

He shifted restlessly. "Can we make sure they don't think there's something here?" he asked, wagging a finger between them.

After that kiss? "Of course." She'd pulled panicked victims from fires and accident scenes. Surely she could project calm, platonic vibes for the duration of a family meal.

"I don't mean to offend y—"

"We're friends, Stephen," she said, cutting off whatever he was trying to say. In her experience friends didn't kiss with that much pent-up passion and she refused to beg him for something he clearly wasn't ready to give. "Don't worry about it."

His scowl deepened, though he seemed satisfied with her reply as he said good-night and walked out.

In bed, Kenzie tossed and turned. His mother and sisters would pounce on the smallest flicker of a personal attachment between her and Stephen. The real worry was making sure his family didn't pick up on her receptiveness to the idea. She was crushing on a man who wasn't ready for anything more than friendship.

Making matters worse, she couldn't get clear on her motives. Was she just vulnerable and he was convenient or had she stumbled over the right guy at the wrong time? Stephen seemed rooted to the idea that his one chance at a long-term relationship had come and gone.

She pressed her face into the pillow, muffling a howl of frustration. Unfortunately, that hot, unforgettable embrace had to be the end of it, despite the alluring potential of trying to change his mind.

* * *

The next afternoon, Kenzie stepped out of the trailer with that generous, friendly smile and Stephen discovered he'd worried all night for no reason. She didn't seem the least bit aggravated or awkward with him, and there was no hint of that exquisite heat he'd felt pulsing between them last night. He told himself he was grateful for her understanding. Getting in too deep would only hurt them both when he couldn't live up to her expectations.

He ignored the niggling voice in his head that pointed out he didn't *know* her expectations. What he knew was that he wasn't cut out for another relationship. He was too hung up on Annabeth.

Dinner with his family was only a slightly smaller affair than last week, since his brother Andrew and his family were out of town on vacation. Like last week and most Sunday dinners, the conversation had meandered around and through a variety of topics, and Stephen had listened, letting the familiar patterns soothe him.

"Did you see the news last night?" Samuel asked Stephen after dessert had been cleared away. Only Stephen, Mitch and their father remained at the table. Everyone else had wandered off to other interests, ranging from cleanup to the swing set out in the backyard. Stephen could just catch a glimpse of Kenzie's bright hair in the kitchen as she dried dishes for his mom. Not that he was keeping track of her.

"Trying to avoid it," he replied, thinking of yesterday's media crews. He and Kenzie had tacitly agreed to let others keep tabs on the media coverage and opinions. It just wasn't worth the frustration. Neither her lawyer nor Grant would let her walk into anything unprepared. Catching the meaningful glance between his brother and father, he had to ask. "What did I miss?"

"There was another shooting at the community center," Mitch supplied.

Stephen swallowed the colorful oath on the tip of his tongue.

"What happened?" If he hadn't been out with Kenzie could he have been there to stop it? His heart hammered against his rib cage. "Did anyone from the community center get hurt?"

"No," Samuel assured him quickly. "The police said a drug deal went awry between dealer and customer. Shots were fired," he continued. "Only one dead, the suspected dealer was wounded, and the cops scooped up everyone in the area."

"The street's clean?" Stephen hoped his interest wasn't too obvious.

"For the moment it seems to be," Mitch said. "I heard through the grapevine that they've had a slew of anonymous tips in recent months that helped them identify the key players." He gave Stephen a long look.

If his brother expected him to admit that he'd been sending in those tips, he was out of his mind. "Good news all around." Stephen relaxed, inwardly pleased that something he'd done out there had gone right. It wouldn't bring back Annabeth, but it eased the guilt plaguing him.

From the kitchen, he heard Kenzie's laughter and then one of his nephews squealed. The back door creaked open and slapped shut again.

"How is she doing?" Mitch asked.

"The hand is improving rapidly," Stephen replied. Over dinner Kenzie didn't share the news about the visit from Murtagh's snooty attorney, so he didn't share that information, either. "She probably won't need the brace for more than another day or two."

"That wasn't what I meant," Mitch said. "Depositions start tomorrow."

Of course Mitch would know that through Julia, if not the PFD pipeline. "She'll get through it," Stephen said with confidence. "Her lawyer impressed me."

"When did you meet him?" Mitch asked.

"He stopped by yesterday," Stephen replied. "After that bad-angle footage from the club hit the news."

"The story Murtagh is trying to peddle is ridiculous," Samuel said. "I'd love to have about fifteen minutes alone with him."

"You think that would help?" Stephen asked.

Samuel muttered an oath. "No, he's too bitter and too willing to blame his problems on others."

"I know you hate having Kenzie underfoot," Mitch said. "You're doing a good thing for her. Staying alone at a hotel or something would've been too risky in my opinion. She doesn't like to admit it, but she needs the support of good friends right now."

Stephen didn't bother replying. If he claimed it was no trouble lending his trailer home to Kenzie, his dad and brother wouldn't believe him. If he grumbled about it that would open a door for one or both of them to lecture him about being too much of a loner. He suspected one of the reasons Mitch hadn't been around the shop as much lately was because he hoped some attraction or romance would develop.

The attraction was there, all right. Just the memory of that kiss sent a hot zing along Stephen's skin. Flirting and romance had never been his strong suit. Kenzie might be open to a light-hearted fling, if he could find a way to fight off the persistent guilt of the idea.

Switching the subject to cars, he gave them an update on the Riley project and told them he had an appointment with a potential buyer for the Charger. It was enough to keep the conversation on safe ground until Kenzie was ready to leave.

"Annabeth would want you to be happy," Samuel murmured, when he pulled Stephen in for a goodbye hug at the door.

"Dad." Stephen shook his head. This wasn't what he needed at all. Annabeth had been everything to him and their plans had been his whole world. Without her he couldn't seem to find his way in anything other than business.

He knew his parents and siblings were frustrated with his unwillingness to move on. Stephen didn't know how he could love one woman with every fiber of his being and then be fair to either her memory or another woman in a new relationship. Losing Annabeth had extinguished something inside him and he wasn't interested in setting himself up for that kind of sorrow again. It would break him.

"If we can do anything to help after the depositions, say the word." His mother pushed a basket of leftovers into his hands.

"This is too much, Mom."

"Not for two and not with stressful days ahead," she countered with a serene smile.

No point in arguing. His family was determined to read more into his hospitality toward Kenzie than necessary. "Got it." When Kenzie went back to her life, they'd understand that alone was how he intended to remain.

Back at the garage, he changed clothes and went into the shop to work, in an effort to keep his mind and hands off the woman living in his trailer. He didn't see her until he walked into the office after his appointment with the potential buyer.

She sent him that gorgeous smile. "Any luck?"

"We might have a deal," Stephen said. "He's thinking it over."

"Is it a money issue or a wife issue?"

Neither concern had crossed his mind. "Does it matter?"

"Only if you want to close the deal," she said, her gaze returning to the computer monitor.

He shrugged. "Everything okay?"

"Yes," she replied absently. "Just tracking down parts for the Nova."

He went to the refrigerator, inexplicably reluctant to leave. "How is the hand feeling?"

"Better." She wiggled the tips of her fingers. "I haven't decided if I should wear the brace for tomorrow's depositions."

Stephen couldn't think of a good reason to leave it off and waited for her to elaborate.

"Is it a sign of my 'frailty' if I wear it or is it a reminder that Murtagh's a jerk?"

"Reminder," he answered immediately. "The man attacked

you in a place of business. Wear it and make sure everyone knows why you're wearing it."

She frowned. "You're probably right," she said, twining the end of her braid around her finger.

He had a sudden urge to see how her hair would look if she left it down. "How do you braid your hair with only one hand?"

She did a double take and then laughed, the sound instantly brightening her face and the entire office. "Practice," she teased. "Seriously, they told me I could leave the brace off to shower and all that."

An image of her in the shower filled his mind, pushing out all other coherent thoughts about cars or parts. Crap. He wasn't as immune to her as he wanted to be. *Needed* to be. His hormones had picked the wrong time to come back online. He couldn't let himself abuse her generous spirit just because she was nearby.

"I'll, ah, just get back out there. Let me know if the guy calls back about the Charger."

"Sure thing," she replied.

Somehow Stephen made it through the rest of evening without going into the office and pulling Kenzie into his arms.

CHAPTER EIGHT

KENZIE WAS UP and out of bed well before her six o'clock alarm on Monday morning. If she'd gotten any sleep at all overnight it was purely by accident. She'd tried reading, meditation and yoga, even a white-noise app on her phone, and still she hadn't been able to quiet the worries that gained strength with every hour closer to deposition day.

She wasn't due at Paul's law office until nine. If Murtagh hadn't messed up her hand, she would be out in the garage burning off this extra energy and indulging in the eye candy that was Stephen elbow-deep in an engine.

Showered, she tied her hair back loosely to give it time to dry. It was too early for her dress uniform, so she chose a camisole top and yoga shorts while she sliced a banana over her breakfast cereal. At the table, she poked at her food while she attempted to review the notes Paul had assembled since taking her case.

Her gaze kept sliding to the class A uniform hanging on the front of the closet door. According to regulations, she could wear the skirt, but she could already picture Murtagh's sneer if she walked in to the deposition with her legs showing. She and Paul had gone back and forth over the wardrobe options and decided the formal uniform sent the most professional and competent message. If Murtagh had his day in court, she'd be wearing the thing far too often during the trial.

She shifted, putting her back to the uniform, and forced down a few more bites of breakfast. When her stomach protested, she dumped the remainder into the trash and took care of her dishes. Her mood lifted a little when she heard the music pumping out from the shop.

Though she had no idea if the desire simmering between her and Stephen would amount to anything, it was comforting to know he would be here when she was done with the legal processes today.

She could get lost in his kisses every day for the rest of her life and still want more. Friendship was a good thing. Loyal, genuine and candid, Stephen was the best kind of friend to have in her corner. If that's all he could give her, she wouldn't be greedy.

Taking care with every aspect of her appearance, she dried her hair and brushed it back into a bun at the nape of her neck. She deftly applied subtle makeup and dressed, thinking about each layer as more armor against Murtagh. Sliding into her patent leather pumps, she patted gloss onto her lips and put the brace on her wrist. With her hat under her arm and a purse that matched her shoes in hand, she left the camper. Whatever happened next, she would handle it with professionalism and dignity.

Stephen stepped outside and she fought the urge to walk right into the shop, lower the door and never come out again. Other than the firehouse, this was the safest place she'd known since her dad died.

"Looking sharp," he said in his quiet way.

He might as well have recited a sonnet, she thought as she felt the heat rising in her cheeks under his serious gaze. "Thank you." She rolled her shoulders back. So many thoughts rattled through her head all at once. Stephen. The case. That kiss. The talking points Paul had given her. Stephen.

"You've got the brace on?"

She lifted it so he could see it better, wishing she could have a hug—or kiss—for luck.

He nodded once. "Go get him."

Oddly enough, those three words were exactly what she needed. She climbed into the loaner and left the yard, heading downtown to her lawyer's office. She'd just found a parking space in the garage two blocks away when her cell phone sounded with the tone she'd assigned to Paul.

She answered on the next ring. "Hello?"

"Where are you?" Paul asked in a low voice, as if he didn't want to be overheard.

"I just parked." She looked at the dash clock. She was on schedule to arrive fifteen minutes early. "What's wrong?"

"Go home."

"Pardon me?" Technically, she didn't have a home until the landlord finished the repair work.

"Do *not* come into this office."

"But—"

"Go straight home. Don't stop anywhere. Keep your phone close."

She tried to ask another question and realized he'd disconnected. What had Marburg and Murtagh done now? It took her only a few seconds to discard the idea of walking into the office and demanding answers. She'd hired him to handle this case and he hadn't let her down yet.

Following directions, she drove straight back to the garage.

Stephen came out, a shop towel over his shoulder, a worried frown pleating his brow. "What's wrong?"

"Paul sent me away," she replied, fuming.

"Why?"

Great question. Too bad she didn't have any answers. "I don't *know*." She had to pause and gather her composure before she could relay what had happened in the parking garage.

"I guess I'll be your receptionist today. Give me a few minutes to change."

"You know I don't need a receptionist," he said, trailing her.

She was amped up just enough that if he stepped a toe inside the camper she'd throw herself at him. Those hot kisses of his would go a long way to vaporizing the crazy scenarios running through her mind. What was going on?

"Then you'd better find something else for me to do," she said. She stomped up the steps and slammed the door.

With her hands trembling and her constant check of her phone display, it took her twice as long to get out of her dress uniform and hang it up neatly. She was angry, with no clear target. For all she knew Murtagh was dropping the case. Or the judge had changed his mind about the frivolous nature of the case. Whatever it was, she wanted to *know.*

She found her favorite cutoffs and a T-shirt she'd picked up for free from one of the bands passing through the Escape Club. Dressed, she double-checked that her phone was set to the loudest alert, with the vibration on. Tucking it into her back pocket, she grabbed a pair of socks. She shoved her bare feet into flip-flops and crossed to the office, where her work boots waited under the desk.

Proving his vast wisdom, Stephen had taken shelter in the shop.

Proving she had a measure of common sense left, she traded the flip-flops for the boots and sat down to work. Whether he needed her or not, she could manage the phones and handle some invoicing with the bum hand. More importantly, those tasks had clear results. She needed that illusion of control while she waited for news from her lawyer.

The day ticked on and the only positive she could see was the lack of media outside. It seemed only fair that she might learn what was happening before the reporters caught wind of it.

At lunchtime, her stomach was too jittery to be of any guidance. She wandered into the shop to ask Stephen what he wanted her to order. Ignoring the Nova waiting for attention she couldn't provide, she let her gaze rest on Stephen. As she breathed in the pungent air of a working garage, a lovely calm unfurled inside her.

"You should have coveralls on," he said, without looking her way.

Just to prove she didn't care about stains, she boosted herself up to sit on the edge of a workbench.

"Feeling better?" he asked.

"A little," she admitted. "You need lunch."

From under the hood of a sedan, he turned, one eyebrow lifting. "You don't?"

She looked away. "Subs or pizza?" Either choice gave her a meal for later, assuming her stomach would settle down once Paul explained things.

"Pizza," he replied. "Add one of those chopped salads to our usual order."

Her gaze snapped back to him, though his attention was on the engine. Was he trying to take care of her or was he expecting someone? "Why?"

"My mother taught me to eat my veggies."

She twisted around and used the phone to place the order for delivery. When she was done, it slowly dawned on her that they did have a usual order. After little more than a week of bumping along, they had a routine that he seemed comfortable with. Did he realize it?

Not that her assessment signified anything between them on a personal level, but he seemed to be relaxing about having someone other than Mitch in the shop with him regularly. Growth was a good thing, especially for Stephen, who showed signs of being stuck too long in his own head.

They didn't talk much over lunch, which was probably for the best. With Stephen hovering, she managed to eat an entire slice of pizza in an effort to avoid a lecture. As she was storing the leftovers in the refrigerator, his cell phone sounded.

He scowled at the display and, in the process of sending a text message reply, walked out of the office. Telling herself it was absurd to be jealous that he was getting text messages, she returned to the desk and willed the business phone to ring.

Desperate to stay busy, she started cleaning every visible surface in the office. She'd just finished mopping the floor when her cell phone shivered and screeched from her back pocket. The display showed it was Paul. "Finally," she said as she answered.

"You're at Galway Automotive?" he asked without any greeting.

"Yes."

"I'm on my way," he said. "Just sit tight."

Her hand gripped the mop handle hard. "What happened?"

"The short version is it's over," he said. "Murtagh dropped his suit. I'll explain everything, but I don't want to do it over the phone."

The call ended and she stood there, utterly stunned, leaning on the mop for support.

"You all right?"

She gave a start at the sound of Stephen's voice. He was watching her from the office doorway, and he looked as if he wanted to smile. Or give her a high five. Or something.

"What do you know?"

"It looks great in here. Thanks."

"Stephen, stop messing with me."

His rare grin broke free and he gave the floor a long perusal before walking in. "Julia said she was on her way over with good news about your case."

If he'd known since lunch and hadn't shared, Kenzie wouldn't be responsible for her reaction. "When did she say that?"

"About three minutes ago."

She was tempted to ask him to show her his phone and prove it. That was too much of a jealous, insecure girlfriend move. "Well, it's a good thing I cleaned up if we're entertaining pricey lawyers again," she quipped.

Stephen made a sound that might have been a laugh. She was too antsy about what Paul had to say to trust her interpretation.

Fortunately, she didn't have long to wait. Julia arrived moments before Paul, but refused to spoil what she referred to as Paul's victory speech. When the four of them were gathered in the office, Paul explained that he was able to catch Murtagh lying about Kenzie's rescue efforts in the deposition. Faced with the perjury, the judge questioned Murtagh further and then tossed out the case.

"Murtagh is supposed to cover your legal fees, too," Paul added.

She felt as if a thousand-pound anvil had been lifted from her shoulders.

"And Marburg has issued a press release distancing the firm from Murtagh," Julia said. "I expect it to break on the early evening news. Though I wasn't on his legal team, I did make sure it was okay if I was here to share the news. As a friend."

Kenzie wrapped Julia in a big hug, swaying from side to side. Next, she embraced Paul. "I can't tell you how happy I am." She looked across the room to Stephen and decided to save his hug for later.

"There's more," Paul said. "Assuming your hand is examined and cleared for duty by a PFD doctor, you can go back on shift as early as tomorrow."

"What?" She was sure she hadn't heard him correctly. Her life was snapping back into place almost as quickly as it had shattered.

"That was the last piece of the puzzle," Paul said. "I've spoken with Chief Anderson and he asked you to come by the firehouse tomorrow regardless of what the doctor says."

She checked the wall clock, wondering if she could wedge herself into a doctor's schedule yet this afternoon.

"Tonight, though," Julia said, "you're expected at the Escape Club for a celebration." She waved her phone. "Grant's orders." She looked to Stephen and Paul. "He's expecting all of us."

"We'll be there," Kenzie answered, before Stephen could make some excuse.

When they were alone, it seemed the moment for hugging him had passed. Shame on her for missing a prime opportunity. "You could take the Charger tonight," she suggested. "Might get some new interest."

"We'll see. You should get over to the doctor's office." With only a hint of a frown on his face, he turned toward the shop.

With a happy gasp, she lunged for the smaller suitcase that had been shoved against the storeroom wall with her other boxed-up belongings.

"What are you looking for?" Stephen had followed her and braced a shoulder against the door jamb.

"My station gear..." She put a little song into the words as she repeated them while she searched. She could proudly wear her uniform again. "I can't go to the doctor for a PFD exam in cutoffs." Hearing him chuckle, she turned around. "Are you laughing at me?"

"Hard not to," he said. "You're as excited as a kid on Christmas morning."

She wrestled out the clothing and shoes she needed, the smile on her face making her cheeks ache in the best way. She did a little happy dance and earned a real laugh from him. Though unpracticed, it was still a great sound. "I'm a firefighter again."

Kenzie wanted to get moving, but Stephen filled the doorway. She wasn't sure she could get by without burrowing into that quiet strength and lingering in an embrace she could easily crave.

"You never stopped being who you are," he said.

There was an odd note of curiosity in his voice and a distance in his hazel eyes that drew her full attention. "What do you mean?"

He stepped back, letting her out of the storeroom. "It takes guts to keep living and believing when your life is torn up. You're an inspiration, Kenzie." He raised her braced hand and kissed her fingertips. Then he walked out of the office and into the shop.

Astonished, her fingertips tingling, Kenzie soaked in the moment.

His laughter and words and the feelings coursing through her and the potential meaning behind all of it... If she didn't have to get her hand checked for work, she would be pursuing this conversation right now. As it was, she made a mental note to discuss it further tonight.

Changed and ready to go, she waved goodbye to Stephen as she climbed into the loaner. She needed some distance to stay on task. She carried the ER report with her to the doctor's office, practically floating while she waited to be seen. Stephen might be right that she'd never stopped being a firefighter, but wearing the uniform made it so wonderfully official.

The doctor cleared her for duty and she sent Stephen a happy-dance text message. Adding the report to the paperwork she would take to the chief in the morning, she headed back to the garage. Stephen was still working, so she scanned the reports into the computer and sent them on through official channels before she went to the camper to dress for the celebration at the Escape Club.

She stepped into a floral-scented camper. Pale pink tulips, vibrant blue irises and bright sunflowers filled a big vase in the center of the table. The card was a simple congratulations written by Stephen personally, if the grease smudge in the corner was any indication.

He surprised her further when she walked outside to see him pull up in the convertible roadster. Combined with the sweet gesture of the flowers, she wasn't sure how much affection she should read into that decision. Refusing to put it off any longer, she wrapped her arms around him, making the hug as platonic as possible.

"Thank you." She stepped back, suddenly unsure what to do next.

"Guess the flowers were the right touch," he said.

"Yes, thank you for those, too."

His warm gaze swept over her. "You look great."

She'd chosen the dress and sandals she'd worn to her first Sunday dinner at his parents' place. He'd opted for dark jeans, a red polo shirt and deck shoes. "You, too. Red is your color."

He arched an eyebrow. "I'll make a note."

She laughed, feeling balanced by the quip. He had a way of steadying her that she would miss once she was back in her apartment. Stubbornly resisting the subtle melancholy that tried to creep into the moment, she moved toward the car and the party that awaited them.

Stephen thought he'd seen every facet of Kenzie in the highs and lows of today alone. She'd worn her class A uniform this morning with stern pride and professional resolve. Seeing her in the cutoff shorts and graphic T with those work boots put a pulse of need into his bloodstream like it did every other day. It didn't seem to matter that her mood had been razor-wire sharp instead of her standard happy one. She'd positively glowed when she was back in her station gear and he'd found that sexy as hell, too.

Not as sexy as the dress, he thought when her arm brushed his as she sipped her champagne. The way that hem flirted with her long legs made his palms itch to touch and slide and tease her until she was as needy as he felt. He took a long drink of ice-cold water and tried to convince himself to let her catch a ride back to the garage with someone else.

Grant had spared no expense on the celebration; champagne flowed as toasts were raised to Kenzie. Everyone she worked with at the club came up to congratulate her on the dismissal of the civil suit, praising her fortitude. Mitch and plenty of other firefighters had been invited, as well, and all of them told Kenzie how happy they were to have her back.

He should go, Stephen mused. Parties weren't his thing. He

didn't move, however, wanting to soak up every last ounce of her happiness. Was that even fair of him, to bank a little of her joy so he would have some later? He toyed with the car key in his pocket. Mitch and Julia should drive her back. If only the idea of letting Kenzie out of his sight didn't make him want to growl.

"You're scowling," she murmured, leaning close.

She made him smile and laugh, two things he'd thought were gone from his life forever. Her hair, woven into a single braid again, carried the scent of flowers. Flowers he'd given her. A sudden rush of possessiveness startled him. He fought an inner battle for perspective and lost.

"How long is your hair?" He touched the end of the braid where it rested between her shoulder blades.

She trembled under his touch. "Pardon me?"

He met her gaze and those lovely blue eyes burned hot with a desire and heat that mirrored his. "You heard me."

The tip of her tongue moistened her lips and he almost kissed her there in front of everyone. "I'm not sure."

He stared at her, waiting.

Her gaze dropped to his lips. "You'd have to take it down to know for sure," she said.

"Is that an invitation?"

"It is." A slow smile lifted her lips. "Do you plan to accept it?"

He couldn't get her out of the club fast enough. It only complicated matters that he was trying not to reveal his desperate intentions to anyone present. Without traffic, he might have broken land speed records on the way back to the garage.

At last they were safe behind the shelter of his security system. He parked the convertible in front of the trailer and pulled her close, indulging the urgent need to kiss her, reveling in the champagne-spiked heat of her lush mouth.

He broke the kiss only long enough to hurry her into the trailer. She laughed, the sound fizzing through his system as he turned her into his arms and picked up where they'd left off in the car.

She was so responsive, matching his ardor and pressing into his touch, his body, drawing out passionate needs he'd never thought he'd experience again. He tugged at the elastic holding her braid and eased her hair loose inch by inch, until it fell in waves around her face, spilling over her shoulders and down over her breasts.

He nuzzled into the pale, silky warmth of her glorious hair, scattering kisses up and down her throat. She'd left off the brace tonight, and when her hands slipped under his shirt to caress his chest and abs, he was lost.

He picked her up and carried her back to the bed. Peeling away her clothing and his, he marveled with every discovery of what made her sigh and gasp and cling. She gave and gave, bringing his body to life with every kiss and touch, every sweet moan and plea for more.

At last he sank deep into the embrace of her body and they were joined intimately. He looked down into her face and her smile held a tenderness he'd never seen. Yet another facet of this incomparable woman.

Something shifted deep in his chest at the gift so freely given, a sweet loosening that flowed through every fiber of his body. Her hands ran up and down his arms, her fingertips flexing into his back as he moved within her and found the sensual rhythm that carried them both to a shattering climax. When he collapsed beside her, pleasantly exhausted, she curled into him without a word, her hand resting gently over his thundering heart.

A few hours later, Stephen disentangled himself from Kenzie's long limbs and scooted out of the bed, immediately regretting leaving her warm, supple body. Her long, silky hair fanned out across the pillows and her eyelashes were dark crescents against her cheeks. Asleep she looked as happy and content as she did awake, as if any minute a figment of her dreams would crack a joke and make her laugh. He would never figure out how she managed it.

God, she was beautiful, inside and out.

He gathered his clothing, pausing just long enough to make sure she slept on. Tiptoeing to the front of the trailer, he tugged on his jeans, tossed his shirt over his shoulder and picked up his shoes. Sneaking away like this was cowardly, but he convinced himself she wouldn't want him underfoot while she readied for her first morning back on shift.

Stretched out on the couch in the office, he decided there would be plenty of time to talk about what last night meant—if it could mean anything—once she came home from the firehouse.

Home. The word tripped him up. Although she was staying in his place this wasn't home for her. It couldn't be. That loose and free sensation in his chest felt wobbly and lost now that he was alone. Clearly, he didn't have the mettle to leave himself open to the inevitable heartache of really sharing his life once more. She deserved a man who could do that.

Her career was fraught with danger. Though he knew the risks were carefully managed through training and teamwork, she voluntarily put herself in harm's way to save others.

Afraid of being broken beyond repair, he wasn't the kind of man she needed at all. Stephen was more than a little shocked by the sting of that realization.

CHAPTER NINE

KENZIE WAS ON such a high being back at the firehouse that she didn't have time to dwell on the awkwardness of sleeping with Stephen last night. She'd told herself repeatedly it was good that he hadn't been there this morning. Trying to come up with breakfast and conversation would've been so much worse. This way last night could stay in its own miraculous little time capsule. Two people capitalizing on a special moment to enjoy a physical outlet for stress.

And what an outlet, she thought, remembering his hands in her hair, on her skin. *Mind on the job*, she coached herself. Though she didn't wish anyone harm, she hoped for a busy shift. It would help her get back into the routine.

Lieutenant Daniel Jennings waited for her to finish pouring her coffee. "Glad to have you back, Hughes."

"Thanks. It feels good to be home." She sipped the dark brew. "Is everything set for the wedding?"

His smile oozed happiness. "I'll say yes, but only because my bride-to-be isn't here to disagree."

She caught up with the rest of the men and women on her shift, pleased no one seemed inclined to discuss Murtagh or why he'd dropped the suit. She suspected they'd heard about his perjury through the grapevine, anyway. Time flew by between answering calls and handling the maintenance details that kept the personnel, equipment and firehouse in peak condition.

Throughout the afternoon she saw the occasional media van roll by, but didn't think anything of it. Since Murtagh's fifteen minutes of fame had expired when the judge tossed out his case, Paul had warned her the media might come looking for a comment from her. She had no intention of providing any sound bites. Even though today was a joyful one, she would continue to direct reporters to her lawyer. She intended to keep all the legal nonsense firmly behind her.

With energy to burn, Kenzie kept so busy that she didn't realize she was at the center of another firestorm until Chief Anderson called her into his office after their latest emergency response.

"What's up?" she asked. There was nothing as awesome as being back at the firehouse with a crew that felt like family. Here, everyone had her back and she had theirs. She didn't have to convince anyone of her ability to act or make the right decisions. Everyone here knew Murtagh had gone out of his way trying to make her look bad. Feeling alone against the world's judgment had been the worst part of being on administrative leave.

"Have a seat," Anderson said, his face serious. "We've been dealing with circling media sharks all day."

"Is Murtagh doing interviews again?" She wouldn't put it past him to keep right on complaining about her, despite the dismissal of his civil suit. Surely she was entitled to more than a twenty-four-hour break from his antics.

"Not exactly." The chief handed her a folder. "This seems to be new trouble and it's too early to tell if Murtagh is connected." He cleared his throat. "These hit the noon news cycle, with more details promised at the evening hours."

"What kind of details?" She opened the folder and gasped. Nude pictures of her in the firehouse showers, her body barely concealed by billowing steam, were accompanied by the vulgar insinuations that her primary role at the PFD was to satisfy her male colleagues.

For a moment the horrible violation stole her breath. This couldn't be happening. Had someone really put cameras in the bathrooms? Gross. She wanted to shred the pictures and then go hide under a blanket or turnout gear. As long as there were layers and layers between her skin and the rest of the world.

Then she looked closer. That wasn't her body in the pictures, just a woman with blond, braided hair posing in a steamy shower. The tilework in the background wasn't the same as the firehouse. "These are faked."

"I know." Chief Anderson cleared his throat. "Still damned awkward to have this conversation. I've sent that information up the line. The media isn't going to know the difference, might not even care as long as they're getting a story. Reporters and photographers from all sorts of outlets are likely to hound you for a comment or reaction.

"Better keep going," he said, his voice grim.

"Pardon me?"

"The file," he said. "Keep going, so you have an idea what to expect."

There were several pages of screen shots where the faked nude images had been tagged with her name and plastered all over social media. The comments were riddled with lewd suggestions.

Outraged, she forced herself to continue. There were more screen captures of Kenzie out with friends at a bridal shower, a bachelor party for Daniel Jennings, and other recent social events with girlfriends or off-shift gatherings with her crew. The captions were crass, implying she was forever in pursuit of a good time or a convenient man.

"Several of these were pulled from my social media accounts."

"Yes," Chief Anderson replied.

She paused at a great shot of her and the chief at one of the PFD family picnics last summer. "I love this picture."

"Me, too," he said.

Now that moment was tainted by whoever was trying to drum up a scandal.

Seeing a picture of her interacting with Jason at the Escape Club, she groaned. "Murtagh must be behind this," she said, handing the folder back. "That photo was from the night he attacked me at the club. He's certainly painting me in the worst light possible."

"On my word that this is another attack against you, the department has launched an investigation. They've warned me it could take some time to sort out the source."

"The PFD can clear up the most offensive part of this by simply posting pictures proving that isn't one of our bathrooms."

"That still leaves people to jump to the conclusion that you posed for the pictures elsewhere."

She hadn't thought of that. "It isn't me." How could she prove the woman blurred by the steam wasn't her?

The chief stacked his palms over the folder. "I know you don't want to hear this, but the department is recommending administrative leave."

"No." She surged to her feet and planted her hands on her hips. "I didn't *do* any of this. It's outright slander." This was becoming the worst summer of her life. "I'm a victim!" She snapped her mouth shut, the words leaving a bitter aftertaste on her tongue.

"I understand you're caught in the middle. The department is following a set protocol. It's a publicity nightmare."

"No kidding?" She turned in a tight circle, trying to keep her temper in check. "Chief, please. I just got back on the job." She struggled to breathe through the sudden panic clawing at her chest. "The civil suit was dropped because Murtagh got caught up in his lies. You and I and the rest of the PFD knew I wasn't at fault to start with."

"This is different. To the department, this looks like conduct unbecoming," he said. "Right now we don't know who set this in motion, only that your name is on the pictures. The fact is, there are enough legitimate postings misrepresented to give credit to the faked photos."

Her stomach pitched. "That's absurd."

"Call your lawyer, and the union rep, too."

Just when she'd thought the days of saving for legal fees were over. "It isn't me!" She reached for the folder and shuffled until she found one of the pictures that had been pulled from her social media accounts. "Your wife was there, along with other wives and kids, too. There isn't a man in these pictures I've ever been with romantically."

"I've told them all of that. I'll make your side of this crystal clear in my written report, as well. We still need to work within the established system."

She bit back an oath as red hazed her vision. "This is the worst form of bullying. The PFD should want to avoid the appearance of giving in to this kind of stunt."

"Public relations are a serious matter, Kenzie. Going through the steps doesn't feel fair to you, but it's necessary for the greater good of the department."

"Right." She closed her eyes, counted to ten, but still couldn't calm down. "I do what's necessary while this miserable bully gets to do whatever he damn well pleases to trash my name and reputation? If you suspend me again you play right into his agenda."

"Lower your voice," Chief Anderson snapped. "I understand your point of view. I know your integrity and work ethic. You're a valued member of this house."

"Not for long, at this rate." She folded her arms over her chest. What would she do if this ended her career? Last week Stephen had joked about hiring her full-time at the garage, though he really didn't want anyone else around. She loved it there. Part of the reason the situation worked was because they both accepted that her invasion of his sanctuary was temporary.

"I'm doing all I can to prevent that," Anderson said. He sighed heavily. "Let me make a call. While I do that, go speak with your lawyer."

"And my union rep," she said. "Yes, sir." Dismissed, she went to her bunk and called Paul. That conversation didn't go much better than her conversation with Chief Anderson. Who knew how hard it was to prove the source of cyberbullying and fake pictures? Oh yeah, everyone.

They might never prove Murtagh was behind this slanderous attack on her entire life. She had to hope they could track down the original source of the nude photos and prove it wasn't her.

Kenzie was sitting on her bunk, wondering what to do next, half wishing for the distraction of another emergency call, when her cell phone hummed in her hand. When the display showed Galway Automotive, she tapped the icon to answer. "Hi."

"Any idea why news vans are circling my place like sharks?" Stephen asked without preamble.

"Yes," she replied, utterly dejected. She could hear his favorite heavy metal group on the stereo in the background. "I know I shouldn't ask you for any more favors. If you could pack up my stuff in the camper, that would be a big help. I'll text you an address to drop it off."

"What?" The background music died. "What are you talking about?"

"Moving out." It had been fun while it lasted and last night had been amazing, but Stephen had no patience for this kind of chaos. She didn't have any illusions that sex meant relationship in his mind. When he did make that decision, he deserved a woman who wouldn't bring media vans along for the ride. "I'm giving you some much-deserved peace."

"Your apartment's ready?" he asked.

The confusion in his voice made her pause. "Well, no."

"Then why would you move out?"

She'd just told him. "Because of the circling sharks," she replied, exasperated.

"You sound tired," he stated.

"I am." Tired of being hounded and hassled by a man who kept getting away with it.

"What's wrong, Kenzie?"

The tenderness in Stephen's voice undid her. She supposed it was better if he didn't hear it from the reporters. "Someone has been on a mission spreading lies and nasty pictures online, demeaning my work and my character. The media is circling your place hoping to get a comment."

"Great."

"They'd be happier if they caught me in the act of performing some sexual service, too."

He swore.

"I agree completely," she said. "The PFD may take disciplinary action."

"Against you?" He slammed something that clanged loudly. "You didn't do anything wrong."

His outraged confidence in her innocence made her feel warm all over. She appreciated that his first reaction was belief in her. "I'm told appearances matter in public and community relations. More process and systems to work through. I haven't been dumped back on admin leave yet. Given enough time, they should figure out I'm not the problem, and any investigation or disciplinary hearing will end in my favor." She wished she believed that.

The silence on his end made her think the call had been dropped. More likely he'd hung up, except her screen showed he was still there. "Stephen?"

"Mitch is on shift with you?"

"Yes."

"Have him take you to his place after work."

She supposed it made sense, although she didn't want to

crash with newlyweds. Especially not after she'd slept with her friend's brother. "What about the loaner car?"

"I'll pick it up from the firehouse later."

"Hang on," she said. "I can't do that. If the media catches me riding home with Mitch it will only add fuel and credibility to the nasty rumors." She understood Stephen didn't want her at the garage, yet staying with Mitch wasn't the answer.

"I don't want you dealing with this alone," he said.

"Thanks. At the moment I don't see an alternative." The alert rang through the firehouse as another call came in. "Gotta go. I'll check in later."

She pushed the conversation and the soft feelings Stephen's concern left behind to the back of her mind. If they wanted to sideline her again, they'd have to catch her first.

Stephen sent a text to Mitch, knowing it would be a while before his brother could reply if they were headed out on a call. It couldn't be as bad as she thought, although... His gaze drifted to the monitors showing media vans completely circling his block. Maybe it was.

At the computer, he typed Kenzie's name into the search box and sat back as the results flooded his screen. The articles and pictures left him shell-shocked. The outrageous claims and ugly insinuations made him want to toss his monitor through the window. This was a blatant attack by a coward hiding behind a keyboard. He closed the various windows and cleared the search from the computer history.

It had to be Murtagh. Stephen fisted his hands on the desktop, wishing he had a direct target.

He agreed with her that *processes* and *systems* were lousy words when she was under the pressure of this obnoxious, damaging bullying. He might not like the media attention personally, but he could ride it out for her sake.

She sure as hell couldn't go anywhere else in town and have the protection his fence and security offered her. He had to come up with a better solution than letting her cope with the chaos alone.

Picking up the phone, he called Grant for an assist. With luck, the former cop knew someone capable of unraveling the cyber side of this mess. A few minutes later, Stephen was relieved to hear Grant had already set things in motion.

Next, he dialed Joey Garcia at the paint and body shop and called in a favor. If he could get Kenzie back home without being harassed by any reporters, maybe she'd understand she really did have someone in her corner.

Although he might not be in the market for a real relationship, he sure as hell knew how to be a good friend.

Kenzie was overwhelmed by the warm fuzzy feelings of being cared for. She was used to doing more than pulling her own weight in any circumstance, and made a habit of handling her life on her terms. Stephen had stepped up in a big way. She still wasn't sure how he'd done it, leaving her one of Joey Garcia's showy street racer mods for the end of her shift, and instructions to drive to Joey's shop rather than Galway Automotive.

At Garcia's warehouse, behind the shelter of a closed bay door, Stephen had been waiting for her. He took her backpack out of her hands and led her to another of Joey's cars, this one with tinted windows. Once he was sure no one from the media had caught on, he drove her over to Mitch and Julia's house.

The four of them had enjoyed a pasta dinner with all the trimmings, complete with gelato for dessert. They played a couple card games, and the only hard-and-fast rule of the night was no one could mention anything about Murtagh or work in general. It had been pure bliss.

After reversing the cars on the way back, he got her safely behind the fence surrounding the garage. When she'd tried to thank him, to let him know how much the evening meant to her, he only gave her a slow, bone-melting kiss at the camper door and told her to get some rest.

What was she supposed to think when he did things like that? She'd known he was one of those rare men in the world who knew when and how to do just the right thing, but this was an unexpected, charming side of him.

As she undressed, she'd found it easier to follow his instructions to rest, after such a relaxing evening. She'd crawled into bed and fallen asleep thinking of Stephen. He was her first thought in the morning, too, even before she checked her phone to see if the PFD had put her back on admin leave.

Not yet.

She hustled through her morning routine, eager to get to the firehouse as early as possible. The Charger was waiting in front of the camper with a big Galway Automotive For Sale sign in the rear window. She'd laughed, happy for him to get some free publicity if the media followed her today. Advertising potential aside, she was relieved to find the streets in front of the garage and the firehouse media-free.

The station wasn't as busy today as they'd been yesterday, and she found she didn't need the busyness with this lingering, overall good feeling. Every hour she was on duty gave her hope that the PFD would see through the obnoxious cyberbullying tactics and let her stay on the job.

Late in the afternoon they were all worn-out from clearing a faulty smoke detector system in a nearby apartment building. As the driver slowed to make the turn to the firehouse, he brought the truck to a stop. Hearing Lieutenant Jennings curse from his seat up front, Kenzie twisted around to see what had upset them.

Hate messages aimed at her had been scrawled across the white garage door in red spray paint. Murtagh, or some knucklehead sharing his views, had made his displeasure with female firefighters quite plain. Her stomach churned at this direct assault on all of them as a house.

Naturally, the graffiti meant the vultures, in the form of news crews, had returned. Vans were stationed across the street, and cameramen and reporters were jockeying for the best angle, no doubt getting prime footage to go along with their endless opinions of her PFD career. Thankfully, none of the reporters seemed to be interviewing Murtagh.

There was no question in Kenzie's mind who had done this. Her first hope was that Murtagh had finally been caught in the act of causing trouble. That would be a far better spin on this bizarre story than the hateful messages against women who served the city with skill and commitment. Secondary to that, she hoped the men and women she worked with and for wouldn't hold this against her.

For the first time, she gave serious thought to moving away. Not wishful thinking because she was discouraged this time. No, as the idea rolled through her mind it gained momentum and substance. She could relocate and find work in another state. Maybe down in Maryland, closer to her mom and sister. She liked that area, although joining another fire department would depend on how well she could clean up the cyberbullying trash.

As the door rolled up and the truck parked in the bay, she joined the rest of her crew resetting everything for the next call.

Mitch rapped her gently on the shoulder. "It'll pass," he said. "We've got your back."

"Thanks." She wasn't sure she believed that it would pass. It seemed like every time things went her way Murtagh did something worse to impede her forward progress. Why was he so damn fixated on her?

"I'll get started on the cleanup right away," she said. Erasing Murtagh's hate would give her time to think through the potentially tough choices right in front of her. She felt like she was at a crossroads and she couldn't see enough to know which direction was best.

Chief Anderson found her in the supply room. "I need a word with you."

"Yes, sir." Misery dogging her, she followed him to his office and closed the door.

"You know you're important to this house, to everyone in it?"

She swallowed. He'd said that yesterday. "Yes." Attempting to say anything more than that single syllable put her emotions too close to the surface.

"We have security cameras, as you know, but the footage isn't clear." Anderson clutched the arms of his chair. "The one camera with the best angle was found broken this morning. We haven't had time to get it fixed. I've spoken with the police and they will canvas the area for any witnesses or leads."

She bit back the urge to toss accusations at Murtagh. The chief knew every lousy thing that had been said about her no matter if it was graffiti on a door, online, or in a formal complaint.

"Those are the facts," the chief said.

"Okay." She pressed her lips together, willing the trembling to stop.

"You're an excellent firefighter, Kenzie."

"Thank you, sir." Using her first name meant he was attempting to soften tough news. Again. She shifted toward the door. "I'll get on that cleanup," she interjected.

"I've already called a professional. You can help if they let you."

She focused on the option to help, clinging to every ounce of positive. That meant he expected her to be here when the professionals arrived.

"I've been asked to put you on administrative leave again."

That last bit of hope burst like a balloon. Kenzie stifled the automatic protest. Chief Anderson spoke plainly. He reminded her of Grant in that habit.

"I negotiated a compromise. You can be here on shift. You just won't go on calls."

What good would that do her, the house or the PFD? "I'll brush up on my cooking skills," she said.

"Everyone up the line believes Murtagh is behind this. This

is *not* a disciplinary action," he said. "We're taking these measures to protect you."

"Of course. I appreciate it, sir."

"If I could haul Murtagh in here and make him scrub those obscenities away with a toothbrush, I would."

She nodded, the image lightening the burden just a little. She wasn't in this alone. With this stunt, Murtagh had attacked everyone at this house and earned the enduring displeasure of the PFD as a whole. Whatever he thought he could gain by forcing her out of her career, this wasn't the way to get it.

She steeled herself to ask her only remaining question. "Chief, if I were to relocate, would the PFD provide a good reference?"

He sat back in his chair, studying her. "You want to leave Philly?"

"Not at all." She straightened her shoulders. "I just feel it's smart to consider the option for the sake of the PFD as well as myself."

The chief pinched the bridge of his nose. "I sure as hell hope it doesn't come to that," he said. "Your exemplary record of service stands on its own and I believe any reference would reflect that."

"Thank you, sir."

She left the office on unsteady knees, inordinately relieved and wondering what Murtagh would try next. In the kitchen she took an inventory, making a shopping list. When the professional cleaning crew arrived she went out and insisted on helping.

By end of shift, Mitch followed her home, and she returned to Stephen's garage too tired to be angry about any of it.

Stephen stepped out of the office as soon as she parked in front of the camper. Did he have to look so sexy leaning against that door? She knew they should talk about what was brewing between them, specifically where they stood after that amazing bout of sex. Surely a conversation like that could wait until tomorrow.

"You okay?"

She paused at the camper steps. "Mitch called you."

Stephen nodded. "Sent a picture, too."

"I don't want to talk about it." Kenzie wanted to scream. She wanted to go inside and indulge in a private, ugly cry to clean the emotional slate so she could go back to being strong and stoic tomorrow.

"There's smothered chicken casserole in the oven," Stephen said. "Salad in the fridge." He gave her another long look and then stepped back into the office.

She gaped at him. "Thanks," she called out belatedly.

"Welcome."

She stared at the closed door, knowing it wasn't locked. He kept it open, as promised, in case she ever needed anything in the night.

She suspected that what she really needed—communication, intimacy, connection—he wasn't ready or able to give. With an effort, she marched into the camper, intending to take a shower before she bothered with food.

The space smelled heavenly with the comforting aromas of garlic, paprika and bacon. She opened the refrigerator and found a bottle of white wine beside the salad. Mitch might have given him a warning, but just like last night, Stephen had stepped up on his own. It scared her to realize she could get used to this... this care and affection. He was inherently kind and thoughtful, and just kept those aspects buried under the scowl and brusque conversations to keep people at arm's length. She loved all those variations of him.

If—when—she moved away, she'd miss this almost-friends-with-benefits thing they were dancing around. Given time and less baggage, they might have a chance at something more. Unfortunately, this was where they were, who they were, and she'd be better off accepting reality.

Shaking off the melancholy, she pulled the plastic container she'd brought from work out of her backpack. She'd had plenty of time in the kitchen after the graffiti cleanup was done, and used the time to bake several batches of chocolate chip cookies, using her new favorite recipe from Shannon, the soon-to-be Mrs. Daniel Jennings.

Kenzie sank into the bench seat at the table. How was she ever going to leave the PFD family she loved so much? This city was her birthright, and she'd earned her place as a firefighter. Contrary to Murtagh's poisonous claims, no one had handed her a spot simply because she was Ken Hughes's daughter. The opposite, really. It hadn't been easy to walk in the wake of a man so well-respected.

Wrapping two cookies in a paper towel for herself, she took the remaining four in the container over to the office and knocked on the door. It opened quickly, as if Stephen had been standing right there waiting for her. It was a nice fantasy.

"I thought you'd like these," she said. "Chocolate chip cookies," she added unnecessarily, as he popped the top and the sweet aroma of dark chocolate goodness wafted up between them. "Thanks for making sure I had dinner."

"You made these?"

"Slow shift," she replied with a shrug.

He braced a shoulder against the doorjamb and his lips gave a subtle kick at one corner. "My sisters call it stress baking."

"They might be right," she allowed. "Good night, Stephen."

Those hazel eyes heated as he studied her. "Thanks for delivering dessert."

"Sure. Enjoy." She took a step backward toward the safety of the camper. That hungry look in his eyes made her want to grab him and kiss him and enjoy an altogether different type of dessert. One mistake of that variety was probably more than enough for both of them, no matter what her hormones and heart were saying about it right now.

Working light duty within the safety of the firehouse was

almost worse than being forced to stay away completely. Almost. She made it through her overnight shift without any additional Murtagh-related antics. Unfortunately, according to her lawyer and Grant, progress was slow on the cyberbullying investigation. Although the nude photo had been found posted on several stock image websites, obviously the source, it was only one piece of that puzzle.

On Thursday, her first day off from the PFD, she hit the garage early because some of the parts for the Nova had come in. Between standard maintenance jobs, she was working through the initial assessment of the classic car.

In the garage, she set an alarm so she would stop work in time to clean up and change for her scheduled shift at the Escape Club. When the clanging bell sound interrupted the heavy metal music Stephen had cranked up, she turned it off and finished up an oil change for one of Stephen's regular customers. "All set here for Mrs. Giaconne," she called. "Want me to make the call for her to pick it up?"

"I'll take care of it," Stephen replied.

"Great." Kenzie stripped out of the protective coveralls, feeling Stephen's gaze tracking her movements. It gave her a charge to know he appreciated the view. And it was a pleasant diversion from the reason she was suddenly underfoot, invading his space again. No one wanted her going anywhere alone right now.

Though the police had questioned Murtagh about the nasty messages spray painted across the firehouse, he hadn't been arrested. Grant had learned Murtagh had an alibi. Kenzie appreciated having such great support, but she wanted her life back.

She wouldn't put it past the craggy old man to have paid a couple kids to tag the firehouse for him. The one person caught on camera moved better than she'd ever seen Murtagh move. Then again, he'd shown some strength and quick reflexes that night at the club when he'd been proving his point that she was too weak to handle trouble.

Which was the act and which was real?

"Are you coming by the club tonight?" she asked, as she traded her boots for her flip-flops.

Stephen stepped back from the brake job in front of him, scowling at the rotor. "We'll see."

She knew that look by now. He'd found something that insulted his mechanic's heart.

"Want me to check for parts?" she offered. "I have some time."

He made a noise she didn't worry about interpreting. "I'll do it," he said.

Working beside him for these two weeks, she'd come to understand how his brain sifted information. He was a genius with engines, with everything a car could throw at him, really, and he did superb, thorough work. Her father would have happily spent hours in this garage beside Stephen, sorting out problems and solutions.

Strange that it took her this long to get interested in a man she believed her father would have approved of. More than that, he would have found a kindred spirit in Stephen. Too bad she couldn't figure out if she had a chance of actually dating him.

She walked out to the camper before she said something she might regret, something that might put him on the defensive. They weren't exactly walking on eggshells around each other since the night the civil suit had been dismissed, but neither of them seemed to know what to do with the other.

Well, she had some ideas she would happily have employed if she could figure out if Stephen wanted to go down that path.

Maybe she had crossed a line, though he'd started it, asking about her braid. And she hadn't been alone as they'd steamrolled right through that friendship boundary. Stephen had been right there with her, through every kiss and touch. Until the morning after, when she'd woken up alone. Other than that one tender kiss and countless thoughtful gestures, he seemed to prefer ignoring the event altogether.

Since she'd gone back to the PFD, they'd settled into this

weird routine of friendly camaraderie with an undercurrent of sexual tension that kept her on edge. Stephen was too stoic to give her any idea what he was feeling. Other than distant.

The situation was something she should sort out with a sister or girlfriend, except she didn't have one of those handy at the moment. It wasn't a discussion she wanted to have over the phone with her mom, who was worried enough about her already. And it wasn't a discussion she felt comfortable having with Julia, his sister-in-law.

In the camper, she pulled all the shades down. It was a paranoid move, yet she couldn't stop herself. The media was still seeking a comment from her about the cyberbully who'd targeted her. Despite the security around Stephen's garage, she struggled against a persistent sense of dread.

"Anyone would," she told her reflection as she tied the end of her braid. "The jerk only wins if you let him."

Once Murtagh had perjured himself in the civil case, public opinion had turned on him. Even without solid proof, she got the feeling the man had no intention of letting up. He'd been cagey about it, but she knew deep down in her gut he was responsible for every attempt to embarrass her and the department.

As much as she wanted to ignore Murtagh, her mind kept trying to figure out what he hoped to gain. It was like trying to find the source of an errant rattle in a car frame.

She glanced at the wedding invitation she'd tucked into her makeup case. On July 4 Daniel Jennings would marry Shannon Nolan and have an instant family with her young son, Aiden.

Kenzie remembered how fast and hard he'd fallen for both the woman and her little boy. Actually, Aiden had won over everyone on his very first visit to the firehouse. The wedding would be amazing and she wanted to go celebrate such a wonderful milestone with friends who were as close as family.

Weeks ago, she'd responded that she'd be attending the ceremony and reception alone. Daniel had made it clear on her first shift back that she could bring a date. Everyone in their circles knew she'd been staying with Stephen since her apartment closed. Clearly, speculation about them was gaining traction.

It wasn't a surprise. In her community people cared about each other. People knew Stephen as the son of a firefighter and older brother of another. They also knew Stephen had become morose and withdrawn since his fiancée's murder. Him letting Kenzie live with him and helping her at every opportunity was raising all kinds of eyebrows.

If she asked him to go with her to the wedding, would that hurt him more than it helped her?

Silly to get too wound up about it before she'd even asked him. Tying her sneakers, she grabbed her backpack and keys. If she didn't get moving she'd be late and that wasn't who she was. Dressed in her Escape Club uniform, she headed back to the garage to tell Stephen she was leaving.

And ask him to go with her to a wedding.

CHAPTER TEN

IN THE GARAGE, Stephen dropped the phone back on the cradle and glanced up to see Kenzie dressed for her waitressing shift at the club. Things had been a little awkward, at least on his side, since they'd slept together. Natural, basic needs, he reminded himself. They were consenting adults and clearly compatible in and out of bed. Still, he should probably make time to *talk* about it. Maybe she'd be open to...what?

Although it felt wrong to suggest they hook up whenever the mood struck, he believed sex could remain a fun distraction for them both, as long as they weren't adding in elements of a relationship. He *liked* Kenzie; he just couldn't go down that road again. She might understand if he found the guts and the right words to explain it.

So why did he keep hesitating?

"You okay?" she asked, her head tipped to the side.

"Lost in thought," he said, patting himself on the back for the clear communication. "You're closing tonight?"

"Hmm? Yes." Her gaze darted around the office. "Are you heading out, too?"

"They need a wrecker on the Schuylkill Expressway. Big accident."

"Is the vehicle coming back here?"

"Not from the sound of it," he replied.

"All right," she said. "Be safe."

With everything going on, those two words had become their form of saying goodbye.

"Thanks. You, too." Should he kiss her? He wanted to, had been missing her lips, the soft curve of her cheek under his palm. The last time they'd kissed was after the dinner he'd arranged with Mitch and Julia. Good grief, with Kenzie around, he felt more like an insecure teenager than a capable adult. If he asked a friend for advice he'd only be setting himself up for those subtle, hopeful glances that silently asked if he was finally moving on with his life.

"Ah, one quick question," she said, trailing him out of the office. "Daniel Jennings is getting married on Sunday."

Stephen paused. Whatever he'd hoped she might say, that wasn't it. "They're getting married on the Fourth?"

His fiancée had been gone three years and still weddings creeped him out. Mitch's wedding had been the only invitation he'd accepted in all that time. Thankfully, his brother had put the best man duties at the reception on their younger brother's shoulders.

"Would you go with me?" She stepped closer as the words tumbled out in a rush. "I know it's July Fourth and last-minute, but with Murtagh skulking around, I really don't want to drive out there alone. Mitch offered to let me ride with them, but I'd rather not if I can avoid it. If you're willing that is. Please?"

When she seemed to run out of words, or oxygen, she stared at him, her blue eyes wide and hopeful and her lips clamped together. How, exactly, was he supposed to say no when she looked at him that way? He doubted any man with a pulse could resist that appeal.

"You just want me to drive you over?" *Please just need a driver*, he thought.

"Well, I was hoping you'd stick around as my plus one."

"As...as your date?" He couldn't remember the last time he'd let a woman ask him out. He stared at her, wondering what she was thinking. Being flattered and confused was his problem.

"Would that be so terrible for you?" she asked.

He pulled himself together. Another woman might have posed the same question like a cornered cat, hoping to save face. Not Kenzie. She was genuinely concerned that he couldn't handle it.

"I'll take you." He told himself it was simply to erase that furrow of worry between her golden eyebrows.

Relief washed over her face and she bounced a little on her toes. "Thanks so much. We don't have to stay long—"

"It's fine." He felt his lips curve as he watched her. "We should both get going."

"Right." She started forward, then rocked back on her heels. "I'll just, um, go now."

He gave in to all that sweet, fiery energy bubbling from her and luring him in. Reaching out, he caught her elbow, drawing her back so he could press a quick kiss to her lips.

A jolt like heat lightning speared through his system and he took the kiss deeper. When he released her, a dazzled smile spread slowly across her face. Yeah, that's what they both needed, an affirmation of this desire thundering like a distant storm.

"Be safe," he reminded her. They walked out and he hit the gate for her to leave ahead of him as he climbed into the cab of the tow truck.

Given a choice, he'd follow her to the club first, but he was needed at the accident site and trailing her would only undermine her fragile independence.

He could see Murtagh's sneaky antics were taking a toll on her. Although nothing new had happened for almost forty-eight hours, everyone was on edge, anticipating who knew what. The man hadn't done anything sensible since she'd pulled him out of that fire.

Stephen wished there was a more direct solution that would allow Kenzie to get her life back on track. In a perfect world, she'd never be out of his sight until the police had Murtagh contained. Hardly a perfect solution, as it would make them both crazy. She had too much energy to be cooped up even in a place as busy as his garage. And he was used to being alone, coming and going as he pleased without any concern for anyone else.

It surprised him to realize he was going to miss her when she eventually went back to her place. That was for the best, he reminded himself. He wasn't the man she needed. He wasn't the man any woman needed. His business and family were plenty of life for him.

Once Kenzie left he could get back to honoring Annabeth's memory by keeping an eye on the community center. He thought of those pictures of Kenzie with the bartender that been plastered on social media sites with derogatory comments. Subtract the nasty side of it and Stephen could see them together. A guy like that, outgoing and friendly, suited her better than Stephen ever could.

So why did he feel anger bubbling by the time he caught up to the traffic jam near the accident site? He had no right to be possessive or jealous over her. They were a couple of people riding out a tough situation. Better to keep it at that.

He liked her because she was a great person. End of story. She knew her cars inside and out, which was as fun as hell. They worked well together, which was rare for him. She tolerated his music, didn't try to talk constantly, and when she had something to say, she said it clearly.

He enjoyed doing things for her. She was always so pleased and a little surprised. So what if he hadn't done those things for anyone in three years? She deserved it, the way she did so much for others, including him.

She was beautiful and sexy with all those subtle curves. That laugh. He felt himself grinning just thinking about her. Man, he never got tired of that sound. His hand flexed as he recalled that quiet triumph when he'd finally got that braid loose. He could weave his fingers through her hair all night. Would she like that?

He was relieved when the police guided him around the stopped cars to the wreck. Stephen swallowed hard, trying to ignore the signs of lives forever changed. Three cars and an 18-wheeler were crumpled as if a giant had thrown a tantrum. He could avert his eyes from the blood on the shattered windshield of a sedan, but the scorched metal and recently extinguished gasoline fire assaulted his nostrils.

One fire truck pulled away as Stephen positioned the tow truck to collect a minivan the same color as Megan's. It had been crumpled like an accordion. It wasn't her car, he knew it wasn't, yet his heart hammered in his chest at the sight of a child seat in the second row.

One of the police officers on the scene was Bob Greely, an old friend from the neighborhood. "Did anyone make it out?" Stephen asked him when he walked over to say hello.

"Only the one fatality," Bob replied. He aimed his chin toward the 18-wheeler. "According to witnesses, the idiot on the bike was zipping in and out of traffic and misjudged the cutback in front of the semi."

Stephen hadn't noticed the motorcycle wedged into the front wheel well of the truck's cab. "Damn."

"Guy wasn't wearing a helmet, didn't stand a chance when he was thrown clear." Bob shook his head. "I think the others will all survive, though there were some serious injuries."

"Good to know."

Stephen hooked up the minivan and secured it on the bed. "I've got room for the sedan if you want," he offered.

"That would help. Everything's going to evidence first," Bob said. "You know the address."

He dropped plenty of cars at the evidence lot.

"Thanks, man." Bob came to the door as Stephen climbed up into the cab. "Hey, is that Kenzie Hughes really staying with you?"

"She is." Stephen braced himself, determined to keep his cool no matter what Bob said next.

"Good. I saw some of that crap on the news. Your security is tighter than Fort Knox, and sounds like she needs it."

Stephen paused. "What do you mean?"

"Just having a rough time, is all."

"Yeah." For a minute Stephen had hoped Bob might know something more "Can't the cops do anything about Murtagh?"

"Not my beat, but you know we try to watch out for our own. Can't believe he went after her that way with the interviews and the, ah, other stuff."

Based on his reddening face, apparently Bob thought the pictures were real. Stephen bristled, barely suppressing the urge to explain that the steamy nude shower photos plastered on the internet weren't actually Kenzie. It wasn't Bob's business. Technically, it wasn't Stephen's business either, and he needed to remember that.

He drove over and loaded up the sedan, then maneuvered out of the area, waiting patiently for the state troopers to make room for him to join the flow of traffic.

He used the voice command to dial Megan's number. Her husband answered, and in the background he could hear his sister and the kids playing. It set his mind at ease and loosened the ache around his heart. He managed some small talk for a minute or two and then ended the call. That was something his family would surely analyze and dissect over Sunday dinner.

He was kind of glad he would be at the wedding so he wouldn't be there to hear it.

While he was behaving oddly, he went ahead and called his mom to let her know why they wouldn't be at dinner. He intended to keep the conversation short and to the point, but her answer derailed his plan.

"Stephen, is Kenzie all right?" she said, as soon as she picked up.

A cold lump formed in Stephen's gut. "As far as I know. Why?" He checked the clock; she'd left for the club two hours ago. If she hadn't arrived, Grant would have called.

"Reporters are all over the pier. Down near the Escape Club," Myra said.

They always were, Stephen thought darkly. It seemed the media was determined to make Kenzie lose her cool. As if being a woman plagued by a bitter old man was somehow her fault.

"The club was evacuated due to a bomb threat," his mom announced.

"Murtagh."

"That's what your father said," Myra agreed. "It's too early for any proof. The fire department and police are still assessing the scene."

"I'll head that way as soon as I can," Stephen said.

"There's more. Murtagh confronted Kenzie outside, during the evacuation. With so many reporters around, it was all on camera and quite ugly."

"What the hell?" Why hadn't anyone called *him*?

"Grant stepped in, and others, too. Murtagh hasn't left yet. Preening for the cameras, trying to claim he's the victim again, being accused of things he didn't do online."

"Shouldn't they be covering the bomb threat instead of pandering to his agenda?"

"You'd think so," his mother agreed.

At this rate the man would cost Kenzie her job. What Stephen wouldn't give for another big drug bust or major car theft, anything to shift attention from Murtagh's campaign against Kenzie. In his mind Stephen entertained violent, satisfying attacks on Murtagh that he'd never be able to carry out in reality. It took the leading edge off his temper.

"If you go down there, be careful."

"If? I can't leave her to deal with this alone." Someone should have called him. He was supposed to be protecting her.

"Well, at least keep your face away from the cameras," she said.

He laughed. His mom had a way with priorities for her children. "I promise."

"We'll be grilling out on the Fourth," she reminded him. "Bring steaks or brats or whatever you'd like to share."

"Oh, right." The reason he'd called. "We won't be there."

"It's the Fourth of July," she said.

"And a Sunday," he added, before she could. "I remember the family traditions, Mom. One of Kenzie's friends is getting married and we're going to the wedding."

For a long beat of silence he could imagine his mother gaping at the phone in shock. "Is that the Jennings wedding?" she said at last.

"Yes."

"Mitch and Julia are going, too. They promised to stop by beforehand. Maybe the four of you can all ride together from here. Your nieces and nephews will be crushed if you don't stop in."

He wanted to call her on the silly, miserable-child ploy, but her heart was in the right place. Myra Galway couldn't suppress her urge to mother people. After this mess on the news, she would want to see Kenzie and reassure herself that everything was fine.

This was the real risk of taking a woman to Sunday dinner: his mom got too interested in the guest. In Kenzie's case, Myra knew her better than Stephen did. Being an attentive, caring mother, she probably had delusions that somehow Kenzie could put an end to Stephen's hermit tendencies.

"I'll let you know how the timing shakes out," he hedged. "I need to unload the wrecker now."

She wished him luck, asked him to tell Kenzie they were thinking about her, and told him she loved him.

"Love you, too, Mom."

He supposed love was the real Galway tradition. It was the cornerstone of the steady foundation Sam and Myra had given their children. Building on love, they'd instilled respect, responsibility and a solid work ethic. With all that in his genes, drummed into his sense of self, he shouldn't be surprised that he felt a need to stand between Kenzie and anyone bent on hurting her.

Chaos swirled around Kenzie. The bomb squad was inside the club with canine units, searching for any sign of explosives. Patrons milled about, pressing the safety perimeter the staff and police had set up. No one wanted to miss a thing. The lights from various media teams flooded the area, washing out the flashing lights of first responder units. Under any other off-duty circumstances, she would go over and visit with the firefighters or offer to help. Tonight, Murtagh had effectively blocked that path. With the right camera angle, she knew it would look as if the PFD welcomed his presence.

Kenzie turned away from his creepy stare, doing what she could to blend in with the rest of the staff, avoiding the harsh lights and judgmental speculation. She'd never been one to shy away from noise or a crisis. Right now, she was anxious for the relative quiet and absolute privacy of Stephen's garage.

Leaving the club wasn't an option; Grant had made that clear, even if the Charger Stephen insisted she continue to use wasn't blocked in. There wasn't anything for her to do.

Jason walked over and rested his arm across her shoulder. "How are you holding up?"

The question made her eyes sting with tears she would not shed in front of Murtagh. She dug deep for cold anger instead. "He's an embarrassment. Why can't he crawl back under a rock?"

She, Jason and Grant had been the last out of the club, making sure the patrons were safely clear. The three of them came outside to find the bands and the rest of the staff had organized the customers back from the club, making way for the first responders.

The media, already documenting the evacuation, had caught

everything when Murtagh ambushed her with his false apologies. His appearance at the club had instantly made him the prime suspect in the bomb threat, though she could never voice such an opinion.

"He's slime," Jason said. "Just hang in there."

She was trying. "Do I have a choice?"

Jason gave her a little shoulder squeeze and glanced past her. "Things might be looking up," he said cryptically.

Before she could ask, he turned her shoulders and she was facing that scowl she found far too appealing. "Stephen?" She glanced around. "I wasn't expecting you. The reports on the accident were dire."

"It was ugly."

For a split second something flashed in his hazel eyes, a shell-shocked emotion she recognized from her mirror after a particularly grueling call. Then he spotted Murtagh and his gaze iced over with lethal intent. She loved him for it.

"We're leaving," he said. "Now."

"I—I can't." At his sharp look, she decided not to argue. "Just let me tell Grant."

"Already did."

That irked her. He couldn't continue to simply *handle* so many things on her behalf. Housing, car repairs, food and transportation, too. At some point she'd have her life back and she needed to take care of herself. "Presumptuous much?"

When he stepped closer she noticed the unmistakable scent of smoke and burned gas clinging to his shirt. He had soot and dirt on his skin and a smudge along his jaw that she wanted to reach up and wipe away.

"You *want* to stay?" He folded his arms over his chest. "Fine."

If there hadn't been so many cameras around, she would have hugged him. "False alarm or not, Grant will need help with this crowd."

Stephen's hard gaze took in the scene around them. "You

don't leave people hanging. I get it." He aimed a far more intimidating version of his relentless scowl at Murtagh.

He did get it, she realized, grateful. He hadn't fixed her car because she couldn't; he'd done it because, like her, he needed to stay busy when things got tough. Sometimes visual, tangible progress was the best defense against all the other uncontrollable stuff in life.

"Thanks."

He glanced down at her, his expression softening. "Had to try."

"I know." She wanted to hug him, and hooked her thumbs in her back pockets to keep her hands to herself. "Look at that." She nodded toward band members clearing a space in the center of the crowd. "Only here," she said with pride. Grant had built something special, and though her part in his business was small, she felt like she mattered.

"Are they setting up to play?" Stephen sounded as impressed as she felt.

She nodded, reluctant to move closer to the music because that would put her—and Stephen—closer to Murtagh.

They didn't have power or full instrumentation, but the headliner band had pulled acoustic guitars from the equipment van and were basically leading a sing-along to keep people distracted. The drummer made do with his sticks and a tambourine.

"Ridiculous," Stephen said.

"Yes it is," she agreed, laughing. "But it's working."

"It's a grown-up version of summer camp," he muttered.

"All we need are s'mores." She glanced in the direction of the car, which was still blocked in. "How much time do you think we have before they let us back inside?"

"You aren't seriously thinking of going to the store for graham crackers, chocolate and marshmallows for this crowd."

"We could take your car." She batted her eyelashes in an overdone and obvious ploy.

His eyebrows flexed into another frown. "I doubt the PFD would let you have an open flame anywhere around here."

His logic popped her fantasy balloon. "True. Still fun to think about."

"If you say so."

Everyone around them was otherwise engaged with the issues inside the club or the impromptu entertainment outside. Though Kenzie and Stephen were surrounded, they might as well have been alone.

"You didn't like summer camp?"

"Not the kind you're talking about," he admitted.

"Why not?"

He shrugged and tucked his hands into his pockets. "It just wasn't my thing."

She wondered if he'd been homesick or if he just wasn't into all the outdoor classic recreational stuff. "No go-cart camp?"

He shrugged. "Fishing with Dad was one thing. Going camping with the family was fine when we did that."

So it was about being on his own. Interesting that he was so comfortable with solitude now. Although his family was rarely more than a few blocks away at any given moment. She caught a gleam in his eye. "You put stuff in your sisters' sleeping bags, didn't you?"

He smirked and she fought the urge to kiss that sly expression right off his face. "Nothing was ever proven."

She smacked his arm lightly. "You were guilty."

"How can you be sure?"

"First of all, the smirk is a dead giveaway. Second, I'm also an oldest child. Did you use the plastic worms or live bait? Frogs, maybe?"

"My sisters squealed over everything. I can't recall exactly what Mitch tucked between their sheets."

"Mitch, right. And if I ask him, he'll blame you. Or Andrew." She folded her arms, reluctantly impressed and a little envious.

"You were so lucky to have a worthy accomplice. I had to create watertight alibis for my pranks."

His smirk smoothed into a smile, but just when she thought he'd laugh, his eyebrows snapped together and his lips went hard.

She twisted around, following his gaze, and caught a glimpse of Murtagh walking toward them. Stephen stepped in front of her and his fingers curled into loose fists. "You don't need to come any closer."

"I just want to talk to Miss Hughes."

"That opportunity passed," Stephen said. "If you have something to say, write a letter and send it to her attorney."

Murtagh's face bunched into a sneer and she braced for another insult. He must have remembered they had an audience, because his demeanor changed abruptly. Too bad for him his hangdog look wasn't very convincing.

"Her indecisive actions hurt *me*, if you recall," he stated in a voice that carried.

Kenzie could feel the nearest cameras aiming toward them. Only a few days of living under this media microscope and she was exhausted.

"She's playing you, Galway," Murtagh continued. "Yeah, I know who you are. She's got you wrapped around her pinkie, fighting her battles. Because she can't win on her own."

"Battles you started," Stephen said, with far more calm than Kenzie could muster.

She didn't say a word, didn't rise to the bait as he tried once more to convince her he was innocent of the online trouble. It wasn't in her nature to hide behind anyone or anything, but right now Stephen was shield and shelter. Murtagh had put her through enough; why wouldn't he leave her alone?

Standing behind Stephen, she could feel the strength radiating through the solid muscles of his back. He'd fight for her if he had to. While part of her thrilled to that idea, she knew it would be worse for everyone if he thrashed a retired firefighter.

"Still can't handle any trouble without a man for backup. You aren't good enough for the PFD."

She slipped her hand into Stephen's and dropped her forehead to his shoulder. Let the media interpret that however they pleased; she didn't care anymore.

"The PFD is a team," Stephen said to Murtagh. "Have you forgotten that's where the real strength lies?"

"A team weakened by females," Murtagh shouted. "If she did everything right, why is she hiding behind you?"

With his encouragement, Kenzie came around to stand at Stephen's side. "Because she can *trust* me," he said. "The real question should be why there's no one standing with you while you continue to attack her."

She saw that strike a nerve as Murtagh started to bluster. Even in the less than ideal lighting, she could see his cheeks turning red. The media was catching all of this.

Stephen turned his back on Murtagh and guided her ahead of him. "I'm sure Grant can handle this without you," he murmured, when they were several paces away. "The jackass won't leave while you're here. He doesn't want you stealing his spotlight."

"So the answer is for me to step aside and let him have it?"

"Hell. I don't know." Stephen rubbed a hand over his face. "Tonight? Yes. Let me take you home. Please. My gut says that's the right move under the circumstances. No one here will let him malign you."

"I'm not a coward," she insisted.

"Isn't discretion the better part of valor?"

"You may have a point," she replied. There wasn't any workable solution here. Logic wasn't effective against the bitter messages Murtagh was trying to sell. Maybe leaving would give the man enough rope to hang himself, as he'd done in the civil suit.

"Let me find Grant."

"Call or send a text from the car." Stephen aimed her toward the parking lot across the street. "He'll understand. Especially after he sees the late news."

"We don't have to watch it, do we?"

"No. We have something better to do."

She shot him a look, wondering if that was some sort of innuendo that they'd be sleeping together, but he didn't elaborate.

He waited in the parking lot only until they got a reply from Grant. Then he left the club behind and took a convoluted route back toward his neighborhood. He stopped at a small grocery store and held her hand as he darted through the aisles, picking up ingredients for s'mores.

"You're kidding," she said, as he paid the cashier.

He grinned down at her and the butterflies in her belly soared. Maybe he didn't grin often because he knew how deliciously devastating it could be. Better to use that kind of power sparingly.

When they reached the garage, he set up two long folding lawn chairs and started a fire in the grill. She unwrapped the chocolate bars and graham crackers and soon they were roasting marshmallows on the tines of the grilling fork.

Though it wasn't quite the same as camping, the s'mores picnic was quickly becoming the highlight of her day, a close second to his agreeing to take her to the wedding.

They stuffed themselves on the sweet treats, laughing about the pranks they'd pulled on their younger siblings back when they could get away with it.

"You miss them?" he asked, as she licked sticky marshmallow goo from her fingers while assembling another s'more.

The chocolate was melting and she caught that drip, too, before it splattered on her work apron. "Every day," she answered. "Mom needed a change of scenery, though."

"You should give her a call," he said, squishing another s'more together.

"I check in regularly."

"I meant because of earlier."

She'd intended to, but had let herself get distracted with this whimsical side of Stephen. As she polished off the s'more and went to wash her hands, some of that Murtagh-induced tension crept into her shoulders, but it lacked the sharp bite and infuriating intensity she'd felt earlier.

She called her mom and gave her a heads-up that she, the club or both might feature on the news.

"I saw a breaking news headline of some trouble at the club," her mom replied. "I knew you'd be okay. You always are."

"Thanks. Grant handled the evacuation well."

"It was a false alarm?"

Kenzie realized she didn't know. "Pretty sure. I left early because Murtagh got belligerent."

"If you didn't sound so calm about it, I'd encourage you to file a restraining order."

Did she sound calm? She felt calm, thanks to Stephen. "Grant's encouraging that, too," she said, trading her waitressing tennies for flip-flops.

"He was a good friend of your father's. I'm glad he's in your corner."

Kenzie agreed, but she was peeking through the camper door, admiring another man who was in her corner. "Just don't believe everything you see or hear on the news, Mom."

Her mother laughed, that rich sound that had always made Kenzie smile through even the worst circumstances.

Feeling better after the conversation, Kenzie took off her apron and dropped it on the bench seat of the camper. Grabbing two beers from the refrigerator, she went back out to the makeshift campfire.

Stephen was pulled from his thoughts when Kenzie waved a beer in front of him.

"Something to cut the sugar," she said.

The soft smile on her face made him want to pull her close

and keep her safe from Murtagh and every other threat lurking out there in the world. "Good talk?" he asked instead.

"It was. Thanks for reminding me to do it."

"No problem." He took a long pull on the beer. She seemed restless, standing there watching the fire rather than sitting back and enjoying it.

"Need to talk about it?"

She shook her head, that long pale braid rippling softly down her back. He couldn't quite get his mind off how silky that hair had been spilling over the pillows.

"Mom wants us to come by the house on our way to the wedding on Sunday," he said.

Kenzie turned to face him, finally sitting down sideways on her chair.

Her lean legs were bare from the hem of her khaki shorts on down, and she'd ditched her tennis shoes for flip-flops. He wondered what she'd do if he stroked the bend of her knee the way he wanted to.

"At some point I have to go home," she murmured. "To my apartment."

He wasn't ready for that, even if it was safe. "File a restraining order against Murtagh and I might let you."

"Let me?" She laughed. "You realize I'm a grown woman?"

He twirled the beer bottle back and forth. "A detail I haven't missed."

She blushed. At least he wanted to believe he'd made her blush. Hard to tell in the weak lighting, so why not assume the positive?

"You've been great..."

He heard the "but" and mentally finished the sentence several ways, all of them unfavorable. "Murtagh clearly isn't done," Stephen said. "It's okay to rely on me until the cops can pin something on him and keep him out of your way. I don't want anything to happen to you."

She stared at her beer bottle. "Thanks." Her voice cracked on the single syllable.

It was as close as he'd seen her come to actual tears. "Come here," he said, making room for her on his chair between his legs.

"I'm fine."

"Maybe I'm not?" It would be nice to hold her close and relax in the knowledge that they were both alive and well. "I could use some company watching the fire die out."

"If only we knew of a way to put it out safely, right now."

He chuckled, the sound startling both of them.

"No fun in that." He patted the chair. "Spoils the ambience."

She moved over to perch at the end of his chair.

"Scared?" he asked.

"Not of you."

"Good." He drew her back against his chest, his legs bracketing hers. He was almost afraid to breathe until she finally relaxed against him.

It was a quiet intimacy he hadn't shared with anyone since his fiancée, and he suspected they both needed the comfort after the things they'd dealt with today.

"Was the accident as bad as it sounded?" she asked, in little more than a whisper.

"Worse," he admitted.

She linked her fingers with his and they didn't talk anymore as they watched the fire die down. He felt like he was going in reverse with her, giving her his home, sleeping with her to burn off adrenaline, and now, resting easy. Maybe it made sense in the context of their odd and sudden friendship. They had so much in common, loner tendencies among them.

The other night, they'd simply found each other, used each other, and now...

Now what? he asked that voice in his head. This was temporary. Kenzie wasn't meant to be a permanent fixture, no matter how well she seemed to fit into his life and business. She was right; at some point she had to go back to her life.

He didn't want that day to be any time soon.

When she was nearly asleep on his chest, he roused her and nudged her into the camper.

He stirred the coals and dumped the last of his beer over them. Certain the fire was out, he retreated to his makeshift apartment in the office. He splashed water on his face and changed into a T-shirt and shorts, but as he made up the bed, he changed his mind.

Returning to the camper, he knocked lightly and waited for her invitation.

"Come in."

He walked inside and caught her standing at the bathroom door, toothbrush in hand. "The office is too far away." He moved to the dinette and started changing it to a bed. "I'm sleeping here tonight."

Her smile was slow and beautiful and loaded with gentle understanding. "Okay. Grab what you need."

He helped himself to a pillow and blanket and stretched out while she finished brushing her teeth. When she came out, she didn't go to the bedroom, she curled up beside him, her back to his chest. When he stiffened, uncertain, she drew his arm over her waist.

From one breath to the next she was asleep. Well, hell.

Breathing in the warm citrus scent of her hair, he decided he wasn't going anywhere before morning. He wouldn't abuse this trust. He might just be the luckiest broken man in the world.

CHAPTER ELEVEN

HE'D BEEN THERE when she woke up on Friday. The overwhelming peace of that just rolled over her, easing the anxiety that had been building until she thought she'd break. Her first thought had been to kiss the burnished gold whiskers shading his jaw, to wake him up slowly with sensual caresses so they could thoroughly enjoy each other.

She'd never be able to keep things light, friendly or simple if she made that move. Her heart was perched, ready to fall into his strong hands. She wasn't sure she could walk away whole if she gave him all she felt right now.

They slipped into a comfortable routine through Friday and Saturday, staying close to the garage and working on the Nova. *Together.* He'd closed the garage for a long weekend in honor of the holiday and they were alone in a cocoon of car parts, tools and music. She loved every minute of it.

Of course, she knew they stuck to the garage in part to dodge the media and to keep her out of Murtagh's sight. It was only Stephen who had to cope with her rant when the PFD moved her back to full administrative leave on Friday afternoon. And only Stephen knew how hard she clung when he pulled her into a reassuring embrace.

On Saturday morning the Camaro came back, and it was

stunning with the silver-and-black paint scheme. They took a quick trip around the neighborhood to test it out, and satisfied, Stephen parked it in the fourth bay, where it would safely wait for Matt Riley to pick it up.

On Sunday morning they shared coffee and muffins she'd baked, while they admired the completed Camaro and work-in-progress Nova. In the afternoon, they enjoyed a few leisurely hours at the Galway house, getting silly with the little ones, giving her time to convince Myra she was coping with the latest debacle. It was all so happy and normal, so easy.

She and Stephen didn't touch at all in front of his family, but she felt his eyes on her and knew he felt her watching him, too. At some point they were going to have to talk or risk exploding from the desire arcing between them.

Dressed for the wedding, they took the convertible out to Boathouse Row. Stephen was model handsome in his dark evening suit and his eyes were hot when he saw her emerge from the camper in her shimmering strapless dress.

Whatever Shannon and Daniel had done to secure this venue on the Fourth of July paid off big time, in Kenzie's opinion. The early evening ceremony was intimate and brief, with guests gathered around an arch of ivy where the couple exchanged vows. The only attendant was Shannon's son, Aiden, standing proudly between them.

The reception spilled outside to the dock and a lovely lawn, and the Jenningses had timed it perfectly so everyone could relax and enjoy plenty of food and cake and dancing as they waited for the fireworks display to start at dark.

Kenzie couldn't take her eyes off the sweet family dancing together in the center of the parquet floor, surrounded by their equally delighted guests. Daniel was practically bursting with pride and love for his bride and stepson.

"I've never seen him so happy," Kenzie said to Stephen.

"Daniel or Aiden?" he asked.

"Both." She chuckled. "All three, really," she added.

Daniel had once vented to her after a difficult breakup that he wouldn't date again until after he retired from the fire department. She understood the sentiment. Outsiders seemed to have this warped image of the job—that they were all bravery wrapped up in fitness and sex appeal—until things turned dangerous. Then the adrenaline-junkie accusations would fly, followed closely by pleas and ultimatums.

Her last boyfriend had been shocked she'd chosen the PFD over him. Being dumped for showing commitment to the job was a fairly common theme among her peers. It took a certain type of person to understand the rigors and the joys of the work they did. Firefighters and other first responders saw more than most people wanted to share and way more than others needed to know. Doing the job well didn't mean doing it unscathed, emotionally or physically.

Her gaze drifted over the other guests. Mitch and Julia were having a blast on the dance floor. Her friend Carson Lane was sharing a dessert with his new wife, Lissa. They'd eloped a few weeks ago and returned oozing joy and contentment. Right now, with foreheads nearly touching, they were clearly sharing an inside joke. Kenzie was so happy for the two of them even as a wisp of envy breezed over her.

Someday. With the right man.

Wonderful events like weddings and the memories being made here were all the more precious because they were on the front lines during their community's most stressful moments. Her day to share this kind of affirmation of life and love with friends and family would come. Her heart clamored that she'd found the right man. Her mind and soul wanted to agree, yet she couldn't bring herself to push him for answers. Not yet.

She glanced at Stephen, wondering what to make of these past two weeks, primarily the past few days. Since waking up together they had shared several kisses, a few tantalizing embraces and lots of laughter, but they were tiptoeing around the bigger issues. Neither of them wanted to talk about the next step and both were avoiding another tumble into bed.

For her part, much of it was the pervasive uncertainty of Murtagh, her career, and where she might have to go to keep doing what she loved.

"Kenzie?"

"Hmm?" Her thoughts had drifted well beyond the wedding reception. Even here she'd let Murtagh creep into her mind like an oily fog. She'd fought so hard to stay on the job despite his antics, yet as she watched Shannon slip into Daniel's embrace for a slow dance, Kenzie wondered if going in a new direction professionally would open things up personally.

Maybe she should talk to Jason about how he'd made the transition.

Stephen covered her hand with his. "Would you like to dance?"

Her body responded to that gentle pressure of his callused palm. Warmth flooded over her from that first point of contact and butterflies fluttered through her belly. With a smile, she stood and walked hand in hand with him to the dance floor.

A serene peace enveloped her as he drew her close, buffering the persistent, sharp desire she felt whenever he was near. That longing had her on edge constantly. Every day was a new test of her willpower to keep things light, when she wanted to explore every hard inch of his body and reclaim that spectacular pleasure they'd shared only once.

His hand rested lightly at her waist, his shoulder firm under the fine fabric of his suit. She remembered the feel of that shoulder, the heat rolling off him as he'd braced himself over her in the bed. It was all she could do not to press her body into his.

Not a good idea to reveal so much with her friends and his brother watching, eagerly hoping for something romantic to develop between them.

"Are you blushing?" His voice was soft at her ear.

"I hope not." She lifted her face and offered him her brightest smile. "It's been a lovely evening."

"It has," he agreed.

The moment stretched and swelled, full of romance and potential with the music swirling around them, the lights twinkling overhead, the scent of lilies in the air. Somehow she managed to keep her lips away from his.

"Thanks for being my plus one," she said, as they swayed together. She found him as enticing in his suit and tie as she did when he was elbow deep in an engine at the garage.

"I didn't think I'd enjoy it," he admitted. His eyes were hot when they met hers and his fingers flexed at her waist. "This makes the effort worthwhile."

She knew the ceremony had been tough on him, but he'd soldiered on with that stoic expression he applied to every uncomfortable task. If he'd been at Julia and Mitch's wedding, she didn't recall seeing him.

"Were you at your brother's wedding?" She regretted the question immediately as his body went tight all over.

"Of course."

"I was at the reception." She leaned back, pretending to leer at him. "I can't believe I overlooked you in the sexy older brother tuxedo."

As she'd hoped, teasing him eased the strain she'd inadvertently created.

"I ducked out early," he replied.

"My loss." She smoothed her hand over his shoulder, offering a small comfort.

He tugged her close. "You think so?"

His husky tone sent goose bumps racing from her hair all the way to her toes. He guided her through a final turn, gave her a squeeze as the band switched to a more lively song. She had to stifle her frustration. She wasn't ready to move on from this more fascinating side of Stephen.

They strolled from the dance floor toward the champagne table and he handed her a glass, taking water for himself.

One more example of the caring, thoughtful nature he frequently hid with a scowl. He'd been generous with everything, going above and beyond to help her. He'd expressed great care for her safety and offered comfort in her lowest moments. They'd even had mind-blowing sex they couldn't seem to talk about. It shouldn't have meant anything, except it did to her. The more time she spent with him, the more she wanted to know what it might have meant to him.

Just ask, she told herself.

She sipped her champagne and tried not to blush again. Her past was peppered with a few short flings to go along with the two serious relationships. She'd been borderline delusional, or possibly too needy, to believe she could keep her emotions out of whatever this was with Stephen.

Maybe the scent of a working garage had gone to her head. That factor didn't hurt, but it was the man who pulled her attention, made her feel safe enough that she could let her guard down and sleep, or shout, or laugh with abandon.

"What are you thinking about?" he asked.

"The Camaro," she fibbed. *Chicken!* "Do you think we can take it out one more time before the buyer picks it up?"

"I can't make any promises. Riley told me he has all of next week as vacation and will try to get up here to pick it up."

"Bummer."

"There are other cars out there." Stephen drew her away from the champagne table just to the edge of the lighting, where they couldn't be overheard. "Tell me what you were really thinking about."

"You," she answered, deciding to stop being a coward.

He cocked an eyebrow, waiting for her to elaborate.

If they were going to delve into feelings, it would be wonderful if he could go first. Too bad she didn't see the conversation going that way.

"You think this atmosphere is getting to me?" he asked.

"No. From my vantage point you're managing just fine." Could he see that for himself, or was his vision still too clouded by his loss?

"You don't sound particularly happy about it."

"On the contrary." She rubbed a hand over his arm. "I'm thrilled. I'd been feeling guilty for dragging you here. All my claims about independence and still I needed a friend to hold my hand for a trip across town."

He took her free hand in his, gave it a gentle squeeze. "I'm glad you asked me."

They both knew it was a cheesy half-truth and she laughed despite the sensations his touch stirred.

A rash of "if only" thoughts went through her mind like a stampede. If only they'd met earlier. If only he could stop blaming himself for the past. If only he was ready to move on and try loving someone else. Someone like her.

Loving.

Yes. That sounded perfect. Her heart gave a kick while her mind flooded with images of what loving Stephen would look like. That was probably light years ahead of where they were tonight. It might even be impossible. Still, it was love, and her heart would not allow her to believe otherwise. She knew it as surely as she knew her name.

Under the spotlight of that truth, her courage crumbled. It was the one thing she wasn't sure she could tell him without hurting them both.

"I should go say hi to Julia." It was a lame and ineffective diversion and she couldn't decide if she wanted him to let her off the hook or not.

"In a minute."

His gaze fell to her lips and her pulse leaped as he leaned in and covered her mouth. The kiss went from tender to blazing in the span of a heartbeat. She tasted the tart lemon of the wedding cake as his tongue stroked boldly across hers. With their joined hands trapped between them, she nearly dropped the glass in favor of holding on for dear life. She wanted to get closer almost as much as she wanted to get him alone.

Stripping him out of this suit would be an erotic pleasure. Her palms were tingling already, anticipating another go at his sculpted body.

Nearby, fireworks began with a heavy *boom* and she gave a start as bursts of gorgeous color sparkled through the trees, danced in the reflection of the river.

His mouth trailed along her jaw and he nipped her ear. "Can we go home now?" His breath fanned the sensitive flesh of her neck and she shivered. "Please."

"Yes." She was wound so tight, she hoped they could get out without having to speak to anyone.

"Don't move." He kissed her, lightning quick, and slipped the glass out of her hand.

A moment later he was back and he tucked her under his arm as they moved around behind the party toward the parking area. He paused several times for deep, lingering kisses, as if he couldn't go two minutes without a taste of her.

She knew just how he felt. The sweet anticipation mounted in the car when they could only hold hands or sneak a kiss at a stoplight. She nearly suggested stopping at the next motel they passed, but checking in would likely take longer than finishing the drive to his place.

When the garage gate closed again after he pulled through, she was tempted to dive on him.

Last time, they'd fallen on each other so fast, all that heat and need. Now she wanted to take her time and savor the process. Savor every lean, sexy inch of him.

He parked the car at the camper steps. Swiveling in his seat, he wrapped his hand around the nape of her neck and pulled her in for a kiss. She kept herself from falling into his lap with one hand on his muscular thigh. Maybe the car could work for round one this time. No, no. She wanted to take it slow.

He shifted, rapped his knee on the steering wheel and muttered an oath against her lips. She laughed. "I'll race you to the steps." Throwing open the car door, she was impressed her quivering legs were up to the task. But Stephen hadn't run for the door. He'd turned toward her and, halfway between the car and the camper, caught her in his powerful embrace, pressing her body to his. His arousal was evident and her hips flexed in an almost painful eagerness for the pleasure ahead.

He groaned, his hands squeezing her hips.

Her lips found his and she slid her hands under his jacket, crushing his perfectly pressed dress shirt as she tried to tug it free of his waistband.

"Kenzie..." He murmured her name over and over as he nuzzled the length of her neck. He leaned her back and trailed more of those provocative kisses lower, along the skin bared by her strapless dress.

"Stephen," she breathed, as the summer breeze and his touch played havoc with her senses. "Inside." Protected by his security system or not, she'd rather not run the risk of this private moment getting caught on a camera.

He didn't hesitate, nudging her toward the camper. His warmth and scent surrounded her as he reached around and opened the door. His fingers skimmed under the hem of her dress, along the backs of her knees as she started up the steps. She froze, mesmerized by those rough fingers.

"Inside," he reminded her, his palms sliding the fabric of her dress over her hips and back down.

She darted into the camper and immediately turned to him, using his tie to bring his lips to hers. Oh, the way he kissed left her breathless and obliterated her self-control.

Her heart racing, she forced herself to slow down as she pushed his jacket off his shoulders. He ran his fingertips back and forth across the top edge of her dress while desire pooled low in her belly. Neither of them spoke; they just watched each other, as if any word would shatter the moment.

She unknotted his tie and started on his buttons, breathing in the clean scent rising from his skin at the base of his throat. When she kissed that vulnerable spot, he groaned again and boosted her onto the tabletop.

Her startled giggle faded as he tugged the fabric back and his mouth closed over her breast. She breathed his name like a prayer. His teeth tugged lightly on her taut nipple and she moaned, shoving her hand into his thick hair.

He wedged his hips between her thighs and she wrapped her legs around his and rocked against him. When at last her hands were cruising along his torso, the slabs of muscle honed by hard work, she remembered why she'd wanted to take it slow.

She drank in the sight of him, memorizing every rise and hollow that defined his body. Burnished gold hair dusted his chest, turning darker below his navel. Her fingers followed the trail of their own volition.

He caught her hands at his belt. "Kenzie. You're too much."

"Same goes," she replied, kissing the hard line of his jaw. "Let's be too much together."

His chin jerked in a nod and he claimed her mouth once more as she reached back and unzipped her dress. The fabric fell to her waist as his hands covered her breasts, teasing and molding her until she was rocking against him, pleading for more.

He lifted her from the table, let the dress fall to the floor, then walked backward toward the bed, bringing her along. She worked his belt loose and he took over, undressing in a rush. No more barriers between them, he fell back on the bed with her sprawled over him.

Oh, this was a fantastic view, and she sat up to enjoy it. To relish all of him this time as she'd promised herself she would. In no hurry now, she feathered kisses over his torso, her hands moving leisurely. This was her chance to give him pleasure, to stoke his passion and hers by reflecting every sensual desire he brought to life in her.

Suddenly, he turned the tables, rolling her under him and

kissing her soundly before taking his skilled lips lower over her breasts, down her belly and lower still to her core. The fast climax bowed her body and he soothed her as she trembled on that delicate edge. When he filled her, thrusting deep, she experienced an indescribable sense of unity.

Love makes all the difference, she thought, reveling in every sensation.

The rest of the world faded, her only thoughts for Stephen and this moment, loving him with all she had right here and now. With her body rather than words he might reject. She gazed up at his intense face, stroking the hard ridges and sinews of his arms. She was too lost in him to hide the feelings roaring through her, and she surged up to steal a kiss.

He laced his fingers with hers, filling her body and soul, and driving them both closer to that sparkling peak. The pressure built and built, and when the climax swept through her he swallowed her cries in a hard kiss as he found his own release.

For a long delicious moment their hearts thundered together. Moving to lie beside her, he drew her in close, and her fingers skimmed through the curls of hair on his chest as she tried to fit all the pieces of herself back together.

It was a lost cause, she thought with a private smile. She kissed his chest, wishing her happiness could fill all the spaces of his heart that had been damaged by grief. The words were there, eager to burst free, and she held them back.

She didn't want him to try to explain away her feelings with the excuse of the romantic wedding or post-sex high. What she felt for him wasn't going anywhere. It was simply a matter of giving him time to discover if he could love her in return.

At just past six, Stephen's phone hummed and chimed. Tangled up with Kenzie in the bed, he quickly silenced it before realizing it wasn't his morning alarm, but a notice from the security system. One of the floodlights on this side of the lot came on, slicing through the dim interior of the trailer. In their fascination with each other, they'd forgotten to pull the curtains.

"What is it?" Kenzie mumbled, tugging the blanket over her head.

"Nothing serious." He knew his security system was making the correct response to whatever had tripped the alarm. Most likely a cat had set off the motion detector. It happened occasionally.

He moved out of the bed as he cycled through the camera feeds, and barely stifled an outburst when he came across the hole in the back fence. It took a precious few seconds to find the angle that showed a man tagging Kenzie's original loaner car with a can of red spray paint.

Stephen pressed the icon to get someone from the security service on the line. He snatched the slacks he'd worn to the wedding from the floor. As he pulled on his pants and searched for his shirt, the service confirmed the silent alarm had been tripped and police were on the way.

The operator advised him to stay in place, out of sight. Stephen wasn't taking any chances. If this was Murtagh, he wanted to provide an eyewitness identification. He found his shirt and slipped it on.

"Stephen?" Kenzie was sitting up now, her hair tumbled. "What is it?"

"Security notified the cops about a breach in the fence. It's handled. Go back to sleep."

"Too late. I'm awake," she said.

"Stay here anyway," he told her. For the first time since she'd kissed him on the camper steps, Stephen wished he'd been sleeping in the office. Then he'd have access to dozens of tools that would make useful defensive weapons.

At the moment, he had only his wits and his phone.

Watching the vandal's progress through the feed on the cell phone, Stephen silently stepped out into the cool morning air. He intended to block the hole in the fence, preventing an escape.

The derogatory message in red paint on the side of the office would have been bad enough on its own. Hearing the vandal attempting to open the bay doors propelled Stephen into action.

No way he'd let anyone destroy client cars, especially not the Camaro that Riley was eager to pick up. Stephen hustled around to the front of the shop, cringing at the sight of wet paint dripping across Kenzie's loaner car.

The message there and on the office wall was identical to the harsh words scrawled across the firehouse, only this time, Murtagh had been caught holding the spray paint can.

"Step away from my property," Stephen said. He held up his phone and pressed the camera icon. Between the phone and the security cameras there shouldn't be any wiggle room for Murtagh.

"If it isn't the boyfriend," he sneered.

"The cops are on their way." Stephen took another step closer. "You won't get away with this."

"Get away with what? I was walking by and saw a kid squeeze out of the fence. Came to make sure you and Miss Hughes were all right."

"No one will buy that. There are cameras covering every inch of the property inside this fence." He'd never been more pleased or satisfied by his decision to beef up his security. "Your lies won't do any good this time."

Murtagh's eyes went wide in his puffy face. "Bull. You have one camera on the gate, that's all."

"Feel free to believe that. Tell it to the cops if you like." He nodded toward the gate. "Here they are now."

Murtagh did an excellent impression of a deer caught in the headlights of an oncoming truck. He froze, refusing to give an explanation or make any comments without his lawyer present. The responding officers had him cuffed and were hauling him to a cruiser when he spotted Kenzie hovering at the corner of the building.

Stephen was close enough to see Murtagh's eyes turn cold

and vicious, his face flooding with angry color. Whatever delusion plagued Murtagh, the man wasn't done with Kenzie.

Stephen blocked Murtagh's view, taking the full brunt of the man's hatred.

Two policemen settled Murtagh into the backseat, while another one questioned Stephen.

"Will you be pressing charges, sir?" the officer asked.

"Absolutely."

"Then come on down to the station. I'll get the paperwork started." The officer turned to Kenzie. "Did you see the man tag anything, ma'am?"

"No," she said. "Will Stephen's statement be enough to keep him off the streets?"

"We can hope," the officer said. "Have a good day."

"When can I clean this up?" Stephen didn't want to leave these offensive messages up any longer than necessary, out of respect for Kenzie.

"Thanks to your security system, we have all we need," the officer replied.

When they were alone, Stephen pulled her into the trailer and just wrapped his arms around her. She was safe. His security measures had worked, protecting her and his property.

"Coffee," she said, withdrawing after a moment. She looked adorable in her worn cutoffs, a tank top emblazoned with the name of a band that recently played the Escape Club, and one of the Galway Automotive caps on her head.

"This will hold him," he said, uncertain which of them needed more reassurance.

"Maybe. Depends on what they charge him with," she said, her normally cheerful features grim. "I saw his face when they hauled him out of here. He blames me for everything that sucks in his life."

"He's wrong," Stephen said, rubbing her back. Kenzie epitomized all the good stuff left in the world. "I'll get started on the fence," he said, when she slipped out from under his hands.

He missed the warmth of her lithe body and the softness of her hair falling loose, but he sensed she was looking for more than physical distance.

"I'll call someone to clean up the graffiti."

"You don't have to do that. It's not like you're a real employee."

She sent him a long, inscrutable look from under the bill of the ball cap. "If you're working on a holiday, so am I."

It took him a second to figure out what she meant. With the wedding, he'd forgotten today was a holiday, since July Fourth had landed on a Sunday. "Right. I'll change clothes and take care of the fence."

When it was repaired, Stephen had to decide whether or not Kenzie should go with him to the police station to make the report. He didn't want to leave her here alone and he really didn't want to run the risk of her bumping into Murtagh.

Grant and his crew had their hands full with another concert setup, so that was out. Though she wasn't expected at the firehouse, maybe they would let her visit. Mitch was on duty and Stephen didn't trust many other people with her safety.

If he explained the situation to his dad, Samuel could stay here while Stephen filed the report. Kenzie might never know how worried he really was for her. His dad wasn't available, but his mom offered to come over under the guise of needing more windshield wiper fluid. Myra could make that small task last hours if necessary.

He was just telling Kenzie to keep the gate closed while he was gone when his mom pulled in.

Kenzie aimed an exasperated look at him. "You called a babysitter?"

"No." He shuffled his feet. "Not exactly."

"It's fine," she said. "I get it."

"You do?" He hadn't expected resigned acceptance of his protectiveness.

"Yes," she said, though she didn't smile. "I wasn't too thrilled about waiting here alone and your mom is great company."

"Kenzie. You should have said something."

She shrugged, leaning back against the workbench. "It was just residual fear. It passes." She'd pulled her coveralls on halfway, gathered at her slender waist in deference to the rising temperature of another bright summer day.

He reached out and curled his finger around the silky end of the braid resting on her shoulder. "It's going to work out," he whispered. He couldn't label the shadows in her eyes as vulnerable, but something was weighing on her. Probably worry, since he'd guaranteed her safety and Murtagh had managed to get in, anyway.

"Why don't I file the report later?"

"If you don't press charges now, his lawyers will have him out within the hour," she said. "Go." She gave him a little shove. He trapped her hands with his and kissed her.

Releasing her, he pressed the button to raise the bay door for his mom's car to pull in. One more layer of protection between Kenzie and the outside world couldn't hurt.

He gave his mom a quick hug and then jogged for his car, determined to make the fastest police report in history.

CHAPTER TWELVE

KENZIE NEEDED SOME time and space to process the myriad emotions flooding her system. Last night had been so beautiful, so much more than sex and physical needs. She'd gone into it knowing her heart was already in Stephen's oblivious grip, and yet she'd been overcome by the experience.

Maybe she *was* romanticizing his basic physical responses due to wedding-effect, or she was using her feelings for Stephen to block out her fear of Murtagh. No. That was insecurity talking. She knew her heart and mind; now she just had to figure out what to do about it.

First, she had to accept that if Murtagh was willing to cut through a fence and vandalize Stephen's business, he might never quit hounding her. Would he drop this pursuit if she gave up her career? Maybe they should get that story out there and see if he gave up the hunt.

With all of that in her head, she gave Myra a warm smile. "Does your car need any service?"

"Probably not." Her own sheepish smile was so like her oldest son's. "The wiper fluid might be low."

"I'll take a look," Kenzie said, heading to the sporty crossover.

"I brought coffee cake," Myra said, while Kenzie raised the hood.

"You know Stephen keeps plenty of coffee around."

"Do you have time to chat?" Myra asked.

"Of course." She didn't have anywhere else to go. She checked the level in the reservoir and added more fluid. Closing the hood, she walked over to the shop sink and washed her hands before leading Myra into the office.

"I know Stephen was worried about leaving me alone," Kenzie said. "Thanks for coming by."

"After this dreadful vandalism, I can understand his concerns."

"Me, too." Kenzie set a cup of coffee to brew for Myra.

She was feeling inexplicably emotional and not at all ready to discuss the real issues with Stephen's mom. Yes, she loved Stephen and she was fairly sure the news wouldn't surprise a mother as tuned in as Myra. Kenzie just wasn't sure love would be enough to keep Stephen. He hadn't given her any real indication that he was ready to leave the emotional safety net of his dead fiancée.

"Samuel tells me Murtagh drank heavily his last year with the PFD. They tried to get him help, but he just wouldn't take responsibility for his actions."

"Some people don't want help." Kenzie pulled a chair closer to the desk so they could use it as a table. "Not until they hit rock bottom."

"True," Myra agreed. She sliced coffee cake for each of them and they sat on either side of the desk to eat. "Mistakes, booze and a bad attitude forced him into retirement."

Raspberry streusel, Kenzie realized, as she bit into the buttery pastry. "This is amazing."

"It's one of Stephen's favorites."

Kenzie took a bigger bite, hoping she wouldn't be cornered into asking for the recipe like a woman planning to stick around. Her wants and hopes were irrelevant if Stephen wasn't ready to make that kind of commitment.

"I didn't make the connection earlier. Samuel reminded me that Randall Murtagh was replaced by the first female firefighter to come into that house."

And then another woman had rescued him. No wonder he'd gone off the rails. "Is he still drinking?"

"I don't know. He's been a loner ever since," Myra said. "The problem with waiting until someone hits rock bottom is never really knowing where that point is."

True. "Are you concerned about someone?"

Myra's lips curved and her eyes, filled with love, crinkled at the corners. "Always. At the moment, I'm concerned you'll get caught in Randall's blind, misplaced hatred."

Kenzie brushed the crumbs from her fingertips. "Stephen is confident pressing charges will help."

"Good. What are *you* confident about?"

"That I won't let him win. His showing up here was definitely a shock," she admitted. "I've wondered if I should announce my resignation from the PFD."

"Do you want to quit?"

"No." She traced the rim of her coffee cup. "My thought was if he thinks I've quit, he'll stop this nonsense."

"And the people you care about will be safe," Myra observed. Kenzie nodded.

"Stephen maintains excellent security. He beefed it up when those car thieves were plaguing the city."

Kenzie swallowed a laugh. "Mitch was miserable when two of the cars the guys had rebuilt were stolen from their customers."

"You don't have to tell me." Myra rolled her eyes. "Sunday dinners were borderline morose for a time."

In more comfortable conversational territory, the two women chattered on. The normality of it was as reassuring and fun as if Kenzie was hanging out with her own mother and her sister. By the time Stephen returned, she had almost forgotten why he'd been gone. It had been a wonderful couple of hours.

* * *

Stephen found his mother and Kenzie in the office, laughing over something they claimed he wouldn't understand. He managed not to point out that he wanted to understand every intriguing facet of Kenzie. Once they'd both said goodbye to his mom, Kenzie went to change for her shift at the club and Stephen prepared for an afternoon in the shop.

"Thank you for pressing charges," Kenzie said, when she walked back into the office dressed in her Escape Club uniform. "I'm sorry Murtagh's issue with me spilled over on you. The cleanup crew should be here by noon."

"It's not your fault, Kenzie. I'm glad he won't be able to squeak through the cracks again. You'll be able to get back to your life."

Once Murtagh was finally buttoned up she'd be safe. As safe as she could be in her career of choice, anyway.

"Back to my life?" she echoed.

"That's what you want," he pointed out. Since the day he'd towed her car, her every decision and action had been moving her closer to getting back on shift with the PFD.

She looked past him to the shop beyond the door and then her gaze roamed the office, including the couch he hadn't slept on since the bomb threat. Had his mother noticed that detail?

Stephen could tell Kenzie expected him to say something more, but what? Of course he'd miss her when she left. He was addicted to her laughter, and when her eyes sparkled as she smiled, all the tension faded out of his body. He hoped she'd make time to keep working on projects like the Nova. Maybe she'd agree to dinner once in a while.

The woman had destroyed his solitude and he didn't even mind.

"What if it worked out?" she asked quietly. "You and me. We're good together, Stephen."

What if?

Every time she returned from a shift at the firehouse or the club, he felt such a wave of joy and gratitude mixed with relief. When she handed him a cup of coffee or a message about an appointment or a potential sale, he felt her presence like his own personal sunbeam. Strong or not, he wasn't ready to put any of that pressure of his past on her shoulders, and he didn't know how to put any of it into words.

"I love you," she said.

Those were the words.

She tipped her head, watching him. "Did you hear me?"

Yes. Of course he'd heard her. The words were bouncing around and through and over the rubble of the wall that had protected his heart since violence had destroyed all his plans with Annabeth. When had Kenzie knocked it down?

"Kenzie." This was too sudden. He still hadn't figured out whether or not he was up for another relationship. *What if?* What if she went to work and didn't come home? He couldn't survive another tragedy. Not now that his heart was all open and vulnerable to her every word and action.

"You know what?" She plucked the keys to her restored compact from the wall hook.

Joey had brought that back with the Camaro, but Stephen hadn't reached out to the buyer yet.

"Forget I said anything," she continued, with an eerie calm. "You've been a great help to me during a trying time. I'll always appreciate that." Unshed tears glistened in her big blue eyes. "Take care."

He'd made her cry? He didn't think that was possible; she was so tough. Tougher than he could ever be.

"Kenzie." She was long gone by the time he jerked himself away from that paralyzing fear and moved to follow her.

He swore and was turning back to grab his keys when his eyes latched on to movement on the security monitor. As Kenzie drove away, Murtagh got into his car and followed her.

Why wasn't the bastard in police custody?

Dread surged through Stephen's system. He snagged his phone and his keys and set off after Murtagh.

In the car he called Kenzie's cell phone, but she didn't pick up. He hadn't held out much hope that she would. Clearly, she was furious and rightly so. He'd screwed up everything. He called Grant next, only to hear another voice mail message. At the tone, he gave Grant the basic information and then he called the police, reporting Murtagh's plate number along with a description of the car.

He stayed on Murtagh's tail, grateful Kenzie was several car lengths ahead of them. If he couldn't do anything right in a relationship, at least he could distract the jerk hassling her. Stephen should have been doing a better job of that all along, per Grant's original request.

He'd gone and fallen in love with her and then chickened out when she called him on it. For the first time, he realized he wanted her in his life more than he wanted to protect himself from further pain.

He couldn't let Murtagh succeed, whether or not Kenzie ever understood his belated epiphany. Although she deserved far more, stopping Murtagh was the first step to keeping her.

They were almost through the cramped streets downtown when Kenzie turned for the club and Murtagh turned the opposite way. Stephen followed him. Using the hands-free commands, he kept calling Kenzie's number, though she continued to ignore him.

Ahead of him, Murtagh sped up and took turns at the last second, clearly trying to lose him. Fortunately, Stephen's street racing skills were still sharp. Murtagh wasn't breaking any laws, though his aggressive driving and Stephen's efforts to stick with him earned them both plenty of honking horns from other nervous and perturbed drivers.

Murtagh gained some space by running a red light, and Stephen chose to stop rather than risk a serious accident. By now Kenzie should be safe at the Escape Club anyway, likely getting an update from Grant that the police had let Murtagh walk.

Stephen tried to pick up the trail again and when he couldn't find any sign of the man or his car, he eventually turned toward the club.

Midday, it was early enough that she had time to talk. Well, time to listen. She'd had the guts to speak plainly and it was his turn. His heart stuttered as he practiced the words he'd never thought to give to another woman. "I love you, Kenzie."

It sounded right in the quiet Challenger. He could only hope she'd believe him and forgive his blunder.

There were a couple cars next to Grant's over in the employee area, including the Mustang they'd sold to Jason. Stephen parked next to Kenzie's little sedan at the kitchen entrance. He walked up and when he pulled on the door, found it locked.

"Come on!" He glared at the security camera. "Let me in."

A moment later the door swung open to reveal Grant, his mouth set in a grim line. "Got your messages."

Stephen shoved his hands into his pockets, his fingers curling around his car keys. "Hopefully, the police will pick him up soon."

"Agreed." Grant's stocky build blocked the doorway. "Is that all you needed?"

"I need to speak with Kenzie."

"She gave me the impression she doesn't want to speak with you."

"Then she can listen," Stephen snapped. "This is personal, Grant." And urgent. He couldn't let her wonder about him any longer.

Grant's salt-and-pepper eyebrows lifted and he stepped back so Stephen could enter. "My guess is you'll need to do some groveling," he said in an undertone. "She's helping Jason prep at the bar."

An ugly surge of jealousy reared up in him. It was hard to

believe at one point he'd wanted to push her toward the assistant manager. He'd been an idiot.

"Is she even on the schedule tonight?" Stephen wondered.

"I'll go check." Grant turned down the hall to his office.

His heart hammering erratically in his chest, Stephen hurried into the empty club. Kenzie sat at the end of the bar, laughing with Jason. Jealousy took another swipe at him, but he ignored it. Kenzie didn't play coy games. She said what she meant, and she'd said she loved him.

He paused, wishing he'd changed out of his grimy garage clothes. Next to Jason, he looked like...well, exactly what he was, a mechanic. "Can I talk to you? Privately."

She tipped her head toward the front doors, which would be open soon. "We need to finish this prep."

"The band isn't even here yet," Jason muttered. "Give him a break."

"I have," she whispered fiercely as she slid off the bar stool.

Stephen soaked up every nuance as she approached, grateful to have another chance. Her eyes were bright, with temper now instead of tears as she stared up at him.

She folded her arms over her chest. "So talk."

"Did you listen to my messages?"

"I deleted them."

"Good." He didn't want her to think he was here only because of Murtagh. "You mean everything to me, Kenzie. I didn't expect to feel this way again."

Her jaw set and her fingertips flexed into her upper arms as if she was trying to keep herself in check. *Again* was the wrong word. His feelings for her were beyond the scope of his experience. He pushed a hand through his hair.

Suddenly, he tugged her into the shadow of the hallway, out of Jason's view. He couldn't do this with an audience. She was stiff under his hands and he released her immediately.

"*Again* is the wrong word, but it's right, too. I did love Annabeth."

"I should hope so," she snapped.

"This. Us." He cleared his throat. "What I feel for you is so much more that it scares me. You are so tough, so vibrant." Wishing she'd let him touch her, he plowed on. "I didn't think I deserved a second chance after..." He left that unfinished.

She blinked, her gaze on the ceiling and her teeth biting into her lip. "It wasn't your fault."

He shook his head. This wasn't about the past; it was about the future. Their future. What could he say to convince her to stick with him? "I screwed up back at the shop," he said, starting over. "I won't make excuses for it and I'll probably screw up a hundred times more by the end of next week."

Her lips quirked up, though she caught the smile before it broke free.

"Only this matters." He tucked a wayward strand of her hair behind her ear. "I love you, Kenzie."

Her lips parted on a startled gasp.

He hated that the ghosts of his past had left her doubting. "I love you so much that I tried to deny it in some ill-advised attempt at self-preservation. Being safe isn't living all out. You reminded me of that essential lesson. Forgive me?"

"Stephen."

That was all, just his name. Those two syllables were as sweet as any touch of her amazing hands. He started to say something more, when an explosion rocked the kitchen.

Shouts of "fire" came a moment before the first belch of smoke hit the hallway. She started toward the kitchen, but Stephen caught her and pulled her behind him.

Murtagh stalked toward them from the emergency exit and the gun in his hand was pointed at Stephen.

"Get out of here," Stephen said to Kenzie. "Go."

"Look, I created a crisis, Hughes. Go fix it," the man dared. "Be the pretty hero if you can."

Stephen felt Kenzie shift behind him. "You picked the wrong target," he said.

"If female firefighters can do anything, prove it," Murtagh shouted. "Prove it!"

"How in the hell do you keep getting into my club?" Grant's voice roared above the sound of the fire and the clanging alarm as he charged up behind them.

Too late, Stephen saw Murtagh's finger squeeze the trigger, and he shouted a warning. The lethal black muzzle of the gun flashed and Stephen tried to shelter Kenzie. He didn't care about her training, only about getting her out of here alive.

Grant swore, skidding to a stop in front of them, his arms spread protectively as Murtagh threatened to shoot again. "You'll never get away with this. Put down the gun and we can reduce the damage here."

"Hand her over." Murtagh coughed as the smoke choked the hallway. "Let her prove what an asset she is to the city."

Kenzie had been with this man in a fire before. If she didn't do something soon, none of them would be walking away. It took a concerted effort, but she wedged herself between the bigger bodies of Grant and Stephen. "What do you need, Randall?" she asked in that easygoing tone she'd used before. "Let's go outside and talk about it."

"You took my job!" Spittle gathered in the corners of his lips.

She swallowed her first instinct to point out that was a preposterous claim. He was beyond logic. She thought about Myra's assessment of rock bottom. Murtagh kept sinking, finding new lows. She'd seen it in the earlier fire.

"Did you set the fire in the kitchen?" she asked conversationally.

"Yes!"

"Why don't you help me put it out?" she offered. The faint sounds of fire engine sirens were growing louder. "We can be heroes together." She shifted toward the kitchen, relieved to draw his attention from Stephen and Grant. "Think how pleased the PFD will be."

The smoke was stinging her nose, burning her lungs, yet she wouldn't quit. Despite his desperate actions recently, Randall Murtagh had once been a valued member of the PFD and community at large.

He snorted "No female can equal a man in a crisis." He waved the gun at Stephen and Grant. "Once again, two *men* have stepped up to shelter you."

She spread her arms wide. "Randall, I'm right here, out front. Let's go do this."

"You will be." Coughing again, he used the gun to gesture for the three of them to move into the empty club. "Go on."

"Run," Stephen whispered, moving between her and Murtagh as much as he dared.

"No." She wasn't going anywhere without him. Or Grant. At least in the club, the air was clearer as the smoke rose to the rafters.

Grant slowed his steps. "Whatever has you upset, Randall, we can sort it out. Just put the gun down."

"It's too late for that," Murtagh said woodenly. He lined them up against the bar.

Kenzie had heard that tone from him before, through the filter of her turnout gear. Suddenly it all clicked. His deliberate resistance in that fire, his focused pursuit of her ever since. "You didn't want to be saved that day."

"Of course I didn't!" Randall screamed.

Crap. This changed everything. He was willing to die, eager for it, and he had no qualms about taking them along with him.

He doubled over, clutching his head. Grant moved in, but Murtagh stood up. "Back off!" He leveled the gun at Kenzie. "You showed up with your idealistic persistence and made everything worse. *You.*"

"It's not her fault you're an arsonist," Stephen said, distracting Murtagh as he squeezed the trigger again. The bullet went wide, shattering the transom over the club's front doors.

Murtagh pressed the hot muzzle of his gun to Stephen's chest. "On your knees."

"No." Kenzie felt tears on her cheeks as Stephen obeyed. "Randall, let him go. Let them both go. This is between you and me."

To her relief, he lowered the weapon, leaving a small burn mark on Stephen's T-shirt. They were hardly out of danger. A telltale sound overhead drew her attention. The fire was chewing through the roof. They had to get out of here.

Though Murtagh lowered the gun, he maintained control. If they tried to run, he could shoot at will. There wasn't enough cover between their position and the front door. The hallway was black with smoke, emergency lights glowing.

"Randall, let's go," she said quietly.

"It's too late," Murtagh was saying. "You can't do anything. This will show the city and the world that females should not be trusted to fight fires."

"I certainly can't do anything when you're holding me at gunpoint. Let these guys go. They don't know how to put out this fire."

"No." Murtagh shook his head, then groaned as if that caused him great pain. "They should know they backed the wrong dog in this fight."

Clearly, reasoning with him was out of the question. "You've made your point," she said, willing to plead, to do anything to save Stephen and Grant. "We need to get out of here."

"Are you scared?" Murtagh leaned close.

"Yes." Though not at all for the reasons he probably believed. She was afraid for the people fighting the fire in the kitchen. She knew real fear that Stephen and Grant were being targeted by a man who wanted only her.

"Good." He was nearly nose to nose with her.

Beside her, still on his knees, she felt Stephen's hand on her calf. The touch steadied her. "What do you want from me?" she asked.

"Just the last few minutes of your life," he said, suddenly calm. "You should thank me for allowing your friend and over-protective lover to join us."

The smoke seemed to be thinning. The firefighters must have the worst of the blaze contained. What would Murtagh do when he noticed? Behind him, she caught a movement at the hallway. Stretched out on his belly, Jason was signaling something to Grant.

"If you want to kill me, just do it," she said, stepping forward, keeping Murtagh's attention on her. "Let these guys go."

Stephen caught her hand in his.

She shook him off. Taking the focus was all she knew to do to give Grant and Stephen a chance to escape. "Come on, Randall. Man up. Let them go and just take the shot. You've tried everything else to get me out of the PFD. This is the last chance you'll have."

"Kenzie, no," Stephen said.

A man shouted from the front doors, identifying himself with the police department, ordering Murtagh to stand down.

"Hostage negotiator," Grant explained. "You should talk to him. Want my phone?"

"There's nothing to negotiate," Murtagh said.

"Sure there is," Kenzie said in a soothing voice. "This can be the end of it. A simple misunderstanding. You and I can start fresh."

Murtagh's shoulders slumped and for a split second, Kenzie thought they were making progress. Then he looked up and she knew he'd gone over the edge. His gaze was blank, his motions stiff as he started shooting wildly.

Stephen yanked her to the floor and covered her body with his. The impact knocked the breath from her lungs. Another gunshot bit into the bar, missing them by inches and sending splinters through the air. Grant swore as one more gunshot sounded. There was a heavy *thud* and then an echoing silence.

She squirmed out from under Stephen, intent on helping

whoever had been shot, but it was too late. Murtagh had killed himself.

She didn't realize she was sobbing until Stephen tucked her close to his chest, hiding her face from the gruesome view. "I'm here. Let it go." He let her cling as waves of sorrow and confusion shook her body.

Voices surged all around them, but he held on, sheltering her while she lost it. She couldn't even pinpoint why she was so upset for a man who'd aimed so much vitriol and hatred at her.

Time seemed to slow as Stephen stroked his hand over her head, down her braid, again and again. She breathed in the earthy, honest scents of the garage and the man underneath.

"Are you hurt?" She peeked under his T-shirt, grateful the gun hadn't burned him.

"Not a bit, thanks to you."

She dropped her head to his shoulder as the emotions began to subside. "I love you," she murmured.

"I know," he replied.

She smiled against his chest, hugging him tightly. He was her lifeline, her connection to the bravest part of herself. "You love me back," she said.

He tipped up her face until she was mesmerized by those steady hazel eyes. "I know."

His lips met hers in a kiss sweeter than their first. Laced with the undeniable passion they'd discovered in each other, it was a kiss full of hot temptation wrapped with comforting acceptance.

It was a kiss between lovers with plans for a long future together.

Stephen finally believed it was over when they were safely back at the garage. They were home. The police statements had been made, the news reporters directed to her lawyer and the assurances given to her family and his. Grant had even told them an initial search of Murtagh's laptop proved he was the source of the cyber bullying.

In the trailer Kenzie had showered and changed into those cutoff shorts and a snug tank top sporting patriotic red, white and blue. He'd cleaned up as well, choosing khaki cargo shorts and a loose, short-sleeved cotton shirt, thinking they might both benefit from a long, leisurely drive tonight.

Right now, she was still too wound up to enjoy much of anything. Stephen caught the tremor in Kenzie's hands as she reached for the tea he'd brewed for her. He understood that quaking, as everything inside him still trembled, as well.

"I can't believe Grant has to close the club," she said.

It was hardly the first time since the fire was contained that she'd expressed that concern.

"Grant's faced far worse," he reminded her. "He'll get through it and have the place open again in no time." Stephen thought Grant and Kenzie had that unflagging spirit and fortitude in common. Traits he'd not seen in himself until Kenzie made him take a closer look.

"Probably," she agreed, her smile not quite up to full power yet.

Stephen kept expecting to hear something stupid come out of his mouth about risks and the benefits of a safe distance. It didn't. He wanted to hold her, to sleep beside her every night and wake up with her every morning. To laugh and curse over back-ordered parts and challenging repairs. He wanted to ask her to take the real risk of tying her future to his. For today, for a lifetime.

"You were amazing," he said, not for the first time.

"You saved my life," she murmured, staring into her tea.

"I panicked," he admitted, sliding into the bench seat next to her and drawing her close to his side. "You had it under control."

Her body hitched on a sound that wasn't quite a laugh. She managed to sip the tea and he felt her relaxing into him.

"He didn't have to kill himself," she said at last.

Stephen sighed. "Murtagh was troubled. Beyond the bitterness of any injury or insult that a woman saved him from a fire." He pressed a kiss to her temple. "He was lost in a dark place."

Kenzie snuggled closer. "Sounds like the voice of experience."

"To a point," he confessed. "I never truly considered ending my life, but I did what I could to increase the odds."

"Picking fights and hunting drug dealers is dangerous," she said.

"Says the woman who runs into burning buildings and calls it a good day." He stopped and stared at her. "Wait. You knew I did that?"

She sat up, brushing his hair back from his face. "I'd been warned about your odd hobbies. Falling willy-nilly wasn't one of them."

Kenzie had set him free, restoring his hope and giving him good reasons to spend more time living his life than haunting his past. Since the narcotics team had moved in and cleaned up the street at last he didn't feel the need to keep up the "odd hobby."

"Grant told you."

She nodded.

"Is that why you stuck around every time I tried to push you away?"

"Please." This time her laughter came much closer to that bold joyful sound. "You did everything except beg me to stay."

"Yeah? Well, I was getting to that when the fire interrupted us." He shifted in the seat and took her hands in his. He really should have a ring, but he didn't want to waste another moment. "Marry me, Kenzie. Be my partner in life and I promise we'll find something to laugh over every single day."

Her blue eyes sparkled and he wanted to kiss her. It took all his willpower to leave her mouth free to give him an answer.

She glanced to the ceiling before meeting his gaze. "If I say no, you'll probably forget how to laugh again," she said, tracing the line of his finger with her thumb.

"So say yes," he murmured.

"Yes." She brought his face to hers and kissed him soundly. "Yes." She peppered more kisses over his nose and cheeks. "You'll be my husband and give me great cars. I'll be your wife and give you great headaches, kids and cookies."

He laughed, backing out of the dinette space and pulling her along with him.

"Plenty of laughter and love, too," she added.

"We'll put that in the vows," he said, his hands sliding under her top and lifting it up and over her head.

Outside, he heard a car horn at the gate. He muttered an oath as he checked the display on his phone. "It's Matt Riley."

She groaned and scrambled for her shirt.

"You could wait here," he said, halfway out the door. The sooner he made delivery, the sooner he and Kenzie could get back to celebrating their engagement.

"I want to meet him," she said. "I'll get the keys."

"All right."

Stephen opened the gate, then jogged over to open the bay door, grinning at the sight of the 1972 Plymouth Cuda he and Mitch had restored for Matt's father.

The driver parked in front of the bay where the Camaro SS was waiting under a protective cloth cover.

General Ben Riley emerged from the driver's side a fraction slower than his son leaped from the passenger side.

"Is she ready?" Matt asked.

"All set," Stephen replied, reaching out to shake hands with Ben. "I appreciate the repeat business, sir."

Ben leaned back. "Something's different about you," he said.

"Oh, it's the smile." Kenzie joined them, a set of keys dangling from her finger. "He's been practicing more lately."

Stephen slid his arm around her waist. "My fiancée," he said, making the introductions.

Ben offered hearty congratulations and wished them a marriage as long and happy as he'd shared with his wife. Stephen noticed Matt was a little more reserved, most likely distracted by the purpose of the visit.

"Go on," Stephen urged. "She's all yours now."

Matt pulled back the cloth and gave a whoop of joy. "Perfect!" He circled the car, then came around and gave Stephen a manly hug, utterly delighted.

Kenzie held out the keys. "She handles like a dream."

"It would've taken me forever to get her into this kind of shape," Matt said from the driver's seat a moment later. "Dad, look at these details."

"Excellent work," Ben agreed.

"We just worked to your son's specs," Stephen said.

Matt started the engine, his face as bright as a kid at Christmas.

"I hope you have a place to run her wide open once in a while," Kenzie said. "It's a great experience."

Over the top of the car, Ben grinned at them. "We know of a few places to open her up."

"Good." Stephen felt Kenzie lean in, her finger hooking in his belt loop.

He accepted the check for the final payment and waved the Rileys and their muscle cars through the gate. He hoped they kept their word to send him even more business. The restorations were a challenge he enjoyed.

Though not as much as he enjoyed the woman beside him.

He reached for Kenzie. "Now, where were we?"

She scooted away, walking backward to the trailer, gathering the hem of her T-shirt, giving him an irresistible glimpse of her midriff. "We might have been celebrating that I said you could be my husband."

Her sassy grin lit him up. "Oh, that's right," he said, chasing her down and sinking into the kiss when she let him catch her. She'd healed him, brought him back into the world, body, heart and soul. Whatever life tossed at them tomorrow or in all the days to come, he knew he could face it with laughter and courage, because Kenzie had taught him how to love.

* * * * *

An Honourable Seduction
Brenda Jackson

WESTERN

Rugged men looking for love...

Also by Brenda Jackson

The Westmorelands miniseries

Zane
Canyon
Stern
The Real Thing
The Secret Affair
Breaking Bailey's Rules
Bane

The Westmoreland Legacy miniseries

The Rancher Returns
His Secret Son
An Honourable Seduction

Discover more at millsandboon.com.au.

Brenda Jackson is a *New York Times* bestselling author of more than one hundred romance titles. Brenda lives in Jacksonville, Florida, and divides her time between family, writing and travelling.

Email Brenda at authorbrendajackson@gmail.com or visit her on her website at brendajackson.net.

To the man who will forever be the love of my life, Gerald Jackson, Sr.

To all of my readers who asked for Flipper's story. This one is for you!

To the Brenda Jackson Book Club/ Facebook fans. Over 4,000 strong and after fourteen years, you guys still rock!

Many waters cannot quench love; rivers cannot sweep it away.
—*Song of Solomon* 8:7

PROLOGUE

The Naval Amphibious Base
Coronado, San Diego, California

"WHAT KIND OF trouble have you gotten into?"

David Holloway, known to his Navy SEAL teammates as Flipper, glanced at the four men surrounding him. They were like brothers to him. More than once they'd risked their lives for each other and they would continue to have each other's backs, on duty or off. That bond was what accounted for the concerned looks on their faces. He wondered how they'd known he'd been summoned to the admiral's office.

"Let's hope I'm not in any trouble, Mac," Flipper said, rubbing a hand down his face.

He had to admit he was wondering what was going on, just like they were. Usually, you were only summoned to a meeting with the admiral when you were getting reprimanded for some reason, and he never got into trouble. At least he *rarely* did. As the son of a retired SEALs commanding officer and the youngest of five brothers—all Navy SEALs—he knew better.

"Maybe there's an event on the base and he wants you to escort his daughter now that you're the single one among us," Coop said, grinning.

Flipper didn't grin back. They'd seen Georgianna Martin, the admiral's twenty-three-year-old daughter. She was beautiful, but they'd heard the horror stories from other teammates who'd been ordered to take her out on dates. According to them, those evenings had been the dates from hell. The young woman was spoiled rotten, selfish as sin and had an attitude that sucked. That's why Flipper didn't find Coop's comment at all amusing. He hoped that wasn't why the admiral wanted to see him.

It didn't surprise Flipper that it was Mac who'd asked if Flipper had gotten into trouble. Thurston McRoy—code name Mac—was older than the other four men on the team, who had all started their careers as SEALs around the same time. Mac had been a SEAL five years before the rest of them. Mac seemed to like to think he was the big brother looking out for them, almost like he figured they couldn't take care of themselves. He was forever giving them advice—even when they didn't ask for it.

In addition to Mac and Flipper, their SEAL team included Brisbane Westmoreland, code name Bane; Gavin Blake, whose code name was Viper; and Laramie Cooper, whose code name was Coop.

Flipper checked his watch. "Since I have a couple of hours to spare before meeting with the admiral, let's grab something to eat," he suggested.

"Sounds good to me," Bane said.

Less than an hour later, Flipper and his four teammates shared burgers, fries and milkshakes at one of the most popular eating places on base. They decided to sit outside at one of the café tables in the front instead of inside where it was crowded since it was such a beautiful May day.

No one brought up his meeting with the admiral again or the notion of him taking the admiral's daughter on a date. He was glad. Instead, the guys had more important things to talk about, namely their families.

Bane's wife, Crystal, had given birth to triplets last year and he had new photos to share, so they passed Bane's cell phone around.

Viper's wife, Layla, was expecting with only a few months to go before Gavin Blake IV would be born. Viper was excited about becoming a father, of course.

Like Bane, Mac had plenty of photos to share; he was married and the father of four.

And Coop had a two-year-old son he hadn't known about until he'd run into his old girlfriend about six months ago. They'd reconnected, gotten married and were now a happy family.

Earlier in the week, the teammates had gotten word from their commanding officer that next week was the start of a four-month leave. For Flipper, that meant heading home to Dallas and he couldn't wait. His mother had a birthday coming up and he was glad he would be home to celebrate.

"I don't care what plans you all are making for your leave, just as long as you remember my mom's birthday celebration. I understand you not showing up, Viper, with a baby on the way. The rest of you guys, no excuses."

"We hear you," Bane said, grinning. "And we will be there."

When Viper ordered another hamburger, everyone teased him about being the one to eat for two instead of his wife. And then everyone talked about what they planned to do with their four months off.

It was two hours later when Flipper walked into the admiral's office. He was surprised to find Commanding Officer Shields there as well. Flipper saluted both men.

"At ease. Please have a seat, Lieutenant Holloway."

"Thank you, sir," he said, sitting down. He was used to being under his commanding officer's intense scrutiny, but there was something in the sharp green eyes of Admiral Norris Martin that was making him feel uncomfortable.

"You come highly recommended by your commanding officer here, Lieutenant Holloway. And the reason I asked to meet with you is that we need you. Your country needs you."

Flipper was happy to step up. He was a Navy SEAL, and the reason he'd enlisted, like his father and brothers, was to protect his country. "And what am I needed to do, sir?" he asked.

"Our investigators have provided intelligence and a preliminary report that says acts of espionage are happening in Key West. Someone is trading valuable government secrets to China."

Flipper didn't respond immediately.

The one thing he hated was a traitor, but he'd discovered that for the right price, a number of American citizens would perform acts of treason. He understood that. However, what he didn't understand was why he'd been singled out for this meeting. He was part of a SEAL team. He didn't work in naval intelligence.

Confusion must have shown on his face because Admiral Martin continued, "The report was given to me, but I don't believe it."

Flipper raised a brow. "You don't believe a report that classified documents are being traded in Key West, sir?"

"Oh, I believe all that, but what I refuse to believe is that this suspect is guilty of anything."

"Is there a reason why, sir?"

"Here is the information," said Commanding Officer Shields, speaking for the first time as he handed Flipper a folder.

Flipper opened it to find a picture of a very beautiful woman. She looked to be around twenty-four, with dark, sultry eyes and full, shapely lips. Then there was her mass of copper-brown spiral curls that flowed to her shoulders, crowning a cocoa-colored face. A pair of dangling gold earrings hung from her ears and a golden pendant necklace hung around her neck.

He knew he was spending too much time studying her features, but it couldn't be helped. The woman was strikingly beautiful.

Reluctantly he moved his gaze away from her face to check out the background of the photo. From the tropical vegetation captured by the photographer, she seemed to be on an island somewhere. She stood near a body of water that showed in the corner of the eight-by-ten photo. Scribbled across the bottom were the words:

Miss you, Godpop 1

Love, Swan

Swan? It was an unusual name, but it fit.

He moved to the next document in the file. Attached to it was a small family photo that showed a tall Caucasian man with sandy-brown hair and brown eyes standing beside a beautiful woman who closely resembled Swan. Her mother. In front of the couple was a beautiful little girl who looked to be around eight.

Flipper studied the child's face and knew that child had grown up to be the gorgeous woman in the first photo. The shape of her face was the same, as were her eyes. Even as a child, she'd had long curly hair.

The family photo was clipped to a profile of the young woman. As he'd guessed, she was twenty-four. Her name was Swan Jamison. She was an American, born in Key West. Presently, she owned a jewelry store on the island. That was all the information the document provided.

Flipper lifted his gaze to find his commanding officer and the admiral staring at him. "I assume this is the person naval intelligence believes is the traitor."

"Yes," Admiral Martin said. "She's my goddaughter. I am Godpop 1."

"She's my goddaughter as well," added Commanding Officer Shields. "I am Godpop 2."

Flipper's gaze moved from one man to the other. "I see, sirs."

Admiral Martin nodded. "Her father was part of our SEAL team and our best friend. His name was Andrew Jamison."

Flipper had heard that Commanding Officer Shields and

Admiral Martin were part of the same SEAL team a number of years ago.

"Andrew was the best. He lost his life saving ours," said Commanding Officer Shields. "He didn't die immediately, and before he died, he made us promise to look after his wife, Leigh, and his daughter, Swan." The man paused and then said, "Over twenty-eight years ago, when we were taking some R & R in Jamaica, Andrew met Leigh, who was a Jamaican model. They married a year later, and he moved her to Key West, where our team was stationed. After Andrew was killed, Leigh returned to Jamaica. When Swan graduated from high school, she returned to the Keys and moved into her parents' home."

"How old was she when her father was killed?" Flipper asked.

"She was fifteen," Admiral Martin said. "Swan was close to her dad. Leigh was so broken up over Andrew's death that she didn't want to live in the States without him, which was why she returned to Jamaica. She passed away two years ago."

Flipper's commanding officer then took up the tale. "Leigh sent for us before she died of stomach cancer, asking us to look out for Swan after she was gone. We would have done that anyway, since we always kept in touch with both Leigh and Swan. In fact, Swan rotated summers with us and our families even after Leigh returned to Jamaica. We took our roles as godfathers seriously. We were even there when Swan graduated from high school and college."

"Did Swan have any American grandparents?" Flipper asked.

He saw both men's lips tighten into frowns. "Yes. However, her paternal grandparents didn't approve of their son's marriage to Leigh," said Commanding Officer Shields.

"So they never accepted their granddaughter." It was more of a statement than a question.

"No, they never did," Admiral Martin confirmed. As if it was a topic he'd rather change, the man added, "We've been given some time to find out the truth, but not much. Luckily, Swan's Godpop 3 has a high-level position at naval intelligence. Otherwise, we wouldn't know about the investigation. We have thirty days to prove Swan is not a traitor and identify the person who is. That's where we need your help. Instead of releasing you to go home as we're doing for the other members of your team, we are assigning you to a special mission, Lieutenant Holloway. You are being sent to Key West."

CHAPTER ONE

Key West, Florida

SWAN JAMISON WAS beside herself with excitement as she opened the huge box on her desk. Although it contained only her jewelry-making supplies, the package served as affirmation that while rebuilding was still taking place in certain areas, the majority of the island had recovered from the hurricane that had hit eight months ago.

"Anything for me?" Rafe asked, sticking his head through the office door.

Her shop was in a very trendy area so she could capitalize on the tourists visiting the island. To help with high operating costs, she leased out one of the large rooms in the back. Rafe was her tenant, who'd converted the back room into a tattoo shop. On some days, he got more customers than she did.

"Nothing for you, Rafe, just supplies for me." She checked her watch. "You're early today." Usually he didn't open up until noon.

"I have a special appointment at ten thirty and I need to ready my ink." And then he was gone. Rafe didn't say a whole lot except to his customers.

The door chime alerted her that *she* had a customer. Jamila, who worked part-time and usually only in the mornings, had taken time off for a day of beauty—hair, nails, pedicure, bikini wax, the works. Her boyfriend worked on a cruise ship that was due in port tomorrow. Swan was happy for Jamila and happy for herself as well. The cruise ships always brought in tourists who wanted to purchase authentic handmade jewelry.

She walked out of her office as a man perused her jewelry display case near the door. That was good. While he checked out her jewelry, she would check him out.

He had a nice profile. Tall, broad shoulders that looked good in a T-shirt and a pair of muscular thighs that fit well in his jeans. He had diamond-blond hair that was neatly trimmed and his hands were the right size for his body.

There was something about the way he stood, straight and tall, that all but spelled out *military man*. And the way his legs were braced apart, as if he had to maintain his balance even on land, spelled out *navy*.

Too bad. She didn't do military men. In all honesty, lately she hadn't done men at all. Too busy.

And then there was the issue of Candy's divorce. Swan knew she shouldn't let what had happened to her best friend darken her own view, but Swan was known to claim whatever excuse suited her and that one did at the moment.

And speaking of the moment, she had looked her fill. She needed to make her first sale of the day. "May I help you?"

He turned and looked at her, and every cell in her body jolted to attention.

Wow! She'd seen blue eyes before, but his were a shade she'd never seen. They were laser blue; the intense sharpness of the pupils captured her within their scope. And his features… Lordy! The man had such gorgeous bone structure! There was no way a woman had ever passed by him and not taken a second look. Even a third, while wiping away drool.

"Yes, you can help me."

And why did he have to sound so good, too? The sound of his voice—a deep, husky tone—made her throat go dry.

"All right," she said, walking over to him. She knew she had to get a grip. Her store had been closed for two months due to the hurricane, and now that the tourists were returning, she needed to catch up on sales.

"And how can I help you?" She didn't miss the way he was looking at her. She saw interest in his eyes. There was nothing wrong with that. She took pride in her appearance because she had been raised to do so. Leigh Rutledge Jamison, who'd been a Jamaican model, had taught her daughter that your appearance was everything.

Pain settled in Swan's heart. She missed her mom so much.

"I'm looking for a gift for someone."

Swan nodded as she came to stand beside him. Not only did he look good and sound good, but he smelled good as well. She glanced down at his hand and didn't see a wedding ring. He was probably buying a gift for his girlfriend or soon-to-be fiancée.

"What do you have in mind?"

"What do you suggest?" he asked her.

"Well, it depends," she said, looking into those gorgeous eyes.

"On what?"

"What the person likes. I make jewelry from stones, but as you can see, there are a number of them, in various shades, colors and styles."

He smiled and Swan felt a tingling in the pit of her stomach when a dimple appeared in one of his cheeks. "I honestly don't know what she likes. Her tastes change from year to year. It's hard to keep up."

Swan nodded. "Oh. Sounds like the two of you have known each other for a while."

His smile widened even more. "We have. I would have to say I've known Mom all my life."

"Your mom?"

"Yes. Her birthday is next month. I was passing by your shop and thought I would drop in to see what you had."

A racing heart for starters, Swan thought. So the woman he was thinking about buying jewelry for was his mother. "Well, I'm glad you came in. Let me show you what I have."

"All right. There looks to be a lot of nice pieces."

She appreciated the compliment. "Thanks. I made most of them myself."

"Really? Which ones?"

She led him to the area set aside for Swan Exclusives. "These. Most of the stones come from India, Argentina and Africa."

He leaned in to look. "You did an excellent job."

Whoever said flattery, especially coming from a good-looking man, would get you anywhere knew just what they were talking about. "Thank you."

"I'm David, by the way. David Holloway." He offered her his hand.

She took it and tried to ignore the sensations that suddenly flowed through her from the contact. "Nice to meet you, David." She quickly released his hand. "And I'm Swan."

"The name of the shop."

"Yes."

"It's a unique name."

"Yes, my parents thought so. On their first date, my father flew Mom from Jamaica to New York to see *Swan Lake*."

"Some date."

"Yes, he was trying to impress her."

"I take it he did."

Swan chuckled. "Yes, because he actually flew them there. He had his pilot's license."

"Now I'm impressed."

She didn't like bragging about her father but there were times when she just couldn't help it. "He served in the air force—that's where he learned to fly. And then he went into the navy after deciding he wanted to be a SEAL. That's when he met

Mom, while he was a SEAL. She hadn't known about his stint in the air force until the night he rented a plane to fly them to New York."

Why was she telling him all this? Usually she wasn't chatty. "What about this one?" she asked as they moved to another glass case. "I call this piece *Enchantment*."

"Why?"

"Look at it," she suggested, leaning closer to the glass. He followed suit. "This is one of my favorite pieces because the teardrop gemstone necklace is pretty similar to my very first piece." No need to tell him that she'd made that one for her own mother.

"It is beautiful."

Something in his tone made her glance over at him, and she found him staring at her and not at the jewelry in the case. His eyes held her captive and their gazes met for a minute too long before she broke eye contact with him.

She swallowed. "So are you interested…in this piece?" She wanted to ignore the way her stomach seemed to be filled with all kinds of sensations, but she could not.

"I'm interested in a lot of pieces, Swan, but I'll start with this one."

Swan Jamison was even more beautiful than the photograph he'd seen last week.

The photographer hadn't fully captured the rich creaminess of her skin. And the shade of red lipstick she wore today seemed to make her lips plumper, more well-defined. Luscious.

He had read the dossier on her. He knew his commanding officer and Admiral Martin were operating based on a personal connection with her. He was not. If Miss Jamison was guilty of any wrongdoing, he would find out. And if she wasn't the one handing out classified data to China, then he would discover who was.

"So you want to buy this particular piece?"

Her question brought his thoughts back to the present. "Yes."

"Wonderful. I think your mother will like it."

"I'm sure she will. What about earrings?"

She lifted a brow. "Earrings?"

"Yes. Do earrings come with the necklace?"

"No, but I can make you some."

He'd been hoping she'd say that. "When?"

"It will take me a couple of days. The cruise ship docks to-morrow, so the shop will be busy. Two days from now will work for me, unless you need them sooner."

"No, I can wait. My mother's birthday is next month."

He would have an excuse to return to her shop.

Flipper watched her open the case and pull out the necklace. He knew his mother was going to love it.

"If you don't mind, please complete this ticket," she said. "And I will need full payment for the earrings before I make them."

"That's no problem," he said, taking the document from her.

After he completed the form, he handed it back to her. She glanced at it. "So you're from Texas?"

"Yes. Dallas. Ever been there?"

"Yes, once. I thought it was a nice city."

"It is. I was born and raised there."

"And what brought you to Key West?" she asked him.

"Work, at least for the next thirty days." That wasn't a total lie.

"Hurricane relief?"

"Something like that."

"You're military?"

"At one point but not now." He would let her think he was no longer military.

"I knew immediately."

He lifted a brow. "How?"

She shrugged. "Military men are easily recognized, at least by me."

"Because your dad is military?"

"He *was* military. Dad died years ago in the line of duty."

"I'm sorry." Flipper was always sorry whenever a fellow soldier lost their life.

"Thank you. Your package will be ready in two days, David. Your mobile number is on the form you completed. If I get to it sooner, I will call you."

"Two days is fine. I'll be back."

"'Bye, David."

"'Bye, Swan." He then turned and walked out of the shop.

As much as he wanted to invite her out to lunch today, he knew he couldn't rush things. He needed to earn her trust, even though he had less than thirty days to prove her innocence and determine who had no qualms about making her look guilty.

Swan was cheerful that night as she let herself into her home. Sales today had been better than normal. A tour group from New York had converged on the island and they'd come to spend money. She'd been happy to oblige.

Opening a jewelry shop had been a risky business move, but one that had paid off. She'd earned a degree in business management from the University of Miami and returned to the island after college to work as a manager at one of the elite hotels on the island. She'd enjoyed her job but had felt something was missing in her life. She hadn't been using her jewelry-making talent.

She'd promised her mother on her deathbed that she would find a way to use that talent.

Even after taking care of all her mother's funeral expenses, there had been more than enough money left to buy a little storefront. It had been a good investment because of its location. Some days were busier than others. This had been one of those busy days.

Now she was ready to wind down for the evening. She pulled her hair back in a ponytail and eased her feet into her favorite flats before heading to the kitchen for a glass of wine. As she did so, she couldn't help but think about her first customer of the day.

David Holloway.

He was a cutie, she had to give him that. And the memory of those eyes had stayed with her most of the day.

David Holloway had come into her shop to buy a birthday gift for his mother. How sweet. His mother was lucky. A lot of men didn't even remember their mothers' birthdays. She'd dated quite a few of those men and never developed lasting relationships with any of them. She figured if a man didn't treat his mother right, then there was no hope for a girlfriend.

As she opened the French doors to step out on the patio, she again remembered those blue eyes and how she'd felt whenever she'd looked into them. No man's eyes had ever made her feel that way before.

The effect was unsettling.

Okay, so what was wrong with her? Cutie or no cutie, she normally didn't get caught up over a man. She dated when it suited her, but she would admit that no one had suited her lately. At least not since her best friend, Candy, had left Key West to go live in Boston. Candy had refused to live on the island with her ex and his new wife—the one he'd married before the ink had even dried on the divorce papers.

Refusing to dwell on how shabbily Donald Knoll had treated Candy, Swan looked out at the water. It was calm tonight. When she had evacuated due to the hurricane, she hadn't known what to expect when she returned. Between her home and her shop, there had been some damage, but not as much as she'd feared.

The thought of losing her home had been devastating. This was where her father had brought her mom after they'd married. This home held so many childhood memories—of her father leaving on his missions as a Navy SEAL, of how happy she and her mother would be whenever he returned.

But then he hadn't returned.

Swan felt a knot in her throat as she recalled that day. She'd never seen that sparkle in her mother's eyes again. Swan recalled her mother telling her once that when you met a man who could put that sparkle in your eyes, then you knew he was a keeper.

Swan often wondered if she would ever find her keeper.

She had plenty of time. Besides, she needed to rethink her opinion about men first. If what Don had done to Candy wasn't enough to keep her single, all Swan had to do was remember William Connors, the businessman she had met while working at the hotel.

At the time, he had convinced her he was a bachelor without a care in the world but claimed that he wanted to make her Mrs. William Connors one day.

For some reason, Candy hadn't trusted him. She had a friend who worked for a private investigator check him out. Swan had been devastated when the investigation revealed there was already a Mrs. William Connors, along with three Connors children.

William had been playing her. He had been a lesson well learned. Her only regret was that she'd shared her body with him. She'd been young, naive and impressionable. He had been her first and he should not have been.

She was not naive now and she went into relationships with caution and even a little mistrust. Her mother once told her that being mistrustful wasn't a good thing. Swan knew she would have to learn how to trust again.

She took another sip of wine. Unfortunately, she hadn't gotten there yet.

"So how did things go, Flipper?"

"Have you met her yet?"

"Does she have a traitorous face or just a pretty one?"

"Do you think you'll be able to prove she's innocent?"

Flipper heard the questions coming at him nearly all at once.

While unpacking, he had placed his mobile call on speaker to engage in a five-way conversation with his SEAL teammates.

"I think things went rather well, Mac. And yes, I met Swan Jamison today, Viper. I went into her jewelry store to purchase Mom a birthday gift."

Flipper eased open the dresser drawers to place his T-shirts inside. "She doesn't have a traitorous face or just a pretty one, Coop. The woman is simply gorgeous. Beautiful beyond belief. And yes, I hope to prove she's innocent, Bane, because Commanding Officer Shields and Admiral Martin truly believe she is."

"What do you believe?" Viper asked.

Flipper leaned against the dresser for a minute and thought about Viper's question. "Too early to tell."

"Did you ask her out on a date?" Coop wanted to know. They could hear Coop's two-year-old son, Laramie, chattering in the background.

"No, not yet." Flipper's attraction to her had been instant. He'd felt it the moment he looked into her face. Discussing her now wasn't helping matters. All it did was force him to recall what a beautiful woman she was—a woman he would have to spend time with in order to discover the truth.

"Then how do you plan to see her again if you don't ask her out?" Mac wanted to know, interrupting Flipper's thoughts.

"I ordered a pair of earrings to go with the necklace I bought for Mom. She has to make the earrings and I'll make my move when I pick up my purchases in two days."

"And if she turns you down?" Viper asked.

"Not an option. I now have less than thirty days to get this all straightened out."

"We should be there with you, watching your back," Bane said.

"No, you guys are just where you need to be, which is home with your families. I've got this."

"Well, some of our families don't appreciate us being home," Mac grumbled.

Flipper rolled his eyes. They'd all heard the complaints from Mac before. After every extended mission, their teammate went home to an adjustment period, where he would have to get to know his wife all over again and reclaim his position as head of the house. Sometimes the adjustment didn't go over well. Mac had a strong personality and so did Mac's wife, Teri. "Do we have to send both you and Teri into the time-out corners?"

"Hell, I didn't do anything," Mac exclaimed.

Flipper chuckled. "Yeah, right. You better get your act together, Mac. No other woman is going to put up with your BS."

"Whatever. So what did you notice about the place today?"

Mac was changing the subject and Flipper decided to let him. "Everything matched the architectural report I was given. Even with the repairs due to the hurricane, there were no major changes. Front door. Back door. High windows. Glass storefront. No video cameras outside. There are several rooms in back. One is being used as a tattoo parlor. I didn't see the person who runs it. I think I'll go out tonight and do a little more investigating," he said, sliding into a black T-shirt.

"Be careful, Flipper," Viper said. "Although you might not have seen any video cameras, that doesn't mean there aren't any."

"I know. That's why I'm wearing my Pilf gear."

Everybody knew how much Flipper liked digital technology. In addition to all the futuristic developments the military used, Flipper had created a few of his own high-tech gadgets behind the scenes. Some had been so impressive the federal government had patented them as Pilf gear to be used by the military. Pilf was the name Flip spelled backward. On more than one occasion, Flipper had been offered a position with the Department of Defense's Research and Development Department and had turned down each offer, saying he loved being a Navy SEAL more.

"We don't give a damn if you plan to parade around naked tonight, Flipper. Be careful."

He knew Mac was in his big-brother mode. "Okay, Mac. I hear you and I will be careful."

"Call to check in when you get back to the hotel tonight," Bane said.

"It will be late and I wouldn't want to wake up any babies, kids or a pregnant woman. I'll text everyone."

A short while later, wearing undetectable military gear under his clothing, Flipper left his hotel using the stairs.

CHAPTER TWO

TWO DAYS LATER, Swan didn't leave the shop for lunch. Instead she accepted Jamila's offer to bring her something back from the sandwich shop on the corner. Although she'd tried convincing herself her decision to hang around had nothing to do with the fact that David Holloway would be returning today to pick up his items, she knew it did.

And her anticipation was so bad that every time the door chimed, her heartbeat would kick up a notch, only to slow back down when someone other than him walked in. She checked her watch. The shop would be closing in an hour. What if he didn't make it before closing time? What if...?

The door chimed, and her heart nearly stopped when David Holloway walked in.

She'd told herself the man hadn't *really* looked as good as she remembered from that first day, but now she saw that he did. In fact, today he looked even better than she remembered. Maybe it had something to do with the unshaven look. Men with a day-old beard had sex appeal. But it could also be his tan, which indicated he'd probably spent the last couple of days lying in the sun.

If he'd been at the beach, there was a good chance he hadn't been there alone. But didn't he say he was in the Keys working?

Why did she care?

She quickly dismissed all those questions from her mind as she continued to watch him walk toward her in a strut that had blood rushing through her veins. His blond hair and blue eyes seemed brighter against his tanned skin. He was deliciousness with a capital *D*.

But then that capital *D* could also stand for *dangerous* if she wasn't careful. Or it could stand for *delusional* if she didn't get control of her senses. Right now, she would play it safe and claim the capital *D* stood for *David*. She couldn't allow herself to think any other way for now, no matter how tempting.

She smiled. "Hello, David."

"Hi, Swan."

"Your tan looks nice."

He chuckled. "So does yours."

She grinned. "Yes, but mine's permanent."

"I know and I like it."

She didn't say anything to that because she understood what he was implying. He was letting her know he had no problem with interracial dating. She didn't have a problem with it either. Neither had her father, although his family had had conniptions about his marriage to Swan's mother. She pushed that thought to the back of her mind, refusing to dwell on an extended family that had never accepted her or her mother.

She reached behind the counter and retrieved a box. "I hope you like the way the earrings came out." She opened it to show him the final earrings.

"Wow!" He ran his finger over the stone that came closest to matching the color of his eyes. "You're very gifted."

"Thank you, and I believe your mother will love them."

"I'm sure she will. I think I've outdone my brothers this time."

She closed the box and placed it, along with the one containing the necklace, into a shopping bag. "You have brothers?"

"Yes, four of them. I'm the youngest."

"My goodness. Any sisters?"

"Not a one. Three of my four brothers are married, so I have sisters-in-law. They are the best."

"And the fourth brother is still single?"

"He's divorced but has a beautiful little girl. And she's my parents' only granddaughter. They have six grandsons."

"Sounds like a nice family. Is your father still alive?"

"Yes, Dad is still alive. He and Mom own a medical supply store."

She nodded as she offered him the bag. "Here you are, David. Thanks again for your business."

He accepted the bag. "Thanks. Now that this is taken care of, there's something I want to ask you, Swan."

She lifted a brow. "What?"

"Would you go out to dinner with me tonight?"

Normally Flipper was good at reading people, but he was having a hard time reading Swan. He definitely needed to remedy that. Although both Commanding Officer Shields and Admiral Martin were convinced of her innocence, the jury was still out for him. He had to remain impartial and deal with the facts, not speculations.

For two nights, he'd searched the area around her shop. Getting inside without triggering her alarm hadn't been easy, but he'd done it. Once he'd picked up the location of the interior security cameras, it was a small matter to make sure he stayed out of their range and within a certain perimeter until he could deactivate them and do what he needed to.

"Go to dinner with you?"

"Yes."

She was apparently mulling over his invitation in her mind and he would give her time to do that. He had no problems studying her while he waited for her answer. Today she looked even prettier than the other day. He figured it had to be the lighting in this place.

"Yes, David. I'll go to dinner with you. You name the restaurant and I'll meet you there."

She wasn't going to give him her address and he had no problem with her being cautious. Little did she know he already knew where she lived and had visited yesterday while she'd been here at her shop. She had a beautiful home on the ocean. Inside it was as neat as a pin with no clutter. She'd even made up her bed before leaving.

"I noticed a restaurant off the pier. Summer Moon. I've heard only good things about it since I've been here." And he knew the place was within walking distance from her home.

"Everything you've heard is true. Summer Moon is fabulous and one of my favorite eating places. I'd love to join you there. What time?"

"What about seven? Will that be a good time for you?" He figured since it didn't get dark until close to nine, he wouldn't have to worry about her walking to the restaurant in the dark. After dinner, he would walk her home or put her in a cab regardless of the fact that she lived only a few blocks away.

"Seven is perfect."

"Good. I'll see you then."

Swan watched him walk out of the shop.

David had the kind of tush that made a woman want to squeeze it...after doing all kinds of other things with it.

She jumped when fingers snapped in her face. Frowning, she looked at Jamila. "What did you do that for?"

"To keep you from having an orgasm in the middle of your shop."

Swan rolled her eyes. Jamila, the attractive twenty-two-year-old green-eyed blonde, evidently thought reaching a climactic state was that easy. "It would take more than ogling a man for that to happen, Jamila."

"I don't know. Your eyes were about to pop out of their sockets and your breathing sounded funny."

"You're imagining things."

"Denial can be good for the soul, I guess. So who is he?"

Swan and Jamila had more than an employer-and-employee relationship. Their friendship had started when Jamila first moved to the island a couple of years ago and patronized Swan's. It didn't take long to discover that Jamila liked nice things and decided Swan's was one of her favorite places to shop. Last year, Jamila had been looking for work after she lost her job as a day cruise ship captain.

As far as Swan was concerned, it hadn't been Jamila's fault when an intoxicated customer had tried coming on to her and she'd kicked him in the balls. Surgery had to be performed and the man had sued the ship company. They'd settled out of court but not before firing Jamila for all the trouble she'd caused.

Jamila had gotten an attorney herself so she could not only sue her former employer for an unfair firing but also sue the intoxicated customer. To avoid negative publicity, her former employer wanted to settle out of court with her as well. The intoxicated customer was also trying to settle since the woman he'd been with on the ship hadn't been his wife. If things worked out in Jamila's favor, she wouldn't need a job at Swan's much longer.

"He is a customer who came into the shop a couple of days ago to buy a gift for his mother."

"His mother and not his wife?"

"He says his mother."

Jamila snorted. "Men lie all the time."

How well she knew, Swan thought. Then she wondered why Jamila was men-bashing today. This wasn't the first comment of that type she'd made since arriving to work. Her boyfriend had come to town a couple of days ago with the cruise ship, right? So what was going on?

Swan decided not to ask. She didn't want to hear another sad story about a man that would ruin her date tonight with David.

It was a date she was definitely looking forward to. She figured going out to dinner with him wouldn't be risky as long as she kept things in perspective.

She knew what could happen if she let her guard down when it came to a man.

Flipper deliberately arrived at Summer Moon early so he could see when Swan arrived. His stomach felt floaty the moment she turned the corner from the street where she lived.

Be still, my...everything.

She was wearing a printed sundress and a pair of high-heeled sandals, but what caught his attention—and was still holding it tight—were her long shapely legs that seemed to go on forever. He would love to see where they stopped under that dress. He forced that thought to the back of his mind.

But the closer she got, the more that thought wiggled back to the forefront. He shouldn't let it. He was on assignment and she was the subject of an investigation. He shouldn't see her as temptation. Letting his guard down around her could be a dangerous and costly mistake. He had to keep his head screwed on straight, no matter how innocent she seemed and how beautiful she was, and she was definitely one gorgeous woman.

Men, even some with female companions, were giving Swan second looks, and Flipper tried to downplay his anger. He had no right to be upset about other men checking her out when he was checking her out himself. The best thing to do to control his crazy reaction was to stop looking at her, so he glanced down at his bottle of beer and thought about the reports he'd finished reading a short while ago on her employee and her tenant.

Jamila Fairchild had worked for Swan for a year. He knew all about her former job as a captain of a day cruise ship, why she'd gotten fired and her litigation against not only her former employer but also the man who'd caused the ruckus in the first place. Naval intelligence hadn't left any stone unturned in

Ms. Fairchild's report and she'd come up clean. Flipper would verify that she was.

Then there was Rafe Duggers, the tattoo artist. Although his parlor was located inside Swan's shop, there was a back door for his customers to use without entering through the jewelry shop. Flipper hadn't gotten a chance to look around the tattoo parlor and he intended to do another visit in a few days. Rafe was too squeaky-clean to be true.

No wonder naval intelligence was trying to point the finger at Swan. After all, it was her shop and they had somehow traced activity as originating there. But how? When? He hadn't found anything.

He had searched Swan's office, the small kitchen in the back, the bathrooms and another room that she used as a workshop where she made her jewelry. He'd come up with nothing, even after checking out her computer. So what were the grounds for accusing her?

Flipper's mind flicked back to Swan and he stood when the waiter escorted her to his table. "Hello, Swan. You look nice."

"Thanks and so do you. I was trying to be early and you still beat me here," she said, sitting down across from him.

"I was thirsty," he said, sitting back down and indicating the beer. Now that she was here and sitting directly across from him, he was more than thirsty. If he wasn't careful, he could have a full-fledged attack of desire. She had a pair of beautiful shoulders and her skin appeared soft and smooth to the touch.

Then his mind drifted to wanting her and he quickly snatched it back. "You walked here. Does that mean you live close by?" he asked, deciding it was best to keep the conversation moving.

"Yes, not too far," she said. He knew she was deliberately being evasive.

The waiter handed him another beer and gave them both menus. "What would like to drink, miss?" the waiter asked her.

"A glass of Moscato please."

When the waiter left, she glanced over at Flipper before picking up her menu. "You're not working so hard that you're not enjoying the Keys, are you?"

"I'm doing a bit of both. I admit the ocean is beautiful tonight."

She smiled. "I think it's beautiful every night."

He nodded as he took another sip of his beer, straight from the bottle. "So are you a native or a transplant?"

"A native. I was born and raised right here on the island in the same house I live in now. My mother never made it to the hospital before I was born."

He raised a brow. "She didn't?"

"No. Mom came from a part of Jamaica where the belief was that when it comes to delivering a baby, a midwife is better than a medical doctor. My father promised to find her a midwife here. Otherwise she would have insisted that I be born in Jamaica and he didn't want that. He wanted me born in America."

"So he was able to find a midwife?"

"Yes, but I was born a few weeks early and the midwife wasn't here."

"So who delivered you?"

"My dad, with the help of three of his closest military friends. They were stationed at the base here and were visiting, watching a football game at the time. Needless to say, over the years I've gotten four different versions of what happened that night. My mother didn't remember a thing other than it took four men to deliver me. Although Godpop 1 claims my father passed out trying to cut the umbilical cord."

Flipper laughed. He then asked, "Godpop 1?"

"Yes, my father's three closest friends, the ones who assisted that night, became my godfathers. That's how I distinguish them. Godpop 1, Godpop 2 and Godpop 3."

Flipper nodded. No wonder the three men felt such strong ties to her. "You're lucky to have three godfathers. I don't have a one."

"Yes, I'm lucky," she said, after the waiter set the glass of wine in front of her. "They were my and Mom's rocks after we lost Dad, especially when my grandparents showed up at the funeral trying to cause problems."

Then, as if she realized she might have shared too much, she asked, "So what do you plan to order?"

Swan thought David had picked the right place for them to have dinner. When he asked for recommendations on what to order, she suggested Summer Moon's crab cakes and, as usual, they were delicious. The mango salad was superb, and after dinner they enjoyed listening to the live band.

When the band played their last song, she glanced over at David to discover him staring at her. The intensity in his gaze nearly scorched her and she took a sip of her wine. "Thanks for dinner, David."

"Thank you for accepting my invitation. The place is about to close. Are you ready to go?" he asked her.

"Yes." Because she knew he would suggest that he walk her home, she added, "If you still have a little bit of energy, I'd like to treat you to something."

He lifted a brow. "What?"

"A laser show that officially kicks off the summer season. It's a short walk from here." Since it was in the opposite direction from where she lived, she would have no problem catching a cab back later—alone.

He smiled as he beckoned for the waiter to bring their check. "Then by all means, let's go."

Once the show began, it didn't take Swan long to decide that David was wonderful company. She could tell he was enjoying the laser lights as much as she was.

She attended the event every year and it seemed the displays only got better and better. Each year, they honored a different state and tonight that state was New York. The New Yorkers in the crowd showed their happiness with whistles and shouting.

And when a huge display of the Statue of Liberty flashed across the sky in a brilliant variety of colors, Swan caught her breath.

After that, the showrunners took the time to honor the servicemen in attendance with a flag salute. She couldn't hold back her tears as she remembered how much her father had loved his country and how, in the end, he'd given his life for it and for her.

David must have detected her weepy state. He pulled her closer to his side.

"Sorry," she said. "I get all emotional about our servicemen and servicewomen, especially those who sacrifice their lives."

"You sound very patriotic."

She pulled back and looked up at him. "Of course I'm patriotic. Aren't you? You did say you used to be in the military, right?"

"Yes, I'm very patriotic," he said, wrapping his arms around her. She wished she didn't think the arms around her felt so strong and powerful.

"I thought you would be, but you said I sounded patriotic as if you thought that perhaps I wasn't."

"I apologize. I didn't mean it that way. I'm glad you're so patriotic."

She nodded, accepting his apology. Scanning the area around them, she said, "They are serving complimentary wine coolers over there. Let's go grab a couple."

"Sure thing." He placed his hand on the small of her back.

The contact sent a rush of desire through her that was so strong she had to force herself to breathe. Swan quickly glanced up at him and noticed he'd been affected by the feeling as well. However, he hadn't removed his hand.

Instead, he pressed his hand more firmly into her back and she felt him urging her away from the crowd and toward a cluster of low-hanging palm trees. Once they stood in the shadows, he turned her in his arms, stared down at her for a long moment and then lowered his mouth to hers.

The moment their lips touched, he slid his tongue inside her mouth, and she recalled her thoughts from earlier that day. He was delicious—and dangerous—with a capital *D*. And it wasn't just because he tasted of the beer he'd consumed at Summer Moon, but because he tasted like a hot-blooded man. All the sexiness she'd seen in him was reflected in his kiss.

When she began kissing him back, he wrapped his arms around her and deepened the exchange by crushing his mouth to hers.

She didn't mind his eagerness. In fact, she welcomed the pleasure of his hunger, his taste, which was getting more provocative with every stroke of his tongue. It had been a while since she'd been kissed, and certain parts of her were reminding her of just how long it had been. Not only that, those certain parts were goading her to keep up with the forceful demands of his mouth. She hadn't been kissed so thoroughly or possessively before in her life. Or so passionately.

Swan wasn't sure how long they stood there kissing. It wasn't until they heard the sound of fireworks that they disengaged their mouths. She glanced up as more fireworks exploded in the sky. Instead of looking up, David trailed his tongue along her neck and collarbone with wet licks.

"Say you'll go out with me again, Swan."

There was no way she wouldn't say it. She looked at him and saw deep desire in the eyes looking back at her. "Yes, I'll go out with you again."

"Good."

And then he lowered his head and kissed her again.

Flipper had tried everything possible to get to sleep. He'd counted sheep, counted backward, rolled his eyes for a full thirty minutes and had even tried hypnotizing himself. None of those things helped.

He couldn't remember ever feeling this tight with need. So here he was, close to four in the morning, and still wide awake.

Nothing he did could erase the taste of Swan from his mouth and the act of kissing her from his mind.

The kiss would complicate his mission, but it hadn't been an act. It had been the most real thing he'd done in a long time. He had wanted that kiss. Needed it. It had been inevitable.

Sitting across from her at dinner and watching the movement of her mouth had caused a throbbing need to erupt in his gut, making him rock hard. There had been no way to ignore the delicious heat of carnal attraction spiking between them.

And the patriotism he'd seen in her eyes when she'd gotten teary-eyed in support of servicemen, and then when she'd told him about her work with the city to find lodging for homeless vets, hadn't helped. Neither had the fact that she'd looked stunning and had smelled irresistibly hot tonight.

Kissing her had made his entire body feel alive. Had revved up his passion to a degree that his libido had him tied in knots and had his pulse tripping. He could feel himself riding the fine edge of intense desire heightened by more sexual energy than he'd felt in a long time.

While kissing her, he hadn't cared that they could have been seen in spite of the low-hanging trees. He'd been beyond the point of caring. He'd been tempted to drag her to the ground right there.

Damn. How was he going to clear her of anything when the only thing he'd wanted to clear her of was her clothes?

He had access to women whenever he needed them. There were always women who went bonkers for men in uniform and he had no problem engaging in one-night stands. Those types of relationships had always been the way to go for him. He liked being single, coming and going as he pleased, with no one to worry about but himself.

It had been a long time since any woman had kept him up at night and that wasn't cool.

Grabbing his phone he texted the message: If anyone is awake. Call me.

Within seconds, his phone rang. It was Bane. "What's going on, Flipper?"

"Why are you up?" Flipper asked his friend.

"Feeding time. Crystal and I rotate."

"Oh? You're breastfeeding now?"

"No, smart-ass. The trio are on bottles now. What are you doing up?"

Flipper stretched out across the bed. "I couldn't sleep. I tried everything. I even tried to hypnotize myself."

Bane chuckled. "I guess it didn't work."

"No, it didn't work."

"So why can't you sleep, Flip?"

He wasn't one to kiss and tell, no matter who the listener was, so he said, "I still haven't figured out anything about the situation down here and the CO and the admiral are depending on me."

"Maybe they're going to have to accept naval intelligence's report that she's guilty."

"I don't think so." Flipper paused. "She cried tonight."

"What do you mean, she cried?"

"Today was the first day of summer and there's an annual laser show to commemorate the change in season. One of the laser displays was a salute to New York, where they did an awesome light replica of the Statue of Liberty and American soldiers. She got emotional and cried. Dammit, Bane, a person who is betraying their country doesn't cry for those in the service. Call me a sucker for tears but I don't believe she has a traitorous bone in her body."

"Then it's up to you to prove it. What about those two people who hang around her shop?"

"The woman who works for her and the tattoo guy? Both seem clean. But I will dig further. I have to."

"Okay, but make sure while you're digging for answers that you're not burrowing yourself into something you can't handle."

"What do you mean?"

"I think you know what I mean, Flip. You were sent there to prove her innocence—not to prove she has a passionate side. Remember that. Good night."

Flipper clicked off the phone and rubbed a hand down his face. Little did Bane know that after the kiss with Swan tonight, Flipper was driven to do more than prove her innocence, or her passion.

He wanted to possess Swan completely.

And he had a feeling the desire wasn't one-sided. He'd seen the look in her eyes during dinner. He'd felt how her body had responded to his touch. He was certain the same sensations that rushed through him had affected her, too. Kissing her had been inevitable, something they both wanted and needed.

The genie called desire was out of the bottle and Flipper honestly didn't know how to get it back inside.

CHAPTER THREE

SWAN PUSHED AWAY from her desk and took another huge gulp of ice-cold lemonade. It had been that way for her all day. Instead of concentrating on the online orders she needed to fill and ship out, her mind was wrapped around that kiss from last night.

All she had to do was close her eyes to remember every single detail, specifically every sensuous lick of his tongue inside her mouth. Even now, the memory sent multiple sensations coursing through her body, causing pleasure the likes of which she'd never encountered before.

She looked up at the sound of a knock on her door. "Yes?"

Jamila stuck her head in. "Mr. Make-you-have-an-instant-orgasm is back."

Swan didn't need to ask Jamila what she meant or who she was talking about. "Any reason you can't wait on him?"

Jamila smiled naughtily. "I could use the pleasure but he specifically asked for you."

Swan nodded. "I'll be out in a minute."

"Okay, I will let him know."

Swan reached over and took another gulp of her lemonade. She didn't want to admit it, but after that kiss last night, David could become an addiction. Besides putting down a gallon of lemonade, she'd been twitching in her seat most of the day, thinking that if his tongue could do that to her mouth, then Lordy...she could only imagine what else he would be able to do...

She quickly stood, refusing to go there even as a naughty part of her mind wished that he would. Leaving her office, she rounded the corner and stopped.

David stood in the middle of her shop wearing a pair of khaki shorts and a muscle shirt. The sight of his muscled abs and strong legs made Swan bite back a groan. Just when she thought he couldn't get any sexier, he'd proved her wrong.

He must have heard the sound of her footsteps because he turned and smiled.

As if on cue, she smiled back. "Hello, David, you came to make more purchases?" Hopefully he would take the hint that she didn't expect him to just drop by without a reason.

"Yes. I'm buying jewelry for my three sisters-in-law and would love for you to offer suggestions."

Swan couldn't help but smile since she liked making sales. What store owner wouldn't? "I'd love to help you pick out pieces of jewelry for them."

An hour later, Swan stood at the cash register to ring up all of David's purchases. With her assistance, he'd selected some really nice pieces, with a number of the stones chosen specifically because that's what he'd said they would like. Then he wanted earrings to complement the necklaces, which he paid for in advance. They decided to select stones for the earrings tomorrow since they'd spent a lot of time on the necklaces today and her shop would be closing in less than an hour.

From their conversation, she knew the Holloways were a close-knit family. He'd even pulled out his phone to show her pictures of his young niece and nephews.

"No pressure for you to marry?" she asked when he tucked his phone back into the pocket of his shorts.

"None. My parents have been married for more than forty years and are still very much in love. They make sure their kids and grandkids know that. They believe we will know when it's time for us to marry without any pressure from them. We'll be the ones to have to live with the people we choose. They just want all their children to be happy."

She nodded. "I like the way your parents think. I want to believe that, had my parents lived, they would have a similar philosophy. Dad used to tell me all the time that he wanted me to grow up and be whatever I wanted to be and do whatever I wanted to do, and that he and Mom would always have my back."

She suddenly felt a deep sense of loss. "Appreciate your parents, David. You never know how truly great they are until they're gone. But in all honesty, I think I've always known I had great parents."

At that moment, he did something she wouldn't have expected from him—he reached out and took her hand. "They sound great and I know they're proud of your accomplishments."

"Thanks." That was a nice thing for him to say. To avoid thinking about just how nice he was, she slid the bag with his purchases toward him and gave him the credit card slip. He signed it and gave it back to her.

"How would you like to go to happy hour at Danica's with me?"

After talking about her parents and missing them like crazy, she could use more than just an hour of happiness. She would love to be able to have a lifetime of that feeling.

It wasn't that she was *unhappy*, because she wasn't, but there were times when she wondered if maybe there was more out there for her than what was currently in her life. Perhaps she was shortchanging herself on some things. What those things were, she had no idea.

"I would love to go but good luck getting a table at Danica's. They have the best hot wings and are always crowded, *especially* for happy hour. I think the entire island heads over there at five."

"Since I know you don't close your shop until five, how

about if we meet over there at five-thirty? I guarantee we'll have a place to sit."

"Um, sounds like you might have connections, David Holloway."

"We'll see." He took the bag and turned to leave, and just like before, she watched his movements until he was no longer in sight.

"Wow. You do have connections, don't you?" Swan said, sliding into a stool at the bar. "I've been here a number of times and the best seat I've ever gotten is at one of those tables outside."

Flipper smiled. Like at Summer Moon, he'd arrived early and was waiting for her. He liked seeing her stroll down the sidewalk looking as beautiful as ever.

Today she was wearing a pair of shorts and a pretty top. Her legs were long and shapely and he could imagine them wrapped around him while...

Whoa, he didn't need to go there. Ever since that kiss, he'd been trying *not* to go there—no matter how tempted he was to do so. Quickly, he changed the direction of his thoughts.

"I know Danica personally," he said, trying hard to keep his naughty thoughts in check.

She lifted a brow. "Really? How?"

There was no way he would tell her the whole story. Danica was the godmother of former SEAL team member Nick Stover. Nick had given up being a SEAL a few years ago to take a job with Homeland Security after his wife had triplets. Instead of the whole history, Flipper gave her a modified version. "Her godson and I used to work together."

"Oh." The bartender chose that moment to take their drink order.

"I know you used to be in the military at one point but what do you do now?" she asked once the bartender had walked away.

Flipper had expected that question sooner or later and had

a prepared answer. "I travel a lot and my job deals with ocean marine work. I guess you can say I'm a specialist in that area."

"Sounds interesting."

He chuckled. "Trust me, it is."

The bartender set their beers in front of them along with a huge plate of hot wings. They dug in.

"Your assistant at the store seems nice," Flipper commented. "I hope she didn't get offended when I asked specifically for you."

"No, very little offends Jamila, trust me."

"You've known her a long time?"

If his question seemed odd, she didn't mention it. "We met a couple of years ago when she moved to the island. The first time she came into my shop she nearly bought out the place. Like you, she has a huge family living up north and wanted to buy holiday gifts for everyone. Thanks to her, I made my month's quota in that one day. She earned a friend for life."

Flipper took a long swig of his beer. What Swan had just told him was interesting. Based on the naval intelligence report he'd read, Jamila didn't have any family. No parents, siblings, aunts, uncles or cousins. She'd been adopted and her adopted parents had been killed in a car accident in her last year of high school. And they hadn't lived in the north but out west in California.

Why had Jamila lied?

"So you hired her that day?" he asked, grinning, trying to make a joke of what she'd told him.

"No, she had a job as a ship captain at one of the day cruise companies in town. When things didn't work out for her there, I hired her on part-time."

He'd read the report and knew why Jamila had been let go and knew about her pending lawsuits. There was a big chance both cases would be settled out of court in her favor. "Is the reason she's part-time because she's a student?"

"Sort of. She saw how much money Rafe makes and—"

"Rafe?" He knew who Rafe was, but Swan didn't know that.

"Yes, Rafe. He rents space in my shop where he operates a tattoo parlor. He's good and always has a steady stream of customers. Some are so pleased with his work that they recommend him to others. I've known people to fly in just to use his services."

She took a sip of her beer, grinned and added, "Jamila decided to give him some real competition by becoming a tattoo artist as well. I have to admit she's pretty good. But Rafe doesn't seem worried. He even allows her to assist him sometimes. I guess you can say he's taken her under his wing. I think that's nice of him."

Flipper took another swig of his beer. "Yes, that is nice of him. Real nice."

Later that night, as they waited for a car at the taxi stand, Swan turned to face David. "I had a wonderful time this evening."

Once again, she had enjoyed his company and hated that their time together was about to end. It didn't come as a surprise to her that the sexual chemistry between them was more explosive than ever. The kiss they'd shared the night before had ignited something within her. From the way she'd noticed him looking at her, she believed something had ignited within him as well.

More than once, her smooth bare legs had brushed against his hairy ones. The sensual contact had sent a gush of desire through her.

The first few times it happened, she'd pulled away. But finally, she'd decided not to pull her legs back and he'd given her one of those *I know you did that on purpose* looks and she had smiled innocently and sipped her beer.

He had initiated the next physical contact and she could envision his mind at work trying to decide how to push her sensual buttons. She doubted he could push them more than he was already.

"I'm glad I got to meet Ms. Danica. After all the years I've been living here, this was my first time meeting her. She's nice."

"Yes, she is."

"And I definitely appreciate this," she said, holding up the bag of hot wings the older woman had given Swan to take home.

"I think she appreciated how much you enjoyed them."

She chuckled. "You're probably right."

"What do you have planned for later?" he asked in a deep, husky tone that seemed to have dropped a purposeful octave.

He had taken her hand when they left Danica's to walk to the taxi stand. The feel of his fingers entwined with hers had stirred something within her, something that grew with every step they took. She was aware of every detail about him as they walked together. Because of his long legs, more than once he had to slow his pace so she could keep up with him.

Swan could have walked home but figured he would suggest walking there with her. She was still cautious about letting him know where she lived. When she left Jamaica to begin living on her own, her mother had drilled into her the danger of letting a man know where you lived too soon. In her heart, Swan felt David was safe, but still...

"It's near the end of the month and I need to work on the books for my accountant." No need to mention she had tried doing that very thing today at work and hadn't been able to concentrate for remembering their kiss from last night.

"How about dinner tomorrow night?" he asked her.

She didn't answer right away. Instead, she broke eye contact with him and glanced down at the sidewalk. Hadn't they seen each other enough these last few days? Where was this leading? Wasn't he leaving the Keys in less than a month?

She glanced back at him. "Why? We've gone out twice already. I wouldn't want to dominate your time."

"You're not. And the reason I want to take you out again is because I enjoy your company."

She certainly enjoyed his. "Can I ask you something, David?"

He nodded. "Yes?" Considering her history with William, it was something she probably should have asked David before going out on their first date. She'd discovered the hard way that a man not wearing a wedding ring didn't mean anything these days.

"What do you want to ask me, Swan?"

She met his gaze and hoped she would be able to see the truth in his eyes. "Do you have a wife or a significant other?"

Instead of guilt flashing in his eyes, she saw surprise. "No. I'm not married and I've never been married. I dated a woman for years but because of my frequent travels, she decided to end things. That was over six years ago." He then leaned against a light post and asked, "What about you, Swan? Have you ever been married or is there a significant other?"

"Of course not."

He nodded slowly. "Then I assume there is a reason you thought that maybe I was in a relationship?"

"I needed to be sure."

He didn't say anything. Instead, he looked at her as if tumbling her answer around in his head. "But like I said, I assume there is a reason you needed to know."

"Yes." However, she didn't intend to go into any details.

"Well, rest assured there is not a Mrs. David Holloway out there anywhere. Nor is there any woman wearing my ring. Satisfied?"

"Yes."

At that moment, a taxi pulled up. "Thanks for dinner again." She was about to move toward the taxi when he reached out, took hold of her hand and tugged her to him. He lowered his mouth to hers and kissed her quickly but soundly on the lips.

"I'll see you tomorrow," he said, his words a soft whisper against her wet lips.

"Tomorrow?" she asked in a daze from his kiss.

"Yes, we're supposed to go over designs for the earrings, remember?"

It was hard to remember anything after a kiss like that. "Yes, I remember," she said.

"Then I'll see you tomorrow."

She nodded, and when he opened the door for her, she quickly got into the taxi and headed home alone.

The moment Flipper entered his hotel room he went to the small refrigerator beneath the wet bar and pulled out a beer. Just then it didn't matter that he'd already drank a couple at Danica's. He needed another. There was just something about Swan that was getting to him, touching him on a level he wasn't used to when it came to women. He had truly enjoyed her company tonight.

He and his SEAL teammates had just returned from a two-month mission in South Africa and more than anything he had needed to unwind. He would be home in Texas doing just that had he not been summoned to the admiral's office.

So here he was, and although he was in Key West on official military business and he was supposed to be investigating Swan, he loved spending time with her.

Tonight, when she'd met Danica, it had been priceless. You would have thought Swan had met a Hollywood celebrity. He had sat there while the two women conversed, immediately as comfortable as old friends.

The sound of Swan's voice had been maddeningly sexy with a tinge of sweetness that had stroked his senses. For the first time since returning to the States, he had allowed himself to uncoil, to loosen up and relax while appreciating the richness of her personality. Her persona was uniquely hers and the sensuality of her very being called to him in a primitive way.

And that wasn't good.

Taking a huge swig of his beer, he switched his thoughts to what he should be focused on—what she'd told him about Jamila and Rafe. Remembering what she'd said, he pulled his phone out of the pocket of his shorts and with one click he connected to his friend Nick Stover.

"This better be good, Flipper. Natalie is taking an art class at the university tonight and I have babysitting duties."

Flipper couldn't help but smile. Like Bane, Nick had triplets and from the sound of the noise in the background, the triplets had him. "Stop whining. Taking care of a trio of three-year-olds can't be too bad."

"Then you come do it."

"Sorry, I'm on assignment."

"So I hear. In the Keys, right?"

He figured for Nick to know that much meant he'd either talked to Bane, Viper, Mac or Coop. "Yes, I'm in Key West."

"While you're there, be sure to stop by Danica's. Give her a hug for me."

"I did that already. Tonight, in fact."

"Good."

"I think she has more photos of the triplets than you do."

"I wouldn't doubt it. So if you can't be a backup babysitter, why are you calling?"

"When you arrive at your cushy job at Homeland Security tomorrow, there are two people I need you to check out for me. I've read naval intelligence reports on them, but something isn't adding up. Call me a suspicious bastard, but after that situation with Bane, when those traitors within the agencies were exposed, I'm not taking any chances."

He then told Nick about the discrepancies between what the reports said and what Swan had told him. "Somebody is lying. Either Jamila lied to Swan or someone falsified the report, and I want to know which it is."

CHAPTER FOUR

"HE'S BAAACK," Jamila said.

Swan pushed away from her desk. She didn't have to ask who Jamila was talking about. "I was expecting him," she said in what she hoped was a professional tone. "He needs to look at designs for earrings."

"If you say so. I'll send him in here."

Swan was about to tell Jamila they could use the computer out front, but Jamila was gone after closing the door behind her.

Standing, Swan inhaled deeply. How she had finished the books last night, she wasn't sure. Thoughts of David had been stronger than ever after their night out. When she'd gone to bed, she had dreamed about him. Okay, she'd dreamed about him before, but the dreams last night had been so hot it was a wonder they hadn't burned her sheets. She had been tempted to do something she hadn't done in a long time, reactivate her vibrator.

She drew in a deep breath when she heard the knock on her door. "Come in."

And in walked David, looking sexier than he had the other times she'd seen him. Last night, to stay focused, she had come up with every reason she could think of for why she shouldn't be attracted to him and why a relationship with him wouldn't work.

She'd even thrown in the race card. But of course that was thrown out when she remembered her parents and how happy they had been together. Yet she also couldn't forget how her father's family had ostracized him for his choice in love. Would David's family be the same way? There was no reason to think they wouldn't. And wasn't she getting ahead of herself for even throwing love in the mix?

"Hello, David."

"Swan." He glanced at her desk, taking in all the folders spread across it. "You're busy."

"That's fine. Besides, I need to get those earrings ready for you."

Now that he'd seen her desk, it would make perfect sense for her to suggest they use the computer out front to design the earrings. But now that she had him behind closed doors, she liked it.

Not that she planned on doing anything about having him here.

"Please have a seat while I clear off my desk." Today he was wearing jeans and she couldn't help but watch how fluidly his body eased into the chair. How the denim stretched across a pair of muscular thighs. She quickly switched her gaze before he caught her looking.

"Nice office."

"Thanks." She closed the folders and placed them in her inbox tray. She then glanced over at him and caught him looking at her. She followed his gaze and soon figured out why he was staring.

She was wearing a skirt with a V-neck blouse, and when she'd leaned over to place the folders in the tray, her shirt had shown a portion of her cleavage. Instead of calling him out for trying to cop a view of her breasts, the fact that he was interested sparked a distinct warmth between her legs.

She quickly sat down. "Now if you would roll that chair over here, I am ready." Too late, she realized how that sounded and quickly added, "To look at designs."

He smiled. "I know what you meant."

He rolled his chair behind her desk to place it right next to hers. When he sat down, their legs touched. Moving away would be pretty obvious so she let the denim of his jeans rub against her bare legs.

"Now, then," she said, trying not to notice how good he smelled. "What do you think of these?" she asked, bringing up a few designs on the computer screen.

When he didn't answer, she glanced over at him and found him staring at her. Sitting so close to him, she could look directly into his laser-blue eyes. It was as if his gaze was deliberately doing something to her, causing a surge in her breath and arousal to coil in her core. She saw the dark heat in his eyes and desire clawed at her even more.

"May I make a suggestion?" he asked in a voice that seemed to wobble in a sexual way.

"It depends on what that suggestion is," she heard herself say.

He leaned in a little closer and whispered, "I want to kiss you again. Only problem is that I don't want to stop until I get enough. And I'm not sure I would."

She had been staring at his lips, watching how they moved while he talked. She slowly dragged her gaze back up to his eyes. She saw need flare in his gaze at the same time that anticipation for his kiss thickened the air flowing in and out of her lungs.

"I don't know what to say."

"Don't say anything, Swan. Just bring your mouth closer to mine."

She knew she shouldn't, but she found herself doing it anyway.

Flipper drew in a deep breath when Swan's lips were almost touching his. He flicked out his tongue and she gave a sharp intake of breath when he began licking her lips from corner to corner with the tip of his tongue.

"What are you doing?" she asked on a wobbly breath.

"Since you asked..." He captured her mouth and when she closed her eyes on a moan, he reached up and cradled her face in his hands while he kissed her with a greed he didn't know was in him.

What was there about her that made him accept the primitive part of himself that wouldn't be satisfied until he made love to her? Was it because she crept into his dreams at night and into his every waking thought? Or was it because an arrow of liquid heat shot straight to his groin whenever he saw her? Or could he blame it on the fact that whenever she touched him, he burned? She made him edgy and aroused him as no other woman could.

It was all of those things and more.

Right now, he didn't know how to back away. So he didn't. Instead he accepted the stream of heat in his gut and the crackle of energy passing between them.

Their lips were copulating in a way that sent blood coursing through his veins like a raging river. It was raw, hot and explosive, causing a hot ache to erupt in his gut. It wouldn't take much to lose control and take her here on her desk. At that moment, his entire body was tight with need, totally entranced by everything about her.

The phone rang and they quickly broke off the kiss, drawing in deep breaths of air. He watched as she reached across her desk to press the speaker button. "Thank you for calling Swan's."

At first, no one said anything and then a deep male voice said, "Swan? Are you okay? You sound out of breath."

He watched as she pulled in another deep breath before a smile touched her lips. "I'm fine, Godpop 1. How are you?"

Knowing who she was talking to on the phone was like a pail of cold water drenching Flipper. He was quickly reminded why he'd been sent to Key West. His admiral would have him court-martialed if he knew what Flipper had just done with his goddaughter. If the man had any idea how many times Flipper had kissed her already and how each time he'd wished they had gone even further...

She turned off the speaker so he heard only one side of the conversation, and from the sound of her voice, he knew she was happy about receiving the call.

Feeling a tightness in his crotch from his still-aroused body, he got up from the chair and walked to the window. If she could have this sort of effect on him just from a kiss, he didn't want to think about what would happen if he were to make love to her. Just the thought of easing his body into hers had his stomach churning and caused an ache low in his gut.

Knowing he needed to think of something else, he glanced up into the sky. It was a beautiful day. Monday was Memorial Day and he wondered if Swan had made any plans to celebrate. He'd heard there would be a parade and unlike some places in the States, where stores remained open on Memorial Day, the laid-back businesses in the Keys closed up for one big party.

He liked the Keys. When he retired from being a SEAL, he could see himself moving here to live out the rest of his days. The island was surrounded by the ocean and they didn't call him Flipper for nothing. He loved water. Being in it and being a part of it. Living this close to the sea would certainly be a plus for him. But then there was the question of how he would deal with Swan if he chose to retire here. Even if he could prove she was not guilty of espionage, there was always that possibility she would hate his guts regardless of the outcome, because he had not been truthful with her.

"Sorry about that, David."

He turned, not caring that she could see his still-hard erection. It was something he couldn't hide even if he had tried. Was she sorry they'd been interrupted or was she regretting that they'd kissed in the first place? He hoped it was the former because he doubted he could ever regret kissing her. "I take it that was one of your godfathers?" he asked, knowing it had been.

She was staring at him below the waist, but after his question, her gaze slowly moved upward to his face. "Ah, yes, that was one of my godfathers. The other two will be calling sometime today as well. It always works out that they all call within twenty-four hours of each other."

He nodded and slowly walked back over to his chair to sit down. "I know you're busy so let's look at the designs."

Had he just seen a flash of disappointment in her eyes? Did she want them to continue what they'd been doing before she'd gotten that call? Didn't she know how close they'd both been to going off the edge and falling into waters too deep to swim out of? Even for him, a SEAL master swimmer.

Somehow they got through the next half hour looking at earring designs. Just as each one of the necklaces were different, he wanted the earrings to be different as well and reflect each one of his sisters-in-law's personalities.

When he was satisfied with his choices, he stood, convinced he needed to rush back to the hotel and take a cold shower. Sitting beside Swan and inhaling her scent without touching her was one of the most difficult things he'd had to do in a long time.

She was so female that the maleness in him couldn't help responding to everything about her. A part of him felt drugged by her scent and the intense physical awareness of her. Even now, desire was racing through his bloodstream.

"I owe you additional monies, right?" he asked. A couple of the designs he'd selected cost more than what she'd originally estimated.

"Yes. I'll let you know the difference after I finish designing them, when you pick up everything."

He hadn't missed the fact that when he stood her gaze had immediately latched on to his crotch once again. Was she still hoping to see him with a hard-on? If that was true, then she wasn't disappointed. He could get aroused just from looking at her.

And why did she choose that moment to lick her lips? She

had no idea that seeing her do such a thing sent the pulse beating in his throat and desire hammering against his ribs.

On unstable legs and with an erection the size of which should be outlawed, he moved around her desk and looked at her. "Yesterday I asked you to go to dinner with me again, but you never gave me an answer."

He figured that seeing how aroused he was, she probably wouldn't give him an answer now either. She surprised him when she said, "Yes, we can dine together this evening."

He nodded. "Okay, you get to pick the place."

She took a slip of paper off her desk, wrote something on it and handed it to him. He looked at it and he must have stared at it too long, because she said, "It's my address, David. I'm inviting you to dine with me this evening at my home."

He broke eye contact with her to glance back down at the paper she'd given him. He looked back at her while trying to downplay the heat rumbling around in his gut.

"Do you need me to bring anything?" he asked her.

"No, just yourself."

Swan glanced around her home and felt the knots beginning to twist in her stomach. She hoped she hadn't made a mistake inviting David here.

Today marked a week since they'd met and if she was going to continue to see him while he was on the island, she couldn't take advantage of his thoughtfulness and expect him to invite her out without ever returning the kindness. However, more than anything else, she needed to keep things in perspective. She needed to remember he was someone she could have a good time with and that's it.

She didn't want anything more than that.

One day, she would be ready to explore her options and consider a future with a man, but that time wasn't now. She liked being single and responsible only for herself.

She knew from Candy that a serious relationship was hard

work. And on top of all that hard work, you could assume you had the right person in your life only to discover you didn't. By then, you would have opened yourself up to hurt and pain in the worst possible way.

The thought that a man had caused her best friend that kind of agony bothered Swan whenever she thought about it. Candy loved Key West as much as Swan did, and for a man to be the reason she had moved away was disheartening.

Swan tried telling herself that not all men were like Candy's ex, Don, or like William. On days when Swan wanted to think all men were dogs, all she had to do was remember her dad.

Andrew Jamison was the yardstick she used to measure a good man. She'd watched how he had treated her mother, had seen the vibrant and sincere love between them. She had not only seen it, but she'd felt it as well. Both her parents had been demonstrative individuals and Swan had often interrupted them sharing a passionate kiss or embrace.

She still felt it here, within the walls of her house and in the very floor she walked on. All the love that had surrounded her while growing up was in this house she now called home.

She was glad her mother hadn't sold it after her father died, when Leigh had made the decision to move back home to Jamaica. Instead, she had kept the house, knowing one day Swan would want to return. It was almost too spacious for one person but Swan knew she would never sell it or move away. This house had everything she needed.

She could see the water from any room, and at night, whenever she slept with the window open, the scent of the ocean would calm her.

Her favorite room in the house was her parents' old bedroom, even though she had not moved into it. It had floor-to-ceiling windows and a balcony she liked sitting on while enjoying her coffee each morning. A couple of years ago, she'd had the balcony screened in to keep the birds from flying into her house, although she loved waking up to the sound of them chirping every morning.

Although neither one of her parents would tell her the full story, Swan knew her father had come from a wealthy family. And she knew he had been disowned by them when he had fallen in love with her mother and refused to give her up. Before dying, Leigh had given Swan a beautiful leather-bound diary to read after her death. That's what had helped keep Swan sane, reading the daily account of her mother's life and love for her father and believing they were now back together.

For weeks following her mother's death, Swan had wanted to be alone to wallow in her pity and read about what she thought was the most beautiful love story that could exist between two people. Her mother had always been expressive with the written word and Swan enjoyed reading what she'd written.

It had made Swan long for such a man, such a love. Maybe that's why she had been so quick to believe in William and why, once she'd found out about his duplicity, she'd been so reluctant to get serious with a man since.

From her mother's diary, Swan discovered her mother's appreciation for her husband's agreement to make Key West their home. The people on the island embraced diversity and tolerated different lifestyles.

Swan had read the account of when her father had been stationed at a naval base in Virginia and had sent for her mother to join him there. In the diary, her mother had written about the hateful stares they would receive whenever they went out together. The unaccepting and disapproving looks. The cruel words some people had wanted them to hear.

Her father hadn't tolerated any of it and hadn't minded confronting anyone who didn't accept his wife. But to avoid trouble, Leigh had preferred to live in Key West, where people's issues with an interracial marriage were practically nonexistent.

However, people's attitudes never kept Leigh from leaving the island to join Andrew whenever he would send for her.

Oftentimes, Leigh would take Swan along and they would both join Andrew in different places for weeks at a time.

When she heard the sound of the doorbell, Swan drew in a deep breath. The time for memories was over. The only plans she had for *this* evening were for her and David to enjoy the meal she'd prepared and later enjoy each other's company.

She had no problem with them deciding what the latter entailed when that time came.

"Hello, David. Welcome to my home."

Flipper pushed from his mind the thought of how Swan would feel if she knew this wasn't his first time here. How she would react if she knew he had invaded her space without her knowledge. If she ever found out the truth, would she understand it had been done with the best of intentions? Namely, to keep her from wasting away in a federal prison after being falsely accused of a crime?

He forced those thoughts to the back of his mind as he smiled down at her. She looked absolutely stunning in a wraparound skirt and yellow blouse. "Hi. I know you said I didn't have to bring anything, but I wanted to give you these," he said, handing her both a bottle of wine and a bouquet of flowers.

He had decided on the wine early on, but the flowers had been a spur of the moment thing when he'd seen them at one of those sidewalk florist shops. Their beauty and freshness had immediately reminded him of Swan.

"Thank you. The flowers are beautiful and this is my favorite wine," she said, stepping aside to let him in.

He chuckled. "I know. I remember from the other night." There was no way he would also mention having seen several bottles of Moscato in the wine rack the time he had checked out her house.

He glanced around, pretending to see her home for the first time. "Nice place."

"Thanks. I thought we would enjoy a glass of wine and some of my mouthwatering crab balls out on the patio before dinner."

"Mouthwatering crab balls?"

"Yes, from my mom's secret recipe. You won't be disappointed," she said, leading him through a set of French doors. The first thought that came to his mind when he stepped out on her patio, which overlooked the Atlantic Ocean, was that it was a beautiful and breathtaking view. This had to be the best spot on the island to view the ocean in all its splendor.

He recalled how, as a boy, he would visit his cousins in California and dream of one day living near the beach. Over the years, being stationed in San Diego had been the next best thing. He owned an apartment close to base that was within walking distance of the beach.

However, his view was nothing like this. All she had to do was walk out her back door and step onto the sand. It was right there at her door. If he lived here, he would go swimming every day.

He glanced over at her. "The view from here is beautiful."

"I love this house and appreciate my mother for not selling it when she decided to move back to Jamaica after Dad died. She got a lot of offers for it, believe me. So have I. Mom said being here without Dad was too painful, but she knew I'd feel differently. For me, it was just the opposite. Being here and recalling all the memories of when the three of us shared this place makes me happy."

Hearing how the loss of her parents affected her made Flipper appreciate his own parents even more. Colin and Lenora Holloway had always been their sons' staunch supporters. Their close and loving relationships had been the reason none of their sons had had any qualms about settling down and marrying. All the marriages had worked out, seemingly made in heaven, except for his brother Liam's.

When Bonnie had gotten pregnant, Liam had done the honorable thing by marrying her. Bonnie had always been a party girl and didn't intend to let marriage or being a mommy slow her down. While Liam was somewhere protecting his country as a Navy SEAL, Bonnie was conveniently forgetting she had a husband.

No one, not even Liam, had been surprised when he returned from an assignment one year and she asked for a divorce. Liam had given it to her without blinking an eye. Since then, Bonnie had remarried, which had introduced another set of issues for Liam. He was constantly taking Bonnie to court to enforce visitation rights to see his daughter because the man Bonnie married didn't like Liam coming around.

Flipper had no qualms about marriage himself, but he had too much going on right now. Namely, resisting the temptation of Swan while he continued his investigation. That was his biggest challenge. The more he was around Swan the more he liked her and the more he wanted to prove her innocence. It was hard staying objective.

"Here you are," she said, handing him a cold bottle of beer. "I figured you would like this instead of the wine."

He smiled. Like he had picked up on her drinking preferences, she had done the same with him. "Thanks. I've never been a wine man."

She chuckled. "Neither was my dad. That's how I knew when it was time for him to come home because Mom would have his favorite beer in the fridge."

He opened the bottle, took a sip and noticed her watching him. He licked his lips, liking the taste of the beer, which was the brand he'd chosen the other night at Summer Moon. When he took another sip and she continued to watch him, he lifted a brow. "Is anything wrong?"

She smiled. "No, nothing is wrong. I just love to watch how you drink your beer."

He chuckled. That was a first. No woman had ever told him that before. "And how do I drink it?"

"First there's the way your mouth fits on the beer bottle. I find it very sensuous."

He tried ignoring the quiver that surged through his veins at the tone in her voice. "Do you?"

"Yes. And then there's the way you drink it like you're enjoying every drop."

"I am."

"I can tell." Then, as if she thought perhaps she'd said too much, she took a step back. "I'll go get those crab balls for you to try."

When she turned to leave, he reached out and touched her arm. He couldn't help it. The air all but crackled with the sexual energy between them. "Come here a minute before you go," he said, setting his beer bottle aside. "Although I do enjoy drinking beer, I've discovered I enjoy feasting on your mouth even more."

And then he lowered his mouth to hers.

Perfect timing, Swan thought, because she needed this. She'd wanted it the moment he tilted his beer bottle to his mouth and she'd watched him do so. And now he was doing her. Showing her that he was enjoying her mouth more than he'd enjoyed the beer. Just like he'd said.

There was a certain precision and meticulousness in how he mastered the art of kissing. First, as soon as his tongue would enter her mouth, he would unerringly find her tongue, capture it with his own and begin gently sucking in a way that made the muscles between her legs tighten. Then he would do other things she didn't have a name for. Things that made desire flow through her like sweet wine, kindling heated pleasure and burning passion within her.

He rocked his thighs against her and she felt him pressed against her. His arousal was massive. Instinctively, she moved her hips closer, wanting to feel him right there, at the juncture of her thighs.

When he finally pulled his mouth away, she released a deep,

satisfied breath. Her mouth was still throbbing and there was an intense ache in her limbs. Right now, their heavy breathing was the only sound audible, and the laser-blue eyes staring down at her sent a tremor to her core.

She licked her lips when she took a step back. "Ready for a few crab balls?"

"Yes," he said, after licking his own lips. "For now."

CHAPTER FIVE

HE WANTED HER.

Flipper knew he shouldn't, but he did. All through the delicious dinner Swan had prepared and while engaging in great conversation with her, the thought of just how much he wanted her simmered to the back of his mind. Now with dinner coming to an end, desire was inching back to the forefront. Images of her naked tried to dominate his mind, the thoughts made him shift in his chair to relieve the ache at his crotch.

"Ready for dessert, David? I made key lime pie."

Right now, another kind of dessert was still teasing his taste buds. "Yes, I would love a slice, and dinner was amazing by the way. You're a good cook. My mother would absolutely love you."

Too late, he wondered why he'd said such a thing. From the look on her face, she was wondering the same thing. So he decided to clean up his mess by adding, "She admires other women who can cook."

Swan smiled. "You don't have to do that, David."

"Do what?"

"Try to retract the implications of what you said so I won't get any ideas."

He *had* done that, but not for the reason she thought. He'd done so because it wasn't right for either of them to think some-thing was seriously developing between them. More than likely, she would hate his guts when she learned why he was really in Key West, when she discovered she was his assignment and nothing more. He couldn't tell her the truth, but he could cer-tainly set her straight on what the future held for them.

"And what ideas do you think I wanted to retract?"

"The ones where I would think we were starting something here, the ones that meant I would be someone you'd take home to meet your mother."

He sat down his glass of ice tea, which she had served with dinner. "Any reason why I wouldn't want to take you home to meet my mother *if* we shared that kind of a relationship, Swan?" Although he didn't think he needed to let her know—again—that they didn't share that kind of relationship, he did so anyway.

"Honestly, David, do I really have to answer that?"

"Yes, I think you do."

She stared at him for a minute. "I'm well aware when it comes to interracial relationships that not all families are accepting."

He chuckled. "My family isn't one of them, trust me. Inter-racial or international, we couldn't care less. My brother Brad met his wife, Sela, while working in Seoul, South Korea, and my brother Michael met Gardenia in Spain. Like I told you, my parents would accept anyone who makes us happy, regardless of race, creed, religion, nationality or color."

She didn't say anything to that. Then she broke eye contact with him to glance down into her glass of tea. Moments later, she raised her gaze back to him.

"My father's parents didn't. They threatened him with what they would do if he married Mom and they kept their word. They disowned him. Still, my mother reached out to them when Dad died to let them know he'd passed. They came to his fu-neral but had no qualms about letting Mom know they still would not accept her. They would only tolerate me since I was biracial. They even tried forcing Mom to let me go back with them. That's when my godfathers stepped in."

Flipper shook his head, feeling the pain she refused to acknowledge, the pain she'd obviously felt because of her grandparents' actions. But he'd heard it in her voice nonetheless.

"It's sad that some people can be such bigots. At the risk of this sounding like a cliché, some of my closest friends are black," he added, immediately thinking of Bane, Viper and Coop. Like her, Mac was of mixed heritage and had a white mother and black father.

"I'm sure some of your closest friends are, David."

He wondered if she believed him. One day, she would see the truth in his words. Then it suddenly occurred to him—no, she would not. There would be no reason for her to ever meet the four guys who were just as close to him as his biological brothers.

"I'll be back in a minute with the pie," she said. Then she stood and left the room.

Flipper watched her leave, feeling that he hadn't fully eradicated her doubts the way he'd wanted to do. That bothered him. He didn't want her to think he was one of those prejudiced asses who believed one race of people was better than another. What her grandparents had done to her father and mother, as well as to her, was unforgivable. Regardless of how she'd tried to come across as if their actions hadn't hurt her, as if they still didn't hurt her, he knew better.

She needed a hug right now.

He pushed back his chair and left the dining room to enter her kitchen. Instead of getting the pie like she'd said she would do, she was standing with her back to him, looking out the kitchen window at the ocean. And he could tell from the movement of her shoulders that she was crying.

"Swan?"

She quickly turned, swiping at her tears. "I'm sorry to take so long, I just had one of those miss-my-daddy-and-mommy moments."

He crossed the room to her, knowing that her tears were about more than that. He knew it and he intended for her to know he knew it. "Not wanting to get to know you—that was your grandparents' loss, Swan."

She gazed into his eyes and nodded. "I know, David, but their actions hurt Dad, although he never said it did. I knew. Mom knew, too. I think that's one of the reasons she loved him so much, because of all the sacrifices he'd made for her. That's why she did anything she could to make him happy so he would never regret choosing her. But it wasn't fair. He was a good man. Mom was a good woman. They deserved each other and should have been allowed to love freely and without restrictions, reservations or censure. It just wasn't fair, David."

And then she buried her face in his chest and cried in earnest. Wrapping his arms around her, he held her, leaning down to whisper in her ear that things would be all right. That her parents had had a special love, one she should be proud of, one the naysayers had envied.

Emotions Flipper hadn't counted on flowed through him as he continued to stroke her hair and whisper soothing words next to her ear. Inwardly, he screamed at the injustice of trying to keep someone from loving the person they truly wanted to love. It was something he'd never understood and figured he never would. And never would he accept such a way of thinking from anyone.

Swan knew she should pull out of David's arms, but found she couldn't do it. Being held by him felt good. His fingers, the ones that were stroking through the strands of her hair, seemed to electrify her scalp. They sent comforting sensations all through her—and something else as well. A need that he was stroking to fruition. As a result, instead of pulling out of his arms, she closed her eyes and enjoyed being held by him while inhaling his masculine scent.

She wasn't sure how long they stood there, but it didn't take long for her to notice his breathing had changed. But then so had hers. His touch had shifted from comforting to passionate. He was using the same strokes, but now the feelings within her were beginning to build to an insurmountable degree of desire.

Opening her eyes, she lifted her head to stare up at him. The minute she did, she caught her breath at the intense yearning she saw in his gaze. That yearning reached out to her, jolted her with a level of throbbing need she hadn't known existed. She'd heard of raw, make-you-lose-your-senses passion, but she had never experienced it for herself.

Until now.

"David..." She said his name as something burst to life in the pit of her stomach. It made a quivering sensation rise at the back of her neck. He implored her with his eyes to follow this passion, as if letting her know he understood what she was experiencing even if she didn't.

"Tell me what you want, Swan," he said in a deep voice while gently caressing the side of her face. "Tell me."

The intensity in his eyes was burning her, scorching her with the sexual hunger that was coming to life inside her. She wanted more than his erection pressing hard against the apex of her thighs. She wanted him on top of her. She wanted him to slide into her body and begin thrusting in and out. She needed to lose herself in more than just his arms.

Suddenly, she felt emboldened to tell him just what she wanted. "I want you, David. In my bed."

Flipper wanted to be in her bed as well. Lord knows he shouldn't want it, but he did. He would have to deal with the consequences later. He felt too tight and hot to try to fight the demands his body was making. Sweeping her into his arms, he quickly walked out of the kitchen and headed toward her bedroom.

"You think you know where you're going, David?"

He slowed his pace, remembering that she had no idea that he knew the layout of her home. Not only did he know where her bedroom was located, he knew the blueprint of the plumbing underneath her floor. He looked down and met her gaze, grateful she wasn't suspicious. "I figured you would stop me if I went in the wrong direction."

"Yes, I would have stopped you, but you're going the right way."

"Good." When he resumed his swift pace, it didn't take him long to reach her bedroom.

Swan had gotten next to him in a way he hadn't counted on happening. Seducing her had not been part of the plan and he should not have allowed things to get this far. He didn't want to think of the major complications involved, and not just because she was the goddaughter of three top naval officers.

But something was happening that he hadn't counted on. His mind and body were in sync and a rare sexual aura was overtaking him. He could no more stop making love to her than he could stop being a SEAL. For him to even make such a comparison was pretty damn serious.

Instead of placing Swan on the bed, he eased her to her feet, loving the feel of her soft body sliding down his hard one. "If you're having second thoughts about this, Swan, now's the time to say so."

She shook her head and then in a wobbly voice, she said, "No second thoughts, David."

Hearing her affirmation spoken with such certainty, Flipper released a low, throaty groan as he lowered his mouth to kiss her again, needing the connection of her lips to his as much as he needed to breathe. Wrapping his arms around her waist, he pulled her body closer to him as he deepened the kiss, wanting her to feel his erection, the hard evidence of his need for her.

He had never wanted a woman with this much intensity in

his life, and he had no idea why Swan was having this kind of an effect on him.

Why she, and no other woman before her, had tempted him to cross a line during a mission. His mind didn't function that way. He had yet to prove her innocence, so technically, she was still naval intelligence's prime suspect, but at the moment that didn't matter. For all he knew, he could be about to sleep with the enemy.

But right now, that didn't matter either because deep down, a part of him believed she was innocent.

What was happening between them was definitely out of the realm of normal for him. He'd known he would have to get close to her, but he hadn't counted on this—his intense desire to do inappropriate, erotic and mind-blowing things to Swan Jamison.

But he wanted her and there would be no regrets. At least not for him, and based on what she'd just said, there would be no regrets for her either.

The moment he ended the kiss, his hands were busy removing her skirt, followed by her blouse, and when she stood in front of him in her lacy panties and bra, he couldn't help but growl his satisfaction. She looked sexy as hell and the rose-colored ensemble against the darkness of her skin was stunningly beautiful. *She* was beautiful.

He reached up and traced a finger along the material of her boxer-cut panties. This style on a woman had never done anything for him. Until now.

"You should have been a model," he said in a deep, throaty voice, filled with profound need and deep appreciation. She had such a gorgeously shaped body.

"My mother used to be a model. I was satisfied with being a model's daughter."

"And a strikingly beautiful one at that," he said, lowering to his knees to rid her of her panties. He couldn't wait to touch her, taste her and do all those erotic things to her he had dreamed of doing over the past few nights. He breathed in deeply, getting more aroused by the second while easing her panties down a pair of long, beautiful legs.

After tossing her panties aside, he leaned back on his haunches and gazed at her, seeing her naked from the waist down. Her small waist, her stomach, the shape of her thighs and longs legs were perfect. She was perfect.

After looking his fill, he leaned forward and rested his forehead against her stomach, inhaling her luscious scent. He loved the way it flowed through his nostrils, opening his pores and causing his body to become even more erect.

And then he did something he'd wanted to do since their first kiss. He used the tip of his tongue to kiss her stomach, loving the indention around her naval and tracing a path around the area. Then he shifted his mouth lower, licking his way down and enjoying the sound of her moans.

When he came to the very essence of her, he licked around her womanly folds before leaning in to plant a heated kiss right there. It was as if sampling her special taste was as essential to him as breathing. His hands held firm to her thighs when he slid his tongue inside of her, loving the sound of his name from her lips.

Then he went deeper, using his tongue to taste her, claim her and brand her. The latter gave him pause but not enough to stop what he was doing. He'd never claimed a woman as his own and had never thought about doing so. But with Swan, it seemed such a thing wasn't just desired but was required.

And he didn't want it any other way. She was the first woman he wanted to claim. Forcefully, he pushed to the back of his mind what it could mean to make any woman his and decided he would dwell on that aspect of things at a later time. For now, he wanted to focus on the delicious, succulent, enjoyable taste that was Swan.

He took his time, wanting her to know just how much he loved doing this to her. He wanted her to feel the connection his tongue was making with her flesh. However, he wanted her to do more than feel it, he wanted this connection absorbed into her senses, into her mind, into every part of her body.

Moments later, Flipper knew he'd achieved his goal when he felt her fingers dig into his shoulder blades, followed by the quivering of her thighs. Tightening his hold on her hips, he knew what would be next and he was ready.

She screamed his name when she was thrown into an orgasmic state. Her fingernails dug deeper into his skin, but he didn't feel the pain because knowing he was giving her pleasure made him immune to it. What he felt was a desire to take things to the next level, to slide into her body and go so deep it would be impossible to detect where his body ended and hers began.

He finally pulled his mouth away and looked up at her, saw the glazed look in her eyes. Without saying a word, he traced his fingers around the womanly mound he'd just kissed before inserting his finger inside of her. She was ultra-wet and mega-hot and he had every intention of capitalizing on both. The orgasm she'd just experienced would be small in comparison to the one he intended to give her.

Pulling his finger from her, he licked it clean, knowing she was watching his every move. "Sweet," he said softly, holding her gaze.

He slowly eased to his feet and reached behind her to remove her bra. When she stood totally naked in front of him, he feasted his gaze on her. "And I'm about to show you just how sweet I think you are, Swan."

CHAPTER SIX

SWAN WAS HAVING difficulty breathing and the blue eyes staring at her made getting air to flow through her lungs even more difficult. Never had she felt this energized from a sexual act. And when David got to his feet and leaned in to kiss her, letting her taste herself on his lips, she felt weak in the knees. But he held her around the waist, holding her up as he kissed her more deeply, making her wish the kiss could last forever.

She released a low disappointed groan in her throat when he pulled his mouth away.

"Don't worry, there's more coming."

He swept her off her feet and carried her over to the bed, placed her on it and joined her there.

"You still have clothes on," she said, reaching out to touch his shirt.

"I know and they will be coming off. Right now, I just want to lie here with you and hold you in my arms."

She smiled at him. "You're not going to fall asleep on me, are you?"

Chuckling, he said, "Asleep? With you lying beside me without a stitch of clothes on? Sleep is the last thing I'd be able to do, trust me."

He'd already pleasured her with his mouth, so she couldn't

help wondering what was next. She soon discovered his intent when he reached over and cupped her breasts.

"You are perfect," he said in a deep husky voice.

The words triggered a memory of overhearing her father whisper the same compliment to her mother, after she surprised him with a special dinner after he returned home from one of his missions.

Swan knew she was far from perfect. Those were just words David was speaking. But still, hearing them filled her with joy. Maybe she shouldn't let them, but they did.

Then any further thoughts dissolved from her mind when David eased a nipple between his lips. She moaned at the pleasure she felt all the way to her toes. Just when she thought she couldn't stand anymore, he began torturing her other nipple.

When he finally eased away, she opened her eyes to watch him undress. When he removed his shirt, she saw the tattoos covering his tanned skin on both of his upper arms—huge dolphins emerging from beautiful blue ocean waters. Another tattoo of even more dolphins was painted across his back in beautiful vivid colors. She'd never been into tattoos but she thought his were stunning.

"I like your tattoos," she said.

He glanced over at her and smiled. "Thanks."

When he lowered his shorts, her gaze moved to the area between a pair of masculine thighs. His shaft was massive and marvelously formed. Just the thought of him easing that part of himself inside of her sent her pulse skyrocketing.

"You okay?"

She lifted her gaze to his. She wasn't sure if she was okay. A thickness had settled in her throat when she saw how he was looking at her. Not only did he intend to join his body with hers, she had a feeling he planned to keep them connected for a while.

"Yes, I'm okay."

Swan continued to check him out, thinking he had a mighty fine physique. His body was all muscle and it was obvious that he worked out regularly. A man didn't get those kinds of abs if he didn't.

She watched as he pulled a condom from his wallet and sheathed himself in a way that was so erotic, she felt herself getting wetter between the legs just watching him. Then he was strolling back toward the bed. To her.

"I'm about to make sure you feel more than okay," he said, reaching down and easing her up to rest her chest against his. Her breasts were still sensitive from his mouth and rubbing them against his chest caused a multitude of arousing sensations to swamp her.

"What are you doing to me?" she asked in a ragged breath, barely able to get the words out.

"Anything you can imagine," he whispered, lowering her back on the mattress and then straddling her. He stared down at her as he gently moved her legs apart. She felt him, that part of him, lightly touch her feminine folds and then he was rubbing back and forth across them, sending even more sensations racing through her bloodstream.

"Trying to torture me, David?"

"No, trying to pleasure you. Ready for me?"

The movement of his manhood against her was making it impossible for her to concentrate. "What do you think?"

"You're wet and hot, so I think you're ready." And then he entered her in one deep thrust.

She gasped at the fullness and was glad he'd gone still for a minute. This gave her the chance to feel him fully embedded deep within her. It had been a long time for her and her inner muscles were greedily clamping on to him, tightening their hold.

"You're big," she whispered.

"You're tight," was his response. "But we're making this work."

And he did. First he began moving again, gently sliding in and out of her. That only lasted a few seconds before he picked up the pace and began thrusting harder.

She responded by wrapping her legs around his waist. Then he lifted her hips to receive more of him. When he established a slow and deep rhythm, touching areas in her body that hadn't been touched in a long time, or ever, she fought back a scream. She grabbed hold of his hair and pulled it, but he didn't seem to mind.

"Rule number one, Swan. Don't hold back."

Was he kidding? It wasn't a matter of holding back. It was more like she was trying to keep her sanity. David was so powerfully male that he was pushing her over the edge with every deep stroke. Every cell within her vibrated in response to his precise thrusts.

"Hold on, baby. Things are about to get wild."

Flipper had given Swan fair warning. When he began pounding harder, making strokes he'd never attempted with another woman—going deep, pulling out and then going deep again—he felt a quivering sensation start at the base of his testicles and move toward her womb with each and every thrust. He had to hold on tight to her to keep them on the bed. He was determined to show her wild.

Simultaneously, he leaned down to have his way with her mouth, licking it corner to corner and then inserting his tongue inside with the same rhythm he was using below.

What he was feeling right now was more than off the charts, it was out of the atmosphere. When she finally let go and screamed his name, the sound vibrated in every part of his body, especially in her inner muscles. They clamped down on him, trying to pull everything out of him while her hands tightened even more in his hair.

"David!"

She screamed his name again. The sound drove him. He wanted more of her. Wanted to go deeper. Throwing his head back, he felt the veins in his neck strain. There was pain but not enough to dim the pleasure.

And he knew at that moment Swan had gotten under his skin in a way no other woman had.

He began rocking hard into her with an intensity that made him go deeper with every thrust. Then he was the one hollering out in pleasure, saying her name as an explosion ripped through him. Then like a crazed sexual maniac, he leaned in to feast on her mouth and breasts. It was like his desire for her could not end.

"David!"

He knew she was coming again and, dammit to hell, so was he. Marveling at such a thing, he tightened his hold on her. His control had not only gotten shot to hell and back but had died an explosive death as the result of the most powerful orgasms he'd ever endured.

This was what real lovemaking was about. No holds barred. No restrictions. Every part of him felt alive, drained, renewed. The room had the scent of sex and more sex. But that wasn't all. Emotions he'd never felt before touched him and swelled his heart.

He quickly forced those emotions back, refusing to go there. Knowing he couldn't go there.

The husky sound of deep, even breathing made Swan open her eyes. She was still in bed with David. Their limbs were entangled and his head was resting on her chest as he slept.

This man had been the most giving of lovers. He didn't come until he made sure she came first. He had kissed every part of her body, some parts more than others, and he had stoked passion within her in a way that had made her reach the boiling point. No man had ever made love to her with such intensity.

He had warned her about them getting wild. As far as she was concerned, they had gotten more than wild, they had gotten uninhibited, untamed. She hadn't known she had so much passion within her. He had brought it out and made her do more than own it. He had made her so aware of it that she doubted she could undo what he'd done.

David Holloway had done more than push a few of her buttons. He had turned on all the lights.

That thought made her smile and pull him closer. Feeling exhausted, she closed her eyes and drifted into sleep.

Flipper slowly opened his eyes, taking in the sight and scent of the woman lying beside him, snuggled close to his body. He was so sexually contented, he could groan out loud. He didn't. Instead he tightened his arms around her.

Things had gotten wild. They had finally fallen asleep after four rounds of the most satisfying lovemaking possible.

While making love with Swan, he had discovered there was a vast difference in making love to her versus making love to other women. He'd known it before but she had made that point crystal clear tonight.

With other women, he'd usually had one goal in mind—seeking sexual pleasure and making sure she got hers. With Swan it had been about that, too, but it had also been about finding closeness. No other woman had made him want to stay inside her. It had only been the need to replace condoms that had forced him from Swan's side. And then he had been back inside her in a flash…like that was where he belonged. Hell, he was still thinking that way and the twitch in his aroused manhood was letting him know just what he desired.

Flipper was known to have a robust sexual appetite. When you lived your life on the edge, engaging in covert operations as his team did, then you needed a way to release.

Usually, unerringly, he found his release in some woman's bed. He made sure she knew it was one and done. Due to the nature of his occupation, he didn't have time for attachments or anything long-term. Some SEALs did; he didn't. He'd tried it once and it hadn't worked out. Now he preferred being a loner.

It didn't bother him that he was the lone single guy among his close friends. To each his own.

So how could one night in Swan Jamison's bed have him thinking things he shouldn't be thinking, especially considering why he was in Key West in the first place?

It had everything to do with the woman he'd had mind-blowing sex with for the past four hours or so. Now he saw her as more than an assignment. Now she was also a woman who had the ability to match his sexual needs one-on-one, something he found invigorating and energizing on all levels. He was a totally physical male and Swan Jamison was wholly, utterly female. Almost to the point that she'd blown his ever-loving mind.

Now she was sleeping peacefully while he was lying here thinking, knowing his honor was being tested. As a military man, he always did what was honorable. On top of that, his mother had drilled into all five of her sons that honor was not just for their country but extended to humans just as much, especially women. Why had that thought settled deep into his mind now?

One reason might be that he'd read the report on her. He knew about those elderly people residing at the senior living complex that she visited on her weekends off and how she'd championed so hard for the homeless. She was working with the mayor to help find funding to build a housing complex for them.

She was a caring person. He'd witnessed her love for her country, for her father, that night at the fireworks and the more he was around her, the more he believed in her innocence.

She made a sound now and he glanced down and met beautiful brown eyes staring at him. Immediately his senses connected with those eyes. She trusted him. He could see it in the gaze staring back at him. Otherwise he would not be here in her bed.

What would she think when she learned the truth? Would she still trust him? He pushed the thought to the back of his mind.

She gave him a beautiful, sleepy smile that melted his insides. Made him wish he had come here to the Keys for a real vacation, a much-needed one. He wished he had entered her shop with no ulterior motive but to do as he claimed, which was to buy his mother a birthday gift. He would still have tried his hand at seducing her, but things would have been different. Specifically, he wouldn't feel as if his honor was being compromised.

"You didn't try my key lime pie," she whispered.

"We can get up and eat some now if you want," he said.

"No, I like being just where I am. We can always eat some later…or even for breakfast."

He leaned down and brushed a kiss across her lips. "Um, breakfast sounds nice. Is that an invitation to stay the night?"

"Only if you want to."

He wanted to. And when he brushed another kiss across her lips, he slid his tongue inside her mouth to kiss her deeply and let her know how much he wanted to stay.

He knew at that moment that his commanding officer and the admiral weren't the only ones with a personal interest in Swan Jamison. He now had a personal interest in her as well.

CHAPTER SEVEN

THE NEXT MORNING, Swan woke up to bright sunlight flowing in through her window and a powerfully male body sleeping beside her.

Last night was rated right up there with *Ripley's Believe It or Not*. It had been just that spectacular. They'd made love a couple more times before getting up after midnight to eat the pie she'd prepared for dessert. After clearing off the table and loading the dishes into the dishwasher, he'd suggested they walk on the beach.

So at one in the morning, they had strolled hand in hand along the water's edge. It had been a beautiful night with a full moon in the sky. The breeze off the ocean had provided the perfect reason for him to pull her close while walking barefoot in the sand. He told her more about his family; namely about his parents' medical supply company.

Then at some point, they began talking about her company and she found herself telling him just about everything about jewelry making. He was curious about her stones and complimented how beautiful they were and inquired how she was able to create so many pieces.

No man had ever taken an interest in her work before and she was excited that he thought what she did for a living was important. She had found herself explaining the day-to-day operations of Swan's. He couldn't believe how she found the time to handcraft a number of the items sold in her shop.

David also thought it was great that Rafe, through his connections with a huge distributor in California, was able to get some of Swan's more expensive stones at a lower cost and had even helped her save on shipping by including them in the packaging with his ink.

She glanced over at him now as he shifted in bed. He kept his arms wrapped around her while he slept. She studied his features and saw how relaxed he looked.

She drew in a deep breath, still amazed at the depth of what they had shared last night. It had been the most profound thing she'd ever experienced with a man. Making love with David had touched her in ways she hadn't thought possible. He had made her feel things she hadn't ever felt before and those things weren't just sexual in nature. While in his arms, she had felt safe and secure. Protected.

As far as she was concerned, what they'd shared last night was more compelling and meaningful than any other time she'd shared with a man, even more meaningful than the time she'd spent with William. She'd never really allowed herself to fully let go with William. Now she could admit to herself that she'd known in the back of her mind that something didn't add up with him.

Yet she'd been so desperate for companionship after losing her mother that she had wanted to believe William was honest, even though he'd seemed too good to be true. She was glad Candy had become suspicious when he'd never wanted them to be photographed together or when he'd insisted that they spend the night at Swan's place instead of the hotel.

At the time, his requests hadn't bothered her because she hadn't wanted her employer or her coworkers to get in her business. But Candy had seen through all that and knew something in the milk wasn't clean, as she would often say. It had been Candy who'd unveiled her own husband's secret affair with a flight attendant. And once confronted, Don hadn't denied a thing. He'd said he was glad she'd found out because he wanted a divorce.

Pushing thoughts of Don's and William's betrayals to the back of her mind, Swan continued to study David. She couldn't help but recall the number of times he'd made her climax. Now that was simply amazing all by itself.

She was enjoying her time with him, even knowing it wouldn't last. Later this month, he would leave the island and she would probably not hear from him again. She knew that, accepted it. She had long ago learned to live for the now and not sweat the small stuff. Especially those things she couldn't change.

"You're awake."

She couldn't help but smile at the slumberous blue eyes staring at her. The dark shadow on his chin made him look even sexier. "Yes, I'm awake. I guess I should be a good host and prepare breakfast before you leave."

"Um, I've overstayed my welcome?"

"No, but today is Sunday and I have a lot to do."

"Maybe I can help you."

"You don't know what I'll be doing."

He reached out and pushed her hair back off her shoulders so he could completely see her face. "Then tell me."

She gazed into his eyes. "The shop is closed on Sundays and I use my day off to visit Golden Manor Senior Place. My mom used to do volunteer work there when we lived on the island years ago. I would go with her on Sundays to visit everyone. I guess you could say it's become a family tradition that I decided to continue."

"I think that's a wonderful thing you're doing. I'm sure the residents there appreciate it."

"Yes, they do, although those who knew my mom are no

longer there. They've passed on. I'm establishing new relationships and friendships."

"Good for you. I'd love to join you."

"You would?" she asked, surprised.

"Yes, and don't worry about preparing breakfast. I'll go home
and refresh and be back here within an hour. We can grab breakfast somewhere before heading over. Afterward, we can spend
more time on the beach. I enjoyed the walk last night with you."

And she had enjoyed it, too. The thought that he wanted to
spend more time with her made her feel really good inside.
"Okay, that sounds wonderful."

"I'm glad you think so, and before I leave…"

"Yes?"

He leaned over to kiss her and she knew where things would
lead from there. She looked forward to getting wild again with
him.

Flipper clicked on his phone the minute he walked into his hotel
room. He noted several missed calls since he'd deliberately cut
off his phone last night. One was from the admiral, who was
probably calling for an update. But first Flipper would return
the call to Nick.

"Flipper, should I ask why I couldn't reach you last night?"

"No, you shouldn't," Flipper said, flopping down in the nearest chair.

"You have heard the saying that you shouldn't mix business
with pleasure, right?"

Too late for that, Flipper thought, running a hand down his
face. Instead of responding to Nick's comment, he said, "I hope
you have something for me. There's another angle I want you
to check out."

"Okay, and yes, I have something for you. I found out the
initial investigation was handed off to a group of civilian investigators, which means naval intelligence didn't rank it at
the top at first."

Flipper was very much aware of the part government bureaucracy played in certain investigations. If someone thought a case should be under naval intelligence's radar, then they made sure it got there. "Why?"

"Not sure yet, but first, let's talk about Jamila Fairchild."

Flipper leaned forward in his chair. "Okay, let's talk about her. What do you have?"

"Not what you obviously think. What she told Swan was the truth. She does have a huge family who lives in the north."

Flipper raised a brow. "Then who made the error in the report from naval intelligence?"

"Don't know, but it's worth checking out, although I don't think it's anything suspicious on Ms. Fairchild's end. Especially when I tell you who her family is."

"And who is her family?"

"Her mother's brother is Swan's grandfather."

A frown covered Flipper's face. "The grandfather who disowned Swan's father?"

"Yes, from what I've gathered. But I can find no record of her grandfather ever reaching out to her."

"Interesting."

"Yes, it is. I take it Swan Jamison doesn't know about the family connection."

"No, she doesn't." Flipper decided not to try to wrap his head around this bit of news just yet. Instead he asked, "What about Rafe Duggers?"

"Personally, I think something is going on with him."

Flipper lifted a brow. "What?"

"First of all, certain aspects of his info are sealed."

"Sealed?"

"Yes. I would think if naval intelligence was checking into something related to Swan and her story, they would see that sealed record for her tenant as a red flag. For them not to have flagged it raises my own suspicions about a few things."

That raised Flipper's suspicions as well. Was Rafe a double

agent? Someone working undercover? Was someone in naval intelligence deliberately setting Swan up as the traitor? If so, why?

"You weren't able to find out anything about him?"

There was a husky chuckle. "I didn't say that. There are ways to find out anything you want when you know how to do it."

And Nick knew how to do it. He'd been an amazing SEAL, but as far as Flipper was concerned, Nick's natural investigative talents were better served at Homeland Security. "When will you let me know something?"

"Give me a couple of days. In the meantime, don't say anything to anyone about my suspicions about Duggers."

"Not even the CO and admiral?"

"Not even them for now. You mentioned Swan had a third godfather who was someone high up at naval intelligence. Was his identity revealed to you?"

"No, it wasn't but then I didn't ask," Flipper said.

"It wasn't hard to find out," Nick replied. "All you have to do is find out who Andrew Jamison's SEAL teammates were at the time he died and do a little research to determine where they are now."

"I take it you've done that."

"Yes, and would you believe Swan Jamison's third godfather is Director of Naval Intelligence Samuel Levart?"

Flipper would not have considered Director Levart in a million years, but it all made sense now. In order for someone to have delayed making formal charges against Swan, that person would have to be someone in power. The admiral had alluded to as much. "Swan doesn't know how favored she is to have three powerful men in her corner."

"Yes, but we both know it wouldn't matter if one of her godfathers was the President. If naval intelligence believes they have enough evidence to prosecute her, they will," Nick said.

Flipper knew that to be true. Now more than ever he had to find the person intent on framing Swan. To him, it was beginning to look like an inside job.

"So what else do you have for me to check out?" Nick asked, reclaiming Flipper's attention.

"It's about something Swan told me." He then shared with Nick the information about Rafe Duggers's association with some huge distributor in California. "I need you to check that out."

"I will. I know time is of the essence so I'll get back to you soon, Flipper."

"Thanks, I appreciate it."

"If you're so concerned about me, then why not return to the Keys and keep an eye on me, Candy?" Swan asked. She moved around her bedroom getting dressed while talking to her friend on speakerphone.

"You know why I won't return, just yet. But I did hear something that's interesting."

"What?" Swan asked as she shimmied into her skirt.

"I talked to Francola the other day and she said Marshall mentioned to her that Don is thinking about moving away from the island."

Swan paused. Francola and her husband, Marshall, had been close friends of Don and Candy's while they were married. The two couples often did things together. Personally, Swan didn't care much for Francola because the woman had been aware Don was cheating on Candy but hadn't told her friend. "I would take anything Francola says with a grain of salt these days," Swan said as she continued dressing.

"I know you still fault her for not telling me about Don and I admit I was angry with her, too, but now I understand her not doing so."

"Do you?"

"Yes. Her relationship with me is not like our relationship, Swan. You and I have been best friends since grade school and we have no secrets. You would have told me about Don had you suspected anything."

"Darn right."

"Well, Francola and I didn't have that kind of relationship. We only met through our husbands, who worked together. Besides, I'm not sure I would have believed her even had she told me. I would have been in denial." Candy paused. "Now, enough about me. Tell me more about this David Holloway."

Swan smiled while putting hoop earrings into her ears. "He's a real nice guy. Thoughtful. Considerate. Handsome as sin." She glanced over at her made-up bed. Although there were no signs of anyone sleeping in it last night, it didn't take much for her to remember all the wild action she and David had shared under the sheets. "And he's great in bed. More than great. He's fantastic."

"Just be careful, Swan. Protect your heart."

Swan slipped her feet into her sandals. "My heart? It's not like I'm falling for the guy, Candy."

"Aren't you? I can hear it in your voice. You like him a lot."

Yes, she did like him a lot. "It won't go beyond me liking him," she said, trying to convince herself of that more so than Candy.

"Can you honestly say that?"

"Yes, because I can't let it. His work brought him to the island and he'll be leaving soon. In less than thirty days."

"Doesn't matter."

Swan knew for her it *did* matter. She only wanted short-term. The last thing she wanted was to do long-term with any man.

CHAPTER EIGHT

"I ENJOYED MY time with you today, Swan," Flipper said, looking down at her.

They'd had brunch at Summer Moon before heading to the senior living complex where they spent the next four hours. She assisted the staff by reading to groups of people and even taking a few of the seniors for walks around the complex. Some, she'd explained, had family who rarely visited so she had become like their surrogate granddaughter.

On the flip side, considering what she'd missed out having in her life, he couldn't help but wonder if they had become her surrogate grandparents.

From the moment she walked into the facility, everyone brightened up when they saw her. It was amazing to him. She knew just what to say to elicit a smile or to get them to engage in more conversation. The majority of the seniors knew her by name and he couldn't help noticing a number of the women wearing what looked like necklaces she'd made.

When he inquired about the necklaces Swan confirmed they were her designs but she had taught the women to make them from stones she'd given them. It had taken longer than normal since a lot of the older women's hands weren't as nimble as they used to be.

After leaving the nursing home, they'd grabbed lunch at a sidewalk café before returning to her house where they'd spent the rest of the day on the beach. Later, after ordering takeout for dinner from Arness, they were back at her place.

No matter how tempting Swan was making it for him to stay longer at her place, he would leave when it got dark. The information about Rafe Duggers's sealed records bothered him and he'd decided to poke around in the tattoo parlor later that night to see what he could find.

He glanced over at Swan as she sat across the table from him eating dinner. Earlier today, when he had returned to take her to breakfast, she had opened the door looking fresh and perky and dressed simply in a pair of shorts and a tank top. Seeing her dressed that way reminded him of just what a gorgeous pair of legs she had, as well as how those same legs had wrapped around him while they'd made love that morning and the night before.

When they had gone swimming, she'd worn one of the sexiest two-piece bathing suits he'd ever seen. He had totally and completely enjoyed his day with her. They would be attending the Memorial Day festivities together tomorrow in town, which included a parade.

Because he needed some investigative time, he'd come up with an excuse for why he couldn't see her a couple of days this week. Time was moving quickly and he had yet to find anything to clear her of wrongdoing.

Because of Nick's warning, Flipper hadn't told Admiral Martin everything when he'd called him back yesterday. Namely, he'd left out the discrepancies between what Nick had found out and the actual reports from naval intelligence. Until Flipper discovered what was going on, he would follow Nick's advice and keep that information to himself for now.

"Although I won't be seeing you for a few days because of work, will you still be on the island?" Swan asked.

It was hard not to be totally truthful about why she wouldn't be seeing him. She was the last person he wanted to be dishonest with but he had no choice. His goal had always been to prove her innocence and now that was doubly true. He would check out the tattoo shop tonight and look around in both Rafe's and Jamila's homes this week while they were here at work. Although it had been established that Jamila was Swan's relative, as far as Flipper was concerned, she was still a suspect.

"Yes, I'll still be on the island but I have to concentrate on this project I was sent here to do." No need to tell her that the project involved her.

"I understand how things are when work calls."

He reached up and caressed the side of her face. "We still have a date for the parade tomorrow, right?"

"Yes."

"What about dinner on Friday evening?" he asked her.

Her smile touched something deep within him. "I'd love that, David."

"Good. I'll swing by your shop at closing time Friday and we can go to dinner directly from there. You pick the place."

"All right."

"What time do you want me to come get you for the parade tomorrow?"

"It starts at ten in the morning and we need to get there early to get a good spot. How about if I prepare pancakes for us in the morning around eight?"

"You sure? I wouldn't want you to go to any trouble."

She waved off his words. "No problem. I told you I enjoy cooking."

After they finished dinner, he told her he needed to leave to read some reports for work, which wasn't a lie. She walked him to the door. He leaned down to kiss her, intending for it to be a light touch of their lips.

But the moment his mouth touched hers and she released a breathless sigh, it seemed the most natural thing to slide his tongue inside her mouth and deepen the kiss. Wrapping his arms around her waist, he pulled her tight against him and knew the exact moment the kiss had changed to something more.

It was no longer a *goodbye and I'll see you later* kiss. Instead it was one of those *I need to have you before I go* kind. And Swan seemed to be reciprocating those feelings as she returned the kiss with equal fervor.

The next thing Flipper knew, he was sweeping her off her feet and moving quickly toward her bedroom. When he placed her on the bed, they began stripping off their clothes.

For him, she'd become an itch he couldn't scratch and a craving that wouldn't go away. There was something about making love to her that made every part of his body ache with need. She had imprinted herself on his soul and in every bone in his body and there was nothing he could do about it but savor what they had for as long as he could.

When she was completely naked, his pulse kicked up a notch and his breathing was forced from his lungs when he looked at her. She was beautiful and perfectly made.

He pulled a condom from his wallet in the shorts she'd helped him remove and toss aside. Knowing she was watching his every move, he rolled it over his aroused manhood.

"I want to do that for you the next time."

He looked at Swan. "All right." So she was letting him know she intended there to be a next time for them. He was glad because he wanted a next time, too.

There was a big chance when she found out the truth about why he was here on the island that she wouldn't want to have anything to do with him again. But he forced the thought from his mind.

"You don't have all evening, you know," she teased.

She was right, he didn't and it was a good thing she didn't know why. He moved toward her. "Impatient?"

She smiled up at him. "Yes, you could say that."

"In that case, I can help you with that problem." He leaned

in. "I've got to taste you again," was all he said just seconds before his mouth came down on hers.

Swan automatically lifted her arms around his neck the moment his lips touched hers.

Capturing her tongue, David drew it into his mouth. Blood rushed fast and furious to Swan's head, making her feel both light-headed and dazed as his tongue began mating with hers. His technique was rousing her passion to a level that electrified every part of her. Insistent need rushed up her spine, spinning her senses and mesmerizing her with his delectable taste.

He suddenly broke off the kiss and they both panted furiously, drawing deep gulps of air into their lungs.

She rested her head against his chest and inhaled his scent as she continued to catch her breath. She knew she was losing herself to passion again when she felt the hardness of his erection brushing against her thigh, energizing the area between her legs.

Then she heard him whispering erotic details of what he wanted to do to her. His words spread fire through her body and when he gently cupped the area between her legs, she moaned.

"You're torturing me, David," she said, before twisting to push him down on his back so she could straddle him. Before he could react, she lowered her head between his masculine thighs and eased his erection into her mouth.

"Ah, Swan," he growled huskily, gripping her hair. She was fully aware of him expanding and felt a sense of triumph in her ability to get him even more aroused than he already was. The feel of his hands locked in her hair sparked even more passion within her and motivated her to use her mouth in ways she'd never done before.

"Swan!"

She felt his thighs flex beneath her hands before he bucked forward. She wasn't prepared when he quickly switched their positions so that she was the one on her back. The blue eyes staring down at her flared with a passion that sent tremors through her.

Before she could whisper his name, he slid inside her. He kept going deeper and deeper, stretching her in ways she didn't know she could be spread, inch by inch.

"Wrap your legs around me, baby," he whispered in a throaty voice.

When she did as he asked, he began thrusting hard. It was as if his total concentration was on her, intent on giving her pleasure. She felt every inch of him as he rode her hard, not letting up.

"David!"

She screamed his name as he continued to make love to her, throwing her into a euphoric state that seemed endless. He was using her legs to keep their bodies locked while relentlessly pounding into her. Her world was spinning and she couldn't control the need to moan, moan and moan some more.

She was unable to hold anything back when her body erupted into an orgasm so powerful it propelled her toward utter completeness. She screamed his name once again as a deep feeling of ecstasy ripped through her entire body.

Flipper eased off Swan to lie beside her. Pulling her into his arms, his nostrils flared as he inhaled the scent of sex. The scent of woman, this woman. A woman he still desired even now.

He was not new to lust. Been there, done that and he figured he would be doing it some more. A lot more. With Swan lying in in his arms, snuggled close to him, close to his heart, he knew something had changed between them.

Bottom line, Swan Jamison was not only intoxicating, she was addictive.

"I don't think I'll be able to move again, David."

A smile touched the corners of his lips. He definitely knew how she felt, but he knew he had to move. He had somewhere to be tonight and as sexually drained as he was, he intended to be there.

"Then don't move. Just lie there. I'll let myself out," he said, reluctant to go, although he knew he must.

"You sure?" she asked in a lethargic voice.

"Positive. I'll be back in the morning for the parade and then we have a date on Friday."

"Yes. I'm going to need it. I'll be working late Wednesday doing inventory. I probably won't leave work until around ten."

"With your worker's help?"

"No. The cruise ship comes in Wednesday."

He released her to ease out of bed and put on his clothes. "What does a cruise ship have to do with anything?" He could feel her gaze on his body. He couldn't disguise the impact of knowing she was watching him. He was getting aroused all over again.

"Jamila dates a guy who works on the cruise ship and they only see each other whenever the ship comes to port. She always requests the day off to spend with him. I guess they made up."

He had planned to check out Jamila's house when he'd assumed she would be at work. Good thing he now knew otherwise.

"Made up?" he asked, pulling his shirt over his head.

"Yes. I got the impression they weren't on good terms last week. Not sure what happened but it's all good now since they've apparently kissed and made up."

He nodded. "How long have they been together?"

"About six months now."

Flipper didn't say anything as he continued dressing. There hadn't been any mention of a boyfriend for Jamila Fairchild in the report he'd read. Another discrepancy. There were too many inconsistencies for his liking and he was determined to find out why. One thing was certain, he didn't like the idea of Swan being at her shop alone late at night.

He moved back to the bed, leaned down and brushed a kiss across her lips. "I'll see you in the morning."

"Looking forward to it."

He smiled down at her and then turned and left.

Later that night, Flipper, dressed all in black, moved in the shadows, careful to avoid streetlights and security cameras. He had scoped out the area and was familiar with where the cameras were located. More than once, he'd had to dart behind a shrub when people were out for a late-night stroll.

He reached the area where Swan's shop was located and when he heard voices, he darted behind a building to hide in the shadows.

Two men stood not far away. One of them was Rafe. Neither of the men saw Flipper. The other guy was a little taller and appeared to be a foreigner. Their conversation sounded like an argument and was in a language Flipper wasn't familiar with and he spoke four. Most SEALs spoke at least that many, except for Coop, who had mastered seven.

When the men lapsed into English, they lowered their voices and could barely be heard. Flipper did make out the words *ink* and *roses*. Was someone getting a tattoo of roses painted on their body? If so, did it mean anything?

Flipper was glad when the men finally moved on. More than ever, he was determined to check out the tattoo parlor. He waited a half hour to make sure the men didn't return. When he was certain they had gone, he went to work bypassing the security alarms and cameras.

Using a sort of skeleton key, he opened the back door and walked inside the tattoo parlor. Using night goggles, he glanced around.

The place looked like a typical tattoo parlor. He should know since he and his brothers had frequented a number of them. He was proud of the images on his body. Luckily, Swan hadn't asked him about them. He was glad because the last thing he wanted to do was lie about why he was into dolphins.

Pulling off the camera attached to his utility belt, he replaced the night goggles with a high-tech camera, which was his own creation. This particular piece of equipment detected objects underground and under water. Looking through the lens, he scanned the room. It wasn't long before the camera light began blinking.

He moved toward the area and aimed the camera lower, toward the floor, and the blinking increased. Evidently something was buried beneath the wooden floor, a portion covered by a rug. The architectural report he'd been given of Swan's shop had not exposed any secret rooms or closets.

Putting the camera aside, he moved the rug and felt around to find a latch. He opened the trapdoor to find a small compartment beneath the floor. He saw more containers of ink. Why? There was a supply case full of ink on the opposite side of the room. Why was this ink hidden?

The first thing he noticed was the difference in the labeling. Was there something different about this particular ink? There was only one way to find out, he thought, taking one out of the cubby. He would overnight one of the containers to Nick instead of naval intelligence.

At this stage of the game, he wasn't taking any chances about who could be trusted.

CHAPTER NINE

SWAN HAD JUST finished the last of her inventory when she heard the knock on her shop's door. Crossing the room, she peeped through the blinds to see who it was. A smile touched her lips as she unlocked the door. "David, I didn't think I'd see you until Friday."

He glanced around her empty shop before looking back at her. "I finished work early and remembered you saying you were working late tonight doing inventory. I wanted to make sure you got home okay."

That was really nice of him. "You didn't have to do that." But she was glad he had. They had spent Monday together celebrating Memorial Day. He had arrived at her place for breakfast and then they'd walked to where the start of the parade would take place.

After the parade, they'd gone to the island festival marketplace where various vendors had lined the streets with booths and a huge Ferris wheel. They had taken one of the boat rides around the islands and had ended up eating lunch on Key Largo.

She had thought about him a lot since Monday, remembering in explicit detail how he'd made love to her before leaving.

"I know you said Jamila would be off today," David said.

"What about your tattoo guy? Is the parlor closed on Wednesdays as well?"

"Yes, but Rafe dropped by earlier. He was expecting a shipment of more ink to come in today but it didn't. He wasn't happy about that."

"He wasn't?"

"No. He said there was a particular shade of blue he was expecting."

Flipper nodded and checked his watch. "Ready to go?"

"Yes, I just need to grab my purse from my office." She was about to turn to get it when there was another knock at the door.

"Expecting anyone?" David asked her.

"No. I'll see who it is."

She walked to the door and David went with her. After glancing out of the blinds, she turned back to David and smiled. "It's Jamila and Horacio."

She unlocked the door. "Jamila, hi."

"Hey, Swan. Horacio and I were in the neighborhood and I remembered you would be here late. I thought we'd drop by to say hello."

Swan smiled at the man with Jamila. "Horacio, it's good seeing you again."

"Same here, Swan," he said in a heavy accent that Swan always loved hearing.

"And this is my friend David Holloway. David, you already know Jamila. This is her friend Horacio Jacinto," Swan said, making introductions.

The two men shook hands. Swan wondered if she'd imagined it but she thought David had tensed up when he'd seen Jamila and Horacio. "Nice meeting you, Horacio," David said. "I can't place your accent. Where are you from?"

"Portugal."

"Nice country," David said.

"Thanks."

"I hope you'll leave before it gets too late, Swan," Jamila was saying.

"I will. David came to make sure I got home okay." Usually whenever she worked late, either doing inventory or making her jewelry, she would catch a cab home even though she lived only a few blocks away. But since David was here, she would suggest they walk. It was a nice night and she would love to spend more time with him.

"We'll see you guys later," Jamila said. "We had dinner at Marty's Diner and now we're going to Summer Moon for drinks and live music."

"Okay. Enjoy. And I hope to see you again the next time the ship ports, Horacio," Swan said.

Horacio smiled. "I hope to see you as well."

After they left, Swan went to her office to get her purse. She returned and noticed David was standing in the same spot where she'd left him, staring at the door. "Are you all right?"

He turned to her. "Yes, it's just that Horacio looks familiar and I was trying to remember when I might've seen him. Maybe I've run into him before, here on the island."

She nodded. "That's possible. He's a chef on the Century Cruise Line that docks here once a week. Whenever it does, he comes ashore and meets up with Jamila. I think I mentioned that to you."

"You did, but I could have sworn I saw him a few nights ago. Sunday. After leaving your place."

Swan shook her head. "It wasn't him. The ship didn't arrive in our port until today. But you know what they say about everybody having a twin."

He chuckled. "You're probably right, but I'm sure you don't have one. I'm convinced there's not another woman anywhere who is as beautiful as you."

Swan knew better than to let such compliments go to her head, but she couldn't help the smile that spread across her lips.

"You, David Holloway, can make a girl's head swell if she's in-clined to believe whatever you say."

"I hope you do believe it because I spoke the truth." He took her hand in his as they headed for the door.

Flipper pulled out his phone the minute he walked into his hotel room later that night. He'd felt it vibrate in his pocket when he was walking Swan home but figured it would be a call he needed to take in private.

Swan had invited him inside but he'd declined, telling her he had a ton of paperwork waiting on him back at his hotel. That wasn't a lie. He'd begun rereading all those naval intelligence reports to see if he could determine why those investigators had failed to do their job and instead intentionally went after Swan as a scapegoat.

He checked his phone and saw Nick had called and Flipper quickly returned the call. "What do you have for me?"

"More than you counted on. All I can say is whoever handled that investigation did a botched-up job."

Or they did the job they'd been expected to do, Flipper thought. "I guess there's a reason you feel that way."

"Yes. That ink you sent to be analyzed isn't what it's sup-posed to be."

"It's not ink?"

"Yes, it's ink, but coded ink. When applied to the skin as a tattoo, it can be decoded by a special light. It's my guess that's how the classified information is leaving Swan Jamison's shop—with people's tattoos and not with any of her jewelry. Guess where the ink is being shipped from."

"Swan mentioned from some place in California."

"Yes, that's right and the distribution company is a few miles from the naval base in San Diego. That means someone on the base must be passing classified information that's being shipped in the ink."

Flipper frowned. "And because Rafe Duggers is conveniently

including Swan's stones with each shipment, it makes sense for her to be suspect."

"Right," Nick agreed. "Someone is setting her up real good, Flipper. They are definitely making her the fall guy."

Flipper wondered who in naval intelligence had targeted Swan and why. "I have another piece of the puzzle I need you to check out."

"What?"

"The guy who was with Rafe Duggers two nights ago. The one I told you he was arguing with. I saw him today."

"You did?"

"Yes. He came into the shop when Swan was closing up. His name is Horacio Jacinto and he's Jamila Fairchild's boyfriend."

"That's interesting. I'll find out what I can about him," Nick said. "I wonder if Ms. Fairchild knows what's going on or if she's being used as a pawn."

"I don't know, but I'm going to make sure I keep an eye on all of them."

"Be careful, Flipper."

"I will."

A few hours later, after taking a shower, Flipper was sitting at the desk in his hotel room suite when his cell phone went off. Recognizing the ringtone, he clicked on and said, "What's going on, Coop?"

"You tell us."

Us meant Bane, Viper and Mac were also on the phone. "I guess Nick called you guys."

"Yes, he called us earlier today," Bane said. "What's going on with Swan Jamison sounds pretty damn serious. Don't you think it's time to call the CO?"

Flipper ran a hand down his face. He glanced at the clock on the wall. It was close to three in the morning. "If Nick told you everything, then you know it's an inside job at the base. There's a traitor somewhere and until I know who I can trust, then—"

"You know as well as we do that you can trust our CO, Flipper," Viper said. "Once you tell Shields what you've found out, if he suspects Martin or Levart of any wrongdoing, he will know what to do."

"Yes, however, the three of them share a close friendship. What if the CO is blinded due to loyalty?"

"We're talking about our commanding officer, Flipper. Shields would turn his own mother in if he thought she was betraying our country. You know that."

Yes, he knew it. But still... "I don't know if Martin or Levart is really involved. Like Shields, they are Swan's godfathers and I would hate to think they are shady. I just know it's an inside job and right now I'm suspicious of just about everybody."

"We figured you would be, so open the damn door," Mac said.

Flipper frowned. "What?"

"We said open the door," Coop said, knocking.

Flipper heard the knock, clicked off his phone, quickly went to the door and snatched it open. There stood his four best friends.

"What are you guys doing here?"

"What does it look like?" Mac asked as the four moved passed Flipper to enter the hotel room.

"We figured ten pairs of eyes were better than two," Bane said, glancing around. "Besides, we need to keep you objective."

"But what about your families? Viper, your wife is having a baby!"

Viper chuckled. "And I plan to be there when she does. According to Layla's doctor, we still have a couple of months, so I'm good."

"And our families are good, too," Coop said. "They know we look out for each other and they agreed we should be here for you."

"Teri is glad I'm gone," Mac said, grumbling. "Maybe when I go back, she'll have a new attitude."

"Or maybe you'll have one," Bane said, frowning at Mac.

"Whatever," Mac said, picking up the hotel's restaurant menu book. "Is it too late for room service?"

Flipper closed the door and drew in a deep breath as he watched the men gather around the table, already rolling up their sleeves, ready to help him figure things out. They worked together as a team and he would admit that whenever they did so, good things happened.

"There's something all of you should know," he said, getting their attention.

They glanced over at him. "What? No room service at this hour?" Mac asked in a serious tone.

"That, too."

"What's the other thing we should know, Flipper?" Viper asked, sitting back in the chair he'd claimed as soon as he came in.

Flipper leaned against the closed door. "Investigating Swan Jamison is no longer just an assignment for me. It's become personal."

The men nodded. "And you think we don't know that, Flipper?" Coop asked in a steely tone. "That's why we're here. Someone is trying to frame your woman and we're going to help you find out who and why. But first things first. You know what you have to do, right?"

Flipper stared at the four men. Yes, he knew. Instead of answering Coop, he picked up his cell phone from the table and placed a call to his CO.

CHAPTER TEN

As far as Swan was concerned, Friday hadn't arrived fast enough. With every passing hour, she would glance at her shop's door expecting to see David walk in. One would think his surprise visit Wednesday would have sufficed. Unfortunately, it hadn't.

She'd had two days to think about how irrational her thoughts about David were becoming. He didn't come across as a forever sort of guy and she wasn't looking for a forever kind of relationship, so what was up with this urgency to see him?

The only reason she could give herself was that she'd been alone and without a man's attention for so long that now that she had it, she was in greedy mode, lapping it up like a desperate woman. And she had never done the desperate thing before.

The door chimed and she looked up to see that it was Rafe who walked in. Lately she'd noticed him using the front door a lot more, instead of the back door to his parlor. They had decided at the beginning of his lease that the entrance to her shop was off-limits so his customers wouldn't trounce back and forth through her shop on the days Rafe worked late.

"Did your box of ink finally arrive?"

He stopped and looked over at her. "Why would you be asking about my ink?"

Now that, she thought, was a silly question. Did the man have a short memory? "Because you came by Wednesday looking for the shipment and left in a tiff when it hadn't arrived."

"I wasn't in a tiff and yes, I did get my box of ink."

Yes, he had been in a tiff, but if he wouldn't acknowledge it, then she would leave it alone. "Good. I'm glad you got it."

She watched him walk off toward his parlor. He hadn't been in a good mood lately. But then, maybe she'd been in such an extremely good mood that she had a distorted view. In fact, come to think of it, it was pretty normal for him to be moody.

Moments later, while she worked with a customer, Swan watched as Rafe walked back through her shop and toward the front door. She decided if he did that again she would remind him of their agreement about which door he should use whenever he went in or out of his tattoo parlor.

After her customer left, she glanced at her watch. Her shop would be closing in a couple of minutes. David usually arrived early. It would be understandable if he'd gotten detained, but she hoped he hadn't been. She was so anxious to see him.

The thought of how much she was looking forward to being with him should bother her, but for some reason it didn't. Like she'd told Candy, Swan wasn't expecting anything from her relationship with David. There had been no promises made, so none would be broken. The only thing she was expecting was exactly what she was getting—a good time. He was excellent company and great in bed.

It had been almost three years since William, and during that time, although she'd dated, she hadn't allowed herself to get serious over a man. Instead she had concentrated on opening her shop and making it a success.

She had put her mind, heart and soul into Swan's. Especially her heart, deciding that if she put it into her business, she wouldn't run the risk of placing it elsewhere. Now it seemed there might be a risk after all and that risk had a name. David Holloway.

A part of her wanted to protect herself from another possible heartbreak by calling David and canceling any plans for
tonight and then to stop sharing any time with him after that.
He had given her his number so she could reach him. She could
certainly come up with a plausible excuse. But did she really
want to do that?

No, she didn't.

David would be her test. If she could handle a casual affair
with him, then she would ace the test with flying colors.

The door chimed and she glanced up and there he was. She
watched him lock her door and put the Closed sign in place before pulling down the blinds. Then he slowly sauntered toward
her wearing a pair of khaki pants and an open white shirt and
holding her within the scope of those laser-blue eyes. There was
his too-sexy walk and a smile that made her heart beat rapidly.

Suddenly seeing him, when she'd been thinking of him all
day, took complete control of her senses. Without much effort,
the man had turned the sensuality up more than a notch. He
had his own barometer of hotness.

Finally moving her feet, she strolled across the floor to meet
him halfway and walked straight into his arms. The moment he
pressed his body to hers, she reached up and looped her arms
around his neck. He responded by wrapping his arms around
her waist, drawing her even closer so she fit against him.

"I missed you, Swan."

She shouldn't let his words affect her, but they did—to the
point where she was having difficulty replying.

"I missed you, too."

And she had, although they'd seen each other Wednesday.
Even when she'd tried to convince herself that missing him to
such a degree meant nothing. Now, as she stood wrapped in his
arms, with her body pressed tight against his, hip to hip and
thigh to thigh, she knew it meant everything.

"That's good to know, sweetheart," he said in a throaty voice.

Sweetheart? The endearment left her defenseless. She was

trying to summon all her senses to regroup. And it wasn't helping matters that his arousal was cradled in the apex of her thighs. Good Lord, he felt so good there.

"Ready?" she found the voice to ask him.

His gaze studied her face as if he was seeing her for the first time. As if he was trying to record her features to memory. And then a mischievous smile touched his lips. "I'm ready for whatever you have in mind, Swan."

Shivers of desire skittered down her spine and Swan wished his words hadn't given her ideas, but they had. Ideas that were so bold, brazen and shameless she felt her cheeks staining just thinking about them. But at that moment, she didn't care. She could and would admit to wanting him.

She should wait until later to act on her desires. That would be the safe thing to do. But she knew she would be tortured during dinner whenever she looked at him. The way his mouth moved when he ate, or the way his hands—those hands that could turn her on just by looking at them—gripped his beer bottle. There were so many things about David Holloway that would do her in if she were to wait until later.

"You sure about that, David?"

"Positive. Do you want me to prove it?"

Did she? Yes, she did. "Where?"

"I will prove it anywhere you want. Right here in the middle of the floor if you like," he said. "But I suggest your office."

Flipper could tell by the way she was looking at him that she was giving his offer serious thought. He had no problems tilting the scale in his favor and he decided to do so. Lowering his head, he kissed her, trying to be gentle and finding gentleness hard to achieve. Especially when her taste made him greedy for more.

He knew she'd ceased thinking when she responded to his kiss by sinking her body farther into his embrace and tightening her arms around his neck.

Some things, he decided then and there, were just too mind-blowingly good, and kissing Swan was one of them. What they'd shared these last few days was a dimension of pleasure he hadn't felt in a long time—or maybe ever—while devouring a woman's mouth. And when his hands shifted from around her waist to cup her backside, he groaned at the feel of her body pressed tightly against his erection.

When he finally broke off the kiss, he buried his face in the curve of her neck and drew in a deep breath. This woman was almost too much. She looked good, tasted good and as he drew in another deep breath, he concluded that she smelled good, too.

"You want to come with me, Mr. Holloway?" she asked, stepping out of his arms.

"Yes." The answer was quick off his lips.

She took his hand. "Then follow me."

He had no problem following her and the minute he crossed the threshold into her office, he recalled the last time he'd been in here. Namely, when they'd shared a kiss that had nearly brought him to his knees.

"It appears dinner will have to wait."

He glanced over at her. She had stepped out of her sandals. After locking the office door, he leaned against it and watched her undress. She was wearing a burnt-orange sundress with spaghetti straps. It looked good on her and the color of the dress seemed to highlight her hair and skin tone.

He had gotten little sleep since his friends had arrived in the Keys. But then they hadn't come here to rest. They had left their families to come here and help him solve a sinister plan of espionage against the country they loved.

And to protect the woman *he* loved.

He suddenly swallowed deep when that last thought passed through his mind. As he watched Swan remove her panties, he knew without a doubt that he had fallen in love with her. He wouldn't try to figure out how it happened but just accept that it had. Now more than ever he was determined to make sure whoever was trying to screw her over didn't succeed.

"Are you going to just stand there?" she asked, standing before him completely naked.

"No, that's not my intention at all," he said, moving away from the door to stand a few feet from her in what he considered his safe zone. If he got any closer, he would be tempted to take her with his clothes on. He removed his shirt and eased both his khakis and briefs down his legs at the same time. Quick and easy.

"I love your dolphins," she said. "I meant to ask you about them a number of other times, but always got sidetracked. So I'm asking you now. Any reason you chose dolphins?"

He decided to be as truthful with her as he could. One day he would have to explain to her why he'd lied about so many things. "Like the dolphins, I love being in the water. But this isn't just any dolphin."

"It's not?"

"No. This dolphin's name is Flipper. Surely you've heard of him."

"Not as much as I know Willy from *Free Willy.*"

He chuckled as he moved toward her. "Willy was a whale. Flipper was a dolphin. That's what my friends call me. Flipper."

"Flipper?"

"Yes. Like I said, I love being in the water."

"You don't look like a Flipper."

He came to a stop in front of her. "Don't tell that to my family and friends. They wouldn't agree with you."

She reached out and touched the tattoo of the dolphin on his arm. Her fingers felt like fire as she traced along the design with her fingertips. "Beautiful. Not just your tattoos but all of you, David."

"Thanks." And in one smooth sweep, he picked her up and sat her on the desk, spreading her legs in the process.

"Did I tell you how much I missed you?" he asked, running his hands over her arms.

"Yes. Just a few moments ago when you arrived here and I

told you I missed you, too. You also told me that you missed me when you walked me home Wednesday night and I invited you to stay."

Flipper heard the disappointment in her voice. If only she knew how much he'd wanted to stay. But once he'd found out Jamila would be out for a while with Horacio, he needed that time to check out her place. "I couldn't, but I intend to make it up to you when we have more time."

He was letting her know this little quickie didn't count. He had something planned for her when all this was over and he could sit her down and tell her everything.

"Not here and not now? What do you call this?" she asked when he reached up and cupped her breasts in his hands, marveling at just how beautiful they were.

"This is an I-can't-wait-until-later quickie."

"Interesting."

Shifting his gaze from her breasts to her eyes, he said, "Let me show you, Swan Jamison, just how interesting it can be." He leaned forward and kissed her while placing the head of his erection against her wet opening. The contact sent heat spiraling through him.

While his tongue mated greedily with hers, he entered her in one hard stroke. Pulling his mouth from hers, he let out a guttural moan when her muscles clamped down on his throbbing erection. That made him push harder and sink deeper.

And when she moaned his name, he knew she could feel the fire of passion spreading between them as much as he could.

Swan wrapped her legs completely around Flipper, loving the feel of him moving inside her. He was giving her body one heck of a workout on her desk. She could feel the heat in his eyes as he stared at her.

He used his hands to lift her hips off the desk's surface for a deeper penetration. When his erection hit a certain part of her, she gasped and arched her back.

"David…"

She whispered his name when she felt him going deeper and deeper. The intensity of their joining sent emotions skyrocketing through her.

She needed this. She wanted this. Like him, she needed it now, not later. This was more than interesting. This was a hot, frenzied, torrid mating. More than a quickie. David was thorough, meticulously so, and not to be rushed. It was as if he intended to savor every stroke.

Suddenly, she felt herself falling. Not off the desk but out of reality when an orgasm rammed through her at the same time as he shuddered with the force of his own release.

They stared at each other, realizing something at the same time. Wanting to make sure he didn't stop, she whispered, "Pill."

It seemed that single word triggered another orgasm and she felt him flooding her insides again while his deep, guttural groan filled the room. His release sparked another within her. His name was torn from her lips when her body shattered in earth-shaking and mind-blowing ecstasy.

As the daze from Swan's orgasmic state receded, she felt David slowly withdraw from inside her. That's when she forced her eyes open to stare at him and accepted the hand he extended to help her off the desk. Once on her feet, she wrapped her arms around his waist, feeling weak in the knees.

"It's okay, baby, I got you. I won't let you fall," he whispered close to her ear as he leaned down.

Too late, she thought. She'd already fallen. Head over heels in love with him. The very thought suddenly sent her mind spinning.

Hadn't she just given herself a good talking to moments before he'd arrived? Told herself he was someone she could enjoy, both in and out of bed and nothing more? That he was someone she knew better than to give her heart to because she hadn't wanted to take the risk?

What on earth had happened?

She knew the answer as she moved closer into the comfort of his warm naked body. David Holloway had happened. As much as she hadn't meant to fall in love with him, she had.

It didn't matter that she had known him less than three weeks. Somehow he had come into her world and turned it upside down, whether that had been his intent or not. When his work on the island was finished, he would move on and not look back. But still, knowing that he would leave hadn't stopped him from winning her heart.

"Ready?"

She lifted her head and look up at him. "You know, David, that lone question will get us in trouble."

He held her gaze for a long moment and then caressed the side of her face. "Or take us to places we really want to go and inspire us to do things that we really want to do."

Then he lowered his mouth to hers and kissed her.

CHAPTER ELEVEN

"GREAT WORK FINDING out about that ink, Lieutenant Holloway. I knew there was no way Swan would have betrayed her country."

"Yes, sir. Those are my thoughts as well," Flipper said. He had placed his CO on speakerphone so his SEAL teammates could listen to the call. "There's no doubt in my mind the persons naval intelligence should be concentrating on are Rafe Duggers and Horacio Jacinto."

"I agree. I met with Admiral Martin and Director Levart this morning and they concur there's a mole within the organization."

"By meeting with them, sir, does that mean you feel certain they can be totally trusted as well?" Flipper felt he had to ask.

"Yes, Lieutenant Holloway. I do. I know that because of what you discovered and what went down with Lieutenant Westmoreland a few years ago involving those moles at Homeland Security, you're not sure who you can trust. I understand that. However, I assure you that you can trust the three of us to protect Swan with our lives if we have to. We knew she was innocent, which was why we sent you there to prove we were right. You have. Now it's up to us to find out who's behind this and bring them to justice."

"And in the meantime?"

"In the meantime, Lieutenant, you are free to consider this assignment completed. Go home to Texas and enjoy the remainder of your leave."

There was no way he could consider this assignment completed, although under normal circumstances it would be once the CO said so. "I think I'll hang around Key West for a while."

"Why?" Commanding Officer Shields asked. "Do you think Swan's life might be in immediate danger?"

"As long as Duggers and Jacinta don't know they're suspected of anything, then no. However..."

"However what, Lieutenant Holloway?"

Flipper had no problem being truthful to his CO. "However, Swan has come to mean a lot to me, sir."

"Oh, I see."

Flipper figured since his CO knew him so well, he did see. "In that case, Lieutenant Holloway, how you choose to spend the rest of your leave is your decision. But keep in mind, since this is an ongoing investigation, you cannot tell Swan anything, including your reason for being in the Keys in the first place. That in itself will place you in what might be perceived by her as a dishonorable situation."

"I'm aware of that, sir, but I refuse to leave her until I have to. How long do you think it will take to wrap up the investigation?"

"Not sure. We will not only be investigating the original investigators but we'll have to restart the entire case, making Duggers and Jacinta the primary suspects. If you remain in the Keys and notice anything I need to know, don't hesitate to bring it to my attention."

In other words, Commanding Officer Shields was pretty much giving Flipper the green light to do his own thing, unofficially. "Yes, sir."

When Flipper clicked off the phone, he glanced up at his friends. "So what do you guys think?"

"Personally, I think you're doing the right thing not leaving here until you're certain Miss Jamison's life is not in any danger," Bane said.

"And since we don't plan to leave until you do, it's time we figure out just who is behind this," Coop added.

"I agree with all the above," Viper tacked on.

They all looked at Mac, who rubbed his chin as if contemplating something. Then he said, "Someone needs to play devil's advocate, so I guess it has to be me."

"No surprise there," Bane said.

Mac shot Bane a glare and then glanced back at Flipper. "Think about what the CO said. You can't tell Miss Jamison anything. Once she finds out the truth, that she was nothing more than an assignment to you, she's not going to like it, no matter how noble or honorable your intentions might have been."

Flipper drew in a deep breath. He knew Mac's words to be true. Although Swan had yet to tell him anything about her affair with William Connors, it had been in the report. The man had betrayed her and there was a chance she would probably see Flipper as doing the same. "So, Mr. Know-It-All, what do you suggest I do?" he asked.

"Start drawing a line in your relationship and don't cross it. In other words, stop seducing her," Mac said.

Too late for that, Flipper thought. All he had to do was remember what they'd done yesterday in Swan's office and again when he'd taken her home after dinner. Especially when he'd sat in one of her kitchen chairs and she'd straddled his body. The memories of what had started out in that chair and ended up in her bedroom made him feel hot. He hadn't left her place until dawn this morning. There was no way he could put a freeze on his relationship with Swan like Mac was suggesting.

"That's not an option, Mac. I'm going to do what I have to do now and worry about the consequences later."

* * *

"What's this about you having a boyfriend? I can't leave you alone for one minute."

Swan smiled when she glanced up at Rosie McCall, one of her frequent customers. Rosie, an older woman in her midforties who'd been away for the past three months visiting her family in Nevada, had returned to the Keys just yesterday. "I see Jamila has been talking again."

"Doesn't matter. So tell me, who is he?"

Swan closed the jewelry case. "First of all, he's not my boyfriend. He's just someone I'm seeing while he's here on the island working, which won't be much longer."

"Um, short meaningless flings are the best kind. What's his name?"

"David. David Holloway."

"Where he is from?"

"Texas."

"You said he's here working. What does he do for a living?"

"Whoa, time-out," Swan said, using her hand for the signal. "You don't need to know all that. David's a nice guy and that's all you really need to know."

She knew how Rosie liked to play matchmaker. She'd been the one who'd introduced Jamila to Horacio. Rosie had met him at one of the nightclubs and thought he was cute, too young for her but just the right age for Swan or Jamila. Swan hadn't been interested in a blind date but Jamila had. Horacio and Jamila met, hit it off and had been an item ever since.

"You can't blame me for being curious, Swan. You seldom date."

"My choice, remember? Besides, you do it enough for the both of us." And that was the truth. After her second divorce, Rosie had made it known she would never marry again but intended to date any man who asked her out as long as they were the right age. Not too old and not too young.

Rosie smiled. "Yes, I do, don't I? But that doesn't mean you shouldn't go out and have fun every once in a while. There's more to life than this shop, Swan. I hope you're finally finding that out."

"Whatever." Swan had heard it before and all from Rosie. She liked the older woman and thought she was a fun person who had a zeal for life. There was never a dull moment around her.

At that moment, the shop's door chimed and Swan knew without looking in that direction that David had walked in. She also knew when he saw her with a customer that he would wait until she finished before approaching her.

Rosie leaned in. "Looks like you have a customer. Let's hope he buys something since he came in a minute before closing."

Swan inwardly smiled. "We can only hope, right?"

"But then he's such a cutie. Look at him."

Swan didn't have to look at David to know what a cutie he was, but she did so anyway. He was browsing around the store wearing a pair of shorts and a sleeveless T-shirt with flip-flops on his feet. He looked laid-back and sexy as sin. "You're right, he is a cutie."

"I love those tattoos on his upper arms. Nice."

"Yes, they are." She knew Rosie was into tattoos and was one of Rafe's frequent customers. The woman had them everywhere, visible and non-visible.

"You need to go wait on him. See what he wants. If he's not sure, offer him a few things."

Swan smiled. Little did Rosie know, but she intended to offer David a lot. "I will. Come on, I'll walk you to the door. I'm officially closed now," Swan said, coming from around the counter.

"You honestly want me to leave you here with him?" Rosie whispered. "For all you know he's not safe."

Swan chuckled and decided it was time for her to come clean. "He's safe, Rosie. That's David and he's here to walk me home. I'll introduce you on your way out the door."

"You mean that gorgeous hunk is your guy?"

Swan glanced over at David again. He was definitely a gorgeous hunk but she couldn't claim him as her guy. "Yes, he's the guy I've been seeing a lot of lately."

"Smart girl."

David glanced up when they approached and gave her a huge smile. "Hi," he greeted.

"Hi, David. I'd like you to meet Rosie McCall. A friend who has been away for the past few months and just returned back to the island. Rosie, this is David Holloway."

David extended his hand. "Nice meeting you, Rosie."

"Same here, David. I like your tattoos."

"Thanks and I like yours," he responded.

"Thanks. Well, I'll be going. I hope you guys enjoy yourselves."

"We will," Swan said, smiling up at David. "I'll be back after seeing Rosie out," she told him.

He nodded. "Nice meeting you, Rosie."

"Same here."

Swan returned to David a few moments later, after putting up the Closed sign, locking the door and pulling down the shades. She turned and studied him as he stood across the room, looking so amazingly sexy. She felt a lump in her throat. She loved everything about him, especially the muscles beneath his shirt, the masculine thighs and his tanned skin.

"Got more sun today, I see."

"Yes, I had to go out on the boat today."

"One day you're going to have to explain to me in detail just what your ocean duties entail."

"I will. But for now, come here. I missed you today."

She crossed the room to walk into his arms. "I missed you, too."

"That's good to know. Rosie seems like a nice person."

"She is."

"She has a lot of tattoos."

Swan chuckled. "Yes, she does. She's one of Rafe's best customers."

"Is that right?" David asked, still smiling. "He did an awe-some job."

She checked her watch. "We can leave as soon as I grab my purse." They would be having dinner at Nathan Waterway and afterward would attend an art show. "I'll be back in a second."

Flipper watched Swan walk off toward her office while thinking of what she'd told him about Rosie McCall. He recalled what he'd overheard Rafe and Horacio arguing about that night be-hind this building. Ink and roses. Or had they said Rosie? Was she a part of the group? If she was, that meant she had an ulte-rior motive for befriending Swan.

Pulling his phone from his pocket he texted Nick. Check out Rosie McCall.

He received an immediate reply. Will do.

He then texted Bane. Excursion tonight.

The reply was quick. On it.

Most of today he and Viper had pretended to go fishing after Mac, who'd been tailing Rafe for the past two days, reported that Rafe had rented a boat and headed in the direction of an-other island close by. Today Flipper and Viper had also rented a boat, making sure they stayed a good distance behind Duggers.

The man had docked in Fleming Key. Bane and Cooper, who'd arrived ahead of them, picked up the tail on Rafe. It seemed the man had gone into a sports shop where he'd stayed for three hours.

Pretending to be two guys enjoying their time out on their boat, Flipper and Viper had waited at the pier and knew when Rafe had left the island to return to Key West. Mac had been there to pick up the tail and reported that the man had been car-rying a package when he went inside his tattoo shop. A pack-age Rafe had gotten from the sports shop, according to Bane and Coop.

"I'm ready."

He looked up and when Swan met his gaze, she quickly clarified, "I'm ready *for dinner.*"

He placed his phone back into his pocket and smiled. "That's all?"

The smile she returned made his insides quiver in anticipation. "For now, Mr. Holloway."

CHAPTER TWELVE

IT WAS GETTING harder and harder to leave Swan's bed, Flipper thought as he and his teammates docked at Fleming Key close to two in the morning. But at least he'd left her sleeping with the most peaceful smile on her face.

Without waking her, he had brushed a kiss across her lips and whispered that he loved her, knowing she would remember neither. But he decided to tell her how he felt when he saw her later today. He couldn't hold it inside any longer. She deserved to know. He wanted her to know. And when all this was over and she knew the truth, he would do whatever he needed to do to win her forgiveness and her love.

He jumped when fingers snapped in his face. He glared at Mac, who glared back. "Stay focused. You can daydream later."

"I wasn't daydreaming," Flipper countered. He then realized he was the only one still in the boat. The others had already gotten out.

"Then night-dreaming. Call it what you want" was Mac's reply. "Just get out of the damn boat."

Flipper didn't have to wonder why Mac was in a rotten mood. Teri had texted him earlier in the day to say the new washer and dryer had been delivered. They were new appliances Mac hadn't known they were buying.

Moments later, dressed in all black military combat gear, the five of them circled around to the back of the sports shop Rafe had frequented lately. Being ever ready and not taking any chances, Glocks were strapped to their hips and high powered tasers to their thighs. Due to Viper's hypersensitive ears—known to pick up sound over long distances away—he would stay outside as the lookout. Flipper, Bane, Cooper and Mac bypassed security cameras to enter the building.

Once inside, they used Flipper's cameras and it didn't take long to find a hidden room. Making swift use of their time, they took pictures of everything. It was obvious this was the group's operation headquarters. More tattoo ink was stored here along with several specific tattoo designs. One design Flipper quickly recalled seeing on the side of Rosie's neck.

Flipper scanned the room with his camera and then opened several drawers in the huge desk and took photos of the contents. When he came across a photo in one of the drawers, he suddenly froze. "Damn."

"What is it, Flipper?" Bane asked.

Instead of saying anything, he motioned his head to the photograph he'd found. Mac, Bane and Coop came around him to see it as well. They looked back at him and Mac said, "We've been royally screwed."

An uneasy feeling settled in the pit of Flipper's stomach. "I need to get back to Swan as soon as possible."

Swan was awakened by the knocking on her door. She glanced at the clock on her nightstand and wondered who on earth would be at her house at four in the morning. Was it David returning? She didn't recall when he'd left but knew it was the norm for him to leave her place around midnight to return to his hotel because of his work. Usually she would be awake when he left but tonight sexual exhaustion had gotten the best of her.

Pulling on her robe, she tied it around her waist as she headed for the door. Looking out the peephole, she saw it was Jamila and

Horacio. What were they doing out so late and why were they at her place? She found it odd that Horacio was on the island when the cruise ship wasn't due back in port again until next week.

From the look on Jamila's face, it appeared she wasn't happy about something. In fact, from her reddened eyes, it appeared that she'd been crying. Swan wondered what on earth was wrong. Had something happened?

Suddenly filled with concern, she quickly opened the door. The minute she did so, Jamila was shoved inside, nearly knocking Swan down.

"Hey, wait a minute. What's going on?" Swan asked, fighting to regain her balance.

"Shut the hell up and don't ask questions," Horacio said, quickly coming inside and closing the door behind him.

Swan frowned. "Horacio? What do you mean, I can't ask any questions?"

"Just do what you're told," he barked.

Swan glanced over at Jamila and saw the bruise on the side of her face. "Did he do this to you?" Swan demanded, getting enraged. At Jamila's nod, Swan then turned to Horacio. How could he have done this when he adored Jamila? "I want you to leave now."

"If I don't, what are you going to do? Call the police? Or call that SEAL you're sleeping with?"

Swan frown deepened. "I don't know what you're talking about. Now leave or I *will* call the police."

"You won't be doing anything other than what I tell you to do. When I get the word, the two of you will be coming with me."

Swan placed her hands on her hips. "We're not going anywhere with you."

A cynical smile touched Horacio's lips as he pulled out a gun from his back pocket. "This says you will."

Swan stared at the gun, not believing Horacio had it pointed at both her and Jamila. She was about to say something when

Horacio added, "I'm giving you five minutes to go into your bedroom and put on clothes. Bring me your phone first. I don't want you to get any crazy ideas."

Swan had no idea what was going on, but from the pleading look in Jamila's eyes, she knew it was best to do as she was told. She went and got her cell phone and handed it to him, but not before she noticed several missed calls from David. Why had he been trying to call her? Her mind was filled with so many questions.

"You got five minutes to get dressed. If you're not back in five minutes or try some kind of funny business, your cousin here will pay for it."

Cousin? Why did he refer to Jamila as her cousin? At what was obviously a confused look on her face, he said, "That's right. Secrets. There are plenty more where those came from, Swan, and you'll be finding out about them later. Now go."

Swan got dressed in less than five minutes. If she hadn't thought Horacio was serious about hurting Jamila, she would have escaped through her bedroom window. That bruise along the side of her friend's face indicated the man was serious.

Swan was walking out of her bedroom fully dressed when Horacio's phone rang. Instead of answering it, he said, "That's my signal that things are ready. We'll go out your back door to the beach. The boat is waiting."

"What boat?"

"Please don't ask him anything, Swan," Jamila pleaded, reaching out and grabbing her arm. "All of them are crazy."

Swan wondered just who were *all of them*. But she decided not to ask.

"Move!"

Following Horacio's orders, she and Jamila walked toward Swan's kitchen to go out the back door.

As soon as their boat docked, Flipper raced through the streets of Key West toward Swan's home with his teammates fast on his heels. He had tried reaching her on the phone but didn't get an answer. He immediately knew something was wrong because she kept her phone on the nightstand next to her bed and the ringing would have woken her up. He had tried several more times with no luck, which was why his heart was beating out of control and fear was gripping his insides, especially now that he knew who was involved.

They had contacted their CO and told him what they'd discovered. He was as shocked as they'd been and they knew Shields would be taking the necessary actions on his end. Flipper hadn't had to tell the man there would be hell to pay if anyone hurt one single hair on Swan's head.

When they reached her house, they found the door unlocked. Her cell phone had been tossed on a living room table and a quick search of her bedroom indicated she'd change clothes.

"Take a look at this, Flipper," Mac called out.

When he reached them in the kitchen, Mac pointed out the window. Flipper saw lights from a boat that was sitting idle in the ocean as if waiting to rendezvous with another vessel.

"I traced footprints in the sand that led to the water. A small watercraft probably took them out to that boat," Viper was saying. "There were three sets of shoe prints belonging to two women and a man. And they left around thirty minutes ago."

Flipper raced out Swan's back door and after putting on his night-vision eyewear, he stared out at the ocean.

"Intercept with our boat," he shouted over his shoulder to the others. Quickly dropping to the sand, he began removing his shoes, T-shirt and pants, leaving his body clad in a pair of swimming trunks.

"Don't try it, Flipper. The boat's too far out," Mac said. "It's too dangerous for anyone, even you."

Flipper glanced up at them while putting the waterproof military belt that contained combat gear around his waist. He then put a pair of specially designed water goggles over his eyes.

"The woman I love is on that boat and I have no idea what they plan to do, so I have to try. Even if I die trying."

Without saying anything else, he raced toward the water and dived in.

Horacio had tied their hands before forcing them into a small boat, which carried them out into the ocean to a much bigger boat. Now they were sitting idle in the waves.

Swan wondered why. She glanced around and noticed that, other than the lights on the boat, there was only darkness. They were so far from land she couldn't see the lights from the homes where she lived anymore.

As if Horacio realized she was trying to figure out what was happening, he said, "I'm waiting for the rest of the gang, then we'll decide what we will do with the two of you."

What he said didn't make much sense. "Will someone please tell me what's going on?" Swan asked, getting angrier by the minute. None of this made any sense.

"I'll let your cousin go first since Jamila has a lot of explaining to do," Horacio said, grinning.

Swan turned to Jamila, who was sitting on a bench beside her. "What is he talking about? Why does he keep referring to you as my cousin?"

At first Jamila didn't say anything. In fact, it seemed she was refusing to meet Swan's gaze, but then she finally met Swan's eyes and said, "Because we are cousins, Swan. My mother is your grandfather's youngest sister."

"My grandfather?"

Jamila nodded. "Yes, Lawrence Jamison is my uncle. I knew for years that Uncle Lawrence disowned your father but I didn't know why until I was much older. Then I thought the reason was downright stupid and told the family what I thought. Everyone else in the family thought the same thing but were too afraid to stand up to Uncle Lawrence."

Swan didn't say anything. She was still trying to dissect the fact that she and Jamila were related. She'd known from her father that Lawrence had a sister and another brother. That was all she'd known.

"When I turned twenty-one and finished college, I decided to come find you. Uncle Lawrence didn't like it but I told him I didn't care. I'm one of the few who stands up to him. He said the family would disown me if I came here."

"Yet you came anyway," Swan said.

"Yes, I came anyway."

Swan glanced over at Horacio. He wasn't saying anything and didn't appear to be listening to what they were saying. Instead he stood at the bow of the ship looking through binoculars as if he was searching for someone. He'd said they were waiting for another boat with the gang and Swan couldn't help but wonder who the gang was.

She wanted to ask Jamila how much she knew and why they were being held hostage but figured that although Horacio was pretending not to listen to their conversation, he probably was.

Swan glanced over at Jamila. "Why didn't you tell me who you were when you first came into my shop that day? Why did you keep it a secret all this time?"

"Because I knew how my family had treated you and your mother. I figured the last thing you'd want was to meet a relative from that side of the family. I decided to let you accept me as a friend and then later I would tell you the truth that we were cousins."

"Now isn't that a touching story?" Horacio said, strolling back over to where they sat.

"Yes, it is touching," Swan said, defiantly lifting her chin. "Why are we here?"

He smiled. "You'll find out soon enough. And I hope you're not holding out any hope that your SEAL boyfriend will be coming to rescue you because he won't."

"Why do you keep saying David is a SEAL when he's not? He was in the military once but he was never a SEAL."

"Sounds like you've been conned by him just like your cousin here was conned by me," he said as if it was something to brag about. "Your lover boy *is* a SEAL and he was sent here to get the goods on you. Whether you know it or not, you've been his assignment."

Swan shook her head. "No, that's not true. I don't believe you."

"I don't care if you believe me or not but it's true. I only found out today what he's been doing and why he was sent here by naval intelligence."

Naval intelligence? Swan glanced over at Jamila, who said, "I don't know whether what he's saying is true or not, Swan, but he told me the same thing tonight."

"Why would naval intelligence suspect me of anything? It doesn't make sense." And more than that, she refused to believe David wasn't who and what he said he was.

At that moment, they heard the sound of a boat approaching. Horacio drew his gun and pointed the flashlight toward the oncoming boat. He put his gun back in place. "Hold on to that question, sweetheart. The person who will explain everything just arrived."

Swan kept her gaze trained on the boat that pulled up beside theirs and saw two people onboard. Both of them she knew. What in the world...?

She watched in shock as Rafe and Rosie came aboard. She was so focused on staring at them that she almost missed the third person who also came on board.

She gasped in shock when the person said, "Swan, you look well."

Suddenly losing her voice, Swan couldn't do anything but sit there and stare. There had to be some mistake. A very big mistake. There was no way the person standing before her was a part of this craziness.

No way.

She finally found her voice. "Georgianna? What are you doing here? What is this about?"

CHAPTER THIRTEEN

FLIPPER REACHED THE boat and attached himself to the ladder on the side. Lucky for him, no one had thought to pull it up. Taking slow, deep breaths, he pulled air into his lungs while ignoring the pain in his arms and legs. He didn't want to think about just how far he'd swum, but like he'd told his friends, he'd had to try.

He quickly eased back into the water when he heard the sound of an approaching boat and was grateful the vessel pulled up on the other side from where he was hiding. He glanced at his watch. It was synchronized with the ones worn by his teammates, and he knew they would do their best to get here soon. In the meantime, there was something he had to do.

Pulling a micro audio recorder off his belt, he moved back up the ladder to peek over the railing and into the boat.

Good. Everyone's attention was on the approaching vessel and no one saw him when he attached the audio recorder that was no bigger than a dime to the interior wall of the boat. He saw Swan and Jamila seated on a bench with their hands tied behind their backs and Horacio was standing not far away. Other than a man in the cockpit, there was no one else onboard. Flipper knew that was about to change when he heard voices.

Satisfied that the conversations would be recorded, he eased back down the ladder. When his watch began vibrating, he glanced down at the text message from Bane. On our way. Had 2 take care of a little problem 1st.

Flipper wondered what kind of problem his friends had to take care of. No matter. They were on their way and that's what counted. He listened to the conversation going on in the boat as he began pulling items from his belt. He intended to be ready to crash this little party when the time came.

He shook his head, knowing Admiral Martin would be heart-broken to discover his own daughter had sold out their country.

"I hate you," Georgianna said, glaring at Swan.

Swan was taken aback by the woman's words. "Why? What have I ever done to you? To any of you?" she asked, glancing around at the people she'd assumed were friends—Rafe, Horacio and Rosie. She hurt more at seeing Rosie than the others because she'd believed the woman had been a good friend.

"They work for me and did what they were told," Georgianna said.

"Work for you?" Swan was even more confused.

"Yes. I'm in charge of the entire operation. But I'll tell you all about that later. First, let me tell you why I despise you so much. I've waited a long time to get this out in the open. When your father died and your mother would send you to us for the summer, my parents thought you were golden. They put you on a pedestal, especially my father. Did you know he called you his little island princess?"

Yes, Swan knew but she also knew her godfather hadn't meant anything by it. It was just a nickname he'd given her when she was born. All three of her godfathers called her that sometimes. "It was just a nickname, Georgianna."

"For you, it might only have been a nickname, but for me, it was Dad shifting his attention from me to you."

"Godpop 1 loves you. He wasn't shifting his attention to me, he was just being nice."

"Too nice, and I despised you for it. He had a daughter, yet any time your mother would call, he and Mom would drop everything and take off. Just because your father saved Dad's life—that meant nothing. They were all SEALs and your dad was doing his job when he died. But it was as if Dad blamed himself and he needed to make it up by being nice to you, like you were somebody special. So, with the help of some friends, I decided to change everyone's opinion of you."

It was hard for Swan to believe what she was hearing. She'd never known that Georgianna harbored such feelings. Granted she hadn't always been overnice and had a tendency to be moody, but Swan hadn't detected animosity like this.

"What did you do?" Swan asked her.

Georgianna smiled like she was proud of what she was about to say. "I set up an espionage operation out of your shop with the help of Rafe and Horacio. Then, with Rosie's assistance, I made it appear that the secret information being sent to China was being done through your jewelry."

"What!" Swan couldn't believe it. Her head was spinning from all the shocks she'd received tonight.

"I have to admit I put together a perfect plan. This guy I was sleeping with at the time assisted me by tipping off naval intelligence with what you were supposedly doing. They did their own investigation and my team and I made sure everything pointed at you. It should have been an open and shut case and you were to be arrested and charged with espionage."

As if she was tired of standing, Georgianna moved to sit on one of the benches. She frowned over at Swan. "Everything was going according to plan until the final thread of the investigation reached Director Levart's desk."

"Godpop 3?"

"See what I mean? You have three godfathers and I don't have a one," Georgianna said in a loud voice, pointing a finger at her. "You don't deserve such love and loyalty, and I intended to tarnish their image of you."

* * *

Flipper's watch vibrated and he glanced down at the text message. Here. N place. Coop got layout of boat.

He texted them back. 1 N cockpit. 4 others. 2 hostages.

He quickly received a reply from Viper. Eliminating cockpit.

Got 4 in scope. That particular text came from Bane, a master sniper.

Flipper knew that although everyone was in place, timing was everything. Georgianna had no idea her words were being recorded so wanted to let her talk before making his move. Then there would be no way she could deny anything.

From listening to what the woman was saying, it was obvious she had mental issues. That could be the only reason to have such a deep hatred of Swan that Georgianna would go to such extremes. Georgianna assumed she'd had the perfect plan for Swan's downfall and Flipper was glad things hadn't turned out the way Georgianna intended.

Before inching up the ladder to listen to what else she was confessing, he texted the message: Will give signal.

Swan shook her head. It was obvious Georgianna's jealousy had blinded her senses and fueled her hatred. Didn't the others see it? Why were they following her blindly? Swan glanced over at Jamila and could tell by the look in her cousin's eyes that she was wondering the same thing.

"When Director Levart saw the report, he refused to believe you could be guilty of anything, especially betraying your country."

Thank God for that, Swan thought.

"He requested a thirty-day delay before agreeing to take any actions against you. Even after we made sure the investigation clearly spelled out your role in everything. There was no reason for you not to be charged," Georgianna said.

She paused a moment before continuing. "Unknown to me and the others, Director Levart went to your other two godfathers and they put their heads together to see what they could do to prove your innocence. They decided to send one of their top SEALs to find out what he could and to prove your innocence."

Swan drew in a deep breath. *Oh no, please don't let what Horacio said tonight be true. Please don't let David turn out to be someone other than what he said he was.*

Georgianna's next words ripped into Swan's heart.

"The SEAL they sent was Lieutenant David Holloway. I guess you didn't know that all the time he spent with you was nothing more than an assignment. You meant nothing to him, Swan." Georgianna laughed as if she found the entire thing amusing while Swan's heart broke.

"Imagine how amused I was to find out just how taken you were with him, while not knowing the true purpose as to why he showed up here on the island. You were played, Swan," Georgianna was saying in between laughter. "But don't worry. I sent some other members of my group to take care of him for you. I think he's dead by now."

Suddenly a deep voice at the back of the boat said, "As you can see, I'm very much alive."

Swan gasped just as the others did. Standing with legs braced apart and wearing only a pair of swim trunks with a utility combat belt around his waist, David looked like a mad badass. It was obvious everyone was shocked to see him, especially Georgianna, who had assumed he was dead.

"Drop your gun," he ordered Horacio, who was still holding his weapon on Swan and Jamila.

"How the hell did you get here?" Horacio asked, enraged.

"I swam from Swan's home."

"That's impossible!"

"Not if you're a SEAL master swimmer," David said. "Now, do like I said and put your gun down."

"And if I don't? It will be a shame if I kill Swan or Jamila before you can get to anything on that belt you're wearing," Horacio sneered.

"Don't try it, Horacio. One of my team members who's a master sniper has all four of you within his scope. Before you could get off the first shot, you'd be dead."

"I don't believe you. There's no one else out here," Horacio said. When he lifted his gun to take aim at Swan, a shot rang out, hitting the man in the chest. The impact toppled him to the floor.

Jamila screamed and Swan understood. Jamila had fallen in love with a man who'd betrayed her and then gotten shot right before her eyes.

Suddenly, Rafe dived for the gun that had dropped from Horacio's hand. Before he could reach it, another shot rang out that hit him in the side. He fell to the floor as well.

"Either of you ladies want to join them?" Flipper asked Georgianna and Rosie.

Rosie looked like she was in shock and ready to pass out.

However, Georgianna looked furious. "You won't get away with this. No matter what you tell my father, he will never believe you over me," she said with absolute certainty. "I'll tell him that you decided to team up with Swan and she turned you against your country."

"I figured you would lie. That's why I've recorded your little confession to Swan detailing everything. I can't wait for your father to listen to it."

Suddenly the boat was surrounded by several naval vessels and sharp beams of light shined on them. A voice through a foghorn said, "Lieutenant Holloway, we are coming aboard."

A dozen men wearing SEAL gear rushed on board with their guns drawn, immediately taking Georgianna and Rosie into custody. Bane, Viper, Coop and Mac boarded the boat as well. Mac rushed over to check Horacio and Rafe. There really was no need since they were both dead.

Flipper rushed over to Swan and Jamila to untie their hands.

More than anything, he wanted to pull Swan into his arms and tell her he loved her. He wanted her to put out of her mind what Georgianna had said about him until she'd heard his side of things. However, he knew when she pulled away from him to give her cousin a hug that she didn't want to give him a chance to explain.

He didn't intend to let her walk away.

"We need to talk, Swan," he said, looking down at her.

She glared up at him. "We have nothing to say to each other. Your assignment is over, Lieutenant Holloway. Now leave me alone."

CHAPTER FOURTEEN

Two weeks later

"How long are you planning to be mad at the world, Swan?"

Swan glanced over at Candy. Her best friend had returned to the Keys after hearing about what happened and she'd decided to stay. Swan was glad Candy had returned home but she was saddened by what had brought her back.

"I am not mad at the world," Swan said, taking a sip of her orange juice.

"But you are still mad at one particular man," Candy said, coming to sit beside Swan on the sofa.

Swan couldn't deny that was true so she didn't. "And what if I am?"

"He had a job to do, Swan. He was given orders. Surely you understand that."

Swan glared at Candy. "I'm sure none of my godfathers' orders included sleeping with me."

"I'm sure they didn't but David didn't force himself on you."

"No, but he deceived me."

"So did the others."

Did Candy have to remind her? "And I'm not talking to them either."

That wasn't totally true since Swan had reached out to Georgianna where she was being held at a federal prison in Orlando. The woman had refused to see her. Swan knew Georgianna was undergoing psychiatric evaluations to see if she was fit to stand trial.

Swan's godparents were heartbroken and she understood how they felt. Like her, they'd had no idea Georgianna harbored such hatred toward Swan, enough to do what she'd done. With both Rafe and Horacio dead, it was Rosie who was singing like a bird, telling everything she knew for a lessened sentence.

According to Rosie, Georgianna had manipulated a number of the men at naval intelligence into doing whatever she wanted them to do. When you were the admiral's daughter, you could wield that kind of power. She had even threatened a few with blackmail. She'd deliberately recorded several of the men having sex with her and then threatened to give the tape to her father and accuse them of rape.

Some of the men were not only married but a number were high-ranking military officers. Fearful of court-martial, the men had done whatever Georgianna asked, including falsifying records. So far, more than twelve men had been named in the scandal.

"I take it David hasn't called."

Swan drew in a deep breath. She had seen him last week when they'd had to show up at the naval station to give statements. "Yes, he's called. Several times. But I refuse to answer. Like I told him, we have nothing to say to each other. His assignment is over."

"And do you honestly think that's all you were to him, Swan?"

"Yes, but it doesn't matter."

"I think it does," Candy countered.

"And you think too much," Swan said, easing off the sofa.

The first week after the incident on the boat, she had closed her shop while naval investigators did a thorough search of

Rafe's tattoo parlor. She had used that time to take care of Jamila, who was still broken up over Horacio. Jamila had loved him and in a single night had seen him become an abusive monster, a man she hadn't known. Then in the end, Jamila had watched him die before her eyes.

Swan knew Jamila was going through something that only time could heal. That's why when Swan had reopened the shop this week and Jamila had asked for extra work hours, Swan had given them to her.

"So what are you going to do?" Candy asked her.

Swan glanced over at her. "About life? Work?"

"No, about David."

Swan just couldn't understand why Candy couldn't accept that David was no longer in the equation. "I'm a survivor, Candy. Although it was hard, I made do after my parents' deaths and I will make do now." She glanced at her watch. "I'm getting dressed to go into the shop today. The cruise ship comes into port tomorrow, so business will pick up. I want to make sure most of my new pieces are on display."

Another thing they had found out was that Horacio had been fired from the cruise ship months ago but hadn't told Jamila. He had moved into Rosie's place while the woman had been gone. The duplicity of the people she'd thought she knew simply amazed Swan.

"And I need to be on my way," Candy said. "I promised my folks we would go out to dinner tonight. You can join us if you like."

"Thanks for the invite, but I'll pass. I just want to have a relaxing evening here tonight. I might go swimming on the beach later."

Swan had called Jamila and told her she would bring lunch from their favorite sandwich café. However, there were no clients in her shop when Swan got there, so she decided to do something she usually didn't do, which was close for lunch.

Normally, the shop remained open and she and Jamila would

alternate lunch duties. But today she wanted to check on Jamila, talk to her to see how she was faring. Although Swan had been there for Jamila last week, they hadn't had a real honest-to-goodness talk since Jamila had admitted to being her cousin.

"What are you doing?" Jamila asked when Swan put up the Closed sign and pulled down the blinds.

Swan smiled over at her. "New store policy. From here on out, we will close at noon for lunch."

"What about the sales you'll lose?"

Swan shrugged. "Sales aren't everything. Besides, it's just for an hour. Come join me in my office."

"All right, let me grab some sodas out of the refrigerator."

A few minutes later, she and Jamila were enjoying their lunch when Swan gave Jamila a long look. "How are you doing?"

Jamila shrugged. "Okay, I guess. Trying to move on. I loved Horacio so much only to find out he wasn't the man I thought he was."

"I know the feeling."

"No, you don't."

Swan snatched her head up, frowning. "Excuse me?"

"I said you don't know the feeling, Swan. David Holloway was nothing like Horacio. David intended to save you and Horacio would have killed me if that woman had ordered him to do so. Big difference."

"But like you, I was betrayed."

"How?" Jamila countered. "Your godfathers sent David Holloway here to prove your innocence and he did."

Jamila put her soda can down and then added, "And another thing. What man takes a chance and swims across the ocean to save a woman? Do you know how far from land we were? Think about that."

Swan had news for her—she *had* thought about it. She could never forget how David had appeared seemingly out of nowhere on that boat, looking tough and ready to kick asses while wearing nothing more than an outlandishly tight pair of swim trunks with a military belt around his waist. Even when she'd been in what seemed like a dire situation, that hadn't stopped the woman in her from noticing how dangerously sexy he'd looked at that particular moment.

"When I mentioned what an astounding feat he'd accomplished to his friends," Jamila said, reclaiming Swan's attention, "they said that's why they call him Flipper. Did you know that's his code name as a SEAL?"

Swan wiped her mouth with a napkin. "Yes, I knew he was called Flipper. But no, I didn't know it had anything to do with him being a SEAL because I didn't know he was one. I assumed Flipper was his nickname."

Swan forced from her mind the day she'd asked him about those dolphin tattoos. He'd told her then they represented Flipper. That had been the day they'd made love in this office. Right here on this desk.

She wished she wasn't thinking so hard about that now.

She looked over at Jamila. "Why are we talking about me instead of you?"

"Because I think you should and because I think I should," Jamila continued. "Talking about your situation actually helps me believe that not all men are jerks and that there are some who still possess real honor, Swan. Whether you want to admit it or not, David Holloway is an honorable man. He couldn't help being attracted to you any more than you could help being attracted to him."

Swan stuffed the wrappings from her sandwich into the empty bag. "Now you sound like Candy."

"Maybe there's a reason why I do," Jamila said, stuffing her own wrappings into a bag. "It might be because Candy and I can see things that you refuse to see. I often think about what could have happened to us had David and his friends not shown up when they did. Do you ever think of that?"

Swan drew in a deep breath. "I try not to."

"I think you should," Jamila said, standing. "Thanks for

bringing lunch. It will be my treat the next time." She then walked out of the office.

Swan stayed in her office after Jamila left, trying to put their conversation out of her mind. She was working on her computer, verifying inventory, when her office phone rang. "Thank you for calling Swan's. How may I help you?"

"Hello, island princess."

She smiled upon hearing her godfather's voice. "Godpop 2. How are you?"

"I'm fine. I just wanted to check on you. So much has happened and I wanted to make sure you're okay."

She had spoken to each of her godfathers and had thanked them for believing in her. They had taken a risk with their individual careers to do that. "I'm fine. How is Godpop 3?"

"He's fine but as the director of naval intelligence, he has his hands full with the investigation. It seems that more names are popping up in this scandal each day."

"And how are Godpop 1 and Barbara?"

"They are as well as can be expected under the circumstances. Learning about Georgianna was a shocker for all of us. We had no idea. When we decided to send Lt. Holloway to prove your innocence, the three of us weren't sure just what he would uncover. The only thing we knew for certain was that you weren't guilty of anything."

"Thanks for believing in me."

"You have Andrew's blood in your veins. You could no more be a traitor to your country than he could. Considering all that happened, I'm glad Holloway remained in Key West when he could have left."

Swan sat up straight. "Wasn't David on assignment?"

"Not the entire time. His assignment officially ended when he sent that ink in to be analyzed and we discovered it was tainted. I told him that he no longer had to stay in the Keys since by then we knew you weren't involved and we would take over the investigation from there."

"Then why did he stay?"

"To protect you."

"He told you that?" she asked.

"Yes. I remember the conversation like it was yesterday. I told him he could consider his job assignment complete and go home to Texas and enjoy the remainder of his leave. But he said he wanted to hang around Key West for a while."

Her godfather paused. "I asked him if the reason he wanted to stay was because he thought your life might be in danger. He said he felt that as long as Duggers and Jacinto didn't know they were suspects, then no, your life wasn't in any immediate danger. He informed me that the reason he wanted to stay was because you had come to mean a lot to him. I told him in that case how he spent the rest of his leave was his decision. And, Swan?"

She drew in a deep breath. "Yes?"

"As his commanding officer, I felt the need to remind him that although he was no longer on assignment, since the issue that had started with you was an ongoing investigation, he could not tell you anything."

When Swan didn't reply, her godfather asked, "You're still there, Swan?"

"Yes, Godpop 2, I'm still here."

"Did you not know how Holloway felt about you?"

"No. I thought I was just an assignment."

"You were at first and I'm glad you were. Otherwise you would be in jail wrongly accused of a crime you hadn't committed. But on the flip side, I'm also glad that when you stopped being an assignment, Holloway had the insight to stay and look out for you because he cared for you."

Long after her telephone conversation with her godfather ended, Swan remained seated at her desk, leaning back in her chair and sitting in silence while thinking about what Candy, Jamila and her godfather had said.

Some people never got betrayed, but she had been, a lot. William, Rafe, Horacio, Rosie, Georgianna and even Jamila. No one had been who she'd thought.

She remembered David and replayed in her mind all the time she'd spent with him since that day he'd first walked into her shop.

Was anything he'd told her true? Did he really come from a huge family? Was his mother even celebrating a birthday? Did he honestly have three sisters-in-law?

One thing was for certain, both Candy and Jamila were right. David hadn't pushed her into sleeping with him. In fact, Swan was the one who'd invited him to dinner at her place with the full intent of having sex with him.

She got up from her desk and walked over to the window. She knew from Jamila that David had left the island with his friends after that first week, after he'd completed all the questioning by naval intelligence. Was he back home in Texas? Did his parents really own a medical supply company? What parts of what he'd told her were true and what parts were fabricated for his assignment?

And why did she still love him so much it hurt...even when she didn't want to love him? Even when she didn't know how he felt about her? He might have told her godfather he cared for her but David hadn't told her anything. Shouldn't he have? But then, had she given him a chance to do so?

The answer to that flashed in her mind quickly. No, she hadn't.

He had saved her life that night, swam across the ocean to do so, and then she'd told him she didn't want to talk to him. And he had honored her wishes...for that one night. Then he had called her almost every single day since, and yet she had refused to take his calls.

He hadn't called today.

Did that mean he'd given up and wouldn't try contacting her again? Was she ready to put her heart on the line and contact him?

She wasn't sure. But what she *was* certain of was that they needed to do what they hadn't done before. They needed to get to know each other. She needed to know which parts of what he'd told her about himself were true and which were false.

She wanted to get to know the real David Holloway.

Then what?

Hadn't she convinced herself she wanted no part of a man in the military? And what about her decision to never to get seriously involved in an interracial relationship like her parents had? Why did all of that no longer matter to her when she thought about her and David deciding to have a future together?

Maybe that's how love worked. It made you see the possible instead of the impossible. It made you want things you told yourself were not good for you because you were afraid to reach beyond your comfort zone.

Taking a deep a cleansing breath, she decided to call David tonight before going to bed. She had no idea what she would say to him but the words would come.

She doubted he would want to come back to the Keys anytime soon, so she would let him know she would come to him if he still wanted to talk. She would see what he said before asking Jamila if she could take care of the shop while Swan was gone. David might very well tell her that it was too late, that they had nothing to talk about. But there was a chance he would embrace her words. Embrace her.

Her mood suddenly lightened, knowing that was a possibility.

Flipper entered the hotel room and tossed his luggage on the bed. Different hotel but same city. He had given Swan two weeks and now he was back. They needed to talk and clear up some things. She hadn't accepted his calls, but now he was here and he wouldn't be ignored.

He shook his head when his cell phone rang. "Yes, Coop?"

"Have you seen her yet?"

"No, I just got here. In fact, I walked into my hotel room less than five minutes ago."

"Okay. And there's another reason I called. Bristol is pregnant."

"Wow, man. Congratulations. I didn't know you guys were trying."

Coop laughed. "We're always trying. But seriously, we figured it was time Laramie had a playmate."

"Sounds good to me."

"I hope things work out with you and Swan, Flipper."

"I hope so, too."

"And do me a favor."

"What?"

"For once, open up. Tell her how you feel. Don't beat around the bush. You have a tendency to do that. Women love a man to get straight to the point and share their feelings. I hate to say it, bro, but you're not good at doing that."

Coop was right, he wasn't. "I never had to do that before. I've never truly loved a woman before Swan."

"I understand. But you do love her, so make sure she knows it. A woman has to believe she's loved."

Flipper chuckled.

"What's so funny?" Coop asked him.

"You're giving relationship advice. Do you know how much like Mac you sound?"

Coop chuckled as well. "You would have to point that out. I guess it comes with loving a woman."

"I guess so."

"No guess in it, remember it. Know it. Feel it. Take care and good luck."

After ending the call with Coop, it wasn't long before Flipper got calls from Bane, Viper and Mac as well, all letting him know they hoped things worked out for Flipper and Swan. All giving him advice. They were married men who had the women they loved and they wanted him to have the woman he loved as well.

He appreciated good friends who not only watched his back but who also cared about the condition of his heart. They knew about the pain he had lodged there and it got worse every day he and Swan were apart.

Flipper glanced at his watch. Swan's store would be closing in less than an hour. He would give her time to get home and relax before paying her a visit. He refused to let her put things off any longer. They needed to talk.

He loved her and it was damn time she knew it.

CHAPTER FIFTEEN

SWAN HAD JUST poured a glass of wine to enjoy while sitting on the patio when she heard the knock at her door.

She knew Candy had gone out to dinner with her family and Jamila had mentioned she would just stay in tonight and chill. Swan had invited Jamila to join her so maybe her cousin had changed her mind.

Her cousin.

That was taking a lot of getting used to but Swan knew her parents would want a family connection for them. Jamila was the only family Swan had and she appreciated their friendship more than ever.

She reached the door and glanced through the peephole. Her heart nearly stopped.

Was it really David? She blinked and looked again and saw it was really him. Back in Key West. And he was standing in front of her door looking like he always did, sexy as hell.

Drawing in a deep breath, she removed the security lock and opened the door. "David? I thought you'd left the island."

"I had but I returned today. May I come in?"

She nodded and stepped aside. The moment he passed her, she caught a whiff of his masculine scent, the same one she was convinced still lingered in her bedroom.

Swan closed the door and stood to face him. He was standing in the middle of her living room wearing a pair of shorts and a sleeveless shirt with a huge picture of a dolphin. *Flipper.* Her gaze moved beyond the shirt to his face to find his laser-blue eyes staring at her.

She cleared her throat. "I was about to sit out back and drink a glass of wine while enjoying the view. Would you like to have a beer and join me?"

She could tell he was surprised by her invitation. She hadn't bothered to ask why he was there.

"Yes, I'd like that."

Moments later, they were sitting side by side on a bench that overlooked the beach. They had been sipping their drinks for a few moments when he said, "I told you that night two weeks ago that we needed to talk, Swan. I think we still do."

Yes, they did. She would let him go first. "Okay, I'm listening."

"I want you to do more than just listen, Swan. I want you to engage by asking questions, giving me feedback, and I would like to be able to do the same with you."

"Okay, that seems fair because I do have some questions for you."

"Ask away."

She took another sip of her drink. "You didn't tell me you were a SEAL and I'd—"

"I couldn't tell you I was a SEAL, Swan," he interrupted to say. "That's why I lied and said I was no longer in the military."

"Yes, I know that now. I want to tell you, because of what happened to my father, I had made up my mind never to get serious about a military man...especially not a SEAL."

"Oh, I see."

She wouldn't tell him yet that she'd changed her mind about that. "Is your mother's birthday really next month and do you have four brothers?"

"Yes. Everything I told you about my family is true. I never lied to you about anything pertaining to them. I just omitted some details and couldn't elaborate on certain things."

She then put her wineglass down and turned toward him. "Why did you sleep with me, David, when I was just an assignment to you?"

Flipper knew this was the time of reckoning and what he told her would have an impact on their relationship for the rest of their days. He needed her to understand.

"You were supposed to be an assignment, Swan. But honestly, I don't think you ever were. From the moment I walked into your shop and saw you, a part of me knew I had to fight hard to be objective and do the job I'd been sent here to do."

He paused. "I tried to keep my attraction to you out of the picture but found it harder and harder to do. Each time I saw you while getting to know you, I fell deeper under your spell. It was hard pretending with you."

He decided to be totally honest with her. "Just so you know, that day you invited me to your place for dinner wasn't my first time there. I'd been to your home without you knowing anything about it. But at the time, it was just a house I was checking out as part of an investigation. The day you invited me to dinner, I saw it through another pair of eyes. Yours. And for me, it then became your home."

She drew in a deep breath. "You invaded my privacy by letting yourself into my home, but that's not why I'm upset. I accept that you had a job to do and I was your assignment but…"

"But what?"

"You still haven't fully answered my question, David. Why did you make love to me?"

David frowned, realizing that he *hadn't* answered her question. His teammates often teased him about beating around the bush, sometimes providing too much context instead of just sticking with the facts.

"The reason I made love to you, Swan, was because I desired you. Everything about you turned me on. Your looks, your scent, your walk...and then after our first kiss, it was your taste. Fighting my desire for you was no longer an option, although I tried being honorable enough not to seduce you."

"But then I seduced you," she said quietly.

He smiled. "No, I think that night we seduced each other. Everything we did was mutual."

"Yes, it was." She took another sip of her wine. "I spoke with Godpop 2 today and he told me your assignment ended but you decided to stay. Why?"

Okay, no beating around the bush this time, Flipper decided. "The reason is that by then I had fallen in love with you. In all honesty, in my heart you stopped being an assignment the first time I made love to you. I crossed the line of what was honorable, and I knew why. Because I felt you here, Swan," he said, pointing to his heart. "I felt you here in a way I've never felt before. No woman has ever been here, Swan. But during the one time you shouldn't have, you got there anyway."

"And now? How do you feel now?"

He placed his beer bottle aside and turned toward her. "Now you are still in my heart. Even more so. I love you so much I ache on the inside when I'm not with you. I love you so much I think of you even at times I shouldn't."

He reached out and took her hand in his. "Now I need to know, Swan, just how you feel about me."

Swan felt the gentle tug on her hand and, surprising even herself, she moved to sit in his lap.

When he wrapped his arms around her, she felt comfort flow through her. She turned in his lap to look down at him. He'd given her answers to all her questions, now she intended to give him answers to his.

"I love you, David. I fought it at first. I didn't know about you being present-day military, but I also had a problem...not with interracial dating...but with allowing anything to come of it. I saw how others saw my parents at times. Not as a beautiful couple in love but as an interracial couple in love. There should not have been a difference. I never wanted to deal with what they had to deal with in the name of love."

She paused. "But then I moved beyond thinking that way after I fell in love with you. Then I realized how my parents must have felt, believing nothing mattered but their love. Even if the world was against them, as long as they had each other, that's what truly counted."

"So you do love me?" he asked her as if for clarity.

Swan didn't have a problem clarifying anything for him or anyone else. "Yes, I love you, David Flipper Holloway." And then she lowered her mouth to his.

Shivers of profound pleasure shot through every part of Swan's body when David slid his tongue into her mouth. Sensations bombarded her as she concentrated on his taste, his scent and the way he pulled her tongue into his mouth to mate with his. And when she felt his hands inch upward and slide beneath her top, his touch made her purr.

Both his taste and his touch were awakening parts of her, making her feel alive in a way she hadn't felt since the last time they'd been together. Here at her house. In her bed.

When his fingers touched her bare breasts, using his fingertips to draw circles around her nipples, she oozed deeper into the kiss, almost feeling like melted butter in his arms.

He slowly pulled his mouth from hers and looked at her. His blue eyes were sharp and filled with the same desire she felt. "Any reason why we can't take this inside?"

She wrapped her arms around his waist. "No, there's no reason."

"Good."

And then standing with her in his arms, he carried her into the house.

* * *

"Just so you know, David, I didn't ask you all my questions," Swan said when he placed her on the bed.

David glanced down at her. "You didn't?"

"No, but I can wait. None are more earth-shattering than this is going to be. And I need this."

He caressed the side of her face with his finger. "I need this, too. I know why I need it, tell me why you do."

She met his gaze and held it while she said, "I love the feel of you inside of me. I've never felt anything so right before. So pleasurable." She smiled. "Do you know I retired my sex toy?"

He chuckled. "That's good to know."

"Um, not too much information?"

"No. Nice to know what used to be my competition," he said as he began removing her clothes. Lucky for him, she wasn't wearing much. Just a top, shorts and a thong. Flipper had discovered outside earlier that she wasn't wearing a bra. He'd noticed more than once that she liked her breasts being free and so did he.

She reached out and tugged at his T-shirt and he assisted by removing his own shorts. Then he rejoined her on the bed. Reaching out, he lifted her by the waist.

"Wrap your legs around me, Swan. I'm about to join our bodies, to make us one."

As soon as her legs were settled around his waist, his shaft touched her core. She was wet and ready. Tilting her hips, he whispered the words, "I love you," before thrusting hard into her.

"David!"

Arching her back off the bed, she provided the prefect position for his penetration to go deeper. They were a perfect fit. They always would be. Not just in lovemaking but in everything they did from here on out. They had become a team.

He began moving, slowly at first and then harder and deeper, over and over again. The only constant sounds in the room were

their breathing and flesh slapping against flesh. The air surrounding them was filled with the aroma of sex.

He felt on fire, like his entire body was burning and the
flames fueled his need, his desire and his love. She was looking up at him, holding his gaze, and he hoped Swan saw the
depth of love in his eyes.

He clenched his jaw when he felt it, the stirring of pleasure
in his groin. The feeling was slowly spreading through his body
and when Swan gripped his shoulders and dug her fingers into
his skin, he continued to thrust inside of her like his life depended on it.

And when she screamed out his name, he knew the same
sensations that were taking him were taking her.

He drew in a sharp breath only moments before calling out
her name. Multiple sensations tore into him, causing an explosion inside of him that had him bucking his body in an all-con-
suming orgasm. The sensations kept coming until he let go and
his release shot deep inside of her.

He knew right then that he wanted her to have his baby. If not
this time, another time. One day, he intended to make it happen.

Moments later, he slumped down beside her and wrapped
his arms around her as he tried to get his breathing under control. After recovering from his explosive orgasm, when he was
able to talk, he said, "I feel like I've been burned to a crisp."

"Hmm, speaking of burning, do you know what I thought
was hot?" she asked, drawing in deep breaths of air into her
lungs.

"No, what?"

"You on that boat wearing nothing but swim trunks and that
military belt around your waist. Now, that was hot."

He grinned. "You liked that, huh?"

She smirked up at him when he straddled her body again.
"I liked it." Then her features became serious. "I still can't believe you swam all that way to save me."

He leaned in and brushed a kiss across her lips. "Believe it."

He then pulled back and looked down at her. His expression was serious. "I'm a damn good swimmer. I'm known to be able to hold my breath underwater for long periods of time. Longer than what most would consider normal. But I wasn't sure I was going to make it to the boat, Swan. I told my friends I had to try even if I died trying because the woman I love was on that boat. That's what kept me going. That's what fueled every stroke I made into the ocean waters. And when my body felt tired, like I couldn't possibly swim another lap, I would think of a life without you and for me that was unacceptable."

He drew in a sharp breath. For a quick minute, he relived the feel of the cold water as he swam nonstop to the boat to save her, not knowing if he would make it in time. "I had to save you."

"And then I rebuffed you. I refused to have that talk you wanted."

"I understood. I had been listening to what Georgianna Martin was saying, the picture she painted. I told myself that once I talked to you and told you the truth that you would believe me. I was just giving you time to think about everything. I figured you would realize that I did care for you."

She reached up and caressed the side of his face. "You never told me you cared."

"I did. Our last night together, when you were asleep, I told you before I left that I loved you. I had planned to tell you the next day when we were together but that's when you were taken."

"And you came back," she said.

"That was always my plan, Swan. I never intended to let you go. I love you that much. And just so you know, my entire family is rooting for me. I told them about you and they can't wait to meet you. My brothers and I are giving Mom a party for her birthday next week. Will you go to Texas with me?"

When she hesitated, he added, "What I told you about them is true. My parents accept people for who they are and not how they look. Will you trust me about that?"

She met his gaze and nodded. "Yes, I will trust you and yes, I will go."

A huge smile spread across his face. "I can't wait to introduce you to everyone. And I've got the perfect thing for you to wear." He quickly eased off the bed.

She pulled herself up. "What's going on? You plan on dressing me that night?"

He glanced over his shoulder, chuckling as he pulled a small white box out of his shorts. "Something like that."

He returned to the bed and pulled her up to stand her on her feet beside the bed. Then he got down on one knee and looked up at her. "I love you, Swan. I know we have a lot of things we still need to overcome. But I believe we will do so together. Forever. Will you marry me?"

He saw tears form in her eyes when she nodded. "Yes, I will marry you."

He slid the ring on her finger and at that moment Flipper knew he was halfway to having his world complete.

He would get the other half the day she became his wife.

CHAPTER SIXTEEN

SWAN GLANCED DOWN at the ring David had put on her finger last week. Seeing it gave her strength and she definitely needed strength now, she thought as she entered a huge ballroom on his arm. It was his mother's sixtieth birthday party.

They had flown into Dallas last night so this would be the first time she met his family. Nervous jitters had tried taking over her stomach but a smile from David was keeping most of them at bay. He was convinced his family would love her and he had told her over and over that she was worrying for nothing. She was the woman he wanted and his family would love his choice.

"There's Mom and Dad," he said, with his arms around her shoulders as she carried his mother's gift. The same gift he'd purchased that first day he'd come into her shop.

A man she knew had to be one of David's brothers whispered something to the older couple and they turned with huge smiles on their faces.

At that moment, Swan knew David had inherited his father's eyes and that the smiles on the couple's faces were genuine. She could actually feel their warmth. David's mom was beautiful and did not look like she was sixty or that she had five grown sons.

When they reached his parents, David made the introduction. "Mom. Dad. I want you to meet the woman who has agreed to be my wife, Swan Jamison."

"It's an honor to meet you," Swan said, extending her hand to his mother.

Instead of taking it, the older woman engulfed Swan in a huge hug. "It's wonderful meeting you as well, Swan, and welcome to the family."

"Thank you. Here's your gift. Happy birthday."

"Thank you."

She received a hug from David's father as well. Then suddenly she was surrounded and a laughing David made introductions. All his brothers had those same blue eyes and like David, they were very handsome men. She could see why when she looked at the older Holloways; they were a beautiful couple. And Swan could tell from the way Mr. Holloway looked at his wife and the way Mrs. Holloway would look back at him that the couple was still very much in love.

A few nights ago, David had shared the fact that because his mother had been married to a Navy SEAL for over forty years and had five sons who were SEALs, she counseled a number of SEAL wives who had difficulties with the frequency and longevity of their spouses' missions. Swan had been glad to hear that since she would become a SEAL's wife soon.

Because David would be leaving in less than four months on anther mission, they hoped to marry within a year. Surprisingly, David wanted a big wedding. She agreed as long as the wedding took place in the Keys.

The logistics of having a big wedding were enormous, given he had four brothers who were SEALs on different teams. Not to mention his closest four friends were SEALs as well. That meant Swan and David had to make sure everyone would be on leave in the States at the same time.

David also introduced Swan to her future sisters-in-law and they loved her engagement ring. The three were friendly and she liked them immediately. She was also introduced to other members of David's family—his grandparents, his niece, nephews, cousins, aunts, uncles—it was obvious the Holloway family was a huge one.

"Now I want to reintroduce you to four guys who are just as close to me as brothers. As you know, they came to the Keys to assist me in proving your innocence. And even when my assignment with you ended, they didn't leave. They stayed."

She had met his four friends that night after the incident on the boat, when they'd had to give statements. She had thanked them for their help but they hadn't been officially introduced.

"Did I tell you how beautiful you look tonight, sweetheart?"

She smiled up at him as they walked across the ballroom floor to the four men and their wives. "Yes, you told me. Thank you." She, Candy and Jamila had gone shopping in Miami. She'd known this was the perfect dress when she'd seen it on a store mannequin.

Within a few minutes, she had been introduced to Brisbane "Bane" Westmoreland and his wife, Crystal; Gavin "Viper" Blake and his very pregnant wife, Layla; Laramie "Coop" Cooper and his wife, Bristol; and Thurston "Mac" McRoy and his wife, Teri.

After spending time with the couples, Swan felt that just like her future sisters-in-law, the four women were genuinely friendly and Swan looked forward to getting to know them better. They loved her engagement ring as well and told David he'd done a great job in picking it out.

"So what do you think?" David leaned down to ask, taking her hand in his and leading her to where his parents, siblings and their spouses were getting ready to take a group picture.

She grinned up at him. "Um, for starters, I think I need to start calling you Flipper, since everyone else does. And then, *Flipper*, I think I am one of the luckiest women in the world right now. I love you."

He chuckled as he pulled her to the side of the room and

wrapped his arms around her waist. "And I, Swan Jamison, think I'm the luckiest man in the world, and I love you."

"A very wise woman, my mother, once told me that when you meet a man who puts that sparkle in your eyes then you'd know he was a keeper. You, Flipper, are a keeper."

He smiled. "You, my beautiful Swan, are a keeper as well."

Flipper then lowered his mouth to hers.

EPILOGUE

A year later in June

BANE WESTMORELAND LEANED close and whispered to Flipper, "Don't get nervous now. You wanted a big wedding and you got it."

Flipper couldn't say anything because Bane was right. He stood flanked by his father, who was his best man, and twelve groomsmen—namely his brothers, best friends and cousins.

Only his SEAL teammates knew Flipper had a tendency to tap his finger against his thigh when he was nervous. He stopped tapping but not because he noticed that Viper, Mac and Coop were grinning over at him. But then he figured both Viper and Coop had reasons to grin since they'd both become fathers this year. Viper was the proud father of a son, Gavin IV, and Coop had a beautiful daughter they'd named Paris, since that was where he'd first met his wife.

It was a beautiful day for a beach wedding and so far everything was perfect and going according to plan. Swan had hired one of the local wedding planners and the woman had done an awesome job. She had thought of everything, including the super yacht that could hold their five hundred guests that they'd be using for the wedding reception. It was anchored in the ocean near Swan's beachfront home. A fleet of passenger boats had been chartered to transport the wedding guests out to the yacht.

A ten-piece orchestra sat beneath towering balustrades draped from top to bottom in thin white netting. Chairs were set up on the beach, auditorium style, facing the decorative stage where Flipper and the men in the wedding party stood waiting.

Suddenly, the music began and all the ladies strolled down the beach and up the steps.

Swan had chosen her wedding colors of purple and yellow and Flipper had to admit the combination was striking. It took all twelve women long enough to do their stroll. His niece was a flower girl and Coop's son and one of Flipper's nephews were the ring bearers.

Flipper almost held his breath when what looked like a huge forty-foot golden swan was rolled onto the beach. When the orchestra changed their tune for the "Wedding March," the swan opened and his Swan appeared in a beautiful, dazzling white gown. She looked beautiful, stunning and breathtaking all rolled into one.

Flipper stared at the woman who would be his wife and felt so much love in his heart. He hadn't known until now just how much he could feel for one woman. They had spent the past year deepening their friendship and their love. He looked forward to returning from his covert operations, knowing she would be there waiting on him.

He watched as she slowly strolled toward him. All three of her godfathers participated in walking her up the aisle, passing her off to the other so many feet along the way. Then all three of them gave her away. When Swan reached his side and extended her hand to him, he accepted it while thinking she was *his* Swan.

His beautiful Swan.

The wedding ceremony began. What Flipper would remember most when he looked back was when the minister announced them husband and wife and told him he could kiss his bride.

Flipper pulled Swan into his arms and lowered his mouth to hers. She was his and he intended to keep her happy for the rest of his days. They would be flying to Dubai for a two-week honeymoon and then return to the Keys where they planned to make their permanent home.

When David released Swan's mouth, the minister said, "I present to everyone David and Swan Holloway."

Flipper knew they were supposed to exit by walking down the golden steps that led to the boat that would transport them to the yacht. But at that moment, he couldn't deny himself another kiss and lowered his mouth to his wife's again.

* * * * *

Captivated By Her Runaway Doc

Doc

Sue MacKay

MEDICAL
Pulse-racing passion

Dear Reader,

I love the idea of French doctors, and to bring one to Queenstown, where he meets my helicopter pilot heroine, Mallory, was so much fun. And once he was here, he wasn't getting away.

Josue Bisset has a big heart but is afraid to share it—until he meets Mallory, and she's so irresistible his world starts to tip off center.

Mallory Baine has the perfect life but she's restless for love and a family of her own. All she has to do is convince Josue to put away his bag and stay on with her.

They work as volunteers in search and rescue, which brings them together in stressful moments and in relief when their mission is successful. All they have to do is make their own mission of love and happiness work out.

Enjoy their story.

Cheers,

Sue Mackay

Sue MacKay lives with her husband in New Zealand's beautiful Marlborough Sounds, with the water on her doorstep and the birds and the trees at her back door. It is the perfect setting to indulge her passions of entertaining friends by cooking them sumptuous meals, drinking fabulous wine, going for hill walks or kayaking around the bay—and, of course, writing stories.

Books by Sue MacKay

Harlequin Medical

London Hospital Midwives
A Fling to Steal Her Heart

SOS Docs
Redeeming Her Brooding Surgeon

Baby Miracle in the ER
Surprise Twins for the Surgeon
ER Doc's Forever Gift
The Italian Surgeon's Secret Baby
Take a Chance on the Single Dad
The Nurse's Twin Surprise
Reclaiming Her Army Doc Husband
The Nurse's Secret
The GP's Secret Baby Wish

Visit the Author Profile page
at millsandboon.com.au for
more titles.

This story is dedicated to all my readers,
especially as we cope with this strange time,
where the future is unknown.
You make me happy with your support.

CHAPTER ONE

AT EIGHT FORTY-FIVE Mallory Baine turned up her bumpy drive and huffed a relieved sigh. 'At long last.' A soak in a hot shower, then into PJs and a thick robe to devour the pizza sitting on the seat beside her while she unwound over a crime show on TV along with it.

Except there was a light on in her living room.

And a car parked by the garage.

Her heart lurched. 'Who the hell...?' No one had said they were stopping by tonight. Scanning back for anyone she might've told to make themselves at home, her memory came up blank. Yet it had to be someone who knew she left a spare key in the meter box. Didn't it? *It isn't an uncommon hiding place.* So, who was inside?

Parking next to the gleaming 4WD she didn't recognise, she snatched her phone from the console and shoved out to take a photo of the number plate. Just in case. She'd probably look like a fool when she learned who'd called in but, still, a girl had to be careful, even in Queenstown.

Woof, woof. Shade's 'Happy you're home, Mum' bark. Or it could be her 'I've smelt the pizza' bark. She obviously wasn't concerned about their visitor. Though any of her friends would've let Shade out of her run to go inside with them.

Crossing to her pet, she unlatched the wire gate and rubbed Shade's head, more for her own comfort than Shade's. 'Hey, girl. Who's visiting?'

Wag, wag, lick.

Some of the tension growing between her shoulder blades backed off. Whoever it was couldn't be all bad. Shade was savvy about people, though she was susceptible to meaty bribes. 'Come on inside. We've got someone to check out.'

A suitcase stood on the small porch near the back door and the key was still in the lock. A relieved sigh escaped Mallory. Woo-hoo. Typical Maisie. No warning, no checking if Mallory would be around for the weekend, her best friend would just fly in and hope for the best. She'd been promising a visit for weeks and after today, with their other close friend ending up in hospital, there couldn't be a better time. Mallory picked up the pizza and headed inside, down the short hall, calling out, 'Maisie, I hope you've brought the wine.' There wasn't any in her fridge, likewise much in the way of fresh food. 'Hello? Maisie? That you?'

A cough came from the sitting room. A masculine cough.

Mallory crashed to a stop in the doorway and reached down to hold Shade's collar with her free hand. A man was unfurling his long body from her couch, rubbing his eyes and yawning. Had he been asleep? Tough. More important was, 'Who are you?' she demanded through the pounding in her chest.

He stood tall, his woollen jersey half hitched up one side, the linen trousers creased and rumpled, dark hair falling into dark eyes. 'Hello.'

Hello? That was it? Not likely. Her hand slipped from Shade's collar as she stood tall and straight, eyeballing him directly. He had no right to be here, no matter what he might think. 'What are you doing here? How did you find the key?' she snapped.

'Your brother told me where the key would be and to let myself in if you weren't home. He said you'd be back sometime tonight.'

He looked such a relaxed mess, and sounded so genuine, that her unease backed off a notch, only to be replaced by anger. *This is my house.* Not once had she come home to find a stranger lounging on her couch like he had every right to make himself comfortable. If he was a villain, he wasn't very good at it, lying around as though he had all the time in the world. Though why would someone with evil intent wait in the house with lights on and his vehicle parked in full view? 'I said, who the hell are you?' she snapped, using the anger to cover concerns about not having a clue what was going on.

'Josue Bisset.'

She stared at him. The tension began cranking up tighter. The name meant nothing. Neither did anything he'd said so far make sense. She kept staring at him.

He finally got the idea. 'The doctor about to start work at the local hospital where you're based as a paramedic? I'm going to board in your house until I find an alternative for the short time I'm here?' Doubt was creeping into his accent, and he glanced around the room. Was he looking for an escape route because it was dawning on him he'd screwed up?

He had. Big time. Continuing to watch him, Mallory drew herself even taller, all of one point six metres, and dug for a *don't fool with me* attitude. It came easily. No one did this to her. Her home was her sanctuary, her safe space. 'I don't have a brother.' With his stunned gaze now locked on her, she continued. 'I am not taking in a boarder. And I'm a helicopter pilot, not a paramedic.'

Something foreign escaped from his mouth.

French? The accent sounded similar to that of the girl from Avignon who worked in the bakery she frequented. 'You mind translating?' she demanded, not ready to play nice. 'Now?'

'I'd better not,' he said. He even smiled. 'It wouldn't translate politely.' He wasn't acting as though he might be on the back foot here and he damned well should be. He was still a stranger who'd walked into her house uninvited, despite what he believed to be a valid reason for doing so.

Beside her, Shade stood straight and firm, her head pointed at their intruder, her muscles tense. But she didn't seem too wary of Josue, more like questioning what was going on. Mallory resisted the urge to pat her because she'd probably relax, and she still knew nothing about this man and why he was in her house. She waited.

'*Désolé.* I thought I'd come to the right address. It's been a long journey from Wellington, crossing over on the ferry and driving all the way down here today.'

That was a helluva distance. Still, 'Don't you use a GPS?'

'I do, and it led me here. I was going to Kayla Johnson's house. Do you know her?'

One of my closest friends. All the air whooshed out of her lungs. Three hours ago, she'd flown out in the rescue helicopter to pick up Kayla from beyond the Cardrona ski field and taken her to the hospital in Dunedin because Queenstown's hospital didn't do major surgeries. Her paramedic friend had two broken legs and was suffering from a severe concussion, having been lucky to avoid a small avalanche from taking her to the bottom of a rocky gully.

When Mallory had held Kayla's hand as she'd been unloaded at the hospital's emergency landing pad, Kayla had been talking gibberish, probably because of the concussion, but she'd said something about a doctor coming from Wellington. Was this man really meant to be staying in her friend's house? Was *she* supposed to go along and let him in because of a few whispered mutterings? It wasn't happening. At least not tonight. Hold on.

'GPSs are usually very accurate with street addresses. Kayla's house is another two hundred metres up the road.'

'Number 142. I have reached my destination,' he said in a monotone as if imitating the voice of his GPS. There was a suspicious glint in his eyes like he was laughing. Yes, his mouth was definitely twitching.

'Number 124. You have not reached your destination.' She retorted in a similar monotone, trying not to glint or twitch. He was beguiling to say the least. Great. Just what she needed at the moment.

'I must've muddled the numbers.'

'I'd say so.' It was getting harder by the minute not to give in to the smile trying to bust out from deep inside now that she was starting to relax. She didn't intend on making him feel too comfortable. Not yet anyway. That'd mean losing the upper hand, if she even had it.

Josue Bisset smiled slowly and easily. 'I'd better take my bags and get out of your way. I've caused enough trouble for one night.' His face softened further, making his mouth even more delectable.

He was probably used to winning over obstinate women. He was built, tall and broad with looks to match. Women would lap up anything he said or did. But surely not a home invasion? Okay, a slight exaggeration now that she understood why he was here, but still. *Still what?* What to do next came to mind. *Nothing.* Let him get on his way and she could take that shower she'd been hankering for over the last hour. But she had yet to explain about Kayla.

Mallory walked through the sitting room to the double doors opening into her kitchen-dining space. 'It's not as straightforward as that.' With Shade nudging the back of her leg, she dumped the pizza on the bench and opened the pantry. Shade seemed to have decided to ignore Josue, which gave her hope he was all he appeared to be, a friendly, honest man who'd made a genuine mistake. Hopefully Kayla had had him checked out before offering him a room in her house. Hadn't he mentioned her brother?

'I take it you know Dean?' she called over her shoulder, and gasped when she saw Josue had followed her and was looking around the kitchen with something like hope.

He locked a steady gaze on her. 'I worked with him in Wellington.'

Fine. Dean wouldn't have sent him to his sister if he'd had any concerns. She filled Shade's bowl with food and placed it on a mat beside the water bowl. 'There you go, my girl.'

Her uninvited guest now stood with his hip against the kitchen counter, his nose crinkling as he breathed deep while looking at the pizza box. The mouth-watering smell of bacon and cheese and mixed herbs was probably getting to him. It was certainly reminding her how hungry she'd been before she'd seen the light on in here.

He said, 'Dean and I get on very well, and he showed me around some interesting places during my time in the capital.'

It was a reference of sorts, Mallory supposed as she filled the kettle. It wasn't her place to change the arrangements, except they might not be the same any more. Kayla's parents would be on the road to Dunedin, if they hadn't already arrived, and they'd surely have contacted Dean about what had happened. But then the last thing that would be on Dean's mind would be the doctor moving into his sister's house.

'I know nothing about what you've organised but unfortunately things have changed. Kayla won't be coming home tonight, or for some weeks.' Kayla's parents would insist she stay with them until she was up on her feet again, and who knew how long that would take? 'She and two other people were caught on the edge of an avalanche this afternoon. Fortunately, they all survived but Kayla's injuries are serious. Both legs broken and a severe concussion at the very least. I was part of the team that airlifted her off the mountain earlier. She's now in a hospital in Dunedin.'

Shock filled those steady eyes. 'That's awful. I'm sorry to hear that. Have you heard any more about her condition since you returned to Queenstown?'

'No, but I'm unlikely to until her parents find out more. The paramedic thought Kayla would need surgery on her legs. They were in a bad way. She's going to hate being restricted by casts and crutches.' So much for getting back on track and recharging her energy, which had disappeared since her husband had died. 'Hopefully she'll be fine once she gets past the shock.' Mallory turned away to wipe a hand over her damp cheeks. Life was so unfair to some people. 'She's one of my closest friends.'

A light touch on her shoulder told her she wasn't alone, that Josue understood she was upset. It felt good, and totally out of place. She might have become a little restless with her life, due to not having anyone special to make a future with, but this good-looking Frenchman who claimed he was only here temporarily wasn't going to help one little bit. A short future was not what she intended next time she got involved with a guy. But it would have been good to download after today's drama. Drama he'd added to, she reminded herself.

He must've sensed her tension because he stepped back, putting space between them, not being intrusive. 'I do hope very much she's going to be all right. Maybe Dean's left a message to update me.' He pulled out his phone and shook his head. 'Nothing, but he's probably on his way south and, to be fair, there's no reason why I should be at the top of his list of people to tell.'

She was grateful for his small gesture of understanding and for not overdoing it. It made her feel she wasn't dealing with this completely alone, which was silly as she could talk to Maisie any time. 'I didn't know about you coming to stay, though Kayla did try to tell me something before the medical staff whisked her inside the hospital. She wasn't talking coherently and I'm only guessing it might've been about you.' *Now what?* Did she offer a complete stranger a room for the night? It wasn't in her to kick him out when he was new to town, though he could probably still go along the road to the other house.

'It was a last-minute arrangement after the accommodation I'd organised was withdrawn due to someone else now not leaving.' Doubt was filtering through the exhaustion coming off the man in waves. 'Maybe I should go into town and find a hotel for the night. I don't want to cause any more worries for Kayla or Dean.' Again, he locked his gaze on her. 'Or you. I am very sorry for this.' His apology sounded genuine.

'Don't worry about it.' She was shattered, her brain whirring all over the place. What were the choices? 'It's not up to me to say, but it sounds like there'd be no problem if you want to go to the house.' The guy was dropping on his feet, and obviously hungry by the way he kept glancing at the cooling pizza. Just as well she'd ordered an extra-large one. There went tomorrow's lunch. Shifting the box to the table, she collected plates and paper napkins, and nodded. 'Let's eat. Maybe you should try to get hold of Dean afterwards.'

'I will.' Hope was filling his eyes and lifting his drooping shoulders.

Mallory yawned, no longer able to hold herself upright, her whole body starting to sag with her own share of exhaustion. The need for a hot shower was becoming urgent, which was a normal response after a tricky rescue flight, especially when it involved someone she knew, something that happened quite often as she'd grown up here. Today's trip, flying Kayla to the hospital, had been particularly gruelling. Her friend was barely getting her life back together and then this. Now Mallory just wanted to unwind, but there was a foreigner in her house who needed help. And a lock on the bathroom door in case he wasn't as genuine as she'd begun to think.

Shade was happily chomping her way through her food, the tinny clicks against the bowl as she tongued up dried biscuits loud in the sudden silence. If she wasn't perturbed by their visitor, Mallory believed she was safe. After closing the curtains in the lounge and kitchen-dining area, she flicked on the heat pump that she'd forgotten to pre-set that morning, and said, 'Let's eat before we do anything else.'

Josue pulled out a chair for her. 'You are being so kind. As I said, I'm Josue, from Nice. I'm working at the hospital for two months before going home. I'm also joining the search and rescue outfit. Can I ask your name?' He held out his hand.

She hadn't told him? Of course she hadn't. She'd been too busy asserting herself. Slipping her hand into his to give a friendly shake, she ignored the heat that spilled into her and said, 'Mallory Baine.' She studied his face more deeply and nearly gasped. Talk about being blind before, or perhaps she had been too focused on him as an intruder and not a man, because now she saw good looking didn't begin to describe him.

A strong jawline, a hint of stubble darkening his chin and lower cheeks, generous lips and those big eyes that seemed to miss nothing. Wow. Then what he'd said dropped into her bemused head, and she tugged free of that warm grasp. 'I volunteer for S and R. That's why I was flying tonight.' So this man would be on her patch over the coming weeks. Seemed they had been destined to meet, which shouldn't be an issue, except for the sudden tapping going on under her ribs that wasn't about finding a stranger in her house, and more about how he was waking up her stalled libido. It had been a while since her last fling, and she didn't want another. These days she was more inclined to want the whole package. And Josue wasn't going to be that. Apparently, he was here short term, while she was looking for someone to share the bed *and* mow the lawns. Someone to have a family with.

'We'll be seeing a bit of each other then,' he replied, unknowingly agreeing with her earlier thoughts.

The accompanying smile went straight to her chest, spreading tendrils of warmth throughout the chill brought on by tiredness and the shock of finding a stranger in her house. Though she was getting used to him already. *Tap, tap*, went her pulse. *Shut up.*

'I guess we will. S and R can be busy.' This was getting out of hand. She'd met Josue less than fifteen minutes ago in the oddest situation and already he had her thinking about him in ways she didn't usually consider men. Two particular horrors having hurt her in the past had, until recently, kept her only wanting the occasional fling. Lately, though, she'd started wanting to find that one person to live with and love and share everything, even when there wasn't much time in her hectic life for a relationship, which was a deliberate ploy to keep her mind *off* what she didn't have and *on* what she did.

When she wasn't working, rescuing or keeping the property up to scratch, she was with her widowed mother at the dementia unit, painting her nails, combing her hair or searching for hidden possessions.

The worst thing Mallory had ever had to do in her life had been to admit her mother into full-time care. It had become necessary when she'd gone for a walk in the middle of the night last winter without a clue where she was. She'd been looking for Mallory's father, the love of her life. Not a safe thing to do under the best of circumstances, and a wake-up call for Mallory about her mother's mental state.

'Have you done search and rescue before?' she asked Josue, more to keep the conversation going than a serious need to learn anything about him.

'*Oui*. In France and then in Wellington. I think it might be physically more challenging in the Wakatipu terrain than anything I've done before.'

'The mountains are tough, the bush as dense as anywhere in the country and the rivers freezing even in summer.' She nodded at her German shepherd now happily curled up on a dog bed. 'Shade works the land searches.'

One brown eye opened at the sound of her name, and Shade thumped her tail.

Josue nodded. 'She has the strong build required to spend hours walking in all sorts of weather and terrain.'

'She loves it.' Opening the box, she nodded at the pizza. 'Help yourself. It won't be very hot now. Do you want me to reheat it?'

'*Merci*. This is good of you. I'm starving. It'll be fine as is. By the time I arrived in Queenstown all I wanted was to get to the house, but I should've stopped to get something to eat. I must've given you a fright, being in your house.' Again, that smile.

'"Fright" was one word for it.'

'What's another?' His smile widened. Used to charming his way through a woman's doubts?

'Disappointment.' Her return smile was tired but cheeky.

One eyebrow rose. 'Disappointment? You felt let down? How did I manage to do that by being inside your house uninvited?' He was still smiling at her.

Mallory surprised herself by laughing. 'I was shocked when I saw the lights on. I wasn't expecting anyone, but when I saw that case on my porch, I hoped my other close friend had decided to surprise me with a visit.' It would've been perfect timing after Kayla's accident. They'd have talked half the night and convinced each other Kayla would be fine.

'Instead you found a sleepy Frenchman on the couch who'd messed up putting correct directions into his GPS.' He nodded. 'Yes, I can understand your disappointment.' His low laugh went straight to her blood, ramping up the pace and heat. 'At least I didn't scare you into considering doing something dangerous to me.'

'You wouldn't be sitting here munching on pizza if I'd had any serious qualms at all. Instead, Zac would be hauling you down to the police station by the scruff of your neck.'

'Zac?'

'A local policeman who lives around the corner.' The advantage of knowing many people in this town was having their numbers just a touch away. 'I'm thinking we shouldn't bother Dean tonight. Obviously, you can go to Kayla's house, but...' She hesitated. What she was about to say seemed pointless when the other house was a minute away, but Josue was shattered and alone, and she knew from experience how debilitating that could feel. Rapidly squashing unwanted images, she drew a breath and said, 'If you want to doss down here for the night and move along the road tomorrow, you're welcome.' Shade would be more than happy to sleep in her room, just in case she was completely wrong about him.

'Doss?'

'Grab a bed.'

'You'd trust a stranger to stay in your house?'

'If Dean's okay about you staying with Kayla then it's all right with me.' Kayla would've quizzed her brother for hours about this man. She took no risks about her safety. Except today she'd obviously got that wrong, but nothing would've indicated she was about to be knocked out by an avalanche.

Mallory knew about bad luck. Hers had come about because of her choice in men. Jasper had been bad enough, but they'd been teenagers, and she'd had a lot to learn. Whereas she'd been twenty-four when she'd moved in with Hogan, who'd turned out to be a right scrounger who had been enough to make her think twice for a long time about getting caught up with another man. A man she could trust with her heart again.

She did want to take another chance, and sometimes wondered if she was like her parents and would find the right match when she was older. In the meantime, she was cautious in a friendly way. But the restlessness over not having her own family was growing harder to deal with as the months went by. A loving man and kids were all that was missing from her life.

Her gaze went to Josue, who was watching her as he munched pizza. Waiting for her to retract her offer? He looked honest and decent, and there was a twinkle in his eyes when he wasn't yawning. Okay, so she might be too trusting, but better that than always being overly careful. Was Josue wondering how to answer her invitation? Had she put him on the spot somehow? 'Would you prefer to stay here or go along the road to the other house?'

'I'll stay, *merci*. I think you're right. It'll be best to get in touch with Dean tomorrow.'

'That's settled.' Taking a surreptitious look at her guest,

she hoped she hadn't gone and done the wrong thing. Fingers crossed he was as decent as he looked.

When Mallory got up to make tea, she glanced down at her overalls. She never wore them inside, and certainly not while she ate dinner, even at her most knackered. She still had her boots on! 'I'll show you the room you'll use and then I'm taking a shower. There's an en suite bathroom attached to your room.'

She'd grown up in this house and still used her original bedroom, which had been enlarged when she'd been a teen. Her dad had died five years ago, which had been the catalyst for her mum starting to become lost in her own little world. Her parents had been so close they'd only functioned 100 per cent when they'd been together. It mightn't have caused the dementia, but her mum had never been the same since the day they'd buried Mallory's dad at the cemetery near Lake Wakatipu.

Mallory knew she'd been a surprise for her parents and, going by the loving atmosphere she'd grown up in, a very welcome one. They'd doted on her, even when she'd messed up big time and become pregnant, then depressed when she'd lost her baby due to an ectopic pregnancy. A stark memory flared of the physical and mental pain of losing her baby, while her boyfriend could only say with relief that they were too young to be parents anyway and that the surgical procedure had not only saved her life but their individual futures.

Her mum and dad had devoted all their time to her until she was back on her feet and then when she'd gone looking for a new career. The nursing course she had enrolled for had no longer been appealing, with thoughts of dealing with other people's pain dragging her down. Her mum had been disappointed as she'd wanted her daughter to follow in her footsteps, but she'd rallied and backed Mallory all the way when she'd decided on flying helicopters and, despite a fear of flying, had been Mallory's first passenger when she'd been allowed to take people up.

Now it was Mallory's turn to give her mother everything she could, including staying here in Queenstown for the foreseeable future, and spending time with her whenever possible. She'd already turned down with few regrets the dream job of flying rescue choppers in Nelson. Family came first, no matter what.

She led Josue to her parents' old room. 'Anything you want, just shout out.' She turned away. Bring on the shower. Nothing like a long, hot soak to ease the kinks in her back. The wind had been strong on the mountain, and along with the worry over Kayla, the thought of starting another avalanche with the downdraught from the rotors had been high on her mind, even though where she'd flown there had been little chance. Exhaustion always came after the adrenaline rush.

As the water pummelled the ache between her shoulder blades, relief at getting Kayla to safety finally pushed out the negatives, giving her that sense of satisfaction she got after a positive retrieval. Not that her friend would be pleased with where she was right now, but better that than at the bottom of the gulley with tons of snow on top.

As Mallory's body warmed, her mind wandered to the man down the hallway. Josue Bisset. Funny how Josue sounded sexier than Joshua. Softer, as though filled with hidden anticipation. And he was sexy, now that she had time to see him not as a problem but a man who had come to her district to work and help those in trouble out in the wilderness. Tall men with broad shoulders tapering down to narrow hips did it for her every time. Throw in a dazzling smile and vibrant eyes and she was a sucker for trouble.

Unreal how quickly she'd gone from anger to this unexpected curiosity about him. It was as though he was pushing buttons hidden deep inside her, reminding her it was time to have some fun again and to nudge the restlessness aside for a while. But to do that with her intruder? She grinned. That might become his name for his time in Queenstown. The Intruder. A darned sexy, interesting intruder at that. She didn't throw herself at men and yet she felt she wouldn't be averse to spending time with Josue. Then again, maybe not. He wasn't staying here forever, and she was.

Having witnessed her parents' deep love for each other, it was inherent to want the same, and so far she hadn't come close. At thirty-two she was starting to wonder if she'd be waiting till her forties, like her mother. *Not till I'm fifty as dad was, please.* Her family had been close, so special, she dreamed of attaining the same for herself. Sometimes she wondered if she was just hoping for too much. She wanted another chance to have a baby and yet was terrified of a repeat of last time. What if she had another ectopic pregnancy? And what if she couldn't conceive at all?

Hogan had accused her of being ungrateful for what they had, saying she wanted her dreams of love to come true when life wasn't like that. He might've been right, but she wasn't giving up yet. She'd gradually fallen out of love with him and he hadn't taken kindly to that, saying she was selfish. When she'd asked him to leave the flat she'd paid for, he'd left the next day while she was at work, transferring online her savings to his account on the way. So much for trusting him.

The water ran cool. Damn, she'd forgotten to tell Josue not to have a shower while this one was in use. Turning off the shower, she reached for a towel. The system didn't work properly when more than one hot tap was on at a time. She really should get around to having the plumber come by, except it seemed like an expense she didn't need when mostly she was the only one living here. Josue was here for one night. He wouldn't be causing problems with the system much longer.

Josue. She stared into the mirror. What did he see when looking at her? Freckles, green eyes, and wavy hair tied back out of the way for work. He'd seen her in her overalls so did that mean he missed the feminine side she kept out of sight while at work because she didn't want the men treating her any differently? It never bothered her what anyone thought of her appearance in heavy duty boots and sensible clothes for all seasons, but when she wasn't at work there was an array of soft blouses and tight trousers hanging in the wardrobe to relax into, shoes with heels and fashionable boots in bright shades of red and mustard and blue.

At home the hair came down to spill over her shoulders, blonde against the sky-blue satin PJs she was about to put on. They probably wouldn't impress a classy Frenchman. His casual clothes might be messed up, but they were stylish. But again, so what? This was home and she was being herself, sexy Frenchman hanging about or not.

Slipping a thick white robe over the PJs, she unlocked the door and headed to the kitchen to make that tea she'd been hanging out for since pulling up to the house.

Josue pulled on loose sports trousers and a sweatshirt. He hoped Mallory wouldn't mind if he made coffee. Being one of his bad habits from the years studying medicine, it didn't keep him awake. Besides, he was exhausted after the long day travelling and needed a caffeine fix. He'd been so happy about coming to Queenstown he hadn't bothered to stop for a night on the way down the South Island.

The scenery had been stunning, but then mountains always upped his pulse rate. They were magical, and dangerous, and he enjoyed any time spent on one. They were the reason he'd decided to spend the last months of his New Zealand trip down here. Getting more insight into search and rescue in such rugged terrain to take home to use if he found a doctor's position at a skiing location, as he intended, was a bonus.

Looking at the bed, he knew he couldn't go there yet. There was too much going on in his head. Mostly about the woman who'd looked ready to boot him out on his backside when she'd first strode into her house and found him on her couch. She'd been equally shocked and angry, and right away had appeared determined he wasn't going to get the better of her. Not that he'd had any intention of trying to best her. He'd been the one in the wrong.

But, wow, she was something else, standing straight, her eyes fixed on him, her voice strong. Intriguing, to say the least. And gorgeous. Those freckles sprinkled across her cheeks she apparently didn't try to hide under layers of heavy make-up like some women he'd known made him long to kiss her gently. They were like a sign saying there was a wonderful woman behind the stance telling him not to mess with her, and that there was another, softer side to her strength hidden away from prying eyes.

He'd messed up completely on arrival, but who'd have thought both women hid the keys to their houses in the same place? And that they were friends? Even then, he should've realised when he'd walked into the house and seen all those photos hanging on the wall he'd presumed were of Kayla and her parents. He'd been so taken with the love in everyone's faces he hadn't realised Dean was missing in the pictures. Mallory and who he now presumed were her parents looked so happy cuddled together that an old envy had filled his heart.

Growing up in foster homes, he'd never known anything like that. In fact, he often didn't quite believe people who said they were so in love the world was permanently rosy, yet those photos told him different. Love could be real. But was it possible for the likes of him who'd been left on a doorstep at twelve months old?

Gabriel always insisted it was and he had shown him great affection since the day he'd taken Josue under his wing to help sort his life out. At fifteen, Josue had been going off the rails in the direction of a life of crime when the policeman who'd arrested him for theft had given him a talking-to like no other, basically saying he had two choices in life and not to blame anyone else for which path he took.

Gabriel and his wife had taken him in a few months later and had stood by him as he'd fumbled his way out of trouble and into study and work, eventually making it to medical school and into a career the boy whose mother had abandoned had never imagined. The policeman and Brigitte had been the first to love him unconditionally and he had given the same back, warily at first and then with all his being.

But he'd never found that kind of love with a woman. Perhaps because he always backed off before they could reject him, like most other people had in the past. He wasn't counting casual friends. They came and went and that was fine. It was the ones who could have loved him, and hadn't, that had him fearful of being hurt again. Gabriel and Brigitte had been the first to show him unconditional love and he had to learn to return it. Twice he'd started to get close to a woman before fearing they wouldn't give him the love he craved and so he'd run.

Josue hauled air into his lungs and sighed slowly. It was an old story and he really should let it alone—especially now when he was in a wonderful country where he'd been welcomed with open arms and was having a great time. He didn't have to juggle emotions over a relationship because he wasn't getting into one.

Looking around, he sighed. This house wasn't where he was meant to be, wasn't number 142. A simple mistake with no serious consequences. If he had reached the right destination he'd probably still be lying on a couch, snoozing or awake, wondering where his hostess was. At least he had the answer to that question. He'd call Dean tomorrow to find out how his sister was and make sure her house was still available. If not, he'd look for somewhere else, no problem.

He took another glance around. It'd be great to stay here but Mallory wouldn't want him hanging out in her space. She came across as independent and not needing company in the evenings while winter raged outside. Then again, she might be a complete softy on the inside. After all she had given him, a stranger, a bed for the night rather than sending him along the road to a cold, empty house.

He was daydreaming. At the moment he had arrangements in place and wouldn't be changing them on a whim. A fascinating, gorgeous whim, though. Mallory hadn't flinched when she'd found him in her house, hadn't been fearful or stroppy. Not that he'd have wanted to push her good nature. He suspected she'd have had him on the floor with a foot on his back while she phoned the police if she'd had any doubts about why he'd come to be here. How embarrassing to be found in a stranger's home, looking like he was meant to be there, though that was probably what had saved him from having his backside kicked.

Mallory might be small, but she was strong. Not once had her shoulders dropped while sussing him out, her gaze had never wavered, and her tone had pierced him with a warning that he'd better be genuine or watch out.

'Josue,' a gentle, kind voice called from the kitchen, showing yet another side to Mallory. She straightened up from petting Shade as he joined her. 'I'm making tea. You want one?'

He gasped internally. Mallory wore pyjamas, the summer-sky shade making her eyes gleam. They drew him in. Dampness, no doubt from the shower, made her blonde hair darker. It fell in thick waves down her back and over her shoulders to her breasts. Her white robe was tied tightly around a tiny waist. Was this the same woman who'd been wearing shapeless overalls and thick work socks inside heavy boots? This version was feminine and lovely.

His breathing stuttered, as though his lungs were confused over taking air in or huffing it out. The other version had been gorgeous, but this Mallory? Gasp. Out of this world. His finger and thumb pinched his thigh. Reality returned through a sudden haze of lust. Why had he put the wrong damned number in the GPS? He was in for a sleepless night knowing this woman was in the same house.

'Josue?' Confusion scrunched her face. 'Tea?'

Tea? What? Shaking his head, he finally got his act together. 'Would you mind if I have coffee?' He crossed his fingers. 'As in real coffee?' Glancing over the benches, he smiled. 'It's okay. I see you have some.' Instant coffee was worse than none at all.

'Help yourself.'

'Merci.' Mallory was already treating him as though he fitted right in, moving around him in the small space as she prepared her tea. It made him feel good, like he mattered in a relaxed way. Even though it was casual and not deep and meaningful, that warmed him throughout. It wasn't something he'd had a lot of. None of the foster families he'd been placed with had been so quick to accept him, if they'd ever even got there. Only Gabriel and Brigitte had right from the get-go, and that had been massive as at the time he'd been the worst kind of brat possible. They were the reason he was heading home after this job, to be there when Gabriel had his heart surgery, to support both of them.

Yet, despite all they'd done for him, the memories remained of how every time he'd met a new family his hopes of being liked and cared about had been dashed. It was as though he had to prove himself every time he met someone, and as a kid he'd turned his anger to hurting others by stealing from them. Gabriel had soon talked sense into him, saying he was hurting himself more than anyone else. It was true, but he'd never quite got over being on edge when he first met someone.

Of course he mattered, as a man and as a doctor. He did believe it, but there was a hole inside that he just couldn't fill. In the two instances when he'd thought he'd come close with women he'd cared for, Colette and Liza, he'd continually questioned his feelings and their reactions to him, eventually leading those relationships to failure. So why was he feeling like he mattered here with this woman in a way he'd not known before? As though he just might be able to find that settled life he craved? It was a foreign sensation. Because she'd shared her pizza? Offered him a room? Or because she wandered around her kitchen as though he'd always been there?

No doubt he was overreacting to her kindness, but a rare warmth was spreading throughout him, surprising and confusing him. Should he be pleased or worried? He obviously wasn't having the same effect on Mallory. Which had to be good, he supposed, if he wanted to get to know her better, as he liked to do with locals wherever he was working. That way he learned more about the area, where best to ski, hike, eat and drink.

Right now he'd like to do all those things with Mallory. Already he knew that? *Oui*, he did, if that's what this unusual sense of anticipation meant. But, like everything he did, if he acted on these sensations waking up his manhood, it would be short term. He knew too well that the itch to move on would strike, as it had done all his life, after going from one foster family to the next, a new school each time, new people to get to know and try to impress.

Gabriel and Brigitte were the people he returned to often and kept in constant contact with when away from Nice. As a teen he'd had his own room in their house, and it was still his. Only with them did he have a complete sense of belonging. There was no family history to hold on to.

The only information he had was that his father had died when he was twelve months old and his mother had never replied to any of the letters he'd written to her as a child. *If she ever got them.* He'd met her briefly when he was fourteen. She had told him she'd started taking drugs soon after he was born and by the time she'd left him, she'd got deeper into the criminal world to feed her habit.

She believed she'd done the right thing by her son and to have visited him at all would have been worse than staying away. After that meeting, she had gone again and not many months later he'd learned she'd died of an overdose.

Mallory brushed past him, steaming mug in hand, as she headed for the lounge.

He was being gloomy. His life had moved on, improved, and there were all sorts of opportunities out there if he let go of the past. Letting the coffee stand, he joined Mallory, settling into a large leather armchair. 'Tell me about flying helicopters. What work do you do?'

A tired smile stretched her mouth wide and lit up her equally tired eyes. 'My full-time job mostly involves flying sightseeing trips up to the snow slopes or around the mountains, out to Milford Sound. Sometimes there are other trips, taking business people to cities up and down the South Island. It keeps me busy, and volunteering for Search and Rescue is an added bonus. My boss is happy for me to help out, but it has to be in my free time.'

Josue could listen to her voice all night. The Kiwi accent was sharper than European ones, but he liked its clarity, especially mixed with Mallory's softness. *Careful, Jos.* It was strange to be feeling a woman's voice, looks, attitude as warm and encompassing so easily. Could he finally be moving past the doubts that usually blocked him from believing anything was possible? Yet he was still overthinking everything. Though he was feeling more relaxed and comfortable than usual, none of that meant he could suddenly settle into a stable life and always be there for a woman he might fall in love with.

'As an S and R volunteer I also do some of the rescue flights, though I'm only the back-up pilot when others are unable to attend.'

'Like today.'

Her mouth dropped, and she blinked rapidly. 'Yes. Any rescue that involves seriously injured people, or worse, upsets me, and not only when it's someone very close to me.'

He wanted to hug away that pain, but they didn't know each other well enough. She might misinterpret the gesture. 'I understand, but those sentiments are why we do the job in the first place.' Was she completely relaxed with him? *Why question it, Jos? Just accept Mallory for who she appears to be.* His heart softened. Not many people in his past had been so accepting of him so fast. They'd wanted to know his history in other foster homes and schools before they'd asked if he liked eating beef, if they asked anything personal.

As an adult, he still looked for that reaction, and found it hard these days to accept that it was normal curiosity that had people asking questions about his job, family, past. His fault, but another old habit hard to let go. It stopped his expectations getting away from him, and stopped him from even beginning to wonder if he could be a good father if he ever got into a permanent relationship.

The TV remote Mallory had picked up remained still in her hand. 'There's also the adventure of heading out on foot into the bush or up a mountain to look for people who've got into trouble.' She spoke faster, higher, and the spark was back in her gaze.

'You're an adrenaline junkie?'

Now a grin came his way. 'As long as I operate safely and carefully, yes.'

He usually liked quiet women, not ones who attacked the world, but here he was, enjoying Mallory's company a lot. Was he more tired than he realised? Or was this the attraction? 'Remind me not to have an argument with you.' He didn't know if the adrenaline junkie ever took over from the careful, safe woman at the controls.

Her laughter filled the room, and his chest. 'Think I'd toss you out of the chopper?'

'Not a chance. I'm not going for a ride with you.' His grin came automatically, as though he was totally at ease with Mallory. At this realisation, his mouth flattened and he went to pour his coffee, trying to stifle the sudden sense there was a storm coming his way, one that would pick him up and shake out the past, open the gates to hope and something far more foreign—happiness. And stability.

His over-tired mind was playing games with him. He really knew nothing about this woman, and certainly not enough to wipe away everything that had kept him strong and safe over the years. Glancing around, his gaze landed on one of the photos that had caught at his heart earlier. Mallory sitting on the sofa she was on now, with her *maman* and *père* beside her, smiles splitting everyone's faces and love filling their eyes. Did she know how lucky she was? Lucky they had been there for her, had kept her with them and loved her so much?

For once he didn't feel the bitterness that rose when he saw families together like this. The air of confidence clinging to Mallory suggested that her family's love had made her strong and kind; the reasons he was staying here tonight and not along the road in an empty house. Envy touched him before it disappeared into a fragile happiness over being with a woman who demanded nothing of him he wasn't prepared to give. Too early to be thinking that, maybe, but he couldn't deny she was getting under his skin, touching him in a way that was foreign to him, but he still seemed to understand.

Tomorrow he'd wake up and realise he was an idiot and that this was all to do with exhaustion and wishful thinking. Not reality with a kind, sexy woman at the centre.

CHAPTER TWO

MALLORY'S PHONE INTERRUPTED the comfortable silence stretching out between her and Josue as they sat in the sunny conservatory the next morning, drinking coffee. Dean had called him to say he could still use Kayla's house as it would be a while before she was back to something like normal and able to get around the house.

Seeing the incoming number on her screen, she said, 'Uh-oh, looks like you're on your own for the rest of the morning. It's Jamie. He's from Search and Rescue, and Chief Fire Officer here.'

'I'm available if an extra body is required,' Josue told her.

She nodded. 'Hey, Jamie. We got a job to do?'

'Two young lads wandered away from their fathers in the hills near Gibbston nearly two hours ago. They were beside the river. You available?'

Why did the fathers wait so long to call for help? It was winter and it would be freezing out there. 'Yes.' She glanced at Josue. 'I've got Josue Bisset here. He's going to join S and R. He's done rescue work and is a doctor.'

'Bring him along.' Jamie gave her details of their meeting point. 'See you ASAP.'

'Got it.' She put the phone down. 'Guess learning your way

around Kayla's house will have to wait. Jamie wants you on board.'

'Great.' He was already standing.

'Get changed into weatherproof gear. We'll get on the road in five. There's some way to travel to join up with the team. Shade, here, girl. You're going to work.'

Three hours later they were climbing through dense bush, following Shade's lead as she headed higher and closer to the river that was pouring down the ravine. 'Come on, girl. Find them,' Mallory said quietly, so as not to distract the dog, who was a little way ahead of them.

Howl.

Mallory stopped in her tracks. 'Shade?'

Howl.

It was what Mallory had been hoping for. Turning to the man behind her, she fist-pumped the air. 'Shade's found something. Hopefully the boys.' Her heart went out to her four-legged girl. *Please have found them.* Mallory strode out, ducking under low branches, following the rough track through the dense bush.

'I can hear the river.' Josue was directly behind her, not faltering in the rugged terrain that was foreign to him. 'Hopefully the boys haven't tried to enter it anywhere dangerous.'

'I doubt it, or Shade wouldn't have found them.' No one wanted to find bodies, not even her girl. 'It sounded like Shade's happy howl, and, yes—' she flicked a glance over her shoulder to her search partner '—she has happy and sad howls.' The radio crackled on her belt.

'Mallory? Did we just hear Shade?' Jamie, the search leader, asked.

'You did. Josue and I are making our way to her now.' She'd given the dog her head when she'd started getting agitated, a sure sign she was onto something. 'I'll send coordinates as soon as we know what we've got.' Slipping the radio back on her belt, she called, 'Shade.'

Woof, woof.

'Through there.' Josue veered off track to the right, taking the lead, ignoring the undergrowth, elbowing branches out of his way, turning back to make sure he hadn't flicked them in her face. *'Désolé.'*

'I'm fine.' She knew not to walk too close behind anyone in the bush. Not even when it was a man with the longest legs filling comfortably fitted black corduroy trousers tucked into trendy hiking boots; trousers that accentuated a tight butt that had her stomach doing loops. They'd automatically been paired up since she'd driven him to the starting point.

Josue broke through into daylight and stopped suddenly. *'Sacré bleu.'*

Mallory banged into the pack on his back. 'Oof. What? Let me see.' Was *sacré bleu* good or bad? She shoved around the man and looked across the riverbank to where Shade stood over two young boys, one prone and the other crying while trying to cuddle his pal. 'Wow.'

She began leaping over the rocks, aiming straight for them, pulling the radio free at the same time. 'Jamie, we've found them. Sending coordinates now.' As team leader he'd call the rest of the searchers, and soon everyone would be here to ascertain the situation. Glancing around, she knew it would be safe to bring in the rescue chopper to hover and lower the stretcher. Because of the proximity of the bush the helicopter wouldn't be landing on the narrow stretch of rocks. She'd call Scott, today's rescue pilot, shortly and give him the necessary details but first the boys needed attention. She wasn't even thinking the prostrate boy mightn't be alive. It wasn't an option.

Josue was already kneeling beside the boys and reaching for the inert one. 'Hello, Timmy and Morgan, we've been looking for you two. I'm Josue, a doctor, and this is Shade. She found you first. And this is Mallory. Shade's her dog.'

Mallory rubbed Shade's head. 'Well done, girl.' Turning to the boys, she added her bit. 'I am so happy to see you two.' The one holding his friend was shivering violently and his little face was white in contrast with blue lips. He didn't talk, just stared at them, eyes wide, breathing rapid and shallow, tears streaking down his cheeks.

Josue said, 'I've got this little man. He's barely conscious, by the look of things. Can you look after the other?'

'Yes.' She reached out to the lad. 'Your clothes are wet.' Saturated. She'd have to get him out of them and wrapped up in a thermal blanket. 'Have you been in the river?'

He nodded once. Then pointed to the nearby edge where the water was flowing slower than out in the middle.

They'd been lucky. 'Are you Timmy?'

He gave a slow headshake from side to side.

'So you're Morgan. What were you doing in the river?'

'Timmy fell on the rocks.'

'And you rescued him. What a great friend you are. That's wonderful.' These two had wandered off while their dads had been making a fire to cook a barbecue and had presumably got lost. That'd be frightening for youngsters, and even for adults inexperienced in the bush.

'He appears hypothermic,' Josue said after a quick glance their way. 'This boy is, too, though he's not wet through like your lad.'

Midwinter in the lower mountains, sunny it may be, but these kids were scared and small so it wouldn't have taken much time to lose body temperature, and they'd been missing for nearly five hours. Mallory leaned close to Josue and pulled the thermal blankets out of the pack he wore. 'Hopefully that's all they're suffering,'

'This boy's got a head wound, and he's not responding to stimulus, though that's possibly due to the hypothermia.' Josue opened the thermal blanket she'd handed over.

'Morgan, I need to check a few things about you. Can you feel it when I touch your hands?' Mallory asked quietly.

Another nod. 'Where's Dad?'

'He's waiting for you at the place where you were going to have a picnic.' She prodded his feet after removing his shoes. 'Feel that?'

He nodded.

Josue said quietly, 'Hello, Timmy. I'm Josue, a doctor. Morgan's right here. You've banged your head but you're going to be all right. I'm going to wrap you in this silver blanket. You'll feel warmer soon.'

More like he wouldn't get any colder, Mallory thought as she tugged at the jeans clinging to her boy like a second skin. Glancing across, she saw Timmy staring at Josue blankly. She nudged Morgan lightly. 'Say something to Timmy so he knows you're here and won't be frightened.'

'Timmy, it's okay. They found us.' Morgan's voice was high and squeaky, but Timmy's eyes opened further.

Pride swelled through Mallory. They had found these two in time. Thanks to Shade more than anyone really, but this was why she did these searches, to bring home the victims of the climate and terrain to their waiting families. Helping people who'd had a run of bad luck gave her a sense of being part of something bigger than herself.

'So,' she said, finally managing to get the jeans off and started to remove Morgan's jacket. 'Are you hurt anywhere?'

He rolled his head slowly from side to side. 'No.'

'That's good. I'm going to check your pulse to see how fast your heart is beating as soon as I've got you all wrapped up. What happened to you?'

'We went for a walk and got lost. We know to follow the river down but it was deep and fast so we stayed on the rocks, hoping Dad would find us. Then Timmy slipped.'

The radio crackled to life. 'Mallory? What have we got?' the incoming pilot asked. 'I'm fifteen minutes away.'

'In a minute,' she muttered as she tugged her jacket off to wrap around Morgan over the thermal blanket for added warmth. The chilly air immediately lifted goose bumps on her skin.

'Okay for them to have water?' she asked Josue. She'd been trained in treating hypothermia, had dealt with it in the past, but Josue was the doctor on the spot. There were water bottles in each of their packs, along with hot chocolate and sandwiches. The warm drink would help the boys' chilled bodies.

'Go ahead.'

Handing over a bottle to Josue for Timmy and one to her little patient, she called Scott and gave him the details he needed. 'See you shortly.'

Josue was talking slowly and quietly to the boys. 'Sip the water, don't gulp or you might cough it back up.' He had Timmy wrapped firmly in the blanket and was fingering the wound on the boy's forehead. 'Did you see Timmy fall, Morgan?' He was studying Timmy's wrist, which Mallory realised was at an odd angle.

The boy pulled a face. 'He was crying and not looking where he was going. He landed on his stomach and then his head banged the rocks. I had to get in the water to push him up. It only came to my ankles but then I slipped and got wet.'

'You're very brave,' Josue said, before turning to her. 'Warming Timmy up is going to cause the pain to return. At least he's a little more alert now so I can give him some ibuprofen.' Josue slipped off the pack and delved into it.

'What about a sling? Or will we be able to keep the arm still by wrapping the blanket tighter around his arm and chest?'

'Let's try wrapping him tight. He needs his whole body in that blanket. How's Morgan's pulse?'

'Low normal,' Mallory told him.

The boy stared at her. 'Why's Dad not here?'

'He's not far away.' Hadn't he heard her answer earlier? Or had he, too, banged his head? She ran her hands over his skull and found no damage.

'I want him now.'

'We're going to get you out of here very soon.' The boys were approximately four kilometres in a direct line from their picnic spot but would've covered a lot more zigzagging through the bush. The fathers had searched for them before calling in help and returning to the spot they'd started out from in case the boys returned of their own accord. That would've been hard for the dads, but sensible. Once the search teams had set out, they'd wanted to go with them, so a police officer had remained with them to keep either man from dashing into the bush to look for the boys and getting lost himself. 'Have you ever been in a helicopter?'

'No-o.'

'Well, guess what? You and Timmy are going to have a ride in one soon. Isn't that cool? Helicopters are so much fun.'

'Will Dad be in it?'

'There won't be a lot of spare room with you two, the pilot and Josue inside.'

'I want Dad to come with me.'

She gave Morgan a hug. 'I know you do. Now he knows we've found you he can meet you at the airport when the helicopter lands.'

Josue said, 'His voice isn't as slurred now, which is a good sign.'

Mallory dug out the flask of hot chocolate and poured Morgan a drink. 'Have you been in the bush before?'

'With Dad. It was scary today.' Morgan was crying now. 'We were having fun looking for weka birds, then we couldn't find our way back. We heard lots of awful noises.'

'Next time, if you get lost, stay where you are. That makes it easier for us to find you.'

'How?'

'We wouldn't have to walk so far in so many different directions. If not for Shade, we'd still be looking now.'

The sound of twigs snapping announced the arrival of Jamie

and Zac, followed shortly after by the rest of the crew, relief the only expression on everyone's face. A good result all round.

'I've called Base. Scott's on the way,' Jamie told them, not realising Mallory had been talking to the pilot. 'Josue, you're to go with the boys. There'll be an ambulance waiting with a paramedic at the airport, and Scott will give you a lift to where you're staying or to join the rest of us for a beer when we get out.' There was nothing more they could do now until the helicopter arrived.

Josue glanced her way, disappointment in his eyes. Why? Did he like hiking in this terrain that much? 'You can let yourself into my house again, if that's what you want.' She smiled now the stress of the search had slipped away. 'It's not as if you don't know where I keep the spare key.'

'I do.' A return smile came her way, making her all warm and happy.

A smile did that? Showed how good those smiles were. Or how quiet her life had become lately. 'Your gear's still there. You haven't had time to go grocery shopping either.' It sounded as though she was trying to convince him to stay another night. Was she? He couldn't stay for ever and Kayla would prefer someone was in her house while she was away.

There was confusion in his expression, probably because of how she'd mentioned him going to her house and not Kayla's. *Welcome to the club. I'm confused with myself too. And with you, Josue Bisset.* He intrigued her when it would be simpler to stay clear. Safer, anyway. 'Let's see what time I'm finished with the boys and that beer Jamie mentioned. Are you going to the pub?' he asked.

'I am. It's always good to wind down and talk the talk after a rescue. Otherwise I lie awake half the night, going through everything.'

'But today we had a good result.'

'I still like to go over it all, making sure there was nothing I could've done better.' Yep, she was a perfectionist.

'Do you discuss all this with Shade?' Another smile.

Another nudge in the stomach. 'Shade's usually happy to have a meal and lie down on her bed.' Or in front of the fire at the pub. 'She seems to think she does a perfect job and doesn't need to drag through the details.'

'Go, Shade.'

Hearing her name, Shade wandered over and rubbed her head against Josue's thigh.

Josue ran his hand down her back before returning his attention to Timmy's head wound and the reddened crepe bandage. 'The bleeding appears to have slowed to a trickle. *Merci.*' Then he added, 'I'll wait in town for you, Mallory, if that's all right? I'll hitch a ride with this Scott.'

'No problem. We'll sort you out yet.'

He gave a deep laugh that tightened her skin further than the goose bumps had managed to do. 'No rush.'

How long did he say he was staying in Queenstown? Two months? She should be able to manage some spare time to get to know him better, *if* she followed through on unravelling the puzzle that was Josue, making the most of the sense of excitement he caused in her.

Josue had an unnatural desire to hug Mallory before he climbed into the helicopter. It was almost as though he needed to say, 'See you soon,' because he didn't want to leave her alone to go back on foot to the vehicles they'd arrived in. Another overreaction, but he couldn't seem to stop them. She was lovely inside and out. And apparently a perfectionist.

Hearing her talk about needing to go through the details of a rescue regardless of a good outcome told him how caring and careful she was. As if he hadn't experienced that with her generous offer of a bed last night. She was refreshingly open and honest. Or was he being more open to her than he was used to being with other people he hardly knew? He and Dean had also hit it off straight away, and he'd found himself accepting people more readily than normal since arriving in this country.

Was that what getting away from his home turf had done? Or only Mallory? Had he started to open his eyes and heart to another way of approaching life after leaving France? Had he begun to change while living and working in Wellington, and now, with Mallory, was he beginning to realise it?

Just the thought excited him. If that was right, then he could finally be stepping into the sort of life he'd once dreamed of. A life of love, with a woman to share everything with. Children to give his heart to along with the things he'd missed out on, growing up. A life where he could trust himself with a home *and* a family. *No.* Not children. That was going too far. He knew nothing about being a good father, and he wasn't putting any kids through the hell he'd known growing up.

Laughter reached his ears from outside the chopper. Mallory stood with Jamie and some of the other rescuers, waiting for the aircraft to leave. She *was* special. Which should have him dancing on the spot. Instead his gut was cramped and his chest tight. Not coming from a steady background ultimately meant he wouldn't know how to achieve one for those he loved. Even if that woman was someone like Mallory, who readily accepted him as she saw him, how could she possibly understand his uncertainties?

While searching for the boys, they'd walked through the bush, up and down slopes, slipping in mud, and not once had Mallory checked to see if he was capable of keeping up, and therefore a competent part of the team. She took it for granted he was. When they'd reached the boys, she'd made way for the doctor and hadn't tried to show how competent she was as a first-aider.

Now he got to fly out, while she'd be walking back the way they'd come, though probably on a more direct route. The doctor in him accepted it was his role to go with the boys and he had no intention of arguing. As a man he'd like nothing better than to walk out of the bush with this woman who'd managed to open his heart a little after only knowing her one night.

Her easy acceptance of him in her home last night after she'd got over the shock and her annoyance had blown him away. She hadn't walked up and said welcome, make yourself at home, but she had taken his explanation and had obviously added it to what little she knew about Dean's sister having someone to stay, and had been okay with his presence. He shook his head. Unbelievable. Not because of his past, but because she'd had every right to tell him to leave and sort the problem out himself. He had erred when he'd put in the street number, but if the two women hadn't hidden keys in the same places, surely he would've finally worked out he was in the wrong place?

'Josue, the boys are strapped in and ready to go. You need to strap yourself in, too.' Jamie stood just beyond the opening on the side of the chopper, bringing him back to reality with a clunk.

Reality in that Mallory may be coming up on his radar as special, but he wouldn't be staying on after his months here were up. He had always intended to return to Nice, the place where he belonged even if his roots were vague and a big let-down. New Zealand had given him a visa for two years, but he'd only planned on staying for one, knowing the inability to settle would drive him away sooner rather than later. Besides, he'd promised to return home for Gabriel's surgery later in the year anyway. 'Onto it. See you shortly.' He reached out to slide the door shut and then focused on the boys in front of him. 'Morgan, are you feeling all right?'

'Why does the helicopter shake so much?'

'That's because the rotors on top are going faster and faster. Soon we'll be off the ground and you won't notice the shaking so much.' He turned to look Timmy over. The boy's eyes were closed again. 'Timmy,' he called quietly.

Timmy opened his eyes and looked around. 'Where's my dad?' he cried.

'Both your dads are heading to the hospital, but we're going to get there quicker. They have to drive all the way.' Hopefully the mothers were already on the way from their homes in town. These little guys were overdue some hugs and loving.

Looking out the window in search of Mallory, he saw her walking into the bush, being swallowed by the thick manuka trees, Shade right on her heels. 'See you soon,' he whispered, before turning back to his charges. 'Hey, Morgan, this is fun, isn't it?'

It was now they'd found the boys and were getting them out to safety. It gave him a thrill and made him happy to have helped. It was one of the best things he'd been doing in this country. He owed Gabriel for convincing him to come here.

'You need to get away and take a long hard look at everything that's happened to you from a distance,' Gabriel had said as he'd driven Josue home from visiting his mother's gravesite for the first time.

'What do you mean?' Josue had asked. 'Nothing would've saved my mother from the drugs but herself, and she obviously hadn't wanted to.' Seeing the grave had raised old emotions that had torn through him like a sharp knife, reminding him of what he'd missed out on.

'Everyone chooses their own path.' Gabriel repeated what he'd said the first time they met. 'It's up to you how you deal with life's obstacles.'

'True. But how would going away change anything?' Josue asked around the bitterness.

'You might find closure. You could see the world through lighter eyes, a calmer mind. You could be so busy enjoying yourself, you'll forget to haul the past along every step of your life.'

'You going to tell me where to go too?'

Gabriel shook his head. 'No, my man, that's entirely up to you.' Then he spoilt it by saying, 'Some place with mountains and not many people where you can be yourself.'

'Next you'll be naming a country.' Josue had laughed then. 'You've always talked about New Zealand.'

'I knew it. You can't help yourself.' Josue stared out the window at the passing traffic, the idea growing as they made their way home.

And here he was—enjoying himself.

'Shade won't be able to walk if you guys keep feeding her like that,' Mallory admonished gently, softness in her heart as she watched her pet lying in front of the large open fire. Shade was a trouper, and today she'd proved yet again just how clever she was at tracking. Now everyone was spoiling her rotten for leading the team to the boys.

'She deserves every steak she gets,' Josue called from the bar, where he was buying another round of beers for the group. Hopefully no more steak for her dog, though. 'She's not exactly overweight.' His French accent seemed stronger in here surrounded by so many Kiwis. Still as sexy, though.

Not that she'd given the doctor, whose black jersey and corduroy trousers covered a body more suited to a basketball player in his prime, a lot of thought this afternoon other than how he worked as a partner in the rescue. He'd known what he was doing, even when the terrain was foreign, though apparently he had done some time helping in searches out of Wellington, which was similar but not as difficult.

He hadn't hesitated at fording freezing creeks or trudging through mud that sucked their boots down and fought letting go. And, yes, she was lying to herself. When he'd gone ahead of her, she'd been fully aware of him as a man. But they'd been in unison about what they were out there for. 'You saying I starve Shade?' She gave him a smile.

'Not after what you fed her last night. Or this morning.'

She'd given Shade an extra meal once she'd heard they were off on a search, as sustenance never went astray when the dog put her heart into finding someone.

Mallory had slept in that morning, which told her how safe she'd felt with Josue in her house, and how much Kayla's accident had affected her. She'd phoned her friend's mother and learned Kayla had had rods implanted in her right leg and that the break in the left one wasn't anywhere near as serious. The concussion was severe and only time would help that. Mallory had passed on her love, explained that Josue had stayed with her last night, and said not to worry about a thing. By the time she'd showered and dressed in trousers and a thick red, angora jersey, Josue had been pacing the kitchen, sipping coffee and talking to Dean on his phone and getting much the same news.

She liked how Josue had put his hand up the moment he'd heard a search was to get under way. He didn't put his needs first, didn't think he should get to the house and unpack rather than go out in the cold and hike through wet bush and mud. He'd also fitted in with everyone immediately when they'd got to the start point. Quietly impressive, came to mind.

He intrigued her with his looks and that accent. She was aware of him whenever he was nearby, which was something she hadn't felt for a long time. Since Hogan. This interest in Josue was different, more grounded in who he might be and how he just got on with whatever was required of him without question, as he had with the boys when they'd found them.

He hadn't expected her to jump at his word. They'd got down to work on the boys together, sharing the jobs, putting Timmy and Morgan before anything else. The past had taught her some painful lessons and yet she barely knew him and couldn't wait to spend time learning more. And getting closer physically? *Why not?* She wasn't disinterested. How could she be when he had her fingertips tingling with only a look?

There was nothing better than occasionally having a good time with a hot man, as long as she'd got to know him a little and felt safe. *Stop.* She didn't have the time for a fling. *Didn't she?* Of course she did. But she wanted more, and that wasn't happening with this guy. This nagging restlessness had come about because she didn't have her family to go home to at the end of the day.

But, in the meantime, what was more important? Looking after the house and grounds, or seeing to her own requirements, as in having fun and meeting a man? Wanting to find the man of her dreams didn't mean celibacy until he came along. Besides, if that didn't happen for another few years, gulp, then she'd be like a dried-up prune.

Josue strode across the room with his hands clutching a load of full glasses.

She couldn't take her eyes off him. Even though she should. He'd pick up on her interest too easily and she didn't need him seeing that. Not until she'd made up her mind—fling or nothing. Nothing was getting more remote by the minute. She tried to concentrate on the men seated around the table, unwinding and telling tall tales as the thought of what the outcome could've been drained out of them. Everyone had been tense, the urgency greater than even the usually high level due to it being two wee lads missing and understanding how desperate their families would've been. Every searcher's nightmare. It was one thing to be out there for an adult who'd had an accident or got lost; a very different story when children were involved.

Placing the drinks on the table without spilling a drop, Josue handed one to Mallory and took the recently vacated seat beside her. 'Bet those boys won't be dashing into the bush again in a hurry.' He stretched his endless legs under the table.

Mallory deliberately looked across the table at Scott to save herself getting redder in the face from sussing those legs for longer than was sensible. But there was no stopping the flush rising in her cheeks. Taking a deep breath, she got on with being friendly while staring at the wet circles left by glasses on the tabletop. 'I doubt their parents will let them out of their bedrooms for a month. They'll want to know exactly where they are every minute.'

'I thought Kiwi parents liked their children to get outside to learn how to manage nature and what it threw at them.'

She glanced at Josue. Shouldn't have. He was laughing softly, teasing her. Turning her cheeks from pink to flaming red. What was it about this man that got her in a flap just looking at him? Good-looking men were a dime a dozen around Queenstown, as they came to ski or partake in extreme sports in droves, so it couldn't be Josue's looks that were rocking her world. Lifting her glass, she took two large mouthfuls and set it back down on the table. 'Is it like that in France?'

'For those lucky enough to have access to the countryside and the mountains.' His face tightened briefly, then he was smiling again. 'I was born in the city, but when I grew up I headed for the mountains as soon as I could afford it. I'd read many books about mountaineers all over the world and I wanted to see what the fascination of mountains was all about. I loved the outside air, the freedom and fewer people being around. There's a certain excitement about just being able to walk a kilometre without meeting anyone else, but I never took to climbing. Didn't have the head required for heights. Staring over cliff edges, knowing I'd have to go back down there, would only turn my gut sour.'

Dipping her head, she smiled. Again. Hell, this man was getting to her. He talked about himself as though he didn't have to prove how great he was all the time, like some of the guys she met through her work did. Sometimes she felt that some of them had to shove out their chests and strut just because she was a female at the chopper controls and therefore in charge of their destiny. As far as she was concerned they needed to get over themselves. 'Anyone would have to be crazy to do that. I'd far rather rely on rotors than my feet in those places. I've airlifted enough injured climbers off mountains to know where I'd prefer to be.'

'I thought you were going to say you don't like heights either and that would've been strange for a pilot.' He was teasing her in the nicest possible way.

'I passed the sanity test for my licence.' She grinned—just in case he was worried she was strange. 'But I agree. There's something special about the outdoors without having to go to extremes, even here where the tourists swamp the place to get a taste of reaching for the limits in as safe an environment as possible.'

'I've been told there're still many areas to go to get away from them, if you're lucky enough to know where they are.'

'Working in the emergency department, you'll meet people who can tell you where to go.' *Keep talking, Josue.* That accent sent warm shivers up and down her spine, and made her shuffle on her chair. Which meant she should shut up with the questions and put a paper bag over her head.

'What about you? Do you get away often?'

'My job takes me all over the district, so I see a lot but from the air, not on the ground, whereas S and R does get me out into country I love, though usually in those circumstances I'm too busy worrying about who we're looking for and not absorbing the countryside. My dad used to take me on overnight hikes to huts and the like when I was younger. I haven't been back to many of them for a long time.'

'Want to show me one or two?' The sizzling smile was again teasing her, sucking her into his aura.

'I guess I can if we've both got free days at the same time.' Would she or wouldn't she try to make certain she did? He was so tempting. This was ridiculous. She never lost her mind over a man so quickly. But she hadn't. Not really. He was hot and gorgeous and great company, but she wasn't going to allow herself to get in deep, knowing he'd pack up and leave well before Christmas.

Anyway, she didn't make rash decisions or actions, didn't ever lose her mind over any man. Since Hogan, she'd become the steady, check-it-out-first kind of girl, even when it came to planning an overnight trip to a town she knew. 'We'd have to do day hikes, not overnight ones.' She wasn't staying alone in a hut with Josue when just sitting here in a group made her blood heat.

'We'll make it happen,' Josue said with a determined nod.

He wanted to spend time with her on hikes? Time up close and personal? Was she warming his skin as much as he was hers? Or was Josue determined to see lots of the district and she was an easy target for a guide? She smiled. What did it matter? She wanted to spend time with him doing anything and everything. Where had the steady, check-it-out-first woman gone? But what was not to like about him? Apart from the fact she couldn't read men any more than she could a book written in Swahili—and that was when she was being cautious. Her track record was short and abysmal. She'd got it so wrong with Hogan and Jasper. Her gaze drifted sideways. She stared at her glass.

All men should be like her dad: honest and gentle. Working in a male environment, she'd met men like that, and some not, but that didn't put her off them. She just didn't always get it right about how their thought processes worked, and expected them to be open and straightforward like her dad had been. Maisie always laughed at that one, saying no woman understood men better than to feed them, love them and let them get on with things.

'I've ordered fries and chicken all round.' Josue spoke loud enough now for everyone to hear.

'No more treats for Shade, please,' she begged. 'I'll have to deal with the bloated stomach for hours to come otherwise.' Leaning back in her chair, Mallory sipped her beer and relaxed. Her legs ached, her head was getting light—beer mixed with the thrill of finding those kids safe—and physical exhaustion was taking over. It was a comfortable sensation, one that came from having done something good with a group of people all in sync.

Plates of hot food arrived, filling the air with delicious fatty, spicy smells that had everyone reaching for the chips and chicken. There was more than enough to go round. Josue obviously understood how ravenous the team got once they relaxed from the hard work of climbing up and down hills and cliffs, of wading through rivers or trekking through thick bush.

'You've gone quiet.' Josue spoke softly.

Nothing unusual in that. 'I'm an observer.' She was seeing too much of those legs again. What would it be like to have them entwined with hers in bed? Jerking her head up, she stared directly into his eyes. Vibrant gold flecks dotted through the dark hazelnut colour. Happy eyes, generous and sensual. Beddable eyes. *Jeepers.* She was way in over her head. After how many hours? She didn't do this. An occasional casual fling with someone she was mildly attracted to was her lot. The exciting physical package she could manage, but not this gnawing sense of wanting more. The getting close and personal was a worry. Something about Josue suggested a fling with him would not be half-hearted. She sensed he might take over her mind, her feelings and she'd become besotted. *Which would be fine, except he isn't here forever.*

Josue *was* different. He didn't rush to talk over her or push his interests before hers. He was genuinely interested in what she did and thought. More than anything she felt comfortable around him in a close way, almost as she felt with Kayla and Maisie, yet she'd known them most of her life and not just since yesterday. But she didn't want to be best friends with Josue. This need filling her, tightening every nerve ending, had little to do with friendship and everything to do with getting absorbed into his life and opening up hers to let him in. 'Damn it.'

'Problem?'

A great big one. 'Not at all.' Not unless she gave in to the intense feelings gripping her. Straightening her back, swallowing hard, Mallory turned to Josue, and fell into the deep shade looking back at her. She was swimming in treacle, going nowhere fast, and so tempted to dive deeper. Snatching up her glass, she gulped a large mouthful, which promptly went down the wrong way and she had to suffer the indignity of having her back slapped by Beddable Eyes's large, gentle hand. More coughing. Time she went home and had a hot shower, and got comfortable in some softer trousers and a thick jersey. *Huh, a cold shower would be more appropriate.*

Something solid plonked onto her thigh. It couldn't be Josue touching her. There weren't any sparks. Anyway, he wouldn't make such a blatant move. Would he? Her hand found Shade's warm, hard head. 'How's my girl?'

This time soppy brown eyes looked at her, filled with love. How come dogs loved without reservation? Without question? They just gave it out and only asked for some in return. And steak and chips.

'How long have you had her?' Josue asked as he began rubbing Shade's shoulders as though nothing had happened. Perhaps it hadn't for him. He probably looked at women like that all the time.

'I got her from animal rescue eighteen months ago.'

'Guess you're into all sorts of rescues then.' His smile was soft, kind and making her stomach tighten.

'I couldn't look at those beguiling eyes and walk away. She had me from the get-go.' She'd better not do the same thing with Josue's own beguiling eyes. She'd never leave her mother to deal with the dementia alone. The nurses were wonderful, but she was the only family her mother had.

Shade lifted her head, nudged Mallory's thigh gently.

'Okay, I get it.' Mallory pushed her chair back. 'We'll be back in a minute.'

Outside Mallory shoved her hands in her pockets and stared through the murky air of the car park as she walked slowly after Shade heading for the trees. 'Damn it. I am so attracted to him.' Her lungs expanded, contracted, pushing air through her lips. 'Too attracted.'

She paused, waited for Shade to join her again. 'Do you like Josue?' Her fingers rubbed between Shade's ears. 'You do, don't you?' That didn't make any difference to the situation. She loved Shade to bits but she had no say in this. Kayla would point out she should have some fun. It wouldn't be hard. He was delicious. But there was more to him than the physical traits that had her enthralled. Enough to take a chance and have some fun? She already felt differently about him from other men. She couldn't let that get out of hand. Yet she was reacting to Josue like she wanted to learn more about him in every way.

Shade nudged her, wagging her tail.

'You're ready to go back inside?'

Wag, wag.

I'm not, because I'm reacting very differently to Josue than I've ever done with any man before, which could kick me in the butt.

Taking out her phone, she pressed Maisie's number. 'Hi, have you heard any more about Kayla?'

'Hi to you too.' Maisie laughed. Then got serious. 'I talked to her mum, and she's having a rough day after hours of surgery first thing. They didn't do it last night because the orthopaedic surgeon wasn't available. I'm still getting my head around what's happened.'

'Me too, though I've been on a rescue today so that took care of some of my headspace for a while. Kayla's supposed to be getting her life back together, not having it torn apart by an avalanche.' So unfair. 'You won't believe what else happened last night. I thought you'd come to visit.'

'Sorry, can't at the moment. Too much work on.'

'I figured.'

'So? Who was visiting if not me?'

'A Frenchman. He's a hunk, believe me.' Mallory filled Maisie in on what had happened. 'It's kind of funny really.'

'Might be karma. It's time you met someone interesting, and hot.'

'He's not staying around for long.'

'Then make the most of him while he's in the country.'

'Thanks, pal. I just might, although I—'

'Blah, blah. I'm not listening to your excuses not to have

some fun. Anyway, who knows what he might do if he thinks you're the bee's knees.'

'Time I went back inside,' Mallory said. 'You're not helping. See you.' She hung up before Maisie could add any more stupidity to the conversation. So much for downloading and sorting things out with friends.

Where would she be without hers?

CHAPTER THREE

JOSUE CHATTED WITH the remaining guys around the table, glancing across to the main entrance every few minutes. Mallory wouldn't have left unless she'd forgotten he needed a lift, and she was too focused to do that. There was still half a glass of beer at her place by the table that she seemed to have set aside.

An intriguing woman, with a heart of gold, who liked helping people. The way she walked through the bush without hesitation and was very sure about following Shade spoke volumes of her competence in a situation many people would struggle with. The local bush was so dense there was no way of seeing through the trees because of all the undergrowth. Dean had told him a story about a Canadian man who went for an hour's walk behind the motel where he was staying and was found three days later completely disorientated and dehydrated. Nothing Josue had seen since made him think his friend had been exaggerating.

The door swung open. Shade trotted across to the mat in front of the fire and lay down.

Mallory started his way, but stopped to talk to a woman who'd called out to her.

Josue studied her, while pretending to listen to Scott talking about flying to a rescue in Fiordland. Mallory was far more interesting. Her wild, blonde hair had begun escaping from the tight knot it'd been in to flick over her shoulders and touch her cheeks. Colour in her cheeks highlighted her all-seeing eyes. Her lips were full and tempting. *Oh, l'enfer.*

He'd better focus on the conversation going on around him. Safer. Not that he was immune to having fun. A fling didn't hurt if both people were keen. He sighed. It had been a while since he'd finished with the petite nurse in Wellington who he'd had fun with and no regrets when it finished. But that had been a fling without attachments. That might not be possible with Mallory since she already had him in knots just thinking about her.

Though, especially following his previous failed serious relationships, he found it hard to imagine he could find a woman he might fall in love with. It wasn't that he didn't want to find a woman to love and cherish forever. He did. But his mother hadn't loved him enough to get her act together and raise him. And not one person in the foster homes had done anything to prove her wrong. Gabriel and Brigitte loved him, and that was the most wonderful thing that had ever happened to him. But they were special. Could a woman love him, faults and all, forever? And could he give the same back without question? Without doubting every move he made? Unlikely.

'Josue, any problems today?' Jamie moved closer to be heard.

'None at all. Once Shade got wind of the boys it was fairly straightforward, if you don't count the sharp climb and then the drop off the edge to the riverside where the boys were huddled together.' The sense of relief when he'd seen them, Morgan staring at Shade as though she was magic, had been overwhelming. He'd surreptitiously swiped at his face while rushing towards them, only to see Mallory do the same as she'd knelt down beside them too.

The air vibrated around him. Mallory was back, sitting down in the same chair next to him. He'd half expected her to take a seat further away. There'd been something crackling between them earlier and he hadn't been sure she was happy about it. Could be he'd got that wrong. *Hope so.* His skin warmed. If only he could bury his fears, he'd be up for a night with her some-time. If she wanted the same, of course. *Only a night?* Had to be, or a few, but no more. Heading home after this contract would save him if he started getting too close. 'Shade looks happier.'

'Shade always looks happy.' Mallory smiled. 'Though she does a good poor-me act when it's time to be fed. Or when *she* thinks it's time for food.'

He'd like to get a dog but with his track record of moving on from place to place it wouldn't be fair on any pet. It was the same with women. He couldn't guarantee loving someone if it would mean settling in one place forever. He didn't know how to do that, so he'd go with his default and make the most of any opportunities on offer. 'Do you ski?' Maybe they could take a day trip to Coronet Peak together.

'Love it, and snowboarding even more. Like I told you, I grew up around here so it's a foregone conclusion I spend time on the snow whenever possible.'

Josue stretched his legs further under the table.

Mallory's gaze shifted and her breathing rate lifted.

So that was how it went. She was interested. So was he. But he wasn't about to act like a jerk and rush in. But—but he wanted to follow up on this attraction. *Slow down, Jos.* Get to know her better first. For a fling? Something was offbeat here. *Him.* His pulse was racing and it was impossible not to watch as she sipped her beer then pulled a face. 'Would you like some-thing different to drink?'

She blinked, pushed her half-empty glass aside, and nod-ded. 'I think I'll get a lemonade. I have to drive home yet. Can I get you something?'

Josue was on his feet, reaching for their glasses. 'I'll get this.'

'You got the last round.'

'*Oui.* And I'll get this one. Want something else to eat as well?' She hadn't indulged much in the fries and chicken.

'I'm going to have a burger soon, then I'm heading home for

a hot shower and some clean clothes.' Another rapid blink, and she was staring across at Shade.

Clothes? It'll be bedtime by then. Bed. Mallory. Josue mentally slapped his head. He'd seen those fancy PJs she wore. 'What sort of burger?'

'Josue, you don't have to do this.'

He loved the way she said his name. Gravelly, sexy. 'It's a thank-you for last night. Your turn next time if you insist.'

'Next rescue we're on together?'

'I was thinking more along the lines of next time we share a beer at the pub.'

Her grin got him in the gut. Hard. It was genuine, carefree, and with no hidden agenda that he could see, no doubts about him. *Impressionnante.*

He spun around and aimed for the counter, turned back. 'Would you like something stronger if I drive us home?' Home? *Non*, he had somewhere else to put his head down tonight. 'I meant back to your place.'

That grin got wider, and hit harder. She dug into her pocket, then her fingers were doing a number on his palm as she handed her keys over. 'A vodka and lemon, thanks.'

He couldn't say if her dancing fingers had been deliberate, but judging by the rose shade filling Mallory's cheeks they hadn't. Feeling confused, he slid the keys into his pocket and headed for the bar, needing to find air more easily breathed.

Leaning against the counter while waiting for the order, he watched Mallory talking to the guys. She was comfortable with them, but then she worked in a male environment so it would come naturally. As was how she made him feel—like a friend already. Except the sensations tripping though his body weren't those he'd feel for any friend. This was dangerous. He didn't do strong need for a woman beyond sex. Yet he suddenly wanted to know everything about her, what was her favourite breakfast, the colour she liked the most, what side of the bed she preferred. *It couldn't happen.*

Why were his lungs squeezing with disappointment?

There was so much to her. She was tough, hadn't been fazed with the men on the rescue when they'd taken over the heavy lifting of the kids on stretchers, wore dull work clothes that fitted neatly but didn't accentuate her sexy shape, and yet her nails were manicured, her curly hair highlighted with dark blonde streaks and her make-up light and perfect.

When he sat down beside her again, he muttered, 'Impressive.'

She stared at him, wide eyed. 'What is?' Eyes he was coming to know already locked onto him. She seemed to be trying to read his mind, that look boring into his head with the temerity of a power drill.

There was no way that he was going to let her know what he'd been thinking. 'Why did you choose flying for a career?'

She continued to stare at him. 'The freedom, which is at odds with how restrictive flying really is. It's like going on an adventure every day of my life. There are so many factors contributing to the job on hand, weather, terrain, the people I'm with.' She was telling the truth, but not all the truth. He could hear there was more behind her words, in the depth of her eyes that had darkened ever so slightly while she'd been talking, in the sudden stiffness in her body.

Knowing there were things about himself he didn't share, he left it alone. 'You've obviously found your niche.'

A thoughtful expression flitted across her face, disappeared as fast as it had come. 'I think so.'

Again, he wondered more about what she didn't say than her reply. Had she ever left Queenstown to work elsewhere, or was this the only place she'd lived? Why this itch to learn so much about Mallory? It was new to him and, frankly, scary. *So put it aside, enjoy the company. Stop overthinking everything.*

Mallory led the way into her house, saying over her shoulder, 'Josue, you're back to where you were last night.'

That low sexy laugh came across the gap between them, turning her stomach to water. 'Nothing new for me.'

She turned to look at him. 'Meaning?' He was used to finding himself in places he hadn't planned on? If so, quite the opposite of her steady life.

Josue shrugged. 'Nothing.' Then he added, 'I'm not obsessive about making plans and sticking to them.'

Again, unlike her, though not obsessive about keeping her life on track, she was careful and focused. If she'd been more in control when she'd been a teenager, she wouldn't have got pregnant and lost her baby, and been left with the fear of never becoming a mother. She would've been a nurse, not a pilot. No regrets about that one. Flying was the best job out there. But losing her baby had left a hole in her heart she'd never completely filled. He or she would've turned fourteen last month, a teenager finding their way in the world.

Sudden longing for a chance to go back and rectify her mistakes swamped her. She understood it was impossible, that there'd been nothing she could've done to save her baby, but there were moments when the yearning was unavoidable. It still gave her occasional sleepless nights, and a desperate need to stay safe and not fail anyone again.

'Mallory? Where have you gone?' Josue stood in front of her, worry flattening his mouth.

Shaking her head abruptly to banish the sadness, she lifted her face to look at this man who'd arrived into her life without warning and was tilting her so far off her heels it was scary. 'I like knowing where I'm headed and how to get there.'

'You're not just talking about a day trip, are you?'

Her mouth dropped open as she stared at him. He seemed to understand her, or parts of her, that most people weren't aware of, as far as she knew. Again—scary. Only last night she'd found him in her lounge, and even then she hadn't been overly uncomfortable around him. 'Not entirely,' she admitted.

'Come on, let's have coffee.' He took her arm to lead the way to *her* kitchen.

'Tea for me,' she muttered through the thickness in her mouth. 'Shouldn't you be getting along the road to Kayla's house?' *And leaving me alone to get a grip on my emotions.*

'I've got all night.' He was taking over, making their drinks as though he'd been here forever. As though he belonged here.

Strange, right? Certainly not something she was used to, or even encouraged with anyone except her closest friends. This was her sanctuary from the world, a place where she'd always felt loved and cared for. No one hurt her within these walls. But the way Josue fitted in *did* feel good. Almost from the start he'd begun causing her to look beyond her hectic life to see if she could make room for him—for a while.

'Milk with your tea?'

An ordinary, everyday question, and she smiled. 'Please.' And went to close all the curtains. At least today she'd set the heat pump to come on when the sun went down before she'd left for the rescue.

'You okay?' He slid a mug over the counter in front of her when she returned.

'I'm fine.' Locking her gaze on him, she added, 'Truly.'

'Good.' He came around to stand beside her, coffee in hand, and looked at the framed photos of her and her parents on the nearest wall. 'When I saw those last night, I was a little envious of the love glowing between the three of you. Your parents?' Then he took another look. 'Or grandparents?'

A common query. 'Mum and Dad. They married when they were forty and fifty and to their surprise I popped along very soon after.'

'They obviously didn't mind.'

'They adored me. Being an only child, I grew up being treated older than I really was, and that was fine, though often I found I was mentally ahead of my peers. And Kayla and

Maisie are like my sisters. We get on so well about most things, so probably better than sisters.'

'You're lucky.'

Yes, she was. There was a hint of sorrow in his voice. He'd also said he felt envious looking at her family pictures. 'You didn't have such a loving childhood?'

'No.' He sipped his coffee, suddenly deep in thought. Then he faced her and said, 'Don't feel sorry for me but I grew up in foster care. When I was fifteen and headed for trouble, I met a police officer who took me under his wing. He saved my butt, and hasn't stopped since.' His smile was wry. 'I'm supposedly grown up now but it's still good to have Gabriel in my life. He's my go-to-for-advice man.'

Mallory tucked her arm through his and hugged him lightly. 'We all need one or two people to download on,' she agreed. 'That must've been hard, growing up in care. Did you get a nice family to live with?' Was the French system similar to the New Zealand one where some kids stayed long term and others moved around a lot?

'There were four families in total and I didn't fit in with any of them.'

Ouch. Not good. In her book, being surrounded by a loving family was the most important aspect of growing up, but then she'd been very lucky and didn't know any other way. 'This cop? You get along with the rest of his family?'

He went quiet for a moment, then put his hand on her shoulder and looked down at her. 'Brigitte, his wife, took me under her wing from the beginning, and wasn't as strict as Gabriel. I loved her for that alone. They never had children so they were very busy with their careers, yet there was always time for me, something I'd been looking for all my life until then. I got lucky with them, though I still struggle with it all after the way those foster families treated me.'

'To be expected.' Standing still, she watched emotions flit

across his face: worry, care, tenderness, fear. 'I can't imagine what any of that was like. *Is* like.'

Placing his mug on the bench, Josue tentatively wrapped her into an embrace, his chin resting on the top of her head. 'We're getting along well so quickly. I hadn't expected anything like this.'

'Neither did I,' she whispered, as her heart thumped once, hard. This togetherness warmed her deep inside. A sensation that didn't happen often. Tightening her hold around him, she laid her cheek against him and breathed deeply, inhaling the masculine smell of his body.

Josue's hands were spread across her back, gentle and endearing. His fingertips began tracing small circles, winding her skin tighter and tighter.

Mallory raised her head, looked up at the strong jawline and on to the dark shadowed chin and on to those eyes that saw so much and were watching her with kindness and a sparkle. She drew a wobbly breath.

'I'd better get along to the house.'

'I guess you should.' Disappointment filled her head, but he was probably right. It would be rushing things to follow through on the urge to kiss him. It wasn't her way. But there was no stopping the heat flooding her, the longing to feel his mouth on hers. What was going on? She liked to know who she was getting close to, know him better than she currently knew Josue. But there was no stopping these sensations knocking at her chest. He was wonderful, and gorgeous, and exciting.

'But before I go...' Josue lowered his head close to hers, his lips seeking hers, covering her mouth gently. Pressing into her, still gently, not demanding.

Mallory was lost. No stepping away from him. 'Yeah.' She was returning the kiss. Not so gently, but opening under his mouth, tasting those lips that had tantalised her since first meeting him. Against his chest her breasts tightened, peaking slowly.

Her hands tightened against his back, pushing into him, feeling the tight ripple of his muscles under her palms.

She felt the instant Josue lifted his mouth away. *No. Come back.*

'I'll see you tomorrow.' There was a hitch in his voice.

'Okay.' She couldn't say any more through the disappointment engulfing her.

'Just one more,' Josue whispered, his mouth reclaiming hers.

Then he took her face in his hands, and pulled back barely enough to look into her eyes. 'Mallory?'

'Josue.' She nodded, running the tip of her tongue over her bottom lip. Her body melted at the desire filling his gaze, desire that matched her own and that she could feel right to the tips of her toes. Everything was happening fast, and it felt right. This had been coming ever since the night before when she'd come out of the bathroom in her PJs and robe and had seen Josue's eyes light up, sending her body into a flurry of desire. What made one man's reaction to her feel so different from others'? Not that she had loads of experience with men's reactions but enough to know Josue was different towards her. He looked at her as though she was spun gold. He touched her as though he'd never touched a woman before—carefully yet firmly, making her feel sexy.

The ensuing kiss was deeper, filled with passion, more demanding, and she gave back as much as she received from this amazing man. His lips were strong and demanding, soft and pliant, hungry—for her. He was getting to know her through their kiss. Tasting her, touching her mouth as though he could read her through his tongue.

Her hands touched him everywhere, feeling muscles through his shirt, ribs under her palms as she slid her hands from his back to his chest. Her mouth couldn't get enough of Josue's as she tried to return the intensity of his kiss, getting sidetracked by the desire firing throughout her body.

Strong hands were on her waist, raising her onto her toes against his full length. And still his mouth didn't leave hers.

Was this paradise or what? She felt as though she'd found a place she might never want to leave. A man she might not be able to walk away from. Ever. Her mouth froze.

Then cooler air crossed her lips. 'Mallory? Are you all right?'

Josue read her too easily. Or perhaps he didn't, because she couldn't be happier. Or more confused, but confusion wasn't getting in the way of sharing a wonderful moment—or more—with this man who seemed to know how to wake her up so gently she almost had to pinch herself to see if it was real.

'Do you want me to stop?' he gasped.

He would stop just like that if she said so? Wow. But it wasn't happening. She couldn't pull away. Not when her blood was pulsing through her veins and her head spinning. 'Please don't.' She raised her mouth to his again, felt him smile under her lips.

'Merci.' The word was drawn out long and slow, and did nothing to dampen her longing to feel his skin under her palms.

Deep down her stomach tightened and heat poured throughout. Her fingers quivered as she slipped her hands under his shirt and onto his back, feeling the tension in his muscles, the warmth of his skin. Then she forgot what she was doing as Josue placed his strong, large hands on her waist again, his palms like rough, cool satin on her hot skin.

Who was this man who was waking her up with a reciprocating need pulsing though his touch to connect with hers? Josue Bisset. French in his looks, in the way he wore his clothes, in that divine accent, and now she was starting to learn French in his touch. *Oui.* She needed him. Now. Pushing his trousers down those muscular thighs sent a shiver through her body as her palms grazed his hot skin and tense muscles.

Another shiver followed as her trousers slid down her legs, assisted by those large, strong, hot hands she already recognised. And he never stopped kissing her.

With his hands on her butt, she wound her legs around that incredible body, raised herself higher. Then she was being turned to lean against the wall as she kissed Josue, kissing as though her life depended upon it. Which it did at the moment. This heat, the need filling her veins, the gripping sense of falling off a ledge into a dream—this was what she'd been looking for, for so long. 'Josue,' she whispered around the need filling her mouth as he touched her, filled her and retreated, filled her, retreated, until her mind blanked except for the explosion that erupted throughout her with sensations she'd never known before.

What happened to taking things slowly? Of learning more about Mallory before getting to know her so intimately? Listening to her gentle breathing, Josue tightened his arm around her waist as they lay spooned under the covers on her bed, where she'd led him after their earth-shattering sex in the dining room. It seemed to have come out of nowhere, even when the atmosphere between them had been winding tighter and hotter for hours. He had meant it when he'd said he'd head away to the other house, and seconds later had returned to kissing Mallory instead. Because he'd been unable to stop. He'd had to kiss and taste, again and again. She'd reacted similarly, returning his kisses with a passion that undid any resolve not to get too involved—too soon, at least.

No. He had to remind himself that there could be no involvement other than a fling. He would be leaving soon and that was that. Unless… Unless nothing. Stopping in one place was alien, and to do that in another country that was not his homeland would overstretch his need to fit in. Or it might work perfectly.

Almost from the moment he'd stepped onto the ground in this country he'd had a sense of having found that something he felt had been missing for as long as he could remember. So far, he'd felt more and more at home wherever he'd gone in New Zealand, as though being so far from his previous life had lifted the self-imposed restrictions on his heart, but that still didn't mean he would settle permanently even if he found a reason to stay. Being constant, stable wasn't in his DNA. Only constantly moving around was.

Mallory snuggled that wonderful body even closer. She was something else. She was strong, focused, and appeared to know what she wanted from life, but underneath that he sensed a need. For what he had no idea, but she intrigued him, and had just blown his socks off with generous and demanding sex. Wild curly hair tickled his face with every breath he took. Those firm backside curves pressed into his groin.

A woman so different from any he'd spent time with. Or was he exaggerating in the heat of the moment? Though the heat was cooling and he still wanted her and liked what he'd experienced with her. Or rather had been stunned by it. Here was a woman he didn't want to roll away from in order to get on with the day, unlike the other women he'd got close to—and he wasn't even close to Mallory. *Yet.*

This new longing to stay put, to find out more about Mallory was taking over his usual safety mechanism of pulling down the blinds on his emotions. She made him feel as though he should let go for once, to try to find out if he really might be able to take a chance on love. *After only knowing her for twenty-four hours?* This was a far cry from when he spent weeks getting to know a woman and constantly looked out for difficulties and found them even if they weren't there. Dread slammed into his mind. This was going too far, too soon. It must never happen, he could not let himself get close. He was returning home soon. *Think, Jos. Back off now.*

But even as he berated himself, he splayed his hand across her stomach, felt the warmth transfer from her to him all down their bodies where they touched and breathed in her scent of sweat and exhaustion and sex.

'Josue?' That sharp accent cut through his meanderings.

'Oui?' How could he deny himself this moment?

'Merci.' Mallory rolled over in his arms and splayed her leg

over him, her knee touching his manhood, awakening him when he'd barely recovered.

Sinking further into the bed, he allowed her to spread across him, smiling freely, without question. Happy. 'Don't thank *me*,' he gulped. Then swallowed. *He was happy?* Yes, incredibly happy. Unusually so. And it was scary. Yet his arms tightened around her.

Mallory lifted away enough to lean on an elbow and fix a gentle gaze on him. 'Problem?'

Oui. Toi. This woman read him too well. He did have a problem. She made him happy without trying, which made her a danger. Looking at her, a wave of sadness rose at the thought of leaving. He swallowed it. She was waiting for an answer, concern starting to fill those beautiful eyes. 'None at all,' he fibbed, then realised it wasn't a complete lie. Everything was perfect if he didn't think about what might happen beyond tonight and into the coming days. Taking her head gently in his hands, he pulled her down for a kiss.

Just a kiss. That went on and on, until their bodies were hot and tight and he was pushing into her as she sat over him, her head tipping back so that crazy mane swung across her shoulders and her fingernails skidded across his nipples, tightening until he thought he'd explode. Driving into her, holding her waist to keep her with him, Josue forgot everything except Mallory and himself, joining together, coming together, dropping into a bundle of damp limbs and falling into safe oblivion.

CHAPTER FOUR

MALLORY GRINNED TO HERSELF. Her body ached in places she hadn't known existed before, and it had nothing to do with yesterday's search in the rugged hill country. The reason was singing in the shower down the hall.

Something in French that sounded off-key and hilarious because it made no sense to her. She'd nearly done the same when she'd been lathering the soap over her body under pummelling hot water fifteen minutes ago, but her singing would've scared the birds out of the garden where they were currently digging for worms amongst the weeds.

She never sang if anyone was around since her friends always gave her grief about the appalling racket she made, and there was no reason to expect Josue would react any differently. She couldn't be good at everything.

She also hadn't wanted Josue to know how alive she felt this morning. He'd probably bolt for Kayla's house, never to be seen again. But it was true, she felt more cheerful than she did normally. It wasn't unusual for her to bounce out of bed, but this morning she'd been walking on air. What a night. Josue was the man dreams were made of. Good looking, hot, tender and he'd put her first when they'd made love.

More than that, he'd been good with the boys in the bush,

kind and caring, medically competent. He'd fitted in with the search team like he'd always been around. He wasn't egotistical. He wanted to be accepted, but didn't try to put it out there that he was clever. Which was all good and well as long as when it came time to finish with him she could do so without getting hurt, and she suspected it mightn't be quite that simple.

There were other men out there who had similar character-istics, but they hadn't pushed her buttons and set her tingling with anticipation. Unable to put her finger on what made him different, special even, the sort of man she'd hoped might be somewhere out there for her, was not a worry at the moment while she was still in the afterglow of a wonderful night. But she knew eventually it would creep in and set her to wondering if she'd made another misjudgement, if Josue would turn out to be all wrong once the glow faded. The only thing she knew for certain was that he wasn't staying around forever, and that was paramount to how, or if, she went about spending more time with him while remaining uninvolved.

Yet here she was, grinning like an idiot. How could she not? Her feet did a little tap dance on the spot. After finally having a shower to wash away the day's grime and the evening's fun, she'd gone to bed and had been joined by Josue, damp from his shower and ready to cuddle her to him as they'd fallen into an exhausted sleep, only to wake and make love again. Spooning together as they'd lain waiting to fall back to sleep once again had been as wonderful as the amazing sex. She'd felt comfort-able with Josue, relaxed and carefree.

Hard to believe she'd found him lying uninvited on her couch the night before. The Intruder. A lot could happen in twenty-four hours. For her it had been a lot of fun and excitement. Even the hours spent searching for those boys and the drinks afterwards to wind down had been different, having Josue be-side her. A bit like he was meant to be with her, and that she'd finally found someone who understood how she loved to use her skills to help people.

Her stomach was complaining of starvation, grumbling loudly, sending signals of hunger up her throat. Breakfast was urgently required, starting with tea for her, coffee for her guest. Guest? Not really. Another grin spread her mouth wide as she hummed out of tune. 'Bacon and eggs, hash browns and mushrooms.'

'Sounds good to me.'

Mallory leapt out of her skin. 'Don't creep up on me like that.'

'There wasn't any creeping happening.' Josue laughed. 'You were completely absorbed in your thoughts.'

'Always lots going on in my head.' Breathing slowly to still the rapid beating going on in her chest, she turned around to drink in the sight of the man who'd given her such a wonderful night of sex and cuddles and just being with her. She felt small beside him, but not weak or incapable. He didn't take anything away from her, instead he gave of himself for her pleasure and made her feel secure in his arms, made her stronger.

Despite his relaxed manner with people, he appeared to be a solitary man, keeping aspects about himself close, which made sense since he'd spent his childhood in care and not knowing family love as she had. That made it doubtful he'd want to get too involved when he was only here for a short time. Which was good. A couple of months of what they'd started last night? *Yes, please.* She began rising onto her toes, about to tap dance again, then got a grip on herself. Amazing sex or not, this couldn't go on willy-nilly. He'd leave and then what? Another broken heart? Her heels landed hard on the floor. *No, thanks.*

Josue placed a light kiss on her cheek then stepped around her to reach for the coffee. 'What have you got on today?'

Thump. That was her heart hitting the floor bringing her back to the stark reality of the thoughts that were running in her head. Today was a normal Sunday, with the usual chores and routines to get through. 'Grocery shopping, a few hours with Mum, and calling into work to fill in some paperwork for

Kayla's flight on Friday night that I was lax about because I was so tired at the time.'

There was a contemplative look on his face as he carefully spooned coffee grains into the plunger.

'Plus the lawn could do with mowing.' Though she'd put that last on the list. Leaving it another week didn't make any difference in winter.

'I'll go along to Kayla's house to get sorted out, and see what I need for meals, and so on.'

Silence fell. Was he waiting for her to suggest he stay here for the next few days—or longer? So they could have more nights like last night? *Oh, yes.* Her hands clenched, loosened. Why not? Her body was almost humming with anticipation.

Her favourite song suddenly rang loud and clear from the kitchen counter.

Josue blinked, looked around to see where the music was coming from.

Smiling, Mallory picked up her phone, then, seeing the caller ID, her smile dimmed. 'Hi, Megan. Everything all right?' she asked the nurse from the dementia unit as she walked over to the window and stared out at the winter-dulled, overgrown English garden that had been her mother's passion, and obviously wasn't hers.

'Everything's fine. Are you coming in to see Dorothy today?'

'I'll be there later this morning. I couldn't make it yesterday as we had a rescue callout.' The staff didn't usually check on her visits. Something was not quite right. 'What's up?'

'Nothing serious, but can you spare me a few minutes when you get here? We've had to up some of Dorothy's meds and I want to talk to you about that.'

Mallory's stomach tightened. She had thought her mum had been less aware than usual lately. 'I had to remind her who I was on Thursday.'

'You've had to do that before, Mallory.'

'I know. But…' The sound of mugs being placed on the bench

reminded her she wasn't alone. 'All right. I'll be there about eleven if that works for you.'

'I'll see you then.' The phone went silent.

Mallory continued staring at the weeds and sad-looking plants in what used to be a picture of colour and shapes in the garden. These days only the sparrows and thrushes were interested in the area. She should get out there and give the garden an overhaul, except what was the point when she'd only let it go again? Her mother wasn't likely to see it again, or, if she did, wouldn't recognise it as what used to be a wonderful, relaxing place to sit in the sun.

'Everything all right?' Josue called from the kitchen.

Her chest rose and fell before she turned. 'Sure. A nurse wants a chat when I go to see Mum later, that's all.' That was information enough.

'Your mother's unwell?'

'Yes.'

'Here's your tea.'

'Thanks.' Talking about Mum wasn't easy since she'd become so quiet, spending hours sitting in her rocking chair, staring at the wall, when she used to be such an exuberant woman who knew so many people. She now barely recognised her daughter. Mallory felt odd having a man in the house making tea while she took that call. It had been a long time since she'd had a man in her life, in her space, like this at all, and this was something personal, almost too personal when she still knew so little about him. 'I'll make the breakfast.'

'You're sad.' Josue was sipping his coffee as he watched her.

Gathering herself together, she gave him a wobbly smile then banged the pan on an element, poured in some oil and dug in the freezer for hash browns. 'My mother has dementia.'

'That lovely lady in the photographs? Mallory, that's awful. How do you cope?'

The next thing she knew she was being hugged tightly against that wide chest she'd often run her fingers over during the night.

A kind hug filled with concern. A hug that warmed her heart. The same, yet different from his sexy hugs. 'I just do,' she whispered, snuggling closer. She could get used to this. *Hello, Mallory? He's not staying.*

'You're one tough lady,' Josue said above her head. 'Come on, let's get breakfast done so you can get on with your plans for the day.' His arms fell away.

Leaving her feeling bereft. Which was ridiculous. They didn't know each other well enough that they'd shared everything about themselves. They'd worked well as a team of two on the rescue, they'd had an amazing night that had her wishing for more along with a whole lot of other things, but two days ago they hadn't known the other existed. Last time she'd met a man and fallen for him, it hadn't been so instant, and it still hadn't lasted a year before she'd realised she hadn't loved him and how little they'd had in common after all. So to think she might find something true and meaningful in a couple of days with Josue was strange, and unlikely to work out.

Sighing, she glanced into the kitchen and gasped, dashing across to turn the heat off and cover the pan before the smoke erupted into a flame. 'That was close.' She'd been too easily distracted, first by the phone and then by those strong arms. A timely reminder that she couldn't let Josue distract her from the day-to-day routines, and that he couldn't sneak in and steal her heart, if that's what was happening. Her mother needed her here, focused, not falling for a man who lived on the other side of the world.

'Here, I'll take that outside.' Josue took the pan, holding the lid in place to prevent a fire, and disappeared out the door.

Another pan and another start on breakfast. Oil splashed into the pan as her shaking hands gripped the bottle. Had she really started falling for Josue so fast? If so, she had to put a halt to everything while she still could. That phone call from Megan had been a timely reminder about where her life was—here in Queenstown, spending time with her mum, flying choppers and helping out with Search and Rescue. It could not be about falling in love with a man who wouldn't be able to become a part of her dream.

A familiar nudge on her thigh had her looking down into a pair of soft chocolate eyes. The confusion dominating her thoughts disappeared in a blink. 'Hello, my girl.' She rubbed Shade's head. 'Be patient. I'll feed you in a minute.'

'Is it all right I let her in? She was waiting by the door.'

'Of course it is. She's hungry.' *Like me*, Mallory admitted. She was thinking food, right? She had to be. Nothing else was happening. Not until she'd thought through everything, at least.

'How much?' Josue was holding up a scoop of dog biscuits.

'That's fine.' She nodded.

He poured them into Shade's bowl, then looked around. 'Your smoke alarm didn't go off with that smoke.'

Another thing she hadn't got around to. 'The battery needs changing.'

'Where do you keep them?'

'Second drawer.'

Within a minute the alarm was beeping to show it was back in use.

'Thanks.' Mallory cracked eggs in the pan.

'You should never let that happen. It could have been serious,' Josue warned.

'I know.' She should have dealt with it the moment she'd known the battery was flat, but she hadn't because it had been another exhausting day at work earlier in the week and she'd come home to shower and eat and had fallen asleep on the couch in front of the widescreen TV.

'I thought you said you liked to be in control.'

Drop it, will you? She'd stuffed up but nothing had gone wrong. 'I made a mistake. How do you like your eggs?'

Breakfast was quiet, almost as though neither wanted to say anything else in case they fell out. Except she couldn't see that happening. Or was that wishful thinking? Because she knew how easy it was to get on the wrong side of someone, no matter how wonderful the night before had been. Her last short fling had finished in a disagreement about Shade and how she allowed her dog inside. Pathetic, but real. She put down her knife and fork, picked up her tea and watched Josue over the rim of her mug. She wasn't enjoying the quiet between them. 'Have you talked to Dean again?' He'd rung Josue while they'd been out looking for the boys and the call had been brief.

'Not yet. I'll do that shortly. I'm thinking I'll drop by the hospital later and introduce myself.'

'What about your plans to check out the skiing and tourist hot spots?' At one stage in the pub last night he'd been talking enthusiastically about bungee jumping and paragliding too.

'They'll keep. It's not as though I'll be working seven days a week.' Josue was watching her with a hint of hope reflected in his eyes.

What did he want from her? She wasn't offering for him to carry on staying here. Not after last night. She'd never get him out of her mind then, or her bed. Used to living on her own, she liked her space and the quiet times. Of course, there were plenty of hours when she wished for someone to be here, talking and sharing a meal, but the moments alone were mostly easy for her.

She slumped in her chair and picked up her tea and glanced across at Josue. Hell, he had her in a turmoil, with her mind throwing up questions about what she wanted. What to do about him, when usually if she met a man who interested her, she got on with spending time with him and letting the fling—if it came to that—run its course? Why not let go of all the concerns about her and Josue and just have a great time? It would be great, no doubts at all. He was sexy as. And fun. And interesting. Those three aspects made her wriggle with happiness.

She gave in—a little. 'We could go skiing next weekend, if you like.' She pointed out the window to snow-covered Cecil Peak on the other side of Lake Wakatipu. She never got tired of the stunning winter view, where the mountain appeared to be within arm's reach, the crisp white reflected on the mirror-like lake. Growing up here, the mountains were in her blood. The months she'd spent with Hogan in outback Australia where the view was brown and dry and flat compared to here for as far as the eye could see had made her feel she was on Mars.

'We can go to whichever ski field you'd prefer.'

His smile was devastating. '*Oui.* Coronet Peak first. I'm looking forward to it already.'

First? There'd be other times? Showed what offering to join him on one trip led to. Excitement tripped through her. Leaping up to get away from that smile destroying her need to remain sensible about Josue, Mallory tipped out the cold tea and started making another one. 'Let's hope we don't get called out to a rescue.'

His smile didn't dim a fraction. 'Then we'll do that and go skiing another time.'

Good answer. Except wasn't she supposed to be drawing back from the temptation that was Josue? The only way to do that was to put some space between them so she could think clearly without distractions like that damned smile. 'Right, guess I'd better get a move on.' *Wasn't I making a mug of tea?* She could drink it while applying her make-up. 'I need to be at the rest home by eleven and there's no such thing as a quick call into work. There're always wannabe pilots hanging around, wanting to talk the rotors off the flying machines.'

'I'll get out of your way,' Josue said. 'See you later?'

It would be so easy to say yes and have another wonderful night. Too easy. Drawing in a deep breath, she told him, 'I'm not sure what time I'll be done with Mum or the other chores I need to do. Maybe another day?' She was consumed with thoughts about what the nurse had to say about her mother. Fingers crossed Mum's placid persona hadn't started changing to something more aggressive, as the doctor and nurses had warned could happen. The last thing imaginable was her mother being aggressive. Not once in her life had Mallory seen her get so angry that she would lose control and hit out verbally or physically, and yet the medics had warned of the possibility.

'Yes, of course.' Josue's smile was gone. The light in those amazing eyes had flicked off. His relaxed stance had tightened. He started walking away.

Somehow, she'd hurt him. A lot. 'Josue?'

He waved over his shoulder and kept going.

No, damn it. Whatever she'd done had not been with the intention of hurting him. It had been about protecting herself. She caught up to him at the front door. 'Stop, Josue. Last night— well, it was wonderful.'

He nodded.

Now what? Try being honest, whatever that was in this case. 'I have never rushed into bed with a man so fast before. I have no regrets.'

Another nod. He wasn't making this easy.

Did he see her words as rejection? Possibly. It was, in a way, because she was afraid where this might lead. 'It's early days, Josue. We don't know each other very well, though I trust you and like what I've seen so far.' *You can do better than that, Mallory Baine.*

'It's all right, Mallory, I understand.' He ran a finger down her cheek so softly it sent whispers of heat throughout her body.

How was she supposed to walk away from that? 'I don't think you do,' she growled through the longing building up inside. 'I'm not saying no to having anything to do with you, but I need to take things slowly.' Heck, when she got honest there was no stopping her.

Now he smiled. 'Bit late for that, don't you think?'

Warmth broke out, pushing away the chill that had begun creeping over her. 'True.' Where to from here? 'I have a busy life that I can't put on hold all the time. Besides, you're not here for ever, Josue.'

'I'm not usually anywhere for long, Mallory. I move on a lot.' The seriousness in his voice was matching a darkening in his eyes. He was giving her a warning. 'I never stop still for any length of time.'

She should be grateful. It matched the warnings she'd been trying to raise within herself. They could continue having a fling and there'd be no expectations of more to follow. While flings were supposedly short term—her few had been—she already felt deep inside that nothing with Josue would be short term for her. Already she'd seen a sensitive side to him that called to her to share herself, to open up to him about her needs and dreams, and hopefully encourage him to talk about his in return.

'Thank you for your honesty.'

Had she just got herself into a deeper quandary? Nothing was going to be solved while standing here talking awkwardly, so it'd be best to get on with the day and let her mind quietly mull over everything. In the meantime, she smiled, she couldn't just walk away without acknowledging he had affected her, and she did want more. Up on her toes, she kissed his cheek, and said, 'It *was* a wonderful night. But...'

'But what?' Driving away from Mallory had Josue grimacing with reluctance. He'd rather be back in her house, talking and sharing another coffee, making plans for going skiing or staying in and cuddling up in bed with their bodies entwined. Except for the sentence she hadn't finished.

Last night had to be one of the most amazing times he'd experienced with a woman, and that came from the way she made him feel so at home with her—if this unusual sense of having found his niche in the world was anything to go by. Not once had she made him feel out of place. *Wrong.* There had been that moment when he'd been lumbering to his feet from her couch that first night to face her steady glare and demanding questions.

But that had passed quickly and last night she'd been as ready for his kisses as he had hers, then when they'd let down the last barriers and he'd lifted her into his arms and up against the wall she'd been more than ready for him.

'But...' she'd said.

Not once had he questioned what they were doing in terms of what Mallory's expectations might have been. Was this to be a one-night stand? Or the beginning of a fling? A relationship? His stomach pulled inwards. That wasn't happening. They'd both end up hurt if that was her expectation. She'd been happy to share their lovemaking. Not that there'd been time to think about anything once they'd started kissing.

He had hauled on the brakes briefly, worried she would change her mind, but his concern had quickly been doused with more hot kisses followed with opening their bodies to each other. It had happened in a flash of need and heat that had scorched the air around them and blanked everything from his mind except Mallory and what she'd been doing to him.

The house he was making for appeared in his vision within moments. No wonder Mallory had been startled when he'd said where he'd been heading the other night. He had been so close. No regrets, however, or he might not have got to know Mallory so well so quickly. The chances of going out on yesterday's search would've been remote as no one had known he was in town, and even if he had and had ended up at the pub with everyone, he doubted he'd have spent much time with her.

Parking in the driveway he looked around at the neat lawns and tidy gardens. Obviously, Kayla spent more time working on her property than Mallory did, unless she paid to have it done. Everything was in its place, not a blade of grass too long, no weeds had dared raise their green heads between the shrubs, which meant inside would be as immaculate. And impersonal, he sighed.

But, then, he wasn't known for making his apartments anything more than somewhere to put his feet up. It might be why he'd felt oddly comfortable at Mallory's with her photos and shelves of books. It was cosy and friendly. With Shade's basket, rug and toys everything felt warm and homely. As far as he understood homely to be, that was.

At the front door he inserted the key he found in the meter box and let himself in. *Oui*, spick and span, not a dust mote to be seen. Hopefully Kayla had someone come in and do the work or he'd be busier here than at the emergency department. Chuckling as he made his way through the house, he found the bedroom obviously allocated to him with a pile of towels on the dresser and extra pillows stacked neatly on the end of the bed. Everything was too perfect, but he had no complaints. He'd have hated to find the home grubby and unkempt. It was the warmth of Mallory's home, as well Mallory herself, that had him looking twice here.

Get out of my head, Mallory Baine.

Like that was going to work. Not even before last night, and now there wasn't a hope in Hades. At first, she'd tickled his interest, and then she'd exploded into his head and shaken him to the core. Throughout his life he'd looked for love—mostly from foster parents because there hadn't been anyone else to expect it from. He'd made two close friends at medical school, but guys didn't admit that a close friendship had an element of love involved. What he'd presumed love to be with the two women he had got into serious relationships with had fallen by the wayside as he'd fought his demons. He'd wanted to fall in love but conversely had kept questioning himself about whether he'd finally found love, pushing away from both women when he'd begun overthinking his inexperience with emotional commitment. He'd hurt them both, and himself, due to his lack of confidence.

Now he'd met Mallory and the same questions were beginning to haunt him, only there was a difference. Never before had he felt anything near the warmth and sense of belonging he already felt with Mallory.

Which was why you warned her you don't settle down anywhere long term. He'd been looking out for her, didn't want to hurt her at all. Yes, and he'd been thinking of himself because he would not be staying on in New Zealand once his time at Queenstown Hospital was up. Would he be able to walk away from here as per normal when there wasn't a lot to hold him in Nice?

When he'd been preparing to fly out of France, Gabriel had told him to be open to opportunities, to grab them with both hands and see where they led. As if Gabriel believed he should be open-minded to another country, another language and a different lifestyle, and to a wonderful, caring and fun woman who might creep under his skin so fast it would be impossible to understand and accept as what he wanted, and needed.

He wouldn't.

He'd get on with what he'd come here to do, and see Mallory when they crossed paths in work or with Search and Rescue. She'd said she was unavailable tonight, but he didn't believe her. She was putting distance between them and he should be grateful, not feel let down. She was doing what he normally did. It felt as though she had rejected him. He was used to doing the rejecting long before his heart was involved, because that kept him safe. But last night had been wonderful, exciting and heartwarming. If Mallory thought they should take things slowly, then what had last night meant? There'd been no slowing down whatsoever.

Hades, but he really didn't know what he wanted. *Yes, you do.* What he didn't know was what to do about it. Risk-taking was not his thing, and getting close to Mallory would be the biggest risk of all.

One day at a time, *mon ami.*

She'd turned down his suggestion of getting together tonight. Rejection stung. What now? Go slowly, spend time with her whenever possible, take the risk she might turn him down again? Was working here and then returning home to France without getting to know Mallory even a viable option? Or would it be best to spend time with her and take whatever consequences arose on the chin?

One day at a time. It was possible. If he wanted this.

Right now, he had his bags to unpack and a department head to meet.

His phone vibrated in his pocket.

His chest expanded as warmth stole through him. *Mallory?*

Dean's name flashed on the screen.

Josue grunted a laugh at himself. Served him right for getting so excited over a phone ringing. '*Bonjour.* How's everything?'

'Come in, Shade.' Mallory's mother's eyes lit up as the dog bounded into her room. 'How's our girl?'

Shade laid her head on Dorothy's knees for the customary pat while Mallory placed the caramel chocolate and oranges she'd brought on the table, before giving her mother a kiss and then a hug she didn't want to stop. This was her mum. 'How's things, Mum?' At least she'd remembered Shade's name.

'I can't find my pyjamas anywhere. Did you take them home to wash?'

'No, I didn't. I'll have a look around, shall I?'

'Megan's done that, and she didn't find them. Someone's taken my slippers too.'

Mallory sighed. This wasn't how she liked the day to start off, though to be fair her mum was sounding quite lucid today. Opening drawers and lifting clothes, she searched for any of the three sets of pyjamas usually there and came up blank. They were most likely hidden somewhere in the room, though Megan had said she couldn't find them anywhere when they'd had their talk. This was not an uncommon problem. Her mother often hid items like a pair of earrings or her favourite books and they inevitably turned up behind other books on the shelf, or in the back of a cupboard behind towels or shoes. 'I can't find them either. Let's do your nails now and I'll take another look later.'

Megan had also told her how her mother had started going for walks in the middle of the night. She'd been found in the staff kitchen, and out in the gardens, sitting watching the stars with only a thin dressing gown on in the bitter cold. It wasn't unusual with dementia and the staff had only wanted to keep her up to date with everything, but it had knocked Mallory. Knowing this was coming and actually hearing about her mother's wanderings were two different things and it upset her. There was nothing she could do to prevent her mother from doing this, and had to accept the staff were doing their best to keep her safe.

Mallory sighed and got out the nail polish remover and a bottle of polish before placing a stool by her mum's feet, ready to get on with making her mother happy.

'What colour this week?'

Mallory rubbed the wriggling feet before her to warm them. 'I've got blue with sparkles.'

'Goody. Reminds me of summer skies.'

It was one of her mother's better days. Despite the missing clothes, she was more alert and there hadn't been an awkward moment when she didn't know her daughter. Mallory smiled softly.

Of all the moments of forgetfulness and agitation the one that always got her in the heart was her mum forgetting her daughter's name. Sometimes it was only her name she forgot, other times she didn't even know who Mallory was. Mallory ranked them together. Hard, painful lumps of sorrow always filled her heart and stomach and brought on a load of memories of growing up and being laughed with, growled at, teased and encouraged by her mother's strong yet sweet voice. *Mallory, you mustn't. Mallory, yes, you can go. No, Mallory, don't do that. I love you, Mallory.*

Her heart swelled. She'd had a wonderful childhood that had followed her into adulthood, giving her the grounding for who she'd become and what she'd wanted for the future. Her future had to contain love. Deep and abiding love. She had plenty to give. It wasn't wrong to expect some in return.

Josue popped into her head. They'd clicked from the beginning. Yesterday's rescue showed how well they worked together. Last night in bed they'd been almost one, had read each other like a book. Already she felt he had a place in her life, as though she couldn't let him go. But he'd warned her he didn't settle anywhere for long, so backing off a bit would be wise. She glanced at her mother, who was watching her paint a nail. She wouldn't be leaving Queenstown to follow Josue anywhere. 'I've met a man I like, Mum. He's staying at Kayla's house and going to work at the hospital.'

'Handy for you.' Her mother's smiles were crooked since having some teeth removed, as though she was trying to hide the gaps.

Mallory had arranged an appointment in a few weeks with an orthodontist in Dunedin to sort out getting false teeth for her. 'He's French, from Nice. And he's gorgeous.' She kissed the tips of her fingers on one hand and spread them wide.

'Les Francais s'embrassent comme le diable.'

'What did you just say?' Her mother didn't speak French. Or so she'd believed.

'Frenchmen kiss like devils.' There was a twinkle in her eyes unlike any Mallory had seen in years.

'You know this how?'

'I kissed a Frenchman once. More than once really. When I was nineteen and went to France with my sisters. We met some men at the camping ground we were staying in. I fell in love with him.'

'What happened?' Mallory asked, the nail-polish brush hovering in the air above the middle toe. She'd never known her mother had once gone to France, let alone fallen in love while there. Was this true or a figment of her imagination?

'We had a good time and then I fell out of love and came home.' Her mother's eyes were flooded with memories. Good ones, judging by the soft smile lifting her mouth. A familiar smile she'd seen her mother give her father often throughout her life. It always softened Mallory's heart to know how in love her parents had been in their marriage. And now she was learning there'd been another man her mother might have smiled at like that. A Frenchman to boot.

But her mum had said she'd fallen out of love. *Like I did with Hogan when he started getting too demanding about how I did the housework or drove the car? Could I be more like Mum than I've ever considered?* Hey, that might mean there *was* someone special waiting around the corner like her dad had been for her mother. Josue? But he wasn't around any corner. He'd been in her house, her bed. She'd met him and they got on brilliantly. She was forgetting—or ignoring—the fact he'd be heading away again. Another thought brought reality to the fore. Even if she and Josue did get close enough to want to be together and she was free to follow him to France, she couldn't work. The language barrier would prevent her endorsing her pilot's licence there, so she'd be unemployable except for possibly a mundane job that brought her no excitement. It would be for the same reason she wouldn't be able to qualify as a paramedic either. The last thing she'd ever want to do would be to rely on someone else to support her, even for the time it took her to become fluent in another language—which could take years.

'Mallory, the polish is drying on the brush.'

It was. 'You surprised me about your Frenchman, and I forgot what I was doing.' Definitely one of her mum's better days. Almost how it used to be between them. 'What was his name?'

'Who? Tell me about your man.' Mischief twinkled out of pale blue eyes that had seen a lot over a lifetime of family and hard work, diverting attention from her past love.

'Mum, he's not my man.' And wasn't going to be if she remained sensible. If she decided to be less sensible, then he'd be her lover until he disappeared on a big tin bird and she'd get back to her normal, gratifying life. Alone. But not lonely. She had her friends and mother. Why did that suddenly make her feel despondent? She loved her job and being a part of the Search and Rescue team. Her home was comfortable, though there was always something needing to be done to it. Now that Kayla had returned home and was living almost next door, and

Maisie was dealing with her own problems but with the potential of also coming home soon, she was happy.

Except it was time to find a man to settle down with permanently and get rid of this restlessness. Josue didn't fit her needs. He moved on a lot. She stayed put. So her heart would be at stake if she fell for him. She'd been there twice, and wasn't looking for a third mistake.

'Mallory Baine, when you get distracted like that, I know something—or someone—has got you in a dither. Now spill. Who is he?'

Forget losing her memory. This was the version of her mother when Mallory had been a teenager, testing her toes in the world of boys. She laughed. 'Josue, and, yes, he does kiss like the devil.' Too much information probably but she was so enjoying this rare moment with her mother that she didn't care.

'We clicked right from the start when I found him in my house, lying on the couch.' She went on to explain what had happened and how Josue had stayed the night. She didn't mention the next night and why he'd stayed then as well. That was far too much information. Not even at her most understanding would her mother have been hearing that.

'I'm glad you've met this man and you like him so much. It's about time.'

'You're rushing things, Mum.' Which was unlike her. Could it be that she wanted to see her daughter settled while she could still understand what was going on half of the time? Mallory's heart bumped. 'I am not falling in love and about to ride off into the sunset with him.'

If only it was that simple. But then nothing worth having was ever straightforward, or so her parents had repeatedly told her when she'd been growing up. So far, she'd chalked up one pregnancy that had ended disastrously and left her fearful of never having children. The relationship with Jasper, the baby's father, had ended equally badly, as had her relationship with Hogan, which, in hindsight, she'd been glad had run its course.

Career-wise, she had few regrets about not following through with the nursing course she'd signed up for as she'd been about to leave school, despite her having planned on becoming a nurse all her life—until the day her baby had died.

Being a pilot was wonderful and took her to places she'd never otherwise see. It also stretched her courage when flying in turbulent weather or retrieving people from rough seas or off sheer cliffs. It had taught her to be confident but wary, to be vigilant and focused. Now she wouldn't trade her career for any other, but she'd never quite let go of the idea of nursing, because it meant helping people. Being a first-aider was the antidote. In a way she was getting the best of both options, helping those in dire circumstances and feeding her need for action and excitement.

As she thought about Josue and her reaction to him, she finished painting her mother's fingernails. 'There you go. Done for another week.'

Dorothy held her hands up to study her nails. 'Pretty colour. Thanks, darling. What about yours? You were wearing that purple shade last week.'

Sometimes there was nothing at all wrong with her mother's memory. 'I'll do mine tonight. Do you want to come shopping with me at Frankton? Megan's okay with it.' As long as she watched her like a hawk. 'We could get you a new jersey to go with those navy trousers you're wearing.' Replacing the pyjamas was the real reason for the trip, but she didn't want to raise the subject and possibly upset her mother's good mood.

'I haven't got any money at the moment. It's gone. I think someone stole it.'

Okay, not a perfectly clear mind after all. 'That's fine, Mum. I've got my wallet with me.' She covered all her mother's day-to-day expenses, while the unit she lived in here at the rest home was covered by the family trust her dad had set up when he'd learned he was ill.

'Then what are we waiting for? Shade, we're going out, my girl.'

CHAPTER FIVE

'THE ONE THING I don't miss from here is this damned cold.' Maisie was curled in on herself in the passenger seat, wearing one of Mallory's woollen coats and a knitted hat. She'd flown down late yesterday from Tauranga so she could visit Kayla today, and had stayed the night with Mallory. They'd sat up talking for hours, catching up on everything they'd been up to, including discussing the Frenchman living in Kayla's house, and getting Mallory to fess up about spending the night with him.

'So you've said at least ten times since stepping off the plane last night. You be careful on the road with my car when you drive it later.' Mallory grinned as she blew warm air on her clasped hands while waiting for the heater to warm up. With a thick puffer jacket over a wool jersey and thick shirt with a merino body-tight top under those, it was still freezing outside her warm house. The temperature gauge read minus nine degrees.

It had been a long, cold week, and not only due to the weather. Deliberately avoiding Josue had been hard. Longing woke her during the nights, and it had been impossible to make sense of the need and emotions and warnings swirling through her head. But she'd felt she had to do it, to at least appear nonchalant, and not dropping at his feet with longing.

'I'm not that out of practice,' Maisie muttered through her glove-covered hands. 'Not like you and men.'

'You want to walk to Wanaka, by any chance?'

'It'd be quicker than sitting here, trying to get warm.' Maisie laughed. 'You know I get homesick every time I visit. No one gives me a hard time like you.'

'Maybe you should think about returning. You can't let the Crim wreck your life forever.' Maisie's ex-husband was doing time for ripping off old ladies of their hard-earned savings.

Maisie was quiet for all of twenty seconds, then blurted, 'I have applied for a job at the hospital. It's in a new department being set up and won't start until next year.'

'My day just got better.' Mallory unclipped her seat belt and leaned over to hug her friend. 'About bloody time.' Yes, the three of them back in town at long last.

Maisie sniffed. 'Glad you agree.'

'You didn't think otherwise?'

'Not really.' The doubt was new for Maisie. But after all she'd been through because of the Crim it was no surprise.

'Cheer up. We'll have the rose petals all over the drive when you arrive. You can stay with me.'

'You might have a Frenchman living with you by then.'

'If you've got nothing better to say, then shut up.' Mallory put the car into gear and began backing out the drive. Her girl-friends got away with saying things no one else could, but Maisie's words hit home, racking up the doubts—should she remain out of contact while she still could?

A yawn ripped through her. The late night was catching up already. Except she'd been tired before she'd picked up Maisie yesterday.

Glancing up the road to Kayla's house, she noted Josue's car parked outside. His headlights had lit up her window as he'd driven home earlier after a night at work and she again thought of him lying in her bed, his body wrapped around hers. Shaking her head, she headed for the intersection, taking her time as black ice became apparent the nearer she got to the corner.

'Watch out,' she yelled as two cars sped past the end of her road in opposite directions. The back wheels of one began to slide. 'Don't brake,' she shouted, even though no one would hear her.

Brake lights glowed red and then an almighty bang reached her inside the car as the vehicles collided. The larger four-wheel drive stopped with its engine crushing the front and driver's side of the car. Two people in the front seats had been thrown forward into the broken mess.

'There's never a dull moment being a nurse.' Maisie was already undoing her seat belt.

Pulling over to one side, Mallory picked up her phone and tapped the most recent number she'd added to her contacts. Climbing out of her car, she felt relief when Josue answered immediately. 'Can you come down the road to the corner? There's been a serious head-on collision and I saw two people being tossed about inside one vehicle.'

'On my way.' And he was gone.

People were coming out of their houses all along the street. Two men were rushing to the accident, phones to their ears.

'I've rung a doctor,' she said when she reached them. 'And Maisie here's a nurse.'

'I'm onto 111 for fire and ambulance,' her neighbour told her.

'I'll hang up then,' the other guy said. 'Holy crap. This is a mess. Did you see what happened, Mallory?'

'The SUV lost it on the black ice.' She approached the squashed sedan and could see it hadn't been a front to front hit, but the side of the sedan was also caved in. Other people were gathering, some already trying to open the doors. Maisie pushed through. 'Excuse me, I'm a nurse.'

A familiar black vehicle braked to a halt beside them and Josue climbed out, a small leather bag swinging from his hand.

It was as though she'd been on a diet for days and now someone had handed her a plate of dessert. He was as stunning as she remembered, and as tall and broad as her body remembered, too. Gulp.

'Has anyone called an ambulance?' he called to her.

'Yes. And Maisie's here, over at the SUV. She's a nurse.' Mallory focused on the emergency as she made her way to the passenger side, where she could see a woman inside slumped against the console.

Josue was striding across to the mangled cars. 'Mallory, can you triage the passenger while I do the same with the driver?' he asked as he took in the details.

Pride filled her. He knew she was capable. 'Of course.' She smiled. Someone had brought a crowbar and was attempting to open the driver's door. At least the passenger door wasn't stuck. As she leaned in towards the woman, she called, 'Everyone, this is Josue Bisset. He's a doctor.'

Josue looked around. 'Anyone injured in the other vehicle?'

'Two tourists and they're are upright but complaining of pains in various places,' Maisie called.

'The fire truck's on the way,' someone else informed him.

Mallory squatted on her haunches, kneeling down to see what had happened to the passenger. 'Hello, I'm Mallory, a first-aid responder. Can you hear me? What's your name?'

'Pam. What happened?' Her eyes opened slowly, and she tried to look around but quickly shut them again.

'You've been in an accident. Can you move your legs?' From what she could see under the airbag it looked like Pam's left one was jammed solid.

The eyes opened again, pain reflecting out at Mallory. 'I can move the right a little, but it gets tight if I try to pull it up.'

'Best not to try any more. You might cause more swelling. I'm going to check your pulse and then look for any other injuries. Is that all right?'

Pam nodded. 'I think I banged my head on the side of the

car. The seat belt dug into my chest hard.' Blood was oozing down the side of the woman's head.

'Josue, have you got sterile pads in your bag?' Mallory asked through the smashed windscreen. 'We've got a head wound here.'

'Yes. Help yourself. I'll take a look at the wound as soon as I can.' He hadn't looked up from examining his patient's face and was lifting her eyelids to check her eyes.

'I've got them,' a man called over the car. 'How many do you want, Mallory?'

'Two, thanks.' The wound reached from Pam's forehead to behind her ear. 'Any dizziness, Pam? Is your eyesight clear?'

'My eyes are a bit blurry. My head's throbbing.'

Her speech was strong and clear, despite the shock that must be setting in. The hit to her head can't have caused concussion then. 'You're doing well.' Fingers crossed. Mallory dabbed at the bleeding area on Pam's head with a pad before placing the second one over the whole wound. 'Right, let's see what your pulse is doing.' She reached for Pam's wrist.

'The fire truck's arrived,' someone announced from behind her. 'Ambulance is nearly here.'

Mallory continued counting the beats under her finger and timing a minute on her watch.

'Need you here, Mallory.' There was an urgency in Josue's voice that didn't bode well for the woman he was attending.

Mallory placed Pam's wrist on her thigh and leapt up, said to the closest person standing by, 'Hold her hand and talk to her, will you?' Then she dashed around to the other side of the car, where the door had been wrenched wide, exposing the injured woman. Mallory gulped at the carnage confronting her, but she didn't have time to stop and recover her breath. Josue had his fist pressed hard into the woman's inner thigh, blood everywhere. 'What can I do?'

'We need to get her out of here so I can put more pressure on this. The femur's fractured and torn the artery. Get those men to help you while I try and keep pressure on this.'

Looking across to the firemen, she called out, 'Jamie, over here fast. We have to retrieve this woman urgently, and Josue can't step away for a moment.'

Jamie instantly issued orders, at the same time surveying the situation. 'Ryan, get a stretcher. Joe, with me. We'll take the shoulders and head. Nick, you take her legs. Josue, I'll tell you when to move and how. Mallory, you squeeze beside Josue and place your arms under her waist.'

She slipped into the minuscule space hard up against Josue and waited for Jamie to give the instructions.

'Take it slowly,' Josue warned. 'If I lose pressure, we have a problem.'

'Right. Ready. Everyone, slow lift now.'

Mallory's legs tightened and pinged with pain as she started to straighten, her arms taking the weight of the woman's torso as Josue struggled to stand up in the confined space while still pressing into that thigh.

'Keep lifting.' Jamie was watching everything like a hawk. 'Higher, Nick, counteract Josue pushing down. That's it. Right, everyone, one step away from the car. Another, another. That's it. She's free. Ryan, where's that stretcher?'

'Right here.'

'Okay, everyone, lower her onto the stretcher. One, two, three.'

Within moments the woman was lying on the stretcher and Mallory was on her knees beside her. 'Josue, want me to take over so you can do whatever else that's needed?'

'Yes. It won't be easy swapping places. We can't stop the pressure or she'll lose more blood. Clasp your hands into a fist like mine.' He nodded when she did so and said, 'Now put them hard against mine and push down at the same time as moving with me to replace my hands. Good. Keep going.

Great. Stop. Now hold that pressure in place. Do not let up at all. Understand?'

'Yes.' She'd learned to do this in her advanced training, but actually doing it and having someone's life relying on her getting it right was frightening.

'You're great,' Josue said quietly.

Surely he meant *doing* great? It didn't matter. He made her feel special whatever he meant. 'So are you,' she replied equally softly. As a doctor, a lover and a man she already couldn't get enough of.

'Let's hope you're right.' He raised one eyebrow slowly and smiled. Then he straightened and looked around. 'Where's that ambulance?'

'Right here. Two more on the way,' Jamie informed them, reminding her she and Josue weren't alone here.

Of course, she knew they weren't but for a moment there she'd felt there was no one else around, even when her hands were pushed into a badly injured woman's thigh to hold back the bleeding that threatened her life. 'You going to hospital with this woman?'

Josue was shining a torch into the woman's eyes and getting no response. 'We need to fly her to Dunedin urgently.'

'Scott will be on standby at the airport.'

'Who calls him in?'

'You can. Or Jamie. My phone's in my pocket.' She held her breath at Josue touched her hip as he found the phone. 'There's a direct number under Emergency Rescue in Contacts.'

'Got it.' Josue punched the number and held her phone against his ear.

Mallory said, 'Tell Scott there's an empty section fifty metres from the intersection. The cops will keep everyone away for him to land.'

He nodded. 'Will do. Scott? This is Josue Bisset. We have an emergency out on the corner of Mallory's road.' He rattled off the street names with a quick glance her way. Checking he was right? Or remembering how he'd got the address wrong the other night? 'I have a woman needing to get to Dunedin Hospital fast—like yesterday. Good. Thanks.' He shoved the phone back in her pocket. 'He's lifting off now.'

Josue placed a hand on their patient's carotid artery, checking his watch. After a minute he lifted his fingers off the artery, a frown between his eyes. 'Low pulse here. And there was no response when I shone the torch directly into her eyes.'

'Head injury?'

'There's a soft area on the forehead I don't like.' His hands were spread over the scalp, his fingers careful as he searched for more damage.

Mallory glanced sideways through the car to Pam, who was now being attended to by the paramedic and first aider from the ambulance. 'Pam's pulse was normal five minutes ago,' she called across to them.

'Thanks, Mallory. Did the doc give her any painkillers in preparation for the engine being lifted away?'

'Not yet.' There hadn't been time, and she doubted if Josue carried restricted drugs with him. Checking she hadn't lightened the pressure on the wound beneath her hands, she looked over the thigh for any indications of other bleeding. Nothing, but there was a sharp shape to the trousers where the femur had broken. She shuddered at the thought of the pain that would've hit the woman at the moment of impact. In some ways it was best she was unconscious.

The heavy thumping of rotors filled the air, announcing Scott's arrival.

'At last,' Josue muttered as he wound a wide crepe bandage around his patient's head that a paramedic from a second ambulance had supplied at his request.

Mallory felt a similar relief, even though Scott had been fast getting here.

Within minutes the woman was being loaded into the chopper, Mallory still applying pressure until Josue could take over for the flight to Dunedin. With the other ambulances having now arrived, a paramedic was accompanying him. As Josue placed his hands over the still-bleeding site he said again, 'You're great.'

Straightening as far as the cramped interior allowed, she smiled and repeated her earlier reply. 'You too.' They were so in sync it warmed her throughout. He was a great doctor, and as for the man, great didn't begin to describe how she felt. If not for him, this woman's chances would be even slimmer. If not for him, her heart would be lying quietly, not beating a little harder and more erratically every time they interacted. 'We work well together.' Along with the other things that they did so well together. Her skin heated, and she had to resist the urge to reach out and take his hand. Wrong place, wrong time.

'Catch up tonight?' A hint of longing flitted through his eyes, quickly replaced with a nonchalance she didn't believe.

'I'd like that.' She'd restrained herself from calling in on him all week and suddenly she was more than ready to spend time with him again. 'I'll text you. I have to take Maisie to the airport.' Then she dropped out of the chopper onto the ground and rushed over to the wreckage without looking back, taking that smile and the warmth in his eyes with her.

'Mallory, I understand you witnessed the accident.' Zac was standing by the wreckage in his police uniform. 'I'll need to get some details when you've got a moment.'

'You can ask me too.' Maisie appeared from behind her. 'Hello, Zac.'

He must've cricked his neck at the speed he turned to stare at his best mate's sister. 'Maisie, how the hell are you?' And he stepped up to wrap her in his arms. 'Long time no see.'

Maisie grinned and leaned back to look up at him. 'If you didn't go bush so often, maybe you'd see me when I come to town.'

Mallory feigned a yawn. 'All right if we get on with this? Maisie and I are on our way to see Kayla in Wanaka.' If only these two would get over themselves and get together, she thought, but they were both stubborn as mules. 'This is what I saw happen, Zac.'

Josue parked outside Kayla's house and leaned back against the head rest. So much for a day off. First Mallory's call about the accident as he'd been about to drop into bed after a long night in the department, and then the flight to Dunedin, where their patient had immediately been admitted for urgent surgery. Despite the woman's heart stopping once due to blood loss and low blood pressure, she'd survived that far, and he was hopeful that once the surgeons had got her in Theatre her chances would rise. They'd promised to let him know later on today how she'd got on and what else they'd found.

He'd been dropped off at home by the paramedic after they'd returned to Queenstown. *Home?* Not the house necessarily, but he still felt comfortable in this town, with the people he worked with, and especially with Mallory. It was as though he belonged here, which he couldn't really. He didn't belong anywhere much except in Nice, and even there he tended to stay on the periphery of the group of friends he'd made through medical college and working in various hospitals.

As much as he'd hankered for caring friends and people to love him, as soon as he'd started getting close to anyone the old fears of being found lacking would start to haunt him.

Had he left some of his hang-ups behind when he'd come to this country? It was almost as though, because no one knew him, he could relax some of his fears of being rejected and therefore felt accepted.

Then there was Mallory. She added to, or was, the main reason he felt as though he'd found someone special that he could bond with. Like with Dean, he'd felt close to Mallory from the beginning. Unlike with Dean, there was a lot more in the closeness than just friendship. She was sexy and gorgeous and kept his veins bubbling just thinking about her.

Was she the reason Queenstown felt comfortable in a way nowhere else had for him? That couldn't be true. He had to be exaggerating the hunger for more to life than work and an occasional fling that had begun filling him from the night he'd met her. Hard to believe only one week ago she'd woken him on her couch, her eyes filled with questions and a warning not to be a smartass with her.

For two nights and two days he'd enjoyed her company over pizza and coffee, out in the bush, and getting very close in her bed. Then he hadn't set eyes on her until this morning. She was as beautiful as he'd remembered, as confident and capable dealing with the accident victims as she'd been with the boys last Saturday.

A sigh escaped. He'd missed her all week, especially when he hadn't been busy at work and had time on his hands. Twice he'd picked up his phone to call her. Both times he'd stared at her number, finger hovering above the screen as he'd thought hard. Should he call when he knew the day would come when he'd walk away? Already he knew he must not hurt her as he'd done Colette and Liza. She deserved better.

One evening he'd even debated walking down to her door and having a chat, sharing a coffee, catching up on what she'd been doing since they'd gone their separate ways after that amazing night in her bed. But she'd said no to seeing him last Sunday night, making him back off and give her some space. His heart had picked up when he'd suggested they get together tonight, and she hadn't hesitated to say yes. Relief had swamped him, quickly replaced with excitement. There was no stopping the sense that this time he might get it right.

As though there was more to come and he couldn't wait for it to unfold. Unbelievable. He hadn't done this in a long time, having decided it was best for everyone that he not get deeply involved. An occasional fling was one thing, safe and easy. This sense of knowing Mallory, of her knowing him, of wanting to find out more was new and exciting, but still scary.

A sharp wind rocked his vehicle, reminding him that his life at the moment included staying in this house while he worked at the local hospital, going on emergency medical flights to various cities and helping search for missing people. And perhaps even making friends, especially with a fascinating woman who lived only two hundred metres down the road.

There were a couple of hours to get through before Mallory turned up. It took only minutes to take off the filthy clothes he was wearing from working with the injured woman and throw them into the washing machine.

'Now what?' he wondered, looking around the immaculate living area. He could go for a drive along the lake and take a look around, but the idea didn't grip him. The day was getting on, cooling down rapidly, and he couldn't find any enthusiasm to go out. Was Mallory flying tourists around the mountains? He hadn't seen any sign of her at the airport when he'd got out of the rescue helicopter. But another woman had been with her at the accident so she could be anywhere. More likely she was probably on a tourist flight somewhere. What a fabulous job, flying around mountains and over lakes and taking people up to the snow-covered slopes.

Grr. He should be doing *something* instead of thinking about Mallory. Hadn't she mentioned mowing her lawn last weekend? It hadn't been done. Was that something he could do to ease this new restlessness winding through his veins?

He now had Kayla's number in his phone, so he texted her.

OK to use your mower to cut Mallory's lawn?

She came back in an instant. Help yourself. It's her mower anyway. You'll be her best friend forever. K

He laughed. Now, there was a good idea. Friends and then lovers? But they'd already made love. And he wanted to do that again, to hold Mallory and kiss her and run his hands over her satin skin. Friends next? Friendly lovers? Time to start on the lawn.

The mower in Kayla's shed was a ride-on and seemed to have as many gadgets as the helicopters Mallory flew. Typical of what he was getting to know about her. She certainly had a mechanical side to her brain. Plus a very feminine one, judging by the soft blouse and trousers she wore when not working, and the sexy lace panties and bra underneath that he'd had fun removing from her soft, warm body.

After a couple of minutes checking out the controls Josue got on board and started up, rode down the road and onto Mallory's lawn. He only hoped he'd got the settings right or there was going to be some explaining to do about chunks missing in the lawn. He hadn't used a ride-on before but it was a simple process once he figured out all the levers and buttons and soon he was driving around the massive lawn, quickly learning to dodge branches of trees strategically placed to take his head off if he wasn't vigilant.

The sun had almost disappeared behind the mountain when he finally rolled the mower into the shed and shut off the motor. The air was cold and crisp with the promise of another frost in the morning and yet Josue was warm with exhilaration. He'd enjoyed being outside in the crisp air and saving Mallory a chore this coming weekend. It also made him feel more at home than ever.

Careful, Jos. A mown lawn didn't make this his home or future. The warning didn't wipe the smile off his face or out of his chest, though. He fist-pumped as he headed inside for a sandwich. The fresh air had made him hungry.

The small stone-walled pub with a large open fire was busy as Mallory and Josue made their way up to the bar. 'Hey, Julie, how's things?' Mallory asked the girl pulling a beer.

'Great. I hear you went on the search for those boys last weekend. A good result.'

'It was.' She nodded to Josue. 'This is Josue Bisset. He was on the rescue too.' *By the way, he's wonderful.*

'Hi, Josue. Let me finish this order and I'll be right with you.'

Josue nodded, then looked at Mallory. 'You always know someone wherever you go.'

'That's what happens growing up in a small district, going to school and then working here. So many people are a part of that.'

'Have you done any travelling? Been overseas at all?'

'Once.' Not one of her favourite topics of discussion, her only trip abroad. She looked around. 'Shall I grab a table while there's one available?'

Josue's eyes narrowed a fraction, but all he said was, 'Sure. What do you want to drink?' So he'd noticed her reluctance to answer his questions.

Hopefully he wouldn't push it. 'A vodka and lime, thanks.'

She moved through the people crowded around tables and snagged one against the wall and hauled herself up onto a stool and rested her chin in her hand, trying to look dignified. The down side to being short was not being able to slip onto a bar stool with aplomb. She crossed her legs. The red leather ankle boots were her favourite winter accessory. They went with most of her outfits, and especially tonight's black fitted trousers and red-and-white shirt and black short jacket.

'Here you go.' Her vodka appeared in front of her.

She looked up into those intense eyes and smiled. 'Thanks.' Josue was so good looking she wanted to tighten her arms around herself and dance on the spot. He was with *her*, and he'd held her hand as they'd strolled through the town from his vehicle to here, making her feel special. Making her regret staying away over the week. It was time she'd never get back and she'd missed him. Strange, but it was how it was.

'I wouldn't have found this place without the GPS app on my phone.' He sat on the stool beside her. 'It's tucked away in such a narrow alley it's as though the owners don't want visitors finding it.'

'We know how good you are with your GPS.' She winked. 'Out-of-towners do find it, believe me. But it's a favourite with locals and we tend to crowd it out on certain nights of the week.'

'I'm glad you brought me here, though I probably won't be able to come back without you to lead the way.' He grinned and once again sent her blood heating. He did it too well.

How had she resisted calling him? Or going along the road to see him, sticking to her decision to take it slowly with him? Her restlessness over the need to find something more to her life had evolved into a need to spend more time with Josue and that had made her back off a little. 'I'll bring you again, promise.'

'*Merci.* I didn't even have to beg.' Josue laughed. 'Are you flying tomorrow?'

Anticipation began rising. 'I'm working tomorrow, but Sunday's mine. At this time of the year I usually do six out of seven days taking tourists on sightseeing flights or up to the ski fields with those who can afford it and prefer not to drive. What about you?'

'I have Sunday free too.'

'I want to go see Kayla again, take some things she asked for today. Would you like to come along and meet her? I could show you around the area afterwards.' It was the first she'd known she was going to make that suggestion. *A damned good one, Mallory.* It was time she got over holding out on having some fun with Josue. One week had been wasted already, and if he turned out to be as wonderful as she already hated to admit she thought he was, then she didn't want to lose any more time. She should get on and make the most of his time in Queenstown and deal with the consequences when they happened because she could no longer pretend she wasn't interested.

Josue leaned over and brushed her cheek with his lips. 'Count me in.'

His aftershave was spicy and light and set her aglow inside. Sipping her cool drink did nothing to chill the heat. Neither did the sudden need to open up to him some more. Wasn't getting to know him meant to include sharing herself and to take some steps towards risking allowing him to know more than she usually put out there?

'About me and travel, I've only been to Australia and then only to the outback. I did spend a few days in Brisbane on the way over, which was exciting, but most of my time was spent north of there on stations or farms.'

Surprise had slipped into Josue's gaze. Not expecting her to return to his earlier question? 'What did you do over there?'

'Crop dusting with a helicopter, and I took cattle owners out over their stations to find stock. The stations are huge, endless really, and flying is the easiest way around when they're not herding cattle, though they sometimes use choppers for that too. The dust can be horrendous and the heat is way beyond anything I'd ever experienced. The flies drove me crazy too.' It'd been an interesting six months, but she wouldn't be repeating it, and that had nothing to do with Hogan even when he'd been the reason she'd come home.

Josue was shaking his head and laughing. 'Anyone else I've asked about their overseas trips has talked about cities and historic buildings or sights like canyons or mountains, not flying in dust and dealing with flies. Mallory, you are something else.' He leaned in for another kiss, this time on the corner of her mouth.

She laughed with him. 'Maybe one day I'll get to travel to your part of the world and be the tourist with a camera around my neck as I take in all the sights I've heard so much about from the tourists I fly around here.'

'Let me know if you want to do that and I'll be your guide.' He stared her, then took a large gulp of his beer. 'I guess you won't be leaving Queenstown in a hurry with your mother here.'

Laying her hand on his thigh, she squeezed lightly. *Too intimate, Mallory?* Or was she getting on with letting go the restlessness? 'You're right. I'm not going anywhere as long as Mum's around. And to be fair, I've not thought a lot about travelling. It's never been something I've wanted to do.'

'So what made you go to Australia?' The steady look coming her way said he knew there was more than a straight-out job offer from a company that did helicopter work, and he'd have picked up on her abrupt answer the first time he'd mentioned her travelling.

Her glass was cool in her warm hand as she turned it in a circle on the table. Hadn't she wanted to let Josue in a little? In that case, she should tell him about Hogan. *All of it?* In order to trust Josue, she would see how it felt to tell him what she'd told no one else except Kayla and Maisie about Hogan's betrayal. 'I followed my boyfriend.'

Josue tipped his head to the side a little. 'This sounds interesting.'

Her smile surprised herself. 'Actually, it was.' As well as infuriating. 'I met Hogan when he worked a summer here on the river jet boats. We got on brilliantly so when he asked if I'd go to Australia with him when he went home, I was thrilled. I got a job and everything was wonderful.' So far so good. She sipped her drink.

Josue was watching her quietly. His hand covered hers for a brief moment. 'It was easy to get work?'

'Hogan's family helped by putting out the word in their district and soon I was busier than I'd ever been. It's an amazing place, being beyond the cities and towns, where everyone has to be strong and rely on each other to get through all that nature throws at them. I did like it, but it would never be somewhere I'd want to live forever.'

'Not even for love?'

'We never got far enough in our relationship for me to have to decide. Yes, I loved Hogan, but he'd often said he wanted to move to the coast and work in the tourist industry. He applied for plenty of positions but he couldn't get one he liked. He didn't want to start at the bottom. That's when his frustration started growing and I became the target for criticism. I didn't cook his favourite meal properly, made the bed wrong, was always at work when he wanted me. I started falling out of love and decided to come home.'

'I'm guessing you've been here ever since.'

She nodded. 'Yes, and no regrets.'

'There's more, isn't there?'

Mallory gasped. 'You're too clever for your own good.' Why not tell him? Usually she locked down on what Hogan had done because it made her feel and look stupid. But really it was no big deal and if she told someone, like Josue, then she might finally forgive Hogan. 'Hogan didn't take my leaving very well. He was furious. When I returned to our flat to pack up I discovered he'd emptied my bank accounts of every last cent.'

'He had your details?'

'We were in a relationship. I trusted him, otherwise why was I there?' Her mouth flattened. 'I won't do that again, I was stupid.' She'd given her trust and expected it to be reciprocated. It had been a painful lesson, and one hard to forget. She doubted she'd be quite so trusting so readily again about anything close to her heart.

Her hand was suddenly in Josue's, his fingers between hers. 'Not at all. You did what you believed was right.'

'That's fine until it went belly up. I didn't see it coming and I should've. He was always complaining about not having enough money for projects and yet spent all his earnings very freely.' She smiled at Josue, feeling happy about having told him. He seemed to understand why she felt so bad about herself, except now she didn't any more. She had made a mistake but it was in the past and she'd recouped her savings by working long hours and had had fun while doing it.

Josue leaned in and placed a kiss on her lips. 'Why am I the first you've told?'

Another gasp. 'How do you do that? Read me like a pamphlet advertising a trip on Lake Wakatipu?' It should be frightening, but it wasn't. She accepted his ability to understand her. Did that mean she was accepting him as more than a man to have a fling with? And why wasn't *that* scaring the daylights out of her if it was true? He had already warned her he'd move on regardless.

'I honestly don't know,' Josue admitted, looking a little confused. 'But I feel I know you. Strange when we haven't known each other long, but it's been like that from the beginning.'

He was admitting that? Did he understand how that was pulling her further into him? Mallory shook her head. There were no straightforward answers and she was tired of thinking too much about Josue leaving. She just wanted to get on and enjoy his company. Get closer and share their free time doing the things they both liked.

'Want another beer?' Then food, a walk around the town, and home to bed. It sounded like a good plan to her, one that warmed her throughout, including her heart. *Careful, Mallory.*

He said, 'Think I'll have a wine and order a steak, then take you for a stroll down to the wharf. After that we'll go home for some rest and recreation.'

Mallory was still laughing at his mind-reading skills when he returned with another round of drinks.

CHAPTER SIX

THREE WEEKS OF shared meals and bed, of laughter and in-depth conversations about everything except where they were going with this fling, and Josue was still smitten. More so. It seemed he couldn't get enough of Mallory.

Now at the top of the ski slope, Mallory looked gorgeous dressed in bright red skiing clothes and matching helmet and gloves. She was grinning like the cat with the cream as she studied the slope in front of her.

Until he tapped his glove-covered fist against hers and said, 'Last one to the bottom buys dinner.' Then he was gone, not waiting for her to agree or even turn to face in the downward direction. She could easily outrun him given half a chance, which he wasn't doing.

'Cheeky bugger,' she called.

'*Oui*, that's me.' He hadn't had such an enjoyable day in a long time. Seemed whatever they did together was fun and made them closer still. The skis skidded under him as he spun around and lunged his poles into the snow to push for more speed. 'I'm not buying dinner tonight.' But he was talking to air, or the other skiers standing around who he had to zigzag through to avoid crashing into someone. A quick glance behind showed Mallory having the same difficulty and had slowed up to dodge an accident. *Good.*

He aimed for the side of the slope where it was less congested, concentrating on keeping his skis parallel and his hips moving in unison with them as he swerved left then right down the steep slope. They were on the top field, where only experienced skiers went, and with fewer people up here and no young children learning to ski it gave a freedom he relished. Up here he could forget everything but the cold air rushing past his face and the glitter of the last of the sun on the snow. It was magic, made even more so today because Mallory was with him. Not right now, though. He was still ahead but not by much.

The urge to let rip and speed straight down, to whizz away, gripped him. Only the thought of losing control on the sharper slope coming up made him hold back and continue as he was.

Whish, whish. That wonderful sound of the snow under skis came from the left. Mallory was closing the gap. He squinted ahead. There was some way to go to the bottom. No way dinner was going to be on him.

Whish, whish. He pushed harder to the other side where the snow was less churned up. He didn't see the small rock until almost on it. Jerking sideways, his balance went from under him and, splat, he hit the snow hard. His skis snapped off his boots, his body sprawled wide.

'Josue?' Mallory swept up to him. 'Are you all right?' Her eyes were full of worry.

Shoving upwards, he stood, clipped his boots onto the skis. 'I'm fine.'

'Are you sure?'

'Two broken legs and a twisted arm.' He grinned as he reached for his poles. 'You going to help me?'

She pulled a face at him. 'You might as well order the pizzas now.' She was off, aiming for the markers for the end of the run now less than two hundred metres away.

'Make mine a Hawaiian with extra pineapple, will you?' Josue swept past her right before the line.

'That sweet tooth won't do you any favours,' she muttered through gasps of air.

'Bad loser?' He stood before her, dragging in air through his smile at a similar rate to her. Good. It hadn't been a doddle for him either. Not after he'd taken that fall.

'Not a bad run for an old bloke,' she quipped.

'An *injured* old bloke.' He laughed.

She suddenly went serious on him. 'You didn't hurt yourself, did you?'

Wrapping an arm over her shoulders, he pulled her close and kissed her cheek. 'Doubt I'll even have a bruise to show for it.' She wouldn't be able to kiss him better. Damn.

'Let's head on down and go home. I'm thinking a bowl of hot soup and steaming bread rolls sound especially good now. Better than pizza.'

The air was cooling rapidly now that the sun was dropping behind the mountain. All around them skiers were making their way down the lower slope to the main buildings and the car parks. 'It's been great having a day to ourselves, no calls from S and R.'

'No emergencies where I was needed at the hospital. *Oui,* a perfect day.' Josue hugged her again. 'And it's not over yet.' He did love being with Mallory. *Whoa.* His arm dropped to his side. *Getting too involved, Jos.*

Then Mallory was leaning into him, those bright eyes twinkling mischievously. 'You want another race down the next slope?'

He couldn't stop the laughter bubbling up and out. Reaching for her, he wound his arms around her lithe body and kissed her long and hard, drinking in all that was Mallory. To hell with everything else. Right now, out here in the fresh, crisp air on the side of a stunning mountain he was happy beyond belief.

Mallory looked up at him, a twinkle in her eyes. 'I like it when you smile like you don't have a care in the world.'

'So do I.' And he truly did.

A shout came from behind them.

Reluctantly Josue broke their eye contact and looked around. He held his breath as he watched a skier speed down the slope too fast, his body hunched in a racing pose, poles sticking out behind him.

'Why do I think this is going to end badly?' Mallory muttered.

Suddenly the skier twisted abruptly and tumbled, rolling over and over, the skis flicking off one at a time as cries were heard. Then the skier slammed deep into the snow on his back.

Josue headed for the person, Mallory right beside him. 'So much for a day off, huh?' He dropped to his knees beside the skier. 'Hello, I'm Josue. Can you hear me?'

'Yes,' a male voice answered. 'What happened?'

'You lost control on your run and fell. I'm a doctor. What's your name?'

'Ian. My leg hurts.'

Mallory was opposite and already checking for signs of injury. 'Josue.' She pointed to the man's thigh. A broken ski pole was sticking into the muscle.

'This where it hurts?' Josue asked Ian as he gently pressed around the pole entry. The pole had gone in quite a way. Best to leave it there until the guy was in the sterile environment of a hospital. Pulling the pole out could also cause more serious bleeding.

'Yes.' The guy was pushing himself up on his elbows.

'Careful. You might have other injuries.' He might have done damage to his spine with all that rolling.

'I'm good.' Ian looked at his bloodied leg and gulped. 'Oh.' He flipped backwards.

'He's fainted,' Mallory said as she continued feeling both legs for more injuries.

People were gathering around. Then a woman stepped up. 'I'm Jane, an instructor here. Do I need to get medical help?'

'I'm a doctor. Mallory here has first-aid skills. We're going to need assistance moving this man down to the main building, where he'll need to be transported to hospital.'

'Someone got lucky, crashing right in front of you two,' said the instructor. 'I'll be back with the mobile sled.'

'I guess he was.' Josue smiled at Mallory before looking for evidence of any other injuries. He found nothing, then ran his fingers over Ian's skull. No signs of injury there either. 'Hey, Ian,' he called. 'Wake up.'

'What happened?' Ian croaked.

'You fainted. Now, tell me, are you hurting anywhere else? Your head?' There could be a concussion or an internal bleed from the trauma of slamming into the snow.

'A bit wobbly, that's all.' This time he sat up slowly, looking everywhere but at his thigh. Lifting the opposite leg off the snow, he grimaced. 'Something not right with my left ankle.'

Mallory began undoing the laces of Ian's boot. 'I'm not taking the boot off, just trying to relieve the pressure. You've got some swelling going on. Whether it's broken or just sprained won't be apparent until you've had an X-ray.'

'Whichever, I won't be skiing any time soon, will I?' Ian grunted. 'My own fault, I suppose, but that run was too good not to race down.'

'You're not wrong there, mate.'

Another man had slid to stop a couple of metres away. 'Is Ian all right?' he asked. 'We're together,' he added quickly.

Josue was saved from answering when a four-wheeled, covered bike with a sled hitched to the back arrived and Jane leapt off. 'I've got a stretcher we can load the man onto and then lift him onto the tray,' she said to Josue. 'One of you want to ride with him? There's room in front for one of you and your gear.'

He'd forgotten about his skis and poles. 'Thanks. I'll go on the sled, keep Ian from moving too much. Let's get him loaded and down to the warmth of indoors.'

'I've notified the on-site medical crew at headquarters and they're arranging for the ambulance to be ready when we get down.' Jane was laying the stretcher beside Ian.

'I don't need that,' he grumbled and tried to stand up on one leg, and sat down abruptly with a groan.

'Let's do it our way.' Josue put a hand on the man's arm. 'Shuffle your butt across.' He looked Mallory's way. 'I'll see you down the bottom?' At her nod, he moved to sit on the bike.

Ten minutes later Jane pulled up beside the waiting ambulance, Mallory and Ian's friend joining them moments later. 'Just in time to help us get your mate aboard,' Josue told him.

With Ian inside the vehicle, Josue and Mallory gave a short account to the paramedic of the extent of the injuries they'd noted and headed towards the car park. Josue reached for Mallory's free hand. 'It was still a great day.'

'I never count helping someone as bad. Even when it disrupts a perfect day.' She grinned and leaned in to kiss him.

The alarm went off at five thirty. Monday morning once more. Another week about to kick off. Mallory groaned as she rolled over and tapped off the irritating buzzing, then yawned hard. She'd been doing a lot of that lately, but then there'd been plenty of nights in bed with Josue and evenings out for S and R meetings and meals at the pub. Her life had gone from busy to busier and she was loving it.

A large hand was splayed over her hip, kneading softly. Her legs were entangled with Josue's. Another amazing night. She'd thought it couldn't get any better after the first time they'd gone to bed yet every time was better than before. 'Why can't it be snowing and howling a gale?'

'You don't want to go to work?' came a low growly question from her shoulder, where Josue had tucked in his chin.

'Can't say the idea's enthralling me even when I'm only doing half a day. I've got my medical this afternoon.' The regular check required by the pilots' licensing board seemed to have come round fast. Hard to believe a year had gone by since the last one.

She tossed the cover aside and sat up, legs over the side. If she didn't move now she might never get up. Not that she had a lot of energy left for getting up close with Josue, but this was more than her body aching from yesterday's skiing on Coronet Peak with this wonderful man. It was odd because she didn't usually feel too bad after a day on skis. Might ask her GP, who did the pilot medicals, if there was anything doing the rounds she might've caught from one of the many people she came into contact with through her job.

'Hey, that's cold.' Josue grabbed back the cover.

'Sure is.' Goose bumps were rising on her skin now that she wasn't curled up against Josue. 'I'm having a shower.' But first she'd put the kettle on.

In the kitchen she paused at the sight on the floor by the bench. The last of the pizzas from last night had disappeared except for some crumbs. 'Shade, naughty girl.' It was her own fault for not tidying up before going to bed with Josue.

Shade lifted her head from her bed and wagged her tail.

'Come on. Outside while I get ready for work.' No point making a fuss about the mess now. Shade would've forgotten what she'd done, or that she'd been naughty. It had been a golden opportunity and she'd taken it. Mallory laughed. Couldn't really blame her girl for that. She'd have done the same.

Holding the back door open, she stared at Shade until she grudgingly got up and walked out. It might be the morning ritual but in winter Shade never leapt off her bed with any exuberance.

In the shower, standing under hot water, arms crossed over her tender breasts, Mallory tipped her head back to wash the sleep away. 'Damn, forgot to put the kettle on.'

The bathroom door opened and Josue strolled in, definitely the man of her dreams in all his naked glory. What a body, with not a gram of fat—he was all muscle. Elbowing the door wide, she moved to one side to make room for him.

He was eyeing her with tenderness.

Her throat clogged. That tenderness for her was...was special and growing on her. She felt as though she was melting into a puddle at her feet. Her eyes were wet, not only from the shower but from the emotions he created within her. This was what she'd been looking for. She looked up at him, her insides all mushy with love. *Really?* Yes, really. It was fast, but everything felt right about this man, different from her previous experiences. He just fitted with her focus on work and caring for people and how he relaxed at home and shared the chores. The list was endless. Regardless of his warning about not staying around, she hadn't been able to avoid falling for him.

'Josue,' she whispered, and reached up to run her fingers over his chest.

He stood still, looking into her as though he was reading her heart. Though his eyes were light, not grave as they usually were when he spoke about leaving, so she hoped he had no idea what was going in on her head.

Her lungs were still, her heart beating in erratic little patters like it was trying to kickstart her breathing. Yes, this was love. Though where could it lead? She had no idea and was afraid to ask in case he ran from the shower and she never saw him again. She'd always known this could happen and she'd chosen to accept the consequences, whatever they were, right from the outset.

'Mallory.' Josue placed his hands on her arms, his gaze still caught in hers, and he leaned in to place a kiss on her chin. 'Turn around.'

She stared at him for a moment. He meant everything to her. It had happened fast. *Now what?* They would carry on regardless, making the most of the time they had together. She turned around.

Josue began soaping her skin with gentle strokes, starting at her shoulders, easing the kinks out of her muscles, and slowly working lower down her back and over her backside.

She began relaxing under his touch. Was this Josue saying how much he cared for her? Showing, not telling her? Had he seen her love in her eyes? Or was he avoiding her truth? Not wanting her to love him?

His hands were on her waist, bringing her around to face him so he could start again on her breasts. His eyes were still light and his mouth soft. Then he stopped and leaned into kiss her.

She was so confused. What did Josue want? Glancing down, she saw he was ready for her, but when she reached for him, he smiled and shook his head. 'We haven't got time.'

Now there was a challenge if ever she'd heard one. Her hand wrapped around him. 'You think?' Josue was ready for her, wanted her, and despite her confusion she was going to show him how much she cared for him.

Josue laughed as he drove into the hospital car park. 'Never say that to Mallory unless you've got spare time, Jos,' he said to himself. Not that they'd needed long, they knew how to bring each other to a climax in an instant. Now he felt on top of the world when he was literally at the bottom of the globe, talking to himself out loud. But how was a man supposed to act when he'd just had another amazing night with a woman who turned him on with a look and followed through with so much more it was almost unbelievable? Almost but not entirely, because time and again he'd experienced Mallory's lovemaking and knew it was for real. And the feelings he had for Mallory were growing all the time. Truly. They were. It felt like love. Not that he had experienced it like this before, but if he was to fall in love this was how he wanted it to be. It felt real. Was he ready? How did he know?

There'd been a moment in the shower when Mallory had gone quiet on him, her eyes darkening as though she'd had something big to say. When she hadn't, he'd felt relieved and disappointed all at once. To hear what might fall from those lips could change his world forever. What if Mallory had come to care for him? Even love him? His heart began racing. Did she? It would be beyond his wildest dreams.

Then she'd smiled, her eyes lightening as she'd laid a hand on his chest. A loving gesture that had softened him. He'd begun soaping her body and they'd made love and he'd been happy. He was fitting in so well with Mallory, with his work and the search and rescue mob that he might really be finding his place. He wanted that, and he was beginning to think this time he just might be able to give as good as he got—with Mallory.

There was so much more than the lovemaking that was special with her. Lying spooned together, his arm around her waist, hearing her gentle breaths as she slept, sharing a hastily put-together meal, yesterday on the ski field, challenging each other. It gave him a sense of homecoming, of having found what he'd been looking for all his life, and that had struck him so deeply he might not be able to let go again.

Mallory was at the centre of everything happening to him. Should he be protecting himself or letting go and diving in? He'd spent his life looking for love and not finding it, Gabriel and Brigitte being the exceptions. Theirs was the sort of love a child required, bringing with it guidance and support and kindness. Until now he'd believed he was too unreliable, wouldn't be able to give stability to any relationship. And now? There was the thing. He had no idea. Except now he wanted to try, wanted to let these loving feelings take over to the point he was starting to think he could do it, could be there for Mallory through all the hurdles that life would throw at them.

The air was cold outside his car. Josue hunched his shoulders and headed inside to the department, his phone pressed to his ear, wanting to hear her voice.

'You've reached Mallory Baine. Please leave me a message and I'll get back to you.' Josue pressed off and then phoned again to listen to her voice, his gut turning into a tight ball as he left his message, 'Hey, it's me. Have a great day. See you later.'

'Josue, you're early,' the department head called from the centre desk as he made his way along the row of empty beds. 'Didn't you sleep last night?'

'No.' Not a lot of sleeping going on where he'd been. 'I woke up early so figured I might as well make myself useful.'

'Your timing's perfect.' John stood up. 'Feel like a coffee?'

'You have to ask?' What did John want to talk about at this hour?

John headed for his office where there was always coffee to be had. 'We've been quiet all night so I've had time to catch up on some paperwork.' He filled two mugs and passed one to Josue before closing the door. 'Grab a seat.'

This was shaping up to be a serious conversation. 'What's up?'

'This is confidential, all right?'

'Yes.'

'Jason's had a cancer diagnosis.'

The older doctor had been looking a bit jaded over the past month. 'I am sorry to hear that. I've heard so much about his cycling exploits it doesn't seem possible.'

'It's been a shock for those in the know. Jason's decided to step back from work—to resign, in fact. It's a serious diagnosis and he'd prefer to spend the time with family and doing a couple of things he's not got around to before.' John sipped his coffee thoughtfully. 'So I'm offering you a permanent position. I know you intend on returning to France next month but you've mentioned that your visa runs for another year. If you accepted the offer and wanted to stay on longer than the twelve months we'd be your sponsor for a resident's visa.'

Josue's chest tightened. Him take on a permanent position? He enjoyed working in this small hospital and had integrated with everyone easily. The work was stimulating so what more could he want? If he said yes it would be for at least a year, and possibly more. Excitement began fizzing in his veins. Then stopped. This would mean settling down, staying put in a town where Mallory lived, even if he got cold feet and called off their relationship. That's how he'd stayed safe in the past. Being able to leave. What if he were to take a chance and let Mallory fully into his life? If she was about to tell him she loved him then this was perfect. She was all he needed, wanted. *What? All I want? As in she really might be the one?* Yes, wasn't that what he'd been trying to tell himself? He loved her. He stared around, looking for a distraction from this blindside, and came up against John's steady gaze as he waited for an answer. He had a job offer that went some way to making this easier. Though it was as if the decisions were being taken out of his hands. A job offer and Mallory seeming to have something important to tell him. He still had to return home for Gabriel's operation, but he could return afterwards, and make a go of it with Mallory. Sharp pain squeezed his chest. If he'd read her correctly, and so far he'd always got it right with her.

'Josue?' John finally asked. 'Are you all right?'

Not at all. Why did the idea of Mallory being the love of his life feel more right than anything he'd ever known? This was too much. He couldn't concentrate, couldn't make any decisions right now. 'I'm surprised.' Surprised didn't begin to describe his emotions. He was overwhelmed, grateful, happy, *terrified*. Not of the job but of finally falling in love. Darling Mallory. He had to get out of here. 'Thank you for the offer.' *Be sensible. Don't rush it.* 'But I do have to be back in Nice next month.'

'Are you at all interested in a permanent position?'

'There's a lot to consider.' He'd love to stay if he could get past the constant fear of rejection when it came to settling down. *Give it a go.* Did he have it in him? He might lose his heart. But anything worth holding onto took effort and determination. Or so he'd been told.

'How about you take the rest of the week to think about it? After that I'll have to start looking further afield, but I'd like you to come on board. You've fitted in well with everyone and our systems.'

Josue nodded agreement. 'Sounds fair. I am keen, but there're things I have to look into.' *Give it a go. Stop overthinking.* He drained his coffee. Fresh air would be great even if it was freezing cold, but walking around the streets wasn't going to bring any answers. Only talking to Mallory could do that and he wasn't quite ready to lay his heart on the line and tell her about this offer. It was his decision to make. And he needed to absorb the knowledge he was falling for her too. Two hits in one go.

The caution he held close had kept him out of trouble before and it could save him from making a complete fool of himself this time. Was he really falling for her? If so, then, yes, he wanted the job. If not, he had to get away fast so as not to hurt her. And himself. *Too late for that one.*

John's phone rang.

Josue stood up. 'I'll get out of your way.'

'Sure.'

Josue's phone beeped as he stepped into the corridor and it took all his control not to rip it from his pocket. It had to be Mallory. No one else would be texting him. Unless it was S and R but they knew he was working today. He reached for the phone and smiled as happiness filled him. Happiness or love? *Both.*

S and R training tonight. Eat out first?

How could he have forgotten the training meeting? Oui. Pick you up at 6.00.

Damn. He'd needed time to work through everything that had happened but he'd answered without thinking. *See?* A knot formed in his gut. Staring at the phone, his heart squeezed. If he admitted to loving her it couldn't be a dabble in the water, he'd have to dive right in. He still had to go to France and help Gabriel. He owed that man so much. But once home would he be able to come back to Mallory, or would he stay away, letting the old fears of failure and rejection win? The knot tightened painfully. He swore.

'Josue, we've had a call.' A nurse appeared from a cubicle. 'The ambulance is on its way with a woman kicked in the stomach by her horse.'

Time to get on with why he'd come to Queenstown in the first place. He put his phone and Mallory back in his pocket where he could reach either of them in an instant. If only he could shove these sudden doubts away as easily. 'I'm coming.'

'Everything is in perfect working order.' Sara folded the blood-pressure cuff. 'I wish all my patients were like you.'

'Then you wouldn't have any,' Mallory retorted around a smile that quickly faltered. 'I'm glad I've passed. But there's one thing.' She hesitated. This was silly. What was a bit of exhaustion here and there? Except it had become so constant over the last few days she was starting to worry something serious was happening.

'Go on.' Sara was typing in her notes.

'I'm so tired all the time. It's getting worse. I have to drag myself out of bed every morning. I went skiing yesterday but most of the time I wasn't exactly speeding.' Except for the last run, trying to outrun Josue.

'Any other symptoms?'

'Like what?'

'Pain, aches, nausea, headaches.'

'None of the above.'

'You're eating all right?'

'Yes.' Ah, no. 'I didn't have breakfast this morning, and last night only two pieces of pizza. But that's no big deal.' She stared at the doctor. 'Come to think of it, I felt queasy on the drive to the mountain yesterday.'

'When was your last period?'

Her eyebrows lifted as she stared at Sara. What was Sara

saying? No. She couldn't be. Nausea rose fast. 'Where's the bathroom?'

'Take deep breaths. It's through that door if you need it.' Sara sat back in her chair, waiting as Mallory sucked in lungfuls of air then huffed them out.

Her hands were tight balls on her thighs, her head spinning. This had to be a mistake. Deep breath. When did Josue arrive? He'd been here over a month. It was possible, but they'd taken precautions. A memory of the first time rose in her mind. 'July. Early July was my last one.' As the words spewed out her body slumped in the chair. This was not happening.

'Then we'd better find out if you're pregnant, don't you think?' Sara asked.

Mallory could only nod as despair took over. She couldn't have a baby on her own. It wasn't right. What would Josue say? If he wasn't interested in staying around for a relationship then he'd hardly want a baby to hold him down.

'Mallory, first things first. Let's do the urine test and find out if it's positive.'

She was. The blue line mesmerised her. A baby. *Her* baby. 'Is this real?' She'd dreamed of this day, and had feared it wouldn't happen. But she wasn't in a relationship. Josue was leaving.

'Yes, it is. I'm going to take a blood sample for an HCG to find out how far along you are.' Sara looked over at her. 'One step at a time, okay?'

'I had an ectopic pregnancy when I was eighteen.' Josue was leaving.

'That doesn't mean you won't go full term with this one if that's what you want. It's rare for a woman to have two ectopic pregnancies and you haven't mentioned any symptoms that suggest this is anything but normal. You'd have known something was wrong well before now if your dates are right. However, I'll arrange a scan for you at the earliest possible time. It'll mean going to Invercargill.'

Mallory's head was spinning with the speed at which this

was happening. She'd come for a pilot medical and was now pregnant and going for a scan. What had just happened to her day? Her life? Within minutes everything had changed radically. 'I'll go. I'm only going to worry myself sick until I know for certain this is a normal pregnancy.' Mallory gasped. Pregnant? Her? 'Am I really having a baby?'

Sara nodded. 'You are. Is that good news?'

'Yes.' The answer was out without any thought. It was true. It might be unexpected, and she had no idea what lay ahead with Josue, but, yes, it was the best news. She was already accepting it. But of course she would. This was what she'd wanted in her future—but her dream had included a man to love too. Not a man who said he wasn't staying around, who didn't believe he was capable of settling in one place and being happy. If that meant she'd have to raise a child on her own then she would. There was already a warm protectiveness for her child growing inside her. Her life had changed in the last few minutes.

Josue. Her heart squeezed with love. How was she going to break the news to him? He cared for her, she knew he did whether he admitted it or not. Yet having a baby was a game changer. Josue would probably take the next plane out of the country, leaving her as Jasper had done with her first pregnancy. Despite his upbringing in foster care she didn't trust him not to make sure his own child never went through that anguish. He might want to, but staying around to be there all the time was a big ask for him. She sank further down the chair. She had to find a way to convince him to stay, to work at being a dad, to accept her love. Could she trust him when Jasper had run in this same situation? What if it *was* an ectopic pregnancy? Would he be relieved, just like Jasper had been, released from his responsibilities?

'Mallory, slow down. I can see the questions spinning through your mind. Take it easy. It's only been minutes since you found out. Let me take the blood, and then I suggest you go for a walk, get some air and just absorb the fact you're pregnant. One step at a time.'

'Sure.' That easily?

It was freezing cold outside and Mallory's nose felt numb within minutes of stomping along the path. A baby. Her hand lay over her belly. *Hello. Who are you? Are you comfortable in there?* At least it'd be warmer in there than out here.

How *was* she going to tell Josue? It would be a huge shock. She'd just been hit with the news and was slowly coming to grips with it. This wasn't something that could be put on hold until she felt ready to deal with it. Josue avoided issues by leaving, it was his go-to reaction. The real question was how to make him pause and consider everything. Her teeth were grinding, making them ache horribly. She didn't have a damned clue how to deal with any of this. Why spend time wondering about what Josue would do? Because she needed him at her side. More than that, she needed him to love her—for herself, not only as the mother of his child.

She stamped her boot on the hard ground and broke the ice covering the grit. *I'm pregnant.*

Unplanned, unexpected and a whole new beginning. Would this really shut down her restlessness now there was something—*someone*—to plan for? Yes, a baby was a wonder. One she'd begun to think she'd never experience when she hadn't found a man to love and be with forever. She'd finally met Josue, and loved him. As for the rest of that picture, that was nothing but a blank at the moment. She had to talk to him. First, she'd need to get used to the fact she was having a baby.

A gust of icy wind slapped her, sending shivers through her. What if the pregnancy *was* ectopic? She hadn't experienced any stomach pains like the first time so it couldn't be. *Don't get ahead of yourself or you might tempt fate.* Enough. She headed for her car. She'd go and see Kayla, picking up Shade from home on the way.

Checking her phone, she saw three texts from Kayla. Apparently she was going stir crazy with boredom.

I'm on my way, she texted, and headed towards Wanaka, where she might tell Kayla her news and have a good old talk about everything.

That didn't happen. Kayla wanted to get out of the house, said her parents were driving her crazy by not letting her do a damned thing during her recovery. Her concussion was long gone, but the left leg ached all the time and the other with a compound fracture gave constant stabs of pain giving cause for her parents insisting on her staying put on the couch. 'I've done nothing but rest for weeks and I'm going to become less active than a statue if I don't do something. Get me out of here.'

After cramming Kayla and her crutches onto the back seat of the car with her legs up and a seatbelt twisted across her body, and leaving Shade at the house, Mallory drove into town and a bar where they eventually sat drinking juice while Kayla vented and Mallory tried to listen and not think about Josue and the baby. When her song started playing, she stared at the name showing on her phone. What did she say? *Hi, having a great day? Wish you were here?* Reluctantly she picked it up. 'Hello, Josue.'

'Mallory, thank goodness. Where are you? I'm waiting to pick you up but there's no sign of you at home.'

She swore. The S and R meeting. Josue had said they'd go for something to eat first. 'I'm sorry. I'm with Kayla. I forgot all about the meeting.'

'You forgot? What's wrong?'

Everything. 'Nothing. Kayla was having a bad day and I came over to cheer her up. That's all.'

'Really?' Silence hung between them. He obviously wasn't satisfied with her answer.

She'd let him down. 'Really. I won't be going to the meeting now. I'll let them know.'

'You sure there's nothing wrong?'

She was hardly going to tell him over the phone. 'Josue, I am sorry.' Yet she'd forgotten they were going for a meal. Not surprising, but he didn't know why. 'I'll make it up to you, I promise.' *With the news that you're going to be a father.* She swallowed hard.

'I'll hold you to that.' His laugh was strained. 'Will you be home tonight?'

She couldn't tell him tonight. She wasn't ready. Once he knew, there'd be no turning back. If he couldn't handle the idea of being a parent because it meant settling down, he'd leave Queenstown early and she would lose more time with him. 'If I do it'll be late.'

'I see.' It was clear from his voice he didn't. 'See you later in the week.'

Mallory dropped her phone back on the table with a sigh. That hadn't gone well. It didn't bode well for the discussion lying ahead of them. Would this be like before? Everything going fine with the men she fell for until the going got tough?

'Problem in the works?' Kayla asked. 'I take it that was Josue?'

'It was.' It would be too easy to spill the truth, put it out there and pick everything apart. It also wouldn't be fair, she realised. Josue deserved to be the first to know. 'I forgot he was going to pick me up for a meal before we went to the S and R meeting tonight.'

'Blame me for wanting you to stick by my side tonight.'

'I will.' Mallory picked up her orange juice and drained it. If only it had been something stronger, but then too many drinks had got her into this situation in the first place. It had to have happened the first night they'd had sex. It had been after the rescue of the two boys when she'd had a couple of beers and vodkas and hadn't thought about protection when she and Josue had got it on. 'When do you intend moving back to your house?'

'After Dad takes me in to see the surgeon next week, I'd rather hobble around on crutches in my own place. Whichever,

I'm going to suggest to Josue he might as well stay on as there's not long to go before he leaves anyway.'

Mallory winced.

'If there's a problem with that I won't mention it. He can find somewhere else.'

'No, it's fine. Anyway, he's a dab hand with the mower now.' Tears streaked down her cheeks.

'Mallory?'

Josue should really be the first to know, but she needed a shoulder to cry on and she could trust Kayla not to say anything. 'I'm pregnant.'

'Come over here so I can hug you.' Kayla shuffled up the couch, awkwardly shifting her legs out of the way. 'Josue?'

Mallory nodded. 'Of course. He's leaving in a few weeks.'

'He might change his mind.'

If only it were that simple. She leaned back to look at Kayla and shook her head. 'It's going to take some work for that to happen.'

'Then you'd better get started. Tomorrow. Tonight you're staying here and we'll drink copious quantities of tea and talk just as much.'

CHAPTER SEVEN

'MALLORY, YOU'RE NEEDED to fly into the hills behind Arrowtown for a retrieval,' Pete called through from his office. 'The rescue chopper's already on an emergency flight so we're up.'

Leaping up from the desk where she'd been filling in paperwork for the tourist flights she'd done earlier in the day, she snatched up her yellow weatherproof jacket and slid into it. Funny how now she knew why she got so tired it didn't affect her as badly. 'Fill me in, boss.'

'A conservation department worker was felling trees by the Kawarau river when he slipped on unstable ground and dropped a tree on himself. He's also sliced his calf with the chainsaw. You're to fly the doctor and Jamie in to collect him and take him to Christchurch. They'll be here in five.'

Josue being the doctor? She hoped so. Even the impending news she had for him hadn't succeeded in downplaying the need he brought on, not only for the amazing sex but spending time with him, talking or not, just being in the same space. It never failed to surprise her. She'd dozed on and off throughout the night, the joy of a baby in her belly going around her head and battling with the fear it might be an ectopic pregnancy. Add Josue and what his reactions might be, and sleep hadn't got a look in. The sooner she told him the better, for both their sakes. Sara had phoned to say her scan was booked for tomorrow morning.

Mallory wouldn't relax until she'd had the scan and the result was good. But right now she had to focus on someone else and getting the man to care as soon as the men flying with her arrived. 'Who's with the forestry worker?' she asked Pete.

'Two other guys from the department. It was one of them who called for the helicopter.'

She'd tidied the chopper at the end of the last flight so all was in order. 'I'll get on board and file flight details with the tower.'

'I've flicked the coordinates through so I'll go and load the stretcher and other medical equipment for you.' Rescue gear wasn't stored on the helicopter they used for back-up emergency flights.

'Thanks,' she called.

Within minutes Mallory had the route and destination coordinates on the screen and was pressing the button on her headset to talk to the tower. 'Queenstown Tower, Tango Juliet Romeo.'

'Come in, Tango Juliet Romeo.'

'I'm filing a flight plan for an urgent retrieval of an injured forestry worker.' She gave the coordinates, their estimated time of departure, number of people on board and the destination after retrieval, which today was Christchurch due to availability of theatre space and surgeon.

'Roger, Tango Juliet Romeo. We'll facilitate your departure as soon as we hear you're ready for lift-off. Over.' As Mallory sighed her relief, the air controller came back. 'Stay safe, Mallory.'

'Will do. Thanks.'

A loud thud told her the men were boarding and then the door closed. Josue popped his head through the gap between the front seats. 'We're good to go.'

She breathed deeply, taking in his presence, feeling the warmth having him near brought on. 'Great.' She began the start-up procedure. 'Want to sit up here?' she asked, without taking her eyes off the dials as they recorded pressure, heat and the increasing rotor speed reaching the levels safe for lifting off the ground. He'd get a fantastic view of the region they were going to fly over to the foothills where their patient was in dire straits, and having him there right beside her would be an added bonus, despite the problem hanging between them. It might even help break the ice.

'Love to.' Josue slid into the seat beside her and buckled up.

Sighing with relief, Mallory focused on starting the flight. Pressing the button on her mouthpiece, she gave her call sign to the tower and said, 'Ready for lift-off.'

The tower came back immediately. 'Cleared for take-off. The A320 at the west end of the runway is standing by for your clearance.'

That had been done because this was an urgent flight otherwise she'd have had to wait a few minutes after the bigger plane took off so as not to get caught in the turbulence caused by the plane's engines. 'Cleared for take-off,' Mallory repeated, as she began increasing the collective and beginning to lift the cyclic for a 40-knot attitude. 'Here we go, guys.'

Another rescue underway. Her eyes skimmed the dials in front of her, then she glanced outside, scanning the area in front of the chopper as it left the ground, moving forward and gaining altitude. Her hands firm on the controls, her mind focused on flying and looking out for dangers, her heart was tight with longing for Josue's acceptance of her and the baby.

He was interesting and exciting, dedicated to his work and when he wasn't in her bed he kept her awake late into the night with the memories of their nights together. Loving him was never going to be easy. Only now she knew those memories weren't going to be enough. She wanted to spend a lifetime making more with him. A long-distance relationship would not work, wouldn't make anyone happy long term. If she couldn't leave Queenstown then she had to find a way to tempt Josue into staying here. That should be as easy as flying the helicopter over the ranges in a blizzard. At least it was possible, she sighed.

Thinking about why Mallory had brushed him off last night and how that had hurt, even when he should've been relieved, Josue couldn't quite believe the smile she'd given him as he'd settled into his seat. He was fully aware of the helicopter lifting smoothly off the ground and rising to the approved height for their thirty-minute flight. He had no qualms about Mallory's ability to fly, even though he'd not been up in the air with her at the controls before. It was just a feeling that anything Mallory did, she did well and with complete focus. As she had on the searches they'd done together before.

He'd never thought about it before but being in an aircraft meant depending on the person or people behind the controls and today that was the woman he was coming to like and respect more and more, and to care about to the point he believed he had fallen in love. She'd got to him like no other and his heart had got involved, whether he'd wanted it to or not. He'd like nothing more than to spend all his spare time with her, be a part of the daily jobs, doing the little things that made up a full, exciting day. Could he stay permanently?

When she'd said she'd forgotten about their date last night, he hadn't believed her. There'd been something in her voice that had said there was a lot more to her being unavailable than merely forgetting. 'Why did you avoid me last night?'

'I told you. Kayla was restless. I went to spend time with her.'

'When you'd already said you'd join me for a meal before the meeting?' He wasn't buying into this.

'I didn't deliberately avoid you. I did forget we'd arranged to get together. And I forgot about the meeting.'

He had to admit she sounded genuine. 'That's not like you.' Mallory was always organised and on the ball. 'Did you leave Shade at home too?'

'No, she came with me.' She placed a hand on his knee and

squeezed lightly. 'Josue, I am really sorry for screwing up. I never meant to hurt you, I promise.'

Genuine again. It was what he wanted to hear. Had he been hasty in his reaction to her not being there for their date? Because he'd wanted to see her so badly when he was supposed to be careful? He took her hand in his and kissed her knuckles. 'Okay.'

She smiled and took her hand back to place it on the controls. 'Thanks.'

Sometimes it was still hard to believe how well they got on. The other day they'd had a wonderful time together skiing, totally in tune with each other. So much so that last night he couldn't accept she might've had a change of heart even when it would've made it easier for him to step back.

'You ready for this?' Mallory sidetracked him.

'I understand I'm to do a quick examination of the injuries, access how cognitive the patient is and decide if we need the stretcher.'

'You're on it. Hopefully it's a quick turnaround. We don't want to be hanging about too long at this time of day, and the other two on the ground still have to make their way back on foot. Luckily it's a benched track but it'll be freezing in the dark.'

Getting out of an aircraft when it wasn't on the ground always felt like a strange thing to be doing. He still didn't know what last night had been about. He understood Kayla's frustration at being stuck on the couch all the time, but not Mallory's reaction to his phone call. Was she gearing herself up for something? Did she also think that they were getting on well and that their fling was coming to mean more? Did she want to tell him she was falling for him?

He growled. This deeper sense of needing her when he couldn't guarantee to be there for her had his hands tightening into fists on his thighs. She gave him hope that he wouldn't always be alone, might finally be able to let go of some of his distrust issues. Was he hiding behind his past? Using it as an excuse to stay alone and remote and safe? If he was then Mallory unknowingly held power over him already, because the questions were rising thick and fast. Could he chance a relationship that might go further than any he'd had before? Go beyond short and fun to forever and happy? To do that he'd have to return from France with his mind fixed on letting his heart rule and not his past.

Josue shivered. If only he had the guts to drop the past and move forward to a future that might hold all the loving scenarios he'd dreamt about as a youngster. It wasn't easy when he'd so often laid his heart on the line with foster families only to have them send him away or treat him like he wasn't there. There'd only been so many times he'd been naïve enough to believe next time would be better. Only so many times he'd let them hurt him before he'd wised up and accepted he wasn't going to find the love he needed. This was why he'd walked away from Colette and Liza. One day they'd have woken up to the fact they didn't love him. Better to get in—or in his case, out—first.

'Nearly there.' Mallory's voice came loud and clear through his headphones, reminding him they were all on a mission to save someone.

Get a grip and stop thinking about yourself. Start focusing on the rescue of a seriously injured man who needs you fully alert to his requirements. But it had been a long time since he'd got so wound up about the past and it had all started when he'd met Mallory. Throw in the job offer, and it looked like his life could come together as he wanted—if he took the chance. 'I'll go back and get prepared.'

'Get that harness ready, Josue. If we have to lower you, I don't want to be mucking around.' Jamie hunched over and squeezed through the gap into the cockpit.

Josue slipped into the harness and altered the straps to fit snugly, twisting his shoulders left and right to make sure there were no snags. Then he got the medical pack ready to put on if they weren't landing. Excitement began streaming through his body. Rescues hyped him up as he prepared to use his skills to help someone. Add in the possibility of stepping off the side of the chopper with only a winch to keep him safe and the excitement was even greater.

'I'll return to the front and be a second pair of eyes for Mallory.'

The moment he appeared beside her she said, 'Look out your side and towards the front.' Her flat tone suggested she was concentrating on flying as much as looking for any signs of the men on the ground. It had to be a lot to contend with and she was so calm about it.

Two minutes later he pointed towards the rocky area in front of the chopper. 'There. Straight ahead.' Relief and excitement filled him as he stared at the waving men.

'Got them,' Mallory replied. 'I can't land there. I'll do a loop to see if there's somewhere close by that's clear of trees and the river.'

Immediately the helicopter banked and began turning in a wide circle. Josue could see down to the river and the high bank on one side. The other side sloped down to the water's edge but there was a lot of scrub curtailing the option of landing. As they flew round, an area of grass and rocks came into view. Would Mallory use that or were the rocks an issue? She coolly manoeuvred her machine above the up-reaching trees, her concentration completely on the job in hand.

The helicopter straightened, slowed to a hover. 'Jamie, I can put down here or we can go with lowering Josue where the men were. What do you think? Josue, did you see a way through that wouldn't be difficult with the stretcher?'

'No, I didn't.' Unfamiliar with such dense forest, he hadn't seen a track of any kind.

Jamie came back with, 'I didn't either.'

'Let's go with lowering Josue,' Jamie decided. 'Otherwise

it's some haul up from the river to this spot, which won't be easy with a loaded stretcher.'

'Josue, you okay with that?' Mallory asked.

'Absolutely.' He'd begun heading into the body of the chopper but glanced back at Mallory, feeling a softness inside at her concern for him. He had the pack on his back within seconds.

Jamie attached the winch to the steel buckle on Josue's belt and checked the pack. He nodded once as he opened the door. 'As soon as you're on the ground unclip the hook. I'll lower the stretcher if required. Otherwise when you're ready to have the patient lifted let us know and raise your right arm and I'll return the winch to you. Keep us informed all the time.'

'Will do.' Josue understood it was important for everyone's sake he got this right.

'Ready?'

The helicopter was hovering above the spot they'd seen the men waving. Josue drew a breath and nodded. 'Yes.' Stepping onto the skid, one hand gripping the edge of the door, he looked down. The air whooshed out of his lungs. It wasn't a long way down, but he was going to have to step off the skid and trust the winch—and Mallory. He'd be fine. Another deep breath. 'Let's do it.'

Before he knew it, he was on the ground, with men grabbing the cable to steady him and get him unhooked. There hadn't been time to think about being in the air on the end of a cable. A smile split his face. Not bad. The noise overhead was deafening. Leaning nearer to the closest man, he shouted, 'I'm Dr Bisset. Josue.'

The guy nodded and pointed upstream towards the trees that followed the river and covered the hillside and set off.

Josue followed quickly, watching where he placed his feet on the slippery ground. It wouldn't do to go and break an ankle now.

Then they were at the edge of the trees, where it was damp, cold and a lot darker. There was a headlight glowing at them.

'This is Russell,' he was told. 'The chainsaw went through his leg above the ankle. We figured not to remove the boot. There's a lot of damage.' The guy pulled a face.

'You did the right thing,' Josue reassured the men. The injury had been described during the call to 111 and the details passed on to him. There was a high risk the foot had been cut off, leading him to ring the hospital in Christchurch to put the surgeons on standby. 'What other injuries has he sustained? I was told the tree landed on him.'

'He's complaining of chest pain on the side and in his right arm, which he can't move. If he says he's hurting, then he's in agony. He's a tough bastard at the best of times.'

Josue refrained from pointing out the obvious and knelt down beside the man they'd just reached. 'Hello, Russell. I'm Josue, a doctor. We're going to get you out of here fairly quickly but first I need to check you over.'

'Just do what you have to,' Russell grunted.

Josue looked at the boot-clad foot. What was left of the boot was helping slow the bleeding. He'd leave it in place. There was nothing he could do to improve the situation out here anyway. Once on board he'd apply tight bandages to help keep the blood flow to a minimum. From what he could see, he didn't like the chances of it being saved, but who knew? Surgeons could work miracles given half a chance. 'What's under that strapping?' he asked over his shoulder. The lower leg had been bound with what appeared to be a shirt torn into strips.

'Russ was bleeding all along the calf muscle up to the knee so we did what we could to stop it,' one of the men answered.

'You've done an excellent job looking after him.' At least Russell's neck and spine appeared to be uninjured by the way he was moving his head and shoulders, though Josue suspected the movement would be causing him some pain. 'Stay still if you can.'

'Reckon the arm's broken. My ribs hurt a bit too.'

Interpret 'a bit' to mean hurt like hell, Josue mused as he

carefully felt along the ulna and radius of Russell's right arm. 'Movement won't be helping either your arm or your ribs.' Under his fingers he felt an inconsistency on the bones. 'You've fractured both bones in your lower arm. I'm going to look at your chest. Tell me about the pain there.'

'Only when I breathe too deep. Reckon that frigging tree got me fair and square.'

'I know this will hurt but take a long slow breath for me.' With a stethoscope Josue listened to Russell's lungs and heart. 'Good. You can stop. You may have broken some ribs but your lungs haven't been ruptured.' He pressed the button on his headset. 'Jamie, we need the stretcher.'

'On its way.'

'How's it going down there, Josue?' Mallory's voice was soft in his ears, and he smiled.

Impossible to stay distant with her when his heart went soft when she was near. 'All good. We'll be out of here shortly. The sooner our man's in hospital the better.' Still smiling, he said to the men with him, 'Can you get the stretcher?'

'On my way,' one of them answered.

'Right. Russell, I'm going to give you a shot of painkiller before we haul you up and on board.'

'Would prefer a bourbon,' the man croaked.

'You can pretend I'm giving you one intravenously,' Josue joked as he filled the syringe. He hoped this tough guy could weather what lay ahead with as much nonchalance.

'They're ready.' Jamie's voice came through the headset.

Mallory brought the helicopter over the men on the ground and slowly descended to ten metres, then hovered. 'Go.' Looking down, she saw Josue standing bent over his patient, protecting the man from the downdraught. Her heart softened for his kindness. She'd seen others do the same thing but from what he'd said Josue hadn't had much experience with chopper rescues and yet doing the right thing by his patient seemed to come naturally. Yeah, he was a good bloke, as the guys in the search and rescue crews would say. But she already knew that.

She read the dials, checked everything was as it should be, looked out and around the location and nodded. All good. The sky was beginning to darken but they'd be well on the way to Christchurch before night took over completely. At least it would be all twinkling stars as the weather forecast was for minus six in the morning. No wind or rain this end of the South Island, but watch out on Saturday. Storms bringing snow and ice were predicted. She shivered at the thought.

'Coming up now,' Jamie warned.

Keeping a firm eye on everything, she waited to be told everyone was on board. The man had to be in a serious condition. When a chainsaw was involved it usually meant horrendous injuries, and then a tree had fallen on top of him too. The injuries wouldn't be pretty.

A light thump, then the winch was dropping the cable down again to Josue.

Leaning against her window, she glanced down at the man who had her longing for things she shouldn't. Josue was attaching the hook that would haul him up, looking well at ease. Why did *he* make her think about love and a long-term relationship? Why not the last guy she'd spent time getting to know, only to decide he wasn't worth the effort?

She hadn't felt this sense of having found someone worth putting everything into, of risking her heart again, in a long time. Not since Hogan, and he'd been quite different, expecting her to change to fit in with him all the time. Josue took her for who she was, and didn't knock her faults. Of course this was early days, when everything was generally rosy, but somehow she didn't think Josue was going to turn out to be a very different man from the one she was slowly—but surely—falling deeper and deeper in love with. Come on, there hadn't been anything slow about it at all. *More like slam, bang, here I am.* She sighed.

Josue had disappeared from sight below the chopper, meaning he'd be on board in a second. Mallory dragged her attention back to what was important right at this moment and focused on being ready to ascend the moment Jamie said they were set.

Josue would spend the flight caring for the injured man, utterly focused on watching for bleeding, making certain the man's breathing was all right and that his heart wasn't faltering, administering pain relief that wasn't going to affect being taken to Theatre for surgery. She knew all this from previous flights with other doctors. He would not come forward and sit beside her to Christchurch, but he might on the way back to Queenstown.

In the meantime, she'd make sure they had a fast but safe trip. 'All set,' Jamie called. He would watch Josue and help wherever he could. That was Jamie. She'd worked with him on enough rescues to know he was always sucking up information, learning what he could as often as opportunities arose. When she thought about it, he and Josue had a lot in common.

'Russell, open your eyes. Look at me.' Josue's sharp command came through the headset and she could hear his worry, like there was a problem going on.

Better not be, Mallory thought. *Our team doesn't like bad results. They cause despair and sleepless nights.* Turning the helicopter in the direction of the river, she flew downstream, ascending until she reached a safe height, and then headed for Canterbury and the hospital in Christchurch, one ear listening out for Josue.

'That's it, Russell. You're in the helicopter and we're flying to Christchurch. Understand?' A pause. 'Good.' Some of the tension had left Josue's voice.

Mallory relaxed. If Josue was comfortable with how his patient was doing, then she was content with flying them all to get help. She hated the trips that were touch and go every minute of the way. She felt pressured to push harder than was safe. Not that she ever did but she couldn't help wondering how she'd feel if that was someone she loved back there with serious injuries.

On today's flight there *was* a man in the back she was keen on. She'd spent a lot of nights with him in her bed now and still wanted more. Her hand slid over her belly. A lot more. Her rare flings had never amounted to more than a few exciting moments before they'd finished, no hard feelings.

Initially that's what she'd hoped she'd started with Josue, despite the niggling feeling that there was more to him than other men she'd dated. As the days had gone by she'd realised she wanted to be with him as much as possible and not only in bed or on rescues. Now there was a baby in the mix. She held her breath, searching for pain in her abdomen and finding none. Bring on the scan and hopefully she could drop this fear that was even stronger than telling Josue he might become a father.

'Feel up to some dinner?' Josue asked from right beside her seat in the chopper parked outside the hangar in Queenstown.

Mallory tugged her eyes open and turned to look at him. Looked right into those eyes filled with wariness. Dang, she was tired. 'Sounds good,' she said through a yawn. Flying to Christchurch and back had taken every last drop of her concentration.

'Sorry to wake you up.'

'Yeah, I know. It's hard to get any peace around here.' Even her smile felt tired. 'I wanted a few minutes to myself. I always do after a rescue flight.' She needed to remember the patient was in good hands and had been all the time. Needed to accept she'd done her best and couldn't have done anything more. Needed to let go and get on with the rest of her night.

'I get like that too,' Josue admitted.

'Where do you want to eat? I'd prefer to stay at home.' Right now, going home and heating something from the freezer was as much as she could contemplate. Pregnancy was turning her into a dull old woman.

His hand covered her shoulder, squeezed gently. 'No problem. I'll sort some food. Let's get out of here.'

Did this mean she was forgiven for last night? 'I'll finish

checking over the helicopter and sign off the paperwork and then head home.'

'I'll see you there in a bit.' His smile looked as tired as hers felt, and he still held himself back a little.

A shower. That's what she needed to ease the kinks in her back and warm away the tiredness in her muscles. *'Merci.'* That and *oui* were about the only French words she knew. Might be time to learn some more. Like *touch me. Kiss me.* 'See you when you're ready.' Learn to say I love you. You're going to be a father. *If* this pregnancy was normal.

Josue leaned in close and kissed her cheek. 'You *were* great today.'

'Just doing my job.' She loved her job and put everything into it. Hopefully she'd be able to fly for a while before the baby got in the way. If the baby wasn't in her fallopian tube. Thud. Her heart stuttered. Tomorrow would reveal the answer she was desperate for. The right answer. Her teeth were sharp, digging into her bottom lip.

'Doing it exceptionally well, or so it seemed for someone not very experienced with being in a helicopter. And stop chewing your lip. I'll feed you, I promise.'

If only he knew. He could, if she got on with telling him. *Tonight?* Yes, it had to be. There was no reason not to, and it would be good if he could go to the scan with her, though he was probably working tomorrow. 'See you soon.'

Breathing deep, inhaling a combination of Josue and aviation fuel, she got on with the checks required at the end of every flight, aware of Josue as he chattered with Jamie in the back as they packed the stretcher and gathered their gear before leaving the aircraft.

Just hearing his accent had her tummy tightening like a small caress. Then she recalled him whispering in French against her skin during the nights they'd spent together and the caress became thick with heat and need. *You've got it bad, Mallory.* Yep, she did. Only one thing to do about that. Enjoy every minute she had, making the most of him while she could and to heck with worrying about what to do when he left because no amount of fretting could change anything.

If only it was that simple. She hoped he didn't walk away from the life-changing news she was about to load on him. She didn't believe he would. No, make that she didn't *want* to believe he would. Josue took responsibility seriously, and this was his child, but he didn't do stopping in one place long term. He had a lot of fears to overcome. She'd do everything possible to help him through those. That's what love was about. She'd seen it with her parents, the support and unbreakable love that had got them through miscarriages and loss of jobs, and knew that's what she would give Josue. If he'd accept her being a part of his life. *If*—such a small word, so many directions it could go.

She crossed her fingers and yawned. Damn, she was exhausted. She was more likely to fall asleep at the table tonight than talk to Josue about the future.

CHAPTER EIGHT

SHADE MET JOSUE at the door, tail wagging and her nose raised to the pizzas he carried in one hand.

'No, girl, they're not for you.' He tried to ignore the hope shining up at him but Shade didn't make it easy. 'Even if you are gorgeous.'

'Shade, behave. You've been fed.' Mallory stood at the other end of the short hallway with a wide but tired grin on her face. 'You're such a sucker for those big eyes, Doctor.'

Forget Shade's beguiling eyes. It was the pair watching him that were devouring him with warmth. Josue's mouth dried. Mallory was heart-wrenchingly pretty. Dressed in a white floaty blouse that had a light blue floral pattern that matched the blue on her nails and fitted rust-coloured trousers that were feminine and accentuated her shape to perfection, she had him in the palm of her hand.

Her wavy hair shone under the light and had his hand itching to touch it. She'd put on new make-up, a little more accentuated than what she'd worn to work. This was Mallory the woman away from the predominantly male environment she worked in. 'You look beautiful.' Nothing to do with the make-up either.

She blinked, shook her head and looked away.

So there was still something bothering her.

Then her focus returned to him, a crimson shade colouring her cheeks. 'Are you going to stand there all night?'

'You think?' Since both hands were full he closed the door with his heel and followed her into the family room, where she'd laid out plates. 'Do you like Pinot noir, by any chance?' He'd stopped in at the supermarket while waiting for the pizzas.

'I do, but then I like most wines. Central Otago's well known for Pinot noirs.'

'Just as well I bought a local brand then.'

Placing the bottle and the pizzas on the table, he went into the kitchen and took glasses out of the cupboard. He was so comfortable here, as though he'd always been doing this. He knew where everything was, and how Mallory liked things to look. He'd brought her a large bunch of roses the second week he'd visited her here and had replaced them every week since because she got so much pleasure out a simple gesture that he did from the bottom of his heart. He'd started believing he could make settling down work, that the urge to run whenever the going got rough might not rear up so quickly, and when it did that he'd be able to manage it.

When Mallory hadn't turned up last night, he'd begun to feel the pain that losing her would bring and already the shutters had started to come down over his heart. The old need to go before she kicked him out had begun ringing loud and clear, reminding him how he usually did things.

His reasoning had been about going home for Gabriel, when in truth if he wasn't afraid of rejection he'd surely find a way to make everything work. He couldn't necessarily offer security to Mallory but he could try his hardest. If she wanted it. Why would she? She was confident in her own life.

Despite the love for her slowly expanding in his chest that he desperately wanted to follow, so was the fear of rejection. It was bigger than before, which told him his feelings for her were also bigger than he'd ever experienced before. The time to make a firm decision to move forward or step back was rushing at him with an incomprehensible speed. As much as he loved her, he still didn't trust himself to do the right thing by both of them.

'Josue?' She was right beside him.

'Let's eat. I'm starving.' For a lot of things. That's what was leading him into trouble. He couldn't let Mallory go, and yet sooner or later he might have to. He *was* leaving. He had to be there for Gabriel's operation so it would be safer to walk away from her while he still could, in case he wasn't coming back. *If* he could. He had yet to tell John his decision. He knew he was stalling. Since when had he got so indecisive? Since his heart had got involved.

'Me too.' Mallory was watching him with a big question in her eyes. 'Will you stay the night?'

That wasn't what was darkening those eyes but he'd go with it for now. He rubbed her back where she often ached after flying. *'Oui.'* His answer had come instinctively from the heart. How could he not spend another night with Mallory? Could he make this the last one? Impossible. *Grow a backbone. You want to look out for her, you've got to make up your mind and stick to it. One way or the other.*

'Are you working tomorrow?' Mallory had moved away to sit at the table and open the pizza boxes, sniffing the air like a hound.

He'd never eaten so many pizzas, and they weren't even a favourite. Another example of Mallory getting to him. 'I've got two days off. Two whole days in succession.' Might be an idea to go away somewhere, stay overnight in another town, do some sightseeing in the name of giving himself some space from his heart's desire.

'What are you going to do with them?'

Quickly thinking of the places he'd been told were must-sees, he went with, 'I thought I'd drive to Fiordland and go for a boat trip. I hear it's quite something.' He sat opposite her and lifted the wine bottle. 'Yes?'

'Yes to dinner. No to wine tonight. It's late and it'll keep me awake.'

'That's the idea.' He smiled and filled one glass. 'You're sure you won't have a little?'

'No, thanks.' She got up to get a glass of water, sat back down and reached for some food.

Needing to fill the gap in conversation before he blurted something awkward, like he wanted to spend more time with her, he said, 'Sometime before I head home I'd like to see the albatross colony at Dunedin. That's more interesting to me than Larnach's Castle. Not saying it wouldn't be interesting but we have plenty of castles in France.'

'Far grander, I'd expect.' Mallory was chewing slowly and her gaze seemed fixed on the family photos hanging on the wall behind him. What was she thinking about?

'What's up?'

Shaking her head, abruptly she bit into her pizza. 'Nothing.'

He never believed her when she said nothing, but he didn't want to argue. He'd done enough arguing with himself to last the week. They finished up dinner and cleared away the dishes in a companionable yet not completely relaxed silence.

Then Mallory made herself tea and said, 'I'm taking this to bed. You joining me?'

'I'll take Shade for a quick walk first, shall I?' The dog had grown restless in the last few minutes. Mallory always took her along the road or around the lawn before she settled down for the night so it seemed odd she was going to bed straight away.

'Would you? I'm exhausted.'

When Josue and Shade returned to the house, he was surprised to find Mallory sitting on the couch, drinking her tea and flicking idly through a magazine. Warmth spread through him. This was just how he imagined couples to be. Sharing the chores, making everything easier for each other and then going to bed and making love. He sighed. He adored Mallory. It no longer shocked him that he felt this way. It was true. He woke most mornings with happiness coursing through his veins and hope for another wonderful day in his heart. Mallory had given him this. Leaning over, he brushed his lips over her forehead. Maybe he could make it work for them.

'I thought you were going to bed.' There were shadows under her eyes, and when he thought about it, they'd been there all day. Hadn't she been sleeping well? Had the tension between them not really disappeared and was causing her to lie awake at night? Had he wanted to believe her so much when she'd apologised for missing their date that he'd avoided hearing something he might not like? Something different to what he'd begun hoping for? He hoped not. 'What's going on?'

Silence answered him.

'The only time you've been distant with me was when you forgot our date yesterday.' He highlighted 'forgot' with his forefingers.

Her shoulders tensed. She was scratching at her trousers above her knee. Not a Mallory action at all. Unless she was worried. Then she looked up and faced him squarely. 'Josue, sit down.'

The last time someone had spoken to him like that had been when he'd been about to be kicked out of school. He folded his arms across his chest and leaned his backside against the back of an armchair. 'What's going on?'

If only they could go to her bedroom and make love, sleep spooned together and then in the morning get up and share breakfast before Josue got organised for a day in Fiordland.

Mallory breathed deeply. That wasn't happening. There'd be no sleeping for her until he knew, and probably none afterwards. She couldn't have one last night when the baby didn't come between them because it was already there, causing trouble for their relationship.

Once Josue knew, nothing would be quite the same. Naturally

he'd be shocked, just as she had been. But for Josue there was so much more to contend with. His past would be a big part of how he reacted. He wasn't going to sweep her up into his arms and tell her it was the most amazing news he'd ever heard and that the three of them would make a great family, even if he wanted to. Not Josue.

She was going to have to be patient and support him while waiting, impatiently, with crossed fingers. She loved him, and for her that meant one thing: together forever, loving each other and their child.

'Mallory, what is going on?' he demanded in a voice she didn't recognise. Was he getting angry with her?

Pulling her eyes open, she stared into Josue's troubled gaze and bit her lip hard to stop herself from crying. He was the most wonderful man she'd ever known, and any minute now she was probably going to lose him forever.

'Talk to me.'

Wriggling deeper into the couch, she gave him a weak smile. Talk to him? *Yes, Josue, that's exactly what I'm about to do. I hope you'll still be able to hug me afterwards.* 'You...' Gulp. 'I...'

Worry was darkening that steady gaze. 'What about us?' He didn't blink, didn't move a finger, his breathing was tight.

I can do this. 'Josue, I'm pregnant.'

Silence answered her.

Shock widened his eyes, tightened his mouth, but he said nothing, didn't cross to touch her, didn't move further away. Nothing.

She waited, breathless, stomach knotted, heart barely beating. And waited.

Finally, 'Is that why you've been so tired?'

Of all the things she'd guessed he might say, that wasn't one of them. He'd put his doctor's cap on. 'I think so. Plus the fact I'm terrified I could have another ectopic pregnancy has kept me from sleeping these last couple of nights.'

'Another? You've been pregnant before?'

'I was eighteen. My boyfriend left me at the time. I'm having a scan tomorrow to make sure this pregnancy is all right.'

Josue winced. 'How long have you known?'

'I found out yesterday, which was why I forgot about the meeting.'

His arms unfolded and lined up with his sides. His gaze was still directed on her. 'You didn't think to tell me then?'

She stood up, moved closer. Reaching for his hand, she wound hers around it. 'I wanted to tell you, but I needed to get everything clear in my mind.'

His hand jerked away. 'Everything? Like what exactly?'

She'd known this wasn't going to be easy but it still hurt. At the moment Josue was turning everything back on her. Probably his way of working through the shock of learning he was going to be a father. She would give him time to get used to the idea. 'Firstly, I want this baby very much.'

Josue's arms went back across his chest, his fingers white against his green jersey. 'I'd have been stunned if you thought otherwise.'

That was a positive sign, wasn't it? Did he feel the same? 'Family is important to me. I'm sure it's the same for you.'

'I don't talk about how I've always done my utmost not to be in this position because, as you know, I don't stay around long enough to be a parent.'

Her shoulders sagged. *Here we go.* She waited to hear him out.

'I can't give a child—or a partner—the stable life they deserve. How can I when I haven't had the experience of a loving family?' He shoved both hands through his hair, leaving it sticking up on end. 'This is crazy.'

'I couldn't fly a helicopter until I was taught.' She glared at him. *Easy, girl. He's taking this hard.* 'You learned to be a doctor, Josue. You can learn to be a fantastic father. And partner.

Think what Gabriel and his wife gave you, how they shared their lives to help you make yours better.'

Josue stared at her as though he didn't recognise her. 'You think so?' He snapped his fingers. 'Just like that they wiped away my fears and pain? I spent my younger life being rejected, only to turn it around so now I do the rejecting. Does that sound like an ideal partner or father?'

'What I know is that my parents raised me with love and care. They taught me to be who I am. I am going to do the same with our child. We can do this, you and I.'

'No, Mallory. You don't know what you're saying. You really don't.'

'You're about to walk out on us?' She was going for the jugular, but being tough was in her blood, and Josue was worth every bit of her strength. She was resilient and would not let him go easily. He needed to understand she'd be there every time he tripped, as he would be for her if he gave them half a chance.

'No, Mallory, I'm going to go along the road to my bedroom to do a whole lot of thinking. I cannot guarantee you or any child a settled life, living with me.' Suddenly he blinked. Tears appeared in his eyes.

'Josue, you don't have to leave next month.' Damn, she'd all but begged there. That wouldn't help her case. 'Your visa has another year to run.'

'Yes, Mallory, I do. I promised Gabriel I'd be there for his surgery.'

'What are you talking about?' Her heart started banging hard. This might mean she'd never stood a chance of winning Josue over.

'He's having a coronary bypass. It was meant to happen in June but he got flu so it was delayed until next month. It's not urgent but his surgeon wants to do it while he's still in relatively good health. After all Gabriel and Brigitte have done for me I have to be there for them. I *am* their surrogate son.' A tight squeeze of her hand and he was back on his feet and reaching for his phone. 'Goodnight, Mallory.'

It sounded like goodbye. 'Wait. Of course you have to be with Gabriel and Brigitte. I understand, but you can come back afterwards.'

'Have you heard a thing I've said?'

Despite his denial, she dredged up a weak smile. 'Yes, I have. All of it, and here's the thing. I believe in you.' Her heart spilled into her words.

He glared at her. 'Laying it on a bit thick, aren't you?'

'It's the only way to get through to you.'

'Believe me, you did that with the words "I'm pregnant". They're going round and round in my head like a broken record.'

Josue was a kind, gentle man who wanted love. Did he not realise how much he loved the couple who'd taken him in and that if he loved them so much, he could love others? Especially his child? And if only he could love her, then they'd have no problems with this.

'I'll see you later on.' He was at the door, looking at her as though he'd forgotten why he'd been here in the first place.

He doesn't love me. The thought slammed into her, took her breath away and stopped her heart. Her hands splayed across her abdomen. *Sorry, baby, but Daddy doesn't love Mummy. I love him, though. With everything I have.* Josue needed to know that. If he threw it back in her face, she'd falter, but she'd stand tall, take the hurt on the chin, and fight for him. What a disaster this was turning out to be. He held on to his feelings too tightly. But he had been relaxing more and more, becoming a part of her life. She'd never told him her feelings for him either.

'Josue, wait.' She raced down the hall and out onto the porch. 'There's something you need to know.'

'Something more?'

She strode up to him and looked into those sad, lonely eyes. 'I love you with all my heart, Josue. You, and only you.'

He swayed towards her, then straightened, all the while looking at her, as though trying to find if she was being honest.

She said it again, with all her heart in every word. 'I love you.'

Then he was gone, stepping quietly along the footpath towards the house he wouldn't be staying in much longer.

I love you.

Mallory's words echoed in Josue's head again and again as he strode up to Kayla's house. He believed her. No one had ever said that to him before, not as clear and unadorned. Not even the two people who'd taken him under their wing.

'I love you.'

He tasted the words, listened to them, breathed them in. They scared him. They warmed him, undermined his worry about not being good enough for Mallory or their child.

A baby. He was going to be a father. Him. Who didn't know the first thing about raising a child with his heart. As a doctor he knew all too well how to change a soiled nappy or feed a hungry tot. As a man—he needed a manual and that was hardly the way to go about it.

Letting himself into the house, he flicked lights on and stared around at Kayla's home, so unlike Mallory's warm comfortable place that had caught his breath the first time he'd opened her front door. He couldn't stay another night here when Kayla was Mallory's best friend. He was the odd one out. Did Kayla know about the baby? They'd had been together last night. Kayla had told him on the phone she was returning home and that he could stay on for the rest of his time here.

Right now he needed to get away from Mallory's friend's space, from Mallory down the road. He'd head into town to find a hotel room for the night. Or he could hit the road and head to Fiordland, get there before the sun rose. Except the last thing he felt like doing now was being a sightseer. There was more than enough to look at inside his head.

In the bedroom he sank onto the bed and tried to decide what to do, but all that came to mind was walking back down the road and climbing into bed with Mallory, to hug her and never let go. Which was irresponsible. He had to make some decisions before anything else.

He was going to be a dad. Yes. Incredible. Unbelievable. To think parenthood had never been a part of his thinking and yet here he was, a father-to-be, with the only woman he'd loved so deeply she had him looking at who he was and who he might become if he found the guts to do it. How was it that the deeper the difficulties the more he found he loved her?

Why not go to her now and say that? Express his love in words. He'd been showing her in small ways, but she needed to hear him say it. So did he. Except he knew if he opened his mouth the only thing that would come out was his fear of failing her, or her rejecting him. He'd tell her he was leaving.

She said she loved you.

He had to go. Grabbing a bag, he tossed in all his gear, locked up the house, put the key back in the meter box, and drove away, slowing as he passed Mallory's house, which was in darkness. *Bet she's not sleeping.*

I love you, Josue.

'And I love you, Mallory, but that doesn't mean I won't hurt you.'

In town, Josue pulled up by the lake's edge, got out and started walking. It was easy going with a full moon to light his way. He wasn't tired. Not enough to go to sleep anyway.

He might never sleep again if he didn't sort this out.

What was his problem? Apart from his fear of letting Mallory and his baby down? Of being rejected despite her claim to love him? Wasn't that enough? She'd said he could do this, but she didn't know how little he knew. She was wrong to believe in him. He had warned her.

Bending down, he picked up a handful of pebbles and one at a time threw them across the calm water to bounce again and again before disappearing underneath the surface. Like him:

he bounced along, meeting women, getting to know them, liking them, and then he sank, leaving only circles of emptiness behind him.

He was about to do that to Mallory.

Turning back the way he had come, his steps were slow. What if he went to the scan with her? Supported her? And then walked away?

That would be worse than not showing up at all.

The scan was important for her. The pain in her face when she'd mentioned the ectopic pregnancy had hit him hard. If this was another of those she'd be devastated. Someone should be with her. If she didn't ask Kayla to go with her, he should. He was in a relationship with Mallory, no matter how hard he tried to look the other way, especially if she carried the baby to full term. They had made this baby together.

If Mallory believed he could do this, then he had to believe in himself. She'd been fierce when telling him they could make it work. Then she'd been so close to tears when she'd said she loved him. Those tears had nearly undone him and had him on his knees, begging for her to take him on, fears and all.

What? Josue scooped up some more pebbles and began flicking them across the surface. *He wanted this child?* Splash. Yes, he did—if he could guarantee him or her a happy, loving life. One where he was always there, always encouraging and supporting.

It wouldn't happen. He would be doing Mallory and the child a favour by getting out of here sooner rather than later, and never, ever coming back or making contact.

He turned back to his vehicle and began driving out of town.

Early the next morning Mallory sat in her car, afraid to put the key in the ignition because the moment she started the engine her journey to the scanning wand would begin.

She couldn't bear to think this might be the last opportunity to be pregnant, to have a baby.

'Stop being negative,' Kayla had growled over the phone last night before offering to go to Invercargill with her. 'The doctor told you everything appeared normal.'

'I'm afraid to believe her,' Mallory had admitted. After all, she had hoped there was a chance Josue would believe her when she told him she loved him. Round three in the love stakes had stabbed her in the heart and was even more debilitating than the previous two. She was on her own in this. Kayla and Maisie would be there for her any time she called for help, but *if* she was going to be a mother then she had to stand tall and strong right from the get-go. It might be the only chance she got and there was no way she was going to get it wrong.

She'd put on heavier than usual make-up to put some colour in her white cheeks and cover the dark shadows below her eyes. It had been a long, sleepless night as hope that Josue might love her faded to despair as reality returned. He'd been stunned by her declaration, but there hadn't been any love coming her way, only bewilderment and fear. Plus the need to get away from her. That had hurt, but she had been warned.

There was a light tapping on her window.

Looking out, she gasped. 'Josue?' She stared at him. He looked as dishevelled as she felt. What did he want? She had to get on the road. Pressing the button, she opened the window. 'Hello.'

'You look like you had about as much sleep as I did. That's not the way to look after yourself, Mallory.'

If that's all he'd come to say, he could go away. 'You think?' She wouldn't mention not being able to force a single mouthful of toast down her throat for breakfast, and that only tea had made it past the lump in her throat, and then not a whole mug full.

'I'm coming with you.'

'Really? Just like that?' She ignored the hope rising inside her chest. It might mean nothing more than he needed to see proof that she was pregnant. Anger began winding her up. He'd come along for his own sake and nothing to do with how she might feel. Then he'd pack up and leave town. 'I don't think so, Josue. This is more than a quick squizz at a scan to see if I am safely pregnant and not going to have a procedure to remove my last Fallopian tube.' This was about her future, whether he was a part of that or not.

'I understand.'

'Do you?'

'Honestly? I'm trying.'

She stared at him long and hard, trying to sort through all the worries slapping around her skull, but there were too many and she was already exhausted. There was a long drive ahead too. 'Get in.'

'Want me to drive?'

Her shoulders slumped. So much for being strong. 'Yes, please.'

Josue opened the door and helped her out of the seat, led her around to the passenger side. Like she was an invalid.

She swallowed that one. They were going to be crammed into her car for a while, no point in getting grouchy. As they buckled themselves in she tried for normal, and asked, 'Where did you spend the night?'

Josue's car hadn't been parked outside Kayla's house when the sun had come up.

'I've moved out of the house.'

If she'd thought there was any hope at all by his turning up to go with her to Invercargill it had just taken a dive. He *was* leaving.

'Warm enough?' he asked as he started up the car.

'Yes.'

'Where are we going for this scan?'

'Invercargill Hospital.'

Josue stopped asking questions and Mallory sank down and closed her eyes. There was so much to say but she wasn't in the mood. All she wanted was to know her baby was where it should be and was going to be fine. Whatever Josue would do had to come second for now.

CHAPTER NINE

'ARE YOU COMING in with me?' Mallory asked as Josue parked outside the hospital. It had been a silent trip.

'Do you want me to?'

'Josue, answer the bloody question, will you?' She vented her frustration. 'What do you want?'

'To be there for you.' He wasn't looking at her.

Did this baby mean nothing to him? Or was this his fear taking control? Well, she'd decided to fight for him. Might as well start now. 'Thank you. I'd like your company, especially if...' She swallowed, unable to go on.

Now he faced her, nothing but concern in his expression. 'One step at a time, Mallory.'

Was that how he was dealing with all this? One step at a time? She'd ignore the tiny bubble of hope that brought on. 'Let's go in.'

Half an hour later, after waiting for the scan and then having the wand run across the goo on her abdomen, Mallory held her breath and stared at the radiologist.

A broad smile on his face brought her another bubble of hope. 'Mallory, Josue, all is well. Your baby is where it should be and looking as it's meant to. That's about all I can say at this stage. But you can stop worrying about an ectopic pregnancy.'

'All is well.' The statement bounced around Mallory's head. *My baby's real. This is really happening.* Her heart was bubbling fit to burst. She was going to be a mother. Bring him or her on.

'That's wonderful.'

Josue. Mallory blinked, looked to him and saw relief mixed with bewilderment coming at her. He didn't know where this left him. He hadn't made any decisions. Swallowing her disappointment, she reached for his hand and held tight. 'Yes, it is. Thank you, Doctor. I've been so scared and now I feel as though I'm walking on air.'

'I understand. I'm glad to have been the bearer of good news.' His eyes flicked to Josue and a frown appeared on his brow. 'I'll leave you both to absorb everything. A copy of the result will be sent to your GP.'

Just like that they were alone in the small space. Mallory shivered in the suddenly chill air. 'Josue, come on. Let's get outside and back on the road.'

'Yes, of course. What a relief for you.'

For me? 'It is the absolute best result I could get.' Her pregnancy really was normal. Phew. Unbelievable. Exciting. She clapped her hands. 'Fantastic.'

Josue said nothing.

'What about you? Does this make you happy?' She watched him think up an answer.

'I was thinking how worried you were this might be a repeat. I am very happy that you're not going through that again.'

'That sounds as though you've decided you're definitely having nothing to do with us. You're heading home, never to return.'

'Is that what I said?' His head shot up, and he locked a fierce look on her.

That was so out of character that she knew she'd gone too far. But she was fighting for him, for the father of her baby and for the man she loved and wanted to spend the rest of her life with. 'You haven't said anything. That's the trouble, Josue. I'd like to know what you're going to do.' Her hands were clenched. 'Sooner rather than later.'

'I'm sorry.' He looked the other way while she got back into her clothes, then took her elbow and started towards the lift that'd take them down to the car park. 'Let's wait until we're on our own before finishing this.'

Finishing this? Not starting or continuing, but finishing. The thrill at learning her baby was safe had been shunted aside with the dread that Josue was leaving them. Knowing how likely that was didn't make this any easier to accept. It'd have been better not to get her hopes up but she'd already given herself that speech weeks ago and hadn't managed to keep him at a distance. She loved him with everything she had and nothing would change that. No amount of pleading, telling him she loved him, asking him to reconsider would change his stubborn mind once he'd made it up.

Outside she waited for Josue to say something.

Instead he headed for the car, head down against the sharp wind, and his hand still on her elbow as though she needed support.

It would've been childish to pull away so she upped her pace to keep up and pretended the slight pressure from his fingers was loving.

Inside the car he turned on the heater and started for the main road back to Queenstown, his shoulders tight as he drove. His lips pressed against each other and his eyes were dark.

Did she give him a break or push for his thoughts?

She leaned back, her hand touching her stomach. A wave of happiness rolled through her, quickly gone. But she'd felt it, knew it to be true. Now that she could relax about an ectopic pregnancy not being a problem she was thrilled about the baby. One step on the way to her future was underway. Funny how when she hadn't been looking for it, it had happened anyway. Now she had Josue to talk to and make him see her love meant helping him overcome his difficulties and be happy too. 'Josue...'

Josue drew a breath. 'I've been offered a permanent position at the hospital with help to get a resident's visa should I want one.'

Her mouth fell open. Obviously she hadn't seen that coming. Why would she have? He'd kept quiet about everything going on in his life.

'Is that a good thing?' she asked.

'I'm still headed to Nice next month.'

'Even now you know about the baby?'

'I don't make rash decisions.' Even to him that sounded like he was covering up his feelings. Which he probably was.

She snapped, 'Rash stopped when I got pregnant.'

'Mallory, it may be straightforward for you to accept you're having a baby, but as I've never contemplated the idea...' He hesitated. Even if he hadn't, how could he not be excited knowing he was going to be a father? First he'd fallen in love, then been offered a job that fitted in with being with Mallory and now they were having a baby. It was too much to take in. It was so far out of his norm he was stumbling. 'You know my story.'

'Tell me more. There're a lot of gaps.'

'I've never considered being a parent and now I've been confronted with the fact that I might have to without a say in the matter.'

'Like me, you mean?' She didn't look at him, just sat watching the kilometres disappearing under the front of the car.

'I suppose it is exactly the same, regardless of our different backgrounds.'

'Background has nothing to do with this.' Breathing deep, she asked softly, 'Then tell me what you're going to do. Stay or go?'

If only it was that straightforward. Josue braked as a truck cut across his line of traffic. Pressing his palm on the horn, he yelled, 'Idiot.'

Mallory looked across to him. 'Easy.'

Which only made him madder. How could he take anything easy when she wanted answers about the future? Wanted commitment from him? More than anything he wanted to tell her he was here forever, would raise their child with her, would buy a house and settle down and get everything right. If only he could say the words 'I love you' without tripping over them, without doubting them. 'Sure.'

He concentrated on driving and let the tension grow because he didn't know how to stop it without letting years of worry explode out of him. His knuckles were white, his stomach tighter than a basketball. To let rip would drive a wedge between them that could take years to fix. Not the way to get into a permanent relationship or to welcome a child into the world. If he was actually going to do it, and he still did not know the answer to that. The doubts far outweighed everything else.

Somewhere during the ride back to Queenstown, Mallory fell asleep. Josue relaxed a little and glanced across at her regularly. Tiredness lined her face but the fear of losing her baby had gone, leaving her as beautiful as ever. *'Je t'adore,'* he said quietly. 'But I doubt it's enough to walk into your life and never leave.'

At her house he went and unlocked the door then returned to lift her out and carried her into the bedroom, where he laid her on the bed and pulled a cover over her. 'Bye, Mallory.'

Whether she heard him he had no idea, but she didn't move or blink so he guessed not. Which meant she'd probably be annoyed when she woke up and found herself alone at home.

But as he stepped out of her room he heard a call.

'Josue? Are you there?'

Returning, he stood at the edge of her bed. *Don't ask me anything. I do not want to answer questions I have no idea about.* 'You've been out for the count most of the trip. I thought it best to let you continue sleeping.'

She wasn't buying it. 'Dodging the bullets?'

Leaning closer, he tucked a stray strand of hair behind her

ear and locked his eyes on hers. 'For now, yes. I have some calls to make. All right?'

She stared at him as though searching deep inside for the truth. Finally Mallory gave him a small smile. 'I guess.'

His legs were shaky as he stepped away. He didn't want to leave her even for an hour but he had to. He was not making any promises he could not keep. Neither was he going to let loose the anger that he'd been holding in all the way back from Invercargill. 'See you later.' *Maybe.*

Not having sorted new accommodation yet, he drove to the same spot by the lake and parked. After staring at the water for a long time he got out and strode along the water's edge again. The water calmed him, as did the view of Cecil's Peak on the other side of the lake. This was a beautiful place and he could see himself living here. After a few kilometres of walking along the lake shore and up onto the road where the lake was inaccessible, he turned back.

He picked up his ringing phone and saw a video-call from Brigitte. *'Bonjour, Brigitte.'* Why was she in a hospital room? His heart dropped. 'What's happened?'

'It's all right.' Brigitte laughed. 'We have a surprise for you.' She moved her phone so he could see Gabriel in bed attached to any number of tubes and cables.

'What the…?'

'Hey, Josue, you worry too much. I'm fine.' Gabriel's voice was croaky, like he needed lots of fluid to lubricate his throat.

'He had his surgery today and has come through very well,' Brigitte was saying.

'But it wasn't scheduled till next month.' What was going on? 'I was going to be there with you.'

'An opportunity come up on the surgeon's schedule so I took it,' Gabriel croaked.

'And you're seriously all right?' Josue asked, even though Gabriel did look fine from here. 'You should've called me. I'd have caught the first plane out.'

'He's tired and sore, but otherwise everything went well.' Brigitte continued, 'We won't talk long or he'll fall asleep on you. But we wanted to tell you so you don't have to come home on our behalf.'

The tension exploded. 'I wanted to be there. Don't you understand?' It had been his excuse for leaving. 'I can't stay here.'

'Why ever not?' Gabriel asked. 'I thought you were enjoying New Zealand.'

'I was.'

'What's happened?'

'Nothing.' Everything. He'd screwed up big time. 'I am coming home.'

'Talk. And stop yelling.'

He hadn't known he was. 'I miss you both.'

'That's good because we're visiting you when I'm up and about.'

'Gabriel, you can't travel for a while after surgery.' What if he got ill on the flight?

'Too late.' Brigitte laughed. 'I booked flights for Christmas to come down to New Zealand. Gab wants to do this more than anything and since he's had a scare I have to agree. Do what we can while we can.'

Suddenly Josue felt as though the world was ganging up on him. A job offer. A baby. And now no reason to have to go home. He couldn't take it all in.

'Josue? You haven't answered my question. What's got you in this state?' Gabriel asked.

'I've got into a mess.'

'And you don't know what to do. Time to stand up and be counted, by any chance?' Gabriel knew him too well.

Josue swallowed his anger. These lovely people didn't deserve it any more than Mallory had. 'I've fallen in love. We're having a baby. I've got a job here if I want it.' The words poured out like he had no brakes.

'Wow.' Brigitte laughed. 'That's our Josue. Doesn't do anything in halves.'

Our Josue. It went straight to his heart. These people *were* his family. 'I've never gone for something so huge before.'

'So what's the problem?' Gabriel croaked, reminding Josue he should finish the call. 'Exactly why are you wanting to return to Nice?'

Josue stared at his mentor and saw the strength that had got him through life this far. Saw the love that went with the strength. And he decided. 'I'm not sure. I'd like to take a risk with Mallory, to stay on and settle down.' Now that he'd put it into words he felt relief settle over him. Had he made up his mind to move forward as easily as that? Impossible, surely?

He had been touching on the possibility for the weeks he'd known Mallory. The time to make up his mind had arrived and he couldn't walk away. He didn't want to. He was ready to take on the future and hopefully enjoy it.

Did this mean he could admit his feelings to her? To take a chance on them as a couple? He had to, otherwise he might as well pack his bags and go. But he wasn't going to. He would stay. He really would.

Mallory sat on the couch with her feet tucked under her backside and Shade's head in her lap. Unable to face anyone, she'd called Pete to ask for the rest of the day off and thankfully he'd agreed. She'd lit the fire, made tea and watched a movie, but she had no idea what it had been about.

When Kayla had rung to see if she needed company and that her dad could bring her over in his campervan, she'd turned her down. There was only one person she wanted to be with and he'd gone off on his own to make some calls apparently. But how long could some calls go on for? It had been hours since he'd left her in bed, looking as though he'd had the world's problems on his shoulders.

He didn't promise to come back, Mallory.

No, he didn't, but she could hope he might.

Shade sat up, her nose pointing towards the front door.

'Who is it, girl?'

The dog leapt to the floor and trotted out of the room.

'Mallory, can I come in?'

Josue. Her heart pounded painfully. This was the moment. She could feel it in her blood. Josue was here to tell her he was going home, that he wouldn't take the job or risk a life with her and their child. He'd be thinking he'd let them down. 'I'm in the lounge.' She pressed Off on the TV remote.

'Hey.' Josue came in and straight over to her where he sat on the other end of the couch. 'You all right?'

She nodded, unable to speak for fear of talking gibberish.

He reached for her hands and enclosed them in his warm ones, his thumbs moving back and forth softly on her cold skin. 'I've had a triple whammy these past couple of days.' He was smiling.

She crooked her head to one side. Smiling. That warm-her-toes smile. 'Sometimes it's best to get everything over and done with all at once.'

His smile widened. 'I'm hoping nothing's over and that this is the beginning of everything I've only ever dreamed about.'

Was she hearing him right? 'You'd better talk in words of one syllable.'

'I love you, Mallory Baine.'

That she could understand. 'Truly?' she blurted. 'It was only hours ago you were telling me how this was a shock and how I didn't understand where you were coming from. That your life had been terrible and I couldn't expect to know why you do the things you do.' She paused, drew a breath. 'Okay, so I've exaggerated, but what I did get was that you weren't interested in staying for the long haul.'

'You kind of got all of that right. I'm sorry for hurting you. I know your trust has been broken before. You can trust me. I've made up my mind to move forward, and that's with you and our baby. I want to give this, and you, all of my heart.'

'Oh, Josue.' She blinked but that didn't stop the tears flowing. She'd waited so long for this moment. A man and a baby. Life couldn't get any better.

'With all my heart, I love you.'

Her skin warmed, her heart changed rhythm to light and zippy. 'As I love you, Josue.'

'Yes, just like that.' He held her gaze. 'I'm going to take the job. I'm not going back to Nice at all. Gabriel and Brigitte are coming out here for Christmas.'

'What about his operation?' There's no way Josue would not be with the man who'd done so much for him.

'All done.' He explained what had happened, and the more he talked the more relaxed he became.

Josue was happy, she realised. 'You're sure about this, aren't you?'

'I am, but there's one more thing.'

Her heart slowed. *Don't make me sad now.* 'Go on,' she whispered.

'Will you marry me? Live with me and raise our child together?'

Mallory flew across the couch onto his lap and wound her arms around him. 'Yes,' she shouted. 'Yes.'

And then they were kissing and pulling back to smile at each other, and the love coming to her through those eyes told her she'd finally got it right and had found the right man to go through life with. She'd found the romance and love her parents had known. 'I love you so much, Josue. I can't believe I found you right here on this couch. It's going with us wherever we live.'

'About that. You need to find a better hiding place for the

key. I don't want any other man wandering in and making himself at home here.'

'There's only one Mr Intruder in my life.' And she went back to kissing him.

The early summer sun streamed onto the lodge's deck, highlighting all the beautiful red and pink roses in their planter boxes lining the carpet leading up to the love of Mallory's life standing watching her as she and her mother began the walk from her single life to the beginning of her shared one, followed by Kayla and Maisie in beautiful cream silk gowns.

The smile lighting Josue's face and the love in his eyes melted her inside. Thank goodness for keys in meter boxes, and a dear friend who hadn't made it home that night. Kayla still teased her remorselessly, saying she was owed plenty for bringing them together.

'Who's that man?' Mallory's mother asked. 'He looks handsome.'

'That's Josue, Mum. I'm marrying him in a minute. Isn't he gorgeous?'

'Yes, darling, he's a stunner. Have I met him?'

Flip-flop went her heart. But she wasn't going to let her mother's condition spoil anything today, and she was determined her mum would have a good time, whether she remembered it or not. 'Yes, you have. He came and asked you if you'd let me marry him.'

'What did I say?'

'When you learned he was from France you said yes, and he hugged you.'

'That's him? Now I remember.'

Some of it anyway. Or maybe Mum was making up bits and pieces. It didn't matter. She was smiling and there was a twinkle in her faded blue eyes. Mallory squeezed her hand tight. 'Love you, Mum.'

They reached the group waiting at the end of their walk and paused. She looked into Josue's eyes and let go of the breath she'd been holding all the way down the aisle. He was here and he looked full to brimming with love for her. This was really happening; it wasn't a dream she was about to wake up from. Josue was real, was the love of her life, and this time she had got it right. Now she understood why she'd stuffed up with the first two men in her life. They had never been the right ones. Josue had always been meant to come along and take away her heart, giving her his in its place.

'Sweetheart, you look beautiful.' Josue leaned in and kissed both her cheeks. 'Stunning.'

Her eyes filled and she couldn't get a word out around the lump in her throat. *I love you.*

He nodded, looked at her mother, gave her two small kisses on her cheeks too. 'Hello, Dorothy. You look lovely, too.'

'I keep telling Mallory Frenchmen kiss like the devil.'

Laughter erupted amongst the seated guests as Maisie took Dorothy by the arm and held her beside Mallory.

Next to Josue, Gabriel and Brigitte laughed too. They were standing up with him, Gabriel's chest pushed out with pride. 'This is the most special day of my life, Mallory.'

Beside him Brigitte cleared her throat, and winked. 'Second most special.'

'Yes, of course.'

The marriage celebrant took over the proceedings. 'Shall we get the ceremony under way?'

'Yes, let's.' Mallory slid her free hand into Josue's and leaned close. 'I'm done waiting.'

'I can't believe I'm here marrying the love of my life.' Josue pinched his skin. *Oui*, it was true. His heart had been blocking his throat from the moment he'd seen Mallory begin walking up the aisle towards him. Bringing him love and happiness, with their baby warm inside her. He'd never have believed that day he'd boarded the plane to fly to New Zealand that everything was going to turn around for him, and that he'd find the most wonderful woman to share his life with.

Gabriel leaned close, said quietly, 'This is real, Josue.'

The man knew him too well. *'Je sais.'* Right from the bottom of his heart he understood how real and true it was and he couldn't wait to marry Mallory and begin the next phase of their life together.

Breathing deeply, he stood tall and listened to the celebrant begin the ceremony. It went by so fast. He was placing the ring on Mallory's slender finger and feeling the band of love she slipped onto his, and kissing her and hearing Gabriel saying that was enough, all before he knew it. When he heard the celebrant declare them man and wife, Monsieur and Madame Bisset, he lifted Mallory up into his arms and kissed her again. *'Je t'aime.'*

'I love you too,' she said through the kiss.

Dorothy's excited voice cut through their kiss. 'See, I warned you Frenchmen kiss like the devil.' His mother-in-law was a bit of a character despite her health.

Mallory stood against him as he held her around the waist. 'I am so happy it's unbelievable.'

'Non, Mallory. It's believable. It's real. We just got married.'

Maisie handed her back the bouquet Mallory had relinquished to exchange wedding rings. 'I'm so happy. It's about time one of us was married.'

Mallory laughed. 'I think you two should have another shot at getting hitched again.'

Kayla smiled. 'Not me. Not yet. I'm coming right, but I'd like time to get settled back in Queenstown before I even think of men and marriage.' She grinned at Maisie. 'Guess that means you're next.'

'Don't even think you can start hooking me up for dates with every male who lands a ride in your ambulance. I am so not interested.' Maisie shrugged her shoulders, but her gaze had wandered out to the groups of friends standing talking and sipping the champagne that was being handed round.

Josue couldn't figure out who she paused on, but he did notice the sudden intake of breath. So there *was* someone she was interested in.

Mallory whispered, 'Watch this.' Suddenly she tossed her bouquet directly at Kayla who had no choice but to catch it.

Kayla glared at the bouquet, and then at Mallory. 'No, thanks.'

She went to hand it back to Mallory, but her friend laughed and held Josue's hands tight. 'Sorry, but my hands are full.'

'Mallory Baine, I swear you are a sneaky piece of work.'

Josue locked eyes with her. 'Kayla, haven't I introduced you to Mallory Bisset yet?' He loved the sound of his wife's name. He spun Mallory up into his arms and kissed her and kissed her some more. 'I promise to kiss you like the devil when you wake in the morning and before you go to sleep at night.' He leaned closer and whispered, 'And to love you forever.' It wouldn't be hard to do. His heart was in her hands now. Safe.

* * * * *

Keep reading for an excerpt of a new title
from the Afterglow series,
THE BOOK BINDER'S GUIDE TO LOVE
by Katherine Garbera

Prologue

"Charm, curse, confluence," Liberty Wakefield said.

"That sounds…" Serafina Conte didn't know how to describe this latest version of kiss, screw, avoid that her friend was trying to come up with to market in their store. It was bold, in-your-face.

Liberty was the most witchy of the three best friends. Their town was sold on the idea, the possibility, that they weren't just friends and business owners…but a coven of witches. It didn't help matters that Liberty had insisted they go to the top of Hanging Hill at midnight on the summer solstice and dance around. More than a few people noticed.

It had been fun, and Sera had always been a no-regrets kind of person.

Oh, who was she kidding. She'd *never* been a no-regrets person. Not once. But Liberty and Poppy were her best friends. And she'd do anything for them. Hence discussing a witchy version of this game that they could possibly create and sell in their shop. Liberty had suggested they make an oracle deck that featured forty-eight different cards inspired by their shop: sixteen cards of authors living and dead from Sera's part; sixteen cards of bakers and famous tea makers from Poppy's; and lastly sixteen cards featuring witches, wizards and magical creatures, both real and fictional, from her own. There would also be twelve blank cards the purchaser could fill in with either people they knew or celebrities or their own category.

"I'm fine with it as long as it brings more customers in," Poppy Kitchener said.

"Me too," Sera said.

The door to their shop opened and they all turned since traffic had been slow on this gray November day. Most locals had hurried home to get ready for Thanksgiving, and tourists were probably doing the same. Sera hadn't celebrated the holiday much. It was for families, and she'd never really had one. Not one of her own. She'd grown up in foster homes, and Thanksgiving hadn't been a big deal.

Poppy was British, so she didn't celebrate, but Liberty did. And they were all going to her mom's house the next day for the feast. Sera was looking forward to it, but trying to be cool in case they canceled on her. Even though she knew her friends would never do that, old habits died hard.

"Hello, are you still open?"

Sera vaguely recognized the woman standing in the doorway. But couldn't place her face. Maybe they'd gone to college together?

"We sure are. Do you need help finding something, or do you just want to browse on your own?" Liberty asked.

"Browse, I guess," the woman said.

"Would you like some tea?" Poppy asked.

"Yes. I'd love it. And I think you have some handmade journals, right?"

"We do," Sera said, getting up and going over to her corner of the shop, which was lined with floor-to-ceiling bookcases stocked with books that she chose, as well as journals she bound by hand. Something about the woman's voice was ringing bells, but for the life of her Sera couldn't place it.

"This is a selection of premade journals," she said, leading her to the display table. "What are you looking for?"

"I don't know. Something that will inspire me."

"To write? This journal has pages that I took from an old manuscript. The writing has faded, but some of the gold leaf they used to embellish the words remains. Want to look at that?"

"I'd love to."

Sera showed her the journals and stepped aside so she could check them out in private when Liberty came over, grabbed her arm and dragged her toward the back room. "OMG. That's Amber Rapp."

As soon as Liberty said the name, everything clicked. The pop singer was known for her catchy tunes and snarky lyrics about her breakups. It *was* her. "I thought she was someone from college."

"As if. What's she doing here?"

"She said she was looking for inspiration," Sera said.

"You should offer to make her a custom journal like you did for Poppy and me," Liberty said.

Sera wasn't sure. That was something private between the

three of them. But Amber did say she was looking for inspiration, and both Liberty and Poppy claimed their journals had helped them meet their goals. "Why not?"

She went back into the room where Amber was still standing at the table. When she looked up, she seemed to know they'd figured out who she was. She waited as if ready to take a selfie or sign something.

What kind of life must that be?

"I guess I'll take this one," Amber said, holding up a leather-covered journal that Sera had made a few weeks ago using a newer binding process she'd learned from her friend Ford.

"I don't know if you'll be interested, but I sometimes make special journals with an intent inscribed."

"She made one for me and Poppy and it led us to opening the store," Liberty said.

"How?" Amber sounded skeptical.

"Well, you write down an intention and then I will emboss it into the cover of the book. You fill out the journal, and when it's full, the intention becomes real," Sera said.

"Really?"

"Yes. It's worked for all three of us," Poppy said, coming over with the tea she'd made.

"Okay. I'll try it," Amber said.

Sera went to her workbench and took a piece of old parchment and a fountain pen and came back, handing them to Amber.

"What should I write?"

"Something you can believe in. I wrote, 'There is magic in

the words in this book, and they will create the life I want,'"
Sera said.

"We did the same," Liberty added.

Amber took a minute to think and wrote a version of Sera's
suggestion.

"Okay, it will take about thirty minutes for me to put this
into the cover."

"Want to have your cards read while you wait?" Liberty
asked.

"Love to."

Sera heard them move away as she went back to her workbench and carefully lifted the cardboard back under the front
cover. She placed the handwritten piece of parchment on the
inside and then closed the cover with glue and reattached the
bindings of the leather. When she was done, Amber told them
she'd enjoyed meeting them and left.

"Wow. We should have asked for a selfie," Poppy said.

"No one is going to believe she was here," Sera said. "But
I think it was probably nicer for her to just be a girl in the
shop than Amber Rapp, megastar."

"Probably. Her cards were intense," Liberty said. "So back
to charm, curse or confluence. What do we think of Merle?"

"Gross. He's my cousin," Poppy said.

"Charm," Sera said. She liked Merle, who bought a lot of
books from her on wizardry and war for his Dungeons and
Dragons campaigns. He was the dungeon master for his group.

"Great, so that leaves curse for me," Poppy said.

"Confluence, then. He's a bit too nerdy," Liberty said. "But
I'd still rock his dungeon."

They all laughed. Sera had found something she'd never had the courage to write about in her manifesting journal. *Sisters.*

One year later, Amber Rapp dropped her new album and it went straight to the top of the charts. She gave all the credit to her visit to WiCKed Sisters in Birch Lake, Maine—which just confirmed for many locals that they were indeed a coven and most likely good witches. Since then, Amber's fans had descended on the town in droves, all wanting to get their hands on the journal Amber had purchased, have tea in Poppy's shop and get their cards read by Liberty.

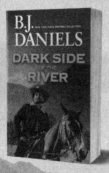

Don't miss out!

LIMITED EDITION COMMEMORATIVE
ANNIVERSARY COLLECTIONS

In honour of our golden jubilee, don't miss these four
special Anniversary Collections, each honouring a
beloved series line — Modern, Medical, Suspense and
Western. A tribute to our legacy, these collections are a
must-have for every fan.

In-store and online July and August 2024.

MILLS & BOON

millsandboon.com.au